BASTION WARS
THE OMNIBUS

Across the worlds of the Medina Corridor, the Bastion Wars rage. As the brave warriors of the Imperial Guard defend the Emperor's domain from the threats of Chaos-tainted heretics and alien interlopers, secret wars are fought in the shadows by the Imperial Inquisition and their treacherous foes, and even the servants of the Ruinous Powers are hard pressed by powers that would see them driven from the sub-sector.

EMPEROR'S MERCY

Inquisitor Obodiah Roth and his henchman Silverstein are sent to uncover the location of a set of ancient artefacts. Meanwhile, a force of Chaos traitors is in search of the treasures for their own nefarious ends. Will Roth be able to find his prize in time and prevent a terrible cataclysm engulfing the Medina worlds?

FLESH AND IRON

On the planet of Solo-Baston, indigenous forces are rebelling against Imperial rule, led by the mysterious 'Dos Pares'. Colonel Fyodor Baeder and the 31st Riverine are sent to reclaim vital weaponry for the Imperium, but are decimated by native resistance. However they find there is much more to the rebellion, and that the forces of Chaos are at work...

BLOOD GORGONS

The Blood Gorgons Chaos Space Marines are called to one of their recruiting worlds as the populace is struck down by a plague of mutation. Facing a hostile environment, shadowy xenos enemies and treachery from within his own forces, their leader, Sargaul, must dig deep into his hatred and determination to leave the planet alive.

A WARHAMMER 40,000 OMNIBUS

BASTION WARS
THE OMNIBUS

Henry Zou

BLACK LIBRARY

A Black Library Publication

Emperor's Mercy copyright © 2009, Games Workshop Ltd.
Flesh and Iron copyright © 2010, Games Workshop Ltd.
Blood Gorgons copyright © 2011, Games Workshop Ltd.
'Voidsong' first published in *Planetkill*, copyright © 2008, Games Workshop Ltd.
All rights reserved.

This omnibus edition published in Great Britain in 2014 by
Black Library,
Games Workshop Ltd.,
Willow Road,
Nottingham, NG7 2WS, UK.

10 9 8 7 6 5 4 3 2 1

Cover illustration by Raymond Swanland.

© Games Workshop Limited 2014. All rights reserved.

A CIP record for this book is available from the British Library.

UK ISBN 13: 978 1 84970 727 5
US ISBN 13: 978 1 84970 728 2

See Black Library on the internet at

blacklibrary.com

Find out more about Games Workshop
and the world of Warhammer 40,000 at

games-workshop.com

Printed and bound by CPI Group (UK) Ltd, Croydon, CR0 4YY

It is the 41st millennium. For more than a hundred centuries the Emperor has sat immobile on the Golden Throne of Earth. He is the master of mankind by the will of the gods, and master of a million worlds by the might of his inexhaustible armies. He is a rotting carcass writhing invisibly with power from the Dark Age of Technology. He is the Carrion Lord of the Imperium for whom a thousand souls are sacrificed every day, so that he may never truly die.

Yet even in his deathless state, the Emperor continues his eternal vigilance. Mighty battlefleets cross the daemon-infested miasma of the warp, the only route between distant stars, their way lit by the Astronomican, the psychic manifestation of the Emperor's will. Vast armies give battle in His name on uncounted worlds. Greatest amongst his soldiers are the Adeptus Astartes, the Space Marines, bio-engineered super-warriors. Their comrades in arms are legion: the Imperial Guard and countless planetary defence forces, the ever-vigilant Inquisition and the tech-priests of the Adeptus Mechanicus to name only a few. But for all their multitudes, they are barely enough to hold off the ever-present threat from aliens, heretics, mutants – and worse.

To be a man in such times is to be one amongst untold billions. It is to live in the cruellest and most bloody regime imaginable. These are the tales of those times. Forget the power of technology and science, for so much has been forgotten, never to be re-learned. Forget the promise of progress and understanding, for in the grim dark future there is only war. There is no peace amongst the stars, only an eternity of carnage and slaughter, and the laughter of thirsting gods.

CONTENTS

VOIDSONG

The evening chill came quickly to the mountains of Sirene Primal. Already, the twilight made shadow puppets of the rumbling vehicle column, transforming them into boxy silhouettes against an ochre backdrop.

Captain Gonan of the Eighth Amartine Scout Cavalry heaved himself above the roll cage of his half-track, panning the pintle-mounted stubber across the deep shadows of dusk. His convoy was rolling through yet another orchard village. Another ruptured settlement of paperbark pagodas, the walls of straw rotting with mildew and the roof tiles bearded with moss. In some places curtains of overgrown tea orchard clung to the frames of empty buildings, hiding any sign of settlement before the Secessionist Wars.

It was the tenth village that the captain's column had passed that day. Through the smoky haze of dusk, boredom and weariness dulled his senses. It was little wonder that Gonan did not see the armoured figure lurking within a rough bank of myrtle reed.

He never saw the shot that killed his driver. The snapping hiss of a lasrifle was followed by a blossom of arterial blood that misted the windshield. The driver, an inexperienced young corporal, began to screech in shock and hysteria, ramming down hard on the brakes of his half-track. Immediately, the slithering file of a dozen vehicles collapsed into an awkward accordion as treads fought for purchase on the mountainous shale.

Above the shriek of brakes and throbbing engines Gonan began to yell. 'Contact! Enemy at left axis of advance!'

By then, the ambush was well and truly sprung. A scattering of lasrifles released their shots into the scout cavalry half-tracks. The AM-10 *Hammer Goats* indigenous to the Amartine 8th were two-ton buggies with rear caterpillar tracks and pintle-mounted heavy stubbers. Also dubbed AM-10 *Scapegoats* by virtue of soldierly cynicism, they were regarded as death traps for the two-man reconnaissance teams that operated them. Immediately, six Guardsmen were killed and two vehicles disabled before they could even react.

The second salvo of las-shots was followed by the thrumming war cry of fifty warriors erupting from ambush. Cold panic seized Gonan and for a moment he was paralysed by neural overload. In their full regalia of war, the secessionist fighters of Sirene Primal were an awesome sight to behold. Three score were Khan-Scholars, tall, fierce-looking men, clad in hauberks of mosaic jade and armed with all manner of lance and flak-musket. Another dozen were pounding through the undergrowth in the tectonic armour of Symbolists, their salvaged lasrifles already discarded for spine sabres. Others still were Blade Artisans, charging with their robes of embroidered tapestry flared, like the wings of some great hunting bird.

Pandemonium followed. When the line of baying warriors collided against the left flank of the vehicle column, it did not in any way resemble the heroic battle murals so vividly brocaded on Symbolist robes. Instead, what unfolded before Gonan was the messy, ugly affair of men killing each other at close quarters.

An Amartine Guardsman was screaming and babbling as a Khan-Scholar beat him to death with the broken halves of his lance. A Guard sergeant grappled with a Blade Artisan for control of his halberd before sinking his teeth into the warrior's neck.

Captain Gonan had barely freed his bayonet from the AM-10's gun rack when a Khan-Scholar surged over the cowling of his vehicle. Gonan had never seen a more vicious predator. The warrior's mane of thick black dreadlocks flowed down to his calves and silver quills were threaded through his cheekbones. Around his torso was a hauberk of interlocking jade scales, worn brown-green in its antiquity, and that was where Gonan aimed his fighting knife.

He thrust thirty centimetres of steel just below the ribs, but the Khan simply stepped into the blow with a carnivorous grace and hooked with an open palm. The first strike smeared Gonan's nose across his right cheek in a burst of blood and mucous. Reflexively the Guard officer stabbed his bayonet into his opponent's kidney, steel puncturing through the ancient jade. If the Khan felt anything, he did not show it. The next punch fractured Gonan's sternum and slammed him against the roll cage of his AM-10.

Gonan had no doubt that in a straight melee, the secessionist would dismantle him piece by piece. The martial sects of Sirene embraced close combat as an art form. He understood now, why the Sirenese culture, so reverent of art and literature, would consider these fighters the greatest artists of all. From glaive dancing to the way of the mauling hand, these men were brutally beautiful to watch. It was suicide to fight them.

Instead the Guard officer drew the laspistol from his chest holster and emptied half a clip to his front. Gonan didn't know what happened next. He may have blacked out temporarily, but for how long he did not know. When the fog of concussion ebbed away, Gonan found himself on the mesh flatbed of his vehicle with a dead secessionist sprawled over him. He felt as if someone had just run a battle tank over his skull and for a moment was content to slip into the velvet black of unconsciousness.

But the sounds of hacking and stabbing soon roused his pain-hazed mind. All around was the killing. Loud and brutal. Gonan heaved the corpse off before pulling himself up behind the mounted heavy stubber. Legs still teetering, he collapsed to his knees before pulling himself upright again and racking the weapon.

'Firing now!' Gonan screamed, voice hoarse.

It was as if a secessionist chose that very moment to rival Gonan's warning with the thick avalanche of his own war cry. Thundering over the AM-10's windshield, the secessionist brandished his spine sabre. Tracking to meet his approach, Gonan thumbed the firing stud on the stubber's butterfly trigger. The stream of high velocity rounds hit his target so hard that the warrior snapped backwards and his sabre spun the other way.

Without pause, Gonan re-sighted the heavy stubber down the column of his convoy and fired again. A long enfilade burst this time. Mosaic armour exploded into chips and splinters as Gonan hosed lambent tracer into a dense maul of Khan-Scholars not more than ten metres to his vehicle's rear.

Despite the devastation wrought by a heavy weapon at point blank range, it was too late to turn the assault. Eight of the Hammer Goats were wrecks, their occupants dragged out and butchered by the roadside. By his estimate, Gonan didn't have more than six men left, too few to mount any meaningful resistance. So he did what any Imperial officer should have done, he juiced out the last rounds of his pintle weapon, drew his laspistol and staggered off his vehicle toward the killing.

By the time Imperial patrols came across Gonan's waylaid convoy, it was well into midnight. They found the body of Captain Saul Gonan horribly desecrated and staked upright on a lance, his men laid out in a neat row before him. They had been stripped of their boots and rifles, yet Captain Gonan still gripped an emptied laspistol in his fist. His eyes were still open.

It was a scene all too common across the wounded landscape of Selene Primal. Imperial and Secessionist forces alike were guilty of inflicting an almost theatrical barbarity towards one another. Entire Guard battalions were crucified while villages and refugee camps would be shelled in reprisal, fuelling a cycle of bitter conflict. Despite this, Imperial historians later argued that events which unfolded toward the latter stages of the war would render the atrocities of the Secessionist Campaign utterly inconsequential.

The mountains were treacherous at this time of year.

The polar equinox was at an end, and the ice caps were melting, sluicing great sheets of water and ice down the mountain paths. Thousands of people were migrating that day. The narrow defiles were swollen with caravans, baggage mules and the crush of toiling bodies. Hordes of refugees, the remnants of haemorrhaged villages and cities, and bands of weary secessionists were toiling over the icy spines of those mountains.

It was here that Inquisitor Obodiah Roth found himself, well into the fourth year of the guerrilla war. He had come here on dispatch from the Ordo Hereticus. The case itself was no matter of significance. The original briefing from the ordo had read – *mild psychic disturbances emanating from Sirene Primal, priority – minor*. It had never seemed like much to begin with.

Initial disturbances had first occurred eight months ago. Sanctioned psykers of the Imperial war fleet had sensed a strong psychic flux from the planet itself. Then reports from the neighbouring Omei Subsector began to surface. Astropaths of a missionary outpost on the tundras of Alipsia Secundus had slashed their throats, writing the name of the planet in blood, and silently mouthing *Sirene Primal* until death claimed them.

The phenomena had initially been dismissed as the psychic backlash of Sirene Primal's war. It was uncommon but not unheard of, for the anguish of billions in suffering to cause to coalesce into psychic disturbance. Scholars had named it a *planetary swansong*. Regardless, senior members of the ordo had deemed the matter worthy of further investigation, an open and shut affair perfect for wetting the noses of virgin inquisitors. Or so it had seemed.

Sirene Primal had not always been like this. Set adrift on the Eastern Fringes of the Imperium, it floated like a muted pearl within the oceanic darkness of the universe. The last of the ancients had died aeons ago, their ossified remains forming mountains of colossal spines and plates. Upon them, Sirenese architects had raised the colonnades and flower-draped monoliths of their ziggurat-gardens.

It was a very different world now. Standing on a jagged tusk of rock, Roth watched the menacing shapes of Vulture gunships, prowling across the Sephardi Peaks as they hunted for targets. Higher up amongst the cloud vaults, Imperial Marauder destroyers hurtled like knife points through the sky.

Beneath him, the mountainous slopes swept into a rocky spur. Among the scree and rubble could be seen the glint of shell casings, and even the odd helmet. Further down the pass, the rusted carcass of a battle tank could be seen, submerged in a glacial melt. The cold air was cut with the smell of fuel.

Despite the icy chill, Roth had suited up in Spathean fighting plate. The form-fitting chrome was coated with a hoar of frost that bled vaporous curls into the air. Over this he framed a tabard of tessellating obsidian. The tiny panes of psi-reactive glass, although a potent psi-dampener, did little to insulate him against the temperature. He was cold and thoroughly miserable.

Yet his shivering condition was just another irritation on his long list of simmering anxieties. He had been on-world for close to a month now and no amount of investigation, research or cross-referencing had yielded any clue as to the cause of the psychic disturbances. While millions suffered, he was mousing about with the nuisances of some psychic irregularity that no one in the ordo really cared about. He felt tired, drained and hopeless. It was, he thought with dry rumination, not a good start to his career.

'They're at it again, sire.' A voice, stern and patrician, jostled Roth out of his brooding.

The man who had spoken was Bastiel Silverstein. One of Roth's best, a xenos game-hunter from the arboreous forests of Veskepine, Silverstein was right of course. A huntsman with augmented bioscope lenses was seldom wrong about such things. Already the target reticles oscillating on the pupils of his eyes had locked on the Marauder destroyers swooping in the distance.

Beneath the banking aircraft, spherical eruptions of fire and ash were accompanied by the unmistakeable rumble of explosives, deep and distant. Even without Silverstein's optic enhancements, he could see that the Imperial Navy was bombing south-west of them.

Roth swore terribly.

There would be more killing today. Not the flattening of Chaos Legions, or the epic banishment of daemon princes that Roth had read about in the Scholam-Libraries of the Progenium. No. It would be the killing of more desperate, scared and malnourished refugees. The bombs would fall, people would die, and by sunset, the war would be no closer to finishing and Roth would be no closer to clearing his damn case.

As if to emphasis his thoughts, the keening hum of distant engines began to build sonic pressure. Looking up Roth spotted a Vulture gunship roaring down from a bar of clouds, two kilometres up and diving steeply. Roth's blood ran colder. He could almost anticipate what was about to occur.

From the surge of panic amongst the refugees down slope, they did too. No more than one hundred paces away from him the mountain defile was congested with a sea of malnourished faces looking skyward in mute fear. Most of the native Sirenese did not know what a Vulture gunship was, but they knew that the ominous shape in the distance was shrieking towards them.

His man Silverstein, however, scoped it clearly, complete with a statistical read-out that scrolled down in the upper left corner of his vision.

+++*Obex-Pattern Vulture gunship, VTOL sub-atmospheric combat aircraft. Organic weapon systems: Nose-mounted heavy bolter – Optional wing-mounted autocannons – Pod-racked double missile systems.*+++

Silverstein looked to Roth, clearly concerned.

The inquisitor turned to his companion and mouthed the word 'wait'.

The gunship blurred past their jutting fist of rock, snorting jet exhaust. It sharply arrested its descent forty metres above the exodus, pivoting on the fulcrum of its tail. There it hovered on the monstrous turbines of vector thrust engines.

From his vantage point up the slope, Roth was almost at eye-level with the gunship. He watched with growing trepidation as half a dozen tendrils of rope uncoiled from the belly of its hold, reaching out like the tentacles of a waiting beast. Troops, bulky with combat gear, began to rappel down the steel cables.

Roth recognized them immediately as men of the 45th Montaigh Assault Pioneers. Great shaggy men, broad and bearded, descending with shoulder-slung lascarbines. Their insulated winter fatigues lined with mantine fur and coloured in the distinctive grey and green jigsaw pattern were unmistakeable.

He had been impressed, years before, when he had first studied the elite mountain troops in the schola progenium. Their engineering of trenches, field fortifications and bridges was renowned. Amongst the death marshes of Cetshwayo in M609.M41, Assault Pioneers had spearheaded their advance through supposedly impenetrable terrain with a system of drainage dams and mobile pontoons. Their ingenuity resulted in a single division of Assault Pioneers overwhelming an estimated eighty thousand orks. Where all battles are won by manoeuvre, the men of Montaigh paved the way.

Roth was not so impressed now, as he watched nine Assault Pioneers hit the ground and immediately form supporting fire positions. Fanning out into a loose arrowhead, they took a knee on the steep slope overlooking the refugees, lascarbines sitting firmly against the shoulder. By his side, Silverstein placed a gloved hand to his mouth in disbelief. Surely they wouldn't. But they did.

When they first opened fire, it was aimed above the heads of the people. Warning shots. Hemmed in between the ledge of the defile and the firers, people began to hurl themselves down the almost vertical slope in desperation. White-hot beams lacerated the air, fizzing and snapping.

'Do something!' Silverstein yelled.

In his shock, it took Roth a moment to realize the huntsman was talking to him. He was caught up watching the catastrophe unfold before him. The panic was total. A caravan was almost scuttled off the edge; a pack mule went over tumbling. The press of frightened refugees was pushing their own people down the pass, gathering momentum like a rolling landslide.

'I know! I know! Just let me consider my options–' he began.

'There aren't any options! Just do something!'

Silverstein was right. He would have to improvise. Of course, making it up on the run was one of the rudimentary lessons taught to all Inquisitorial acolytes. His masters had called it *aptitudinal adroitness*, but it amounted to much of the same thing.

Brandishing his Inquisitorial signet in an upthrust hand, Roth broke into a run. The mountain sediment slipped and slid beneath him, pitching his run into a violent descent. He slid half of the distance and slammed his knees and elbows into the shale several times for good measure. Roth ended his skittering plummet with a flying leap over the scree bank, flailing briefly in the air before landing with a shuddering impact. He was right in the thick of it now.

'Cease fire! Cease fire!' he roared.

To the credit of the Guardsmen, their well-drilled fire discipline showed through. The whickering fusillade died out, but they didn't lower their steaming muzzles. Roth was suddenly very aware of nine lascarbines trained on him.

'Lower your weapons, I am Obodiah Roth of the *Inquisition*.' Roth stressed the significance of his last word, thrusting his badge of office towards the troops.

As all soldiers would have done, they looked to their sergeant, a grizzly beast with the well-nourished build of a lumberjack. The sergeant, levelling his gaze on Roth, didn't move.

'Don't listen to him lads,' snarled Grizzly.

Roth breathed deeply. The still air was now heavy with the smell of burnt ozone. The gaping maws of nine las-weapons filled his vision. He didn't realise when exactly the Sirenese behind him had stopped screaming, but they didn't utter a sound now. He could tell the sergeant was staring at the stout chrome-plated plasma pistol in his shoulder rig, daring him to make a move.

Roth drew it.

'Lower. Your. Weapons.' Roth repeated.

'Don't be stupid now. We wouldn't want there to be any accidents between us,' replied Grizzly, his tone cold and even.

'I have the authority.'

'And I have my orders, inquisitor. This isn't your war.'

Roth's pulse felt like a war drum. He could tell they were not going to see reason. They were forcing him to play his final hand and Roth had hoped it wouldn't come to this. The inquisitor clenched his jaw and pointed up the mountain slope.

'Sergeant. Up there, three hundred paces behind you, is a huntsman with a Vindicare-class Exitus rifle. Don't bother looking, he's well hidden. What I can tell you, is that he was trained by the lodge-masters of Veskepine and I've seen him shoot the eyes off an aero-raptor in mid flight. Give him four seconds, he'll put down half your squad. It's your call Sergeant.'

'You're bluffing,' said Grizzly, but his voice wasn't so calm. This wasn't his game anymore.

'If you say so.'

There was a pause. Then the sergeant looked to his men and nodded reluctantly. Nine lascarbines were lowered to the ground. Far up the slope, a crop of slate rock and gorse weed juddered then moved. Bastiel Silverstein, in a fitted coat of dark green piranhagator hide unfurled himself from concealment. In his hands was a rifle, long and lean. Roth flashed his man the hand signal for *stay alert* and turned his attention back on the sergeant.

'Sergeant…'

'Sergeant Clais Jedda, Second battalion Airborne Sappers of the Forty-fifth Montaigh Assault Pioneers.'

'Sergeant Jedda.' Roth repeated, letting the name hang heavily in the air before continuing. 'What the hell are you and your men doing?'

'Clearing a path, until you got in the way,' he replied, still defiant.

'A path to where?'

'Urgent priority mission. On orders from my battalion colonel. It's none of your concern, inquisitor.'

'You made it my concern, sergeant. If you tell me nothing, I will charge both you and your colonel for collusion of criminal activity. He would be very displeased, don't you think?' Roth had cornered him. He knew Jedda was the type of soldier who would rather risk ire from the Inquisition than the wrath of his commanding officer.

'There's nothing criminal here. These people are all potential threats. Two days ago we lost a patrol of Pioneers on their way to an AOI. Gone. Wiped out. I'm not taking any chances with my boys.'

AOI. Guard terminology for *area of interest*. Roth raised an eyebrow, 'What area of interest, sergeant?'

'An off-world landing craft. A four-man patrol picked up signs of a large metallic object in an ice cavern two kilometres west of here. Their last transmission confirmed it was a lander, frozen solid with snow. Must have been right under our noses since before the winter months.'

Roth was definitely interested now. The snow entombment meant it must have slipped past the planetary blockade at least six or seven months ago. Perhaps it was linked to the psychic disturbances, perhaps not, either way he would need to know more.

'Sergeant Jedda. You will cease terrorising these people immediately. Furthermore, you will not fire at all, unless permission is granted.'

'Permission...' he was really caught off guard now.

'Yes sergeant. Permission from me. I'm coming with you.'

The ship was a merchant runner, entombed under a tongue of glacial ice. The burnt sepia of its painted hull appeared incandescent under the striated ice, almost aglow with lambent energy. A cavern formed its cradle, where it slumbered in the throat of a frosty maw, framed by fangs of icicles.

The ship itself was a blunt-nosed cruiser about two hundred paces long, the hammerhead of its prow pockmarked with the scars of asteroid collision. Roth surmised by its squat boxy frame that it was a blockade runner, similar to the type favoured by illicit smugglers and errant rogue traders.

Roth and his team approached the ice cave down a narrow gorge, advancing slowly down the rock seam. The inquisitor led the way, auspex purring in his grip. Behind him, Silverstein and the Montaigh Guardsmen formed a staggered file with weapons covering every angle of approach. They reached no further than the shadow of the cave entrance when the auspex chimed three warning tones. A solitary target flashed on the display, half a kilometre from their position, almost right on top of the beached cruiser.

Roth signalled for a halt and lower. Sinking to a wary crouch, he squinted into the cavern with his plasma pistol primed. He took in the vastness of the cave, its immensity dwarfing the colossal docking hangars of Imperial battleships. Before him, towering colonnades of ice buttressed a vault ceiling of shimmering white-blue. Arroyos of melt water reached like veins across the cavern floor and forked through the grooves of snow dunes. Roth couldn't see a damn thing.

'Bastiel,' he hissed, almost at a whisper. The huntsman hurried to him, keeping low to the ground.

'Sire, what did you find?'

'Nothing. That's the problem. See what you can make of this.' Roth showed the huntsman his chiming auspex.

Silverstein lowered his Exitus rifle and scanned the cave, optiscopic eyes whirring and feeding data. He achieved a lock-on almost instantly.

+++Solitary target, stationary. Height 1.5 metres. Mass density approx. 40–50kg. Target identification: Female, human 98% – Female, xenos 57% – Humanoid, other 36%. Target distance: 298.33 metres. Status temperature – ALIVE.+++

'Sire, I'm reading what appears to be a lady sitting on a snow dune, about three hundred metres to our front. What would you like me to do?' Silverstein asked.

'Nothing yet. Good job Bastiel.' Roth then turned around to face Sergeant Clais Jedda and clicked once for his attention. 'Sergeant, were there any women in the patrol which was lost here?'

The sergeant shook his head. 'There aren't any women in the Assault Pioneers, sah.'

Roth chewed his lip, a nervous habit he had never quite shaken off. Finally, he stood up and gave the hand signal for his team to do likewise. 'Bastiel, we're going to press on as before, but I want you to cover that target with your rifle. Make sure it never leaves your sights and tell me what you see. Clear?'

'Clear, sire.'

With that, the team resumed its cautious advance, prodding through the snow. The ship's ice mesa loomed closer and so did the lone figure at its base.

'Sire, it's definitely a woman. She's seen us too and she has stood up.' They were less than two hundred and fifty metres away now.

'What do you see Bastiel? Tell me what you see.'

'She's young; I'd say no more than thirty standard. She has a weapon too. Some sort of polearm. Could be a secessionist, sire.'

Two hundred metres and closing. Roth's eyes darted across the icescape, seeing a possible ambush behind every crest, every ridge. Despite the relentless cold, Roth was suddenly very glad for the frictionless trauma-plates that hugged his body.

'She's looking straight at me sire,' reported Silverstein.

They were within one hundred metres now and Roth no longer needed Silverstein's relay to see the young woman on the snow dune. He could tell she was slim, made slimmer by the brocaded sapphire silks that cascaded down her frame. Where the broad painted sleeves ended, her forearms were tattooed with verse after verse of war-litanies. She was unmistakably a Blade Artisan.

'Kill her!' urged Sergeant Jedda.

'No! Stand down!' Roth turned and snapped ferociously at the Guard squad.

Ahead, on the crest of the dune, the Blade Artisan had anchored her weapon in the snow: if not a sign of peace, then at least a gesture of armistice. The weapon was as exactly long as she was tall. It was a thin glaive, half of it leather-bound staff, half of it straight blade.

'Come forth and announce yourself,' she commanded firmly.

Roth was wary but recognized diplomacy as the greatest faculty at his disposal. He emulated her gesture by inserting his plasma pistol back onto its shoulder rig.

'I am Inquisitor Obodiah Roth of the Ordo Hereticus, and these–,' he said, gesturing to the men behind him, '–are servants of the God-Emperor.'

'Tread lightly, inquisitor. I am Bekaela of the Blade and this ship is mine to guard.'

'Was it you who slew the soldiers, who came here two days past?'

'Nül. The ship killed them.'

At this reply, Roth heard the thrum of lascarbines as the Guardsmen racked their weapons off safety. Their blood was up and unless Roth could extract some straight answers soon, the situation would be out of his hands.

'Blade Artisan, these men will shoot you soon, unless you tell us what happened.'

Bekaela did not seem at all daunted by his warning. 'Shoot then, if you wish. But I have foresworn my oath to the Sirene Monarch. I have no quarrel with your soldiers.'

'Very well then. What lies in that ship?'

'Nothing. Everything. Sixteen moons ago, they came here to Sirene and claimed to be the Monarch's children – his scions.'

It was not an answer he had been expecting. The Sirene Monarch, Roth knew, had been a cultural figurehead of Sirene, a tradition that harked back to the pre-Imperial history of the planet. It had been the Sirene Monarch who had renounced Imperial dominion and ousted Lord Planetary Governor Vandt. Pre-war records had shown that when the isolated Imperial outposts and missions had been overrun, the natives certainly had no access to interplanetary travel and there had never been mention of the Monarch's offspring.

'Scions?' Roth asked.

Bekaela nodded. 'Yes, his children came in this ship, sixteen moons ago. The Monarch embraced his children and welcomed them home. It had been a grand ceremony; many clan-fighters had feasted there. I know because I was there too.'

'The Sirene Monarch has been in hiding ever since the war began, if not dead,' Roth countered. He could sense something poisonous was at work on this planet and part of him did not want to believe it.

'He is not dead. I know where he hides,' Bekaela said.

That was almost too much information to digest at once. Since the beginning of the campaign, Imperial forces had been driven in relentless pursuit of the fugitive Monarch, slated as the spiritual leadership of the guerrilla insurgency. Hundreds of aerial bombing runs, thousands of infantry patrols had all amounted to nothing. But now this.

'Why would you give us this information?' Roth pressed.

'Because I've seen what lies in that ship and if they are the Monarch's bloodline, then he is no Monarch of mine!' she proclaimed.

It only dawned on Roth then, that Bekaela was not guarding the ship from intruders. She was guarding against whatever lay within from getting out.

Sergeant Jedda, however, was not one to be convinced. 'It's a trap. That witch probably gave my boys the same speech before they got off'd,' he growled. His men chorused in assent.

Roth was not so quick to make his conclusion. The significance of her story, if true, was far too monumental to dismiss. His duty as an inquisitor compelled him to investigate deeper. Stepping forward, slightly away from his team, Roth summoned a subtle wisp of mind force and gently probed her mind. Bekaela tensed visibly from the intrusion.

'What did you just do?!' she hissed.

'I was testing your intentions.'

'Don't do that again, or I'll kill you and make it painful.'

Roth nodded sincerely. He would not. Besides, he already knew all that he needed to know. She was telling the truth, on both accounts.

'My team and I, we must explore this ship.'

'Then I will come with you,' she said. Her tone brokered no argument.

'So you are willing to aid us?' Roth mused. 'As an ally?'

'No. I hate you. But I will help my people. They do not know what I know. I've been in that ship.'

'What's in there?' Roth asked.

'You will see,' was the answer.

The ship was alive.

Or at least that was what Roth first thought. Wet ropes of muscle and pulsing arteries groped and twisted along the walls and mesh decking of the dormant ship. The air was nauseatingly warm and humid. It was as if something infinitely virulent and shapeless was incubating within the cruiser's metal chassis.

Roth's team had entered via a breach in the ship's hull and found themselves in a disused maintenance bay. Banks of workbenches lined the walls where raw tendrils of flesh had begun to creep over them. In the upper-left corner of the ceiling, an enormous balloon of puffy flesh expanded and contracted rhythmically like a monstrous lung.

Further exploration of the ship's corridors, deck and compartment revealed only more of its pulsating innards. The deeper into the heart of the cruiser they progressed, the thicker the infestation. The walkway that led to the ship's bridge funnelled into an orifice of ridged cartilage. They could see no further, as a pink membrane of tissue expanded over the entrance.

'Do you know where we are?' Roth asked Bekaela.

'Nül. I have never been beyond the first compartment. This place is cursed, it's all bad following.'

Roth was not sure the Blade Artisan's prognosis was the correct one, but it was apt enough. He moved toward the membrane, careful not to step in the pools of semi-viscous liquid that collected on the deck plating. He holstered his pistol and was in the act of gingerly reaching out to touch the organic membrane when all three auspexes in his team chimed simultaneously. Roth froze.

'What's the reading?' he asked.

'I'm getting multiple rapid movements converging on this corridor intersection,' one of the Assault Pioneers reported.

'Yes sir, I'm getting the same readings,' another trooper echoed.

Roth about turned, drew his pistol and trained it on the inflamed flesh cavity that was once a t-junction.

'Readings are too fast. I suspect we're just picking up latent electrical currents from the ship's circuitry,' a third trooper added. They waited in tense silence.

'Trooper Wessel, double time ten paces back and get me a new reading. We could be standing under an electrical hub,' Sergeant Jedda barked.

With his eyes on the auspex and carbine hard against the shoulder, Trooper Wessel approached the intersection. He peered into the gloom, sweeping his auspex about to get a better reading.

The thing slashed out of the darkness so fast it severed Wessel's spine and bounded off his corpse. Streaking through the air in a shower of blood, it landed on another trooper crouched within the corridor and eviscerated him too. An eruption of wild las-fire crazed the spot where the thing had been, but it was moving again.

'What the hell is that?' Roth shouted at Silverstein as his plasma pistol unleashed a mini-nova of energy down the corridor.

The huntsman tried to get a lock on the creature as it slammed into its third victim. He barely registered the profile of its blurring outline.

+++*Target analysis: Xenos, Hormagaunt. Subspecies: Unknown. Origin: Unknown. Hive fleet: Unknown – Data Source: Ultramar (745.M41)*.+++

'Tyranid,' Silverstein replied. With a spectacular shot that anticipated the creature's next running leap, he blew out its skull carapace with an Exitus round.

Another two shapes shrieked into the corridor, straight into the storm of fire laid down by Roth's team. The inquisitor aimed his pistol, ready to fire when it seemed like the world exploded behind him. The membrane plugging the ship's command bridge burst, and from the darkness surged a monster so tall it was almost bent double in the corridor. From its segmented torso, four bone scythes connected to hawser cables of muscle slashed like threshing sickles. As an inquisitor, Roth was privy to knowledge otherwise deemed heretical for others. Yet knowing the enemy and its power sometimes replaced ignorance with fear. Roth recognised the thorny frame of sinew and plate hurtling towards him and froze in shocked awe.

It was a genestealer broodlord and it was on him so fast he had no time to react. The only thing that saved him was Bekaela's glaive singing through the air to intercept the beast. The Blade Artisan pirouetted with a twirling downward stroke that severed one of the monstrosity's upper limbs. In reply, the tyranid speared her into the wall with a battering ram of psychic force.

Roth wasted no time in engaging the broodlord. He activated his Tang War-pattern power gauntlet and moved inside the broodlord's guard with a thunderous right-hook. The creature snaked back its torso with serpentine grace, evading the blow and swept in with its three remaining hook-scythes. Roth ducked, feeling an organic blade skip against the frictionless shoulder plate of his armour.

They fought on two separate planes. While their bodies raged, so too were their minds locked in a psychic duel. The tyranid was much stronger, its mind a tidal wave of raw, seething force. Roth was not a potent psyker, but what ability he had, he utilised well, sharpening and tightening his will into a poignard of deliverance. Although the broodlord's mind was like the staggering force of a blind avalanche, Roth's was the clean mind-spikes and mental ripostes of a Progenium-trained psychic duellist. It was like a death struggle between the kraken and the swordfish.

On the physical plane, Bekaela struck again. She was barely conscious and fought purely from muscle memory. Spinning her glaive like a lariat she hoped she was aiming for the right target. The paper-thin blade sliced deep into the broodlord's flank, snapping through the corded muscle. The creature shrieked at a decibel so high, the ship quavered in empathy.

It was exactly the distraction Roth needed. Sensing the sudden gap in the genestealer's mental defences, Roth tightened his will into an atom of focus and surged through the slip in its psychic barrier. Once through, he exploded into a billion slivered needles, expanding infinitesimally outwards.

The broodlord died quickly. With it, the last of the hormagaunts in the corridor lost all synaptic control and were literally disassembled by gunfire. Yet as it expired, the broodlord's mental shell collapsed, plunging Roth into its mind, like a spearman breaking through a shield wall headlong through the other side. Roth was utterly unprepared for what happened next.

He saw a hive fleet, at the furthest edges of his mind's eye. He saw it looming larger, so ravenous and hungry. He felt, no, heard the psychic song that was drawing it closer, like a pulse, like droplets of blood rippling outwards in the ocean. The song was coming from Sirene Primal, a poisonous ugly sound that drove spikes into his psyker mind. A swansong. All at once, it fell into place like a crystal fragmenting in rewind. He saw the ship, and its genestealer brood, the children of the Sirene Monarch. He saw their minds pulsing in unison, calling to their hive, calling for salvation. The psychic vacuum shut down his nervous system and Roth's heart stopped beating.

'Sire! Can you hear me?!'

The voice wrenched Roth back into consciousness, wrenching him to the surface like a drowning man. The first thing he saw was Silverstein, the yellow pupils of his bioscope implants wide with concern. Had it not been for the huntsman's voice, he would have died standing up.

'Sire? You look bloodless,' said the huntsman reaching forward to steady Roth. The inquisitor, in a daze, brushed Silverstein off and fell against the cartilage tunnel, sliding down to his knees.

'Kill it... kill him. Find him. Kill him,' he murmured weakly.

'Kill who?'

'Kill the Monarch,' Roth called, a little louder as he pulled himself up. 'The Monarch. Father of the brood.'

Beyond the Sephardi ranges, Imperial artillery was pounding the mountains to rubble and the rubble to dust. The steady *krang krang krang* of the batteries sounded like thousand tonne slabs of rockrete in collision. In the tomb-vaults below the mountains, deep within the arterial labyrinth, billions of ancestral caskets tremored under the brutal bombardment. Finally, down amongst their dead, the Sirene Monarch's hidden legions would make ready for their last battle.

The assault on the Sirene tomb-vaults had started before dawn. To their credit, Imperial high command had been quick to react, with Lord Marshal Cambria personally overseeing the mobilization of a quick reaction force within six hours. Inquisitor Roth's discovery had hammered a shockwave through the campaign's war-planners and they were eager to seize the initiative. The stalemate, it seemed, was about to be broken.

By the time the Sirenese sunrise had tinged the night sky a bruised orange, Assault Pioneers of the Montaigh 45th had breached the tomb underworld. Combined elements of the Kurassian Lance-Commandoes and five squadrons of the 8th Amartine Scout Cavalry, alongside three full battalions of Assault Pioneers had been committed to the operation.

It was all a decoy. The decisive strike of the assault had been the insertion of a kill-team directly into the Sirene Monarch's last refuge, once secessionist forces were pre-engaged. Led by Inquisitor Roth and guided by Bekaela of the Blade, a platoon of Montaigh 45th and a squad of bull-necked Kurassian Lance-Commandoes had penetrated the cerebral core of the tomb complex. Precision breach charges rigged up by airborne sappers had seen to that.

The kill team now prowled beneath a monolithic vault of basalt. According to Bekaela's hand-sketched schematics, which Roth had committed to memory, it was the Monarch's atrium. The walls were so thick and black with age they seemed to absorb sound and light. Of the distant sounds of combat, Roth heard nothing. Even their long-range vox-sets were dead.

It was the oceanic silence that unsettled him most.

The atrium was so very still, dark and quiet. A white bar of sun lanced from the soaring heights of the ceiling, laying down a smeared ghostly light. But it wasn't just the silence that was unsettling, there were those damned pools of water too, Inquisitor Roth seethed to himself. There was water everywhere.

From enormous bowls to dishes, troughs and ponds, basins and urns, everywhere Roth looked he saw stagnant bodies of water stretching into the deepest shadows of that chamber. Most of the pools had developed a slick surface of green algae, and others were scattered with pale lotus blossoms; all of them sat stagnant and silent.

'When the Sirene Monarch meets the boys of the Montaigh Forty-fifth, I want it to be the most traumatic experience of his life!' Sergeant Jedda's call clapped through the still air. The Guardsmen all roared in unison.

Despite his failings, Jedda was a natural troop leader. As an inquisitor, Roth was glad the Imperium had men like Sergeant Clais Jedda to unleash upon its enemies. The kill-team broke into a run now, cutting for the throne chamber that lay beyond.

Falling in step behind Roth was Bastiel Silverstein. He toggled the target lock of his hunting crossbow to active and loaded a prey-seeker missile. The light polymer sleekness of a Veskepine *arcuballista* was ideal for tunnel assault. Running point was Bekaela, who was now dressed in the Sirenese regalia of vengeance. Her face was painted a leering mask of white and crimson, symbolising the witch-ghosts who claimed the dead. Her sapphire robes were cinched tight by a waist belt, woven from the hair of slain enemies and a flak-musket was slung over her shoulder.

Racing down the thousand-metre walkway, Roth's retinue finally emerged into the Sirene throne chamber. The room was vast, humbling even the impressive scale of the antechamber. Basalt walls and pillars of thickly veined marble soared up into the heavens, the ceiling completely lost from sight. A path of jade flowed down the centre of the throne room, flanked on either side by legions of water-bearing vessels. Once again, Roth noted there was water everywhere. He didn't have time to ask Bekaela why.

'The patient court of the Sirene Monarch bids you welcome,' a smooth androgynous voice announced. The source of the voice came from powerful vox-casters set into the arms of the Monarch's jade throne. Upon that throne sat the Monarch himself.

He wore a high-collared gown of ruby red silk, the hem and sleeves spilling out for several metres from his throne. His hands, folded demurely upon his lap, were capped with long needles of silver. None could look upon his face for a veil of pearls shimmered down his onion-domed crown. The Monarch's ten dozen scions were arrayed below his throne in seated tiers, a chilling calm instilled by their impassive stares.

The aura of ethereal dignity was so great, Roth noticed, that some of the troops lowered their guns and gazes involuntarily. Roth, on the other hand, raised his chin and stared deep into the pearl veil.

'The Ordo Hereticus is here to bury you,' he shouted in reply.

The choir of sons arrayed below the Monarch rippled with shrill chortling. They were exactly as Bekaela had described in the pre-op briefing. Eunuchs, all of them. Slim and effete, all were clad in ankle-length gowns of pastel silk, pinks and purples and creamy jades. They appeared human enough, but even at a distance Roth could see their coral pink skin, semi-opaque and laced with delicate red veins.

Curiously, all of their left hands had been amputated. The gold-capped stumps of their forearms were attached to thick tendrils of silk cord. The long braids forming a muscular rope of fabric over a metre long. Like some bizarre pendulum, at the end of each length interwoven knots formed a fist-sized sphere of silk.

Roth could not gauge the symbolic significance of these amputations. Dimly, he remembered archival files regarding the Tyrant of Quan, on the fringes of the Tuvalii Subsector. Such was his fear of assassination, the Tyrant had ordered all who entered his court to don fluted gauntlets of glass. The flutes of those fragile gloves had been chased with acid and shattered under the slightest force. So great was his paranoia the Tyrant had even forced his three thousand wives to wear them in his bedchambers. Alas, Roth remembered with a glimmer of dark humour, those gloves did not save him from the mouth dart of a Callidus assassin.

However, if the Monarch was offended by his brazen threat, his veiled visage offered no sign. Instead his soft sexless voice emitted through his throne-casters, emotionless and measured.

'I cannot allow that,' he stated, rising from his throne.

The air immediately grew brittle and cold. To Roth's right, Bekaela's glaive went slack in her grip and her eyes glazed over. To his left, Bastiel Silverstein moaned softly.

'Witchery!' Roth raised his plasma pistol a millisecond too late. A psychic bolt exploded from the Monarch, warping the air around it into an oscillating cone. It tore through Inquisitor Roth and threw him thirty feet down the ivory path in a spray of blood and black glass. The psychic aftershock rippled through the room like a stone in a pond, coating every surface in a thick rime of frost.

The mind blow would have liquefied any normal man. But Obodiah Roth had a trump card. The glinting hauberk of psi-reactive crystal had absorbed the brunt of the psyker's power. As shards of black glass scattered in a blizzard around him, Roth realised the armour would not survive another psychic attack. And neither would he. Blood and bile oozed from his mouth and nose in thick strings. His head swam and he could barely see.

Dimly, he could hear the chatter of gunfire, as if very far away in the distance. He could hear Silverstein yelling but he couldn't make out the words. The only coherent thought in his mind was that the Monarch psyker must be temporarily weakened from his tremendous mind blast. That gave Roth a few seconds to nullify him before he gathered the strength to finish them all off.

He looked up, fighting down the urge to vomit. The world appeared at a slant. The Monarch's scions had formed a phalanx around him. As one, they dipped their long silk pendulums into the many water vessels in the chamber, letting the water soak into the fabric. The innocuous silk spheres instantly become heavy flails.

'Sly bastards,' Roth hissed through a mouthful of broken teeth. To his flanks, the Guardsmen continued to rake a steady stream of las-rounds at the Monarch's scions. 'I'll bet my balls that they're wearing armour under those gowns too,' Roth laughed darkly to himself. Some of the scions were slammed off their feet by the kinetic force of the shots, only to get back up and continue charging the inquisitor's team.

'Fix bayonets!' someone, somewhere, shouted. The voice was washed with distortion to Roth's trauma-shocked ears.

The Assault Pioneers did as commanded, forming a staggered rank of fighting blades. The Kurassian Lance-Commandoes drew their serrated short-swords, howling and clashing the weapons to armoured chests. Together they met the charge of the scions.

Roth staggered to his feet, fighting to regain his balance as a eunuch stormed down the ivory path toward him. Bastiel Silverstein's polished boots suddenly filled Roth's vision, as the old retainer stood over the dazed inquisitor. The xenos game hunter aimed his crossbow. He had swapped to a rapid-fire cartridge, designed to bring down swift moving game. On automatic, Silverstein could empty all twelve bolts into his assailant in three seconds. He needed only one. A salvo of bolts tore out the eunuch's face, the neural toxins causing the assailant to spasm so hard his spine broke. He dropped to the floor, his one hand locked into a flexing claw.

'Are you good? Are you good?' Silverstein screamed at the inquisitor.

Roth finally found his footing and nodded vaguely.

'Stop fussing over me and snipe that psyker bastard already,' Roth managed to gasp.

'Can't draw a bead. He's got some sort of force generator. The kill-team almost bled their ammunition dry trying to crack him open. We'll have to get in close,' said Silverstein.

Roth grimaced and ran a hand over his bloodied face. 'Well he's thought of everything then, hasn't he? Cover me.' The inquisitor shook his head once more to clear it. There was a dark spot in his left field of vision and he hoped his brain wasn't haemorrhaging. Casting all doubt aside, he lifted his right hand. The one clad in a slim-fitting gauntlet of blue steel. A Tang War-pattern power gauntlet. The weapon hummed with a deep magnetic throb, the disruption field sparking like a blue halo.

Breaking into a run, he made straight for the throne. Assailants appeared in the corners of his vision but Silverstein's covering fire was lethally efficient. The streaks of grey slashed over his shoulder and head, one passing so close to his face he could feel its passing and hear its viper-like hiss. The bolts intercepted the scions as Roth ran their deadly gauntlet, down the ivory path towards the throne.

The inquisitor kept a mental count of each bolt as they flew past until finally, he counted the full twelve. Silverstein would need to reload. He was only a scant ten paces away from the throne; the Monarch still slumped in his seat recovering when a eunuch threw himself at him.

Roth turned, his reflexes still sluggish from his mind thrashing. Howling, the eunuch whipped the silk flail into his lower ribs and Roth exhaled a painful jet of air. He tried to bring his plasma pistol to bear but the flail lashed in again, this time snapping into his hand. *My hand's broken*, Roth thought numbly, adding it to his long list of injuries as the pistol slipped from broken fingers.

Eager for the kill, the eunuch pressed his advantage. The silk flail's trajectory arced toward Roth's head. With more luck than timing, the inquisitor slipped under the blow and drove his power fist into the eunuch's chest. The gauntlet's disruption field flared into a bright corona of light as he drove his hand clean through the Eunuch's chest. His assailant simply dropped onto his rear and slumped over backwards.

Knowing he had no time to spare, Roth spun on his heels and turned on the Monarch. The psyker was almost at full strength. Already he had forced himself onto his feet, his eyes turning into milky orbs as he gathered his will for another psychic bolt. The temperature was dropping like a countdown timer. Roth had all of one second to react before he was dead.

'Now!' cried Inquisitor Roth as he launched himself at the psyker. Extending his power fist, he rammed the weapon into the Monarch's invisible force bubble. As disruption field met force field there was a static shriek and a blossoming wall of blinding light. Then the jade throne's force generator blew a fuse. The force field shattered, air filling its void with a low thunderclap. Roth flew himself flat before the throne.

Bastiel Silverstein emptied all twelve bolts into the Monarch in three seconds flat. At fifty paces, every bolt found its mark and pinned the psyker to his throne like a broken marionette. Almost as an afterthought, Bekaela's flak-musket spat a cone of flechette at the corpse, stitching it with smoking holes.

Then it was over, as quickly as it had begun. Except for the cordite hiss of gun smoke, and the baying of the Kurassian Lance-Commandoes as they took the eunuchs apart, the battle was over. The metallic scent of blood and gunfire filled the chamber.

Inquisitor Obodiah Roth picked himself up and brushed himself off. He coughed and spat a bloody tooth at what was left of the Monarch. Bending down, he slapped the Monarch's veiled crown with a backhand.

A face of sharp alien angles stared back at him with dead eyes. Dead dark xenos eyes. The ridged forehead was streaked with blood and his slack mouth was a nest of teeth, like translucent needles.

'Genestealers,' said the inquisitor.

Wearily, he turned to his team and the carnage before him. During his tenure as an interrogator, Roth had survived a clutch of firefights. His mentor, Liszt Vandevern, had been a prolific field inquisitor who believed a raid would always reap more answers than clinical investigation. Before his thirtieth year, Roth had skirmished with half a dozen heretic cults, and even besieged the compound of a narco-baron on the death world of Sans Gaviria. But none of that could compare to the brutality of a close-quarter firearms assault.

The throne room was a butcher's hall. Most of the bodies were dressed in gossamer silks, thrown in disarray like crushed butterflies. Dozens of immense water vessels had been upturned or shot through, flooding the chamber with a pane of rosy, blood-tinted water. Other bodies scattered about were in either Montaigh or Kurassian battledress. Nearest to Roth, a Kurassian commando had died sitting up, the fingers of his gauntlet locked around the throat of an enemy. The Guardsman had been shot over a dozen times, but he had not released the chokehold.

Around Roth, his kill-team moved quickly from body to body. It seemed to him that they were but going through the motions, high-powered weapons at close proximity rarely left survivors.

'Sire – we have a live one sire,' Silverstein said.

Roth snapped out of his post-conflict daze and realised Silverstein had been standing at the base of the throne for some time, calling repeatedly. He followed the huntsman, sloshing through the pink water towards a huddle of Guardsmen with their weapons raised. As the circle parted for the inquisitor, they revealed a scion sitting wounded on the chamber floor.

It was genetically more man than xenos, Roth recognized that immediately. Yet nestled within the brow of its orbed forehead, its eyes were like iridescent pools of black oil devoid of any human quality. Most startling of all was the creature's parody of symbiote weapons. Up close, the silk flail, damp and glistening was not unlike a muscled mace appendage. Its right sleeve was torn, unveiling a hand fused to an obsolete machine pistol, brown with well-worked grease. The flesh and fingers were smeared like wax into the heavy calibre pistol, whether by coincidence or design to resemble some organic biomorph.

'It can talk, sire,' said Silverstein, nodding towards the creature.

The scion had taken the stray round of a Kurassian shotgun. Its left leg was peppered with bleeding perforations and pockmarked with powder burns. It looked up, met Roth's gaze and smiled mockingly, revealing clusters of quill-like teeth.

Perhaps if Roth had been older, wiser and more patient he could have dealt with the matter by more tactful means. But as it was, Roth was none of those things. The inquisitor simply pounded forward and snagged the scion's collar in his fist.

'How long has this planet been infected?!' Roth screamed into the creature's face.

'Why does it matter?' the scion replied, his vocal cords cut with a coarse alien inflection.

'Because I asked you!' shouted Roth. He hauled down on the scion's embroidered collar, slamming its head into the marble floor. The creature came up snorting water out of its nostril slits and started to laugh, a thrilled harmonic peal that bounced around the chamber walls.

Bekaela appeared by Roth's side and laid a hand on his shoulder. 'Kill him. Just kill him and be done,' she said.

'Not until it answers me!' hissed Roth. Still tight in his clinch, he manhandled the creature, jerking the scion from its seated position and forcing it down on its wounded side. The action elicited a shuddering exhalation of agony. Satisfied, Roth repeated the question again. 'How did it start?'

'Three generations ago,' the scion snarled through its teeth. 'Our fathers came to Sirene as missionaries to spread the seed of the great family and his blessed children.'

In truth, the admission did not surprise Roth. It was almost elementary. Sirene was a frontier world and missionaries had been the only true Imperial outposts on the planet. Incidentally, those clerics and ecclesiarches were also the only ones to access warp-capable vessels.

'It was perfect,' crooned the scion. 'By seven winters of equinox, Sirene's firstborn prince was of blessed blood. He was the father of fathers. When He ascended the throne, this world was ours for the taking.'

'When did the taint spread to the rest of Sirene?' Roth asked through gritted teeth.

'Patience, patience. I'm getting to that,' chortled the creature. It was clearly enjoying the narrative, drawing itself up theatrically. 'We did not need to, you see. The martial sects had always chafed under Imperial occupation and when our Monarch declared rebellion, they were our herd and we their shepherd. With the sect warriors under our banner, the rest of the Sirenese followed quietly enough.

'We set about purging all Imperial influence from this realm.

Sect-Chieftains who were resistant quickly became silent when their wives were poisoned and denounced as conspirators. There were a thousand public executions of Imperial loyalists each day for many years. The Sirene renaissance was endemic.

'The local militia did not even try to fight but we cleansed them anyway. Soft and idle, they were civic militia drawn from the ranks of poets, sculptors and merchants, for no sect fighter would ever debase himself by devotion to the Imperium. Any Sirenese in the militia uniform of tan brocades and gilded tall-helm was a traitor. When the executions started, they barely knew how to operate their autorifles. Most of their weapons were still wrapped in the soft plastic covers they were delivered in.

'They died so quickly. On the Isles of Khyber the blessed children killed an entire division of them in one day. Can you believe it? Twelve thousand loyalists lined up and buried alive. Oh, it was a golden age.'

At this Bekeala interjected, her eyes red and watery with rage, 'Enough! We do not need to hear this. Let me kill him!'

'One more thing,' growled Roth as he pulled the scion's grinning visage close to his face. 'The psychic backlash, the planetary swansong. Your brood is responsible...'

'I am surprised you belittle yourself by asking,' it said smugly.

Roth released the scion and took a step back. He let the answer settle heavily on his chest and sink into the pit of his stomach. Like the final stroke of an oiled brush, the painting was complete. He had resolved the matter for the ordo, but it would be a pyrrhic victory. It was already too late for Sirene Primal.

'Absolutely correct psyker. It is far too late. Our choir has been singing to the family, calling out to the warp and the family answered our call.'

Looking down, Roth drew his sidearm in anger. He had slackened his guard and the xenos breed had gleaned his surface thoughts. 'How long do we have?' asked Roth, reasserting his question with an octave of psychic amplification.

The scion simply rolled back his head and laughed. His laughter came in great shrieking bursts, resonating with the thunderous acoustics of a cyclopean hall. It was all too much. Roth took aim with his pistol. His finger slipped inside the trigger. Yet before he applied pressure, the scion's face threw out a great crest of blood.

Roth lowered his weapon, breathing heavily. Bekaela was by his side, her silver glaive streaked with strings of crimson gore. She was terrifying. The paint on her face smeared with sweat and fury, a daemonic visage melting down her cheeks. At her feet the scion lay, a cloud of bright red hazing the water and forming a halo around its skull.

But the laughter did not abate. Long after the scion was dead, the laughter continued to toll through the chamber.

* * *

The annals of Imperial history would not be kind to Sirene Primal. It was recorded in M866.M41 that a xenos armada known collectively as a hive fleet entered the Orco-Pelica Subsector. On the most urgent warning of an Inquisitor Obodiah Roth, all senior officers and dignitaries were evacuated. The Imperial Navy was ordered to withdraw, regroup and re-engage. Sporadic reports from retreating naval forces described the incursion as a *seething wave of oblivion*.

On Sirene Primal, seventy thousand Guardsmen of Montaigh, Kurass and Amartine dug in on the rugged Sephardi ranges to stall the xenos advance. It is said, that within three months the mountains had been transformed into a sprawling network of artillery palisades, tunnelled barbicans and interlocking firing nests. Once the xenos made landfall, the Guardsmen were expected to hold out for eight weeks. They lasted less than five hours.

The ensuing campaign to reclaim the subsector is itself a historic epic worthy of narrative, but of Sirene Primal there was no more. In the end, the lonely jewel on the Eastern Fringes became little more than a smudged ink record in the forgotten archives of Terra.

EMPEROR'S MERCY

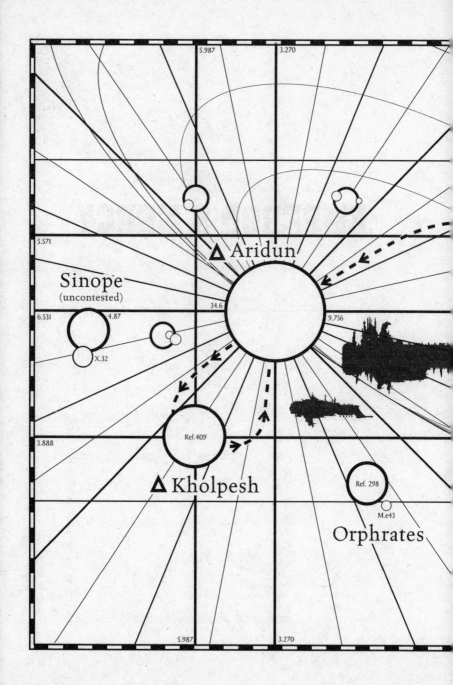

5.987   3.270

5.571

△ Aridun

Sinope
(uncontested)

6.531   4.87   34.6   9.756

X.32

Ref.409

3.888

△ Kholpesh

Ref. 298

M.e43

Orphrates

5.987   3.270

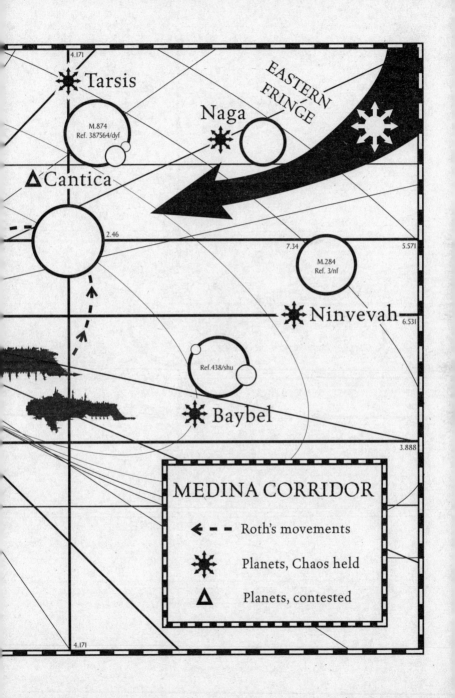

PROLOGUE

The first projectile thundered into the tenement bazaar. It hit with a percussive blast that could be heard in the terracotta valleys far beyond.

Carving a plume of debris, the vessel ploughed into a picket of tea stalls and spice carts, its fifty-tonne bulk skipping with momentum. Finally it penetrated one of the tenements that flanked the commercial district, demolishing the entire bottom tier.

Jolted by the seismic collision, human congestion in the narrow market lanes sounded a shrill chorus of panic. Streets began to flood with hurried, confused foot traffic, like a sprawling river system. The stacked buildings and overhanging roofs gave them no room to flee or see the commotion. Dust clouds of ochre yellow, the powdered stone of ancient buildings, formed a solid wall around the crash site.

Vinimus Dahlo had been toiling at his tea cart when it happened. He had been nursing urns of sweet black tea over an iron griddle with expert hands, and had not seen the collision at all. Rather he had felt it, a sonic tremor that shot up his spine and rocked the base of his skull. When Dahlo looked up, the locals perched or squatting on the stools around him were all pointing in one direction and exclaiming in shrill agitation.

They were pointing down the narrow avenue. Down past the canvas awnings and the rafts of grain sacks, silk fillets of various hues, porcelain and dried fruits. Down to where the mezzanine avenue had been ruptured by some colossal cartridge from the skies.

Dahlo left his tea cart unattended, an uncharacteristic act for a man of his sensibilities. Suddenly seized by fear, he pushed and prodded his way into the crowd, craning to catch a glimpse of the destruction. Traders, labourers and flocks of women in shawls faltered in their work, gravitating towards the crash site.

When the rolling blossom of dust began to wilt, it revealed a long iron pod nestled within the rubble. It resembled some beached ocean submersible, its metal hide flaking with rust and oxidised scorching.

No one knew what to make of it. Naga was a frontier world of the Medina Corridor, and the only aeronautical vessels that frequented these ports were the Imperial ships that claimed their tithes of textiles, ceramics and spices. Perhaps because of this, when the belly of the vessel popped free with a hydraulic hiss, the throng only edged closer.

Dahlo, however, began to back-pedal against the tide. He was not one to be swept up by an inquisitive herd. Something, whether it was the hot prickling in the nape of his neck or the coiling sensation his stomach, warned him that all was not right.

An armoured figure clawed out of the hatch, like the birth of some ghastly newborn. Its head emerged first, humanoid in shape yet wholly bound with bars of some ferrous alloy. It then dragged its armoured torso over the lip of the hatch, a cuirass of chainmail and iron petals. Simultaneously, turret hatches began to peel away on both sides of the beached vessel. Armoured silhouettes began to surface. That was when the killing started.

It began with a solitary shot that echoed in the awkward stillness of the bazaar. A las-round crumpled a young girl. She slumped lifelessly against the press of bodies behind her as panic began to ripple outwards like capillary waves. Screams of outrage and confusion interspersed with the whickering snaps of rifles broke the calm that had existed mere seconds before.

High above the tenement bazaar, more vessels pierced the clouds. Against the ochre sky a dozen vessels turned into hundreds, the hundreds turned into thousands.

Less than two kilometres from the bazaar, high up on the garrison walls, the 22nd Naga Air Defence Squadron stood sentry. Even at extreme optical zoom with their sentry scopes, they could not see the killing in the markets. But the soldiers could see the pulsating lights of pink and purple las throbbing in the distance, and it made their palms sweaty and their jaws tense. Around them, like autumnal shedding, craft similar to the speck which had plummeted into the commercial district, were falling in thick sleets.

The monstrous rigs of their quad-linked autocannons nosed out over the haphazard tiers of terraces and tenements. Like most military hardware on Naga, it was obsolete and had been harboured behind an abandoned chariot shed almost as an afterthought. The weapons themselves were Onager-pattern anti-aircraft platforms. A primitive yet reliable indigenous design, each 50mm barrel was pneumatically driven. The combined rate of fire was typically six thousand rounds per minute of low-altitude air deterrence. Mounted on the flat-tiled roofs and minarets of most Nagaan cities, it was a workhorse of the Naga Militia Combine squadrons against both ground and air targets.

Major Meas Chanta of the 22nd Naga Air Defence Squadron wanted nothing more than to unleash those six thousand rounds as he watched strange foreign objects fall from the sky. Standing on the disc platform high above the cityscape, the major squinted through his magnoculars as the distant specks plummeted with an eerie grace.

'What orders from the division HQ?' asked Chanta.

'Stand by until further direction, sir,' replied his vox operator. It had been the same answer for the past forty minutes, and in truth Chanta had not expected anything different. A curtain of vessels were dropping down, bruising the amber cloud bars an ominous black, but still they waited.

The squadron company were arrayed in an overlapping fire pattern, batteries of Onager anti-air platforms anchored on the highest points across the city. They were one hundred and twenty men in all, clad in quilted gambesons of khaki twill – the uniform of the Naga Combine. The padded flak coats had high collar guards that shielded the lower face from the biting perennial dust storms. These part-time citizen soldiers had been summoned to their ready stations less than forty minutes ago, when the first vessels had entered the atmosphere. But the mobilisation had faltered there, milling into the disordered confusion of a hesitant defence strategy.

Chanta chewed on his lower lip, a habit of anxiety that he had not indulged in since childhood. This time he drew blood. He was a ledger clerk by trade, and his commission had been passed down from his father on account of his high education and public standing. But Chanta was not a soldier; his hands were uncallused and inked from years of wielding the quill. This was no place for him. Around Chanta, the 22nd squadron were braced in tense silence, some looking up vacantly at the sky, others looking to him for direction.

He had none to give them. Naga was a tiny rimward world in the Lusitan Sub on the Eastern Fringe, and military prowess was not a defining feature. The military seniors were in disarray and unable to provide decisive leadership to the soldiers that manned Naga's increasingly obsolete military arsenal.

For most of his men it was the first time the klaxons had summoned them to their stations for anything other than a drill. They were looking to him and he had nothing to give them. Still the vessels continued to fall.

'Tell me again in exact words why we are to hold fire,' Chanta asked his vox operator. He had asked him before, but he needed to hear it again.

'Sir, long-range signal instruments have failed to identify the incoming objects. Although they appear to be landers, preliminary defensive measures cannot commence until proper identification can be ascertained, sir,' came the reply.

Chanta wasn't really listening any more. To describe Naga's signal instruments as archaic would be a generous assessment. The corroded array of listening stations strung up across the dune spires of the western Naga continents would be hard-pressed to pick up a ship's presence let alone its source signature.

He looked up into the sky as if searching for some divine guidance. Whether he found it or not, the galaxy of landers swarming across his field of vision made him resolute.

'Corporal, commence vox orders to fire,' Major Chanta ordered.

'Sir?' asked the squadron vox operator, his features creased with confusion.

'Commence firing orders. Please, corporal, do hurry,' Chanta said as he cinched the padded khaki of his collar guard tight across his lower face. He did not want his men to see his bloodied lower lip, already clouding his ivory uniform a vivid pink. Major Chanta had never been so wracked with fear in his entire life. If he was wrong there would be hell to pay, but if he was right, then it would not matter either way.

In the subterranean depths, the repository trembled. Tunnels and vaults, networked beneath the continents like coiled intestinal tracts, were not spared the cataclysm, despite their deep insulation. Grit shook from the rafters as multiple impacts from the surface continued the rhythmic pounding. The aftershocks travelled through the catacomb libraries and were felt even in the archives. The script silos too were trembling violently. It seemed that Naga would collapse from the inside out.

Elhem Meteadas, senior archivist, was beginning to fear the worst. A buttress of books three hundred metres high began to shiver precariously, rocking on wooden supports so old they were ashen. A volume of *The Movement of Stars*, a nine-hundred-year-old almanac, was dislodged from its shelving seventy metres up the northern vault face. It came whistling past Meteadas and exploded on the tiling next to him in a fluttering swirl of parchment.

'Meteadas! Meteadas! What is happening?' shrieked Scholar Amado.

'I–' he began. But the senior archivist did not know how to finish the answer. Meteadas was well into his one fifties and had been a keeper of the texts for almost all of those years. Some would consider him a polymath, a man with encyclopaedic depth of knowledge. If anyone on Naga understood the catastrophe that was occurring on the surface above, he would likely be one of them. Yet Meteadas did not want to incite panic.

'Earthquake of course,' he lied.

'That cannot be! This section of the repository does not lie under any planar fractures or subduction zones,' yelled the scholar as he gripped the sleeves of Meteadas's linen shift.

'Are you familiar with the works of Aloysius Spur?'

'No...'

'Excellent. Then you have absolutely nothing to worry about,' Meteadas quipped as he shrugged off Amado.

'But Meteadas, some of the others say it is fighting! Are they fighting? Why would there be fighting?'

Elhem Meteadas sighed deeply. Perhaps the others already knew, or perhaps they had already read the same texts he had. The labyrinthine libraries tightly woven beneath the surface of Naga served as the central repository of the Medina Worlds. Although they archived everything from the war poetry of pre-Heresy to subsector trade outputs of last month, it was a possibility. The writings of Aloysius Spur may have been a lesser-known work, but all archivists were at heart hoarders of obscure knowledge.

'Why would anyone bother fighting for the Medina Worlds but for the Old Kings of Medina?' Meteadas admitted solemnly.

At this Amado threw back his head and laughed. 'The Old Kings of Medina are one of the great mythical tales.'

'Then for what reason, Amado? You are a learned man, a polymath. Have you learned nothing? Naga is a minuscule planet of a frontier sector. It has neither strategic relevance nor resources of note.'

It was the elder's turn to seize the younger man's cotton chemise. 'Aloysius Spur warned us about the Old Kings of Medina. He foretold that they would bring war from the stars. Why do you laugh about it?'

'Because, Elhem, they are children's stories! Relics from the Age of Apostasy, buried and lost on one of the Medina Worlds? There is not even a plausible account of what or where they may be! Pure fabrication!'

'Aloysius Spur did not fabricate; he observed the laws of inevitability. If the Old Kings were lost in the Medina Worlds, it is inevitable that someone will try to claim them, now or in a hundred thousand years' time.'

'Who was Aloysius Spur? A prophet?'

'No. A military tactician. A lord general during the Age of Apostasy.'

'Ah,' nodded Amado, suddenly taken aback.

Meteadas released the man from his fervent clutch. His postulating was interrupted as more archivists spilled into the northern vaults from the myriad catacomb entrances. Some were shouting, some were crying, others still were petrified with glassy-eyed shock.

'They are here! Naga is at war!' Through the confusion, that much was clear.

Before Meteadas could discern any more, a rumbling tremor from the surface punctuated the cacophony. Three buttresses of texts collapsed, two on the northern vault face and one adjoining the western silos, as the tortured wooden supports could hold no longer. The hundred-metre stacks swayed preposterously before they liquefied into a rolling tidal press. The avalanche of prose, poetry and epic history came down and decimated the repository chamber.

Mercifully, Elhem Meteadas blacked out. He did not have to hear the dying screams of his colleagues or the deathly quiet that followed.

In the slamming, teetering crush of people, Vinimus Dahlo had lost his abacus. His tea cart had been upturned too, but that could be repaired. The abacus was precious to him. It had been carved out of a fragrant red wood and bought for him by his wife. His wife, who had scraped together two years' worth of her own savings in a dented tin hidden in his daughter's bassinet.

He foraged on his hands and knees, covered in a sienna dust kicked up by the stampede. Bodies surged around him, trampling down the picket stalls, pushing and falling. A merchant balancing decorative bird cages on a carry-pole trod on Dahlo's heel. Close by, a potter wailed piteously as her raft of earthenware was stomped into fragments. And through all of this, the steady snap of gunfire remained a constant.

Dahlo's scouring led him against the human current until he finally glimpsed a wink of carved wood in the chalky ground ahead. Staying low and shielding his head with his forearms, Dahlo drove himself against the crowd. He stumbled through the remains of someone's rouge stall; the little pots of colours – red for the lips, purple for the eyes, cream for the cheeks – were all crushed underfoot. At one point the swell of the stampede was so great that he was lifted bodily off his feet and dragged backwards for several metres.

Forcing a wedge into the stampede, Dahlo spied his abacus on the ground. The varnish had scuffed but it was otherwise intact. He lunged for it, seizing the prize against his chest. Then, as he turned to run, a rough hand seized the beaded collar of his jacket and snapped him flat onto his back.

He landed hard on his spine. Dazed, it took Dahlo's vision several seconds to swim into focus. What he saw next almost froze his heart with sheer terror. Standing over Dahlo was one of the armoured killers.

Its frame was tall and raw, swathed in weighty layers of chainmail, scrap and gunmetal plating. It was a monster, wild and savage. Across its chest were slung multiple bandoleers of ammunition and grenades.

But it was the head that terrified Dahlo the most. Its head was bandaged in iron. Strips of metal enclosed it from skull to jaw, with a slight gap for the mouth and narrow slits for vision. Up close, Dahlo could see the pus that wept between the gaps of each iron slat.

Slowly and deliberately, the Ironclad killer raised a gauntleted fist. A thirty-centimetre spike was welded to the backplate, and the Ironclad traced a slow arc with it. Dahlo was certain that behind the metal bindings, it was smiling at him.

'Shoot me instead, please,' Dahlo gasped and immediately wished he hadn't. He had always fancied that his last words would be profound and measured.

Tracer fire hammered into the stratosphere, scuds of flak darkening the sky like ashy condensation. Despite the florid resistance, the vessels continued their bombardment. Dozens were snared by screens of shrapnel, disintegrating in their burning, tumbling descent. Dozens more continued to scream through the orange twilight and land in great mushrooming clouds on the surface below.

Major Chanta crouched behind the mantlet of an Onager. He traversed the iron-sights, hosing up quadruple streams of firepower. His primary gunner had been shot. They had been receiving enemy fire from positions on the ground for some time now. The invaders had advanced into Central Naga, overrunning the Militia Combine ground units. The vox-links were dead. Much of the city was burning.

As far as Major Chanta could tell, he was the highest-ranking officer in the region by default. His air defence squadron had done all they could, but it would not have been enough, even if they had acted earlier. The seething aerial deployment was absolutely overwhelming. The training manuals had never prepared him for anything like it. Against the horizon of the cityscape, enemy formations were amassing.

It was so loud, so brutal. The clatter of guns had reduced his hearing to a constant ringing. Across his field of vision the searing flashes burned afterimages into his retinas. It was little wonder then, that Major Chanta never saw the flanking force that swept across the rooftops and engaged his heavy guns in hand-to-hand. He didn't even notice the Onager platforms being picked off, one after another. To his immediate left, thirty metres away, an Onager of Delta Squadron was overwhelmed by Archenemy soldiers, the gunners and loaders being thrown off the platform onto the rooftops below.

'Corporal, vox to all units and report back the ammunition levels. Are they depleted?' Major Chanta ordered as he continued firing.

There was no answer from his vox operator.

'Corporal. Affirmative?' he repeated. Still there was no answer.

The hairs on his neck prickled with chills. Major Chanta slowly turned to look behind him. What he saw was singularly the most terror-inducing thing he had ever experienced.

Corporal Anan was dead. His corpse was being cradled by one of the

Archenemy. The Ironclad rocked back on its haunches, humming tune-lessly. He was playing: tracing geometric patterns on the ground with the corporal's blood.

'What do you think you are doing?' bellowed Major Chanta with a bravery he did not truly feel.

The Ironclad looked at Chanta. His metal-bound skull was featureless and betrayed no emotion. The Archenemy raider tilted his head, almost quizzically, and rose to his feet. From the bandoleers festooning his chest, this one unsheathed a hooked machete.

The major leapt off the Onager's bucket seat and seized the closest weapon. It was a discipline rod. A fifty-centimetre truncheon of polished hardwood, issued to all officers of the Naga Combine. It was not really a weapon but he hoped it would suffice.

Breathing hard, Chanta lashed out with the rod. The Ironclad parried with his machete and stepped inside Chanta's guard. The enemy revealed an embedded razor running the length of his forearm. Pressing hard with the machete, the Ironclad ran his bladed forearm across Chanta's abdomen.

The paper-thin blade scissored into the twill gambeson, eliciting a bloom of blood against the ivory fabric. Chanta gurgled. He took a step back and his knees buckled underneath him. It was all over. The Archenemy soldier pounced and straddled him, hacking down with the machete again and again.

It could have been the rubberised crump of combat boots that woke him. Or it might have been the harsh voices shouting orders in a clipped military tempo. Either way, Elhem Meteadas slowly regained his con-sciousness to the sounds of intruders in the repository.

He could not move. His spine was bent in such a way that, with every laboured breath, his shoulder blades spiked his lungs with agony. Books, thousands of them, had buried him. The *Horticulture of the Western Naga Archipelago* nudged into his kidney. He knew it was that book because the elaborate copper curling on the tome's edges was unnecessarily pointy. A good archivist remembered such things.

Around him voices barked back and forth in a language he did not understand. It was a human tongue, but nothing he had ever encoun-tered in his studies. Meteadas could only assume, through tone and inflection, that it was the tongue of Chaos.

The thought that Chaos was ransacking his duty region of the laby-rinths plagued his mind with impending dread. He did not fear for himself – his old arthritic bones were well past their prime and he had come to accept his fate with a mellow reluctance. Instead, his rational mind began to fear for Medina.

War, at least on an absolute scale, had not scarred the star cluster for four thousand years. Yet the earth-shaking ferocity of this assault bespoke of more than a cursory raid. This was war.

Meteadas knew wars were not fought on miniature rimward worlds such as Naga without pretence. No, wars were ghastly affairs only waged when the prize exceeded the costs. The Medina Corridor was not a strategic route in the subsector. It did not collate in Meteadas's rational mind.

Within seconds, Meteadas's brilliant intellect had reached a conclusion. Whatever the machinations behind the conquest of Naga, it would only be a means to an end. That notion pumped more dread through his veins than anything else.

He knew what he had to do. Deny the enemy their prize, whatever that may be. *'Scorch the land and leave no seed or fruit in passing,'* was a quote from one of Meteadas's favourite military philosophers. He had no choice.

With laboured gasps of pain, Elhem Meteadas wormed a hand through the debris of the book avalanche until his fingers brushed his belt. Immobilised as he was, it took Meteadas's fingers some time to hook onto the shuttered lamp at his waist. Easing it free, Meteadas slid open the hinge plate and sparked the gas condenser. A tiny flame fluttered into being.

At first nothing happened. But then, the naked flame began to catch on the sheaves of brittle manuscript that pressed down upon it. After the combustion, it did not take long at all for the lapping flames to erupt into a whirling pyre, sixty metres high.

Old Elhem Meteadas, senior archivist, died without much pain. He had burnt ten thousand years of Imperial history and literature, some irreplaceable and lost forever. But in doing so, he had struck a body-blow against the invasion. Naga would die, but perhaps Medina could live to write the histories again.

CHAPTER ONE

The dispatch to Inquisitor Obodiah Roth was urgent, couriered directly from the Ordo Hereticus. It had reached him, by way of clockwork pigeon, in a waxed envelope sealed with the highest order of authority, the scarlet seal.

The letter had been a cordial invitation to convene with a Conclave of Medina, for a matter of 'no small calamity'. It was the Inquisition's way of informing him that he had no choice in the matter. In Roth's experience, the more understated the situation, the more apocalyptic it would likely be. The very fact that the message had been sourced from the Medina Corridor, three weeks of non-warp travel by frigate, attested to its importance.

As it was, the request could not have arrived at a more inopportune moment. For months, Roth had been embroiled in a treasonous scandal concerning the oligarchy and the governing administration of the Bastion Stars. For the most part, it had been dry, paper-sheaving work, endless hours of cross-referencing tax ledgers and metric data. Now his investigation was on the cusp of fruition. He had narrowed down the conspirators to a clandestine circle of elites within the Bastion militocracy.

But now Roth would not be participating in the raid. The message arrived, as most messages do, in the most inconvenient of times, as Roth was cleaning his weapons, surrounded by gruff, growling Interior Guard troops who were eager to exact retribution on the political conspirators. The guardsmen had laughed, consoling the inquisitor with claps on the back and heavy handshakes, but it did not change the fact that Roth would not bear witness to the fruits of his labour. No amount of cursing and ranting would change that. Regardless, it didn't stop Roth from cursing or ranting.

By the time Roth embarked on his three-week journey from the Bastion Stars to the Medina Corridor, the invasion of Medina had been seething for five months. By that stage the war had, in the words of Inquisitor Roth, reached an apocalyptic scale indeed.

Archenemy forces had swept through the system, dismantling the unprepared Imperial resistance. They were the Ironclad, corsairs of the Eastern Fringe that had plagued Medina shipping lanes with sporadic small-scale attacks for the past six centuries. But now they fought with cohesion and in unfathomable numbers under the command of a Khorsabad Maw. Conservative reconnaissance estimates placed enemy numbers at seven million.

The regiments of the Cantican Colonial, the primary Imperial Guard formation of the Medina Worlds, numbered no more than nine hundred thousand, including auxiliary support units and non-combat corps. By the first month the CantiCol had suffered a successive series of staggering defeats in the frontier planets. Their noses bloodied, the Imperial High Command had recoiled, the entire front on the verge of collapse.

Far more troubling was the constant stream of intelligence that the Ironclad were only a vanguard force. Khorsabad Maw's seven million Ironclad were the spear-tip of a Chaos armada en route from beyond the Fringe.

For this reason, Imperial reinforcements amassed in the neighbouring systems of the Shoal Clusters and the Bastion Stars. Medina had little strategic value for the subsector. Despite a combined population of sixteen billion, the Medina Corridor was, for all intents and purposes, a sacrificial lamb.

Amidst the elliptical crescent of the Medina Corridor, the Imperial 9th Route Fleet moored at high anchor.

They were five dozen ships submerged by pink sparks of starlight, floating like a trillion motes of dust. The barbed, knife-like frigates and ponderous spears of Imperial cruisers clustered in protective formations. As fleets went, this was by no means a large one. Against the depths of space, the flotilla seemed almost vulnerable, so absolutely eclipsed by the smoky infinity of galactic nebulae.

The *Carthage*, the nucleus of the 9th Route Fleet, was a grand cruiser over nine kilometres in length. It was an old ship, even by Imperial standards. From its gilded arrowhead prow to the fluted reactor banks of its warp drives, the cruiser displayed a decaying elegance of ages past.

Since the Chaos offensive on Medina, the *Carthage* had been the military nerve centre of the dogged Imperial resistance. On board the cubic kilometre expanse of the *Carthage's* docking hangar, Lord Marshal Varuda Khmer waited. He did not like to be kept waiting, especially aboard his own ship. It irked him that a man of his rank should have to swelter in the oppressive heat of the docking bays alongside the common ratings.

Underneath the vertical lancet arches of the hangar, fork-loading servitors with chirping sirens ferried supplies from cargo carriers. Labour crews toiled and sweated at repair bays and fuelling stations. Throughout the organised pandemonium of blaring alarms, shouted directions and choking heat, the recycled oxygen of the pressure vents added a burden of drudgery that chafed the lord marshal no end. The fuming anger rising out of Khmer was tangible like a shimmering curtain of heat, and crewmen and servitors alike gave him a wide berth.

The stratocraft he had been waiting for had touched down on the cradle clamps almost six minutes ago. But still no one had emerged. Khmer checked his chron, a timepiece affixed by a gold chain to his breast pocket, for the sixth time.

'If he doesn't haul himself out of there by the time I count to ten, I'll shoot him when he does,' growled the lord marshal. His bodyguards around him, tall and powerful provost marshals, chuckled meaninglessly. Some did so out of fear.

Lord Marshal Khmer was not a physically imposing man. He was on the short side of average, with a lean build for a man in his sixties. Yet he carried his authority like a mantle about his shoulders. Despite his size he had an alarming presence. It was everything about him, down to the smallest detail. His movements were surgical, every gesture swift and intense. Khmer was so intense that when he clasped his hands behind his back, he clasped them together so hard the leather gloves emitted a low creaking groan.

It seemed too much energy and vehemence had been concentrated into such a small vessel, so much that it sparked and hummed like an overcharged powercell.

Finally, the gangway of the stratocraft detached from its fuselage with a hiss of steam-driven hydraulics. Lord Marshal Khmer stiffened. His two score bodyguards, flexing muscles beneath their rubberised sheath armour, rose like guard dogs.

Inquisitor Obodiah Roth sauntered out of the hatchway. He appeared unhurried. He was a young man, young for an inquisitor. His face was handsomely equine. Even though he had just transited into a war zone, he eschewed the vestments of combat. Instead he was stripped to the waist in white jodhpurs and leather ankle boots, his torso taut and wiry. His knees were still strapped with thick leather kneepads, his hands still bound in sparring mitts.

Khmer hated him immediately.

'Lord Marshal! I was just indulging in some fist-fencing. I hope I did not keep you waiting,' Roth said as he brushed past the forest of bodyguards.

The lord marshal, bristling in ceremonial finery, complete with gold frogging, war honours and embroidered velvet, eyed the down-dressed inquisitor with a look of abject revulsion. Khmer had expected more. Obodiah Roth had been requested by the Inquisition's Medina Conclave to aid the war effort. Previously, the lord marshal had serious doubts as to the relevance of Inquisitorial actions during the war effort. This new arrival just cemented his suspicions.

'You did. Is this going to set a precedent in relations between the Imperial High Command and the Inquisition?' Khmer retorted.

'Have it as you take it, sir.'

By this stage, Roth was less than an arm's length away from the lord marshal. At two metres tall, the Inquisitor reared well above the shorter Khmer. The phalanx of provost marshals squared up and edged in. Their tower-length ballistic shields and shock mauls were held low but ready.

'You needn't have brought me a welcome party, lord marshal.' Roth nodded at the provosts. The bodyguards were a subtle insult and one that the inquisitor could not let slip.

'Just as you've brought yours.' Khmer gestured at the man who had followed Roth down the ramp.

Bastiel Silverstein gestured back with a nonchalant wave. He was man on the spry side of forty. Whippet-thin and dressed in a waistcoat of finely tailored pirahnagator hide, he cut a sternly patrician figure. A scoped autogun was nestled in the crook of his left arm, a self-loading rifle painted in a camouflage of stylised foliage.

He stalked across the decking, looking unimpressed at the slab-shouldered provosts.

An Inquisitorial agent, thought Khmer. Probably another one of the many specialised pawns employed by the Conclave. As far as he was concerned, they weren't soldiers and therefore weren't to be trusted. He'd already had enough of the Inquisitorial circus troupe on board the *Carthage* to suffer any more.

'I'm here to make one thing clear, inquisitor. I did not want you here. Nor did I want other members of your Conclave,' the lord marshal stated.

'Oh, very clear,' Roth replied, unfazed.

Khmer continued. 'Yet Warmaster Sonnen ordered the collaboration of the Medina Conclave with my general staff. In turn the Conclave has requested you. Keep out of way, and our cooperation will be smooth, clear?'

Obodiah Roth wiped the perspiration from his wire-frame shoulders with a square of linen. He appeared uninterested. Finally, he looked the Lord Marshal of the Medina Corridor square in the eyes and winked.

'Can you fetch me a fresh towel?'

Lord Marshal Khmer stiffened. Unseen to anyone else, he gripped the timepiece in his hand hard, spider-webbing the glass lens. Both men, soldier and inquisitor, were guilty of a monumental temper, and things might have played differently had Forde Gurion not appeared at that moment.

'Obodiah! Welcome, welcome,' called Inquisitor Forde Gurion as he strode towards them, his augmetic legs clapping out an irregular rhythm.

'Master Gurion,' said Roth, bowing deeply to his elder.

The lord marshal cleared his throat. 'Gurion. I was here to welcome our esteemed guest. We have come to a mutual agreement,' he said with a reptilian smile at Roth. 'I expect to see the Conclave at our command briefing this evening at sixth siren. Do not be late.' And with that, Lord Marshal Khmer turned briskly with the practiced ease of a parade officer and marched away, flanked by his provosts.

'I can see the partnership is blossoming,' quipped Roth once the Imperial commander had disappeared into the roiling press of the docking bays.

Gurion shrugged wearily. 'Diplomacy is not one of the lord marshal's strong points but his efficiency is beyond reprove. We need officers of his mettle if we're to see out this campaign.'

'That bad?'

Gurion looked solemn. 'Come, Obodiah. There is much you need to know.'

The stateroom assigned to Gurion might once have been lavish. A large apartment in the officers' quarters, sections of the room had not been refurbished since the *Carthage's* maiden voyage six thousand years ago. Inside, the light was a smoky orange from lanterns. The walls were draped with elaborate floral velvet, which were once vivid primary colours but had now faded to creams and tans. Towering wardrobes, recliners and chairs had twisted columns, broken pediments and heavy carvings. A harpsichord dominated the centre of the room, its wood hand-painted with thousands of nesting birds and stylised botany.

Inquisitor Roth paced over to the harpsichord where a map of the Medina theatre had been spread-eagled across its decorative lid. It was a cartographic antique, centuries old, depicting the three core worlds of Medina – Cantica, Kholpesh and Aridun – alongside their various satellite planets. Gurion's handwritten notes and annotations marked the vellum surface.

'We are losing the war,' Gurion said from across the room. He placed a wafer plate onto the phonograph. Francesci's *Symphony of the Eldest Season* crackled out of the flared trumpet cone. It was the same concerto that Gurion had played from their APC when they had incited the loyalist Counter-Revolution on Scarbarus eight years ago. Roth had only been freshly ordained then and Gurion had led the joint ordos operation. The strident compositions of Solomon Francesci reminded him of past loyalties.

'Losing, or lost?' Roth asked.

'The rimward world of Naga was conquered five months ago. Since then, Chaos forces have pushed their advance onto the satellite and core planets of Medina.'

Gurion joined Roth by the strategy map. Under the smoky light of reading candles, Roth noticed for the first time how much his ordos senior had aged. Gurion looked drawn and grey. To Roth, the man had always been the scarred veteran of almost two centuries of service to the rosette. His spine had been broken and reinforced during the Fall of the Fifth Republic in the Corsican Subsector. Below the hips, his legs had been lost during the Orpheus Insurgency and replaced by augmetics of fluted copper skin and fibrous muscles of wiring. Yet he looked older than Roth remembered.

'Naga is conquered. Ninvevah, Baybel and Tarsis. All satellite planets taken by Chaos,' said Gurion as he indicated each planet on the map. 'Imperial forces have retreated to a war of attrition on the core worlds of Medina – Cantica, Aridun and Kholpesh.'

'How is the campaign faring on the core worlds then?'

'Judging by manpower, supplies and enemy disposition, Imperial forces cannot hold the core worlds for more than three months.'

Roth's expression darkened considerably. 'Seems like we are wasting our effort here. Why doesn't the military retreat and consolidate in the Bastion Stars?'

'So High Command keeps telling me, but no. I am clearly of the opinion that if the enemy sought to claim the Bastion Stars, they would have circumvented the Medina Worlds entirely. This cluster of planets has no strategic relevance to the subsector.'

'Then I don't follow you,' Roth admitted.

'The Archenemy is fighting for a reason. It wants Medina for a reason. That's why the Conclave was formed. Circumstance, logic and intelligence indicate that the Archenemy is seeking to claim the Old Kings of Medina. Come now, Roth, I don't need to explain this to you.'

At this, Roth nodded slowly, raising an eyebrow. '"The Old Kings of Medina. Here be the relics of the Emperor's cause. Wielded for the dominion of worlds and lost in the aperture of civilisation",' Roth recited, an old verse from Medina's historical annals.

'Yes, Obodiah. Our objective here is to gather and collaborate on a network of intelligence which will hopefully unveil the nature and exact location of these relics, and present them to the Imperial High Command,' said Gurion.

Roth was not convinced. It seemed like they were clutching at straws.

The sliding screen of Gurion's stateroom rolled back. A young woman entered, taking slow and measured steps across the carpet. She was suited in an egg-yellow bodyglove, an Inquisitorial rosette worn as a choker on her throat.

'Ah, she arrives on time. This is Inquisitor Felyce Celeminé,' said Gurion, introducing the newcomer with a welcoming sweep of his arm.

Roth bowed deeply and offered his hand.

'Inquisitor Roth, it's a pleasure. Lord Gurion has had nothing but praise for you,' she said, folding Roth's hand in both of hers.

Roth studied the newcomer with a gentleman's appraising eye. She was not tall, nor was she beautiful in the conventional sense. Rather, Inquisitor Celeminé was delicate, almost girl-like in stature. Her copper-blonde hair was cropped stylishly short and a lip ring tugged at the centre of her pout. She was, Roth decided, handsome in a demure and eccentric kind of way that verged on the bookish.

'Oh he has? I think he's been too liberal with his liquor then,' Roth dismissed lightly.

'Not at all. And a body's got a right to be curious.'

'Maybe you should keep that body in check, and remember to let go of my hand,' smiled Roth.

Celeminé started and slid her hands away, chewing her lower lip in slight embarrassment.

Gurion cleared his throat. 'Inquisitor Celeminé is newly ranked. I am confident in her abilities, but I hesitate to send her to Cantica and investigate alone. I want someone with experience with her, as we can't afford to take chances. She will be your second.'

'Settle down, sir. I haven't agreed to this yet,' said Roth.

Gurion, looking crestfallen, didn't say a word as he crossed over to the harpsichord. He studied the map closely. Under the yielding light, his face looked weary and battered. It was a face of flat planes and corners, brows polished by fists and forceful blows. Slowly, it dawned on Roth that Lord Gurion was scarred and sharpened through two centuries of service to the Emperor. And yet, Roth had never seen his colleague so filled with such barely suppressed fear.

'There will be a war council tonight. You will be there. After you know what I know, I trust you will do the right thing. I wouldn't have brought you here if I didn't,' said Gurion with conviction.

CHAPTER TWO

The Council of Conclusions was the plenary organ of the entire Medina Campaign.

Present were the senior commanders of the Imperial Guard and Navy, representative officers of neighbouring regions and, of course, the inquisitors. Even the titanic form of a Space Marine was present, an envoy of the Stone Gauntlets Chapter as denoted by the markings on his shoulder plate. The Astartes settled in his dusk-red armour like a dormant fortress.

Far removed from the opulence and grandeur of a congressional council, this was a regular assembly of briefing and intelligence dissemination. The representatives of the Governate and other political bodies were not invited. It was no place for bureaucrats.

For this reason, the Council of Conclusions assembled in the war vault of the *Carthage*. It was a tactical chamber constructed specifically to house the most powerful military and political chieftains of the subsector.

The war vault was a domed chamber, armoured within the hammerhead prow of the cruiser. The walls and ceiling were of ribbed ceramite, sparse and spartan when compared to the haughty elegance of the *Carthage's* design. The seating galleries were steel benches, forming U-shaped tiers around a hololithic projector. The chamber was unlit except for the ethereal glow of the projector. It was raw and reflected the blunt, unrelenting attitude of military leadership. Truly, this was the nerve centre of the entire war effort.

Inquisitor Roth had suited up in his Spathaen fighting-plate. He

57

decided it would be prudent, considering the occasion. The chrome trauma-plates afforded him a degree of buoyancy against the disapproving glares of blade-faced military seniors.

The Council began with a detailed briefing of the war situation: production output, fuel, ammunition, food, a comprehensive analysis of casualties. The officers debated with each other in a terse, clipped military fashion, their words coming in tight bursts like gunfire. Roth was content to listen. From what he could gather, the situation was very bad indeed. It seemed the general consensus amongst the Council was that Medina was, for all intents and purposes, defeated. The remaining Imperial forces should be re-routed to shore up defences in the strategically vital Bastion Stars.

At one point, a Naval admiral stood up and brandished a scorched wad of papers for all to see.

'This is the war journal of a captain of infantry, salvaged from the trenches of Ninvevah. It contains intelligence of Archenemy tactics prudent to our discussion.'

The officer opened the papers, tracing the words with his finger until he found the entry he was looking for.

'"Day sixty-two. The Archenemy, perhaps by design, parade the captured civilians of Ninvevah before our positions daily. They execute them within sight of our trenches, arranging the bodies in ranks. By my count, the entire city is dead and arrayed before us. Among those who are not killed, stout, healthy young men are marched in slave columns towards an unknown fate. This is appalling, I very much want to go home."'

As the admiral finished reading, there came a murmur of unease from the gallery. Even Roth, who had travelled widely, had never experienced war on such a scale.

'The captain and his 161st were overwhelmed shortly thereafter. This journal was retrieved as the remaining Cantican forces withdrew from Ninvevah following a surge of Archenemy aggression,' the admiral announced flatly before returning to his seat.

Then it was Forde Gurion's turn to speak. The inquisitor rose slowly, looking imperious in a long cape of carbon-ceramic polyfibres. The loom-woven armour glowed brass under the light of the hololith.

'Gentlemen, as you are well aware, our respective ordo have drawn together a Conclave in order to reveal and deny the objectives of the Archenemy in this subsector. Today, our Conclave is complete with our final member – Inquisitor Obodiah Roth.'

For a brief second, several dozen unfriendly eyes focused on Roth. Their distaste was palpable.

Gurion continued smoothly. 'Further, our Conclavial Task Groups on Kholpesh and Aridun have been toiling ceaselessly these past months in analysing intelligence regarding the Old Kings of Medina.'

A voice called from the assembled officers. 'And are you any closer to finding out what these mythical pieces are? Or where we can start digging them up with shovels and spades?'

Gurion shook his head politely. 'As of yet, we know not their exact nature or location. We have, however, obtained new findings from collated data over the past several months. According to the sources, the origins of the Old Kings began no less than twelve thousand years ago, and no more than twenty. Across the span of the Pre-Imperial galaxies, many lost outposts of man were bequeathed with visitation from what the sources described as "Early Sentients". The visitors brought with them their worship of the stars and constellations, as well as mathematics, astronomy and technology. In return, man adopted their worship of astronomical bodies.'

A Naval staff officer raised his hand. 'What sources are these?' he asked flatly, clearly unimpressed.

'Old scriptures, folk literature, but most importantly intelligence briefings gathered during the initial War of Reclamation, when Imperial fleets first moved to reclaim the Medina Worlds. The fleet acknowledged that when the Early Sentients left the Medina Worlds for whatever reason, they left for their subjects a parting gift. It was a monument of worship. The gift was known by many names – the Old Kings, the Star Ancient, the Guardian of Medina. According to the intelligence gathered by the Naval Expeditionary Fleet, this monument would strike down the enemies of Medina, at a time of dire need.'

'These gifts certainly didn't help the Pre-Reclamation Medinians from fighting the Imperial Crusade. This is Imperial territory now, is it not? Didn't we smash these barbarians thousands of years ago?' another officer retorted.

Under the barrage of scepticism, Gurion kept his composure. 'We can only ascertain, from archived scripture, that the Old Kings rest on one of the three core worlds. Historical experts postulate that the Old Kings were worshipped by Pre-Imperial Medinian culture, and to this effect it is believed that when the stars and the magnetic properties of the star system are in alignment, the Old Kings can be woken from their dormant state and be reborn as the "Star Kings".'

There was a ripple of derisive laughter. Gurion, however, remained unfazed.

'I have also come into possession of orbital reconnaissance photos detailing the mass excavations which have taken place across the surface of conquered worlds.'

He cued the grainy high-altitude reconnaissance pict. Roth squinted at the black and white hololith of excavation quarries that, judging by the comparative size of nearby terrain features, were a kilometre deep.

Gurion reviewed a slideshow of various picts. 'It is our belief that the slaves collected post-invasion, are utilised in an immense mining effort on these worlds. This leads us to believe the Archenemy are actively searching.'

He zoomed out to show a high orbital shot of the several subjugated worlds. The Archenemy had been so voracious in their digging that they had gouged into the equator lines of the planets, like a series of zagging claw marks. Most of the excavation quarries seemed to navigate the entire circumference of a planet.

After a moment of contemplative silence, the lord marshal himself stood up. The scar tissue on his face was alive, twitching and livid as he spoke.

'This is Chaos; they act without pattern or logic. We cannot hope to understand them, and certainly we cannot base our own campaign strategy around their madness. You mean to ask us to clutch at straws? To formulate a war plan because of some historical narrative?'

The marshal's rebuttal was met with a raft of applause. Roth noticed that even the giant in power armour – the Space Marine – shifted his massive weight and leaned in, his broad features eager to hear Gurion's response.

Roth would have brandished his Inquisitorial rosette then and there to remind Varuda of his authority. In truth, his fingers twitched to do so. But Gurion's response reminded Roth how young and unlearned he was in comparison. There was no substitute for two centuries of experience or the cold, steady head of a veteran. With his composure unswayed, Gurion turned his wrists out in placation.

'Gentlemen, please. I only ask to re-establish my case again. We know the Medina Corridor is of little strategic merit in the context of subsector conflict. We know the Archenemy are utilising slaves in mass excavations. We know all this.' Gurion paused, panning his eyes across the gallery, waiting for a challenge.

'Regardless of the Old Kings, the question remains why the Chaos vanguard would choose to attack Medina. At the very least, Imperial forces must defend core worlds until we can define Archenemy objectives and neutralise them. That is all we ask.'

Varuda opened his mouth to speak but was cut off by the resonant collision of metal on metal. It sounded like a forge anvil, slow and rhythmic hammering.

The gallery all turned to see the Space Marine clapping gently. The ceramite gauntlets that sheathed his massive paws reverberated through the chamber. Nodding his shaven head in approval, the Space Marine even dipped his head in respect to Gurion.

The lord inquisitor bowed once and retreated back to his seat next to Roth. As another officer took the stage to make his report on fuel supply, Roth whispered to Gurion, 'Do you think you've swayed them?'

Gurion snorted. 'Definitely not. But I've made my point. Besides, if all else fails I'll force this down their throats.' He dangled his rosette from a chain on his wrist.

Roth arched his eyebrows with equal parts surprise and revelation. He should have known. It was a fundamental principle taught to all ordos candidates – move in soft, then bring their whole damn world crashing down around their ears, if you have to. His mentors had coined the term 'being a smiling pirahnagator'.

Roth's reaction summoned a chuckle of amusement from Gurion. 'Oh my Roth, you have a lot to learn regarding Inquisitorial diplomacy.'

Inquisitor Roth racked the slide against the receiver of his stripped-down plasma pistol, checking for slick lubrication.

The parts of his MKIII Sunfury were laid out neatly at the foot of Gurion's bed. Barrel, cocking cam, trigger assembly, bolt assembly. The weapon was a monster, a gas-operated cyclical pistol, carapaced in plates of insulating brass.

Despite its firepower, the pistol was subtle and that was what Roth admired the most. It was a gentleman's Parabellum with the bark of a military-grade cannon. He holstered it in a shoulder rig and continued with his equipment check.

He limbered up, checking the smoothness of his Spathaen fighting-plate. The fluid interlocking plates of chromatic silver were fitted in such a way as to allow complete fluidity of movement. Everything from the shoulder domes to the sleek shin greaves were designed to slip and turn the ballistic properties of an attack.

Satisfied with its condition, Roth then donned a knee-length tabard of tiny tessellating obsidian scales. As he moved, the tiny panes of psi-reactive glass clinked like the scales of a sea serpent.

Finally he checked the feedback of his power fist. His right hand hummed with a low magnetic drone. The weapon was a Tang War-pattern power fist, a slim-fitting silver gauntlet. Lighter and smaller than the standard designs issued amongst Imperial officers, this elegantly slender power fist had been seized from the armoury of a narco-baron on Sans Gaviria during Roth's tenure as an interrogator. An artist, a gentleman and a connoisseur, the narco-baron had been like Roth in many ways. He had had a fine taste for artefacts of both utility and style.

Bastiel Silverstein was likewise making his own preparations. He had upended his luggage next to Gurion's well-stocked sideboard, chasing shots of oak-aged bramsch as he sorted through his array of hunting equipment. For Silverstein, it was a matter of selecting the proper tools for the job.

Repeating crossbows, hunting autos, long-las, needle pistols and even a harpoon-throwing rig were piled up around him. From his carry cases, the huntsman selected a bullpup autogun, slender and spidery in frame. He played the weapon in his hands, feeling out its balance and its weight. Shaking his head, Silverstein placed it back in its case and took out a scoped autorifle. This one was much longer, its stock painted in dashes of greens and greys. Silverstein tested the trigger with a click, toggled the safety and racked the bolt. He fired again with an audible click. Satisfied, Silverstein slammed back a shot of bramsch and placed the weapon aside.

Ever conscious of style, the huntsman was still dressed in his tailored coat of green leather, with jackboots polished to gloss-backed sheen. Over this, he grudgingly struggled into a flak vest, a basic piece of Guard kit that Silverstein had hand-painted a woodland camouflage onto. The huntsman did not trust the tools of his trade to anyone else.

Strapping on a utility belt, the huntsman began to stuff items into the various pouches – composite-polymer cord, auspex, tranquillisers, bolos and a large serrated skinning knife. Looking pleased with his preparations, he stood up and bounced on the balls of his feet, listening for loose straps or rattling pouches. He was as quiet as a hunting cat.

Wordlessly, the inquisitor and his hunter continued to adjust buckles and load magazines, latching and unlatching various large and ominous luggage cases. Neither of them looked up as Gurion, Celeminé and a CantiCol officer entered the stateroom.

'Are you planning on starting on a war?' asked Gurion.

'No. Joining one,' replied Roth without looking up. He was working out a knot in the release latch of his harness with his teeth.

Gurion nodded sagely. 'You will head the Task Group to Cantica then?'

'If that's where I'm needed.'

'I knew you would.'

As he spoke, Roth glimpsed the newcomer in his peripheral vision – the young staff officer who had accompanied Gurion into the room. Although he wore the rank-sash of a captain, he was too young. The brown felt of his jacket was loose on him, and his white kepi hat sat oddly on his head.

'Who is the young scrapper?' Roth said, nodding towards the captain.

'I am Captain Leyos Pradal, sir,' announced the boy, his eyes staring straight ahead in severe military discipline.

Gurion smiled apologetically at Roth. 'Captain Pradal will be your adjutant. He is a fine marksman and has seen combat experience.'

'What experience?' Silverstein snapped from across the room.

'Oh... I... uhm, limited skirmishes with rogue bandits on Cantica,' Pradal said.

'What kind of bandits?' Silverstein pressed.

'Hinterland raiders,' said Pradal.

'You mean Cantican bandits who shared one autorifle between five men,' Roth called to Silverstein.

Pradal puffed his chest and piped up again. 'I also score ninety out of one hundred on our graded shooting classes,' the young captain said.

'Hitting a target at a shooting range is one thing. The game is different when you have explosives going off overhead and the enemy is rushing you with a large axe,' Silverstein explained as he slipped rounds into a curved magazine.

'I see what you are saying,' Captain Pradal said. 'I am not here to boost your combat capability, but to liaise on your behalf with Cantican command staff. I can look after myself.'

Roth sighed. Gurion did not look pleased either. The last thing Roth needed was an inexperienced field officer on his task group. But if it would help smooth over some of the friction with High Command, then perhaps he could accommodate. Roth nodded curtly at Captain Pradal, then returned to his preparations.

Gurion picked his way around the clutter of spilled baggage and settled down in his armchair. 'Before you do go, I should tell you that there is already another Conclave Task Group on Cantica headed by Marcus Delahunt. They have been there since almost the beginning.'

Roth spared Gurion a look as he counted out fusion canisters for his pistol. 'I know Marcus. So why are our services still required? Or perhaps I am missing something?'

'We believe they are dead.'

'Ah,' said Roth, his expression unchanged.

'High Command has not established any comms with Cantica for the past twenty-seven days. Likewise, the Conclave hasn't been able to make astropathic contact with Inquisitor Delahunt for that same time.'

'Convenient.'

'Roth, please listen to me. If you still choose to go ahead onto Cantica, we need you to find Delahunt and to extract intelligence about the state of Cantica.'

'This keeps getting better, sir,' smiled Roth.

'I will contact you during the Cantican dawn on the fifth day, by astropath. Have Celeminé prepare herself for conveyance. In the event I am not able to reach you, I will repeat the conveyance once every second day, for a week. After that…'

'You can assume we're dead,' Roth finished for him.

'Be serious, Obodiah,' Gurion said, assuming his paternal tone. 'We cannot afford any chances here. You will be carving your path into the lion's den. Are you certain you are prepared to do this?'

Roth unholstered his Sunfury and loaded a fusion canister into the pistol grip. With habitual ease he expelled a tiny spur of gas from the venting assembly, toggling the weapon to *dormant-safe*.

'Well, Master Gurion, of course I'll go. Dressed as I am now, it would be terribly embarrassing of me not to.'

CHAPTER THREE

Byrsa Prime had fallen. Sibboeth had fallen. Iberia had fallen. The city-states of Cantica were collapsing and Central Buraghand would be no different.

Although Cantica was the defensive buttress of the Medina Corridor, its military had fallen under the invasion. Within the subsector, Cantica was strategically insignificant, yet within Medina the planet was a lone sentry. The archeo-world, its ancient geography appearing as an orb of yellowed parchment from orbit, had been assaulted with the full force of the Archenemy invasion, a heavy blitzing attack that had allowed the Cantican Colonial Regiments no time to formulate a cohesive defence. The CantiCol, a formation of light infantry spread thin over the entire star system, had not been enough to even temporarily slow the Archenemy momentum.

The invasion had begun with a surgical, probing attack. It had started four months previously with an aerial deployment of Archenemy Harrier-class raiders that perforated the Imperial Naval pickets.

Corsairs of Khorsabad Maw – the Ironclad, raiders well versed in the art of amphibious warfare – stormed the beachheads of the Cantican Gulf. An enemy force, primarily infantry numbering some one hundred and fifty thousand.

In the eleventh week of invasion, Lord General Dray Gravina wrote in his journal, 'The Archenemy, having resolved to make an amphibious landing, have amassed their forces in a stalemate along our coastal defences. It is our intention to deny the Archenemy access to inland routes. This shall be achieved by concentrating our resources in the sea-forts of the eastern and northern Gulf. It is a favourable opportunity to allow the enemy to disperse themselves like waves against our curtain defences.'

In that event, it was precisely what the Archenemy pre-empted. The Cantican Guardsmen were stretched thin across the coast against a diversionary assault. In the sixteenth week, the Ironclad began aerial deployment into the undefended Cantican heartland. Legions of mecha-nised and motorised infantry and fighting vehicles were inserted, almost directly into population centres. Significant urban sprawl covered the majority of Cantican continents, yet these low-lying clay forts and sprawl-ing terracotta cities were prime targets for high-altitude deployment.

What followed would be remembered as the Atrocities. Estimates made at a later date indicated that the total number of civilians and prisoners of war massacred during the first two weeks of the Archenemy occupation was well over four million.

An Imperial missionary by the name of Villeneuve made pict-recordings and first-hand spool reels of the Atrocities. He died but his recordings were later retrieved by Imperial intelligence. The infamous Villeneuve recordings revealed mass live burials, and slave columns marched into the wastelands, presumably for excavation. Lord General Gravina was publicly executed. The Archenemy unceremoniously dragged his body, in full military regalia, through the streets of the government district.

The journal entries and letters of dead civilians uncovered from the ashes were the worst. Within the scorched pages of a diary, one man wrote, 'I fear I have gone mad with the obscenity of these circumstances. Yesterday the occupiers discovered the language scholam where the local children have been hiding. They were loaded onto trucks and driven to the outskirts of the city. I do not know where those children may be. They were screaming "save our lives" as they passed my house.'

The conquest of Cantica, the largest core world of the Medina Corridor, heralded the beginning of the end for the Imperial war effort.

Roth could see the plumes of smoke that rolled off the shattered spine of Buraghand from the high altitude of his stratocraft. The panoramic wilderness of bomb-flattened debris and impact craters made him realise he was in the land of the enemy now.

The stratocraft swept in on an arcing descent. It hurtled low, hugging the ocean surface of the Cantican Gulf to reduce its auspex signature. The servitor pilot skimmed so close, its turbine burners hollowed out a tail of steam and boiling water in its wake. On the horizon Roth could see Buraghand, the central city-state of Cantica, rise like a thousand-tiered pyramid.

Snarling hard on thunderous thrusters, the stratocraft skimmed along the western coastal ridge of Buraghand. The craft was a modified Naval sixty-tonner, its armaments stripped to carry exhaust dampeners, counter-stealth generators and extended fuel capacity. Had it been spotted from the ground, the craft would have appeared as a dart, its needle-like cockpit perched on massive quad-engines. Toothless, sharp, its profile had a minimal auspex cross-section and its dampeners reduced its thermal footprint, rendering it almost invisible to Archenemy surveillance.

It traced the seawall, a towering curtain of mosaic that fortified the seaboard for fifty kilometres. They trailed it for forty, until the servitor pilot found a breach within its defences. The stratocraft shot in through the opening, flying no more than twenty metres above sea level.

They were going so fast, Roth was overcome with inertia. The visual blur was too fast for his eyes. He barely caught glimpses of the Cantican city, structures of terracotta and heavy copper shaped in ascending tiers.

The city was defined by its masonry. Shaped without plumb lines or spirit levels, the masons seemingly improvised as they built. The buildings were teetering affairs, with blunt edges, curvaceous parapets and leaning walls that lent the city a dizzying effect. Between the structures, webs of open-air staircases connected the multiple city strata from the minarets of the upper tiers to the fossilised ruins many kilometres below the ground.

Still maintaining a recklessly low skim, the stratocraft entered the stack ruins of lower Buraghand. An archaeological wasteland spilled down the slopes from the city-state's apex in a rambling scree. Broken-toothed ruins chopped past them, so precariously close they whispered past their wingtips with subsonic sighs. Finally, the stratocraft banked hard, rolling almost belly up before it decelerated underneath a mess of exposed wooden frame supported by crumbling pillars. Roth could not tell what the building had once been, perhaps a shrine judging by the copper dome that dominated the roof. Regardless, the rusted ceiling would shield the craft from enemy radar sweeps.

The stratocraft's monstrously snorting thrusters settled into a soft purr as the servitor-pilot powered off. He deactivated the stratocraft into hibernation. Slowly and wordlessly, the members of Roth's task group emerged from the lander, weapons ready.

Inquisitor Roth stalked out of the craft first, hunched low, the chrome of his Spathaen fighting-plate frictionless and silent. With a running crouch, he sprinted for cover behind a revetment of rubble. Drawing the plasma pistol from his chest rig, Roth took up a firing position and scanned his surroundings. Turning to the stratocraft, the inquisitor signalled the all-clear.

Captain Pradal and Silverstein appeared next. With practiced precision they sprinted down the ramp, boots crunching on the carpet of crushed stone as they went to ground, taking up firing positions on Roth's uncovered flanks. Celeminé was the last to emerge, clad in her egg-yellow bodyglove that seemed at odds with the desolate environment.

'Get on your guts!' Roth hissed from his position. Celeminé settled into an awkward crouch, suddenly aware that the wilderness of disintegrating masonry could hide any number of unseen gunmen.

'Silverstein, I need you to fix me a position,' the inquisitor said as he squinted into the ragged flames on the horizon. To Roth, Upper Buraghand was just a silhouette of ragged spine-like buildings, but to a huntsman with bio-scopic lenses it was a different matter.

The xenos game-hunter reared up, the yellow lenses of his pupil augmentations narrowed to targeting reticules as they homed in on distant targets. A tabulation of data began to scroll down the periphery of his vision, analysing the distance, climate and movement signatures.

+++Buraghand, Upper city state – Cantica: 7255 metres distant.

Visibility Spectrums: Noon Visible Heat/Wind: High/High Movement Signatures: 41%.+++

'Sire, I'm picking up a lot of movement, probably enemy patrols. If we stick to a north-east route, we should avoid the majority of it,' said Silverstein.

Roth nodded and turned to the others. 'Delahunt's last known position was a garrison fort in Upper Buraghand, roughly seven kilometres due north. That's our destination. This is enemy territory now, so stay sharp and keep moving. Good?'

The others primed their weapons and nodded. As one, they rose and picked their way through the ruins towards the burning metropolis. Far away, the echo of sporadic gunfire and the screams that followed were carried on gusts of wind and wisps of blackened ash.

They edged into the desolate, shell-scarred remnants of a fortress compound. Within the terracotta walls, the marshalling ground was pockmarked with shrapnel and shot. An artillery shell had found its mark in the central keep, caving the command tower inwards like a collapsed ribcage. Blood and death had seeped into the porous earth and a pall of gun smoke still hung heavily in the air.

Silverstein was running point, his bioptic pupils dilating and contracting as they tracked for targets. His autorifle was braced loosely against his shoulder, the camouflaged weapon blending hazily with his long coat of reptilian hide. Crouched and running as he was, Silverstein resembled a hunting hound seeking his quarry.

Fifteen paces behind, Roth and Celeminé followed. Roth looked long and lean in his fighting-plate and obsidian scale, his most favoured regalia of war. He ran with long loping strides, the fighting-plate seeming to facilitate, rather than hinder, his grace of movement.

Beside Roth, Celeminé gripped a bulky two-shot flame pistol in both hands. Extra fuel canisters were secured to her chest webbing, along with her med-kit and other utilities.

Bringing up the rear was Captain Pradal, lasrifle held at the hip, spike bayonet socketed in its lug. The weapon was CantiCol-pattern, distinctly longer yet thinner than standard, with a stock and grip of low-grade comb wood. His uniform was Cantican standard issue – a brown cavalry jacket and widely cut grey breeches, tapered around the calves by canvas binding. Upon his swarthy head was the distinctive regimental kepi cap with its circular flat top and forager's bill.

The captain turned around and panned his rifle at the empty marshalling square every few paces. He held a wad of tabac in his lower lip. His eyes were wide and wired as he chewed slowly.

Inquisitor Roth had researched the Cantican Colonials prior to entering the star system. It would have been rude of him not to. Although a little-known regiment, the CantiCol were the Medina Corridor's primary troop formation. According to census, four hundred thousand Guardsmen were garrisoned thinly across the Medina system alongside indigenous PDF elements. But like the planets they defended, their heritage was swathed in antiquity. The regiments had been raised six thousand years ago from the Cantican loyalists of the Reclamation Wars. They had been the few warring dust tribes to aid the Imperium during the Reclamation and were thus the only regiment granted the right to defend the entire region. Unified under Imperial colonisation, these soldiers had only seen intermittent actions against frontier raiders and minor xenos incursion on the Eastern Fringes. Nothing in their long and lengthy history had prepared them for an absolute war against the millions-strong legions of Chaos.

Of Delahunt, there was no sign. The main barracks block of the inner bailey was empty. The team crept into the blockhouse, silent except for the grinding of broken glass beneath their boots. There was no movement there, nor had there been any signs of life anywhere in the compound.

Inside the barracks, slashes of dried blood stained the walls and congealed in the corners and crevices of the tiled flooring. Spent casings and power cells littered the area. Ranks of bunk beds had been toppled over, some had evidently been used for defensive cover, their metal frames twisted and scorched. The fighting had been heavy here. In one corner of the housing unit, nestled behind an improvised barricade of granary sacks, a heavy stubber had fired its last rounds. The barrel was heat-warped from continuous firing and a bed of brass casings covered the area around it. Evidently, the Guardsman here had put up a dogged resistance.

Roth looked out the broken window into the outer courtyard. He saw the bodies of the entire garrison company, a hundred and twenty men in all, strung up across the battlements. As a member of the ordos, Roth had seen brutality before but he was thankful that he had not yet become inured to it. The massacre was painful to see and he knew it wounded Captain Pradal even more. Those were his men up there, swinging in the humid breeze. Even though the captain had not known them personally, they were his brothers in arms nonetheless. It saddened Roth immensely.

'Live target! South-east corner of the compound,' Silverstein called. Immediately, the four of them dropped to their stomachs.

Roth hit the tiles with a clatter. His cheek pressed against the semi-dried blood. Some of it was still viscous and felt like oil on his skin. Cursing softly under his breath, he leopard-crawled towards Silverstein, who had been watching from the window.

'How many?'

'Three movement signatures, at least. Maybe more. Want me to look again?' Silverstein asked.

'No, I will,' said Roth. The plasma pistol in his gauntlet began to vibrate as he thumbed it off safety. He hazarded a peek through the sepia-stained shards of the glass window.

Sure enough, the huntsman had been correct. Roth spotted a ghost of movement, darting between two squat storage sheds no more than fifty metres away. Then another flicker of movement, this time closer still, heading for their barracks block. Roth had seen enough; he ducked back down and gestured to the others.

'Enemy. They've got us cornered. We can either make a break from the barracks across the open marshalling grounds. Or we wait.'

'I say wait, at least until we know how many of them there are. They'll flush us out and cut us down otherwise,' replied Captain Pradal fearfully. The others nodded in agreement.

'Fine. Celeminé, Pradal, cover that window. Silverstein, with me.' Roth said as he scrambled behind an upturned bed frame. He made a quick assessment of the entry points to the barracks. Besides the main door, and a central window on the courtyard-facing side of the housing unit, there were no other entrances.

The four of them settled into a tense silence, eyes darting, jaw muscles clenching. Roth kept his eyes fixed to the main entrance. It was a thin metal door, so warped and perforated by small-arms fire it tilted on its hinges, unable to close. It hung there, slightly ajar, as Roth waited for the slightest creak of movement. To his left, Silverstein had stabilised his rifle on top of a storage trunk. He had settled into a pattern of rhythmic breathing, slowing his pulse and easing out his muscles. He aimed down the scope of the weapon and briefly closed his eyes before opening them again to check for realignment. Roth wished he too had the same hunter's poise.

'Do you hear that?' Celeminé whispered. Her voice suddenly seemed so loud, Roth flinched inwardly.

Sure enough they could hear the scuffling crunch of boots on a dirt floor. They were barely audible at first, but increased in pitch and rhythm rapidly. Something was starting to sprint towards the barracks block. Several somethings.

Then the door began to swing outwards. Roth's index finger slipped into his pistol's trigger guard. He raised the weapon with both hands. A figure appeared in the doorway, a dark silhouette framed by the harsh sunlight that flooded into the room and haloed around it. Roth aimed for the centre of mass, his synapses firing the impulse for his hand to squeeze the trigger.

'Hold fire! Hold fire!' Silverstein screamed. At the same instant, the huntsman had instinctively made his shot. He shifted the weight of his rifle at the last moment, bucking the aim upwards and unleashing his round into the ceiling. The noise was deafening.

Roth faltered, paralysed with confusion. His brass-plated plasma pistol wavered in the air. He paused... drew a breath. Slowly his vision adjusted to the influx of light, and the figure in the doorway swam into focus. It was a Cantican soldier.

The Guardsman stared back at him, frozen in the doorway. At that moment, Roth imagined their expressions of shock would have mirrored each other. The soldier was no more than seventeen or eighteen standard; dirty and dishevelled as he was, he was not old enough to have nursed a growth of beard. His brown felt jacket was missing a sleeve and his grey breeches had no leg wraps, so they flapped voluminously. Roth noted the sash around his abdomen denoted him as a corporal.

'I'm a friendly,' the young Guardsman finally stuttered. He lowered his CantiCol lasrifle. Several other men appeared behind him, tired and ragged and all dressed in Cantican uniforms. Another soldier slowly nudged the surprised corporal out of the way. He was a much older man, with a thick handlebar moustache. The rank sash stretched taut across his abdomen denoted him as a sergeant major. He looked at Roth, unsure what to make of the situation until he spotted the Inquisitorial rosette embossed on Roth's left shoulder guard. The sergeant expelled a soft gasp of hope.

'Praise the Emperor. You are inquisitors,' he muttered under his breath.

Roth holstered his pistol back in its shoulder rig and rose up to his full height. He was an impressive head and shoulders taller than all the Canticans. Several of the Guardsmen retreated a step or two.

'I am Inquisitor Obodiah Roth of the Ordo Hereticus. This is my field team,' he said. As he spoke, Roth noticed in the periphery of his vision that Silverstein and Pradal had not relaxed their weapons. It was a necessary precaution considering the circumstances.

'I am Sergeant Tal Asingrai. Formerly of the Cantican 6/6th Infantry.'

It was Captain Pradal who spoke next, rising from his position by the window. 'Sergeant. Are you deserters?' he asked with his lasrifle gripped in both hands.

The sergeant's jaw hardened visibly. 'No, sir. We still fight.'

'Cantica fights? Cantica has fallen,' Captain Pradal stated flatly.

'Cantica has fallen, yes. But some of us still fight. Resistance cells have formed in the under-ruins. We don't do much, but we do what we can,' the sergeant replied.

The reaction in Captain Pradal was overwhelming. He dropped his rifle, letting it droop on its sling, and squeezed the old soldier in a heavy bear hug. Roth could only guess how it must feel for the captain to realise his home was not dead, that its people still lingered. Perhaps they had a fighting chance yet.

The Cantican Colonials surged into the room, exchanging names and handshakes; it was unusual for an officer to act with open candour with enlisted men, but this was an unusual situation. Roth allowed the atmosphere of jubilation to wane before he spoke.

'Gentlemen, this is the first glimmer of positive news I have heard for weeks. The Archenemy, have they subjugated the surface?'

Sergeant Asingrai stole a furtive glance out into the courtyard where the garrison company had been butchered, and over the walls into the enemy-held city beyond. 'It's not safe here. Follow us to the under-ruins. We can talk there.'

CHAPTER FOUR

When men had colonised the Medina Worlds so very long ago, they had raised cities from the arid plains. These were ancient structures of clay, mortared with the crushed sea shells of long-extinct ocean-dwellers. Over the centuries, these cities were eroded by the seething dust storms and relentless suns until new cities were raised over the skeletons of the old. This natural cycle of construction had continued over the course of millennia, strata upon strata of ossified structures, growing as vertically as it did laterally, forming a mantle of architectural under-ruins, a labyrinth of archaeology that went five kilometres deep.

It was here, driven four kilometres underneath Upper Buraghand, that Inquisitor Roth came upon the isolated pockets of Imperial resistance. Down through an arterial maze they descended, groping their way through structures so old that natural rock growth and man-made construction had fused into one organic cavern. Crops of fungal growth grew wilder and more monstrous the deeper down they went.

Roth lit his way by the dull blue glow of his activated Tang War-pattern power fist. At one stage, Roth tripped and pushed his power fist through an ashlar wall. He found himself peering into a house that had not been visited by a human presence in at least seven thousand years. The structure was empty but for the petty ornaments of everyday living that lay undisturbed under swathes of dust and white mould – ceramic urns and plates, a crumbling copper-framed cot that had verdigrised to deep turquoise. The thing that seized Roth's attention, however, was an aquila shrine mounted on the far wall. A stylised double-headed eagle of black ore, housed within a shrine box of porous, flaking wood.

Roth was seized by a desire to brush the cobwebs from the shrine but thought better of it. If something had remained such a way for millennia, it was not up to him to disturb it.

After two hours of black, dusty, claustrophobic descent, Roth assumed they had reached their destination. He saw a stratum of ancient structures that had collapsed, forming a natural valley two hundred and fifty metres in length. The shoulders of the ravine were clustered with buildings so old and ossified they had fused with the planet's geology into a honeycombed warren. Overhead, rock pillars supported another stratum of ruins like the buttressed ceiling of a cathedral. As they entered the underground valley, Roth smelt rather than saw the signs of a camp first. He smelt boiling broth, chemical fires and the stale warmth of humans.

'This is it,' Sergeant Asingrai said as he gestured at the rock cubbies that rose up around them.

Judging by the number of drumfires and the refugees that huddled around them, Roth estimated there were over a thousand people seeking shelter in that small underground enclave. Men, women and children shuddered in the subterranean cold, swathed in blankets and rags, their faces hollowed by starvation. A small-bore autocannon, bronzed and ageing, was manned by a Cantican Guardsman and an armed volunteer. Sandbagged within a nest overlooking the mouth of the valley, it provided the enclave's only defensive hard point.

Roth rubbed his face wearily with his hands. The situation was woeful. He had hoped for something more, perhaps an underground command bunker, or at the very least some semblance of effective resistance. As far as he was concerned, his mission to gather intelligence on the Cantican warfront was over before it had begun. Cantica was utterly defeated.

'Sergeant. I don't want to waste any more time. I need answers about the nature of the defeat on Cantica. I need you to tell me what you know,' Roth said.

'You look disappointed, inquisitor. But we haven't been defeated, not like that,' Sergeant Asingrai replied. 'There will be a time for questions once you speak to our senior. I know he would like very much to talk to you.'

He led them through the settlement, and as Roth walked amongst the people he began to see what the sergeant meant. Despite the almost sub-zero temperature and lack of nourishment, women in beaded shawls danced and clapped on tambourines. Tired-looking men warmed their hands over drumfires while sharing the ashy stubs of tabac sticks. Although their clothes were shredded and greased with dirt, the people still carried themselves with an air of quiet dignity. As they walked, a boy of no more than fourteen ran alongside Roth. His cheeks were hollow and his hair was matted but a stern fury smouldered in the boy's eyes. Although he wore no shoes, he cradled a lasrifle in his arms.

'Cantica lives!' the boy shouted, hoisting the rifle above his head.

'Indeed it does,' Roth smiled. He was beginning to understand.

They finally came upon a man ladling broth to refugees. He was an elegantly dishevelled fellow, especially so with his leonine mane of hair and sternly ferocious eyebrows of black. A neatly trimmed beard edged the determination in his jaw line and when he met Roth's gaze, his eyes were a flinty grey. The man reminded Roth of the sort of rough face an Imperial propagandist might model for a conscription poster.

'This is our elected senior, Shah Gueshiva.'

Roth had expected a military man, but Gueshiva was a civilian. A civilian who nonetheless wore a leather jerkin slung with ammunition belts and slung a drum-fed autogun across his chest with accustomed ease. Upon seeing the newcomers in his camp, Gueshiva carefully passed his pail and ladle to a nearby woman. He approached Roth slowly, his face furrowed with incredulity. It was as if Gueshiva did not believe the inquisitors to be real. He first scrutinised Roth up and down before turning his attentions to Celeminé, studying them both from odd angles. He shook his head and ran a hand through his snarling mane.

'Master Gueshiva, I am of flesh and blood and so are my colleagues. You have my word on it,' Roth said, proffering a hand in greeting.

'Doctor. Doctor Gueshiva. I was a physician before this, but please, just Gueshiva will do,' he said as he gripped Roth's forearm. 'It is good to know the Imperium has not forsaken us,' he said, more to himself than Roth.

Roth bowed. 'I am Inquisitor Roth of the Ordo Hereticus. This is my colleague, Inquisitor Felyce Celeminé.' In turn, Celeminé also bowed low, smiling her bow-shaped smile.

'This is momentous indeed. Please, I have so many questions and need so many answers. Will you and your companions join me for tea?'

'Lead the way,' said Roth. His only concern was that Gueshiva did not have unrealistic expectations. Expectations that two inquisitors, a huntsman and a good captain could not hope to meet.

Doctor Shah Gueshiva's tent was nothing more than a tarpaulin erected over a rock shelf on the valley gradient. Hooded sodium lamps powered by a ballast generator kept the perpetual night at bay.

Roth slid cross-legged onto a sandbag. His team did likewise, settling down onto sandbags arranged around a plank of wood set across an ammunition crate. A taut sheet of canvas had been erected overhead, strung with beards of hemp and medicinal sundries. As was the custom, Gueshiva began to set out food for his guests – hardtack boiled with water into a creamy sludge, a ration tube of salted grease and tinned fish.

They were desperate rations and Roth hesitated, unwilling to erode their evidently dwindling supplies of food. Although he was hungry Roth nonetheless considered declining the meal, until he saw Gueshiva smiling broadly at him.

The man made shovelling motions with his hands towards his mouth. 'Eat, eat!' Gueshiva bade enthusiastically. He himself did not eat and looked like he had not done so for several days.

Roth reluctantly added a smear of salt grease to his cup of tack porridge. He exchanged a concerned glance with Celeminé, who clearly shared his sentiments. She sipped softly on her battered tin mug. Nobody touched the prized tin of fish. The team ate what was in their bowls appreciatively but did not reach for seconds. Roth swallowed the last of his cereal and nodded his thanks. When they had finished the Cantican custom of breaking bread, Gueshiva cleared his throat.

'Will the Imperial Guard save us?' Gueshiva started.

'Forgive me, Doctor Gueshiva, but at this stage the Imperial High Command are at a loss regarding Cantica. We do not even know the situation. All contact between this world and the Ninth Route Fleet ceased twenty-seven days ago. I must answer your question with a question and ask you – what has happened here?' Roth replied in measured tones.

'Look around you, inquisitor. This is Cantica now. The enemy took it from us and drove the survivors into hiding. Vox systems are dead. Communications are non-existent. For all we know, we could be the last and only survivors.'

Roth paused, digesting the information. 'The defeat has been so sudden, so total. How did the enemy overwhelm us? Was it…' Roth hesitated, trying to find the right words, 'was it… the Old Kings of Medina?'

At this, Shah Gueshiva leaned forwards almost as if he did not hear the inquisitor properly. 'You mean the mythical relics of the Old Kings?' He chuckled. 'If that is what you mean, then no.' He leaned back and shook his head softly.

'The Archenemy had been fighting hard but our soldiers fought harder. Morale was good and we did what we could for the war effort. Knitting blankets, pickling foods, rationing. We thought we would pull through.' Gueshiva paused, a lump in his throat making it hard for him to continue.

'But a month ago hundreds of thousands more came from the skies, deploying column after column of armour and mechanised infantry. The depleted garrisons didn't last out for more than two days.'

'Then they have not found the Old Kings yet,' Roth muttered under his breath.

'Pardon my candour, but the Archenemy will break apart the Medina Worlds just to find them,' said Gueshiva.

Roth was taken aback. He was surprised at the good doctor's uncanny insight. He looked to Celeminé but she too was too astonished to ask anything.

'Don't be surprised, inquisitor. I'm not a fool. Why else would war of such a scale be brought to rimward Medina, if not for some grander pretence?' Gueshiva smiled humourlessly.

'Which brings me to my next question – Inquisitor Marcus Delahunt was an ordos operative dispatched to Cantica six months ago, in order to investigate the Old Kings of Medina. His last known location was a distress beacon from the above-ground entrance to the garrison fort where Sergeant Asingrai found us. Is he perhaps within your camp?'

'I'm sorry, inquisitor, but no. Thousands of above-ground portholes, tunnels and hatchways lead into the under-ruins. If he is still alive he is not here.'

Roth let everything he had been told seep and settle. The situation was grave, but the revelation that Cantica had been subjugated by conventional warfare was reassuring in an ironic way. He and his Task Group would have time to establish a temporary base of operations within the enclave until they could ascertain Delahunt's fate. There would still be much to do.

'Do you hear that?' Celeminé asked, leaping up from her seat. Her sudden enthusiasm intruded on the contemplative mood.

At first Roth thought Celeminé, a kappa-level psyker, had felt something he did not. But slowly he realised he heard it too – the distant barking of dogs. Roth turned to Gueshiva but the doctor had already risen from his sandbag, racking back the cocking handle of his autogun. The gesture did little to assuage Roth's sudden concern.

'Were you followed?' Gueshiva asked.

Before Roth could answer, the physician had dashed out of the tent. The barking was louder now. Louder and closer.

'With me,' Roth said to his team. The rattle of loading ammunition and hollow clacks of primed weapons was his reply. Without looking back, Roth pushed aside the tent flap and emerged into the subterranean valley.

Outside, panic was total. Fires were doused and tents were flattened. Refugees scrambled into the rock warrens, snatching up their children and carrying the old. Roth spotted a dozen armed volunteers sprinting in the opposite direction towards the steep entrance of the valley. Roth followed, heading for the autocannon nest at the lip of the defile.

He heard someone shout an order to cut the lights. Immediately, the enormous floodlights that lit the settlement were powered down. Roth dived onto the ground beside the gun nest just as darkness dropped around him like a black curtain. He landed hard on his stomach.

Just as abruptly as the commotion had begun, the settlement became quiet. It took Roth's eyes a moment to adjust to the darkness but the fluorescent glow of subterranean flora allowed Roth to make out murky shapes. He found himself lying prone next to Gueshiva, the man distinctively outlined by his wild hair and beard. On his left was Silverstein, his bioptic vision unaffected by the absence of light as he aimed down his scope. Together they formed a static firing line that stretched for perhaps fifty metres if not more, covering the notch entrance and western flank of the valley depression.

Roth squinted into the depths and traced out vaguely humanoid shapes cresting a hog-backed mound of rubble to their front. The figures stood atop the mound and peered directly down at him, well within shooting distance. Roth swore that they were staring at each other. They were so close Roth could hear them snarling at each other in a slurred guttural tongue heavy with awkward consonants.

Gueshiva leaned in close and whispered. 'Archenemy murder squads. They've been sweeping the under-ruins for signs of Imperial resistance. Don't move a frakking muscle.'

Roth held his breath and pressed himself further against the gritty sediment of the underground. Several of the figures had moved away from the squad on the ridge and were stalking cautiously down the scree.

'Sire, I count fifteen men. Five approaching,' Silverstein whispered.

'The dogs. What about the dogs?'

'Just untrained maulers, not scent hounds. I've targeted seven of them, one hundred and twenty-two metres away up on the ridge, and I don't think they've got a scent. No wind currents or circulation down here.'

'Stay put and wait out then,' Roth hissed back.

The approaching figures were climbing over a tumble of masonry and blunted pillars. They were so close now, Roth could make out the razor-edged lines of their armoured silhouettes, metallic petals and corollas sweeping from their shoulders and arms. Three of them aimed lasguns as the other two probed at the boulders and rock slabs with long metal pikes and roving torch beams.

Roth closed his eyes and clenched his fists. Perspiration beaded his upper lip. The white beams of light oscillated wildly and several times flickered dangerously close to their hidden positions. Finally, after an agonising eighty-five seconds, by Roth's count, the intruders turned to go. They prodded their way back up onto the ridge, growling in their language. Whether they were cursing or reporting to their squad leaders, Roth could not discern. After a few more glances in the direction of the collapsed ravine and the hidden settlement, they disappeared over the ridge.

Roth let out a prolonged breath. Without consciously doing so, Roth had held his breath almost the entire time. They waited for a few seconds, straining to see into the darkness before climbing off their fronts.

'Routine patrol,' Gueshiva observed.

Everyone else had risen to a crouch, yet Silverstein stayed prone. Roth shook his friend by the shoulder. 'Bastiel, are you good?'

The huntsman looked up at Roth, stunned, blinking his bioptics. 'They had no faces,' he said.

'Bastiel?'

'I saw them. They had no faces,' Silverstein repeated as he rose. For the first time in almost ten years of service, Silverstein was visibly shaken. For a xenos game-hunter, who pursued bone kraken and carnodon unperturbed, the visage of the Archenemy had truly unnerved him.

CHAPTER FIVE

He was trapped and he was done.

When Inquisitor Marcus Delahunt awoke, those were the first thoughts that came to him. He tried to sit up, but pain lanced up from his broken femur. Rolling over onto his side he vomited onto the cold, wet flagstones.

Delahunt tried to remember where he was. Panning around, he could see he was in a darkened hall of some sort. The floor was lined with polished wood and cylindrical leather bags hung in rows like gutted carcasses. A fresco along the far wall painted in crude pigment depicted stylised athletes, naked, punching and kicking. A training facility, thought Delahunt.

Yet he had no idea how he had got there. His last conscious thoughts were of being hounded by murder squads through the streets of Buraghand. Vaguely he remembered colliding with a heretic raider mounted on some sort of motorised bike. That was how he had broken his leg, of that he was sure.

Delahunt eased himself up on his quivering arms and spotted a water basin, just out of reach. It was an earthenware oblong, undoubtedly placed there for the athletes to sup. But the athletes were dead now. Delahunt flash-backed to their barracks cots, red with blood as he had made his way to the training hall. That memory had stayed vivid above all else.

With slow agony, Delahunt reached out a hand and dragged himself towards the basin. But the splintered ends of his bones grinding against each other almost blacked him out with pain. He collapsed in a heap on the floor, his throat too dry to vomit.

Utterly defeated, the inquisitor lay down for a while, not even blinking. He considered killing himself with the autopistol at his hip. It was a thought he nursed for some time. Finally, he came to a resolution. Lifting his left hand, he pressed his signet ring to his lips and began to speak. The ring, although bronze and unadorned, bore the authority of his Inquisitorial seal. As he spoke, his words were crystallised into data and conducted along microscopic veins of quartz within the signet. The current of information flowed through the circuit and was encrypted, transforming sound waves into codified symbols.

In his state, it was a trying task. Despite lapsing in and out of consciousness, slowly and with great deliberation, Delahunt began to record everything he could remember since he had set foot on Cantica.

It was morning as far as Roth could tell. It had only been his second day in the under-ruins and already he had lost all sense of day and night, dark or light. The only reason he knew it was morning, was that he was fatigued. His eyelids felt caustic with lack of sleep and his head was throbbing.

He and Celeminé had been awake all night attempting to establish psychic communion in order to find Delahunt, with little success. Not only had the psychic strain been totally draining, it had been dangerous too. They had taken turns to disembody themselves, soaring their psychic entities high above the minarets of Buraghand. The threat of being ambushed by other psychic entities, especially on a world subjugated by the Archenemy was all too imminent. While one of them was disembodied, the other had kept constant vigil ready to intervene, psychically if need be. Yet as their night wore on, their efforts had floundered as exhaustion set in. Roth had ingested three tablets of melatonin, but even that did not kept his mind fresh.

Celeminé was asleep now, laid out on the freezing stone floor. She was still clad in her yellow bodyglove and boots, her hair tussled and falling into her face. Celeminé's raw psychic potential could be eta-level but she was still young, and at best she currently skimmed a very potent kappa-level. As a consequence, she had borne the brunt of their efforts. By the third attempt, Celeminé was so spent, her speech was barely coherent.

They had taken up residence in a sheltered cove, a flat-topped house of Cantican design that had collapsed into the ravine aeons ago. It had accumulated so much chalk and calcium deposits that it resembled a rocky shell of natural flowstone. Considering their circumstances, the ruins at least provided the tranquillity and shelter necessary for psychic meditation. Gueshiva had also been a gracious host, giving them a plastek groundsheet and a coal stove to keep the temperature affable.

Roth pulled the groundsheet over Celeminé's sleeping form. Sleeping as soundly as she was, Roth did not want to wake her. He took up a perch in the tiny rock hut, sitting cross-legged on the millennia-old flagstones. He swallowed another two melatonin and mentally steeled himself for another communion. This time he would do it alone.

Roth let his mind drift like a dinghy unmoored from its pier. He floated up as an invisible mote of light, looking down on himself and Celeminé. He was already tired, and the ebb and flow of spirit winds threatened to carry him away into the abyss. It took all of Roth's focus to buoy himself against the current. Hardening his mind's eye into a knot, he began to ascend.

It was slow at first, wafting up through the honeycombed strata of the under-ruins. Roth tasted the lingering ghost-prints of each ossified strata. He moved through the earliest stages of Cantican history, passing a domed palace of the dynastic Imperial governors. He empathised with the guilt of a governor-general who had suppressed a rebellion of horse nomads. The governor-general had ordered their steeds and menfolk executed by live burial six thousand six hundred years ago. The guilt lingered as a sour aftertaste.

He soared up through a layer of single-storey houses stacked from mud brick and covered in mosaics of red, brown and turquoise stones. Although the seismic pressure had crushed the structures into flattened rubble, Roth could smell the vigour of hearth and home. The oily scent of cooking was so strong; he was tempted to stay a while. But up and up he went, gathering in velocity.

Soon the under-ruins flashed past in an overwhelming surge of sensation until he erupted onto the surface. Roth braced himself. Immediately, the turmoil of a city at war threatened to flay open his mind. A tidal wave of brutality and sheer paralysing terror impacted hard against his mental defences. Had it not been for the many hours of tutelage Roth had received under the ordo's finest psychic-duellists, he would have died. Roth recoiled, spiralling inwards into a helix shell as he concentrated internally. Four kilometres below the surface, Roth's physical body tremored momentarily and his left lung fibrillated.

He could feel the terror of families hiding in cellars and basements, the suffocating hopelessness of many who were just waiting to die. Worst of all, he could feel the addictive rush of Ironclad murder squads on a rampage. He could see their black auras, hideous and nauseatingly evil. They haunted the city like a plague of laughing ghosts.

He knew he could not last long. Roth flew low and fast, skimming the haphazard stacks of the tenement quarters. He cut across ornate structures of terracotta and heavy copper and reached the major Buraghand canal. He cast his mind snare wide, hoping to catch any tentative sign of Delahunt – a thought, an ornament, a cry for help, anything.

He searched as best he could. Compared to Celeminé, Roth was not a powerful psyker by any means, but what he lacked in raw potency, he made up for with a singular will to focus. Like the body, the mind could be vigorously trained. Meditation, psychic sparring and even the simple puzzle book could all be tools for psychic prowess, as much as weights, callisthenics and nutrition could build the body. Roth regularly honed himself, and was considered omicron-level by his peers.

Combing the city block by block was a torturous effort. Delahunt was nowhere to be found. Instead Roth glided over the central plaza of Buraghand, a flat hectare of unbroken ground paved with a billion sea shells to resemble the stars and planets of the Medina Corridor. Once the central basilica and forum of Buraghand, it was now a mustering field for Ironclad slavers to herd their Cantican captors for the excavation quarries. The misery and hopelessness of those people, beaten and prodded into the plaza, was so poisonous that capillaries in Roth's physical form began to bleed, threads of blood lacing down his eyes and nose.

It was all too much, and momentarily Roth almost lost control and lapsed into a coma. He strained hard to anchor himself, a single flower against a gale. One more sweep, Roth decided. Narrowing his search area down to the region surrounding the garrison-fort where Delahunt had last transmitted his distress beacon, Roth flew in a concentric circle.

Many thousand of metres below, Inquisitor Roth's body became wracked with seizure. Blood poured from his face. It poured from his nose, his eyes, his ears and from every pore in his cheeks. The atmosphere of holocaust was consuming him.

Unable to maintain his psychic form any longer, Roth decided to return. He recoiled from the conical metal caps and bronze roofs of Upper Buraghand. But as he did so he snagged a glimpse of a sign, the sparkling wink of an Inquisitorial seal being activated. Roth halted, holding his ethereal breath. He searched for it again and sure enough, it was tangible. Down amongst a vast amphitheatre in the commercial district of Upper Buraghand, Roth could almost reach out and touch it. It had to be Delahunt.

Throwing caution aside, Roth shot in like a bird of prey. Assuming the form of a psychic spear, he lanced into the amphitheatre and aimed for the training barracks attached to the western wing of the complex.

Streaming through the stone columns, the psychic manifestation rocketed into the sparring hall. There, crumpled against a wall, lay Inquisitor Delahunt. He was unconscious and his despair was palpable, but he was alive.

Roth roused Delahunt with a brisk mental probe.

+Marcus Delahunt.+

'That is I,' wheezed the inquisitor. He squinted up towards Roth like a man staring into the sun. Delahunt was not a psyker and he could see nothing. Despite bleeding and spasming, Roth drew into his mental reserves and summoned a visage that Delahunt would recognise. It was of a much younger Roth, from their youth as orphans of the schola progenium. The image was painted into Delahunt's eye, a spry lanky Obodiah Roth in his mid-teens, lost within the folds of a scholam robe several sizes too large.

+Marcus. It's me, Obodiah.+

'You old bastard. How long has it been, sixteen, seventeen years?' chuckled Delahunt through a mouthful of broken teeth.

+Too long, Marcus. I knew you'd be here, you always were too tough to die, the warp would only spit you back out.+

'If only. I don't know how much longer I have. This whole city is crawling with Archenemy. I can hear them banging on my door.'

+I know, Marcus, I've seen it. Tell me quickly, where exactly are you?+

Delahunt shrugged. 'I think I'm in the Gallery of Eight Limbs. It's an old training facility and tournament pit for maul-fighting. Buraghand commercial quarters. I think I crawled here somehow.'

+Hold on until sunset, old friend. We'll be coming to fetch you.+

'Wait, Roth,' Marcus started.

+Marcus? Quickly. I'm slipping.+

Roth had already stopped breathing for over a minute. Hypoxia was setting in and carbon dioxide began to poison his blood.

'Roth. If I don't make it, I've recorded everything I know in my signet,' said Delahunt.

+Did you find the Old Kings?+

Delahunt shook his head. 'I don't even know what the Old Kings are. I'll explain when you get here, unless the Archenemy get to me first.'

+We'll find you first, Marcus. We will.+

And with that Roth had nothing left. He broke his psychic link, too fast and too abruptly for his weakened state. Asphyxiated and seizuring, he collapsed onto the ruined flagstones.

When Bastiel Silverstein found Inquisitor Roth, he was folded backwards over a kneeling position. Arching his spine with his stomach pushed outward, his face was smeared with a film of blood.

He looked like he had died. At least that was what Silverstein thought until a cursory scan with his bioptics revealed a pulse. The huntsman rushed forwards and handled him by the underarms, easing Roth's weight into an upright position.

'Sire, what happened here?' asked the huntsman.

Roth blinked blearily, his words slurring into each other. 'I'm fine, just psychic communion.'

Silverstein propped the inquisitor up against the wall and handed him a steaming tin cup. 'I came in to bring you some tea.'

'Thank you.' Roth wrapped his hands around the warmed metal appreciatively and took a moment to gather his breath. He sipped the tea slowly. It was only a watery Guard-issue infusion, but the earthy bitterness did much to mend his spirit.

By this stage, their conversation had awoken Celeminé. She shrugged off the groundsheet and began to instinctively smooth down her hair. When she spotted Roth, her eyes widened.

Roth raised a hand to halt the questions before they left her mouth. 'Relax. I'm well, but that's not important right now.'

'Roth–' she began.

'Hush. Delahunt is alive and I know where he is. Fetch Gueshiva for me and gather what aid he can spare. We move out at nightfall.'

CHAPTER SIX

Esaul usually didn't mind roof sentry. It was a chance to shoot down any stray flesh-slaves who were lax enough to wander the streets after dark. From his position on the highest tenement roof, he felt like a god. But tonight was a cold night and he was impatient to join his unit. Since the invasion he had almost collected enough ears and teeth to decorate the sling of his newly looted lasrifle, and he was hungry for more.

The prayer towers struck twelve and began to mark the hour. Speakers nestled in the minarets and temple alcoves had once crackled with the flat-toned warble of holy Imperial prayer. Chaos had changed that. Now, on the hour, they broadcasted the incantations of Khorsabad Maw in a guttural Low Gothic. It was a ghastly sound, with its wailing inflection and sinister drone of voices all muted by a static crackle.

Such electronic incantations reverberating through a silent city were a great demoraliser to the dissidents and resistance cells. The trembling acoustics were conducted so well by the conical copper roofs of the city that the echo lingered for many minutes after. Esaul revelled in it. He drew a stick of obscura from one of the many loot pouches harnessed across his breastplate and lit it. Taking a moment to savour the ghoul's gospel, he inhaled deeply on the opiate.

Smoke wafted from his mouth slit and coiled from the gaps of his iron headpiece. The hot desert days and dry freezing nights had irritated the raw facial skin underneath. With a bayonet, Esaul nonchalantly scraped and prodded into the gaps between the slats to satiate the itch.

Suddenly there was a ripple in the shadows on the streets below. His boredom and discomfort were quickly forgotten and Esaul leaned over the ledge of the roof. Drawing another lungful of obscura, he squinted through the vaporous smoke at the darkness below. Again he saw it: someone detached from the shadowy walls and broke into a sprint. For a brief moment Esaul wondered if it was the hallucinogenic obscura playing phantoms with his vision. But no, sure enough the second was followed by a third figure.

Esaul flicked aside the obscura and nestled down behind the scope of his lasrifle. The gun had been set on a tripod mount and placed over a ledge overlooking the main boulevard. By the way they scurried, they must be live-plunder. He wriggled into a comfortable firing position and tapped his metal cheek against the stock of his weapon. Tracking through the scope, he hunted the jogging figures down the length of pavement. The target reticules wavered onto the back of a running live-plunder. He made ready to ring a shot out into the night and make known his presence. He was a god again and they were his play-things.

The sudden impact to the back of his head jolted Esaul out of his delusion so hard he almost lost his rifle over the edge. Surprised and off-guard, the Ironclad rolled onto his back and placed his forearms over his head, taking the next blow on his rusty vambraces from sheer muscle memory. His assailant pressed the initiative, straddling the prone Ironclad and striking again.

Up close under the pale moonlight, Esaul could see his attacker clearly. It was a man, dressed in civilian clothing but equipped with the military paraphernalia that marked him as a resistance fighter. He had killed enough of them to recognise one in the dark by now.

'*Eshulk!*' barked the Ironclad. He came alive in the surging panic of close combat and unhinged a flick razor folded beneath his left wrist. It was just one of the many blades he had in his possession. Bridging up on his neck, Esaul rolled his attacker off his chest and reversed their positions. Without pause, he gripped the throat with his free hand and brought up his flick razor.

An unseen knife cut his throat first. Rough hands seized Esaul from behind and a forearm cranked the Ironclad's head back as the bayonet plunged in.

High up on the roof ledge, the guerrilla hand-signed the all-clear. The sentry had been silenced.

Roth signalled back and his Task Group fanned out to secure the main street. It was an arterial lane that ribboned up towards the commercial district, narrow, tight and winding. Roth and Silverstein sunk into a crouch behind the remnants of a little blue fruit cart, hand-painted and gilded. As the pair covered the street ahead, Celeminé and Captain Pradal ghosted past them on the opposite side, hugging the terraced workshops that flanked the thoroughfare. They passed the terrace of a tailor, a barber, a clocksmith – all empty and abandoned. On the overhanging eaves above, birdcages clustered like lanterns, once filled with songbirds. The birds were dead and drying now.

Behind the Task Group came the resistance fighters, running low with their weapons tracking the rooftops. Gueshiva had been gracious enough to volunteer a fifteen-man escort of his guerrillas. They were resilient men who knew the city well. Even though most of them had been civilians who had once plied their trade in this very district, the recent months of war had scarred and sharpened them into fighters.

One of the volunteers, a youth who had lost his hand to a grenade, padded softly next to Roth. The inquisitor knew his name was Tansel, a boy who had once been an apprentice rug weaver. He could not weave rugs any more, even if Cantica were to be liberated. Now ammo pouches had been sewn onto a vest far too big for his coat-hanger shoulders, and he gripped a stub-pistol in his remaining hand.

'Beyond this lane, we come to an open bazaar and past that is the Buraghand Amphitheatre,' whispered the boy.

Roth nodded and waved the resistance fighters on, past them to cover the next section of the street. Celeminé and the good captain then leapfrogged the next secured area. The Task Group maintained this cautious advance for some time before reaching a junction in the lane.

The volunteers prowled ahead, half of them nuzzled down with their weapons to give suppressing fire as the other half-dozen disappeared around the winding bend. They waited for some time before re-emerging. Roth could not discern what was happening but the volunteers appeared to be arguing in hushed voices amongst themselves.

'Can you see what they're doing?' Roth asked Silverstein.

The huntsman shrugged. 'We'll see soon,' he said, nodding in the direction of Tansel who was crouched over and running back towards them.

The boy waved the stump of his arm and shook his head. 'It's blocked off, we can't get through.'

'What do you mean it's blocked off?' said Roth.

'Barricaded. The Archenemy have barricaded the avenue into the plaza. Tires, rubble and razor wire about twenty metres high. I think we're going to have to double back the way we came and find another entry point.'

Roth swore colourfully under his breath. Then repeated himself for good measure.

'It's not too far, inquisitor. My old weaver merchant had a workshop five hundred metres back. There was a rear door that would take you straight onto an adjacent alley. We can reach the amphitheatre that way,' Tansel assured them.

'That's quite all right. You lead the way then,' Roth replied.

The Task Group began the agonisingly slow advance back the way they had come. They had not gone far when their tactical caution was validated by the low rumble of engines. The string of guerrillas began to hiss sharp, urgent words down the line.

At first Roth did not recognise the bass tremor that shuddered through the stillness of night.

'Enemy patrol, break track,' whispered one of the volunteers. The warning rippled down the column.

There was nowhere to hide in the cramped confines of the lane. Roth spied headlamps and searchlights thundering in. Spears of white light pierced the darkness. The silky darkness of the night was suddenly penetrated by a brilliant flush of incandescent white. They were caught.

Roth turned to a nearby window with a lattice-work screen of ageing wood. He shouldered his way into it and came crashing through the other side, rolling onto his knees in a fog of dust. Silverstein came spearing through the window after him. The terrace was a humble bookshop. The shelves had been overturned and most of the texts had their pages torn out and carpeted the floor. A bank of narrow arched windows faced out onto the street. The two of them ripped the latticed shutters off their hinges and rested their weapons on the sills.

The outriders appeared first, raiders astride motorised bikes that shrieked like chainsaws. Two light trucks followed behind, patrol vehicles painted in off-white enamel streaked with rust and grease. On the flatbeds, two Ironclad murder squads and braces of attack dogs rocked on the shrieking suspensions.

Most of the resistance group had been caught out in the open. They exchanged stray shots as both sides sought cover or went to ground. The patrol trucks pulled up just short of the group and their troops dismounted. The attack dogs came off first, slab-chested mastiffs bounding and snarling. The Ironclad clambered off after them.

Roth opened fire with his plasma pistol. The mini-nova of energy pulverised an Ironclad as he was dismounting, liquefying his breastplate into molten metal and fusing him to the truck chassis. From an alcove opposite Roth, Celeminé and Pradal exchanged small-arms fire as they bobbed and ducked behind cover.

Someone shot out the searchlight on the leading patrol vehicle and visibility winked out instantly. The sudden loss of light turned everything black. Roth could see nothing except for the flickering exchange of lasbolts and sporadic muzzle flashes. Vaguely, he could hear the slavering growl of dogs as they tore into something wet and fleshy.

'We're as good as dead unless I draw them away,' said Silverstein. He had moved next to Roth, his vision unfazed by the night.

Before Roth could disagree, Silverstein clasped his forearm. 'I'll see you back here before dawn. Open your vox-link for contact.' And just like that the huntsman vaulted over the windowsill into the street.

He paused briefly, picking off two outriders with two clean shots. The soft-point rounds poleaxed the riders off their bikes. Barely breaking stride, he cut across the narrow lane to where the resistance fighters had been pinned down by fire underneath a tympanum arch. Several more well-aimed soft-point rounds in the direction of the enemy patrol gave them the respite they needed. Silverstein and a handful of Canticans broke from cover and sprinted directly towards the murder squads. The remaining guerrillas sprinted back towards Roth and signalled for him to follow.

It was the decoy that Roth needed. Wasting no time, the inquisitor leapt back onto the street. He didn't really know what happened next. He could barely see the back of the man in front of him. Somehow, in the confusion, Celeminé's hand found his and he held on hard to make sure he didn't lose her in their flight. They crashed through plywood boards, hurtled up flights of stairs, stumbling blindly. At one point, Roth put his foot down through something that gave way with a snap, almost turning his ankle. He hoped the men in front knew where they were going.

After another headlong lurch up a rickety flight of steps they spilled out of a trapdoor onto a roof landing. The resistance fighters began to climb across the rooftops but Roth pounced onto the limestone ledge to peer down the street below. The murder squads were still directly below him. Further up, he saw what could only be Silverstein and his volunteers, the muzzles of their guns barking in the night. Even further away, more headlamps were converging on their position. With pained reluctance, Roth turned his back on Silverstein and began scaling the rooftops.

Cutting across a snag-toothed row of terraces, they finally shimmied down a drainage pipe onto a stack alley. The pedestrian lane was no more than ninety centimetres wide and tapered up into a mess of irregular stairs. A sodium vapour lamp strung up on wire lit the way. The place stank of bile and urine.

'Quickly now, up this way,' said Tansel.

The remnants of the Task Group drew out into a staggered column and followed the boy. Close by, far too close, could be heard the angry rev of engines.

The *Carthage*'s congressional chamber was a vaulted hall, the ceiling crowned by a canopy of tapestry and banners. Heavy leather benches were arranged in a geometric octagon, ringing the central dais. The walls themselves were the most remarkable triumph of Imperial grandeur – glazed tiles, mathematically arranged, rendered the historic battles of pre-Unification in shades of brilliant blue. There were three hundred thousand tiles all told, no two the same, a task that had taken the prodigious painter Jorge Seville the better part of half a century to complete.

Here, Lord Marshal Khmer addressed an assembly of the most powerful men in the star system. Present were nineteen generals, stately and resplendent, twelve divisional commanders, two score Naval officers of the highest order, chosen regimental officers and a representative of the Officio Assassinorum. In all, they were men with enough power to destroy galaxies.

Staff cadets mingled in the congressional benches, serving light refreshments. Despite the pomp and dignity of the war council, luxuries were eschewed for basic rations. The officers ate what their men ate, they did not expect anything less of themselves. Staff bore silver trays piled with hardtack, and salvers of the finest sterling containing nothing but raw onions and tinned fish. Even the crystal decanters held barley wine of the standard half-pint ration. These were dire times indeed.

Lord Marshal Khmer waited until the drinks were dispensed and the officers were settled before speaking. The address was pronounced in measured tones, the fluid acoustics carrying his voice around the chamber.

'Brothers-in-arms, I have ordered a military council today to reassess the grand strategy pertaining to the execution of the Medina Campaign. For too long, military command has been indecisive, inadequate and hamstrung by external elements.'

There was a polite raft of applause from the military council. Some of the commanders stomped their boots on the ground in approval. The lord marshal raised his hands for silence and continued, 'Our men have fought bravely and beyond reprove. But we cannot deny the fact that our strategy of attrition will lose us this war. Our one clear objective is to halt the Chaos advance. To achieve such an objective, a tactical retreat is our only option at this point. It is in my informed opinion that it is the Bastion Stars we must hold. To this end, I declare we withdraw and consolidate with gathering Imperial reinforcements in the inner subsector.'

The declaration caused no small degree of consternation amongst the delegates. Khmer had expected this. Among those seated, many were loyal to him, but many could be considered rogue dissidents, intent on complying with the Inquisitorial edict to defend Medina.

To this end, Lord Marshal Khmer had already arranged for a plan. He had made certain to order the presence of several outspoken rogue officers, men not loyal to him. It would be a chance for Khmer to make examples of them.

As if on cue, a gaunt, shaven-headed officer scarred from scalp to chin stood up from his bench. The rank sash around his waist denoted him as a brigadier of the 29th Cantican Light Horse. The cavalry officer cleared his throat elegantly. 'Sir, if I may say, we are restrained by the edict of the Inquisition. We must, according to the Conclave, hold the Medina Worlds with all available resources until they can discover what objectives the Archenemy have in securing Medina. Is it not a fundamental objective of war making to deny your enemies their objectives so as to satisfy your own?'

'No you may not *say*, brigadier! I will not have my soldiers suffer defeat, for some mythical old wives' tale. The Medina Conclave does nothing but hamstring our efforts to secure the subsector. Sit down, brigadier, before you embarrass us all,' scoffed Khmer.

'Sir, with respect. The edict of the Inquisition is clear. Hold the Medina Corridor. As much as it pains me to say, they are the highest Imperial authority here,' replied the scarred officer.

The fool was playing straight into his hand, Khmer thought to himself.

'I am the highest Imperial authority here! These men are my men, this ship is my ship. I will deal with Gurion and his travelling troupe, is that clear?'

'Sir,' said the brigadier through clenched teeth. He folded his cap to his chest and sat back down.

It seemed the air in the chamber had cooled several degrees. The military seniors growled amongst themselves. Some glowered, seeming to agree with the brigadier.

'My fellow soldiers. Understand that I do not wish to abandon our home, our planets. But it is not a choice any more. Civilians do not have to make the choices we make. It is our duty to protect the Imperium and to do so we cannot give our lives needlessly here. We must reinforce the defences in the Bastion Stars for the major Archenemy advance.'

Khmer waited for the dissenters, knowing full well he was about to lure them out. Indeed, the brigadier stood back up. 'This is our home, sir. What you are telling us to do is to allow Chaos to destroy our planet, and defy the edict of the Inquisition, the work of the God-Emperor. I find it abhorrent and I will not have any part in it.'

It was exactly what Lord Marshal Khmer had hoped for. Now came the denouement. The chamber hushed. Lord Marshal Varuda Khmer said nothing for ten long seconds. He even counted them precisely himself. Finally, his hand reached into his pistol holster and he drew his laspistol and shot the brigadier through the sternum.

The cavalry officer's face lit up in shock. He was dead before he slumped back into his seat, his eyes and mouth still wide. No one said a word. These were the senior architects of war; there was little they had not seen but even this shocked them.

The lord marshal finally broke the silence. 'Remember. I am the highest Imperial authority here.'

He delicately drew a silk cloth from his breast pocket. Calmly, he wiped down his pistol before holstering it. The gallery was still silent as Khmer strode to the front gallery and held out his hand to the officer of the Assassinorum.

Gloved in a cameleoline bodyglove that shifted with every spectrum of grey and black, the man appeared like a deathly spectre. The Assassin clasped Khmer's hand in allegiance. Again, it was another brilliantly orchestrated affair that sent a clear message to the Imperial High Command.

'Brothers-in-arms. For the sake of this campaign, I declare myself the highest regional authority in the name of the God-Emperor. If anyone sees otherwise, please speak now.'

As Khmer expected, nobody did.

CHAPTER SEVEN

It was only three hours past the middle of night but dawn was approaching. Already the triple suns were bruising the horizon from dark blue to amber, shortening the shadows and airing out the dark. It would not be long before the sticky pall of the day's heat turned the cool of night into condensation.

By Roth's calculations, that meant they had thirty minutes to reach their objective and return to the under-ruins. Forty at the most. Fortunately, the Gallery of Eight Limbs already rose into view. It was a natural amphitheatre, a crescent-shaped stadium built into a precipitous curve of red, white and orange rocks. The stepped seating overlooked an oval arena covered in a mixture of sand and salt. That had been where the maul-fighters in their prime had fought for the entertainment of thousands. It was also where they had been rounded up and executed during the initial Atrocities.

The team swept around the perimeter of the stadium into the gymnasia of training barracks attached to the wings of the Gallery. These were spartan quarters, a gridwork complex of palaestra and fighter-stables where the athletes trained and slept.

Tansel and Captain Pradal led the way, followed by Roth and the rest of the team in a herringbone formation. They entered through the central yard of the palaestra, essentially a rectangular court framed by colonnades. The columns ran along all sides of the court, creating porticoes that led into spacious training halls.

They cleared each hall with methodical precision. The team moved quickly, silhouettes flickering through the colonnades as they prowled through rooms dedicated to steam baths, striking bags and weights. Beautiful friezes were chiselled into the stone walls, depicting the athletes and their patron saints. The Ironclad had evidently already raided here, desecrating the artwork with vulgar graffiti, almost juvenile had it not been daubed in blood.

Roth recognised the striking figures as practitioners of Medinian maul-fighting. As an avid theorist of the unarmed arts, Roth's interest had been piqued at a young age by the gentlemanly pursuit of fist-fencing at the progenium.

As a pugilist, Roth respected the brutal art of Medinian maul-fighting. The combat sport of maul-fighting prohibited the use of hands or feet. Fighters instead sought to strike with forearms, elbows, knees and head-butts. Most bouts were short, scrappy affairs usually concluding in a knock-out. It was a shame his first encounter with the sport was under such trying circumstances.

The rest barracks were the worst to see. The fighters had slept on straw mats, their living spaces cluttered with the personal effects – books, blankets, clocks, prayer ornaments and even the detritus of dead relationships.

Yet as the team filed past the mats, they saw the gore and shrapnel that feathered the area. Flashes of blood dripped from framed photo-picts and curtains. The barely recognisable remains of humans festered on the floor, the stench cloying the sinus passages and lingering forever behind the palate. Roth's rudimentary grasp of forensics revealed the story – the maul-fighters had tried to hide in their barracks and the Archenemy had filled the hall with grenades. The destruction was gleefully excessive and not much had remained intact.

'See that, inquisitor?' Pradal said, pointing to the ground.

Roth looked down, seeing nothing at first. But sure enough, he followed Pradal's pointing finger until he saw a fresh trail of blood, brighter than the browning crust around it. Amidst the drying carnage, fresh, perfectly circular dots of blood left a speckled trail across the gallery into a side portico. It was barely perceptible.

'Delahunt?' asked Celeminé, crouching down to inspect the sanguine trail. Her voice came muffled through the kerchief she held against her face.

'A rather astute observation, madame. One can only hope,' Roth observed. The pattern of blood-fall indicated light wounding, perhaps sub-dermal incision or puncture. It might not have been life-threatening but, in any event, Delahunt needed aid. Urgency got the better of him and Roth sprinted the last several metres through the tetrastyle columns.

He rounded the entrance and saw Inquisitor Delahunt, flayed open on the clay tiles.

Roth halted, his breath caught in his lungs. Someone had got to Delahunt first. From the way the inquisitor had been laid out, someone had left him there to be found. It had to be a trap. Someone was playing their game and staying one step ahead. Eyes wide in sudden realisation, Roth spotted ghosts in the periphery of his vision, shapes and silhouettes moving on his flank. Roth opened his mouth to shout but the word *ambush* never reached his team.

The concussive stutter of auto-weapons engulfed his warning. Roth went to ground as the resistance fighter closest to him was poleaxed off his feet. High-velocity rounds shrieked overhead. A single slug impacted into his shoulder pauldron, piercing the fighting-plate and mushrooming within the armour. Spinning shrapnel bounced around, lacerating his shoulder. Hollow points for tissue rending, was the only thought that ran through Roth's mind. Cursing, spitting and scrambling on his hands and knees, Roth dived behind a salt basin. He hazarded a look at the ambushers, detaching themselves from the columned shadows.

Expecting to see soldiers of the Archenemy, Roth instead recognised something else entirely – the most feared mercenary formation of the subsector if not the entire Ultima Segmentum: the Orphratean Purebred. Eugenically bred humans with their long lean frames poured into snakeskin bodygloves, there could be no coincidence in them being here. In the gloom they moved like diamond-backed spectres, shifting through shades of brown, mauve and crimson. A harness of chest webbing carried the tools of their trade, ammunition, pistols, wire cord, field dressings and other military kit. Torch beams underslung on their weapons dozed through the lightless room in blinding circles.

Each mercenary shouldered an EN-Scar autogun. The matt-black carbines cut the air with snapping barks of fire. They fired single well-aimed shots in overlapping arcs of fire as they manoeuvred into position.

In one corner of the training pit, behind a stack of wooden mannequins, a heavy stubber had been set up on a tripod. The Purebred gunner raked enfilade fire in a diagonal cone, pinning Roth's team in the open. Lambent threads criss-crossed the air creating a solid lattice of tracer.

Panic was not something inquisitors were accustomed to. Acting as the hands of the God-Emperor, the Inquisition were seldom placed in compromising situations so utterly out of their control, influence and preparation. But compromising was an understatement right now. Celeminé huddled behind a stone sparring post, bullets gnashing into the stone and biting off the wooden arms and legs. Shot slammed into mural carvings behind Roth, showering him in chips of rock and a fine powdery talc dust. Two of the six resistance fighters had been shot dead. Pradal was nowhere in sight.

But more than the shock and ferocity of the ambush, the one thing that really rattled Roth was the simple fact that these were not Archenemy.

Genetically superior men of the warrior caste on Orphrates, the Orphratean Purebred had seen limited action since the beginning of the Medina Campaign. Utilised by Imperial forces to augment the special operations capacity that the Cantican Colonials so severely lacked, these mercenaries had been and still were, as far as Roth was aware, under the employ of Imperial High Command. But now they were freelancers contracted to kill Inquisitorial agents. Whatever their motives, they were damn good at it.

So fierce was the suppressing fire that Celeminé could not gather her mental faculties to generate a concerted psychic counter-attack. She hesitated, strangely undecided. Popping a buttoned pouch on her chest webbing, she slid a grenade into her hands. The device was stencilled 'fragmentation' in a yellow munitorum script. Celeminé wrenched out the pin and rolled the grenade out like a croquet ball before bobbing back behind cover and pressing both hands to her ears.

+Duck for cover!+

She jettisoned the urgency directly into the mesocortical pathways of her comrades.

Roth, emptying his Sunfury into the pillars directly to his fore, barely managed to swing back behind the stone basin before the grenade erupted. The detonation was felt with a physical rumble. Roth felt like someone had slapped his back, hard. The enemy fire abated for several seconds.

It was all the time Celeminé needed. She immediately threw up an illusory wall at her enemy, hazing the darkness into a formless, nauseating depth of vertigo. It was her favourite trick, and in the low visibility of night it was enough to throw off aim and destabilise equilibrium. Even sheltering outside the radius of her focus, Roth was seized by rolling inertia.

It was only then that Celeminé vaulted from behind the sparring post. She announced her presence with a hand-flamer. The jet of liquid fire roared into the shadows, flushing the Purebred from their cover. She killed five before the flames lost pressure and licked back into the muzzle. Her second squeeze of the trigger sent the Purebred scuttling for cover. An incandescent spear lit the hall in dazzling shades of amber.

+Holy Throne, woman. You never told me you were so dangerous!+ Roth telepathed.

+If I had, would you have believed me?+ She ended the thought-speech with a brush of girlish laughter.

No, Roth admitted to himself. In fact, he still found it hard to believe. Under the exaggerated shadows and extreme lighting, Celeminé in her yellow bodyglove and harness of heavy-duty military gear looked like a scholam-child playing soldier.

But there she was, a virgin inquisitor, alone and slight of build, scattering at least forty killers of the Orphratean Purebred before her path of war.

'Fall back and disengage!' shouted Captain Pradal. He had reappeared, firing his lasgun on full auto. Seizing the initiative, the remaining resistance fighters followed him out the portico they had entered from, firing as they went. The last two to leave took a knee by the portico, laying down suppressing fire for Celeminé and Roth.

+Time to go,+ she called.

Inquisitor Roth unfurled from his crouch and made ready to sprint for the exit, but halted in mid-step. +No! Wait, not just yet!+

He pivoted on the balls of his feet and dashed towards Delahunt's body. Psychically, he could feel Celeminé urging him to leave. The Orphrateans were recovering, shouting fire drill and target coordinates in precise military inflections. Their shots were building in tempo and accuracy.

Roth was not far from Delahunt. He could see his old comrade, supine against the wall, his neck cranked in an absurd backwards angle, his arms prostrate like a martyr. In the background, he could hear Celeminé's flamer, snorting and choking out its last coughs of fire. It would not be long before the three dozen Orphrateans caught the both of them in the open. Ludicrously, Roth wondered what six hundred rounds of sustained fire would do to his body.

That was when the Orphratean speared out from behind a pillar and collided with Roth. They went tumbling over and hit the ground hard. Barely recovering, Roth was pinned by the Purebred's raw-boned frame. Up close, Roth could understand how the planet of Orphrates had made an economy out of killing. The man was bred for combat. His father and his father before him, interbred with the warrior caste. In that way, the genetic purity maintained a dynasty of long, lean and ruthless killers.

The man astride Roth betrayed no emotion on his equine features. He simply reached up to a cord on his shoulder strap and extended a fine thread of razor wire. In one well-practiced motion, the Purebred looped the garrotte around Roth's neck. Gripping hard on the mercenary's wrist to prevent him from tightening the noose, Roth raised his Tang War power fist.

It hummed to life with a corona of static.

The razor wire slitted down onto Roth's epidermis, slicing so clean it didn't draw blood. Before his carotid arteries could be severed, Roth shovel-hooked his power fist into the Purebred's floating ribs. Power fists, Roth knew, were primarily developed as anti-armour devices. From experience, a power fist could rend the flank armour of a battle-tank, scooping out great handfuls of molten steel. Against human flesh, the results did not bear thinking about. Roth was literally covered in Orphratean Purebred within a matter of seconds.

He heaved the eviscerated body off him and dived the last few metres to Delahunt. The dead inquisitor's eyes were still open and glazed, almost accusatory. They had not found him, as promised.

'I'm sorry,' mouthed Roth. He reached down towards Delahunt, deactivating his power fist as he did so. The signet ring gleamed at him. Roth plucked at Delahunt's hand and the ring, slick with blood, popped into his palm.

As he did so, Celeminé's flamer depleted its fuel canister with an oxygenated burp. +I'm out!+ she cried.

Roth pivoted hard on his heels and powered towards the portico. In the corner of his vision, bristling phalanxes of EN-Scar autocarbines steadied their aim. Three rounds almost scalped his head. He shouldered into Celeminé, hooking an arm around her waist, and just kept going. A round slammed into the segmented trauma plates of his abdomen. The ballistic apron tensed on impact, absorbing the kinetic force. Although the deep tissue bruising would be severe, the round did not penetrate.

Less than ten sprinting strides away from the portico, Roth saw a shot find its mark on one of the resistance fighters covering the exit. The young man, a former administrative clerk of the Governor's palace, spun completely around. His face hit the wall behind him, his neck spurting out arterial crimson in a three metre stream. Roth ran through the portico and kept going.

He emerged in the rest-barracks. The survivors, Captain Pradal and young Tansel, sprang up from their firing positions as soon as they saw him emerge.

'This way, we can cut through the gymnasia,' beckoned Tansel.

Roth acknowledged with a frantic motion for them to keep going. Behind him, he could hear the last surviving resistance fighter following close behind, turning to snap off several last defiant shots into the chamber of ambush. No doubt, the mercenaries would give chase. The Orphrateans lived by their reputation. Roth just kept running, focusing on Tansel's darting form before him.

'You can put me down now,' Celeminé said. Roth had forgotten that Celeminé had been thrown across his shoulders, her head bouncing on his back. He quickly lowered her back down.

'My apologies, madame. I didn't mean–'

Celeminé put a delicate finger to his lip. 'Not the time for your verbosity.'

'But I–'

'Shush. You talk so much all the time.'

The resistance fighter bringing up the rear waved his arms frantically, motioning for them to keep moving. They headed from the gymnasia down an arched tunnel.

When they emerged from the complex, the night had receded and day had come. Roth found himself in the arena proper. The suns were already out in full, low and swollen embers that crested the skyline. Gasping for breath and dazed in defeat, the Task Group slogged across the stadium and back out into a conquered Buraghand.

CHAPTER EIGHT

Bastiel Silverstein slotted the last round into the chamber. The thought crossed his mind to save the last shot for himself. But he was too stubborn. With an almost weary resignation, Silverstein raised his weapon and fired his last shot.

The bullet hissed down from the minaret fifty metres above street level, cutting diagonally over the jostle of tenement roofs. It traced towards the blockade of Ironclad that had sectioned off the city block and found its mark on an Archenemy raider hunched down behind the flank of his patrol vehicle. The round entered his forehead. With an explosive spray it exited out the back of his skull, his iron headpiece opening up like a flower in bloom.

Silverstein ducked back under the balcony of the prayer tower. The expected volley of return fire clattered overhead in fierce reprisal. Placing down his empty autorifle, he sat his back against the smooth red clay of the balcony and sighed.

'Anyone have any rounds left?' he asked.

The six resistance fighters around him shook their heads. They had emptied their canvas pouches and webbing. They were tired and spent. It was early morning, but the Medina suns were already searing the city with intense shimmering heat. Dehydration and latent heat exhaustion were beginning to set in.

The siege itself had already taken the better part of five hours since the group had splintered away to run decoy. It had been a tight run and they had lost three on the way. At one point, it seemed like there were dogs and patrols waiting them for them around every bend. They had fled into the highest prayer tower in commercial Buraghand and there they had held the Archenemy at bay. To their dismay, the accuracy of their fire had driven the Archenemy into a protracted siege, cordoning off the block and gathering nearby patrol units.

For the last hour, as ammunition had run low, they had resorted to simply giving up their spare rounds and allowing the huntsman to snipe away at the encircling foe. They guessed that Silverstein had fired at least two hundred rounds in that time. Many of them had been kill shots.

They waited a while. The enemy fired no more shots as if testing, no, taunting them into firing back. But they had nothing left and it would not be long before the Archenemy realised that.

'How long do you think it will be before they roll up a tank to flatten this whole thing?' asked Goa, a foundry worker in his late sixties. Sunstroke had affected him the worst and he spoke with his eyes closed, his head lolling.

'Death by artillery would be lucky. They won't give us that luxury,' Silverstein replied matter-of-factly.

As if on cue, they heard the gate at the base of the tower being breached with some sort of a piston ram. Voices began shouting harsh words in the dark tongue.

'Here they come,' shrugged Silverstein. The six others began to fumble for their spike bayonets but Silverstein sat without a sound, hands on knees.

The huntsman was feeling strangely morose and eerily complacent. He wished he could feel the same motivating fear that the others felt, but he couldn't. The sounds of the Archenemy ascending the spiral staircase of the shaft should have elicited some panic if not terror, but he didn't feel either. Perhaps his three decades of Inquisitorial service had deadened his nerves. Perhaps his adolescent years as a 'beater', driving out large carnivores for his senior huntsmen on his home world of Veskipine, had hardened him. Boys tended to mature fast when they spent their youth flushing tusked lupines from their dens with little more than a switch cane. Most things just didn't affect him. Instead he popped the ivory button of his top coat pocket and drew a rolled stick of tabac. He ran it under his nose, wishing he had time to smoke one more.

The Ironclad thundered up the upper gallery landing. They surged out from the stairwell, baying and snorting for blood. For the first time, Silverstein saw them in the daylight. They were wild, bestial men roughly shod in a disarray of hauberks, breastplates, jack plate, brigandine or splint. Some brandished machine pistols, others lasguns. Silverstein even spotted a flak-musket somewhere.

They crashed onto the balcony. Silverstein closed his eyes, unwilling to examine them so close with his bioptics. He didn't want the last thing he saw to be a statistical analysis of the Archenemy.

'*Tung etai!*'

The killing blow did not come. A voice had barked them to a halt. Silverstein had coordinated enough times with the Imperial Guard to recognise an officer's authority when he heard it. Slowly, the huntsman opened his eyes.

The Archenemy stood at bay within arm's reach. They towered around him like a curtain of iron. Silverstein was not sure why, but his bioptics flickered and washed with static. His augmetics had never failed before, almost as if the circuitry could not bear to siphon such insidious visual imagery into his brain.

Staring into the eyes of Chaos, the six Canticans dropped their rifles and sank to their knees. Without the adrenaline of battle to fortify them, their nervous systems just gave out. It was just all too much.

'Kehmor avul, Kehmor eshek avul,' ordered the Chaos officer in a strangely lilting, free-flowing dark tongue. The minor warlord was a monstrous creature. Tall and sinuous, he was clad in a cuirass of nailed splint that tapered down into an armoured apron, giving him the frame of a rearing viper. Unlike his subordinates, the metal banding of the skull-piece that enclosed his head was patterned. It formed a symmetrical braid that ran down the centre of his head, some sort of rank, Silverstein surmised, that placed him as leader of this raiding party.

The underlord leaned in to examine them, tilting his head curiously. Without warning he lunged forwards and gripped Goa's throat. The elderly resistance fighter didn't react, even as he was dragged up to his feet. With one swift overhand motion the Ironclad hurled the man over the balcony.

Silverstein stood up. He did not want to die sitting down. The commander turned on him. He snagged the huntsman up by the lapels of his leather coat and forced Silverstein's torso over the balcony railing. Silverstein looked down at the fifty-metre drop. On the pavement below, Goa was laid open in a halo of blood.

But the Ironclad did not throw him. Instead, he paused, running his thumb along the collar of Silverstein's coat. The Inquisitorial service badge, a delicate little pin of silver, winked under the sunlight.

'You are a watchdog of the dead Emperor?' the Ironclad leader slithered in Low Gothic.

Silverstein clenched his jaw and said nothing.

'Orday anghiari inquiszt', the underlord said to his men. Judging by the crestfallen reactions, Silverstein surmised that they had just been denied the privilege of summary execution.

'I am Naik Ishkibal. Naik is my rank. Ishkibal is my blood name. You may not call me by either. To do so is sacrilege and I will have to kill you.

I tell you this because I do not want to kill you yet. Understand?' His voice had a metallic resonance that carried the threat well.

'Stick your fist up your own rear,' spat Silverstein.

'Good. Good. You learn quickly, watchdog. Let's see how long we can keep you around for. I think my warlords may want to have a word with you.'

'I'm not an inquisitor. I'm a game hunter,' replied Silverstein.

'All the same. You wear the pin, you have the answers,' chuckled the underlord. He turned to his subordinates and rattled off a series of orders in the dark tongue.

The Ironclad seized up the resistance fighters, laying in with punches and kicks as they did so. With heavy hands they began to bind hands and feet with wire cord.

'Amel buriash!' snapped the underlord. 'I need them in one piece for interrogation. I will eat the face of anyone who bleeds them without my permission.'

It was the third night they had spent in hiding. Roth was laced in blood, some of it his own, most of it not. Brick dust, grit and grime coated his armour in chalky enamel the colour of filthy teeth. Exhaustion had exceeded his physical limits, his tendons felt disconnected and his muscles throbbed.

Of his whereabouts, Roth was also vague. He guessed that he was hiding in the ventilation shaft of some semi-demolished tenement in Upper Buraghand. He couldn't even be sure of that, as they had dared not stay in any one location for too long. The roving murder squads were thorough in their patrols. Once, on the second day, they had nearly been caught. Desperately hungry, they had ventured into a semi-demolished granary processing plant in search of provisions. Instead they walked straight into an Ironclad patrol. They had barely escaped. Roth had canine bite-marks on his greaves to prove it.

Yet his suffering was purely physical. Roth's mind was still reeling from the system shock of his past seventy-two hours. Within that time he had lost Bastiel Silverstein, his unit of Cantican guerrillas had been decimated and now he was hiding in the crawl-space of a tenement basement, hoping he would not be discovered and shot. To add venom to his laments, he could not fathom who would hire the Orphratean Purebred to orchestrate such a premeditated ambush. He had been down every cognitive path, trying to piece together an answer, but nothing logical or even remotely rational could be gleaned. The only plausible explanation was betrayal. Betrayal from within his own cadre. In Roth's current state, that didn't bear thinking about.

Through the pandemonium of his thoughts, the only clear decision was that he could not flee Cantica aboard his lander. Although Celeminé had been adamant about withdrawal, Roth had refused to leave the planet, thoroughly defeated and no closer to the truth than when he started. Roth was stubborn when he wanted to be, and the Task Group was under his command. They had stayed, if only to salvage some semblance of a mission objective.

'I've brought you some soup to share,' said Celeminé. She was crawling along the tunnel towards him, one hand running along the overhead drainage pipes for balance. In her other hand she proffered a steaming cup canteen. 'It's only dehyd but it's cold tonight.'

Roth nodded his thanks and cradled the cup. He sipped it and rested his head back. The warm metal felt so good in his frost-numbed hands. The soup, despite being Guard ration, was not bad either. Thick and salty, it just reminded him of a rich grox consommé. But only just.

Celeminé settled next to Roth, wedging her boots against the opposite wall as she rested her back against the cramped confines. Perhaps it was his fatigue, but under the phosphorescent glow of gas burners she looked especially beautiful. The chemical lighting made the profile of her face positively porcelain. Even the ring in the centre of her lip, something Roth had never been fond of, gave her mouth a particularly innocent pout. Roth didn't even realise he was staring.

'We can't stay like this, you know,' Celeminé urged.

'Twelve more hours. If Silverstein hasn't voxed us by then...' Roth trailed off.

'Roth. We can't stay here. I'm sick of running and hiding. We have no food, we're low on water. We transit back to the *Carthage* and allow the Conclave to decrypt Delahunt's signet. It's reasonable and it makes sense.'

'In any other time or place, I would be inclined to agree with you, madame. But with so much at stake, we cannot leave Cantica until we are certain that the Old Kings will not fall into Archenemy hands. We haven't done enough here.'

Roth was not sure how much of his reply was false bravado and how much of it was simply his stubborn streak. But he just could not allow it. His mentor, the late Inquisitor Liszt Vandevern, had disparaged Roth as being too impetuous and far too possessed by emotion. Initially, Roth's lack of the rhythmic rationality so common amongst inquisitors almost cost him his sponsorship to full inquisitor. But throughout the years, Roth's gut instinct had stood him in good stead. Now his instincts told him he could not flee back to the Conclave with his tail between his legs, on account of two demoralising gunfights. Infiltrating a Chaos-held world, Roth had expected to be shot at. Indeed, it was part of his Inquisitorial duty to be shot at. Or maybe he just wasn't thinking straight.

'Roth, this is idiocy. I'm sorry but it is and I won't tell it any other way. At the very least, we have to move because we can't stay here,' Celeminé protested.

Roth noticed that when she was upset, she could not look Roth in the eyes. Instead she looked away and bit the tips of her fingers.

'I promised Silverstein I would wait for his vox in the tenement district. I can't move out of vox range.'

'Roth. Please. You said it yourself, we haven't done enough here. As much as it pains me to say it, this can't be about Silverstein. The Conclave has ordered us to establish whether the relics exist on Cantica.'

At her words, Roth expelled a ragged breath. She was right, and Roth knew it. They could leave now, or push on with the original mission. Roth could not leave, so that left him with only one option. 'We'll go,' he relented.

'I'm glad you've said that, because Captain Pradal has a wonderful plan!'

Roth laughed for the first time in four days. 'Please, do tell.'

'Have you heard artillery in the past few days?'

'No,' Roth admitted.

'Well I have. And so has the good captain. Which meant the Archenemy were still fighting. Evidently this would suggest Imperial forces are still active in the region. Captain Pradal risked raising vox contact on an Imperial frequency. He's very clever with comms and I don't think the Archenemy were able to tag on our location for long enough to get a fix. Unless we want them to.'

'And?'

'And he made contact. There is a battalion of Cantican Guardsmen, fighting hard about twenty kilometres north-west of Buraghand city.'

'So we proceed on foot for twenty kilometres through enemy territory?'

'No. Here's where the plan gets good.'

The murder squad thundered down the empty street, predatory machines roaring from brute engines of diesel. Two trucks painted off-white, escorted by two fighting patrol vehicles growling with throaty exhaust. The FPVs were squat, hog-nosed four-wheelers with an open passenger side chassis. A side-mounted heavy stubber panned out from the exposed opening, the gunner hunched down behind a mantlet. Since the Atrocities, the distinctive shuddering scream of an FPV engine was the most feared sound of the night. Resistance fighters and refugees were right in coining them 'preds and prowlers'.

Ripping down the war-torn streets of tenement quarter nine, the vehicles rolled to a juddering halt outside a tenement stack. The whole frontal façade of the building had sagged away from its structural frame like wet paper, exposing girders and twisted struts.

Someone had been broadcasting a distress signal on an Imperial frequency. A frequency that had been compromised since the Ironclad had overrun CantiCol forces. The signal had been pin-pointed to that very building.

The murder squads dismounted from their vehicles, checking weapons and cinching ammo belts the moment their boots hit the ground. The full complement of two squads, twenty killers in total, sprinted up the short stoop of steps towards the front entrance. Ironically, even though the wall around it had been demolished, the door in its door frame stood intact and alone. The squad leader – a Naik – bashed off the lock with his mace-gauntlet and the others formed a tactical column after him, weapons raised.

Inside, shafts of moonlight lanced in between the puncture wounds of masonry. A third of the tenement had fallen away like a cross-section cut. On the seventh storey, a child's bassinet balanced off a jagged edge of flooring, one wrought iron leg suspended over empty space.

The Naik homed in on the signal with auspex in hand. The signal was vibrant and clear, no more than a fifty metre radius away. Soon, he expected another dissident cell would learn the error of sustained broadcasts in an enemy zone. The Naik trained a heavy-calibre machine pistol into the geometric shadows ahead.

The murder squad sloshed down a communal corridor. Somewhere, a drainage pipe had ruptured, filling the bottom level with ankle-deep water, a soupy mixture of ash and sewerage. Most of the tenement doors had been torn off their hinges, the insides thoroughly ransacked. Furniture spilled out into the hallway, soggy, brittle wood crunching underfoot.

The auspex's chirping reached a shrill crescendo. Ahead, a locked utility door barred the way into the tenement's boiler basement. The vox beacon was broadcasting from within there, of that they were certain.

A piston ram, thirty kilograms of solid metal, was brought up from the rear of the line. The murder squads made final weapons checks. They were hungry for the kill, so much so that agitated clicking sounds came from behind their face bindings. An Ironclad swung the battering ram back with both hands and drove it into the door. The wood gave way like crunching bone.

The murder squad stormed the boiler room. The Naik entered first, swinging his pistol back and forth for a target. But the second he stepped into the room he noticed two things.

One, the room was empty except for a single military vox set. It was planted underneath a pool of moonlight, chattering away on the highest vox channel setting. Two, the door had been rigged up to a rudimentary pulley trap. A thread of wire fastened to the door had been hooked up to an overhead cinch, which in turn pulled taut on a brace of grenades. The stoved-in door, which now lay a good ten metres away, had snapped the pin loose with an audible clink.

By the time the Naik noticed, it was already far too late. He didn't bother to call out a warning, he just turned on his heels and tried to push his way back out through the door. He was nowhere near fast enough.

The grenades exploded with the sound of clapping concrete. Sixty thousand anti-personnel ball bearings shredded the boiler room. In an instant the plastered walls eroded into a perforated sponge. Of the Arch-enemy who had stormed the room, most were caught in a solid curtain of expanding shrapnel. The after-shock blew out every window of the tenement block that had not already been broken, and the windows of tenements several streets way.

The shattering windows gave them the signal to move. Roth rushed from his hiding place in a drainage ditch adjacent to the tenement's communal courtyard. The remains of his team followed close behind.

Scurrying low, hugging the walls of the building, they spotted the vehicles of the murder squad parked outside the front of the tenement. Roth ran towards an armoured truck, convinced he would be downed by an unseen shot before he reached it. No shots came and he hurled himself into the open door of the vehicle. Once inside, he turned and pulled Celeminé into the cab after him. In the rear-view mirror, he saw Captain Pradal and the two resistance fighters clamber onto the flat-bed.

The belly of the truck stank of machine grease and ammonia. He was glad it was too dark to see in detail. Reaching down underneath the heat-warped dashboard he fumbled for the keys. They were still warm in the ignition. He cranked it and nursed the truck to life like a winter-waked bear. Two spears of white light stabbed from the headlamps, pale and incandescent.

The truck began to roll, heavy and sluggish at first. Roth edged the vehicle forward, pressuring the accelerator. In the side mirror, Roth spotted an Ironclad stumble from the tenement entrance, dazed, wounded and brandishing his lasgun wildly. Captain Pradal put him down with a well-aimed shot. He then shot out the over-sized wheels of two stationary FPV Prowlers in quick succession.

'Go sir, now now now!' Pradal shouted. He slapped the back of the cab frantically.

Finally roused from its gear-seizing sleep the truck found its rhythm and surged away, trailing a cone of exhaust. The cracked speedometer clocked a high seventy, leaving the tenement quarters far behind.

Lord Marshal Khmer was brooding in the depths of his armchair when an adjutant announced the arrival of the Orphratean emissary.

The silk screen panels of his stateroom door slid smoothly open on intricate cog rollers. Aspet Fure walked into the chamber, bowing respect-fully at the threshold of the entrance. Like the others of his clan, Fure had the bronze skin and pale olive-green eyes that marked him as Purebred, a product of human eugenics. The bodyglove of snakeskin sepia did little to hide the hard muscular lines of his limbs. He was evidently a fighting man, and even though he had shed his wargear out of etiquette, a Lugos Hi-Power autopistol was holstered at his hip.

Khmer was not impressed. He did not even bother to rise out of his chair. To him, they were little more than uncultured freelancers. Indeed, the lineage of the company could be traced back to the barbarian soldiers of the Ophratean sub-arctic, during the lost times of pre-Unification. These were the very same savages who had worshipped sky pythons and raised pillars from the painted jawbones of their enemies only ten thousand years ago. Now the entire economy of Orphrates relied on the capital inflows of its famed mercenaries.

'Salutations, lord marshal. You seem morose, so I will keep this brief and civil,' began the Aspet.

The lord marshal raised an eyebrow. Obviously the barbarians had chosen an emissary who could string together sentences without growling between words, he mused.

'I'm listening,' said Khmer.

'An attack was orchestrated for the priority targets on Buraghand, Cantica, eighty hours ago. Your informant from within the target group was able to contact my company with ample intelligence. Unfortunately, the attack met with limited success. The priority target still lives–'

'Shut your mouth!' roared the lord marshal. He had sprung up from his chair, veins of anger popping livid against his neck. He stomped over to a dresser of chocolate satinwood. It was a masterpiece carved by the late Toussaint Pilon in the early Revivalist style. The furniture was inlaid with a veneer of pearl; the iridescent patterns resembled cherubs at play when viewed from a distance. Khmer put his boot straight through the lower cabinet.

'Do you know what this means? Your incompetence, the incompetence of your men may cost me everything! Do you know what we are dealing with here? We are dealing with the damned Inquisition. There was no room for error!'

'Which reminds me, lord marshal. You did not inform us prior to contract that the initial bait-target was a sworn member of the Inquisition. Such a high-risk killing brokers an eight hundred per cent increase on the initial amount.'

Khmer almost drooled with fury. 'I hired you idiots expecting full competency. Now you expect me to deal with this garbage?'

The Orphratean shrugged. 'We don't ask questions. We fought, we bled and we expect full payment. That's the way it works, lord marshal.'

'Not this time. You think I needed you to tell me of your failures? I already knew. I've known for some time that your men fouled up.'

The Orphratean was slightly taken aback. For once, confusion creased his noble features. 'Then why the facade? Why did you request a brief if you knew the answer?'

A cold slivered sneer crept up the corners of Khmer's mouth. 'Because I wanted you here when I told you the news of my own. I wanted you here so I could savour your reaction.'

The Orphratean took a step back. His fingertips rested lightly on his holstered pistol. Behind him the screen door rolled open and a full squad of provosts greeted him with a wall of shotguns and shock mauls.

The lord marshal cleared his throat theatrically for all to hear. 'I want to tell you, Aspet Fure, that twelve hours ago CantiCol garrison forces stationed on Orphrates raided your company holdings. They have broken your network, and what little remains of your enterprise have scattered into hiding. Your crimes, which include collusion with the Archenemy and murder of an Inquisitorial authority, have given me the right to terminate dealings with the Purebred across the subsector and process punishment accordingly.'

The Orphratean mercenary shook his head in mute disbelief.

'I'm sorry it had to be this way. But silence is a heavy price worth paying,' said Khmer as he turned his back on the Purebred.

CHAPTER NINE

The last battalion of the 26th Colonial Artillery had been fighting for the past thirty-one days. Since the Atrocities, twelve hundred men of the 26th had fought for the cave temples twenty kilometres west of Buraghand city.

They had held, even as the meat-grinding advance of Ironclad mechanised columns had crushed ninety per cent of CantiCol forces. Every day the Archenemy had assaulted that pale, coarse-grained intrusion of igneous tusk over three hundred metres in height. Every day the warren of caves within the batholith had repelled them with guns and artillery.

Strategically, the low-lying scrubland provided limited enemy cover. Erosion had weathered the surrounding ruins and trace fossils into sculptural rock. Bulbous succulents and taproot knotted in the gaps of man-made geoforms. Ever since the Guard had been stationed at the cave temples they had coined it the 'Barbican'. The three thousand Archenemy dead that littered the dry prairie attested to that.

Spitting up great plumes of smoke, sixty-pounders had bombarded the Archenemy positions, harassing them and taunting them into suicidal charges. The great guns vibrated the caverns with their recoil, lobbing shells beyond the Erbus canal five kilometres out.

Although sustained enemy assaults had inflicted five hundred and ninety-two casualties, the battalion kept fighting. The 26th fought on almost in spite of the fact that they had nothing left to defend. Before the conquest, they had been tasked with defending the only motorway that connected Buraghand to the western outlands, but that didn't matter any more.

It was during the early hours of the thirty-first day that Inquisitor Obodiah Roth and his retinue sought refuge within the Barbican. Their captured truck had been left beyond the perimeter defences of the cave temples. By virtue of superstition the vehicle had been set ablaze beyond the razor wire.

Lurching up the escarpment, the inquisitor and his men looked bloodied, ragged and delirious with fatigue. They stumbled towards the nearest cave bunker, an outlying sentry post that could fit no more than three or four men.

It was camouflaged with prairie grass and fortified by a breastwork of mud and basket-woven sticks. From the cave, Troopers Prasad and Buakaw rushed out to meet them. At the sight of the Guardsmen, in the brown jackets and rank sashes of the CantiCol, the inquisitor fumbled out his rosette. Exhaustion tarred the words in his mouth. Instead he cast the rosette onto the ash before him, as he collapsed onto one knee.

Roth did not know how long he had been sleeping for. He could not even remember falling asleep. When he awoke, the high-noon suns filled his vision, flaring from the cave mouth in a prickling wash of white light.

He found himself in a small cave, asleep over a bed of packing crates. The cuirass of his Spathaen fighting-plate had been shed like a metal husk on the ground. He was still armoured from the hip down, but on top he had been stripped down to a loose cotton shirt that was stiff with sweat mineral. Somehow he still holstered his plasma pistol in its shoulder rig.

Squinting against the light, Roth eased himself up. He winced as his stiff limbs stung with lactic build-up. A cursory inspection yielded bruised ribs, minor lacerations and stress fractures in his lower legs. Given his circumstances, Roth considered himself extremely fortunate.

He took stock of his surroundings, realising he was in a hand-carved cave with a smoothed floor and low ceiling. Dimly, he remembered he was in some sort of cave temple complex, a place of pilgrimage before the war. Small shrines and votive offerings to the God-Emperor cluttered one side of the grotto – crude clay aquilas, painted candles, beads, scriptures on parchment strips feathering the walls.

Shuffling over to the cave mouth he peered down at the Barbican, which sprawled out beneath him. It was a shelved cliffside of grey and ivory stone, smeared with banks of thorn-bush, reed and toothy stumps of cactus. The slope was broken by almost vertical cliffs in some places – rocky, bare, precipitous and irregular. At its plateau, batteries of field artillery bristled like a roc's nest, heavy Earthshaker barrels saluting the horizon.

'Sleep well, inquisitor?' asked Captain Pradal. Roth turned to see the man emerge from a stooped tunnel at the rear of the cave. The officer had shaved and scrubbed most of the bloodied filth from his face. His head was bandaged and so was his left wrist.

'Like a beaten-up child,' said Roth, rubbing his face with his hands. Flakes of dried blood and filth dislodged into his palms.

'Welcome, inquisitor. It's about time we had some conscious activity out of you.' A second man had appeared beside Pradal. His rank sash denoted him as colonel, but he was young for a man of such rank. Thick-necked, square-jawed and shaven-headed, the officer looked more like gang muscle than a colonel of the artillery. When he spoke his voice was sandy and coarse, whether from chain-smoking tabac or gun-smoke inhalation, Roth could not tell. Both suited his rough-edged demeanour.

'My thanks, colonel–'

'Colonel Gamburyan, battalion commander of the 26th,' he said.

They briefly shook hands. The colonel's grip was hard and callused, from years of gripping awkward shells and pulling artillery pieces. It made Roth ashamed of his own well-manicured hands.

'Captain Pradal here has given me a full briefing of your situation. I wouldn't have a frag's clue how we can help, but if there's anything you need, I can try my hardest to accommodate,' rasped the colonel as he drew a stick of tabac from behind his ear and lit it in one deft, well-practiced movement.

In truth Roth could have done with some sustenance, or even some water and a rag to scour the solid filth that caked his body, but he had his priorities.

'I need a cipher machine, a cryptographer. Military-grade will do, you must have one somewhere.'

The colonel savoured a mouthful of smoke and nodded. 'I thought you would. The other inquisitor, Sella-meanie I think her name is. She said you might need one. I've got it set up in the main command bunker.'

'Excellent. You are quite on the ball, colonel,' said Roth as he struggled to his feet.

'Have to be. We're alive aren't we?' He shrugged with a grin, tabac stick clenched between his teeth. 'Anything else I can do for you?'

Roth sighed wearily. 'Yes, colonel. May I be so frank as to ask for a smoke?'

When Roth had requested a military-grade cryptographer, he had forgotten that military-grade often stood for obsolete, un-serviced and possibly broken.

The cipher machine was a heavy-duty cogitator set up in the sandbagged belly of the Barbican. Its porcelain casing was furred with dust, the spindles and keystrokes cracked and faded. Several hundred rusty cables spooled out from underneath its skirting like the tentacles of an undersea leviathan. Roth had never in all his years of service seen a cogitator like it.

With neither patience nor an inclination for technology, Roth left most of the work to Celeminé. She was a natural, tapping on the loom pedals as she adjusted the bristle of cogs and dials. The machine purred, and a flower of ivory set above the mantle of the machine began to gyrate, signalling the decoder's activation. Roth tried to busy himself with the cables, trying to look useful.

'The sooner you stop fussing over my shoulder, the sooner we can begin the decoding,' admonished Celeminé.

Roth mumbled an apology and sat himself down on a bench improvised from plywood and ammunition trunks, content to watch. Celeminé plugged Delahunt's signet into the cipher's central feed, winking data pulses into the machine's logic engines. Her other hand began to spool paper out from the mouth of a porcelain cherub's face set into the machine's side casing.

'Is it done?' asked Roth, craning for a look from his seat.

'No. This signet is magenta-level encryption and this decoder is garbage-level *de*cryption. Its logic engines have to penetrate the data's enigma coding and polyalphabetic substitution. You can figure out the rest.'

Roth stared at her blankly. Celeminé stood, one hand on her hip, her suede boots tapping in reprove. She had changed out of her bodyglove and procured a cotton shirt and some baggy CantiCol breeches. The trousers fit her so loosely that she had to double them over and cinch them tight around her tiny waist with a silk scarf. Likewise, the shirt was so voluminous that she knotted the hem up above her midriff. Roth thought she looked like some sort of hive dancer. She rolled her eyes at him.

'It means this might take a while.'

'That's quite all right. We can wait,' said Roth.

As if to prove him wrong, the cave bunker suddenly shook with a low tremor. Grit loosened from the rafters in a dusty downpour. Roth felt the percussive heave in the depths of his diaphragm.

'Are we under attack?' Celeminé said. Her playful demeanour vanished in an instant. Her chest webbing, sloughed off and hung on the rafters overhead, was snatched down.

'I don't think that's incoming artillery,' answered Roth. The cavern shook again, jarring the sand-bagged walls.

'What is it then?'

'Outgoing, of course. The Guard are firing on targets.' His reply was punctuated by a rhythmic trio of blasts, the decibels echoed by the acoustic warren of the cave temples.

Soon enough, Cantican officers began clattering into the command bunker. The bank of vox arrays that encompassed an entire wall of the cave began to hiss and chatter with multiple open stations. The sound of distant gunfire and commands, washed with static began to grate out of the speakers.

Roth snagged a passing captain by the sleeve as he ran by. 'What's the situation?' Roth asked.

The captain looked at Roth like he had been just asked a rhetorical question. 'Uh… well we're fighting, of course. Again. Ironclad infantry offensive, crossing the Erbus canal and making another break across no-man's-land.'

'Does this happen often?'

'Every damn day,' came the reply.

Captain Pradal sighted the Archenemy first. He had volunteered for sentry in one of the forward observation caves overlooking the northern approach when he saw them – Archenemy foot scouts silently scouring up the steep scree slope no more than two hundred metres away.

Through his magnoculars, he saw them skulking low against the tumbled wedges of igneous rock, slowly rustling through the crops of mountainous flora. They made good use of the sparse cover, crawling on the loose gravel and hugging the dry, stunted vegetation. At first he counted no more than ten, but then he saw twenty, fifty, perhaps more. A full company advancing in open file.

Pradal turned to the two Guardsmen in the gunpit alongside, handing one of them his magnoculars as he reached for the vox-set. There was no need. The Archenemy fired first. A flak rocket, most likely from a shoulder launcher, screamed overhead, trailing a ragged spine of smoke. It spiralled wildly before exploding forty metres uphill in a scatter of rock fragments.

And just like that, the Archenemy announced their presence. With a bestial roar that swelled in volume, the Ironclad surged to their feet and charged. All told, Pradal counted four, maybe five, full infantry companies, most emerging from cover. They thundered up the slope in a staggered line, closing the two hundred metre distance fast. But beyond the infantry screen, kicking up a curtain of dust, mechanised columns rolled across the Erbus canal in support. It was the fighting vehicles that terrified Pradal most of all.

All at once, the three perimeter positions, two cave bunkers and a concrete pillbox opened fire. Captain Pradal had bellied down behind the gunpit's lone heavy bolter. The forty kilogram gun bucked like an industrial drill, even when Pradal threw his weight behind it. Fat nosed bolt shells slammed out of the barrel.

'Command one! This is forward observation eight. Enemy infantry advancing at north bank!' barked Private Chamdri into the vox-set. He was hunkered down next to Pradal, one hand over his kepi hat as he screamed into the mouthpiece.

By now the Archenemy had reached the first line of defence, a cordon of razor wire three coils deep. Pradal hammered rocket-propelled bolt shells into them at a range of fifty metres, throwing up a mist of blood and fragmented metal wherever he raked the gun. The enemy answered with spikes of las-fire.

Pradal's vision began to tunnel. He smelt the methane stink of fyceline as his weapon ejected steaming-hot cartridges. A las-round punched through an empty ammo pallet by his side. Smouldering splinters of wood drizzled the air, prickly warm against his cheek.

'Come on you fraggers. This is my house!' Pradal shouted. He clenched the spoon trigger hard, the long burping bursts of fire muting his words into angry grimacing.

Through the cross hairs, Pradal shot an Ironclad pawing through a clutch of brush-tail reed. The shell's mass-reactive payload ruptured its target, throwing up a fan of blood and dry brown grass. His next shot went wide, hitting an arrow-headed slab of scree. It didn't matter. The rocket-propelled round exploded into a boulder, sending fist-sized fragments of rock shearing through the air. It killed more Ironclad than a direct hit. On and on he fired as Private Chamdri fed a looping belt of ammunition into the chamber. Throwing out an automatic stream, Pradal was ignoring the standard Guard doctrine of tightly controlled bursts. There were too many enemies for that.

Further up the incline, other cave temples fired within their interlocking arcs, throwing up a solid curtain of fire. Bolters, autocannons and heavy stubbers, their elemental roars combining into decibels so deafening it reduced Pradal's hearing to a soft tinnitus ring.

'–fun without me–' came a voice, muffled as if spoken through water. Pradal only caught broken snatches of it. Turning to his side, he saw Inquisitor Roth emerge from the connective tunnel at the rear of the gunpit and slide next to him.

'Not yet, sir! You've only missed the prologue,' Pradal yelled back. At least that's what he thought he said. He couldn't hear a damn thing.

Nonetheless he was correct. The infantry advance had only been a screen. Ensnared in razor wire and pulverised by heavy weapons at close range, the Ironclad infantry assault had withered. Now half a kilometre off, the mechanised assault was only just closing in. Growling, fuming, howling – no less than fifty fighting patrol vehicles, gun-trucks and Chimeras supported by a full lance of KL5 Scavenger-pattern light tanks. The eight-wheeled tanks, gleaming white and up-armoured, loomed like ghosts.

'–light tanks are going to ruin our day–' mouthed Roth. The Guardsmen cramped in the gunpit echoed the inquisitor's sentiments with colourful language. In a way, Pradal was glad the weapons had dulled his hearing.

'Can you crack them?' Roth screamed, practically directly into Pradal's ear.

Pradal shifted the heavy bolter and lined up one of the fast-approaching KL5s under the iron sights. He unleashed a long sustained blast that sent shockwaves rippling up to his shoulders. The heavy rounds *spanged* off the tank's frontal hull, erupting in a chain of small explosions. Underneath the coiling smoke and punctured plating, the tank was not affected.

Despite their sustained fire the mechanised assault rumbled on. Now only three hundred metres away, the columns began to fan out into a cavalry line. Tracers flashed into them, the shriek of solid slugs impacting on metal. A handful of FPVs and gun trucks caught fire as fuel tanks combusted, shedding peels of flaming wreckage as they spun out of control.

Enemy fire intensified, chopping into the Guard positions. The Archenemy were upon them now. Ironclad infantry dismounted from their motorised convoy, struggling up the hill against the teeth of Imperial fire. To Pradal's right, a light tank rolled in line with the forward pill-box. Its turret slowly traversed, lining up the fortification with a chain-fed autocannon.

'We have to move!' shouted Roth. He grabbed Pradal by the collar and dragged him away. Pradal didn't see what happened next. He didn't need to. The KL5 fired and he felt rather than heard the cataclysm, as sixty kilotonnes of kinetic energy split open thirty-centimetre thick rockcrete.

Half a kilometre up, a whickering salvo of enemy fire belted the highest defensive line. Defensive breastworks of interlacing logs, sticks and clay mortar bore the ruptured scarring of heavy-calibre rounds.

Celeminé threw herself flat as a javelin of las-fire fizzed into her cave bunker. It dissolved a neat hole into the pilgrim's shrine at the rear of the cave. Jugs, candles and blessing dolls clattered off the rock shelf.

'Anti-armour weapons, over there, give it to me!' Celeminé shouted at the two troopers sharing her gunpit. In the panic of war, she lost all semblance of grammatical eloquence.

'Are you sure? The enemy are too far out of range, inquisitor, it would be a waste,' Trooper Jagdesh shouted back.

'Yes, yes! Just hand it over,' Celeminé beckoned as Jagdesh bellycrawled over with a shoulder-launched missile. He was right of course; at five hundred metres, the frag missile would likely propel away in a wild spiral at two hundred. She had a different idea.

'Load me,' she said, chewing on her lip in contemplation. Jagdesh held the launcher tube upright as Trooper Gansükh fixed the shaped-charge warhead. As they handed her the weapon they gave her a look that implied she was totally mad.

Shouldering the rocket, Celeminé peered over the breastworks. She saw tinder sparks flashing from camouflaged gun-holes, weapons nests and fortified cave-temples. She saw Ironclad dismount from their transports to storm the defences like tiny silver beetles below.

Celeminé adjusted the cross-hairs for angle and distance. She armed the fire control lever and took aim. A solid slug cracked past her shoulder but she was too deep in psytrance to notice. Resting the launcher over the edge of the breastwork, she aligned the sights on a KL5 light tank, two hundred metres and closing.

'Watch for the back-blast!' she warned.

The weapon clapped with a hollow bang. A cone of pressurised exhaust jetted into the rear of the cave, the thermal gas destroying what remained of the pilgrim's trinkets. The warhead itself trailed a coiled serpent of smoke in its wake, stabiliser fins snapping. For over two hundred metres it stayed on trajectory, until the rocket lost momentum and crazed off target.

Celeminé concentrated hard and reached out with her mind, snagging the warhead and forcing it back on path. She could feel the whirr of the gyro motor, jumping against her control as if she were cradling the rocket in her hands. It flew up in a catapulting loop before spearing back down on the KL5. Celeminé hooked it down onto the turret and the missile did what it was designed for. Its copper rocket sheath punched through the enemy plating and high explosives rocked the tank from inside out. The turret flew off. Wheels collapsed. A side hatch popped open and flaming figures staggered out of the tank, before collapsing on the rocks. They writhed like tortured beetles before lying still.

'That's one,' breathed Celeminé. As if in reply, a salvo of impact slugs chopped overhead. The inquisitor and her soldiers ducked into an exit tunnel, just as a volley of autocannon rounds hammered into the cave-bunker they had held scant seconds ago. The cave collapsed behind them with a seismic bellow and a mournful shudder.

In the central command bunker, deep within the heart of the Barbican, the command post pounded with activity. Signals officers hunched at vox-bays, screaming into headsets, each louder than the next. Battalion commanders surged back and forth, relaying orders and communiqués, scraping knees against supply crates and yelling over each other's shoulders. Overhead, explosions throbbed through the thick stone. The single sodium lamp swung on its cord, casting wild claustrophobic shadows.

Roth and Pradal dashed into the command post through one of its many connective tunnels. Between them they dragged Private Chamdri, who was crying with fear, his hands held up above him like he was already surrendering.

'Colonel Gamburyan!' Roth bellowed. He juiced his words with psychic amplification, so he could be heard above the pandemonium.

From a circle of officers huddled around a map table, Gamburyan looked up. The colonel had shed his cavalry blazer and his braces hung from his breeches. Crescents of sweat soaked the chest and arms of his undershirt. The officer excused himself from his peers.

'Inquisitor. How do you do?'

'I've just had an autocannon almost rearrange my gentlemanly graces. But I'm otherwise in perfect health, thank you. What's the situation?'

'The situation is under control. Nothing we haven't seen before,' replied the colonel as he dragged on a tabac stick.

'Sir, the perimeter bunkers are being overrun,' Pradal interjected.

'As is expected, captain. Defensive nests on the north and west banks are scrapping with a mounted infantry offensive. I've already ordered artillery to flatten the perimeter as our forces withdraw deeper into the Barbican. Trust me, we've seen much worse than this.'

As if to reiterate the colonel's assurance, the low bass rumble of artillery thrummed like muzzled thunder. Deep within the cave complex, it sounded like an avalanche rolling down the escarpment.

The fighting continued well past sundown, ebbing and flowing in intensity. Three more times that day, the Ironclad mounted a concerted offensive of mixed-order advance – mechanised columns scattered with infantry platoons. They met tenacious resistance, scythed down in ranks by the furious torrent of Imperial fire. More than once, the Ironclad overran the first-line defences, breaching the bunkers with grenades and flamer. At one stage, a squad of Ironclad had even penetrated up into the tunnel network, massacring an artillery crew before they were put down.

The Canticans had manned their posts in short shifts, fingers tense, eyes glazed and shaking with adrenaline. They had fired a total of over sixty thousand shells, missiles, las-charges and solid slugs. By evening the enemy had receded, slinking away into the dusk-bruised horizon.

Sustained assaults on the north and western banks had inflicted sizeable casualties. Major Aghajan, the battalion's deputy commander, had been one of those killed. He and five other senior officers had been on routine inspection during a break in the assault when a single enemy mortar had claimed them all. It was an irreplaceable loss to the battalion. In all, forty-one men of the 26th were killed in that day's fighting. Many more were wounded.

CHAPTER TEN

For now the field was quiet. The following morning had passed without further enemy movement, or even gas or shell attack. Yet the weariness of battle was still fresh in Roth's mind, while his ears were ringing with the hum of post-battle. At night the ringing had become so persistent that Roth had not slept, and now he welcomed the quiet. The fighting at the Barbican was by far the most confrontational and desperate siege he could have imagined.

He stood on the flat mesa plateau of the Barbican, watching the sweeping expanse of knotted rock that fell away like a stretched grey blanket. So high up, the wind fluttered against Roth's plating, a stirring buffet that numbed the tips of his ears and nose. It carried with it a fine ashy dust from the tomb flats between Buraghand and the western coast, coarse and cold. Before the war, the ascent of the cave temples had been known as the Pilgrim's Stairway.

It was not that any more. The bodies of the Archenemy littered the slopes like beached carcasses, tangled in razor wire and scattered between stones. Dark, scorched rings and jag-toothed craters scarred the earth. The scene was still and grey, trailing curls of smoke like every battlefield Roth had ever surveyed. But in its own way Cantica was also different. There was no hope here; the fighting was done, like the curtains had already fallen. The atmosphere was quiet, contemplative and deeply morose.

This was where he was going to die.

Roth picked up a wedge of flint and threw it towards the horizon where the Archenemy amassed. Out there, four hundred thousand soldiers of the Ruinous Powers prowled the landscape, burning and butchering. His work here was done. He would give the Conclave what he found and he would be allowed to die here, at least with some dignity and defiance.

He heard footsteps clapping up the tunnel steps that led onto the plateau. Roth presumed it was Celeminé, returning with the readouts from the cipher machine. But it wasn't just her.

The hatch door, camouflaged with a nest of thorn-bush, slid aside. Colonel Gamburyan climbed from the hatch, dragging on tabac as always. Celeminé emerged after him, clutching a sheaf of wafers.

'Marvellous view from here,' said Roth, turning back to stare into the distance.

'Always good to see the results of a hard scrap,' Colonel Gamburyan nodded as they moved to join Roth at the edge of the precipice.

'How many did we lose today, colonel?'

'We lost Corporal Alatas in the infirmary just five minutes ago. He lost a leg from a tank round and bled out, poor bastard. That makes forty-one today.'

'Oh,' said Roth, his shoulders visibly sagging.

Gamburyan proffered a little envelope of waxed paper. 'Would you like a stick of tabac? You look terrible.'

Roth laughed at the soldier's blunt observation as he drew a stick. Roth had not seen a mirror in so long. He dreaded what he would look like, if he ever saw one again.

'Where do you keep finding these anyway?' sighed Roth.

At first, the big man almost looked sheepish. 'Votive offerings. You'd be surprised how many pilgrims had left tabac for the pleasure of the God-Emperor.'

The inquisitor snorted. 'The Emperor provides.'

A rustle of paper behind him reminded Roth of Celeminé's presence. His mind had grown absent of late. It was not at all like him. He turned to her and bowed deeply.

'How rude of me. I'm sorry, madame, was there something you wished to speak to me about?' Roth asked.

She nodded, oddly straight-faced. Celeminé handed Roth the sheaf of papers. 'I have the decrypted text from Delahunt's research log.'

Roth took the papers and flicked through them absent-mindedly, not really reading anything. 'What does he say?' Roth asked, looking up from behind the wafers.

'Delahunt seems to have thought the Old Kings cannot be on Cantica.'

Roth shrugged. 'I thought as much.'

'You did?' Celeminé asked.

'If they were, do you not think the Archenemy would have found them by now? Cantica has been their playground for well over a month.'

'I did find something of importance in his research,' said Celeminé. She rifled through the pages until she found it and held it up for Roth to see.

'Here. He writes that, "It is with some degree of certainty, judging by historical evidence and geological composition, that relics from the War of Reclamation do not reside on Cantica. Rather, the myth of the Old Kings became a pillar of institutional identity, so embedded within the historical collective and creational narrative of the planet, that it has become difficult to separate myth from reality."'

'What does that mean?' Colonel Gamburyan asked.

'It means our work here is done. The Old Kings must reside on one of the other core worlds, colonel, one of the core worlds under the jurisdiction of another Conclavial member.'

'So where do we go from here?' Celeminé interjected.

Roth thought for a while. It was not that he needed to work out what he needed to do. No, he had given that much thought already. It was how he was going to propose it to Celeminé.

'We stay here, madame. The colonel could do with our help, I am sure.'

'We… stay?' Celeminé repeated. She found it hard to roll the words off her tongue. Even Colonel Gamburyan was surprised. He let the stub of his tabac slip out of his fingers to be carried away by the wind, spinning and tumbling.

'Yes. Of course. We are inquisitors. We fight the enemies of mankind until we die. That is our role. We accepted that the moment we became what we are. What good would fleeing do?' said Roth. He couldn't look into Celeminé's eyes. Instead he kept his gaze level with the horizon.

Celeminé stopped talking. By the expression on her face, she was not prepared for his answer at all.

'Inquisitor. You do not have to do this,' the colonel began.

'But we must. What other choice do we have? We cannot reach the stratocraft. Not surrounded as we are. Better to die here fighting than to be shot like dogs running.'

'This is about Silverstein isn't it?' Celeminé snapped.

Roth didn't say anything.

Celeminé shook her head softly. 'Let me convene with Gurion.'

'If you must. But I do not think the choice is ours anyway. Out there, the four hundred thousand killers disagree with your prognosis.' Roth gestured into the distance.

'I-I see your logic. But I will ask Lord Gurion as I relay him our findings,' Celeminé replied in unconvinced, yet soft deference.

'As you wish,' said Roth finally. He took a drag of his tabac and turned away without another word.

At one hour past midnight, when the night was at its coolest and quietest, the Ironclad attacked again. A line of infantry waded out from the shadows of the prairie, flanked by fast-moving FPVs in a sweeping pincer. The forward observation bunkers, barely repaired from the previous day's fighting, engaged the Archenemy at a range of no more than fifty metres. Above, the artillery banks on the crest of the Barbican did not fire, their muzzles threatening but silent. Ammunition was low as it was, and far too precious to squander on anything short of enemy armour.

By all accounts of the Guard at his side, Inquisitor Roth fought furiously. He led a thirty-man platoon on a counter-attack, bayonets fixed. They hooked around wide to pinch the flanks of the Ironclad pincer, disrupting their advance with enfilade fire. The Canticans under Roth's command fought like men with nothing to lose. It should have been suicide, unarmoured Guardsmen on open terrain exchanging shots with Ironclad fighting patrol vehicles. They hammered away with shoulder-mounted rockets, and when those ran dry, they charged. It was rough, dirty fighting. Hand-to-hand, face-to-face.

Men of the 26th witnessed Inquisitor Roth drive his power fist through the engine block of an FPV. The inquisitor tore the light-skinned vehicle right down the middle and gunned down the occupants in the cab. Visibility was poor and the men fought blind, gouging and flailing at heavy black shapes.

Despite their small numbers, the counter-attack blunted the momentum of the Ironclad push, halting them just short of the razor wire. At eight minutes into the assault the Ironclad withdrew, chased back into the shadows by drizzles of las-fire.

Celeminé settled into a cross-legged lotus posture, drawing deep, relaxing breaths. It was severely difficult to concentrate with the constant fighting outside her cave bunker. Since her arrival, the fighting had almost been incessant. There was nothing she could do about that.

She had tried her best to find the most suitable cavern for her needs. After a little searching, she had come upon a shelved pocket deep in the heart of the Barbican. A gaudy papier-mâché saint slathered in garish pastels had once dominated the chamber, draped with garlands of grain and prayer beads. Since the Atrocities, the saint shared her shrine with ammunition pallets and stacked drums of fuel. Cantica had once been beautiful, and wistfully, Celeminé wished she could have visited it before the Medina War. If only.

Slowly, Celeminé drew herself into a meditative state. The distant drumming of gunfire faded. She was trancing. The temperature in the cave plummeted. Candles arranged in geometric patterns flickered out all at once. Celeminé's breath, steady and rhythmic, plumed frostily.

A gentle calm pervaded throughout the chamber. The saint, kneeling with hands in benediction, watched over Celeminé with glassy eyes. Condensation formed on the saint's cheeks, curling the paper skin and melting the pigmentation from her face. As Celeminé's consciousness drifted from her body, the last thing she saw was the gaudy saint crying in prayer.

From the port side of the *Carthage*, the satellite suns of Medina glimmered through the glare-shutters of the tall, arching viewing bays. Judging by the alignment of the suns, it would be hazing dawn on Cantica.

In his stateroom, Forde Gurion's chron, synced to Cantican time, struck three in the morning. He sat in a deeply cushioned high-back. Because of his hoofed augmetics, Gurion seldom needed to sit, but he often did out of courtesy and to make his guests at ease. It was very important to make the man, sitting in the chair across from him, very much at ease indeed.

'Would you like a drink?' Gurion said, gesturing at the thimble of ambrose in his hand. He did not need to gesture, however: the man was blind.

'No, my thanks. Liquor distorts mental clarity,' said the man with the sunken, hollow eyes. The embroidered robes, spilling over the armrests in a radiant sheen of emerald, marked him as an adept of the Astra Telepathica.

'Oh but of course. I ask you every time, don't I?'

'The last two times we have tried this. Yes.'

'Let us hope we are more fortunate this time,' said Gurion, webs of worry crinkling the corners of his eyes.

'If the Emperor wills it,' replied the astropath in his monotone voice.

With this, the astropath sidled down deeper into his robes, sinking back into the chair. His head tilted forwards and for a long time he was very still. It almost looked as if the psyker had nodded off to sleep. Then, despite the wrought-iron heating grille set into the stateroom fireplace, it grew colder by a dozen degrees. The air took on a scent of residual ozone.

Gurion felt uncomfortable, but not because of the chill. It was the astropath. In over a century of service to the Inquisition, Gurion had dealt with astropaths many times, but it never made it easier. It was the way they writhed and squirmed in their trance, their faces twisting and leering in pantomime agony. Or perhaps, it was the fact that their minds were swimming through the warp. Gurion had always believed that the only barrier between the warp ghosts and him were the astropath's eyelids. That if the man were to suddenly arch up his stomach, with his mouth partially open, then his eyelids would snap open and all the warp would come streaming through.

Gurion slammed down the thimble and shook his head vigorously to clear it. The tart spice and earthy terroir of the Mospel River vintage anchored his senses. Just in case, he placed a small nickel-plated autopistol in his lap and waited while watching his chron.

'Gurion…' the astropath murmured after a long period of silence.

Gurion started inwardly. When the man spoke, it was not with the monotone he had grown accustomed to. Instead, it was the soft, canting lilt of Felyce Celeminé. It never failed to disturb him. Someone had once explained to Gurion that through the psychic connection, the mediator became one with the messenger, mimicking emotions, voice patterns and even body language. That did not make it any less disconcerting to an old non-psyker.

'Gurion…' called Celeminé's voice.

The old inquisitor leaned forwards, the servomotors in his hip whirring. 'Yes. Yes, Felyce, I am here, it's Forde Gurion.'

'Gurion. I don't know if it's safe to commune. It's very loud here. Very violent and colourful. I need you to listen to what we know,' mouthed the astropath.

'Of course. Tell me, dear,' nodded Gurion. He picked up a data-slate from an adjacent stand and made ready to scribe with a gilded stylus.

'Where do I start?'

'From the beginning, please, dear.'

Word after word, Celeminé began to recount their findings. She told him of Delahunt's fate, his research, and the fall of Cantica. Most importantly, she told him that the Old Kings were not on the conquered planet. That it must be, by reason of deduction, hidden on one of the other two core worlds. By the time the astropath finished talking, Gurion realised his augmetic left hand had clenched so hard it had gouged small crescent moons into the leather armrest of his chair.

'And what of you two? Are you well? Is Obodiah well?'

'Roth is… I am well. But Inquisitor Roth wishes to stay and die on Cantica. He says we have nowhere to run, so we should die fighting… I–' began the astropath.

Gurion shook his head. 'No no no. That will not do. The Conclave still needs you.'

'I thought as much,' said the astropath. Gurion was not sure, but it seemed the man actually breathed a sigh of relief.

'No. Celeminé, listen carefully. Inquisitor Vandus Barq on Aridun has uncovered something crucial to our work here. We can't risk transmitting the information by vox or astro-telepathy so I need Roth and the Overwatch Task Group to travel to Aridun. It matters not how you get there, just depart with all possible haste. Vandus Barq is in the Temple of the Tooth, on the Antillo continent. That is all I can tell you and I fear I may have already said too much. Can you rendezvous with him?'

'We can try,' said the astropath, shrugging his shoulders up high like Celeminé would.

'That's all I expect, Celeminé. Try to arrive within two weeks' time. Vandus will wait for you.'

'Yes, Lord Gurion. I have to go now,' said the astropath, octaves wavering between a female and male voice.

'Take care of yourselves,' Gurion pleaded. He gripped the astropath's hand earnestly, then immediately felt foolish for doing so.

Roth had been waiting for news from Celeminé for some time. Anxious with anticipation, he had attempted to occupy his mind with other activities. At the behest of Colonel Gamburyan, Roth and the battalion commander elected to conduct a general assessment of the forward defences.

He followed Gamburyan from bunker to bunker, conversing with soldiers at their posts, praising them for a job well done and sharing tabac. It was the standard officer's inspection. But it also served to give them a realistic assessment of their situation. The Guardsmen were tired, their nerves frayed from ceaseless fighting. Some took it well, becoming inured to the threat of constant enemy attack; others less so, their hands trembling, their faces offering only blank stares. Supplies, especially clean water, were running low and dysentery was becoming endemic. If the Archenemy didn't kill them, starvation and infections would.

At designated cave bunker two-two, a mid-line gunpit housing a heavy stubber draped with camouflage netting, they came upon a dying man. His name was Corporal Nabhan, and he was feverish with gangrene. Wrapped in a blanket and clutching his lasrifle, the Guardsman had volunteered to hold bunker two-two on his own until he died. Dehydration and infection had leeched the corporal into a pale wisp of a man. Colonel Gamburyan knelt by the Guardsman and administered him several tablets of dopamine. There was little else Roth could do.

As Gamburyan nursed capfuls of water from a canteen for Corporal Nabhan, Roth heard a knock on the support frame of the cave tunnel. Celeminé entered the cave, ducking low to avoid bumping her head on the support beams.

'Lord Gurion's astropath contacted me,' she said, biting her lip.

'Very good. What does the Conclave say?' Roth asked. For a man who seldom flinched when being shot at, Roth was suddenly nervous.

'Well, in light of our recent findings, Gurion orders us to make for Aridun and–'

'Absolutely out of the question,' Roth interrupted.

His answer evidently jarred Celeminé. Her eyes took on that particular tint of rose before tears, a sad ruby kohl that made her seem suddenly vulnerable. Roth felt a spike of guilt.

'Apologies for my lack of courtesy, madame. I simply mean that it is not possible for us to leave. We have been hunted ever since landfall. Better we make a stand here.'

Celeminé's eyes hardened. 'In truth, Roth, I don't want to die here. There is still much to do.'

'I understand how you feel, but we have little choice. We've finished what we needed to.'

'Roth, I'm sorry but I really don't think you do. I'm too young. I have more to accomplish.'

But Roth did understand. He remembered his virgin deployment to Sirene Primal in 866.M41. Caught between a secessionist insurgency and an alpha-level xenos threat, that first assignment had almost killed him. The fatalistic part of him always believed he should have died on Primal, and that every moment since was an extension granted by the God-Emperor. An inquisitor could not function to his fullest capacity if he was preoccupied with self-preservation. That was what he had always believed, anyway.

Roth walked close to Celeminé and touched the tips of her hair. He was not sure why he did it. It was an awkward gesture but it had a calming effect. 'Be as it may, Celeminé, we can't leave. Look around you. We are under siege. We are surrounded and nowhere close to our transport. Our work here is done. There is nothing left to do.'

'There is one thing, inquisitors,' said Colonel Gamburyan crisply. He stood at the cave mouth, trying to light the frayed end of a tabac stub. Taking his time, he walked towards Roth with his rolling officer's gait and paused contemplatively before continuing.

'The 26th can conduct a ground assault from the Barbican. All of us, every last one. You and your Task Group can make your escape under the cover of our offensive,' announced the colonel in slow, measured tones.

Roth considered himself a scholar with a rogue's wit, seldom at a loss for words. But he quite simply did not know how to react. Colonel Gamburyan continued to speak before Roth could muster any protest.

'Let's be realistic for a moment, inquisitor. We are running dry of food, water and most critically ammunition. Every day I lose more good men. How long can this go on for? Two weeks? A month? It wouldn't matter. What you could do for the subsector would far outstrip anything my battalion could potentially achieve here.'

'I cannot have your men die for me,' muttered Roth weakly.

'We're already dead, Roth. No one will remember us here, unless you go. Let us have one last moment under the stars. A strident last charge, wouldn't that be grand?' laughed the colonel.

Roth paused, hesitant to answer. They were right of course; they were both right, damn them. An inquisitor should not live in fear of death, or he could not serve the Emperor, Inquisitorial doctrine had taught him that. But his mentor, old Inquisitor Liszt, had also taught him no service could be done for the Imperium if he died a stupid death. Roth's reflection was interrupted by a weak voice from the gun-post of the bunker.

'Sir... if there is a last charge can I please go with my unit?' rasped Corporal Nabhan, his eyes staring at the dripstone on the cave ceiling.

'Son. If there is a last charge, I would not be the one to deny you,' answered Colonel Gamburyan. At this, he levelled his gaze on Roth and smiled broadly.

The last charge was scheduled for 06:00 hours on the thirty-sixth day.

At 05:00, the five hundred and twenty-five men of the 26th Colonial Artillery began last equipment checks. At the foot of the Barbican, a sombre line of soldiers locked their bayonet spikes and adjusted their canvas webbing in silence. They loaded up their equipment satchels with musette pouches, grenades and exactly two spare cells each.

By 05:30, Colonel Gamburyan made last inspections. In close order rank, his five hundred men stood to attention in the brown blazers and tall white kepi hats he had grown so accustomed to in his twenty years of service. They stood in the open prairie, waiting for the enemy to see them, taunting them with their presence. The colonel thought of his wife, the wife he had not seen since the Atrocities and who would never again tease him for his scowl, or pick the loose threads from his uniform. He thought of her because it steeled his resolve.

At 06:00, it was Gamburyan who sounded the charge. Strung out in an open line, the battalion broke into a steady cant that rolled momentum into a roaring charge. Bugles sounded, officers blew on tin whistles. Guardsmen screamed themselves hoarse as the regimental standard was borne aloft. The wind caught their colours: the sabre and stallion of the CantiCol regiment, embroidered with the chain-link wreath of the 26th Artillery, snapped high on a brisk easterly.

It was during all this that Inquisitor Roth, Celeminé and an understandably reluctant Captain Pradal made their escape. They threaded west, hugging the Erbus canal towards the coastal headlands. During their flight, they went to ground many times in order to avoid the Ironclad elements moving in the opposite direction, storming towards the cave temples. By the time the battle was over, Roth and his group were clear of the red zone. Regional Archenemy commanders were so preoccupied with the last stand of the 26th that a lone stratocraft powering up on the western shores did not warrant their attention.

Roth never saw the last stand on that hot, brittle plain of undulating grass husk and dog-tooth stone. In the thick of the fighting, the battalion formed a large defensive square, two soldiers deep. For the first time the Ironclad engaged the Imperial Guard point-blank. The Archenemy were seized by a predatory glee, eager to pounce upon the Guardsmen who had held them at bay for so long. They were eager to claim heads and ears. Even the crew of light and heavy armour clambered from their vehicles with blades and weapons of blunt trauma. Every Ironclad warlord and underlord within a twenty-kilometre radius mustered his forces for the attack. No less than eight thousand Ironclad foot-soldiers and as many armoured and light-skinned fighting vehicles converged on the Barbican plains.

Despite the shock of the Ironclad charge, the Cantican Colonials seemed like a bulwark that could not be moved. They stood firmly, shoulder to shoulder, forming a bristling phalanx of lasguns, heavy weapons, cannon and rocket. They laid down a furious killing zone two hundred metres out, hewing down the churning press of Ironclad.

Despite sustaining las-rounds to the leg and upper torso, Colonel Gamburyan continued to rally the battalion. At the battle's apex, when the CantiCol phalanx was punctured, ragged and beginning to fracture, Gamburyan attempted to hold a breach in the line alone. The colonel died behind the post of a smoking heavy bolter. He was shot a total of thirteen times, but it was a ricochet slug entering beneath his chin that finally claimed him.

In all, the Guardsmen withstood the assault for eighteen minutes even though the Archenemy several times broke into the interior of the Cantican square. Many years later, this scene would be rendered in oil pastel by the revered muralist Niccolo Battista. Awash with vivid colours on the ceiling of the Saint Solomon Cathedral on Holy Terra, it gave the men of the 26th CantiCol a voice in history.

CHAPTER ELEVEN

The holding cell was a cold, rusted, disorientating affair.

Silverstein no longer knew how long he had been captured for. He spent his days wrist-chained to the grate alongside the Cantican five. Their cage was no larger than a Munitorum shipping crate, and hung like a pendulum from the ceiling of a docking berth. By the nature of its design, there was no room to sit or crouch and the constant shifting of his companions to ease their joints caused the cage to swing nauseatingly. His captors sporadically dealt them scraps of sustenance, at odd hours and without any semblance of pattern.

All that Silverstein knew was that he was aboard some kind of frigate in transit. It was a bloated Archenemy troop carrier en route to somewhere. The Elteber had promised Silverstein that they were being taken to 'dine' with Khorsabad. Who or where Khorsabad was, Silverstein did not know. Regardless, the huntsman had vowed to escape at the first opportunity. He and his fellow captives discussed the escape endlessly. It was the only thing that kept them sane.

Sometime into their journey, whether it was days or weeks, an Ironclad slaver lowered the suspended holding cell by means of a clanking lever. The slaver was swathed in chainmail and a frilled mantle of feathery scrap iron. Slinging a two-handed mace casually across his shoulders, he entered their cage and chose Varim, a clocksmith with steady hands who was a keen shot with the las. Without warning the Ironclad lashed the studded maul into Varim's head. It was one swift brutal strike that lathered everyone in a mist of blood.

Then, just like that, the Ironclad latched the cage and left. There had been no reason, no provocation, no warning. Creaking on cabled chains they were hoisted back up, along with the bleeding corpse of Varim. Throughout the ordeal, no one made a sound. Silverstein, pressed against the body, could not look away. His bioptics watched the heat signature slowly fade, and the pulse signs taper flat to nothing.

Aridun, the smallest of the Medina Worlds, was at once both ancient and new. Six thousand years ago, the planet had suffered mass extinction. The atmosphere was eroded and its alignment to its satellite suns had bleached the planet, evaporating the great ocean basins and baking the soil with a shimmering curtain of heat. This change birthed new flora and fauna, evolving to flourish under the primordial environment. It was a new dawn only six thousand years old.

Across the ash plains were the remnants of prehistory, the crushed bones and fossil dust painted in hues of faded sepia. Where oceans once lay, vast tracts of evaporite deposit sprawled into salt flats.

On the southern belt of the horizon, a dry savannah of dunes formed the core of Imperial settlement. At least there, the seasons were temperate enough to sustain thousand kilometre reefs of cycads, ferns and ginkgoes.

The structures of settlement here predated Imperial colony. Known as the Fortress Chain, the cities formed a line of strongholds, strung out across the southern savannah. They were twenty-three city-states in all, Percassa, Argentum, ancient Barcid, dead Angkhora and nineteen others, each twenty kilometres apart in a line of squat stone chess pieces. A rampart wall four hundred kilometres long connected the walled cities in a defensive grid. The wall itself, an earthen rampart of lime and sandstone, was simply known as the Fortress Chain. Bombasts and mortars peered from embrasures that stretched across the horizon like a stone rind. It was the only bastion of civilisation and, indeed, fertile life on Aridun.

Sparsely populated and lightly garrisoned, it was odd that Aridun was the least ravaged by war. Thus far and for reasons unknown, the Archenemy incursion had been probing and sporadic. The deployment of the Ironclad was limited; CantiCol reconnaissance estimated seventy thousand enemies at most, judging by drop-ship disposition. Even then, most had been driven away from the inhabited southern belt by the chain's aerial defences, into the Cage Isles and scorching wastelands many kilometres out.

It was on the temperate belt in the ninth chain-fortress of Argentum that Roth and the Overwatch Task Group found the Temple of the Tooth.

Roth straightened the sapphire folds of his brocaded silk robe, a fine piece of attire he often wore at rest. It had been less than a week since they had arrived on Aridun, but it was remarkable how a bath, a shave and few days of sleep had made the conflict on Cantica seem decades past. Roth stepped out into the elevated temple rooftop, his toes warmed by the soft, loamy clay tiles. Over the low parapet of the temple walls the roof offered an expansive view of the southern savannah belt. For the past two mornings, the temple priests had suggested Roth seek meditative solace on the temple walls, to recuperate himself. It was sage advice, as the landscape seemed to banish doubtful thoughts and the sharp worrying stones of his mind. Out there, bars of floral green wreathed the outskirts of the Fortress Chain. Narrow canoes meandered from the swamplands and up the city viaducts, wending towards the market districts. Further out, herds of sauropods, grey reptiles long of neck and thick of limb, grazed on the sprawling vegetation. Silverstein would have loved to hunt here, Roth thought.

The temple itself, as befitted its namesake, resembled the cusp of a human molar. An edifice constructed entirely of mud, it was a circular monument crowned by a ring of minarets some forty metres in height. Every year, before the mild rainy season, new mud would be smeared over the old walls. The city's plasterer guilds were the only masons deemed worthy of this task.

Work started only on an auspicious day, determined by star-gazing, religious debate and when the mud in the canal channels was of the right consistency. The foundations would be blessed amid holy prayers, a mixture of Imperial verse and local incantation. Each phase of reconstruction was marked by ritual.

Once a monastic retreat, the Temple of the Tooth was now a convalescence run by the priesthood of Saint Solias. It was a genteel facility, the gymnasium and courtyards filled with the murmuring, resting infirm. Inquisitor Barq could not have selected a more suitable location for their rendezvous. After the ordeals of the past month, it was the least he could do in order to function in his official capacities. Roth had spent only two days at the convalescence, most of it in deep sleep. Nourished by the restoring meal of potted rice simmered in poultry broth, his vigour was already renewing and his wounds healing.

'Are you feeling better? You look morose.'

Roth turned and saw Celeminé emerge from a brass door at the conical base of a minaret. Much like Roth, she had shed her battlefield attire days ago and had not donned it since. She now wore a chemise of alabaster, her throat chased with white lace. Freshened, rested and reposed, Roth thought she looked absolutely radiant.

He bowed deeply. 'Celeminé. I am fine, thank you.'

She glided in close and pretended to pick a loose thread from his collar. 'Don't lie, Roth. You're certainly not very good at it. What's on your mind?'

Roth sighed. Although he had first thought Celeminé too young and too green to be an inquisitor, he now knew better. She was sharp, perhaps much sharper than he. More than that, despite her demeanour she was a hellcat in a firefight. Gurion had selected his colleague well.

'It's the ambush,' he began. 'The enemy, they were not the Archenemy. But more than that, they knew where we were going to be.'

'You suspect an infiltrator,' she said flatly.

'I suspect,' Roth said, choosing his words carefully, 'that someone very high up in Imperial Command wants us dead. By all accounts, the Orphratean Purebred have been deployed in surgical strike roles by the Imperium since the onset of the Medina Campaign.'

Celeminé crinkled her nose and bit her lip-ring thoughtfully. It was a gesture Roth had grown strangely accustomed to.

'You suspect Captain Pradal is the leak?'

'He would be the most likely suspect, yes.'

Celeminé thought about this. 'Or perhaps me? There *is* me, you know.'

Roth chuckled. He realised Celeminé was standing very close. So close that he could smell her cosmetic fragrance, hints of citrus and fresh milk.

'If it were you who wanted me dead. Why don't you kill me now? You could have shot me any time you wanted.'

She crinkled her nose again. 'Or perhaps Silverstein? I mean no offence, Roth, but the puzzle fits. I'm sorry.'

The suggestion startled Roth. It had not occurred to him that Silverstein, old Bastiel, his primary agent, could have been the one to betray his whereabouts to the mercenaries. He had departed before the ambush, perhaps not on circumstances of his own choosing, but he had departed nonetheless.

'There is a distinct possibility, yes. But–'

'But?'

'It would be immoral of me to regard a lost friend in such light without the Emperor's own verification. I'd be a lesser man for it.'

Celeminé nodded. 'I'd think less of you too. Don't make me do that.'

Roth looked away. In the distance he spied a flock of winged reptiles, circling lazily on the solar currents. When he turned back he had recomposed himself.

'Was there something you wanted to see me about?'

She smiled. 'Yes. Inquisitor Barq has been waiting to see you since you arrived here. He said you both have much catching up to do in the gymnasium.'

'The gymnasium?'

'Of course,' she said, taking him by the hand, 'He's been waiting for some time.'

* * *

Tugging him by his hand, she led Roth down the spiralling stairwells and helix corridors of the temple.

They finally entered a cloistered court adjoining the main structure. Although the temple was four thousand years old at last census, the cloister was a recent addition of the plasterers' guild. Balance beams, vaults and pommel horses sprouted from the packed dirt flooring while still rings and high bars swung from the ceiling like wooden fruit. They all served as excellent instruments of recuperation, but this early in the morning the courtyard was largely empty.

Empty but for Inquisitor Vandus Barq, limbering up at the centre of court. Although it had been decades since the progenium, Roth recognised him immediately – a young man with a wrestler's build. His bull-neck and hulking shoulders tapered into a narrow waist wrapped in a lifting belt. The wrestler's leotard he wore exposed forearms ridged in sinew and inked with tattoos. If Roth didn't know him better, he might have mistaken him for gang muscle.

Barq looked up from his stretching as Celeminé drew Roth into the court.

'Obodiah! My Throne – you've become ugly,' smiled Barq as he clinched Roth in a crushing hug.

'I haven't had the same luxuries you have had for the past months, no,' acknowledged Roth, still clasping forearms with his old friend.

'By all accounts, no you have not. Gurion has thoroughly briefed me on your misfortunes.'

Roth shrugged, almost dismissively. He looked around at the gymnasium and realised he could not remember the last time he had indulged in his daily routine of fist-fencing and callisthenics.

'What is the situation here? On Aridun, I mean,' asked Roth.

Barq flexed his wrists and rolled his jaw to warm it up. 'I'll tell you all about it while we spar.'

In a way it was their ritual. It was almost but not quite a rivalry that had developed ever since they were twig-limbed progena at the academy. In his day, Roth had been the champion tetherweight fist-fencer for his age group. He was slim but he was whippet-quick. Roth's multiple knockouts over anchorweight fencers several years his senior were still the stuff of legend within the progenium dormitories.

On the other hand, Barq was a scrapper. He was well versed in the linear system of military self-defence developed for the Cadian regiments and its surrounding subsectors. His rough brawling style was complemented by progeniate-level wrestling. Chokeholds, leg-locks, armbars and neck cranks composed the core of his unarmed arsenal.

'It's been years, Vandus. Either you've got better or you've too much confidence,' remarked Roth. He adopted a low fist-fencing stance, wide-legged, springing on his toes like a dancer. The lead fist was held straight forwards, poised like a swordsman in en garde. Across the dirt floor, his opponent Barq coiled up into a wrestler's half-crouch, hands held up in front of his face.

'Still practising that wimpy punch-fencing nonsense, I see.'

'It is a gentlemanly pursuit,' chided Roth. 'Now, are you just going to taunt me or will you tell me how Aridun fares?'

Barq stepped in cautiously. 'Aridun is at war. But with the slaughter across the region, Aridun is low-scale in comparison. The Archenemy have deployed mass aerial landings but the numbers aren't anywhere near as overwhelming as on the other core worlds.'

'How about the Ironclad motorised elements? They ran roughshod through Guard infantry back on Cantica.' Roth punctuated his question by pirouetting off his back foot and snapping his fist into a double jab.

The blows stung Vandus on the nose, catching him off guard. Growling like a wounded bull, Vandus circled off to the right. 'Archenemy forces have been mainly infantry. Vigilant aerial defence have limited their drop zones to the wilderness at least some three hundred kilometres out from the Southern Savannah.'

Seizing upon his pre-emptive blows, Roth glided forwards and uncurled his right hand in a straight cross. The blow connected with a satisfying snap against Barq's upper jaw. In reply Barq lunged out with a looping overhand punch, throwing all his weight behind it.

Roth took a pendulum-step backwards. With forearms raised like pillars, Roth trapped Barq's punch. It was a technique known as 'sticking hands'. Besides its array of fist strikes, fist-fencing also contained a thorough syllabus of fifty-one hand blocks and trapping techniques. Roth believed he had mastered forty of them by the last count. Pulling Barq off balance with his trapping block, Roth disengaged and pedalled away.

'What of the Medina Campaign? Does the defence hold across the system?' Roth asked between sharp intakes of breath.

'Worse than we'd feared. Of the half-dozen satellite worlds, only Sinope remains free and even then, recent weeks have seen some heavy fighting there. Kholpesh has mired to a war of attrition that we do not have the numbers to win.'

Barq shot in for a wrestler's takedown, dropping to his knees with his arms outstretched. Roth had been waiting for his tackle – Vandus ate several more sharp punches. Tap-tap on the jaw and nose.

'Which leaves me to ask. Why is my task group here? Gurion said I was needed,' said Roth, his breath becoming more laboured. To give himself space, his feet glided in radially symmetrical spirals, confounding his opponent.

'Because I requested you.'

'I'm flattered, old friend,' said Roth as he scored a jab right between Barq's eyes.

Livid red welts were beginning to appear on the cheekbones and bridge of Vandus's nose. He shook his head to clear it and continued to speak as if unscathed.

'I've been here six months and I've unearthed a lot. I have a contact, a xeno-archaeologist who tracked down an item of interest being held for auction by a relic collector on Kholpesh.'

'You think you've found the Old Kings?'

Barq shrugged. 'Most likely not, but the relic dates back to the War of Reclamation and we may have a lead. Inquisitor Joaquim's agents have contacted me and seem to think it's important enough. I trust them, so it's the most solid lead we have thus far.'

Barq took a big penetrating step and tried the tackle again. This time Roth pivoted on the balls of his feet and whipped a flurry of punches at Barq's head. Six punches in under a second. Despite Barq's thickly corded neck, the wrestler was visibly rocked. He bulled forwards, striking with a series of knees, elbows and looping punches. The two fighters traded, exchanging a barrage of haemorrhaging strikes.

'Kholpesh – why not have Inquisitor Joaquim pursue it? He heads the Conclave Task Group on Kholpesh, does he not?' panted Roth as he circled away.

Barq closed the distance between them with a sweeping low kick. He lashed explosively in a wide arc with his shin but missed as Roth quick-stepped. Suddenly vulnerable, Barq shelled up his torso as Roth snapped his lead fist at the now-exposed head. Body head, body head, just like he had been taught in the textbooks.

'Haven't you heard?' Barq huffed between Roth's shots. 'Inquisitor Joaquim is dead. Three weeks ago, Archenemy mechanised forces made a concerted push for the outer shelf continents on Kholpesh.' Barq paused briefly as a crisp hook cracked his ribs. 'The Cantican Fourth and Twelfth division were routed. Joaquim was amongst those killed.'

Roth was shocked. The grave news startled him so much he didn't even see Barq's takedown. Roth was slammed around the midriff. His feet cleared the air before his body came crunching down hard on the packed earth below. Momentarily dazed, the air stunned out of his lungs, Roth blinked. The equilibrium in his ears swirled with vertigo. Celeminé shrieked something in the background, but Roth couldn't make it out.

Then he began to choke. Barq was applying a forearm across the side of Roth's neck, jamming his weight behind the blade of his ulna. The chokehold was cutting off his carotid arteries. Blood pressurised in his head, thrumming so hard Roth could feel the tremor behind his sinus passages. He was blacking out.

'One for me,' growled Barq with laboured breaths. 'That's an Ezekiel choke. The Kasrkin taught me that one.'

Abruptly the pressure eased. Barq eased his hand off Roth's neck and the blood seeped back into circulation. Rolling off him, Barq slumped onto his back, breathing hard.

'Joaquim is dead?' Roth croaked. Propping himself up by on an elbow, he coughed.

Nodding, Barq gestured to Celeminé. 'The three of us are all that Gurion has at his disposal. As far as the Conclave goes anyway.'

'When do we leave for Kholpesh?'

'As swiftly as possible. Tomorrow I will be travelling by sauropod train into the Eridu Marches and linking up with the xeno-archaeologist. You can accompany me if you're feeling better.'

As she heard this, Celeminé stood up from the pommel horse she had been leaning against. 'Sauropod train? I've never been on one of those,' she said.

Roth shook his head. 'I need you to stay here and keep close scrutiny on Captain Pradal.'

Celeminé looked decidedly crestfallen, but acquiesced.

'Vandus, can we not travel by locomotive? I've heard Aridun has an excellent overland transit rail,' asked Roth.

Inquisitor Barq's mood darkened several shades. 'The steam locomotives have been decommissioned. The railways are far too susceptible to Archenemy attacks.'

'Aren't the Ironclad forces stalled beyond the demarcation line beyond the Cage Isles and western wastelands?' asked Celeminé.

What she said was true. The heavy concentration of las-silos and other anti-air defences had driven enemy deployment out beyond the Cage Isles. By reconnaissance reports, the fragmented islands were now teeming with Archenemy nautical forces. Shoals of iron submersibles, sea-barges and plated galleys filled the Cage Isle channels, their bellies swollen with cargo and enemy troops. Imperial outposts on the demarcation line harassed them with heavy ordnance, but the vessels sailed largely unchallenged, deploying forces freely across Aridun.

'Most of them. But the Ironclad are raiders. Rogue bands have continually harassed Imperial supply lines. At least by sauropod we won't be immobilised by a destroyed section of track. Since the outbreak of invasion, the Archenemy have detonated twelve hundred kilometres' worth of locomotive railway.'

Roth nodded grimly. They were dealing with a different sort of enemy. The Ironclad were raiders first and soldiers second. Even when they did not have the advantage of numerical superiority, as was the case on Aridun, they inflicted disproportionate damage on civic and military infrastructure.

'So, armoured and armed for the trip then?' Roth asked.

'I wouldn't leave the southern belt without anything short of serious firepower,' Vandus answered flatly.

Roth was about to laugh until he realised that his old friend was very serious.

CHAPTER TWELVE

They descended from off-world in their holding pen, transferred onto a brig-lander and escorted by a squadron of Archenemy interceptors for landfall. On board the brig, they were guarded by a hundred veteran Ironclad – scarred, knotted fighters bedecked in the collected trophies of war. As prisoners went, they were a valued prize indeed.

When their captors herded them off the landing ramp, Silverstein winced at the unaccustomed glare of searing sunlight. He had lost count of how many days he had been caged, and his augmetics reacted badly. Lens shutters flared for low-light reception, and the sudden flood of sun almost blinded him.

When the apertures of his bioptics recalibrated and his vision flickered back, Silverstein almost wished he had been blinded permanently. He found himself in a war camp of the Archenemy.

The scene before him was a vivid nightmare in flesh. A vast gridwork of parked vehicles covered the scorched and salted earth. They had laid waste to a square kilometre of ground, burning the land into a blackened wound. Amongst wheels and tracks of their vehicles, bivouacs and camouflage netting were erected as shelter. It was a muster yard of mechanised machinery – Scavenger light tanks, Chimeras, Hellhounds, FPVs and eight-wheelers, dormant like sleeping predators. They marshalled under the watchful gaze of sentry towers erected on skeleton girders.

A pall of chemical smoke, fuel and burning plastek cut the air. Presiding over the encampment were two crude wooden idols, seven metres

in height. Carved with rough, blunt strokes, the idols depicted a leering
daemon, its tongue hanging past its waist, carving an infant from the
belly of a pregnant woman. In their own crude, supernatural way, the
idols were the most deeply disturbing things Silverstein had ever seen.

The prisoners were frog-marched around the perimeter of the camp,
a snaking earthen embankment raised to chest height. Soldiers of the
Archenemy stared at them. Just the thought of so many tainted eyes
boring into his back coated Silverstein in a film of cold sweat. Some of
the Ironclad chuckled, in evil, delighted little burbles, running a finger
against their throats.

To ignore them would have been impossible. He feigned disinterest,
indignantly straightening the gold piping on his filthy, decaying jacket.
When he had been a gunbearer for his father's hunting trips, he had often
thought that by closing his eyes and not seeing the prey, then perhaps
the prey would not see him. He reverted back to his childhood instincts
and squeezed his eyes shut. It wasn't that Silverstein was a coward, no;
he was just trying to keep his sanity intact.

'Uhup uhup,' an Ironclad snarled into Silverstein's ear. He was shoved
as his tormentor pointed at the back of an armoured transport truck.
Silverstein smoothed his collar and levelled his gaze at the Ironclad. For
his defiance, the Ironclad punched him hard in the kidney and hurled
him up onto the back of the truck by his lapels. Doubled over in shock,
Silverstein felt rather than saw his fellow captives pile onto the truck after
him, crushing him with their weight.

The hatch of the panelled truck was shut, eclipsing the light like a closet
door. Cloyingly hot, suffocating and pitch-black, Silverstein strained to
hear the low rumble of other engines grumbling to life. A convoy escort,
he surmised. They were being transported elsewhere, to whatever fate
awaited them. Outside, someone pounded the side of their truck with
hard, reverberating slaps. It was followed by a peal of muffled laughter
as the truck kicked into gear.

There was nothing Silverstein could do but wait and see what became
of him.

It was, as expected, a bright, humid dawn as the two inquisitors tramped
through the reef-lands. Roth placed a hand to shield his eyes against the
suns as he peered at the rather peculiar mode of transport that awaited
him. Despite his travels, he had never seen anything like it.

The sauropod train was saddling up on the humid mud flats, beyond
the outskirts of Aridun Civic. The reptilian beasts were great and grey,
some of the male bulls growing to six metres tall at shoulder height.
Down the cabled length of their long swaying necks ran a plume of dull
feathery spines.

Roth counted eight of the beasts tethered by harness, seating platforms swaying from their backs. When they brayed, they emitted a sonorous trumpet from the hollows of their cranial crests. Roth found the sound at once both eerie and majestic, like a suite of brass horns resonating from some deep ocean.

Fussing around the stomping pillars of their feet, caravaneers adjusted caparisons of gaudy beaded fabric, tassels and jingling silver discs. Shaded wicker sedans swayed upon their backs, some beasts already carrying a dozen handlers, musterers and guards. On the decorative platform of the lead caravan beast, Roth recognised the distinctive outline of a belt-fed heavy stubber.

'Vandus, you always did remember to travel with elegance,' Roth said sarcastically as he plugged the polished boots of his fighting-plate deep into mud.

'You can always walk if you wish,' Barq retorted as he hauled himself up a hemp ladder that dangled down a sauropod flank.

Inquisitor Barq, ever the eccentric, was clad in wargear of a sort Roth had never seen before. It was, in a way, typical of the Ordo Xenos. Barq was suited in an olive-drab bodyglove, but from the abdomen up he was shod in a hulking armoured rig. His torso, shoulders and arms flexed with thick, cabled plating. The pugnacious outline was reinforced with sledgehammer fists and piston banks along both arms. Multiple heavy-calibre barrels arrayed in racks of eight lined the back of each armoured fist. Despite its armament, it was the milky green of the enamel and the oddly organic curves of Barq's rig that caught Roth's attention.

'Xenos-tech?' said Roth as he scaled the ladder.

Barq laughed breezily. 'Not quite. I procured this suit from a pompous house of a particular upper-tier hive.'

'Would it be prudent of me not to ask you which noble house this was?'

Barq winked. 'It would be for the best. I had suspicions that they may have had limited dealings with xenos – but benign enough for me to let it slide. They were very grateful and gifted me this marvellous suit.'

'You're getting soft.'

'And you're getting stiff in your old age,' retorted Barq.

Roth shook his head as he settled in the creaking wicker of their sedan. 'You're dancing with devils, Vandus. I could have you martialled before the ordos for that act alone.'

'Not if I silence you first,' chortled Vandus, flexing his segmented paws.

Roth was poised to riposte but the crack of the musterer's whip and the resonant bellow of sauropods drowned his words. With a lurching, lolling rhythm the great beasts began to move and the winding rampart of the Fortress Chains receded into the distance.

* * *

By steam locomotive, the trip would have taken less than three hours but conflict had forced the decommissioning of locomotive rail. By sauropod it took the better part of a day. But Roth didn't mind the time spent. After the catastrophes of the preceding weeks, he appreciated the open country.

Everywhere, Roth experienced the new era of a planet in evolution. They plodded through biotic reefs that purportedly sprawled out to the coastal basins – endless kilometres of whispering horsetail fern, cycads and clustered conifer. But he saw too the vestiges of a past ecosystem. Monolithic salt flats, once thermal oceans, lined the horizon with bars of crystalline white. Shale rifts, red bed sandstone and calcite plains marked the graves of a former environment.

Most startling of all were the abandoned city-states that kept silent sentry on their trail. When the suns shifted axis, thousands of years ago, Aridun had been besieged by hurricanes, floods and temperatures that had boiled the moisture from the earth. Long since abandoned, these cities crested the horizon as hollow skeletons, black with age and neglect.

At least twice during their trek they encountered packs of dog-sized carnivores. Attracted by the warm musk of humans and the ground tremor of sauropods, the reptiles paralleled the caravan at a cautious distance. Caravan guards fired lasguns over their heads to scatter them.

'Those are just heel-biting scavengers. It's the Talon Squalls you should be afraid of,' said Barq. He handed Roth a gilded telescope with his ponderous hands and gestured to the distance.

Roth had indeed heard of them already. The animals had quite a reputation amongst those inclined to study fauna. Naturally, Roth was a curious and learned individual, although the biological sketches did not invoke the true ferocity of such animals. Peering into the telescope, Roth spied gangs of flightless birds powering across the southern horizon on long loping strides. Even at a distance they appeared large, far larger than any avian had the right to be.

'And what of the Archenemy?' Roth enquired.

'The aerial defences have driven enemy deployment far out beyond the wastelands. Splinter raiding parties, however, are a real threat,' Barq said.

Roth could understand how Aridun had escaped the worst of the Archenemy attentions, at least for now. The environment was not exactly conducive in supporting the large-scale movement of troops, especially raiders with poor supply lines. It was hot, it was barren and it was open ground.

Roth sat back, wiping his brow. By late afternoon the air was dry and quiet. Even under the shaded pagoda of their sedan the temperature was in the low forties. He was not acclimatised, and what's more he was beginning to seriously regret wearing his Spathaen fighting-plate. The metal was incubating him in a cocoon of prickling heat.

'This xeno-archaeologist, what ungodly effort would draw him out here, to a desolate warzone?' Roth muttered, mostly to himself.

'Actually, as part of the bargain in aiding us I've promised her a secure transport out of the Medina conflict zone. She came to Aridun in order to study the new cycle of history and was trapped by the initial Archenemy offensive.'

'A she?'

'Oh yes. Professor Madeline de Medici of the Katon-Rouge Universitariat.'

At the mention of her name, Roth clucked his tongue. He was entirely familiar with the works of Professor de Medici. She was a prominent xeno-archaeologist, a leading scholar in her field within the star system if not the entire subsector. Her works were prolific, including *A Treatise on Pre-Imperial Man* and *Reflective Studies of an Early Eastern Fringe*. Roth admired her dedicated approach to field research as much as her eloquence in script.

Had Roth not been a servant of the Imperium, he had often fancied that he would have become a scholar. Indeed, he took his academic fascination past an amateur hobby, and his large estate on Arlona was more of a dedicated library than a manor. To Roth, study was a compulsion. He had been smitten by the concept of the warrior-scholar ever since he read of the Gojoseon Kingdom on ancient Terra, and their caste of Flower Knights or Flower 'youths'. Such youths were socialised from a young age in the arts of calligraphy, archery, theatre and horsemanship. They were the symbiosis of martial and mental prowess, and a symbol of spiritual balance amongst the ancient Asiatic realms. Roth had long held a romantic fascination for these knights and despite being older now, a part of him continued to extol those virtues.

The petrified forest of Eridu lay eight hundred kilometres from the Archenemy demarcation line. The wilderness was located exactly half-way between the southern savannah of Aridun Civic and the Archenemy amassing beyond the wasteland rim. Roth and Barq dismounted the sauropods at the edge of the woods and proceeded on foot.

The geosite resembled a sculpture garden of melted, wrinkling rock. Pillars of argon cobalt and organic mineral rose like titanic chess pieces. Everywhere Roth looked, he caught fleeting glimpses of frozen time, the fossilised imprint of a leaf on a stone, fronds and whorls against bedrock, the spinal column of some extinct beast surfacing above the sediment.

Overhead, wilting, leafless trees some sixty metres tall created an arterial web with their frail, feathery branches. Some of the trees had been opalised, trailing glistening seams of pearlescent gems. Sun dappled through the bowers, cutting stark patterns on the mosaic floor.

Under the bowers of bearded wood fungus, Roth found Madeline de Medici's excavation team toiling in a narrow little gorge. The labourers were local, bronzed from constant sun exposure. They must have been desperately poor rural workers, considering most other Aridunians had refused to stray far from the southern belt since the invasion.

As the inquisitors approached the excavation site, half a dozen men rushed to intercept them. Instead of the khaki overalls of the excavation crew, these men wore dark linen morning coats with black three-piece suits. Instead of hauling picks and shovels, gilded hand-las pistolletes were suspended by gold chain from their belts. Pinned to their lapels was the crest of administrative office on Aridun – the Governor's seal.

'Halt! Stop where you are!' they shouted.

It almost made Roth burst out laughing. The armed group were a pompous bunch – svelte, mincing men completely out of their element. They tried to look intimidating and professional, but were far too sunburnt and miserable to be taken seriously. They were little more than technocrats playing soldier.

Putting his hands up in mock surrender, Roth cast a sidelong grin at Barq. His old friend shrugged his power-armoured shoulders with a mechanical whir. They were alike in many ways, in mischief especially.

'Disarm yourselves. Lay your weapons on the ground and lie face down. Immediately!' ordered one of the armed men, levelling his pistol at Roth. He appeared to be their leader, a tall man with the long, haughty face of an Administratum clerk. This clerk, however, had obviously chemnourished the muscles of his arms to be more aesthetically intimidating. Neither of the inquisitors were overly impressed.

'You're joking, right?' snorted Barq. He held up the heavy-gauge boltracks on the back of his hands. Roth wasn't sure whether Barq was indicating the idiocy of their request, or whether it was a subtle threat. Either way, Roth found it immensely entertaining.

'I don't know who you think you're talking to, but I am Lorenzo Miaz Hieron, envoy and security specialist of Madame de Medici,' he trilled with a measure of shrill indignation.

'I'll talk to you however I please,' Roth goaded, stringing the man along.

'Do you want to die? Are you stupid? Do you know Aridun is at war? State your purpose or suffer the consequences!' Hieron cried. His fellows agreed, heads bobbing like token birds.

'Lorenzo! Laslett, Hamil, Piotr, the rest of you! Mind your manners!' came a voice from behind Hieron. It was a woman's voice, imperious and stately without even having to shout.

Roth did not immediately recognise the esteemed Madame de Medici. She was far younger than he had expected. He had envisaged a wizened, perhaps motherly academic; instead the woman before him had the porcelain skin, high cheekbones and delicate figure of a well-bred noble's daughter.

Madeline de Medici ducked out from the flap of her canvas tent. She balanced a lace parasol delicately in gloved hands. Given the climate, her attire was entirely inappropriate: a modest pencil skirt and double-breasted coat of twill. Her face was blushed with subtle rouge and her hair curled into loose chestnut ringlets so fashionable amongst the upper-spire aristocrats. Anywhere else but on an archaeological site within the heart of a warzone, Roth would have mistaken her as a spire heiress.

'Madame de Medici?' said Roth, still unsure if it were truly she.

'Madeline Rebequin Louise de Medici. But please, do call me Madeline,' she said, curtsying.

The inquisitors both bowed graciously.

'Madame Madeline, I am Obodiah Roth. I must admit I am a great admirer of your works. *On the Natural Cycles of War and Conflict* was an impeccably researched collection of essays.'

Madeline tilted her nose up. 'Inquisitors, you flatter me,' she said.

'Inquisitors?' spluttered Hieron, backing away. He ushered his colleagues aside like chastised children.

When the guards were out of earshot, Madeline strolled closer to the inquisitor. 'Excuse them. I am sincerely embarrassed by their behaviour.'

'Call this a casual observation, but those men are not fighters,' Roth said.

'No indeed they are not. But they claim to be. So let them. The Governor of Aridun provided me with some of his household custodians. The Governor insisted.'

'Was the Governor trying to get you killed? The Archenemy are held at bay less than a day's travel from here. You should not come out this far with those fools as protection.'

'Don't tie yourself in knots, inquisitor, I can look after myself,' she sniffed.

She was perhaps correct, thought Roth. Of all her texts, the one which stood out to Roth was her recently documented field study of ancient pylons scattered across rimward planets of the Eastern Fringe. The book was in limited circulation and included woodcut illustrations of an eldar attack on her excavation team. She had evidently escaped, and her resultant accounts of the tale caused quite a stir, even amongst the ordos.

'Be as it may,' Barq interjected, 'it is time for you to send those fops back to the Governor's estates and come with us. We are pressed for time.'

'I've got several trunks of field equipment and research I will be needing,' Madeline called over her shoulder as she twirled away. 'Have my crew load them onto your vehicles.'

'We don't have vehicles, madame. Only sauropods,' Roth called after her.

She halted, turning slowly. Her lips pursed, her heart-shaped face florid. 'I cannot ride by sauropod! A lady does not travel by pack beast!' she implored.

'You can always walk,' chuckled Roth.

CHAPTER THIRTEEN

Lord Marshal Khmer plucked a pistol from the tiered cabinet. It was a heavy hammerlock pistol of dark wood, as long as his forearm and fluted with a sweeping grip. Acorns and leaves of crisp topaz inlaid the pistol grip while vines of silver filigree chased the barrel. A weapon of its calibre had not been used since the Hadrian Emergency in the Bastion Stars, circa 762.M41.

Khmer had collected this particular hammerlock as the trophy of a duel many years ago. The Navy admiral who had lost his pistol had also lost several fingers to Khmer's sabre. It was fortunate, Khmer mused, that one of those severed digits had been the officer's trigger finger.

Inserting a cartridge into the chamber, Khmer sauntered over to his shooting gallery. It was his own gallery, his very own on board the *Carthage*. The hall had once been a troops barracks, which could have housed two platoons of sixty. Now it was a lead-lined hall, latticed shooting booths facing a target gallery at varying ranges of twenty to two hundred paces. One entire wall of the gallery was devoted to the magnificent vault of Khmer's antique weapons display. It had glass-paned racks containing fusils, flak muskets, hand-crafted solid sluggers and ancient rifles as long as a man was tall. There was even a sleek assembly of military-grade lasgun variants.

The marshal squared up in a double-handed shooting stance and took aim at a painted canvas target at eighty paces. The canvas was painted with an almost child-like caricature of a daemon, eyes bulging, teeth gnashing. He drilled three rounds into the target, the kinetic impacts whipping the target pad like a kite in high wind. The hammering snap of shots was echoed by the lead-lined acoustics of the hall. For Khmer there could be no better sound.

'Clean this for me,' said Khmer as he tossed the pistol into the waiting hands of a junior officer. 'If I find a lick of carbon in the working parts, I'll have your hide for guncloth.'

The marshal strode over to his antique arsenal and selected an auto-gun. The piece was nondescript as far as his collection went, an obsolete rifle of stamped metal and ageing wood. Well over a metre in length, its characteristic iron sights, scythe-shaped magazine and hardwood stock bespoke of its age and previous owners. The autogun was crude but it had history.

Khmer was a great appreciator of history. Each of the weapons had a different tale to tell, a different war front experienced, from the up-armoured lasgun of the Bastion Ward Interior Guard, to the revolving hand cannon plundered from the techno-barbarians of the deeper Shoal Clusters. History was written by those who shot fast, and shot true.

'Lord marshal! A word, please.'

Khmer placed the autogun back in its velvet cradle and looked up to see Forde Gurion storming into his chambers. Judging by the galloping clank of his augmetic legs, the inquisitor had not come for personal reasons.

'Forde Gurion,' Khmer acknowledged with an air of nonchalance. He turned back to inspecting his weapons.

'I must speak with you, lord marshal, now if you please,' Gurion said through clenched teeth.

Almost wearily, Marshal Khmer looked at Gurion. The inquisitor lord stood before him, the muscles in his jaw twitching, a document brief viced hard in his mechanical hand. Khmer dismissed his attendee with a wave.

'Gurion, what seems to be troubling you?'

The inquisitor shook the parchment in front of him. 'This. This states that as of 06:00 yesterday, Imperial reinforcements from the Lupina chain-worlds were re-routed away from the Medina war zone. Seventy-six thousand riflemen of the Lupinee 102nd were diverted to shore up defences for the Bastion Stars.'

'I don't see the problem,' said Khmer, as he began to polish a flak-musket with the sleeve of his dress uniform.

'The problem, lord marshal, is that you authorised this diversion.' Gurion spat the last few words like venom.

'That is true. I did what would be best for the long-term objectives of the campaign.'

'Need I remind you that the Council of Conclusions has decreed our objectives? We are to hold the line at the Medina Worlds until such time as the enigma of the Old Kings can be dealt with.'

Finally, Khmer put down his musket and turned to face Gurion. He cleared his throat.

'Those are your objectives, Gurion. My military objective is simple – to deny Chaos forces the space, coordination and ability to conquer the subsector. In this context, a concentrated defence in the Bastion Stars is how I will achieve this.'

'That decision is not yours to make. My Conclave has conclusive evidence that suggests the Old Kings myth is of threat-level alpha.'

'You are not a soldier.' Khmer said, sincerely lamenting. 'You do not understand war. We do not win wars by suggestive evidence. We win wars by logic and strategy. Can you not understand that?'

Gurion shook his head, not because he could not understand, but because he realised that Khmer was too hardened in his ways. Peeling aside the lapel of his coat, Gurion let his Inquisitorial rosette tumble from its chain. 'Lord marshal, the Inquisition works in its own ways.'

If Khmer understood the symbolism, he paid it no heed. Instead the lord marshal wandered down the aisle of gun racks until he found what he was looking for. He took up a lasgun, peered down its scope and balanced the rifle in his hands.

'Do you see this rifle, Gurion?' he asked. It was a soft gun-metal grey all over, with a collapsible stock and a shortened muzzle that gave the weapon a squat, brutal profile.

'Yes. That is a lasgun. Evidently, I am not as well versed in the specifics as you,' replied Gurion, clearly uninterested.

'This is not just any lasgun. See this picatinny rail here?' said Khmer, pointing to the grooved carry handle. 'And the shorter length of the barrel and handguard? Modified for airborne deployment?' he continued, indicating towards the polished barrel and the smooth grey polymer of the body.

'I see it,' Gurion answered cautiously.

'This is a Guard-issue weapon of the Bravanda Centennial regiments. But more than that, this weapon saw action during the reclamation of the Bravanda Provincial Palaces. In 870.M41, the elite wealth-barons, a dissident faction known as the Revolutionists, imprisoned the Regent of Bravanda in his own palace. The ruling elite and the landed gentry established their own governance, and the rural masses of Bravanda lamented but could do nothing.'

'I am familiar with the Revolutionist uprising on Bravanda. Please continue.'

Khmer shouldered the rifle to aim at a phantom enemy in the distance.

'You have to understand, the Imperial Guard, we represent the people. And the Regent was the people's Regent. On the first day of the revolution, without specific orders, a small group of loyalist Guardsmen stormed the Provincial Palace.'

Lowering the weapon, Khmer racked the charger bolt and stripped the barrel in one liquid motion.

'This very gun was in the possession of a Sergeant Natum Quarry, 7/7th Centennial. He held the gates alone for forty-five minutes against Revolutionists. He was one of five brothers, all of them Guardsmen, and the son of a manufactorum father who often worked through his rest shifts in order to feed his boys as they were growing up. Sergeant Quarry cost the dissidents some forty casualties. Do you know what the Revolutionists did to him once they got him? Many of the dissidents were convicts, condemned men that the wealth-barons had freed from the penal colonies. When they finally got him they mutilated him and paraded parts of him on pict. His posthumous Medal of Valorous Citation was awarded to an empty grave.'

'That is a stirring tale,' Gurion admitted. 'But I fail to see the connection to our issue at hand.'

'The point I'm trying to make should be self-evident. War is conducted by guns and behind every gun, a man. Medina is of no strategic value and I will not waste the lives of my soldiers here, when we could make a stand on the Bastion Stars, alongside the Lupinee Rifles, the Bastion Ward regiments, Montaigh, Arpadis Mortant.'

Gurion sighed deeply. This was Lord Marshal Khmer at his best. For all his egomania, his political viciousness and his pomp and flair, the man was a brilliant leader of men. He would not be wearing his rank if he were anything less. It wounded Gurion to think that he might have to resort to Inquisitorial authority and dethrone the lord marshal. The Medina Campaign was demoralised as it was without the loss of its highest-ranking officer.

'Lord marshal. Let us, for a second, forget about the Old Kings of Medina. Even then, you would be abandoning the Medina Corridor, and leaving billions of Imperial citizens to die at the hands of Chaos.'

'You may think me a monster. But I do what I must to deny the Archenemy. It takes a monster to do what I do. I am a lord marshal. I command killers in the act of killing. You stick to what you know,' bellowed Khmer. His introspective persona fell away like a curtain and his face seeped with veiny red. Khmer's legendary temper was building pressure.

'I understand. But I have my reasons and I would not be here if I did not think it was crucial. My Conclave is hard at work in achieving the same objectives you do. The forces of Chaos are not irrational, why do they want Medina if you don't? Why?'

'I don't know. I don't need to know. We choose to fight our battle in the Bastion Stars. Not here!' snarled Khmer. He threw Sergeant Quarry's lasgun across the chamber. The gun skipped across the marble floor and crashed into a display stand of long-arms, bringing down a forest of muskets.

Unflappable, Gurion betrayed no emotion. 'You can rage all you wish, Khmer. But I am the Inquisition. Do not force me to wrest control of the operation and your Canticans away from you. You are a fine general and it would be a tremendous loss to the campaign.'

Teeth bared, his face utterly bestial, Khmer leaned in close on Gurion. The inquisitor lord remained stony faced, his augmetic hand hovering over his Lugos. Gurion knew he could not be complacent: Khmer was far too unpredictable. A raging lord marshal with an arsenal of weapons in arm's reach made for a volatile combination.

'It doesn't matter,' Khmer spat. 'Your Task Groups on Aridun are finished.'

It was the only thing Khmer had said so far that elicited a tremor of shock in Gurion. No one was supposed to know his Task Groups were on Aridun but the Conclave. Gurion had kept no written data of their status, had discussed their situation with no one. Yet the inquisitor said nothing. Gurion had been at this game too long to betray his emotions. In his time serving the Inquisition, he had lost sixty per cent of his body to conflict. A man so scarred became honed to a rough edge. He had learned to keep his face passive, his mouth shut and his eyes open. He would watch the lord marshal, because that was what he did best.

Recoiling, as if he had said too much, the sudden change in Khmer's demeanour was startling. Loosening out his shoulders, the lord marshal turned away from Gurion as if they had not spoken at all. He loaded a fresh power cell into the lasgun and drifted almost absent-mindedly towards his gallery booths.

'Before you go,' Khmer called to Gurion over his shoulder, 'I would like to remind you that I am the last piece of sinew holding this entire campaign together. Take me away, and Medina will come crashing down around your ears, inquisitor.'

Night was always a time of calm at the temple. But tonight, an unexpected visitor stalked through its empty corridors.

Ghostly and swathed in shadow, her long limbs moved so fast, so awkwardly, that she seemed to flit between positions. Not really walking, but almost flickering between the alcoves to the columns, from column to underneath the stairs.

The priests had taken their evening supper. The patients had returned to their wards and infirmaries. The arterial corridors were lambent with the monochrome light of the moon. In the central prayer hall, a single shaft of moon slanted from the atrium ceiling, the translucent pillar swimming with motes of dust.

Everything was so utterly still that the spectral shifting of the shadow seemed brutally intrusive. She had entered through the atrium, detaching from the vaulted ceiling like a liquid droplet. Then she had darted her way from shadow to shadow, hugging the inky depths of architecture.

As she skimmed past the light, she revealed glimpses of her form. Sweeping, corded limbs shod in vambraces and greaves of hardened leather binding. The flash and flicker of naked blades.

The intruder scaled the walls with effortless ease, limbs rippling like an arachnid. Vaulting over the lip of a third-storey landing, she prowled down into what appeared to be a temple kitchen.

It was lighter here. Flat stone benches and clay ovens dominated the open space. Cauldrons, copper pots and ranks of clay jugs arranged in neat rows like an army of terracotta.

Three priests in their vestments of stark white hospitalier tunics were scrubbing clay platters at a water trough. They were deep in murmurs of conversation and did not see the shadow that crept in behind them.

She slid out three throwing needles and flicked them casually at a distance of fifteen metres. The piercing slivers entered the base of the victim's skull, between the second and third vertebrae. Two of the priests collapsed, their nervous systems shutting down, their legs folding. The third priest spun around, in time to have a throwing needle enter the hollow beneath his sternum.

As he died the last thing he saw was the face of his murderer, the stylised mask of a grinning jester – its teeth long and leering, its eyes slitted in perpetual laughter.

The assassin whispered away from the murder scene and drifted down a tight, winding ribbon of steps. She emerged in the northern ward. It was a long hall where the mentally infirm would spend their daylight hours, wandering absent-mindedly and conversing in a sporadic fashion.

It was almost empty, the narrow arched windows casting long strips of alternating light and darkness into the hall. At the far end, sunk into a rocking chair, was the still form of a patient who never moved from his perch. A veteran of the Guard, the man now spent his waking hours staring blankly at the wall, his nails digging crescents into the armrests of his chair.

The assassin dispatched him quickly with a narrow blade and moved on.

The northern ward opened into the infirmary. A line of brass-plated doors were set into the clay walls that housed the individual dormitories of the psychiatric patients. The windows that banked the corridor were barred.

Drawing a spine-saw, the assassin entered the dorms in methodical succession. She worked quickly, flickering in and out of the rooms, attending to each patient. Twice, the night-shift priests accidentally came upon her. Twice, she garrotted them, dragging the corpses into the dorms and locking the doors.

The assassin emerged from the last door at the end of the corridor. Her spine-saw was feathered with long strings of blood. The jester's mask of black and white was now contrasted with perfect droplets of red.

Unlatching a pouch from her utility belt, the assassin checked her chron. She was dead on schedule. Sheathing her spine-saw, she ghosted into the western ward. By dawn, the Temple of the Tooth would be truly empty.

CHAPTER FOURTEEN

Roth was awakened by a scream.

Even through the hazy fog of sleep, the cry was unmistakeably chilling. The timbre was shrill, agonised, and almost plaintive. He could recognise the sound of death anywhere.

Kicking himself off the bed in a tangle of linen, Roth groped for his plasma pistol. The candles in his room had thawed to sludge as he slept, and it was pitch black. His palm grazed the cold, heavy metal of a pistol grip and his frantic heartbeat slowed to a controlled feather. The ascending hum of gas fusion as he powered the Sunfury off safety made him feel secure, like a torch in the night.

Then came another scream, closer this time, a long drawn-out warble that ended abruptly in a hacking gasp.

Roth briefly considered suiting up in the fighting-plate, scattered in pieces across his dormitory floor. Once he steeled his resolve, his realised the idiocy of such a notion. Instead, he slid into the blue silk robe that he had shed at the foot of his bed. He made for the door, but doubled back and donned his tabard of reactive obsidian. Just to be safe.

He burst out of his room, pistol leading, but stopped short at the threshold. Roth was not sure if what he was seeing was real. The scene before him pulsed from his pupils to his retina and into his visual cortex, but part of his brain refused to accept it. It was all too ludicrous.

The door opened into the atrium, an open-air tiled courtyard. From the arched columns and tympanums, several corpses were hung. In the centre of the atrium, where a stone fountain babbled gently, the water was crimson. Propped up around the fountain, four dead priests sat upright. One was missing his hands, another's mouth gaped without a tongue, the third had no ears and the last one seemed to stare at Roth with raw, empty eye sockets.

The symbolism was not lost on Roth. It was the closing scene from Methuselah's tragedy *The Four Hells of a Heretic King*. The fourth act of the piece traditionally involved the hubris of King Messanine and his final punishment in the one hundred and nine layers of damnation. It was, for lack of a better interpretation, a warning against the impious and unfaithful. Back on his home world of Sancti Petri, Roth had seasonal passes to all the local theatre companies, and this piece had been his favourite. But any previous rendition he had seen could not compare to the visceral horror of the vision before him.

'Heretic…' a voice whispered, almost into his ear. The voice was silky, smoky and shrouded in shadow.

A lesser man would have hesitated, perhaps even turned to find the source of that voice. Roth knew better.

He launched himself into a headlong tumble as something cord-sharp and whisper-fast sliced the air above his head. Rolling into a crouch, Roth pivoted and took aim with his plasma pistol.

His assailant kicked the weapon cleanly from his grasp. It was, Roth thought with self-admonishment, too easy.

'Be still heretic, we'll make this quick.'

Roth rolled onto his arse in a backwards tumble to create distance. The assassin stalked him into the courtyard. Out there, under the watery light of the moon, Roth saw his killer clearly.

She wore a black-grey bodyglove, the polymer fabric swirling like iridescent petroleum, blending in and out of the shadows. Roth estimated at least a dozen various types of blade, hook and shuriken were attached to her various slings and harnesses although he couldn't be sure – his head was pounding with adrenaline.

The assassin stalked towards him, hunching like a coiled feline. Her face was an inscrutable mask painted in the macabre form of a laughing jester. Roth recognised a death cult assassin when he saw one. She did not possess the techno-wizardry of a temple trained Assassinorum agent, but what she lacked she made up for with ferocity. For a death cult assassin, it was not a matter of eliminating a target; she was less calculating, less programmed than a Culexus or a Callidus assassin. Instead, she used her rudimentary arsenal of blades with a creative splendour that heightened murder into the realm of theatrics.

Kicking backwards across the tiles, Roth sprung up onto his feet, adopting a fist-fencer's orthodox stance. He would not lie to himself: unarmed, he was as good as dead.

The assassin flicked something at him.

A throwing needle pierced his forearm, sinking deep into his muscle spindles. The pain sent sparks of shock down into his elbow.

'No poison?' Roth mused, trying to maintain his wavering composure.

'I said keep still. You didn't. So we can make this slow and painful,' she replied.

Slowly, purposefully, the Assassin unsheathed a razor's edge from her back. It was not a murder implement; this was a weapon for close-quarter combat. A slivered oblong of metal, the wafer-thin slice of monofilament blade was exactly a metre in length and a uniform one finger's width wide. In the night, it somewhat resembled a broken sword with a two-handed rubberised grip.

As the Assassin slashed the air with it, the razor emitted a shrill humming resonance. It was so sharp it was splitting the air, Roth mused.

'At least humour me, tell me who sent you,' said Roth, backing away and biding for time.

'I am doing the Emperor's work,' she hissed. Without telegraphing her movements, in a single mercurial surge of energy, the Assassin aimed her razor at the gaps between the tessellating panes of his obsidian tabard. The blow was so fast, so precise, without an iota of wasted effort. One stroke, one kill.

Roth moved forwards on his opponent, his fist-fencing instincts possessing him. Had he tried to slip backwards, the razor's edge would have surely taken off his trunk, cleanly above the hip. As it was, he moved inside of her blow. The razor teethed into the black glass, glittering fragments exploding into the air. The tabard was not armour, not against physical attacks anyway, but it was enough to deflect the weapon's finite edge.

Roth would not get another chance like that. He seized on his fleeting advantage, grabbing the hand that wielded the razor's edge. It was all he could do to delay her. Like a coordinated chess game, the Assassin somersaulted out of his grip, landing four or five paces away.

Then the air erupted with the hammering report of gunfire, sparking and roaring into the still night air. Both Roth and his assassin went to ground as tracers lit up the atrium. The shots almost seemed indiscriminate in nature.

On his stomach, Roth peered up at the muzzle flash. He saw Madeline de Medici, under the atrium arches, standing in her chiffon nightgown, firing away with a greasy machine pistol. Her marksmanship was enthusiastic yet poor, the gun bucking under her barely contained grip.

Judging by her frantic rate of fire, her gun would be spent in several seconds. Roth had to act quickly. Shimmying on his hands and knees, he retrieved his Sunfury from the base of the fountain.

He gripped the pistol just as Madeline's weapon clicked empty. The

Assassin was already up, sprinting towards Madeline with long, floating strides. Her razor's edge was raised like a scorpion's sting, coiled to strike.

'I am Inquisition!' Roth bellowed, emphasising his announcement with a shudder of psychic will.

He could not see the reaction beneath her jester's mask. But judging by the slight shift in her shoulders, the tiny recoil of her step, it was not something she had known. The Assassin halted, her mask peering impassively at Roth.

It was her mistake. Roth fired four successive shots, a steady draw of the trigger – *tap tap tap tap*. It unleashed a pillar of incandescent energy, trailing threads of atomic afterburn. The Assassin was vaporised, her constituent atoms dispersing into the curtain of heat and steam. Within seconds, all that remained were the molten puddles of metal blades, cooling rapidly on the atrium tiles. The wall of consecrated mud behind her was now a crackling web of burnt, flaking clay.

Madeline dropped her gun, her hands and expression frozen in a mixture of terror and shock. A door swung open. Vandus Barq, a sheet wrapped around his naked self, stumbled from his room.

'Where in Throne's name were you?' growled Roth, adrenaline still glanding hot through his veins.

'Sweet merciful…' Barq gasped, his eyes wide as he took in the carnage.

The others of the Task Group rushed into the atrium in their sleepwear, evidently roused by the skirmish. Celeminé and Pradal stopped as they neared Roth, wordless. Neither could do anything but stare at the meticulous arranged corpses. Celeminé's shoulders began to tremble. Pradal hugged his lasrifle close to his chest.

'Where were you?' Roth repeated, shouting this time.

Barq shook his head slowly. 'I'm sorry, Roth. I must have slept through it,' he admitted guiltily.

'Look around,' Roth snarled, pointing at the dead, at the jagged seams of bullet-holes, the blood that laced the tiles in glistening starburst patterns. 'You slept through this?'

'Yes. I did. What happened?'

Roth shook his head. He didn't know who to trust any more. Someone close to him had marked him for death, marked his Task Group for elimination. Someone with tremendous Imperial authority. He wished his old mentor, Inquisitor Liszt, were with him to soothe his fears, to tell him what to do. Or even Gurion, to lend him guidance. For the first time in his career, Roth thought he might have been too young for a task of such magnitude. For the first time, he realised there were those who did not fear the Inquisition.

'Vandus. I'll be making for Kholpesh come dawn. Do not follow me.'

'Obodiah, please, tell me what's happening?'

'I can't. But I think it would be best if you did not accompany me to Kholpesh. I fear betrayal.'

Barq blinked in disbelief. 'You do not trust me?'

Roth steadied his breath and levelled his gaze first on Celeminé, then Pradal and finally locked eyes with Barq. 'There is a betrayer amongst us. It's not that I think it is you, Vandus. But that I do not want to kill you if you are. I'm sorry, old friend.'

CHAPTER FIFTEEN

The truck rolled to a shuddering stop. Trapped though he was, Silverstein felt the lurch of deceleration and heard the squealing protest of the brakes. He did not know how long they had been travelling for. Perhaps two hours, perhaps eight. It was impossible to tell.

'No, Silverstein, don't try,' Asingh-nu pleaded in the dark. Silverstein couldn't see him but he could recognise the drawling Cantican vowels of a former rural labourer.

'Perhaps, if we wait a while, we will have a better chance for escape,' Temughan stuttered. He did not sound so sure. For a former clocksmith with steady hands, steady rifle-firing hands, the guerrilla fighter lacked a steadiness of nerve, Silverstein noted. He would be a liability in the event of escape.

'Silverstein, you decide what to do. I will follow you,' said Apartan. He was a former soldier, a sergeant in the CantiCol Second Division. Despite the over-enunciation of his syllables in the Cantican accent, his terse staccato speech was unmistakeably military. Nerseh, a dust-hunter and trapper from the Outbounds of Cantica, nodded in agreement. In their time together, Silverstein knew both men to be coarsely dependable and he was glad that of everyone, those two were with him.

'You do what you want. I have no intentions of meeting the warlord. I don't think it sounds particularly pleasant. Do you?' Silverstein said, addressing the others.

Aghdish, the oldest of the captives, a coarse labourer with heavy hands from the ports of Cape Cantica, made the decision for all of them. 'Do what we said we'd do, Silverstein. It's that, or we die,' he said flatly.

The hatch swung open on its hinges. Unrelenting sunlight streamed into their temporary prison. Silverstein shuttered his augmetics and went over the plan in his head for the hundredth time, visualising it in minute detail.

An Ironclad leaned into the lorry. 'Aram gadal, aram! Aram!'

Silverstein replied by slamming his jackboot into the throat of the Ironclad. He aimed his heel into the soft point between the soldier's gorge plate and his face-bindings. The Ironclad gurgled wetly behind his mask, stumbling with rearward steps as he clutched at his crushed windpipe.

Without a second thought, Silverstein hurled himself out of the truck. It would be his only chance. His fellow captives piled off after him. The huntsman landed awkwardly on his shoulder, his hands still bound. He looked up, assessing the situation.

They were in dense wilderness. Colossal trees with thick craggy trunks like inverted mountains branched up around him. Banks of gingko and fern clustered in tiered shelves amongst the tremendous root systems. Silverstein was a huntsman and the wilderness was his trade, but he did not recognise this place.

Around the disorientated captives, the vehicle convoy had stopped to refuel. Ironclad hauling battered jerry canisters of fuel stared at him. They saw him. He saw them. In the scramble to draw weapons, several of the Ironclad dropped their fuel containers. Shots, angry and hissing, snapped at the edges of his clothes. A las-round dropped Aghdish, puncturing the Cantican as he made a dash for the trees. Another shot punched clean through Nerseh's abdomen, folding him over. Now there were three.

Silverstein dived for the fallen Ironclad, still writhing on the ground, blood and froth seeping from his face-bindings. He wrenched a laspistol from the Ironclad's hip holster.

The huntsman aimed as he steadied his entangled wrists. Las-shots fizzled next to Silverstein's ear, so close he could feel the prickling heat of its afterburn. He aligned the shot at the toppled jerry cans, gurgling fuel onto the hard-packed earth. One precise round was all he needed.

The tightly focused beam of las sparked into the fuel. The effect was instantaneous. Swooning fire rose into multiple growths of searing gas clouds blossoming into the air. There was a low crump of pressurised oxygen, an expanding shell of corrosive heat. It ignited a chain reaction.

Smoke, solid and black boiled in gagging clouds. Fire washed on the wind, sheeting in orange swirls. Men staggered about, blinded and choking. It was exactly what Silverstein needed. With a click, his augmetic shutters opened and his low-visibility vision revealed the scene before him in shades of monochrome green.

He locked onto an Ironclad outrider, astride his bike, pawing at the air with blind, groping hands. Silverstein dispatched him with a snap of his laspistol. One after another, in vivid two-dimensional optics, Silverstein searched out the outriders, took aimed and killed them with headshots. He put down six of them in about as many seconds.

Turning to his fellow captives, Silverstein pushed them in the direction of the fallen outriders. 'Seize the bikes, grab as much fuel as you can!'

Rendered senseless by the inferno, the guerrillas fumbled against the heat and fumes. 'Go! Faster!' Silverstein urged, pushing them along. A las-shot fizzed over his shoulder, dangerously close.

The huntsman rolled the corpse of an outrider off his mount. It was a quad-bike, with deeply treaded all-terrain wheels. Silverstein slid onto the seat and gunned the throttle, his wrists still bound. The quad-bike snarled in response.

'Follow my lead,' Silverstein called out. With a sharp lurch, the bike shot off into the rocky wilderness, weaving between the ossified trees. He looked behind to see the bikes of his guerrillas storming out of the oily smoke, tracer and las chasing them.

The heating grate in Gurion's stateroom fluttered low, exuding its dim murky warmth. The tittering woodwind symphony of Cavaleri's *Summer Garden Allegro* drifted softly in the background. The old inquisitor was asleep at his desk, pillowed by mounds of tactical readouts and war reports. The last weeks had been hellish; the campaign was faltering. Intel reported that the invasion had begun on faraway Sinope. His nights were marked by endless war conferences and urgent debriefs as the High Command agonised over their successive defeats. Gurion snatched irregular naps when he could. At two hundred, he was not the young man he used to be.

It was during his slumber that Roth came to him. Or rather, an astropath appeared in the eye of his mind in the visage of Inquisitor Roth, a mere mouthpiece of psychic conveyance. The astral projection broke through a physical distance of three hundred thousand kilometres, painted directly into his frontal lobe.

'Lord Gurion,' said the ghost image, his voice reverberating with mind echoes.

Gurion's subconscious woke with a start, although his physical body sunk into deeper sleep.

'Roth. What time is it?'

'Late. Is that Cavaleri I hear?'

'Oh yes. Of course. Music is the only thing that keeps me sane these days,' Gurion chuckled gently.

'Then I think I must be already mad, Gurion. Things are very bad here. Soured up, as you would say.'

'Is anything the matter?'

'Where do I start?' Roth uttered with a watery sigh. 'There is a betrayer within my ranks. There have been too many close attempts on my life so far.'

'How do you know it is betrayal? You are, after all, in a warzone that is nothing if not on the edge of conquest.'

'Because my murderers are Imperial agents. A death cult assassin, local mercenaries last under the employ of the Medina war effort. The nicest kinds.'

'I see,' Gurion reflected thoughtfully. When he was thoughtful, he rolled the words on his tongue like he was evaluating a complex wine.

'I can only assume that the location and the activities of my Task Group remain a secret of the Conclave?'

'Yes of course. Only I know the status of the Conclavial Task Groups–'

'Which would mean I have an infiltrator in my ranks, leaking out my intelligence and keeping two steps ahead of the game grid,' Roth finished.

'Are you safe now?'

Roth's astro-vision shrugged its wispy, translucent shoulders. 'I will continue on to Kholpesh tomorrow. But I will not be leaving with Inquisitor Barq's team. I cannot afford to…'

'I understand. You are caught in a vice. Transiting between battlefields with a betrayer at your side warrants a special kind of caution,' Gurion mused.

'I suspect Varuda,' Roth admitted bluntly.

'Well then you are not alone. He does everything short of admitting foul play. But I cannot act without premise. Not at a time like this. The campaign hangs by a thread and summary punishment of its highest-ranking general is a risk I cannot take. Not without solid cause.'

'Of course. Do one thing for me, Lord Gurion.'

'Anything.'

'Follow Varuda, and you'll find the rat.'

Gurion nodded thoughtfully. 'I won't let him out of my sight.'

CHAPTER SIXTEEN

Kholpesh, geographically and architecturally, had much in common with Cantica and the grapevine worlds of Medina. Civilisation clustered on a dispersed chain of archipelagos, mid-ocean ridges immersed in a churning sea of milk. The triangle suns of Medina pivoted constantly in the bleached sky. As a consequence, the protein-rich water that covered much of the planet was subject to mass condensation and the formation of attendant thunderstorms. There was no night or day on Kholpesh, only the searing glare of sun and the boiling black clouds of tempest.

It was for this geographic reason that the Archenemy conducted war on Kholpesh in a different way. Through the absence of open ground to facilitate mass aerial deployment, the Ironclad heralded the invasion with aerial bombardment. Squadrons of Archenemy interceptors and bombers skimmed on the shrieking turbines of slam-propulsion engines. They slashed through the sky like bats in formation. Archenemy escort cruisers, ones that had slipped through the Imperial Navy picket, lurked in the sky like ghostly floating continents.

The bombing had laid waste to Kholpesh. It left a trail of blast-flattened destruction from the citrus groves of the sandy coastal plains to the tiered domes and minarets of the Kholpeshi city-states.

The enemy strategy had been to disrupt, disorder and wound. It had achieved this objective within just three days of sustained bombing. Roads and transit systems were destroyed, rural districts were isolated, cities were burning and four million citizens became displaced and homeless. The death toll reached one hundred and twenty thousand.

In a way, the initial bombardment fortified the morale and spirit of the Kholpeshi people. In Mantilla, the axial city of Kholpesh, the streets became congested with citizens rushing to donate blood and food to the outlying regions. So thick was the congestion that the Governate issued an unprecedented mandate for citizens to return to their homes, lest they hamper the organised relief efforts.

Unable to wait idle, isolated companies of CantiCol infantry marched seventy kilometres in one day, in order to initiate a rescue effort to the ravaged southern rural districts of Astur and Valadura. The Kholpeshi Governate was in disarray and senior officers of the Cantican Colonials organised independent rescue efforts.

Twenty-four hours later, a column of sixty thousand Guardsmen, shovels on their rucksacks, banners of the Kholpeshi Garrison fluttering, began the long trek to the outer provinces.

Military trucks with supplies attempted to cross the burst dams and irrigation systems between shallow archipelagos with a cavalier disregard for their own safety. Many made it through to the refugees stranded amongst the ruins of their villages, delivering much-needed medical and food supplies. But dozens of trucks, along with their occupants, were lost to mud sinks and landslides.

Further from the city reaches, in the provinces, settlements became isolated in their own little pockets of suffering. A husband bound the body of his wife to his back with string, as he rode his bicycle thirty-five kilometres to the funereal caves.

In the cities themselves, many wandered amongst the rubble and smoke in a daze. In Orissa Minor, a young mother and father shrieking with distress flagged down and pleaded with a passing industrial dirt-miner to find their son, lost underneath the collapsed folds of their tenement building. The parents had been on manufactorum shift when it happened. Despite a death toll that reached the hundreds of thousands, a crowd gathered in breathless silence as the sheets of rockcrete were lifted. For many hours they dug, passers-by joining in with shovels, pails, even bare hands.

When the debris cleared inside, they found three bodies. A young child, two months shy of six. He was cradled in the arms of his grandfather, his grandmother holding her husband from behind. Even amongst the destruction, the crowd wept openly.

Axial Mantilla, the ruling seat of Kholpesh, had always been the domain of the aristocrats, oligarchs and upper tier of Kholpesh. It was thus the only city-state sheathed in the semi-sphere of a void shield. Like a shimmering bubble of oil-slick water, the shield dissipated the worst of the Archenemy bombardment. It was precisely because of this that Mantilla became the focus of the Ironclad's major ground offensive. Having secured a deployment site following their brutal aerial campaign, the Archenemy besieged the city-state with the entirety of its Kholpeshi invasion force – fifty deca-legions of Ironclad, five hundred thousand strong, supported by the motorised and mechanised battalions so prevalent amongst Ironclad doctrine.

By the fourth month of the siege of Mantilla, the battle had mired into a grinding trench war of attrition. The Imperial trench networks were three hundred metres deep, the high mosaic walls and shield pylons of Mantilla rearing up behind them. Entire sections of the sand-bagged entrenchment were within grenade-throwing distance of Archenemy trenches. It was vicious, it was close and the firing never stopped.

It was here that the Task Group made their descent. The stratocraft scraped an evasive landing into the defensive bulwark, tailed by enemy flak and tracer. It was the welcome they had all expected.

Once on land, the Task Group understood their obligations and they went about them with determined efficacy.

Liaising with Cantican senior officers through Captain Pradal, Inquisitor Roth made a thorough assessment of the siege. He inspected the flak-board trenches, ankle-deep in sour filth, slogging through kilometres of zigzagging fortifications. The Cantican Guardsmen on Kholpesh were the most desolate body of fighting men he had ever seen. Their uniforms were ragged and worn thin; many were wounded and indiscriminately bandaged. Disintegration seeped into the very eyes of those men.

Madeline de Medici, escorted by Inquisitor Celeminé entered the city of Mantilla proper. They were to establish communications with one of Madeline's contacts, a minor broker of the underground and often very elite network of private collectors.

The atmosphere within the capital was like nothing they could have imagined. Two million refugees crowded the streets, shuddering in blankets and bundles of their last possessions. They clustered in throngs, sleeping openly on the pavements, in alcoves and crevices, and congregating in miserable huddles down side lanes and one-ways.

Under the protective veil of the void shield, the aristocrats and wealthy bourgeois flaunted their position with a defeatist debauchery. They revelled as the planet burned. In their pavilions and theatre-houses, they saluted endless rounds of liquor with the cry, 'They are coming!'

There was no rationing. No sense of responsibility or inhibition amongst the elite. Mantilla had accepted its fate. It was only a matter of living as much as they could with the time they had left.

The auto-sedan, cigar-nosed and open-topped, was chauffeured by a young transport corps lieutenant. The Cantican officers, in their peculiarly cavalier fashion, had insisted that Madeline and Celeminé travel into Mantilla by staff car.

Mantilla was an old and powerful city-state. Tall terraces of soft pastel – pinks, jades and powdery blue – lined the slab stone roads. The city grew in tiers, and to Madeline, it reminded her of an ancient pre-Imperial text documenting the Tower of Babel. Plum minarets and flaking, gilded domes dominated the skyline. In all, Mantilla had a haughty cosmopolitan charm that was unmatched by any other city-state on Kholpesh.

Not too far into the hab districts, their staff car became mired in refugee congestion. The desperate and the hungry tapped at their tinted windows, hands held out, pleading. The young lieutenant blasted his horn as he eased the vehicle forwards. Behind the soundproofed windows and armoured chassis, Madeline felt strangely distant from their distress. Their voices were muffled. The air in the staff car was cold and recycled. It made the outside world seem surreal. Unbearably so.

Madeline and Celeminé alighted from the vehicle, much to the protests of their escort. The two ladies, both dressed in the demure cultural garb of Medinian women, proceeded through the city on foot.

They cut across the municipal park of the district. The neat lawns and geometric footpaths had become a designated refugee camp. Makeshift tents strung up from ration sacks lined the square in densely packed rows. People resorted to using the sculptural fountains as drinking water, and disease spread rapidly. Everywhere they looked were the jaundiced faces of cholera and dysentery.

Beneath the columned arches, Madeline noticed small malnourished children track her with dark, sunken eyes as she went by. They lolled in the arms of their parents, too tired and too sickly to move.

'This is horrible. This place is so wretchedly filthy. And the smell. Is this what all wars are like?' Madeline asked.

'These are the lucky ones. Millions of refugees, some coming on barges from across the archipelagos, some trekking for days on foot. For every one refugee you see here, they shut the gates on a dozen. Hundreds of thousands of people were caught out in the open as the Archenemy mounted their initial ground offensive,' Celeminé said.

'Oh please. Stop!' Madeline said, not wanting to hear the rest.

The pair of them walked on in silence for some time.

They followed the pedestrian bridges that would take them into the commercial district. The four-storey terraces that faced onto the streets, with their painted railings and tiled steeples, were shut off from the world. Only the very privileged lived here. The refugees huddled for shelter at their doorstep, foraging through their debris bins for edible scraps.

Many times during their walk, Madeline saw the sled-chariots of minor dignitaries or bourgeoisie rattle past. Their occupants were more often than not blind drunk, sometimes yelling obscenities at the refugees who did not scurry fast enough away from the path of their horses. Once, a bodyguard riding on the running board even began unleashing a lasgun into the air to scatter the people before him.

As they walked closer to the upper tiers of Mantilla, the atmosphere began to gradually change. In the exclusive commercial and administrative quarters, the refugees began to thin out. Ape-faced private house guards stood sentry outside the gates of estates and manor houses. Women with painted faces, probably aristocrats by virtue of their tall hair and suggestive bodices, cavorted openly in the streets. Dishevelled noblemen mingled amongst them, their breath sour with alcohol, laughing the laugh of the mentally diminished. All were wreathed in beads and dry, wilting flowers.

Madeline was disgusted.

A soft-middled aristocrat grabbed her from behind, cackling as he buried his face into her neck. 'Please, where are your manners?' Madeline protested, trying to shrug him away.

The man was persistent. Still snorting his intoxicated laugh, he encircled Madeline with sweat-slick arms.

Celeminé put him out with a palm to the base of the skull. She moved fast and Madeline barely had time to register the movement. With a grunt, the man sagged to his knees, cupping the base of his neck.

The pair trotted away quickly, melting into the lascivious crowd.

The tea-house was created as a splendid aviary.

It was a fan-brimmed pavilion, its wrought-iron scrollwork and railings painted sea-green. Tripod tables and chess stools clustered under the veranda and meandered down the sidewalk. In the centre of the tea-house, a birdhouse crafted as a fenced palace contained hundreds of songbirds, flickering flashes of emerald, sapphire and magenta.

Here, the Mantillan elite could go about their daily business of trade, politics and social obligation without the unsightly distraction of war or refugees. A dozen private guards shouldering flechette shotguns saw to that.

It was also where Madeline would rendezvous with her broker. She recognised him immediately. He had no name of course, brokers worked on a strictly need-to-know basis; the black market of relic smuggling was an exclusive network and the patrons took this very seriously. But Madeline had acquired his services enough times to recognise him by face.

The broker was a mad bear of a man, shaggy and genial. Yet on occasion he wore periwigs of absurd pomp, flowing, curled and beribboned. A tiny waistcoat was stretched to splitting point across his shoulders and a lace cravat adorned his bullish neck. Combined with his looping pencilled eyebrows and white-painted face, he was once the most curious yet repellent individual Madeline had ever been acquainted with.

'The client is always right,' Madeline said as she took a seat at his table.

'Oh, the client is never wrong,' answered the broker with the prearranged cue.

'This is a friend of mine, Lady Felyce Celeminé. She is the client inter-ested in purchasing.'

The broker extended a heavy paw gloved in lace. 'Pleasure to meet you, Lady Celeminé. You can call me Little Cadiz.'

'Oh of course, Little, what a delightful name!' squealed Celeminé, feigning interest. Madeline could see the repulsion that threatened to manifest as a gag reflex well up in Celeminé. But the inquisitor kept her poise.

Little Cadiz promptly ordered a round of herbal infusions before dis-cussing business, as was the etiquette.

'At your behest, I have devoted a good deal of time and energy to thinking of the patron. To this date you have not identified any of these patrons specifically, nor have you outlined the content of their character, forcing me to draw certain conclusions about them from your tone of voice,' tittered Cadiz in his strained alto.

'I refer to the patron Hiam Golias. A collector, I believe, who is offering a relic from the Age of Apostasy?'

'I have inferred from your confident tone that these relics are at the very least quite important, as you seem to be in a hurry to locate them. Were these relics of a more mundane nature, say a rather expensive clock or xenos jewellery, I believe you would sound more relaxed.'

+Is he mad?+ Celeminé projected into Madeline.

Madeline nodded slowly, biting her lip.

'But no, your tone has been one of abstract concern, and seemed to be directed at the wellbeing of yourselves. I can certainly sympathise with your point. We live in a dangerous world and at a dangerous time. I would be hard pressed to come up with a group of people more at risk in this world than us, other than perhaps smaller children.'

+This has got to be a ruse to throw people off,+ Celeminé sighed.

'If it is, he does his job well,' Madeline whispered under her breath. 'When can you arrange for us to meet with Master Golias?' she inquired, jotting down a tidy sum on a paper napkin as her broker's fee.

Little Cadiz slid the napkin over to himself and peeked at the numer-als. He appeared satisfied.

'For the sake of the completeness of our deal, I would say – imagine a grand social gathering for recreational purposes, to be held on the Golias Estate. A celebration of liberation! That is where you shall find Master Golias.'

+Ten seconds. I'll give him ten seconds before I cross this table and put him to sleep,+ Celeminé commented with a searing tinge of half-hearted aggression.

Madeline laughed out loud without realising.

'I'm sorry, was it something I said?' Cadiz enquired, clearly concerned.

'No no, not at all. When is this celebration to be held?'

'Every night of course! They are coming, there is no time left to squander,' he cawed theatrically.

'Of course,' said Madeline flatly.

'But tonight is when Golias is willing to see you. The both of you. He is very eager to do so.'

Slipping a vellum fold from his breast pocket, Cadiz daintily slid it across the table. 'Invitations to the Golias Estate. I wish you all the best with your purchasing ventures.'

With that, Madeline and Celeminé rose from the table, curtsied and left the madman.

CHAPTER SEVENTEEN

Roth stalked up to the observation deck of the command post bunker. A flock of staff officers trailed him, ghosting him so hard they trod on his heels.

The bunker was set at the foot of Mantilla's fortress walls, ringed by the apron of trenches that spider-webbed the terrain around it. An ugly structure of prefab boarding and sandbags, it resembled a fat-bellied urn, piled high with kev-netting and hessian sacks. Yet from the observation tower, the bunker afforded a clear enough view of the battlefield.

At first survey, the terrain was barren and undulating. What little vegetation that might have clustered in that sandy soil had long been churned away by artillery. The Imperial trenches encircled the city with a twelve kilometre stretch of razor wire, tank traps and gun nests. Facing them, almost interlocking amongst them, were the trenches of the Archenemy. Tactically speaking, the enemy held the higher undulating hills. It was a bad position for the Imperium, as the Ironclad artillery in those hills had been able to rain down ordnance with almost clear line of sight.

'This is terrible,' Roth said. 'Absolutely untenable.'

'What right have you to say that?' growled one of the officers.

The man who had spoken was Major General Sihan Cabales, commanding officer of the Mantillan siege. He had been caustic with Roth since the inquisitor had made landfall. He was a tall gentleman in his late seventies, with a broad, imposing frame that stretched the shoulders of his cavalry jacket.

'Major general, why, is it not an elementary mistake to allow the enemy to claim their high ground unopposed?'

Cabales joined Roth at the sandbagged ledge. The field before him was smoking, like the soil itself had soaked up the heat of the bombs that pounded it. 'Because,' he began, 'these men are the most demoralised troops I have ever had under my command. Absolutely useless.'

'General, wars are not lost by men, they are lost by officers. I'm not a military man, but even I know that,' Roth said. The inquisitor couldn't help himself, he realised he was being entirely too pompous, but the general could do with some unwinding.

'Then you do it,' Cabales grinned wolfishly. 'You can take command of that far section of the Magdalah trenches.'

The general snapped his fingers and a young lieutenant bearing his snuff box and a handful of maps stepped forwards. Cabales slid one of the map tubes from the pile and unfurled its flapping corners across the ledge. 'Here, the Magdalah foothills. If you think you can claim any of these hills, claim that one.'

Roth found the foothills on the map, and then made a sweep with his telescope. It was not a good area. He adjusted the mag-scope and zoomed in on a blast-withered patch of flat, rocky ground. A lattice-work of trenches covered most of the low-lying ground. That in itself was a military blunder.

What's more, the Archenemy to their front had claimed the Magdalah hills. They rose up half a kilometre away, a series of hump-backed ridges, wrinkled with crevices, crannies and the natural cover of rock and gorse. The enemy had established static firing positions from up on high, shelling and pounding the flat, open trenches below. It was, in Roth's opinion, the worst possible tactical plight.

'Will you accept?' Cabales said, loud enough for all the assembled officers to hear.

It was a ploy of course, for Cabales to regain face and knock the upstart young inquisitor off his pedestal. Cabales knew this. Roth knew this. An older, reserved commander, perhaps a veteran with less to prove, would have thought it folly. The voice of his mentor Inquisitor Liszt would have been lecturing him. But Roth's mind was already made.

'I accept,' Roth shrugged. 'Take me down to the Magdalah section and allow me to meet these fellows.'

The defensive lines around the Magdalah foothills were called the 'The Pit' for good reason.

Casualty percentage rates here were in the low forties. Elements of the Ninth and 16th Infantry, Seventh Light Horse and 22nd Lancers who had been deployed here were known as those who 'drew the backend straw' amongst comrades.

Roth stepped down into the trenches and his boots immediately settled into five centimetres of gluey scum. It was a thoroughly wretched mixture of mostly mud, precipitation, human waste and no small amount of blood. He waded through the trenches with Pradal close behind, following an escort of NCOs.

It was humid here, the moisture clinging to his sinuses like a steaming film. The temperature in the low thirties did not bode well for the corpses, some of which were stacked stiffly horizontal to the sandbags and flakboards that reinforced the trench walls.

Roth stepped carefully, resisting the temptation to bring a hand to his nose and mouth. It would not lend a good impression to the troops he would have to command. The inquisitor moved amongst them, giving them curt nods when they caught his eye. But they rarely did. Many of the Guardsmen sat blank, with the glazed stare of exhaustion and some measure of shell shock.

Altogether, they were some of the most demoralised soldiers Roth had ever encountered. They had shed their proud brown jackets, squatting about in breeches and braces. Most huddled on crates, muttering darkly and smoking. Many others still wore their rebreathers, as the threat of poison gas was constant.

It was perhaps a slight detail, but what concerned Roth the most was the way they carried their rifles. One could always discern the morale and training of a soldier by the way they carried their arms. Well-trained troops had good trigger discipline, fingers coiled loosely outside the guard ready to fire, or straight by their shoulders like spears. Others still, carried them close to their chests, cradled in their arms as if about to rear. The variations were many, but the intentions were the same – the guns were always ready to discharge at the enemy.

The men of the Magdalah defences settled on their lasguns like crutches, leaning on them with weary resignation. It seemed they had given up the thought of fighting, they just wanted the time to pass less painfully.

Roth crouched down next to a bearded soldier whittling sticks with a bayonet. He couldn't tell what rank the man held, as his rank sash was soiled and bloodied beyond recognition. 'Soldier, where can I find Colonel Paustus?'

The man didn't respond. Roth repeated himself twice before he realised the man was deaf from shelling.

Captain Pradal caught the man's attention by placing a hand on his bayonet. The man looked up and Captain Pradal signed up a deft series of field signals. Something in the order of 'look for the colonel'.

The man spoke, his voice unconsciously loud. 'The colonel is dead. Mortared yesterday. Major Arvust commands this section now. He should be in the comms station if he's not dead already.'

Pradal signed his acknowledgment and Roth moved on, trying to step on the duckboard path laid over the worst of the collected filth.

They found Major Arvust in a hollowed section of the first-line trench, under an improvised command post. A vox set was mounted over a stack of ammunition pallets and a plastek groundsheet was pitched overhead to keep the rain from damaging the comms system. The major hunched over the arrays bay, staring blankly as a tabac stick melted down to grey ash in his hands.

Major Arvust was a Guard-lifer. Roth could tell by the set of his jaw and the way the index finger of his free hand was constantly flexed, as if coiled to squeeze over an invisible trigger. The man was rough-edged, his face handsome in that rugged, sun-battered way. Looking to be in his late forties, Roth knew a career in the Guard was severely ageing. Most likely the man was no more than mid-thirties.

'Sir, Captain Pradal, military liaison of the Medina High Command, sir.' Captain Pradal snapped a stiff salute.

The major's eyes never left the vox array. He flung his hand up to his head in the most half-hearted salute short of being a fly swat and took a draw of his tabac.

'Major General Cabales already voxed through your arrival. You and the inquisitor. What do you need here?' Arvust said, not bothering to look at either of them.

'To bolster command staff in this area. From what we've heard the casualties among officers have been appalling, sir,' Pradal said.

The major shrugged. 'Be my guest.'

Roth took one carefully placed step forwards. 'Let's cut to the point, major. This section is dying; I've never seen Guardsmen in such a state of disrepair. I don't want to tread on your toes. Either you'll help us reclaim this section, or you can leave.'

Startled by Roth's candour, Major Arvust ashed his tabac and turned to regard Roth with a slow, appraising eye. Roth knew immediately that the major was a solid officer, a good navigator placed into a sinking ship.

'I've tried. HQ staff want us to sit tight in a static defence. My hands are tied,' the major said with resignation.

Roth squatted down in the mud next to Arvust and studied the officer's notes and tactical spreadsheets. 'My hands are not tied. I have authority to command the defences here as *we* see fit. Provided you wish to facilitate this arrangement.'

'We'll see.' A genuine smile twitched at the corners of the major's forlorn scowl. 'If you mean to do what you mean to do, then I hope you have some sort of plan.'

'Let's see what we can hammer out,' Roth said, tracing the grid map with his finger.

* * *

The Golias Estate was a four-storey villa daubed in powder-pink pigment. It was a villa of Kholpeshi design, taller than it was wide and severely asymmetrical. It teetered above a mezzanine gallery with long winding stairs that speared fifty metres to the commercial district below. Six hundred-odd steps was no easy climb, and Madeline had to fuss about her face with a kerchief, lest her sweat dampen her cosmetics. Perched so high up on the tiers of Mantilla, the Golias Estate was decidedly impressive with its haughty, antiquated air.

'This place is marvellous!' shouted Celeminé as she bounded up the steps. She was dressed in a petal frock of cream linen with a hooded scarf of soft wool, an outfit Madeline had personally selected. The inquisitor spun on her heels, the long tails of her scarf dancing with her. The heights did not seem to bother her at all.

But the heights bothered Madeline. The steps were narrow and of worn, uneven stone that spiralled down into the dizzying depths below. On stiletto-heeled buckle boots, she precariously edged up, pausing ever so briefly between each step. Like Celeminé, Madeline had dressed for the occasion in a chemise.

'This Hiam Golias, what sort of character is he?' Celeminé called down.

'He's a minor game piece. See these workshops and boutiques along the commercial galleries? He owns quite a few of them.'

'Uh huh. And you know him how?'

'We... have history,' Madeline concluded and left it at that. It was no fault of her own that in the two times she had dealt with Master Golias, he had exuded a blasé, dispassionate charisma that she had not been able to resist. It was better to let Celeminé find out about Golias herself.

'And how does the network operate?'

'Well, the relic trade is a mix of enthusiasts. Historians, investors, collectors...'

'Cultists?' Celeminé added.

'I suppose, if the right item was on offer. But it's clandestine – don't ask, don't tell. Everything is based on word of mouth and reputation. If your dealings aren't clean no one will operate with you.'

'And what would that mean?' Celeminé asked, bounding three or four steps closer in one leap.

'You lose your network. Your source, the smugglers, the brokers, the clients. Everyone meshes together on a need-to-know basis. It's a fraternity to keep away the undesirables.'

'What do you mean by undesirables?' asked Celeminé, although she already knew.

'The Inquisition of course,' laughed Madeline.

The celebrations had already begun by the time they had arrived. Or perhaps the previous night's festivities just hadn't ended. Either way,

Golias's guests lounged about the antechamber. Many had the slack, sweaty faces of surge-heads and the rest were evidently drunk. They lazed about in various stages of undress, lost in a fugue of self-indulgence.

It was a shame, since the chamber itself was breathtakingly beautiful. Hand-woven Cantican rugs and cushions were strewn about the floor. The walls were red velvet, floral detailing picked out in gold thread. Exotic stuffed beasts, off-world felines and horned, hairy herbivores were locked in a stiff pantomime in the corners of the chamber, their out-stretched paws draped with lingerie. It was a beautiful house and a shame that it had to be despoiled by those with no appreciation for it, thought Madeline.

As they trotted past the antechamber, sleepy, whispery voices called out to them, yearning for them to join the writhing limbs. Others called out the Mantillan toast of the hour – 'They're coming!'

'Go frag yourself,' Celeminé muttered under her breath.

A porter in servant's robes led them into the dining area. Divans were set around a marble table so that the guests could recline as they ate. On the table were platters of raw shellfish, aquatic delicacies and gelatinous desserts. Without a doubt, these were not the rations decreed by governing mandate.

'I appreciate the hospitality, but we have already eaten. Would you be able to lead me to Master Golias?' Madeline asked.

'Master Golias is occupied at the moment. If you will help yourself to refreshments, he will attend to your needs as soon as he is able,' the porter recited.

+Tell him if he doesn't drag Golias out here, this little birdie will start blasting a heavy-cal pistol into the ceiling,+ Celeminé whispered into her mind.

'My client has an appointment with Master Golias and she is in a terrible hurry,' Madeline interpreted smoothly.

'Is my presence required?'

They all turned to see Hiam Golias stride out of an adjacent chamber, his house robes unashamedly open. Two females, aristocrats judging by their pouty cos-implant lips and heavy eye make-up, followed him guiltily, clad in boned corsets.

'Master Golias. It is I, Professor de Medici, and this is Lady Felyce Celeminé.'

'Of course, how could I forget such a delicious face!' laughed Golias, stepping under the light of the chandeliers.

He was a distinguished gentleman in his late seventies who had aged immensely well, on account of his pampered lifestyle and no small amount of juvenat treatments. He was tall and broad, with chem-nourished muscles and a long mane of silver hair. His face was greasily confident if not handsome, with a tall, prominent forehead and a sternly set jaw. Although he was not a fighter, he had an aristocrat's fascination with adventure and had tattooed the emblem of an obscure Guard regiment onto his abdominal muscles. Of course, Golias had never served, a man of his status did not, but it certainly sparked conversation with females.

'I'm surprised you remember me, Master Golias,' said Madeline. She found herself hating him yet flushed in the cheeks at the same time.

'I'm surprised you believed I'd forget. And this, this is Felyce? She has a wonderful curve in the small of her back. If only all my prospective buyers were so athletic,' Golias said. He appraised the girls as he would a fine piece of antiquity, or perhaps stock in an auction yard.

+Revolting. Absolutely revolting.+

Madeline started, subconsciously putting a hand to her florid cheeks in embarrassment. She hadn't intended her surface thoughts to be so obvious. Such transparent behaviour was quite beyond the bounds of etiquette.

+It's fine. I can see what you mean. If only I didn't hate him for his confidence, his wealth, his tastes, his fine mane of hair...+

With a single clap of his hands, Golias dismissed his guests from the dining chamber. They drew away sheepishly to seek other vices.

'Shall we find more private arrangements to conduct business?' Celeminé said coyly, playing every bit into the persona that Golias wanted her to be.

'That all depends, my lady, on what sort of business you would like to conduct,' Golias laughed with an unsettling silkiness.

Roth and his officers worked long into the days and nights. There was much to be done. Battle plans were drawn and scrapped, timings were coordinated and many tabac stubs were collected in the ashtray. Roth had never realised the minute details that contributed to a strategy, even down to the order in which his men would march.

The triple suns never set on Kholpesh and their time was marked by the regularity of gas attacks.

Almost on the hour, the tin whistles would relay down the trenches. Men would tug goggled rebreathers out of musette bags, pressing cumbersome masks over their faces. Rolling banks of ochre and creeping tendrils of mustard would wash over the trench systems, billowing in a slight easterly. The gas was a dense respiratory irritant, and movement only worsened its effects. Instead the men would stand up on the firing steps or parapets, allowing the dense fumes to sink and settle. It happened so often that the men often continued to play cards or clean weapons, almost unperturbed.

Admittedly, Roth found it difficult to plan tactical strategy and discuss battle plans through the filmed lens and filtration hoses, but he managed. Roth managed because he had known his strategy the minute he laid eyes on the men under his command. To him, they were thoroughly demoralised Guardsmen, sitting about withering under constant enemy aggression. What was needed was an offensive, an all-out push into the enemy-held Magdalah hills. Roth would give them what the overly cautious HQ staff had denied them for so long. He'd try to give them the good fight. On a personal level, it was what Roth needed to occupy his mind while the Task Group went about their networking. It gave him purpose after the events on Cantica.

The fight itself would be an uphill battle. According to the readouts provided by Major Arvust, the geography, enemy disposition and their own resources did not leave them with many choices. The Archenemy were dug in amongst the foothills, roughly four hundred metres across no-man's-land.

From his magnoculars Roth could spot the Ironclad's large number of static armour: light tanks, tankettes, bombards and Basilisks, mostly hulled down in static firing pits. The silvery glint of their turrets buried under camo-netting resembled studs riveted into the soil. They would be hard to dislodge and the Ironclad would not expect the besieged Imperial forces to mount any form of counter-attack. It was an assumption that Roth intended to exploit to its fullest.

These vehicles had been devastatingly effective from their high vantage points but Arvust and Pradal firmly believed they would be vulnerable to a well organised infantry advance. Roth was inclined to agree if only by dint of their sheer confidence.

To this end, Roth had rallied the combined companies of the Seventh Light Horse and 22nd Lancers, leaving the Ninth and 16th infantry in reserve to hold the trenches. Numerically, with less than four hundred Guardsmen for the offensive, the numbers did not favour them. Yet these Guardsmen were the elite Cantican Horse Cavalry. The lancers especially were fighting men of no small repute. The Cantican Colonials lacked the heavy armour prevalent amongst other Guard formations, and the lancers bridged the gap between infantry and vehicle. While the primary role of the light horse was to escort the few precious tanks in the Cantican arsenal as mounted infantry, the lancers were the shock troops.

In particular, the lancers wore chest bandoleers clustered with fuse bombs. Mounted on nine-hundred kilogram destriers, the lancers would even charge headlong into enemy formations, leaving a trail of fuse bombs in their wake.

Unfortunately, having been relegated to trench warfare, the Cantican cavalry had parted with their steeds in Mantilla. Roth commandeered what horses he could. He voxed for the reacquisition of their steeds but was informed that of the several thousand well-trained horses left inside the city of Mantilla, hundreds had been slaughtered for food in order to fuel the aristocratic celebrations. Roth met this news with a series of choice expletives and very real threats to the well-being of the entire Mantillan upper class.

After his temper had simmered down, they re-adapted. The Magdalah offensive would become a mixed mounted infantry advance. Under the cover of rain, the Seventh and 22nd would storm the Magdalah foothills, each man loaded with as many explosive charges as he could carry. Their targets would be the ponderous beasts of static armour, the very same engines that had rained down tonnes of ammunition onto their lines for the past months. Lacking the proper supplies, many Guardsmen even resorted to creating their own improvised trench-fighting devices with what equipment they had at hand.

Given two days to prepare, the Canticans proved the inventiveness of Guardsmen in the art of dealing death. Stick grenades were defused and studded with nails to make hand clubs, knotted balls of rope were embedded with .68 calibre rounds to make studded flails. The simplest weapon Roth noticed during his final inspection was the sharpened entrenching tool. Even the thin metal plates supplied to reinforce firing steps in the trenches were hammered roughly into tin sheet breastplates. The process of industry and the preparation of war infused the Canticans with a vigour they had not felt since the beginning of the conflict.

The charge would be straightforward. It was a simple plan but was by no means flawless. But for the Guardsmen, it was better than waiting in the trenches for the unseen shell with their name on it.

CHAPTER EIGHTEEN

The atrium ceiling captured a shaft of sunlight in a single slanting pillar of gold. Motes of light, soft and dancing, coalesced across the surface of the impluvium pond below it.

The indoor atrium garden of the Golias Estate was by no means large, but what it lacked in grandiose scale it far exceeded with Neo-Medinian design. The atrium was three times taller than it was wide, the soaring heights allowing for a cradling canopy of imported trees, mostly tall finger palms and fern-tailed fronds. Trellises of carnivorous flower vines and potted succulents in poisonous colours jostled for attention in a vivid display of off-world flora. To complete the interior, a stone bench and upright harp were arranged at an angle from the central pond, a pocket of ambience beneath the subtropical surroundings.

'This is impressive, Master Golias,' Celeminé whistled. A mechanical nectar bee crafted from golden clockwork buzzed onto her shoulder and misted the air with an artificial fragrance before darting away.

'Oh this? This is nothing. It's all worthless once the Archenemy take this city,' Golias shrugged. He plucked several permellos from an overhanging bower swollen with fruit and handed one to Madeline.

'This is why you need to offload your item in such a hurry?' Madeline asked.

'Offload is an inaccurate term. I have plenty of prospective buyers for this item. Particularly from the Imperium, if the rumours are to be believed,' said Golias as he shed his robes and slipped into the pond.

'Rumours?' said Celeminé, her face suddenly serious.

'Indeed. Rumours abound. Have you ever heard of the Old Kings of Medina?'

'In passing.'

'You know the children's tales. Artefacts from the War of Reclamation, something like the Emperor's own balls or what have you. Either way, I have something valuable in my hands.'

'You have the Old Kings in your possession?' Madeline exclaimed, loudly enough to lose any pretence of bargaining power.

Golias snorted as he floated on his back. 'Perhaps not. But what I have is a relic that reveals much about the nature of the Old Kings, most likely sourced from the same origins.'

Celeminé dared to press. 'Master Golias. The Imperium could have much to benefit from that. Especially during such a time of war. Is it right for you to keep it?'

'Who are you, the Inquisition?' he cackled crisply. 'It's exactly because they want it so badly that a private collector from the Alypsia Subsector offered me half a continent worth of holdings for it.'

Golias waded to the edge of the pond and licked the water of his lips with a predatory smirk. 'If you have what the Imperium wants, that is power.'

'That's treason,' Celeminé said flatly.

'Who is this bitch and why is she in my house?' snapped Golias, pointing at Celeminé. His demeanour changed with a volatile reaction, on no small amount of alcohol and residual narcotics.

'Please, Master Golias,' Madeline stepped in. 'She means no offence by it.'

Golias glared dangerously at Celeminé, his pupils dilated and his breath snorting his nostrils in ragged jags.

'We can surpass your highest offer. What Lady Celeminé means is, why you would wish to sell such a valuable item so hurriedly?'

That seemed to placate Golias somewhat. For a moment Golias's temper wavered before his features softened. 'Because I enjoy a fine life. Kholpesh will not live forever and I have something the Imperium may find very valuable.'

Golias hauled himself out of the impluvium, shaking down his wetted mane from side to side. 'Better I take what I can now and live than die waiting for the highest bidder. Let me show you this.'

Naked, Golias crossed over to them and parted the waxy folds of vegetation. He led them through the garden, rustling through the curtain of fronds and leaves until they reached an alcove in the atrium, previously obscured. Beyond the alcove window on a rooftop landing pad could be seen the hook-nosed beak of a military flyer.

'This is why I need to liquidate my assets,' Golias proclaimed proudly.

He led them outside to his landing pad, so high up that they could see the pulsating flashes of war in the horizon.

Outside, like an eagle in its roost, wings folded and landing struts clawing the ground was a Golem-pattern cargo flier. Thirty metres long, it was turbine-nosed and round-bellied, ugly in the utilitarian way that only military logistics equipment could be. The Golem was a supply craft, ferrying cargo within fleet cruisers and more than capable of short-distance space flight. Madeline was not the least bit surprised that Golias had been able to procure one.

'I take it I should not ask you how you obtained this?' Madeline said.

'You wouldn't believe the things I had to do to pilfer one of these from the Governor's facilities,' Golias laughed as he patted the cannon-mouthed propulsion thrusters on the Golem's wing. Where Golias's hands rested, Madeline could clearly see the scraped-off paint scars of a Munitorum serial number.

Madeline and Celeminé circled around the craft, prodding at the fuse-lage pretending to be impressed. Golias had balls, they gave him that. Since the Medina Campaign, Imperial mandate had decreed a ban on all non-Imperial military fliers. Refugee barges transiting off-world were few in number and even then, most placements were allotted to Impe-rial authorities and military chieftains. Most on Kholpesh simply did not have the means to escape.

'As you can see, I am well prepared once the void shields come down. I have a chartered trade frigate waiting to ferry me beyond the Bastion Stars. What you choose to do with the artefact once I am gone is no concern of me. Most of my prospective buyers will probably want to sell it for magnified profits to the Imperial war machine.'

'If you could lever a greater price from the Imperium, why do you sell to private buyers knowing they will sell on?' Madeline questioned warily.

'Because I have no desire to deal with the Imperium. None. You can do whatever you want. I'll be on my vineyard several subsectors away by then,' Golias grinned.

'Can we see this relic?' Celeminé asked.

Golias looked at her incredulously before a burble of laughter snorted from his nose. 'Absolutely not. Are you an amateur at this business?'

'How do I know what I am paying for?' Celeminé protested indignantly.

'Again, who is this bitch? Does she know nothing of the network? Who was your broker?' snapped Golias.

Celeminé pushed Madeline aside.

'I have rank and authority,' she said, before Madeline could restrain her.

Golias looked incredulous. 'Who are you?' He snapped. 'Military? Ecclesiarch? What in Throne's name is going on?'

Madeline tried to mediate, cupping her hands in supplication. It was no use. Celeminé had said too much. Golias was heading towards the door. Madeline gripped the inquisitor by the arm and pulled her away.

'Guards! Guards!' Golias began to shout.

Madeline and Celeminé turned and fled. They clattered through Golias's finely appointed home, shoving aside his many dismayed house guests. Hiam Golias chased after them. His guards were with him now, toting shotguns that they dared not fire into the clusters of house guests.

'Seize them!' Golias called from the upper-storey landing of his staircase as Madeline and Celeminé reached his entrance foyer. A noble in an avian mask and costume made a clumsy swipe to grab them as the two reached the door. Celeminé struck him on the side of the neck, digging her wrist into his carotid artery. The bird-faced man crumpled, and with that they dashed out the grand double doors of the Golias Estate.

The rain swept in horizontal sheets.

It was some time in the haze of afternoon, and pre-dusk always brought rain on Kholpesh. Like pressurised steam, the whirling pattern of storm clouds would build up throughout the day until finally the sky would burst into a torrential downpour.

The Seventh and 22nd advanced at a despondent trot, their horses drooping under the downpour. Out here, the poison gas remained active in the soil for several days given the constantly humid weather conditions, and the ground was a solvent yellow. Rebreathers were a necessity in order to move through the tainted soil. Men and horse alike had faces shod in the bug-eyed sheathing of Cantican MK02 gas filters.

Before them, the open mud flats that separated the warring trenches had become a morass of sink soil. The dragon's teeth of tank traps and coils of concertina wire rose out of the mustard-grey bog. In some places, half-submerged corpses lolled like hump-backed marine life.

Roth and Captain Pradal, along with a platoon of lancers, moved ahead of the main line of advance. They dismounted and crawled forwards on their stomachs, cutting breaches in the cordons of concertina wire, of which there were many. It was a slow and arduous process, probing the soil around the barbed coils for mined explosives before signing the all-clear for the battalion advance.

Roth slithered close to an Archenemy trench. It was so close, Roth could have spat into it had he wished to. A lone sentry stood on the firing steps, squinting into the grey curtain of rain. He was manning a drum-fed autocannon; both he and his weapon were draped underneath a pattering plastek sheet.

Once the way was clear, the forward advance party slithered back towards the main line of advance. Four hundred horsemen mounted on slab-muscled destriers were waiting patiently in the rain. Their horses pawed at the soil, snorting and shaking their heads. Of the men, some were praying while others stared in silence at the enemy lines they could not see. Their sabres were drawn and their lances were steadied. They had been briefed by their commanders to ride in a staggered line. Upon contact with the enemy trenches, the Seventh Light Horse would dismount and engage the Archenemy positions. The Lancers would continue on using their momentum, their speed and the shock of cavalry to seize upon the undefended rear-echelon armour. It was simple enough, and the Archenemy would not expect such aggressiveness from the thus far soundly defensive Imperial positions.

Roth's steed was a fine specimen of war horse, twenty-five hands tall with rolling, mountainous muscle. The horse shifted its bulk underneath Roth's legs, teetering him precariously. Roth had been a fine leisure rider but of combat riding he knew little. Besides, it had been many years since he had ridden.

Roth looked up into the sky. The clouds were a solid ashen grey and he could barely see the riders to either side of him. It was not, he reflected, the best way to reacquaint himself with the equestrian arts.

Major Arvust trotted over to Roth. 'We're all in place, signal the charge,' he whispered as he handed him a tin officer's whistle.

Roth shook his head. 'No. They're your men, you do it.'

They waited breathlessly for several more seconds, savouring the heavy staccato of rainfall. Then the major blasted the whistle.

With a tidal roar, the CantiCols rose from the mud flats and charged towards the enemy trenches. They charged into the heavy fog of grey mist, seeming for all the world to be charging at phantoms.

The Archenemy fired blindly at them. Rods of las-fire hissed from the murky mist to their front. A spear of light hit a lancer to Roth's left. Rider and horse bucked backwards, their forward momentum suddenly arrested. The last Roth saw of them as he galloped past was the silhouette of hooves flailing in the air.

They were close now. If Roth squinted against the lashing raindrops he could see the ominous silhouettes of Archenemy soldiers, prowling on the firing steps of their trenches. At fifty metres out, the enemy saw them and the fire became accurate. Thudding tracers began to bowl over the Cantican cavalry. But by then, the horsemen were already on them.

Abruptly, the foggy grey was lit up by flashes of searing orange. The Guardsmen announced their presence by lobbing grenades into the unwary trenches. A fluttering chain of detonations pounded Roth's ear drums into a tinnitus ring.

To the credit of the Lancers, they executed their battle plan to the letter. The first wave of cavalry, once having unleashed their explosives, dismounted and assaulted the trenches on foot. The second wave continued on mounted, clearing the trenches with jarring crunches of hooves on soil, galloping for the secondary defences.

Roth stood up on his stirrups, screaming as he ignited his power fist.

His horse sprinted the last few metres into the enemy lines, and Roth rolled off the saddle into an ungainly dismount. Grenade flashes hazed his vision, and the inquisitor half-charged, half-fell into the enemy trench.

It was utterly disorientating.

Dirt and debris swirled about him. Detonations sprayed the entrenchments with feathery streaks of gore and shrapnel. Archenemy soldiers reeling from the aftershock of explosives were struggling to fight back. Looking up, Roth spied a Cantican Guardsman teetering above him on the edge of the trench, his face collapsed by a las-shot. The man was dead but still sat upright in his saddle.

Roth struck out with his fist on instinct, rendered senseless by smoke, rain, blood and the sheer aural assault of close combat. They could not use firearms for fear of friendly fire, and the cramped confines did not allow for the use of fixed bayonets. They fought with whatever was at hand.

An Ironclad wielding a rectangular cleaver circled around to Roth's left, hacking at his thigh. The blade sparked off trauma-plate as they connected. Another enemy soldier swung a barbed trench pike into the back of Roth's head. Blunt, brutal pain spread in the back of his skull. Roth bit his tongue and blood began to drool from his chin.

Dazed, Roth leaned down and threw out his hand in a backfist. It was a wild, desperate technique but the enemy were too close, too pressed to avoid it. The back of his power fist clipped into his unseen assailant's jaw and catapulted the entire head clean out of the trench. Still snorting like a wounded bull, Roth hammered his palm down on the cleaver-wielding Ironclad. The Archenemy folded at a crisp ninety degree angle and hit the mud without further movement.

Roth looked around, blood cascading from a gash at the top of his head into his eyes. It was a deep cut, he could feel it by the way it was numb instead of painful. He only hoped his skull was intact. Blinking the oily crimson from his eyes, Roth tried to gather his senses.

Captain Pradal lurched into his field of vision, slashing the air with his trench club. His right hand hung at his side, blood soaking the sleeve up to the elbow. He was missing two fingers from that hand.

'What happened to your hand?' Roth yelled above the rattling clamour.

Pradal looked and his mangled fist and laughed, almost surprised. 'Didn't even notice,' he cackled.

Their rage was up now. That was dangerous, Roth knew. They could not become mired in a protracted engagement in the trenches. It would not be long before the Archenemy began to filter in through the trench networks and overwhelm them with numbers. They had to keep moving.

'Keep advancing, targets on our axis of advance,' Roth screamed. He pointed up the undulating slopes and the enemy armour that dotted them.

Major Arvust blasted his whistle. 'Fuses! Fuses!' he cried, ordering them to disengage with more grenades.

To their credit, the Cantican discipline held and they broke away from their staggered enemy. Leaving their horses panicking on the other side of the trenches, they surged up the hill on foot. The Guardsmen tossed delay-charged fuse bombs in their wake to deter pursuit. Having cleared the first line of trenches, the Cantican cavalry moved to join the second wave in the skirmish on Magdalah.

Roth pounced onto the front cowling of a KL5 Scavenger.

He climbed onto the tank, boots slipping against the smooth plating as he fought for purchase. His power fist gouged deep molten holes into the sloping frontal hull as he hauled himself up.

The turret hatch swung out and an Ironclad writhed out. Roth backhanded him back into the vehicle. A Cantican Guardsman climbed atop the turret and dropped a frag grenade into the opening. It clattered into the cab with a metallic echo. Roth slammed the hatch shut and both men leapt off as a muffled crump shook the tankette.

All around, the men of the Seventh and 22nd swarmed over the Archenemy war machines. The hull-down vehicles snarled back with thunderous 105mm shells and the chain rips of cyclical cannon fire. Many of the Canticans had dismounted, weaving amongst the vehicles and sowing explosives.

The fuse bombs and frag grenades cut through the downpour of rain as miniature claps of thunder – incessant, sparking up like water being poured onto electric circuits. The most devastating were the PK-12 drill-charges. A small clamp mine, the drill charges could be magnetised to the side of a vehicle. Upon ignition, the charge propelled a molten core of copper with an armour penetration of ten centimetres. Each Cantican carried at least three or four.

Roth circled around to the periphery of a Leman Russ. The behemoth was a ransacked Guard vehicle, its old camouflage blistered and scraped down to a burnished metal hide. The Leman Russ was hull-down in a wide earthen pit, the monstrous snout of its turret cannon trying to track its sprinting human targets. PK-12 in hand, Roth slapped the charge onto the gap between turret and chassis. He was moving again before the heavy guns could track him. Behind him, an expanding shockwave chased his heels and a sheet of flaming wreckage slashed overhead.

It was a brief, brutal clash. The Ironclad infantry were in disarray and many abandoned their positions as the cavalry penetrated their front-line trenches. The wave of flashing hooves and incendiary explosives were too much for them. These were not the same broken Guardsmen who held the Magdalah trenches by the skin of their teeth. The Ironclad were not prepared for it.

Roth saw a light horseman land behind the mantlet of a Basilisk. The Cantican laid into the Ironclad crew with lance and sabre, killing two before being dragged off his steed. To Roth's immediate right, a lancer Guardsman unleashed his rocket tube at an oncoming FPV. The hood of the Ironclad vehicle peeled back like blistering skin. It ran over the lancer and kept going, a fireball carried on by wheels of melting rubber.

A tankette went up in a star of exploding pieces. Spikes of las sizzled past Roth, so close he could feel the steam of rain drops as the rounds punched through them. A grenade went off close by.

'Regroup! Regroup!' Roth ordered, pulling hard on his reins. In their fury, the cavalry charge had dispersed, chasing individual targets and scattering the enemy. It was to be their undoing.

The momentum of the cavalry charge was faltering. Ironclad infantry were regrouping and fighting back. Fast-moving FPVs were converging on them, making their presence known with pintle-mounted heavy stubbers.

'Tighten the formation!' Roth screamed, his voice stolen by the wash of rain storm.

A cone of flame rippled across his front, consuming several horsemen and the wreck of a KL5. Like a ghost, the sinister form of a Hellhound flame tank emerged from the rain curtain. Its turret was licking with tendrils of fire.

Roth turned his horse and spurred it into a gallop. He had to find a vox-operator before the Archenemy, clashing their war drums and howling for blood, managed to encircle and overwhelm them all.

He found a vox-caster, but the operator was no longer alive. His horse was nowhere to be seen, and his body was laid out on the soil, stiff and jawless. The vox system was submerged in mud several metres away.

Vaulting off the horse, Roth sunk to his knees and scrabbled for the handset. A line of tracer stitched the mud in front of him, kicking up plumes of grit. Roth forced himself to steady his pulse and hands before dialling in on all vox frequencies.

'This is the Seventh and Twenty-second Magdalah Cavalry. Request immediate reinforcements in the Magdalah foothills, we are pinned by anchor fire. Over!'

'Magdalah Cav, this is command HQ. Reinforcements denied. Magdalah hills is red zone, what in the Emperor's name are you doing out there?'

Roth fired several plasma rounds from his pistol in the general direction of enemy muzzle flashes. He doubted he hit anything.

'HQ Command, we are reclaiming the foothills. Request immediate assistance to consolidate captured ground.'

The voice on the other end, despite being fuzzed with static, was clearly incredulous. 'Consolidate captured ground?'

'Are you stupid? We've shaken the Ironclad loose. I am–'

Roth was cut off as a solid slug punctured the vox-caster. The next shot slammed into Roth's chest just below his ribs, putting him straight onto his arse. The kinetic force was so great that he sunk slightly into the mud. Roth wheezed for constricted breath. Beneath the trauma plates, he could feel the small bones of his floating ribs popping and grinding.

A second shot hit him at the armoured strong-point below the sternum. A rounded segment of abdominal sheathing just above his breastbone collapsed inwards. At best, it would be a hairline fracture and severe bruising. But Roth feared the worst – deep internal haemorrhaging.

He tried to roll onto his knees but the hot brittle pain flickered his consciousness. Blacking out repeatedly, the next few moments became a stuttered series of events as Roth slipped in and out.

He saw Ironclad troopers march out of the enshrouding smoke – a long line, their silhouettes bladed and sharp.

He saw the corded pillars of equine limbs appear around him. The Canticans must be regrouping.

A shell ploughed into the cavalry. He didn't know how close. But it was close enough for him to see at least one horse and rider thrown five metres into the air, limbs skewed in impossible angles.

There was a lot of shooting. Many of his men were dying.

When he finally came to, rainwater had collected in the gaps of his armour. The cold seepage on his bare skin brought him some clarity. Looking around, he saw some of the Seventh and 22nd still fighting, the riders standing high on their stirrups as they fired their lasguns. But most were casualties. The bodies of horses, upended, their legs in the air like in a slaughterhouse, littered the battlefield. Guardsmen hunkered down behind the bulk of fallen steeds, firing sporadic shots as they tended to wounded comrades.

There was no real cover. The Ironclad went to ground, firing from prone positions. Visibility was almost non-existent.

'Can you hear me?' a voice lanced through the wall of gunfire, and a heavy hand gripped the back of Roth's shoulder rig.

Roth rolled his head back and saw Major Arvust. A gash had opened over the officer's eyebrow and diluted blood leaked down his face. Roth managed a weak nod.

Arvust began to drag him back towards the defensive position. Cantican Guardsmen, probably less than company-strength, were huddled down behind the broad flanks of dead horses. They faced outwards in a ring taking single well-aimed shots to conserve ammunition.

Of the remaining Imperial force, they had one heavy weapon at their disposal. It was a wheeled rotary gun – a heavy stubber with multiple repeating chambers towed by Cantican cavalry. It was not much but it was all they had.

Connecting a wedge of coiled ammunition into the cartridge cylinder, Major Arvust set down behind its butterfly trigger, peering over the brass gun-shield.

'How many spitters do we have for this thing?' Arvust called to his troopers.

'Six hundred jacketed lead and about four hundred boat-tails and tracers, sir,' a young corporal replied in between shots.

'Get rid of the tracers, I don't want to give away position. How many do we have then?'

The corporal immediately began to slot out the interspersed tracer rounds from a wedge of ammunition with the tip of his bayonet. 'No more than nine hundred rounds all up, sir.'

Major Arvust cranked the rotary handle. 'Well then, we better make these count.'

Rocking back on its spoked wheels, the heavy weapon began hammering out a steady *cham cham cham*. Spent cartridges, steaming in the downpour, ejected from the side port. Roth counted them as they spun, arcing through the air.

CHAPTER NINETEEN

The scarlet letter was the most basic of Inquisitorial methods. But throughout the centuries it was always one of the most effective. Gurion had used it to great effect throughout his career and it had never once failed him.

It was the most rudimentary method to reveal infiltration. False intelligence, or the bait, was deliberately slipped off to the enemy. In this case, Roth had specified Lord Marshal Khmer.

From then on, it was a mechanism of human manipulation. The enemy would pass the bait on to the infiltrator. The infiltrator would act on false intelligence, thereby revealing himself to possess knowledge that no one unaffiliated with the enemy should know. It was a simple trap and one of the core tenets of Inquisitorial method.

It was simple, but its complexity lay within the artistry of execution. A perfectly orchestrated scarlet letter was a trap of subtlety.

Gurion had delighted in the pantomime. He had even agonised many days over it. Something special and particularly intricate would be reserved for Khmer.

First, he had selected the corpse of a crewman from the morgue. The man had died of natural causes; as natural as could be when a hawser cable in the docking hangar had snapped loose, whipping eighty kilograms of tension cable into his chest.

Gurion had dressed the body in a grey storm coat and tactical vest, and even holstered a bolt pistol to the hip. Most crucially, he slipped an

Inquisitorial rosette around the corpse's neck and ordained him 'Inquisitor Gable'.

The bait, in this case, was documentation placed in the pocket of Inquisitor Gable. It simply stated that the Conclave suspected an infiltrator in Roth's Overwatch Task Group. Further, it stated that Delahunt's encrypted rosette contained the identity of the infiltrator and that Roth was working to decrypt the rosette. Of course, it was conveyed in code, but it was a basic code that Gurion had purposely made sure Naval Intelligence could analyse.

The irony was that Gurion had no concept of what was contained within Delahunt's log beside his contact with Celeminé. But Khmer was not to know that. The seed would already be planted.

The corpse of Inquisitor Gable was placed onto inbound cargo, left specifically for subordinate officers of High Command to discover. Gurion did not doubt that High Command would examine the corpse and secretly pilfer any intelligence before tasking the body to Gurion's care.

It happened exactly as Gurion predicted. The corpse was repatriated to the Conclave, minus the documentation on its person. It would be in the military bureaucracy's hands now. To have attempted to directly feed the false intelligence to Khmer would have been far too obtuse. Instead he let events take their natural course. Without a doubt, Lord Marshal Khmer would be briefed on the corpse if he did not directly search the body himself.

As the finishing touch to his scarlet letter, Gurion wrote a post-mortem report on Inquisitor Gable. He reported that the inquisitor had been killed on Kholpesh by subversive elements. At the following Council of Conclusions, Gurion debriefed the war council with great solemnity. Inquisitor Gable had died in the service of the Conclave, and the officers, including Khmer, had participated in a minute's silence.

The trap was laid. The rest, he knew, was up to Khmer.

A tank shell landed in the midst of the Imperial ground assault.

It was a splintered sabot projectile. The way it skimmed low across the terrain, screaming like an unleashed banshee, was unmistakeable.

The shell exploded on impact, its bursting charge expelling shrapnel in a streamlined forward direction. The effect on troops in the open was terrible, shredding uniform from flesh and flaying flesh from bones.

Most likely, Roth thought, it was fired from a Leman Russ. He had to move before the Archenemy gunners could realign and reload.

Roth rolled out from behind the cover of a fallen horse and began to crawl through the mud towards where the Seventh and 22nd were reforming. His ribs throbbed with a deep bone pain and his dented sternum plate dug into him, but he kept moving. The lancers and light horse were a disciplined lot, and they kept movement constant, firing and reforming before the Archenemy could draw an accurate bead. Disciplined fire and movement was the only thing that kept them alive.

That and the rain. Precipitation continued to shaft down in whickering grey pillars, hard enough that Roth could barely see twenty metres in any direction. If it abated, they were as good as done.

Major Arvust dived into the mud slick next to Roth. His kepi hat was gone and mud was on his cheeks. 'Inquisitor! We have to withdraw! I can't afford any more casualties,' he shouted.

To reiterate his point a high-powered las-round, more than likely from a lascannon, scorched the ground ten paces away. The sudden pillar of energy left a vacuum in its wake that refilled with a thunderclap.

Roth was torn. To withdraw now would relinquish all the gains they had made in the foothills. Although they left a trail of burning vehicles in their path, the enemy would reclaim the high ground and they would be strategically in the same situation as before. It would turn their tactical victory into nothing more than a fleeting act of defiance.

'Withdraw then, while we still can,' Roth said. He would have liked to believe that his injuries played no part in his decision, but he was not so sure.

'Listen for my signal. We'll veer to our east and circumvent the Ironclad's frontline trenches in the event they've regrouped to cut us off.'

'Clear enough!' Roth cried, rainwater and blood trickling into his mouth.

Major Arvust rose into a crouch and took two steps. A solid round punched through the back of his head. The exit wound sprayed Roth with a sudden, shocking burst of steaming blood.

Arvust froze. He looked at Roth, his eyes wide. The major's mouth was moving, trying to work words but nothing came out. His brain was no longer connected to his spine. In a slow, syrupy motion, the major toppled backwards at an angle.

Then the Ironclad exploded out from the mist curtain.

They came, shrieking down on them, materialising out of the threshing rain like smoking ghosts. Water vapour curled off their scrappy, plated silhouettes. Their combat instruments were brandished. Maces, flails, warhammers and cleavers glistened with the sheen of wet metal.

For the first time, Roth found himself face to face with the raiders of Khorsabad Maw. He saw their masked, featureless faces and their crudely barbarous attire. He felt outraged that such savages could threaten the fabric of civilisation. Roth realised he hated them. It was not fear or adrenaline, but a bland baseline hatred. He hated them for the inconvenience it caused him. It was absurd that he was squaring up with the Archenemy, but was driven by a cavalier disregard for his own life. He didn't care, he was just angry.

The Ironclad splashed through the mud. The first Canticans they met were still crouched, firing lasguns over the ribcages of fallen steeds. Their forceful, brutal instruments of war clove into yielding flesh and brittle bone. The impact of the Ironclad charge threw up vertical sheets of blood. Guardsmen toppled as heavy pieces of metal broke them apart.

Roth rose to his feet, his rage overriding his pain. 'Up! Form up and at them!' he bellowed. 'Fix bayonets and at them!'

There was no real direction in attack any more. Roth could not distinguish forwards, nor rear or flank. The battle was a clashing mess. An Ironclad with bulky shoulder pads forged from tank-treads slid in front of Roth. Roth pressed his plasma pistol against the Ironclad's hulking shoulder rig and blew it off. At point-blank range, the Ironclad fell aside, his upper torso incinerated. The superheated gases blistered Roth's face with steaming backwash, but he was glanding on far too much adrenaline to notice.

Roth fired more shots. The fusion-boosted trails of energy ruptured three more Ironclad. Solid matter was rendered into gas, forming dense fountains of bloody steam. Roth drained his entire cell and reloaded.

Captain Pradal floated in Roth's peripheral vision, his lasgun chopping away on semi-auto. Roth had thought he was dead too. The sight of him urged Roth to fight on.

'Getting us all killed wasn't part of the original plan, captain, I apologise,' Roth yelled as he fired at targets no more than striking distance away.

'We did what we came to do and we're doing it well!' Pradal shouted back. He nailed an Ironclad through the vision slit in his textbook shooting stance.

'Nonetheless, I sometimes think I put myself in unnecessary danger,' Roth yelled as he side-stepped a flanged mace.

'You really think so?' replied Captain Pradal. Roth couldn't tell whether the captain was being sarcastic. A mace slashing across his field of vision warranted most of his attention.

One of the Guardsmen close by fell to his knees, his forehead stoved in by a ball-socketed hammer. Roth lunged with his power fist, splitting weapons and pounding aside the Ironclad who pressed in around him.

He was so lost in the frenzy of punching, bobbing, weaving and tearing that he didn't see the sledgemaul that slammed into his lower back. Electric agony shot up his spine and his legs buckled. The pain was so real he could taste it in his mouth, harsh, bitter and sulphuric. He was hit again but this time he didn't feel it. He only found himself laid out on his back, staring at the sky.

The world around him seemed to shut off. Scenes of fighting became stilted and fragmented. He remembered thinking that pain was a good thing. Pain meant his body was still working the way it was meant to. No pain at all was never good.

He saw the sledgemaul swing up like pendulum. Roth watched its trajectory. He waited for it to come down on his head. He wondered if he would feel anything.

But he never did.

The sledgemaul never came down. A round poleaxed its wielder away, in a direction that Roth couldn't see.

Other shots followed the first. Clean, precise shots. Glowing white, las-rounds like rays from the Emperor's halo. Several Ironclad close by were hit. They went down soundlessly.

Dimly, as if very, very far away, Roth could hear the sound of tin whistles. At first he thought it was the sound of pressurised blood escaping his ears but it was not the case. The sound of CantiCol command whistles was distinct. It was the most beautiful sound Roth had ever heard.

Captain Pradal's face fell across his vision of the sky. 'Keep breathing, Roth, keep breathing. Can you move?'

Roth shook his head, not knowing if he could. Then he realised his foolishness and raised a leg. He could.

'Are they here?' Roth said as Captain Pradal shouldered his arm and guided him back to his feet. The captain fired several more shots from his lasgun, one-handed.

'They're here. They're here in force,' Pradal replied.

The rain was abating now. Across the mudflats, advancing across their flank, churning on segmented treads, came a full squadron of Leman Russes. The smooth-plated hulls were painted in the brown, grey and gold of the Cantican regiments. Their pintle mounts were spitting tracers with overlapping regularity.

Advancing between the rare Cantican tanks came six, eight, perhaps ten companies of Cantican infantry. Arrayed in close-order march ranks, they fired as they advanced, a withering lattice of enfilade fire that scythed down the enemy's exposed flank. Drummers rolled out a strident percussion, officers conveyed orders on their tin whistles and regimental banners fluttered.

'They answered the call then,' Roth muttered.

Pradal didn't answer. He fired several parting shots one-handed as the Ironclad broke away. The impetus of their counter-attack was gone, chased down by las and solid shot. The torrent of fire stitched up the Magdalah hills, following the Archenemy over the crest. Firepower like thousands of glowing darts following the fleeing enemy, tagging and dropping them face-down into the terrain.

Someone shouted 'Magdalah is ours!'

The survivors of the Seventh and 22nd did not cheer. They simply collapsed into the mud, exhausted, their faces mute. Many closed their eyes and just went to sleep. They knew, for now, they were safe.

* * *

The Magdalah foothills had been the first real Imperial victory for many months.

Elements of the CantiCol field artillery and other infantry battalions reinforced the Seventh and 22nd on the Magdalah. Wading through the after-smoke of defeat, the Ironclad retreated, losing a two kilometre stretch of defences. The Imperial standard was raised on the hills.

News spilled onto the streets of Mantilla, and for a while even the refugees danced and laughed. A hasty artist's rendition of the Imperial standard being raised on Magdalah, borne aloft by a noble-chinned officer, was plastered all over the city walls. Although no such officer existed, the image became the prevailing face of Imperial resistance for many weeks after.

CHAPTER TWENTY

Silverstein watched the Ironclad from concealment.

He was coated in red earth, a sandy film of dust that grazed even the lenses of his bioptics. He stayed low, splayed out against the rim of a dry riverbed. His breathing had been regulated, slow and shallow. A layered cloak, mantle and shawl of matted taproot, tangle stem and other stringy desert foliage splayed from his figure. Like him, the guerrillas were also shambling with camouflage. Had it not been for Silverstein's expertise, the Ironclad patrols, which had hounded them for the past five days, might have already found them. Bone dust and salt had been rubbed into the camouflage to conceal his smell. It had thrown the Archenemy attack dogs off their scent during their initial escape, and Silverstein had insisted on maintaining the ritual. The guerrillas did not argue. Under the cover of night, they were just another wrinkle in the ridges and ribs of the rock basin.

Less than twenty metres away from them, three fuel tankers, caterpillar-tracked beasts with snaking carriage bays, were draped in camouflage netting. In the dark, the eighteen-metre long vehicles formed swollen silhouettes, but Silverstein knew from experience that aerial reconnaissance would only discern three long banks of shrubbery.

Apartan, the ex-sergeant, rustled over to Silverstein, the shrubbery of camo-shawl nodding gently. 'That's the eleventh fuel cache we've come across in the past three days,' he hissed urgently into Silverstein's ear.

'This one is a source depot,' Silverstein said to the guerrillas spread out around him. 'See the extraction tower?'

Asingh-nu shook his head. The rural Cantican had never seen an extraction tower before. The skeletal structure of steel girders before him looked awkward and vague. 'What is it used for?'

'Plumbing fossil fuel from the shale deposits. The Archenemy are collecting resources for a massive campaign, discreetly I might add. Spreading out their caches and amassing their forces in the wilderness, far away from Imperial auspices.'

'Why? Why don't they just attack and claim it like they have with Orphrates, Tarsis, Ninnevah...' Apartan paused and swallowed. 'And Cantica.'

Silverstein had no answer.

The Ironclad had been operating this way for some time. They were amassing resources, rearing their supplies for invasion, all the while carefully concealing their movements from Imperial reconnaissance. Silverstein's optics had picked up the distinct outline of Naval scout Lightning soaring high overhead, no doubt on aerial surveillance. The Archenemy were going to great lengths in order to hide themselves. It was a most methodically clandestine preparation, distinctly removed from the Ironclad's mass aerial deployments. It was too unusual to ignore.

'Get low!' Apartan hissed.

They all went low, pressing their faces into the rock. The stone was still warm from the residual heat of the previous day. Silverstein counted backwards from ten, slowly, clutching his looted laspistol. He looked at his hands and saw that white spots of discoloration dotted the back of his hand. Then he realised it was the other way around. The tiny white specks were the colour of his natural skin, otherwise caked in a scabby bark of dirt, grease and too much dried blood. His hands were mauve and so too was his face. It had been weeks, if not months since water had cleansed his skin. Five days since their escape, and for how long before that?

'Enemy, down below,' Temughan whispered to them as he peered over the ridge with a rifle scope.

Silverstein looked and affirmed that fact with his bioptics. Ironclad sentries were posted around the petro-extraction tower. More Archenemy soldiers were stripped to the waist, hauling barrels and connecting clamp hoses to the waiting caterpillar carriers. It was a bizarre contrast between scarred, pallid torsos and the faceless iron masks. Until now, Silverstein had often doubted whether they were truly human beneath the jagged sheets of metal.

+++*Distance: horizontal 17 metres – vertical depression 6 metres.*
Heat/Movement Signatures: 8 Human/Sub-Human (85% Variation)
Temp: 31 degrees Visibility: Low.+++

'Eight hostiles in view,' Silverstein said, relaying the information to his companions as he processed the data. 'This is how we're going to play, I want the ex-Guardsman and the farm boy with me,' Silverstein said, indicating to Apartan and Asingh-nu. 'Temughan, hold this ridge and cover us, pick them off if anything goes... awry.'

Temughan, the clocksmith with his steady hands, nodded in acknowledgment. He racked the lasgun, the only real weapon they had managed to salvage since their escape five days ago. The others slithered over the ridge line on their hands and knees, clutching looted weapons and braces of munitions and improvised explosives.

They moved with agonising slowness, sometimes not appearing to move at all, creeping forwards with small, controlled shifts of muscle fibre. They moved in a wide circle around the encampment, sweeping out to come in the flank. The silhouettes of Ironclad flickered ever-present in their periphery. Silverstein tried not to look at them. It was an old hunter's myth that looking at your quarry would give them the kindling, warn them they were being encroached on. It was like children who believed if they covered their eyes they could not be seen. There was some truth in that. A good huntsman was guided by other senses.

It took them twelve minutes to sweep around to the side, and a further ten minutes to close the distance towards the extraction tower.

'Stop!' Apartan hissed urgently at Silverstein.

The huntsman was already still. With his left foot, Silverstein quivered the camouflaged reeds around his ankle softly, to match the nodding movements of the dry rush grass that he had crawled over.

An Ironclad staggered into the darkness towards them. It was dark and Silverstein could see only the silhouette of broad, boxy shoulder guards. The huntsman chose not to analyse the trooper in any greater detail. He did, however, notice that the Ironclad had the unmistakeable outline of a heavy stubber yoked across his shoulders.

The three of them lay very still. The Ironclad came closer. A metalshod boot complete with bolted ankle plates stamped onto the ground a mere five metres or so from Silverstein's face. The Archenemy trooper began to prod the strip of dry rush grass with his foot, as if searching for something.

Slowly, Silverstein's hand slid towards the trigger of his EN-Scar autogun. The Ironclad stepped closer, prodding the grass with one boot. Silverstein placed a hair of pressure over the gun's trigger.

With a grunt of satisfaction, the Ironclad found what he was looking for. The trooper fumbled with his chainmail tabard, muttering under his breath. Silverstein heard the drizzle of hot liquid hissing against dry grass and breathed a sigh of relief. The trooper had been searching for the latrines.

They waited until the trooper was finished, then for several minutes after that. Finally, Silverstein flashed the hand sign for them to continue.

Bellying forwards on their elbows, they crept on to the Archenemy fuel depot. Here, the enemy's need for concealment meant the camp was unlit except for the light of the moon. The darkness was to Silverstein's advantage.

The huntsman made one more scan of his area with his bioptics. He counted eight Ironclad, no more. Rising onto one knee, he signalled for the others to take aim at targets to his far left. Looking down his own iron-sights, Silverstein sighted the six others. He searched for a fluid pattern of fire that would carry him seamlessly from one target to the next. He considered firing at the sentry by the base of the extractor, but realised that by the angle of his position, it would leave the furthest target, lounging by the cab of a fuel carrier, open to escape. He could begin firing from the middle outwards, at the two Ironclad smoking tabac at the centre of the camp, but the variance of visibility might alert the enemy to the angle of his muzzle a fraction of a second too early.

After much deliberation, Silverstein settled on a linear pattern of fire, from right to left, darting from one target to the next. If the wind did not affect his aim, which it probably would not, he could put down all six of them in under three seconds.

There was a crackle of shots. Frantic and urgent. The guerrillas reared up, firing on full auto.

'Hit the trucks!' Silverstein shouted.

There was another stutter of barking muzzles followed by a tremendous explosion. For a brief second, night became harsh white day. A roaring mushroom of angry red gas erupted from the ruptured tankers.

Under the belching smoke and confusion, Silverstein rushed towards the drilling rig and hurled a single fragmentation grenade down the drill pump. The huntsman then ran and did not turn back. The resultant explosion would likely have scorched the hair from his face.

Silverstein and the guerrillas exited the area swiftly, their quad-bikes long gone before Ironclad units could be alerted. As they fled, the horizon fluttered a satisfactory yellow against the deepwater sky. It was the ninth oil well that they had set fire to in just five days.

Roth was retired to the officers' infirmary, kept quite separate from the hospice tents of the enlisted men. In the aftermath of Magdalah, combat medics tied him to a horse and led him back into Mantilla for treatment. Had he not been numbed by metadine and hyproxl, the shuddering trot of horseback would have been agony to his battered body. The inquisitor was billeted in Bocob House, once an orphanage within Mantilla and far away from the fighting outside its walls, and there he was allowed to rest.

Bocob House was a large, double-winged Imperial building, as austere as Kholpeshi design would allow. Despite this, the structure was still a domed collaboration of glazed tile, mosaic and coloured glass inlay. The clay earth court which surrounded the orphanage was scattered with wooden structures of children's play. There were slides, teeter-saws and climbing rings, structures that resembled the skeletal carcasses of animals picked clean by scavengers and bleached by sun. Of the children, there was no sign. No one seemed to know where they had gone.

No one thought to ask.

Wounded officers were cycled through here quickly. They didn't have enough beds, and the frontline combat exacted a heavy toll on the officer cadre. Officers with anything short of a grade-two injury were sent back to the front after a maximum of three days at Bocob House. Those who died were taken to the cellars that had once been used for food stores. The pallets they had vacated were hosed down with water and new occupants assigned to them. Blood and waste collected in the sheets and soggy mattresses. It was the reason why Bocob House now smelt of decay.

Roth was a grade-four injury.

The pain was probably at least a grade three. He had sustained blunt force trauma to his sternum and chest, enough to cause minor internal bleeding. The medics had also braced his spine with iron rods to limit movement in his back. The sledgemaul had slipped a disc and almost herniated a fluid sac in his seventh vertebrae. His collection of injuries most likely warranted more than a grade four, but the medics had deemed his injuries 'non-life threatening/absence of bodily severage'.

Rather, Roth had languished for the past twenty-four hours in a semi-comatose fever. He had developed an infection that was more likely the result of poor infirmary hygiene. The medics hooked him up to a fluid drip with a halo of tubes. Amongst the inflow of war casualties, no one noticed he was an inquisitor. In Bocob House he was simply a grade-four patient and they let him ride it out.

'This is just an opinion. But I think you want to get yourself killed.' A voice roused Roth from his heavy slumber.

Roth woke with the heated flushness of a man on the tail-end of sickness. Groggily, Celeminé swam into his vision. She was still clad in her petal dress. Heavy eye shadow of iridescent green gave her eyes a feline slant. She was also wearing long fluttering faux eyelashes and had removed her lip ring. Roth barely recognised her.

'What in Throne's name are you wearing?' Roth murmured weakly.

Celeminé crossed her arms and pretended to be angry. 'This was for the Golias meet. But you wouldn't know because you were too busy trying to make a name for yourself amongst the Guard,' Celeminé chided.

'I think she looks quite pretty,' Madeline said, drifting to his bedside. Likewise, she too was clad in her festive garb. Her chestnut hair was worn long and straight with a blunt, severely fashionably fringe. Her lips were ruby-red.

'You both look like street walk–'

Roth was cut off in mid-sentence by a hard cuff to his shoulder.

'That's no way to talk to a lady,' Madeline admonished.

'Maybe you both should go back to the Golias Estate. He seems to know what a lady should be,' Roth said, still juddering with a delighted burble.

'I don't think we are welcome there any more,' said Celeminé.

Roth stifled his humour. 'How did the meeting play out?'

'Bad,' Madeline said. She shot a look at Celeminé, but said nothing.

'How bad?'

'He tried to have us killed,' Celeminé replied.

Roth shot up. His spine brace was awkward and cut into him but Roth didn't care. 'He did what?'

'Tried to kill us both when the transaction went sour. He's playing the deal cautious. I didn't think he was going to let us even examine the merchandise.'

'But you know the relic is genuine?'

'I don't see why he'd try to kill us over it, if it wasn't,' Madeline concluded.

Roth began to tear out the tubes from his wrist, unplugging them from his flesh with a frantic fury and then unbuckling his spine brace. The exiting needles left puckered welts of purple.

'Roth, what are you doing?' Celeminé cried out in protest. They tried to push him back down onto the pallet.

But Roth's temper was up. He brushed their fussing hands away and tore off the last of his bandages. 'Find me Captain Pradal. I want him to hand-pick a platoon of Cantica's best. We're going to pay that bastard Golias a visit. Tonight.'

The Lancers were one of the founding units of the Cantican Colonials. They were an elite formation that had been a Regiment of Origin, amalgamated from the fractious colonies of Medina. Even during the Reclamation Wars the Lancers had fought with sword and halberd as the loyalist Frontier Auxilia. That had been six thousand five hundred years ago.

As a poorly equipped force, Cantican Guardsmen were defined by the quality of their men not the superiority of their equipment, and the Lancers were the apogee of this philosophy. Much like the Kasrkin of Cadia or the Commandos of Kurass, selection into the Lancers was limited and highly selective.

A minimum height of one hundred and eighty-five centimetres was enforced and physical demands were high. The regiment largely selected its own. Candidates could be drawn from any unit within the Cantican Colonial regiments and thus selection was egalitarian in a rough, uncompromising way. They were a hard bunch and the company, not the officers, decided who was permitted to wear the Lancer pin.

Recruits, referred to as 'Ponies', were hazed mercilessly regardless of background. They were constantly beaten by up to five fully fledged Lancers at once in a ritual called 'Callusing'. Ponies were mentally and physically broken. It was a process much like the sharpening of a stick. Stripped down to nothing but a jagged mess, the real mettle of a man could be seen and judged by his peers. Those who did not break were welcomed into the fold. For those who did, the Lancers joked, they could always join the Mounted Infantry.

Roth could not have asked for a better selection of soldiers for his raid on the Golias Estate. Captain Pradal had taken him to the Lancer billet, a commandeered building known as the House of Jealous Lovers. It was a courtesan's hall on the fringe districts of Mantilla, illicit and since the war, closed. The House's front façade cascaded with silk drapes of a red and the interior was much the same. Expensive off-world textiles in shades of red, black and tan rippled down the walls, fanned by the open-framed windows.

He found the Lancer reserves cleaning weapons and making kit checks beneath the voluminous gauze curtains. It was a strange visual composition – lean, hard-faced Guardsmen, clacking and snapping rifles with focus, while silk drapes billowed around them. Most of them sat on large oval beds, their gun parts and kit laid out on the linen in greasy black lines.

'This is Captain Almeida, he will be the commanding officer of Two Platoon. Call sign Jackal,' Pradal introduced proudly. Although they were of equal rank, it was evident that the younger Pradal was in awe of the Lancer officer.

The captain shook Roth's hand. The skin of his palm was hard and horned and Roth noticed the skin of his knuckles was coloured dusty white. It was the sign of a bare-knuckle fighter.

'Inquisitor. Your command of the Magdalah offensive was magnificently daring, I applaud you and so does my camp. But I hope your reputation does not give you the wrong ideas. We're Lancers, and these are my Lancers. You work with us, understood?'

So Almeida was the archetypical special duties officer, Roth thought. He warmed to his gruff candour immediately. It was not every day a field officer spoke so openly with a member of the Inquisition.

'Perfectly understood, captain. We storm the Golias Estate and we're done. In and out,' Roth said.

Almeida didn't look at him. His face was creased with focus as he strapped the trademark bandoleer of fuse-bombs and frag grenades across his chest. The explosives clustered in their leather harnesses like swollen metal fruit.

'Captain Pradal has already briefed me on the operation. There will be civvies on the estate so my boys and I will be using low-calibre submachine rifles. I don't want any stray las going through walls and killing mothers, elders and loud children. Any questions?' Almeida asked.

He brandished a T20 Stem autogun, gummed with grease and probably more than several centuries old. The weapon was of stamped and pressed metal, its profile spidery, resembling nothing more than a pipe with a metal T-bar for a stock. Its magazine was distinctly side-fed and horizontal. Without a doubt, it was the most awkward and unimpressive gun Roth had ever seen.

'A Stem T20, captain? Is that weapon going to suffice?'

Almeida clicked a magazine into its side-feed and released the cocking handle with a metallic snap. 'What difference does it make whether the round is .75 cal from a bolter, or a 10mm slug from an autogun? If I drill you between the eyes, it's all the same.'

The captain made a valid point. The Cantican Colonials were certainly not a highly equipped regiment, but if forty angry Lancers could not storm the estate, then they might as well not try, thought Roth.

Tactical entry of the Golias Estate was a delicate matter. The quaint charm of the terrace lent it a certain measure of tactical advantage. Being perched high above street level denied the platoon any option for multipoint entry. The winding stone steps created a natural bottleneck so a frontal assault was out of the question. According to Madeline and Celeminé, the terrace's multiple bay windows housed an overlapping array of alarm systems.

To make matters more precarious, the triple suns cast their light indiscriminately, chasing away shadows and betraying their presence. Stealth would not be an option.

Rather, Almeida ordered a shock raid on the estate. Roth did not object. Jackal One, a team consisting of twelve Lancers, would storm the main entrance, breaching the brass entry door with explosives. Jackal Two, a twelve-man fire-team led by Celeminé and seconded by Pradal, would enter through the roof-top garden by way of Vulture flier.

That left Jackal Three, led by Almeida and Roth who would enter the terrace through the courtyard at the rear. It was straightforward and uncompromising in execution, just the way Roth preferred.

The wind was coarse and heavy, carrying grains of sand on its warm current.

The outside wall of the courtyard was of smooth terracotta. Roth hugged it, harnessed to a climbing cable that bumped him rhythmically against the walls with every gust of wind. They were high up, on the highest residential tier of Mantilla, a cluster of fabulously wealthy estates reserved for those who had the funds to invest.

Roth checked his wrist chron. According to the winking digitised display it would be starting soon.

On cue, his vox headset spluttered with static. 'All call signs, this is Jackal One, entry team in place. Stand by for countdown. Over.'

Almeida squeezed the bead of his wraparound vox between thumb and forefinger. 'One, this is Jackal Three. Rear entry team in place. Over.'

Digitised, Celeminé's voice echoed his call over the vox system. 'One, this is Two. Jackal Two ready for descent. Over.'

Roth looked up to check. Indeed, the speck of a Vulture gunship was sweeping in, the thumping howl of its turbine thrusters still quiet enough to go un-noticed.

'Fuses ready!' Almeida commanded, his voice amplified by the gusting wind.

Like the Guardsmen in his fire-team, Roth selected a frag grenade from his borrowed bandoleer. He tested the grenade in his hand, rolling the weight on his palm. As one, the fire-team twisted the pins out and squeezed the grenades hard, holding the catch release in place. They waited.

There was no mistaking the signal when it came. A deep earthly tremor of multiple explosions, travelling from the front of the terrace. Even muffled by walls, Roth felt the energy pass through the back of his spine like a wallop of solid wind. Jackal One had breached the entrance.

'Breaching now!' Almeida bellowed as Jackal Three tossed a volley of grenades over the wall. There was a shuddering blast that sent up puffs of dusty debris along the edge of the wall.

Roth was the first to scramble over the courtyard. His T20 Stem was already cradled in his hands, aimed across the tiled garden at the terrace house. The aching joints and injuries of the previous days were forgotten as adrenaline pumped hard through his system. Lancers dropped down around him, crouched with their weapons ready. They met no resistance.

There was no one in sight.

They had come over the wall expecting a fight. Household guards at the very least, but nothing. The fire-team seemed stunned, as if momentarily at a loss with what to do with the weapons they held if not to kill.

'It's clear. Where the hell is everyone?' Roth hissed to Almeida.

The captain shook his head, clicking his vox headset. 'Jackal One, this is Three. Report status, over.'

Silence over the channel.

Some of the Lancers looked at each other uneasily. They realised there were no sounds of gun-fighting in the house. Just an eerie calm and the tittering of clockwork insects in the garden.

'Jackal One, this is Three. Report status, over,' Almeida repeated.

Then, with a shriek of static, Jackal One flooded all channels with their report. It was so loud that several of the Lancers close to Roth winced and tore at their headsets.

'Emperor! Oh damn, oh damn, oh damn–'

There was a rush of static.

'I'm bleeding everywhere! I'm spilling out–'

The vox abruptly cut out. It had been the voice of Sergeant Chanchyn, leader of Jackal One. The frantic terror in his voice burned itself into Roth's memory. Several Lancers tore off their headsets, swearing blackly.

Then Jackal Three was hit.

Trigger mines buried in the subtropical plants went off with a searing flash of white. Roth never heard the explosion, just an overwhelming ring in his ears. Anti-personnel shrapnel shredded the garden, whipping up a blizzard of scrapped vegetation and human meat.

It took some time for his senses to return. For a while, he saw only white and heard only the ringing in his ears. When his senses flooded back like a vacuum he took in the scene before him. Almost half of the fire-team lay on the ground, their limbs twisted and split, their blood pouring out in gulping spillages. The explosives had evidently been hidden beneath the roots of a knot-bole cycad and those closest to the tree had been the worst hit. Bodies lay around the splintered stump.

'Are you good?' Almeida shouted directly into Roth's ear. The captain was bleeding from a split in his right cheek, a deep cut that revealed the whiteness of bone beneath.

Roth checked himself over, patting his limbs. His fighting-plate had absorbed the damage. Pock-marked dents showered up his left calf and torso, small and multitudinous like a galaxy of stars. The anti-personnel mines would have pulped his flesh otherwise.

'I'm good, I'm good,' Roth said.

'Fraggers pre-empted us. Who the hell told them we were coming?' spat Almeida.

We were betrayed, Roth wanted to say. But now was not the time. Instead he looked around and made a quick assessment of the situation. Of Jackal Three, four of the Lancers were evidently dead and two of the wounded would be in no shape to fight. One wounded Lancer was cupping his upper arm, the entire bicep muscle having been stripped away. Another was screaming horribly, his face scoured away by gravel and woodchips into one large graze.

That left seven of them including Roth and Almeida. It might not have been enough, but there was no turning back. Almeida was already up and running, signalling for the others to follow.

Roth crossed the courtyard, kicking over a bird-fountain out of spite on the way. Almeida reached the back door, a lattice screen of fragrant wood. He kicked it in with a boot and hurled a grenade into the dark interior.

Roth sprinted after Almeida. Adrenaline pulsated through his temples. He fired his T20 Stem. The weapon shuddered as he released a burst of semi-automatic fire. It lacked the wrist-jarring recoil of his plasma pistol, but the streak of orange tracer was strangely satisfying. Roth stopped at the threshold of the house, firing a three second burst into the smoke-filled room before hurtling in after the captain.

Golias's private guns waited for him on the other side. They all looked to be ex-gang muscle. The elites of Mantilla had a patronising fondness for hiring slummers as their private guards and escort. There seemed to be an impressive fascination with the chem-nourished biceps and tattoos of a ganger. It made the bourgeois feel like they were flirting with danger. It injected some edge into their otherwise pampered lifestyles. These men were no different. They were all pug-faced and shaven-headed. Tattoos crawled up their necks.

Hiding behind divans, settees and overturned bookcases, the Golias militia handled their street weapons with amateur bravado. They fired wildly, not so much concerned about aim as with laying down an inordinate spray of firepower.

It was in this close-range firefight that Roth truly noticed the difference between well-trained Guardsmen and street gunners. The Lancers went to ground, calm, some even hand-signalling for targets. Their return fire was precise. A house guard was struck in the sternum, spinning him around. The next shot caught him in the back and sprawled him out. Another guard clutched at his throat, frothing at the mouth. The Lancers played well-aimed squeezes of the T20s, rounds hitting the centre of mass.

Within a handful of seconds, the Lancers had cleared the room. Five Golias militia sprawled on the fine carpet under the clearing haze of smoke.

'Clear!' Almeida yelled.

'Clear!' His men echoed.

Then they were up and moving again.

A function hall took up most of the first-storey building plan. Private guards of the Golias household were waiting in ambush there.

Roth felt their minds, crouched behind pieces of ornate neo-colonist furniture. He smelt their anticipatory fear like sour musk in the air. He could sense their lethal intent.

Halting the fire-team before the function hall's sliding lattice doors, Roth warned them of the enemy in wait. Almeida did not question it. He punched a wide, ragged dent into the latticework and the fire-team lobbed a series of grenades underhand into the room.

There was the detonation. They waited for an exact two-count before storming into the function room, the muzzles of their T20s flashing spears of flame into the coiling smoke.

Roth chased the fire-team into the room, weapon raised. The grenade fog was lifting, and the Golias guards were fighting back. The heavy period furnishings of ivory, ebon and solid, well-made wood had protected them from the worst of the fragmentation. They answered back with shotguns and loud solid sluggers.

The sheer volume of projectile and trace fyceline in the room was a tangible smog. They were firing at men less than ten paces away. Roth staggered behind an upturned armoire, seeking cover behind the dense ebon-wood furnishing.

No more than arm's reach away, a Golias gunman rose up from behind the other side of the armoire. He fired a loose shot and missed, his aim thrown as he hastened to duck. The shotgun perforated a bookshelf behind Roth.

'Frag it,' Roth swore. He dropped his T20 and tugged his Sunfury from its holster. Exhaustion was robbing Roth of his momentum, and he could feel the pain from his previous injuries ebb like a creeping tide. He needed to end it quickly. Roth's first plasma shot melted a perfect hemisphere over the lip of the cabinet. The next shot bisected the offending gunman on the other side.

'Jackal Three, this is Jackal Two,' Celeminé's voice crackled over the frequency.

'Two, this is Three, come in, over,' Almeida reported. His command was punctuated by a raking volley from his T20.

'Our entry point is denied. Repeat, entry point for Jackal Two denied. Our craft scanners have picked up heavy weapons and explosive traps on the rooftop. This is going to be harder than we thought,' she yelled.

'Two, this is Three. Abort entry,' Almeida said. He fired another burping burst from behind a divan. Turning to Roth he shouted, 'It's done. We're playing on our own now.'

Roth tucked his head as shotguns barked over him. They were alone, that much was true. But these were the Cantican Lancers, and their enemy were nothing more than hired muscle. Roth wasn't the least bit fazed.

'Fire pattern Ordnance,' Almeida instructed over the squad-link.

It was the one training drill that the Lancers had run through with Roth before the operation. They had only shown him the rudiments in passing but it was a simple enough drill. Everyone in the fire-team had been assigned an odd or even number.

On Almeida's command, the evens rose and lay down a screen of covering fire forcing the enemy down. Roth was one of them. He rolled to his knees and hammered a series of plasma shots down the length of the chamber. The shots atomised fabric and calcified wood on contact, laying out fist-sized holes of destruction at the far end of the function room.

The odds primed grenades, and as the evens ceased fire, they uncoiled into a semi-crouch, hurling the grenades across the chamber with a leaning wind-up. The explosives bounced off the walls, landing behind the makeshift barricade of the enemy.

Sheets of sparking explosions engulfed the furthest end of the room.

The walls shook and loose plaster drizzled from the ceiling. A bookcase collapsed.

The heated exchange of fire died away. The enemy were screaming, moaning. They were street scrappers, young ganger braves with enough scars to impress the closeted aristocracy into employment. Some knew the business end of a knife or pistol, but they were no match for trained soldiers.

The survivors emerged from behind their barricade, hands raised in surrender. Almeida rose too, picking them off with one clean shot each. There was not enough time and too much at stake to process prisoners.

Roth rested for a moment, breathing hard against the battered, splintered and scorched remnants of the heavy armoire. He looked at the dispatched gunmen, their bodies draped across the barricade. Despite himself, Roth pitied the corpses. They had simply been desperate men, men who found themselves in a business way over their heads.

'All call signs, this is Jackal Three, first storey is clear. Proceeding to second level. Over,' Almeida broadcasted into his vox headset. In all likelihood, Jackal One were all dead and Jackal Two would be a long time coming. He might as well not have used the link at all.

They were moving again. Almeida and his sergeant ran point. They ran with a synchronised efficiency, Almeida bent double in a running crouch, his sergeant aiming a T20 over the captain's hunched back. Together, the seven men of Jackal Three made for the railed, corkscrew staircase to the upper levels.

They met dogged resistance at the connecting corridor of the second storey, with Corporal Aturk being downed by a headshot on entry. There was a ferocious exchange of fire but the Lancers pushed the house guard back. Private Aman, the fire-team's surviving assault specialist, took to the fore with a flamer. His weapon unleashed a tornado of fire down the corridor, incinerating a twenty metre stretch of hall. It was over in a matter of seconds.

They found Golias's house guests, herded together like frightened sheep in some of the upstairs guest rooms. Perhaps fifty or sixty Mantillan elites, huddled in the chambers, crying and frightened to the point of hysteria. The black rouge ran down the faces of women in dripping rivulets and the men were even worse, their shoulders racked by uncontrollable sobs. Some were still crashing on narcotics, their delirious terror amplified by opiates.

At one point, Sergeant Calcheed gripped the silk lapel of a wealthy oligarch and pulled him close. The man was obviously under the influence of obscura, spurse, alcohol or some combination of the three.

The sergeant leaned in until they were nose to nose, and grinned. 'So you want to ignore the war by revelling hard, huh? How about ignoring this?' Sergeant Calcheed pressed the barrel of his T20 to the man's head. The merchant audibly soiled himself and his knees buckled. Calcheed dropped him, disgusted.

Roth looked to Almeida but the captain did not reprimand his sergeant or tell him to stop. The captain said nothing. In a way, Calcheed was only acting out how they all felt. For too long the nobles had gone about their business, ignoring the war at the expense of all others. It felt good; it felt like the Emperor's justice to snuff their debauchery.

They locked the panicked guests in their rooms, barring the doors with heavy antique chairs to prevent any interference, before pressing on.

It was not until they cleared the second storey that they heard the Vulture gunship of Jackal Two overhead, pounding the rooftop garden with autocannons. It sounded like an industrial drill dismantling the upper storeys.

'Jackal Three, this is Two. Permission granted from Central Command to use aerial weapons in a civilian zone. Neutralising rooftop obstacles. We'll be down to play shortly. Out,' Celeminé reported.

Golias was trapped between Jackal Three storming up the corkscrew staircase from the lower levels, and Jackal Two sweeping down from the rooftops. Golias militia attempted to intervene in the rooftop garden, but soon learned that their street-fighting held no credibility up there either.

'Two, come in Two. Third storey all clear except for the atrium and his launch hangar. Report status?' Almeida growled. The fire-team was crouching low now, wary. Their guns flickered from corner to corner. Golias would be close.

'This is Two. Rooftop all clear. No place left to run. Over.'

'Loud and clear. Stay sharp on the rooftop and be ready. We might flush him out yet. Out.'

This was when Golias would be at his most dangerous. Roth knew it all too well, that when the quarry was cornered, he was the most unpredictable.

Jackal Three found Hiam Golias in his atrium. The man was not armed. He did not appear to be. He was naked, lounging silkily by his impluvium pond.

The fire-team fanned out, training their submachine weapons on him while auspexes scanned for trip-wires, trigger bombs and motion sensors. Golias didn't seem to care much for them. He splashed the pond surface with his palm, watching the wrinkles in the surface ripple outwards.

Roth approached the collector, slowly.

'Hiam Golias. This is Inquisitor Obodiah Roth. I have heard a lot about you. I thought you would have put up more of a fight, considering.'

The collector looked up lazily, pushing his silver mane upwards and away from his face. He shrugged, nonchalant. 'And I thought you would all be dead by now. Sometimes plans don't go our way.'

'You're a bastard, do you know that?' Roth remarked.

'I was just protecting my interests. No one told you to come looking for me,' Golias shrugged.

'And who told you that we would come looking for you, Golias? Who told you?' asked Roth, standing over Golias.

Golias didn't look at him.

'Someone with my interests in mind. Someone who doesn't like you, inquisitor.'

Roth decided to change tack. He brandished his plasma pistol, and drew it across Golias's field of vision.

'This is a Sunfury MKIII plasma pistol. Its fusion reactor core fires an ionised gas nova that will melt ten centimetres of plasteel. Do you have any idea what this will do to your face?'

Golias said nothing.

'Let's start with some questions,' Roth said, evening his tone. 'Who told you I would be coming for you?'

Finally Golias levelled with Roth's gaze. 'I don't know. I was warned by a Cantican officer. He did not indulge me with who sourced to him. Don't ask, don't tell. It's how we operate.'

Roth probed him with a gentle mind spike, intruding on the man and making him startle visibly. Roth was perhaps more forceful than he could have been. He simply rifled through his emotional receptors, roughly. Golias was telling the truth.

'Next question. Where is this relic?' Roth asked.

'What will you pay me?' Golias replied brazenly.

'I have three choices for you, Golias. We can kill you now, if you're stupid enough. Or you can work with us, and live. Third option, you play me the fool, and we air-evac you and drop you into Archenemy territory.'

'You won't kill me, you need me for the relic,' Golias said confidently.

Roth slapped the haughty merchant on the back of the head. He dealt him a second humiliating slap. 'Are you stupid, man? Auto-séance. Heard of that? I'd love nothing more than to put a round through your skull and drag your soul kicking and screaming from the abyss for answers.'

Golias was less confident now. There was a tremor in his lip, slight but noticeable.

'Be a good man. Show us where it is,' said Roth, crouching down next to Golias in an almost benign manner. 'I don't want to have to waste a shot on your stupid head.'

CHAPTER TWENTY-ONE

'I've never seen anything of such scale and preservation,' Madeline said.

She had joined Roth's fire-teams via escorted Vulture gunship. Her expert opinion had, in Roth's words, been warranted out of utter necessity. The Task Group, steering Golias with the muzzles of T20 autoguns, were led down a mineshaft. That was what it appeared to be at first glance, once Golias had opened a vaulted blast door concealed behind an oil portrait of a Golias ancestor.

'This place is a mine in every sense of the word,' Madeline continued breathlessly.

The elevator trolley, a wire mesh cage of flaking red oxide, clattered as it lowered the team. Its keening metallic screech echoed down the abyssal depths, screaming back up at them from below. Down and down they went, for six thousand metres until they hit the bottom.

'Holy Throne,' Roth muttered, as the phos-lamps of the conveyance trolley illuminated the subterranean dark.

'Yes, every bit as majestic as you expected,' Golias said.

In truth the collector's relic was not what Roth, or indeed what any of the Task Group, had expected.

At first it appeared to be a mining seam, at least eight thousand metres in length. Striations of ore and red ironstone ran the length of its sheer, scoured face. Anchor bolts buttressed the monstrously cavernous heights where rock had been sheared away in precisely cut horizontal and vertical sheers.

Yet as they approached, they could make out finer details. Crenulations and fleche spires melded from the rock-face like unfinished sculptures. In some parts, repeating pointed arches seemed to be carved into the geo-strata, long orderly rows that played the entire length of the mining cut.

'This is Imperial Gothic architecture, Ecclesiarch design, perhaps?' Madeline murmured.

'No. Dictator-class design,' Roth said.

'Dictator? I'm not familiar with that era of architecture. Is it of Fringe cultural origin?' Madeline asked.

'What he means,' Celeminé began, 'is that this is a Dictator-class cruiser. Can you see the lance-decks there? The gargoyle steeples there?'

Golias's relic was a fossilised Imperial cruiser. A patina of mineral growth sheathed its exposed parts, simple salts and silicate deposits glittering like a rime of gritty ice. Geo-forms clustered across the ship's flank like a hide of barnacles. It was as if the cruiser itself had become a part of the planet's mantle, a tectonic wedge of quartz, mica, calcium and ironstone sediment.

Golias guided them up a ramp that led into a blast-cut opening in the ship's broadside. The wound in the ship resembled a mining tunnel. Support beams created a framework beneath the sagging rock where demolitions and mining drills had punctured its surface.

'This is the *Decisive*, a Dictator-class cruiser of the Second Naval Expeditionary Fleet,' Golias proclaimed proudly. 'The ship itself was downed on Aridun at some point during the War of Reclamation in Medina. There was nothing in the ship's data to reveal the cause of the ship's demise but judging by this entry wound in the ship's hull, it had not been primitive barbarians that the Imperium had been fighting.'

Roth paused at the threshold of the cruiser's wound. The jagged cross-section of the ship revealed a hull that was almost five metres thick. Whatever had damaged the *Decisive* had been powerful indeed.

'Golias, if you've got any more aces up your sleeve, forget it. I want nothing more than to finish you, so don't give me a reason. Understand?' Roth growled.

The collector nodded mutely as Roth vented his plasma pistol with a vaporous hiss. Celeminé lit the ignition on her hand flamer. Captain Pradal slid the bolt of his T20 to semi-automatic. Even Madeline cocked the hammer of a slim, revolving stub-pistol.

'You first,' said Roth, waving Golias into the shaft.

Slowly, the Overwatch Task Group entered the ossified cruiser.

The vast interior of the cruiser was barely recognisable.

Over the millennia, beards of stalactite drip from the upper gantry formed an undulating warpage of ground rock across the surface flooring of the vessel. Roth led the way, the beam of his stab-light probing over broken shapes of ship instruments and cavernous corridors.

House Golias had strung up dim, phosphorescent lamps to light the way. Under the pallid light, Roth could see that age had changed the ship in strange ways. The belly of the vessel was vast, painted in hues of rotting teal, brown and mostly black. Many interior walls had collapsed, or had melted seamlessly with stone. Veins of opal glimmered in fissures. Thermal springs had formed in some corridors, vomiting intermittent geysers of toxic gas. The air was bad, and the wet, humid fumes cultivated bacterial strains of fungus on the walls.

'Don't touch anything, some of the microbials here are quite infectious,' Golias said as he expertly led them down a path he had obviously trodden many times. The ship had been the sole reason that the ancestral patriarchs of the Golias house had levied their estates in its location. They knew its worth, and invested in it. An investment that spanned forty-five generations.

'Slow down, Golias.' Roth commanded. 'Where are you leading us?'

'To the ship's bridge, where else? Unless cave exploration is what you were after,' Golias said in an irritatingly off-hand manner.

'Golias, I'm very close to headbutting your nose inwards,' Roth said flatly.

They climbed rather than walked for some time until finally emerging in a communications hall. Thirty metres to their front, the blast doors to the bridge yawned open like the ruptured shell of a rotting crustacean.

'There's the bridge, undisturbed since the Reclamation Wars,' Golias said, suddenly rushing forwards over a crest of calcite deposit that might have once been a broken support strut.

Roth tightened the grip on his pistol and signalled for several of their CantiCol escorts to stay guard outside the command bridge.

Unlike the rest of the cruiser, the reinforced vault of the cruiser's bridge was remarkably well preserved. It was like a piece of history, crystallised in time. A tactical spreadsheet was still spread on the tact-altar, its small chess-like pieces still pinned in place. The ship's command throne was untouched, its neural plugs placed in a neat row on the leather seat.

'Servitors?' asked Madeline, pointing to the trio of frail cogitate-logicians standing around the command throne. They were strange creatures, with despondent human faces and ornate box-shaped torsos. Keys and wires spilled from a hatchway in their abdomen.

Golias nodded. 'We purchased them to maintain this vault. They can power up the ship's main databanks.'

Roth waved his pistol at Golias. 'Be a good man, and power up the databanks.'

Golias, for once, was obedient. The servitors began their work, their bald heads bobbing up and down in rhythmic unison as their fingers trotted across the ivory keystrokes. Some of the cogitator screens had been damaged during the initial crash-landing six thousand years ago. Many of them had also fallen into disrepair despite the efforts of the House Golias servitors.

'Over the course of several thousands years the cogitators had lost physical memory,' Golias explained. 'Disintegrating logic-engines and withering circuitry have corrupted much key data, but what I have here is invaluable. You'll be so pleased, inquisitor.'

With a mechanical groan, the cruiser's data banks started. The monitors that still functioned flickered a lambent green as the servitors dredged up the ageing data.

It had been there the whole time.

When the hololithic map of the Medina Corridor was projected, the six-thousand-year-old image reviewed Medina as it was – a cluster of globes each marked with clearly visible orbit lines and equatorial ley-lines across the planet's surface. As the three-dimensional map made its orrery revolution and the planets shifted, the puzzle, for Roth at least, fell into place.

It was a moment of fleeting clarity, the exact breath between accepting reality and the blindness of not knowing.

The Medina Corridor was, in the old proverbial, a treasure map. The equatorial ley-lines formed linear markings across the globes. They appeared as thin razor scratchings visible from orbit. The alignment of planets in the Medina Corridor formed a stellar map, and the equator lines formed patterns. Patterns that were complex and interlocking yet primitively minimalist in concept.

Roth was dumbfounded that they hadn't seen this earlier. It had been so evident, literally before their eyes. The Medina Corridor formed a series of links with the axis of the equatorial planar lines all meeting at a central location.

The centre of the Old Kings.

'The Archenemy isn't digging blindly at all...' Roth began.

'No. It's forming the old equator lines and schematics required to awaken the Old Kings,' Madeline said.

'Awaken?' Pradal asked, taking off his cap and running a hand nervously through his hair. The young captain was obviously confused.

'I'm not sure. But ley-lines have existed for as long as human civilisation. Geodesy was an old Terran discipline of studying a planet's magnetic fields, polar motion, tides and so forth. Early man postulated that such lines were extraterrestrial in nature, along with a heavy dose of geomancy. What I am sure of is that these lines across the Medina Worlds are related to the Old Kings.'

As the map spun on its three-dimensional axis again, dense blocks of script scrolled up the length of the monitors, revealing the extent of

Imperial war-making intelligence during the Reclamation campaigns. It seemed even during the Reclamation, the Imperial military machine had given some focus on the existence of these Old Kings and their potential for changing the course of the campaign.

According to the sources, the origins of the Old Kings began far back in the antiquity of pre-Imperial Medina. What the ship's data described as 'Early Sentients' had come to Medina, bearing with them the influences of a highly advanced xenos culture as well as their worship of the stars and constellations. This Roth already knew from Gurion's briefings, but there was much more lodged in these databanks.

When the Early Sentients finally left the Medina Worlds, they left for their subjects a parting gift. They bequeathed them an embryonic star. Through their worship of the stars, in effect, the Sentients had gifted Medina a god. It was the Old Kings, or the Star Ancient or the myriad other names that had passed through the generations. The star was held in a form of dormant stasis described as a *Tomb Bell*, to forever watch over the people of Medina. Or so the databanks would have Roth believe. There was so much detail, so much scripture. So much to take in.

The intelligence report continued, 'During a great time of strife, at the precise alignment of the magnetic conduits of the ley-lines with the astronomical bodies, the star could be released from its stasis and unleashed. The star within the Tomb Bell can be thus removed from its resting place and unleashed where strife is greatest.' The report became vague thereafter, postulating various theories as to the significance of the ley-lines and the destructive magnitude of an expanding star.

'A star kept in stasis?' asked Roth.

'This worship of astronomical bodies has happened for all time since the history of man,' Madeline said.

Roth understood. On Ancient Terra, he knew of lost tribes that had carved similar lines visible from orbit. These lines were the geological conduits of magnetic energy. Roth had read about these before, although the true meanings and practices soon became lost to ritual and symbolism. Man did not truly understand the teachings of the Early Sentients. But they trusted themselves to a blind following of the schematics ordained by the elder races. They carved great helio-lines, swathes of geometric markings across the surface of their planets. The data did not elaborate any more as to the nature of these xenos or their practices. Roth humbly conferred with Madeline for answers.

'Early Sentients, madame?'

The professor shook her head as she read. 'Probably a disambiguation of the term. It would not be the first time that an alien race has played its hand during the early formative years of human development.'

'And these lines? These ley-lines, have you studied them at length?'

'I've seen them before. The composition of globe lines was called "*Pedj*

Shes" in the earliest languages. It literally means "stretching of the cord". It's a process of marking long linear geometry across the surface mantle of planets, so that during a specified point of the astronomical revolution, the equator lines would align and create shifts in magnetic polar energy.'

'And the early Medinians understood all of this?'

'Probably not. An isolated society's first contact with others often results in attempts to emulate and mimic without reason or understanding. According to anthropologists, symbology and fetishisation became more important than knowledge.

Roth had known that primitive civilisations when contacted by the Imperium often resulted in such behaviour. Primitives had constructed canoes in the shape of Imperial ships. The Tukaro culture of the Mephius subsector even shaped spears in the crude outline of lasguns, and made their warriors brand themselves with a stylised aquila, in order to mimic the power of the Imperial Guard.

Indeed during the Tukaro Civil Wars, the Imperium had deployed onto the primitive planet with a great deal of unknown equipment. The vast amounts of war materiel that were airdropped onto these archipelagos during the subsector campaign necessarily meant drastic influences to the Tukaro people, who had never seen the Imperium before. Manufactured clothing, medicine, canned food, textiles, weapons and other cargo arrived in vast quantities to equip soldiers. Some of it was shared with the Tukaro indigenous. Following the resolution of civil strife, the Imperium abandoned the primitive planet. It had no strategic or resource value to the Imperium, and planetary governance was ceded to the Ecclesiarchy. The cargo lifters no longer visited.

In attempts to receive cargo, the indigenous Tukaro imitated the same practices they had seen the soldiers use. They carved headsets from wood and wore them while sitting in fabricated control stations. They waved dried-leaf landing paddles while standing on the runways. They lit signal fires and torches in the abandoned starports.

The difference here was that the Early Sentients ordained mankind to worship the stars. They promised that during the proper alignment, the Old Kings would wake from their dormant slumber and strike their enemies down with wrath should their civilisation ever be threatened.

Suddenly it all made sense to Roth. He did not require the rest of the databank history to connect the remaining pieces. The insurrectionists who had fought the Imperial Fleet during the Reclamation Wars had attempted to release their embryonic star. Of that there was no doubt.

The Medina Corridor's unique stellar alignment, orrery orbit and axis angles, and most importantly the constant shifting of its axial cycles, meant that the helio-lines that had once marked the planets would shift into alignment. But they had failed. Evidently, the Imperium had reclaimed the Medina Worlds.

'Do you think that the natives tried to release the embryonic star? Do you think that is what caused the mass extinction on Aridun?'

'I've never thought of that,' Madeline admitted. 'But it would make sense. If the star was still dormant, releasing it from stasis would at least have caused a radioactive flare.'

'Which would mean...'

'Which would mean an erosion of the planet's atmosphere, causing turbulent climate changes.'

Roth breathed out with the weight of revelation. He realised the only difference between the six-thousand-year-old projection before him, and the cartographer's charts he had studied in his pre-operation briefings, was the absence of those global markings. As the millennia worn on, Cantica and Kholpesh built their cities on cities and the lines were buried under civilisation. The same geodetic lines that the Archenemy were unearthing. It was a matter of filling in the gaps, retracing the zenith, the nadir, the azimuth points. Measuring for elevation and meridian planes and thus rebuilding the schematics of these Early Sentients.

'These scratchings, these ley-lines, how do they awaken the Old Kings?' Roth asked.

'I can only answer in terms of pre-history. It was common amongst the prehistoric tribes of Terra to believe such lines channelled the magnetic energy of planets. There must be some correlation between magnetic equator lines, the alignment of astronomy and the stasis field of the Old Kings. The timing seems key here,' Madeline surmised. 'Once the stasis field is disrupted, I'm guessing this violent star can then be transported within its Tomb Bell to *wherever the strife is greatest*, as this scripture suggests. The Archenemy have timed this well.'

And indeed it was all executed with impeccable timing. According to the orrery of the hololithic map, the constellations were already in perfect alignment. The Old Kings would be active now, roused from their dormant sleep and thrumming with the magnetic sustenance channelled by the conduit ley-lines spanning an entire star system.

But the worst, the very worst was the revelation that they had all deceived themselves. They had underestimated the enemy. Khorsabad Maw's vanguard assault had not been a blindly roving treasure hunt. It had not been the sporadic plundering of planets. Rather, it had been a methodical process of preparation.

They had not, as Imperial intelligence believed, been using the slaves to excavate in some vain attempt to locate the Old Kings. The quarries, so visible from orbital reconnaissance, had been the geodetic constructs.

What terrified Roth even more, the one thing that was most horrifying, was that the Archenemy had known where the Old Kings slept all along. They had simply chosen not to play their hand too soon and reveal it to the Imperium. Instead they prepared their conduits, leaving the Old Kings on Aridun untouched.

The Archenemy had been waiting until the lines had been laid across Medina from Naga to Tarsis, and the embryonic star was ripe to release from stasis. From there on, the Archenemy could remove the star contained within its vessel, and utilise its destructive potential at any strategic location within the Imperium. Lord Marshal Khmer had been wrong. Very wrong. Chaos had not been irrational. It had been so entirely logical that the Imperium had missed it.

With the revelation of the Old Kings, the Task Force moved quickly. Preparations were made to transit off planet immediately. Mantilla was crumbling and the minor victory at Magdalah, although morale-lifting, did not abate the inevitable. The void shield was stuttering in places, and Ironclad gas artillery was beginning to pound on the city proper. Of Hiam Golias, the collector, Roth made sure to confiscate his cargo-flier for the war effort. The collector, under the auspices of Cantican military provosts, was then sent to the front-line trenches as an auxiliary labourer. Of his fate, Roth knew not.

The inquisitor was already preoccupied with the next phase of his mission and his mind was elsewhere. As pressing as it was to act swiftly on Aridun, Roth was a man of priorities and he could not leave Kholpesh without flushing the traitor from within his ranks.

The scarlet letter was a trap of two folds.

Once the quarry took the bait, it was up to him to reveal himself through error. An error that an innocent man would never have made.

The error here would be Delahunt's log. The jewel of his signet ring was plugged to a decryption machine like a crumb of food in a spring-loaded rodent trap.

Roth had made it clear, in no uncertain terms, that he had found something of interest on Delahunt's log that the previous encryption scan had not relinquished. He'd put it down to poor system function; the device used in the tunnels of the Barbican had been rudimentarily crude.

It was all a ploy.

Now Roth lay in wait, sequestered within the panelled walls of their military billet. His room had been purposefully left in a state of disarray. He had informed the Overwatch Task Group that Major General Cabales had requested his immediate assistance regarding an issue of tactical significance. Roth had ordered the Task Group to prepare their equipment for transit to Aridun in his absence.

Now he, and ten hand-picked Canticans, men he had personally drawn from the trenches with no prior contact to his staff, lay in wait.

He had even left the linen on his pallet bed unmade, and the drawers of his dresser ajar, as if he'd left in haste. The decryptor was in the corner of the room, beneath a glass-shaded lamp, its gilded keys chattering quietly.

The figure padded down the barrack's billet. It was late in the evening and although the Kholpeshi suns were still searing, the rest shutters had been drawn along the corridor. Slatted bars of fiery amber sun played along the plyboard walls, bending the shadows into exaggerated shapes of black on a canvas of fiery orange. The figure slinked along the shadows, veiled in inky blackness.

Roth's room was easy to find. It was the only room along the corridor with the door ajar. Evidently, Roth had left in a hurry.

There was no need for stealth. It carried with it unwarranted suspicion. Rather, a hand pushed the door open, brazenly.

'Roth, Roth are you here?' called the voice.

The figure stepped into the empty room. Their billets were spartan, the sleeping quarters of a gas mill where the workers were allowed their daily six hours of rest shift. That had been before the war.

Roth's room contained nothing more than a single iron-framed bed. Gas canisters in rusted cylinders lined the plyboard partition walls, towering over the bed in a way that suggested utility room rather than sleeping quarters. A single ventilation fan stuttered overhead. It squeaked on its wiring, its blades lashing fast-running shadows continuously across the room. These quarters were not known for their comfort.

In a far corner of the room, nestled between a gas cylinder and a sheet-metal spit bucket, a decryptor was at work. The machine looked at odds with its surroundings, its ivory keys tapping, sinking and releasing of their own accord. Mother-of-pearl panelled the casing and a series of whirling gyroscopes timed the rhythm of its work. A golden cherub's face mounted at the centre of the console released a paper tongue of readouts, its decrypted data collected in a spool of loose parchment.

The figure locked the door and stalked towards the decryptor. Delahunt's ring was attached to a pulse data link, the cord winking a cold blue light. The figure knelt down before the machine and halted its process with a few deft strokes of its ivory keys. The decryptor gunned down with a reluctant groan of cogs, the paper tongue ceasing to lengthen.

Unfolding a flask from beneath a belt, the figure began to douse the machine with a slick, oily liquid. The stale, humid air of the room was suddenly cut with the sharp sting of naphtha. Particular attention was paid to the signet ring; that had to burn first.

Producing a small book of paper tinders, the figure struck one. A small flame guttered into being, producing a small halo of light around the hand that held it.

Something was not quite right.

Under the light of the teetering little flame, the decryptor's data slips could be read clearly. They did not say anything of worth. Rather they said nothing at all. The signet ring had been emptied of its data cache and replaced with a sequence of scramble patterns and sequenced nonsense.

Scarlet letter caught – caught scarlet as now – letter spilling scarlet – caught now –

'Oh Throne,' said the shadowy figure.

Roth had seen enough.

He laid open the plyboard with a kick of his metal-shod feet, sending the partition board flying in separated parts. Gas canisters toppled, collapsing in a domino chain with hollow metallic rings. Cantican Guardsmen, their lasguns held up to shoulders, came barging in from all sides, kicking down the dormitory partitions.

'Cease and surrender! Inquisition!' Roth yelled.

He lined up the target kneeling in front of the decryptor with his pistol. He steadied his aim and stopped.

He froze, his mind stalled as it struggled for rationality.

Celeminé stared back at him. Her eyes were so far open her pupils were surrounded by white.

Roth hesitated. His mind tried to invoke some logic into what he saw. He tried to find some way to explain what was happening that did not lead to confrontation. Roth's mouth was so dry, and his mind was so blank. Fumbling for reasoning, he found none except that it had been Celeminé all along.

The hesitation was all she needed.

An expanding ring of psychic energy fluttered from Celeminé. It was partly powered by her mind, partly driven by her intense instinct to fight back. The wall of solid force hit the Cantican Colonials closing in on her, striking with the impact of a fast-moving freight vehicle. The last of the partition walls and gas banks were bowled over like loose skittles. Guardsmen were poleaxed off their feet, their entire skeletal structures rendered into splintered fragments on impact.

Roth was blown half-way back across the adjoining dormitory, sliding across the floor before his momentum was arrested by a storage locker. His psi-reactive tabard calcified, some of the obsidian panes around the hem turning to a dusty, brittle white. It was a forceful mind blow, but Roth had taken worse. He staggered back onto his knees.

Celeminé stalked towards him. The sudden explosion of psychic force left her weak and off balance. She lurched drunkenly towards him, a thread of blood running down her nose. 'I should have known, Roth, you can't work a decryption to save your life.'

'I just did,' Roth said. He reached for his pistol and realised it had spun out of his grasp. He bided for time. 'Why did you betray us?'

Celeminé almost smiled. 'Come on, Roth, you sound hurt. You should have seen this coming. I'm surprised it took you as long as it did. Aren't I ambitious enough for you?'

'What did Khmer give you? How did he turn you?'

'I am a woman, Roth. The ordos, it's a patriarchal game. Khmer gave me something you wouldn't understand. He promised me he had the pull to give me greater authority.'

'You had authority. You were an inquisitor.'

Celeminé laughed. Even now, Roth found it a pretty laugh; she curled the corners of her lips up like a broken bow.

'Not like that. He would have given me things you wouldn't have.'

'Me? What are you–' Roth began.

'You insensitive ass,' she laughed. Roth flinched at her stinging words. 'You still don't understand. I would have the opportunity to advance more rapidly as an inquisitor.'

'He lied.'

'Everybody lies,' Celeminé shrugged.

Roth squeezed the trigger.

She beat him to it. Her psychic form, a rushing bow-wave of tidal energy, surged up and towards him like a tsunami.

Roth's psychic power could not hope to match her strength for strength. He played the intellect's game. He shifted his mind into an empty bubble, allowing the crashing tide to carry him.

Celeminé's attack swept them away, taking them high above the Mantillan skyline within the span of half a second. Roth knew he was in deep now. He was playing her game.

Celeminé attacked hard and furiously. Sea serpents, wide of jaw and many-headed, uncoiled from her mind's eye. Seven, seventy, eventually seven hundred sea serpents like tendrils of hair writhed and intertwined as they reached out with snapping, translucent maws.

He wasn't strong enough to counter anything like that. Roth refused to play her game. He curled up into an abstract shape, too many corners to be a triangle, far too multi-dimensional to be a polygon. The lashing serpents hammered him, knocking him about. It hurt Roth, threatened to break him, but it confused Celeminé, denying her a tangible target.

But her intellect directly correlated with her psychic ability. She adapted quickly, fusing her hundreds of serpents into a single horned fish, its grinning maw bristling with spikes. The leviathan engulfed Roth, swallowing him whole. Roth dispersed himself like droplets of water just as the maw snapped shut. He survived, but barely. The fish blew out every shingle of the gas mill roof like a storm of broken teeth in its psychic backlash.

Roth was tiring now. His mind wasn't sharp. Part of him was still in disbelief, and the doubt had a tangible effect on his psychic ability.

Sluggish, he crawled away, seeking escape. He fled in the only direction he could go – out beyond the trenches towards the Archenemy. Taking the form of a streamlined bolt, Roth streaked out across Mantilla. The Imperial trenches, throbbing with small-arms fire blurred beneath him. Celeminé pursued. He could feel her mind-snare, reaching out for him. Several times she almost touched him, the whispering fingers of her pursuant form sending shocks of fright through him.

+Celeminé. Why?+

+Shut up, Roth. I'm tired of explaining already. Let's just finish this.+

She chased him far from Mantilla into the battlefields. Out beyond, in the fields of the enemy, the psychic planescape was different. The sky was darker there, the light filtered and silty. The plague of Archenemy minds below him seethed like a pit of violence, aggression and ignorance. The things he could see there, the ambient memories of so many murderers, were strong enough to completely destroy his sanity.

Roth dived in amongst it.

It was akin to plunging into a cauldron of boiling water. The shock almost killed him. His physical body, many kilometres away, convulsed with enough force to cause hair-line fractures in his spine. He tried to shut out the minds of the Archenemy but they were all around him. He suddenly knew what it was like to kill a child. He knew the wild elation of watching others die from slow poisoning. He knew what it was like to slide a razor into the belly of a sleeping man.

Worst still were the ghosts. They were vaguely humanoid shapes, smoke-black and faceless, they clutched onto the Ironclad, hugging their backs, riding on their shoulders, holding their legs with a tortured, vengeful grasp. They were the dead – souls of murder victims, unable to leave the world. The followers of the Ruinous Powers had an ability to blur the line between the warp and the world, allowing the spirits of the dead to manifest in strange ways. Here, they clung to those who wronged them, hanging over them like a dark aura.

Roth tried to shut it out, throwing up layers and layers of mind blank. He reduced his psychic signature and buried his face in the soil.

Celeminé swept in after him, trailing psychic magnificence. She took the form of a radiant avian, wings flared. Her confidence was to be her undoing.

The spirits, if not the resonance of the warp, then the angry ghosts of those the Ironclad had killed followed their armies like an aura of vengeful suffering. They were attracted to Celeminé's psychic brilliance.

The sudden swarming of despairing spirits snared Celeminé. She fought back, the wild lashes of her psychic will actually haemorrhaged the brains of several Ironclad sentries in a nearby tent. The ghosts leered at her, clawed at her, pulled and pleaded for her to stay with them. To join them in their suffering.

Roth seized his moment. He would not have another like it.

He surged back into his body. A fraction of a second before Celeminé realised he had gone.

Roth awoke back in the gas mill. The metaphysical shift was disorientating. The room spun in helical spirals. He staggered and righted himself. The room was covered in a thick crust of frost and the temperature was well below zero. Roth pawed through the ice, clawing at a T20 autogun on the frozen corpse of Guardsman. It dislodged, sleeting panes of thin ice as Roth picked it up.

Celeminé returned to her body as Roth's bearings returned. Her psychic discipline was good despite the distraction Roth had inflicted upon her. Celeminé's eyes tore open, immediately ready.

But Roth's trigger discipline was better. He squeezed the trigger. The first shot hit Celeminé below the ribs, buckling her onto her knees. His next round entered her below the chin, jetting a thin stream of crimson onto the white ice.

Inquisitor Felyce Celeminé lay, face-down in the snow. Strings of blood stained her yellow bodyglove orange.

Roth stared at her. His laboured breathing spiralled up in frosty plumes. A tension headache constricted his cerebellum, sending nerve tingles into his right elbow. He felt intoxicated, his mind dulled in what psychic-duellists termed *post-duel stupor*. It was his brain trying to recuperate from the confrontation. Blood pounded in his temple, its beat irregular.

As he sat, he thought about the vengeful ghosts that latched onto the Ironclad, following their killers into eternity. It was an unsettling thought. He could still feel the tortured thirst for revenge that those spirits had for their murderers. Roth wondered if Celeminé would follow him, her ghost latched onto his back for all eternity. A part of him hoped she would, to absolve him of guilt. And although he should not have felt guilt, try as he might, he did.

CHAPTER TWENTY-TWO

'I will not commit my soldiers to Aridun. I will not commit my soldiers to this war,' Lord Marshal Khmer announced to the assembly of senior commanders.

Those were the historic first words for the last Council of Conclusions of the Medina Campaign.

There was a stir of unease but none of the officers objected.

The lord marshal, naked of his medals and ceremonial trappings, wearing the starched uniform of a Cantican rank-and-file, stalked across the podium, playing his audience like a grand thespian.

'As Aridun has fallen quiet, the last of the core worlds of Medina are potentially lost.' He paused, allowing this fact to sink and settle.

He continued imperiously. 'There is nothing left for us here. Gentlemen, let us not forget the first rule of military engagement. Fight with objective. We have lost any and all objective in Medina.'

Polished boots clapping across the grated decking, Khmer walked to where Forde Gurion sat in the front bench. He levelled his gaze on the inquisitor and said with great clarity, 'For us to stay, we would be fighting out of emotional ties, out of moral obligation. We would not be fighting as military architects, but rather men blinded by loyalty to our home. We would not be generals, we would be guilty of being *civilians.*'

The last words were twisted and spat at Forde Gurion. The implication was clear.

There was some truth to Khmer's words. The silence of Aridun had been brutally abrupt.

The last message, received by long-range vox, was transmitted from a listening station in the Cage Isles of Northern Aridun directly to the Ninth Route Fleet. That had been at 13:00 hours, on the first day of the new Medinian moon. The transmission had reported low-level enemy activity across the demarcation line, nothing out of the ordinary.

By 14:00 hours that day, communications ceased. All vox systems were down and astropathic signatures in the Governor's palace on Aridun were dreadfully cold and empty.

General Cypus Tanbull of the CantiCol 12th Division remarked that the planet had, for lack of a better term, 'fallen quiet by providence of the God-Emperor.' It was a sanguine way of saying something sickeningly dreadful had occurred on Aridun, and High Command had no intelligence to go by.

The Council of Conclusions was called, but conclusions had been the antithesis of what they had achieved. They had no intelligence to align their debate. Orbital reconnaissance showed nothing across the continental plates. Nothing at all, not even the twinkling constellation of lights that illuminated a city at night. Just blackness. It was as if Aridun had been wholly abandoned in the span of several hours.

That had been four days ago. Ironically, and truly by the providence of the God-Emperor, the situation had changed.

With a hydraulic hiss of his legs, Gurion rose from his seat.

'Lord marshal, there is logic in your words,' he mused. 'But the situation, I believe, has changed dramatically. I have come as swiftly as time would allow, to report to the Command a critical piece of intelligence unearthed by my Task Group.'

Something hardened behind Khmer's eyes but he allowed the inquisitor to continue.

'The Old Kings have been discovered.' It was Gurion's turn to play the theatrical role. He even sharpened his words with a touch of his mind so it reverberated in the minds of those seated around him.

'The Medina Corridor, the very star system, forms the fabric of the Old Kings. It has been before our eyes the whole time if we had bothered to see it.'

Gurion pushed past Khmer, ignoring him and addressing the assembly as he touched the hololithic projector. An orrery orbit of the Medina System flickered into grainy translucence, the image hovering like an inverted pyramid from the projector lens.

'If we study the equator lines and surface markings of the planets, we can see wide globe-spanning lines on most of the planet clusters,' Gurion said, indicating each of the planets in turn with his finger.

'Now, if we allow the planets to shift through their cyclical rotations, the equator lines form distinct patterns.'

Steadily, the planets spun on their heliocentric axis. The equator lines, like scars across the planets' surfaces, shifted until finally Gurion paused the projection. The projection showed the planets in the first moon cycle, with the triple suns at contrasting angles.

There was a rustle of discussion amongst the officers.

Although some of the equator lines were broken, and some planets bore none, a lattice of overlapping lines, oddly abstract but startlingly apparent, seemed to link the planets of the Medina Corridor. There was a symmetry and order to them, but at the same time there was a fluid yet alien regularity to the planetary markings. Gurion had already taken measuring instruments to them and the angles were razor edge in precision. It was extraordinary considering the true scale of those planets. Almost like a series of curving script had been sliced into the skin of each planet, overlapping and dancing.

'Mathematics and patterns, inquisitor?' Khmer snapped impatiently.

'Let him speak,' the Space Marine envoy said, his bass voice rolling with thunderous authority.

Gurion remained placid. 'This was an orbital map of pre-invasion Medina. I now invite you to study an orbital surveillance of the star system, after the Archenemy conquest.'

An orrery projection replaced the first. There was little difference, except the monolithic excavations and quarries of the Ironclad were clearly visible. In their new context, the massive quarries and excavation sites lined up with the pre-existing ley-lines seamlessly. On the planets of Ninvevah, Baybel and Cantica, where no lines had existed before, the excavations surfaced new ones, at exact angles with the old.

At the centre of the symmetry, during the first day of the moon cycle, was the planet of Aridun.

This was, perhaps, the greatest revelation to High Command since the conflict had begun. The assembly erupted. There was a tumultuous babble of shock. Even a two-hundred-year-old admiral of the fleet, a veteran who had seen everything in his centuries of campaigning, held a hand over his mouth.

Gurion did not need to explain it, the orbital picts said everything. The Archenemy had never been conducting a blind treasure hunt of the relics. They had never been acting with the irrationality that Khmer and many officers had predicted.

No. Rather, they had been re-creating the broken equator lines, and finishing the perfect symmetry of new ones. It was a monumental task that spanned the star system. They were recreating the ritual of the Star Ancients with chilling precision and the Imperium had never even known.

Chaos had been acting with logic and precision. That was what frightened the assembly of warriors so much.

For the first time, Khmer relented. 'What does this forebode?'

'Let me explain this precisely. The Old Kings, or rather the Old King, is an embryonic star held in stasis. Aridun marks the central axis. That is where the Old King lies. It has been placed there in line with astronomical and magnetic properties. We believe that is what the old tales refer to when they say the stars will rouse them from dormant slumber. The old mathematical geodesists of Terra would suggest that the magnetic fields and polar motions have disrupted the dormant star's stasis field,' Gurion replied.

'And so the Old King has been, in a way, activated...' a Naval officer from the assembly murmured, loud enough for all to hear.

'Perhaps. Perhaps not. The only way to know is if we deploy an expedition force onto the planet,' Gurion declared.

'What if they are activated? Then what?' Khmer pressed.

'Although we do not know what form this star exists as, more than likely, the Archenemy will not unleash an embryonic star on Medina. It's strategically insignificant. From all our sources, this star seems to be dormant within some sort of a containment vessel. Now we don't know what this is, but it's intuitive enough. Once activated by the ley-lines it would suggest that this vesselled container can then be removed and utilised elsewhere.'

'I don't follow you,' Khmer said stubbornly.

'Let me put this in terms you will understand. This is a star within a vessel. Think of it as a bomb. Except this bomb, when unleashed, will likely consume an entire star system and expand outwards with radiation and enough kinetic energy to rend rifts in the warp,' said Gurion. 'As an example of course. We won't know until we send an investigative team to Aridun.'

'Out of the question. I will not send soldiers as sacrificial lambs. You said yourself, the Old Kings may already be roused from their dormant state,' Khmer interjected. 'This does not change our strategy to reinforce the Bastion Stars.'

'Logical, lord marshal, logical,' Gurion conceded. 'Which is why I volunteer to deploy my last remaining Task Group to Aridun.'

Khmer ground his teeth, ready to speak again when Gurion halted his words with a mechanical hand. 'As I speak, Inquisitor Obodiah Roth and his task force are en route to Aridun. Once they make landfall, they have forty-eight hours to contact us by long-range vox.'

'And then what?' Khmer asked.

'If they are able to contact High Command, we will deploy all available military resources to secure Aridun. I do this by mandate of Inquisitorial authority. If they do not, then you can have your withdrawal, lord marshal.'

Above the piped collar of his uniform, Khmer's carotid arteries throbbed like hose-pipes. The scarred skin of his face turned a pressurised red. The lord marshal nodded once, very slowly. 'Excellently played, inquisitor.'

Gurion snapped the CantiCol salute to the assembly of commanders, clashing a mechanical fist to his chest in the gesture of solidarity. 'This is the one chance you have to fight for your birth worlds. Have the fleet and the Guard prepare for rapid deployment. You have forty-eight hours, followed by a six-hour notice for mobilisation.'

Gurion strode out of the war vault, halted at the blast doors, then turned to regard the assembly one last time. 'This is our time, gentlemen. If we fail now, you will be remembered for it, regardless of the victories and triumphs you have already bled for.'

CHAPTER TWENTY-THREE

The orbital reconnaissance of Aridun had been accurate regarding the abandonment.

There were no signs of life, at least in the human sense. The stratocraft skimmed low across the southern savannah belt of Aridun Civic, to avoid radar detection and to survey the city. The maze of streets was empty, and although it was only a bruising dawn, no lights were visible along the skyline.

What the reconnaissance had revealed were the burning pyres that smoked into blackened embers out in the thousand kilometre reefs of cycad and gingko that surrounded Aridun Civic.

The pyres were monuments, some as high as sixty, seventy metres tall. The pyres resembled gas nebulae, blackened and swollen and crowned with gaseous flame. The stratocraft had veered in, trying to snatch close observation.

As they flew through the pillars of smoke, Roth had ordered the pilot servitor to vent atmospheric oxygen and allow air into the cabin. The sour, acrid stench of burning flesh and hair that seeped into the vessel confirmed Roth's suspicion. It was indeed corpses of Aridun out there in those fields, heaped up and burning. The smell was so pervasive, Captain Pradal had vomited three times before the stratocraft's venting systems repurified the oxygen and locked down the atmospheric seals.

But the oily taste still lingered at the backs of their throats.

'I've seen the Archenemy do this before but never on such a scale,' Roth admitted. 'Once on a mining station in Helm's Outreach, the Juventist Cult there had murdered almost everyone. They had been desperate enough for the people not to contact the Imperium. The desperation had tallied almost thirty thousand lives.'

'That's obscene,' Madeline said, looking out the starboard ports, the flames of the evening light reflecting dancing shades across her face.

'Mmm,' murmured Roth listlessly.

'Something is eating away at you, Roth. You look morose.'

'I'm fine about Celeminé.'

'I didn't say anything about Celeminé...' she said, letting the statement hang in the air.

'Madeline, don't start. Celeminé and I, we had a working partnership. We were inquisitors. At best we would have stayed together in coop-eration for maybe several years, who knows maybe several decades. But eventually the Inquisitorial calling would take us apart from each other. By ideology or by personality we would eventually go our separate ways. For Celeminé, this happened much sooner... and much more regrettably.'

'Very detached perspective, Roth. It's not like you.'

'That's because now is not the time to have my head between my legs, figuratively speaking.'

In truth, Roth had not been well. Most times he kept it together, but at times Celeminé and Silverstein seemed to haunt him. He thought he heard them talking sometimes, but reminded himself it could not be. Yet it was also a time when he could not afford to be anything less than mentally precise, and it was only the fortitude of an inquisitor that had allowed him to go on. Inquisitorial fortitude and chems. He had glanded endorphin pills, dopamine injections and had not eaten properly in months. He barely recognised the blackened hollows around his eyes and pale, gaunt cheeks that sulked at him in the mirror.

The peals of a tri-tone over the intercom system shook Roth from his contemplation. 'Preparation for landing in six hundred seconds,' the servitor pilot announced in his monotone voice over the speakers.

It was time.

Roth led Madeline to the shuttered landing ramp where Captain Pradal was securing a vox array to his backpack with locking straps. His lasrifle was slung muzzle-up across his shoulder and a bolt pistol from the stra-tocraft's arsenal bay was tucked into a thigh holster.

'You look ready to start a war, captain,' Roth smiled.

'I'm ready to end one, inquisitor. Do you think this could really be the end game?' the junior officer asked. He struggled to shoulder the bulk of his equipment.

'No doubt,' Roth said, helping the captain weave his arms under the straps of his load-bearing pack.

'Once we touch down, this craft is moving off-world. I don't want it to betray our presence. Either we make contact with High Command and initiate the grand offensive, or we die here.'

Captain Pradal nodded contentedly; he jumped up and down to test for loose equipment before flipping his white kepi onto his head. 'Either way, I'll die on my home world.' He moved to the landing ramp ponderously under the bulk of a vox array and webbing, his musette bags of ammunition, magnoculars, rebreathers and water bottles clustered from his hips and thighs.

'Are you sure you're ready for this, Madeline? This is your last chance, the offer to ferry you off-world still stands. It's not too late to stay on this craft,' Roth asked Madeline.

The xeno-archaeologist had eschewed her finery for more climate-appropriate gear. A frock coat of loom-woven ceramic polyfibre cascaded down her narrow shoulders, winking like fish-scales of opaline green. A scarf of fine chainmail was wound about her neck and head like a coif.

'I've made up my mind, Roth, it's my scholarly duty to see this through,' she said as she pulled on a pair of kidskin gloves.

'In that case, get rid of that irritant,' Roth said, pointing to the revolving stubber holstered at her waist belt. 'It will just annoy the enemy.'

Roth crossed over to the stratocraft's arsenal bay and popped open a locked trunk. He retrieved a compact carbine, matt-black with a ribbed foregrip and blunt-muzzled profile. Silverstein used to call it a shard carbine, but the common name was simply ripper pistol. He reversed the weapon and handed it pistol-grip first to Madeline.

Roth then dumped a brace belt of magazine cartridges into her arms. 'This gun belonged to an old friend of mine. It fires a concentrated coil of metal shards at a target, highly accurate up to eighty metres. The recoil is smooth but it can dispatch a tusked mammoth with one shot.'

Madeline tested the weapon awkwardly, wedging a magazine into place. She looped the belt of spare mags over her arm like a swinging satchel.

'Good enough?' she asked.

'More or less.'

The stratocraft made a sharp descent, its steep, curving flight taking them across the reef plains. The insertion point was a matter of mathematical formula. The axis of a stellar map, despite its star-spanning length, had been calculated down to a variance of several degrees. The pilot would land them eight kilometres west from where the Old Kings were believed to rest in buried dormancy.

Roth nodded to Pradal and Madeline. 'Whatever happens, know we were doing the Emperor's work.'

Angkhora was not an Imperial name.

Like the names of all the Medina Worlds, their administrative protectorates and city-states, the name was a vestige of the early Medinian tongue. The language had long been suppressed, by dictate of Imperial decree, but names were all-pervasive. Names bespoke history, recognition, a single word that conjured the sentience of a place.

Angkhora was a place of abandonment. It was one of the forgotten cities of the previous dynasty, a broken link of the Fortress Chain after the millennia-long drought and flood cycles of M36. The rampart wall, which connected Angkhora to the Fortress Chains, was sagging and moss-eaten.

Perhaps its desolation was fitting. For as long as man could remember, Angkhora, the axial centre of the Fortress Chains, was a place for burial. The unique reverence of ancestors had devoted an entire city to the interment and rest for those who had passed.

In the early tongue, Angkhora literally translated as 'The house that the first creators built'. It had been built to represent the island in the sky that deities of pre-Imperial Medina had come from, an early myth of creation.

On the horizon, Angkhora appeared to levitate above the earth on a shimmering mirage of heat, although that was an illusion. Its profile was dominated by a quincunx of sandstone towers, ogival in shape like tightly furled buds of flowers. Stairs were a dominant feature; the city had no walls, only ziggurat steps that tiered the outer cruciform terraces. The design gave Angkhora a harmonious symmetry that seemed strangely inhuman in the precision of its arrangement.

Roth's insertion point was exactly eight kilometres out from Angkhora, the minimum distance in the event of signature detection. They made landfall on an apron of reef mangrove that sprawled out before Angkhora's monument gates. The region was a glistening plain of muddy water and bulbous, shallow-rooted hydrophytes.

Slogging under the weight of thirty kilograms of surveillance, survival and military equipment each, the trio waded through the shin-deep mangrove. Their weapons were cautiously shouldered as they advanced, scanning the surroundings for signs of enemy or natural predation. Madeline had warned them the primordial creatures that inhabited the low lands were small but they could be quick, darting out of mud burrows with snapping, lashing jaws.

Moving at a stealthy, wary creep, the task group reached the three-hundred-metre tall gates of Angkhora in just under four hours. They halted several times during the advance, allowing Pradal to make intermittent signal burps on his vox, broadcasting to low-frequency Imperial channels across the southern belt. There was a chance the frequencies had already been compromised, but it was a gambit Roth was willing to make. Yet they received no answer by the time they reached the monument gates.

Up close, Roth could see the narrative scenes etched into the stonework. Each dancing character – animal, flower or astronomical body

– was no bigger than Roth's thumb, yet the cavorting figures were carved across the entire surface of the gate pylons.

'These gates here, they depict the interment of the dead in their final resting place – the garden in the sky. Angkhora was never a place of domestic living, it was an extensive tomb-city,' Madeline said, reaching out to touch the stone with her gloved fingertips for protection. It was a Medinian superstition she had acquired in her studies.

'They built this place for the dead? All of it?' Roth asked.

'Yes they did, but that was a long time ago. For the past several centuries, the climate has become more habitable, temperatures here have lowered and a substantial part of this city had been converted to urban hab, mostly for the destitute, the poor, the ones less missed, so they lived here amongst the dead. The population for this city should be at least eight thousand,' she said but then checked herself. '*Should be...* eight thousand.'

'That's a bad omen,' Captain Pradal said, making the sign of the aquila before thrice tapping the stone with his knuckles. Cradling the lasrifle slung across his chest for comfort, his other hand resting on the bolt pistol at his thigh, he crossed the threshold into the dead city.

Within, the streets were a rambling maze. The flagstones were worn smooth by flood and silt deposits, and then baked into a cracked finish by the searing heat. Black run-off like dried tears ran down every surface of stone, what Roth could only imagine as being the evaporated essence of time itself. From what Roth had seen, ancient structures were often blackened through sheer dint of age.

Of the population of eight thousand, there was no sign.

'No life signs at all,' said Pradal, reading an auspex that was attached by a wire cord to his hip webbing. 'Not in proximity at least.'

'Signal-burp again,' Roth bade him.

'Sir, I've been transmitting on sustained long-range frequency for the better part of four hours, emitting contact to listening stations across the entire southern belt. If anything, we'll bring every Archenemy within the southern savannah on our tracks.'

'I know, captain, but we need this,' Roth said.

They went down into cover, moving towards a line of stone apartments. Whatever purpose the terraces served in the city of the dead, it had been converted to a tenement block. They entered one of the small habs, noting that all the apartments were missing their doors.

Inside, they could see signs of recent habitation. A stone pallet bed was unceremoniously upended, its thin mattress half-thrown across the apartment. Tables and lockers of a cheap mass-produced alloy were dented and ransacked, the meagre possessions strewn across the floor. If Roth's forensic reasoning was anything to go by, it seemed that the occupant had been dragged out of bed as they had slept.

'Sustained signal-burps, captain, keep them brief and clear,' Roth ordered.

The inquisitor moved to one of the low square windows cut into the thick sandstone. He surveyed the city quietly as the captain went about his work. The tightly coiled streets were empty and heavily shadowed by the ogival towers at their cardinal points above.

'So this is where the Old Kings sleep,' Roth whispered under his breath.

A giant, lurking within the deep folds of stone that formed the architecture of Angkhora, watched the three little humans.

It watched them with the same malevolent interest that a predator would regard its frail, cumbersome prey.

As the giant moved, the shadow of late afternoon rippled across its glossy hide. Where the sun shone, its hide was a hard black enamel, so glossy it was slick with a film of red. Like blood on the surface of black oil.

And how it moved! As overwhelming as the tide, it surged on plated limbs through the crumbling masonry. The brutal speed and controlled power with which it cut across the rooftops and streets was terrifying.

It could, if it chose to, warn the others of its kind. But the giant chose not to disturb them. It lived by the rhythm of killing and eating and it would be better not to share its prey.

Leaping from roof to roof with a simian lope, the giant paralleled the movements of its prey, constantly keeping them under its watchful eye.

According to the complex geometry of the equator lines and if their mathematics were anything to go by, the Old Kings of Medina would be buried in the central tomb complex, deep within the womb of Angkhora's central ziggurat.

'At least another twelve kilometres to our north-east unless we can find some way to circumvent these dead-end avenues and maze stair-wells,' Pradal said as he checked his auspex.

Referring to his map-sleeve, Roth traced the route with his finger. It was an imperfect map, an old piece they had acquired from Madeline's own scholarly collection. In the time since its making, the galleries and step-mazes of Angkhora had been subject to collapse. Even conservative estimates put them half a day's trek from the site.

Roth shrugged off his canvas bergen and rolled his neck, easing out the acidic knots along the muscles of his shoulders. 'Drink some water and grab some food while you can, we've got a long way to go yet.'

With a sigh of relief, Captain Pradal sunk down under the shade of a mausoleum and unlocked the strap of his webbing and equipment, keeping them within easy reach. He stretched out his leg and began to unwrap a block of compressed grain ration.

'We're being followed,' Madeline said, moving to join the others under the alcove of balustrades. She turned and played her carbine across the garlands of stone flowers that uniformly edged the pediment rooftops.

Roth looked up from his map and swore quietly under his breath. 'I thought so. I've known for some time but I didn't want to cause distress until someone else concurred.'

Roth looked across the silhouette of Angkhora. The city of the dead stared back at home, utterly quiet, refusing to give up its secrets. For the first time, Roth noticed that not even the leather-winged lizards roosted here, nor flocked to the skies.

'What do we do?' Madeline groaned, suddenly despairing.

'We wait,' Captain Pradal said confidently. 'Let's find a defensible position and bait him out.'

'Elementary bait ambush. What could go wrong?' Roth winked. With delicate care, Roth folded the map into its plastek sleeve and folded that into a side-pocket in his bergen.

'This will do,' Roth said.

The chosen site of their ambush was not ideal but it would suffice. It was a stair pillar, or rather that was what Roth called it; Madeline assured him they were called *gopurams* in the ancient Terran lanuage of Anglo. Its foundations were a rectangular slab of sandstone, likely more than some fifty tonnes. The structure tapered up, each stepped tier diminishing in size as they swept upwards, in acquiescence to the heavens. The song birds, chariots and horned animals that dancing along the bas-reliefs of each tier represented the sky gardens of the dead, a reminder that Angkhora was a cemetery for the past. Song birds and horned animals had not danced on Aridun for thousands of years.

'Whatever it is, it's coming closer,' Madeline whispered without turning to look.

Roth nodded softly. He too had seen a ghost of movement in his periphery, just a vast and very sudden shadow that was no longer there when he turned. Their hunter was getting careless – either that, or it was getting bolder.

'I've seen the hostile too, several times now,' Pradal said. He stopped plodding up the ziggurat and checked on the course of the suns. It would be dusk soon, one sun was already dipping along the horizon as an amber rind, another sun making a heliodonic arc over the first, turning the deepwater sky from blue to black. In Pradal's military training, dusk was the most opportune time to attack, when the mind was hard-wired to rest at the break of light.

'Don't look down, but I think it's slinking at the base of the ziggurat,' Madeline said, hurrying up the last few steps to the shrine at the top of the gopuram.

If what Madeline said was correct, it meant that the hostile was no longer tracking them; it was simply stalking them in the open. It meant the hostile had no need for stealth, perhaps even deliberately induced the fear of attack by flitting in and out of view. Roth gritted his teeth, resisted the temptation to look down the steps and followed Madeline.

'Pradal, cover the north, Madeline, cover the south, I'll take the east. The suns are coming down west so keep your backs to them,' Roth commanded.

The top of the gopuram was a flat square about twenty metres wide along each side. The three of them crouched down, back to back, their weapons pointed directly ahead. Their position afforded them a magnificent view of Angkhora; as the suns set, they chased the yawning shadows. The sunlight gleam of sunstone fading to a dim purple.

The hostile did not need to wait for dusk.

Roth heard steps, dulled and quietly menacing. The sound of grit and loose earth crunched underfoot.

'Here it comes, up the north face,' Pradal said, thumbing his lasrifle to its highest setting.

Roth spun on his coiled crouch to face the approach. He felt the familiar surge of adrenaline, building like a spring coil in his bladder.

The slow, deliberate steps sounded like war drums. The Tong cannibals of the Punic subcontinents used war drums to psychologically assault the enemy, Roth remembered. A deep, almost ritualistic rhythm that put the 'fears in the bellies of their foe'. Roth imagined it would be quite similar – he certainly felt the fears.

'Throne, I hate this, I hate this,' Madeline hissed under her breath.

The steps stopped.

Pradal slid a frag grenade from his belt loop, tensing to hook the pin with his thumb and throw one-handed.

Vandus Barq surfaced over the edge of the ziggurat. He looked a mess. His armoured rig was blackened with ash and his face was marred with speckled bruising. In his steel-gloved hands, he clutched a vox-signaller, the tracking array guiding him up.

'Roth! You bastard! When I snagged those vox transmissions I knew it was you.' The inquisitor was trembling, quaking.

Roth rose to his feet and placed a hand on one of Barq's heavy shoulder guards. 'Look at you, Vandus. Calm down, you look a mess.'

Barq shrugged off Roth's hand, his shaking head. 'Not now, not now. You're being hunted.'

'Hunted? By whom?' Captain Pradal said, still aiming his rifle along the northern edge.

'I said not now!' Inquisitor Barq snapped, almost irritably.

Barq's breathing was irregular and laboured; a nervous tic was seizing the entire left side of his face. Roth recognised the latent stage of shock when he saw it. Something was terrifying an Imperial inquisitor, terrifying him enough to send an inquisitor's formidable mental faculties into neural overload. The fear in his belly, as the Tong cannibals would have said.

'Barq, you have to explain what is happening. Intelligence before action, the first principle of the Inquisition. Come on now, old friend, breathe, breathe,' Roth said.

'Roth. I'm coherent,' Barq jagged through gritted teeth. 'I've got a vehicle waiting in the causeway. We have to get out of this region, you don't understand. We have to go – if the vehicle is still there.'

Roth was reluctant. Travelling at night in the dead city did not appeal to his sensibilities. He looked at the horizon; the suns were sinking into hazy crescents and tinting the city a murky purple.

But then he saw it again. The silhouette of a giant, rising across the rooftops. It was backlit by the twilight, like a shadow puppet. It was there and then it wasn't.

This time they all saw it. Madeline exhaled sharply.

Roth made up his mind. 'Okay, Vandus, show us to your vehicle.'

Quickly, before night falls, Roth thought to himself silently.

Barq's vehicle, thankfully, remained where he left it, underneath the lengthening shadows of a lotus shrine.

It was a V-8 Centaur, a small military tractor. Its square-framed, boxy hull was painted in the russet-brown of the Cantican Colonials. The rearing horse, sabre and cog crest of the CantiCol Sixth Logistics and Supply dominated the welded frontal plates.

Clambering into the Centaur's open-topped cab, the Task Group nested amongst the neatly stacked rows of ammunition and the disassembled parts of a 75mm mortar.

Barq snuggled down into the operator's seat, hunching his shoulders so he could lean forwards and peer through the narrow, visored vision slit.

'Are you fit to drive?' Roth asked.

'Oh please…'

Barq fumbled at the ignition. Finally, with a guttering metallic chain rip, the Centaur coughed into shuddering wakefulness. The Centaur rolled forwards, picking up speed, little by little.

It wasn't fast enough.

The stalker exploded from the shadows. He was enormous. From the plated pillars of his legs to the towering turret of his torso, he throbbed with primal power. His armour was of the deepest red, so red it was almost black. In metal-shod hands he swung a double-handed chainsword, the venting pipes at the hilt grumbling with exhaust.

Captain Pradal screamed. It was the first time Roth had heard a trained soldier scream with such fervent, almost plaintive panic. It was a horrifying sound and Roth did not ever wish to experience the organic fear again. He looked to see what Pradal saw and froze.

It was an Astartes of the Chaos Legions.

'Blood Gorgon!' Barq roared, without turning to look. He gunned the Centaur, taking its engine to protesting limits.

Roth was the first to react. He leaned over the edge of the vehicle and let loose a plasma shot. The Traitor Marine took the hit on the tower of his shoulder plate, before accelerating fast towards them. It was so explosive, like the gliding footwork of a champion fist-fencer, utterly in control of his body, thought Roth. Except this monster weighed half a tonne.

'Throne's sake, come to your senses!' Roth bellowed at Madeline and Pradal. His shouts seemed to rouse them from their paralysis of shock. Captain Pradal, still screaming in wide-eyed panic, began to hose his weapon in a rearward direction on full auto. Madeline fired her carbine double-handed; the first torrent of shrapnel went wide as their vehicle thumped over a loose flagstone. The second expanding coil of splintered metal hit the Blood Gorgon across the thick slab of his chest. It barely arrested his sprint.

The Blood Gorgon closed the distance. How fast were they going? Perhaps forty kilometres an hour? And still the Traitor Marine was gaining on them, pumping his armoured legs with seismic force, blading his arms as he closed in. Like the pirahnagator, he was utterly explosive in a single direction.

'Turn! Keep jinking!' Roth called to Barq.

The Centaur peeled off from the causeway down a walled viaduct. The evasive manoeuvre left the Blood Gorgon careening away, albeit briefly, at a perpendicular direction.

A plasma shot ate a broken, calcified puncture in the Blood Gorgon's upper thigh sheathing. Las-rounds bubbled the waxy enamel of his ceramite. Flechette shells puffed like smoke against his hide. The Blood Gorgon pounded down on them, undaunted.

Barq turned them down a broad boulevard, ornate headstones flanking the avenue like cathedral pews. It was difficult to navigate in the dark, the headlamps bobbing and shaking, revealing only a blurred path of illuminated ground that streaked by beneath them. Roth didn't know if Barq knew where they were going.

The Blood Gorgon was close enough that one of his enormous, armour-clad gauntlets could almost graze the tow bar of their Centaur. Close enough that Roth could see the Traitor Marine's face plate, snouted and equine with flared nostrils and a shrieking mouth grille.

In his desperation, Roth seized one of the mortar rounds from the stack. He banged the percussion cap against the plating of the Centaur and lobbed it overhand from the back of the vehicle. The round clattered, bounced and skipped against the cloven boots of the Traitor Marine and exploded.

The Blood Gorgon actually staggered, briefly. He growled through the bassinet grille of his helmet. The sound amplified through his chest speakers, wet and tremulous.

'Mortars, use the mortars!' Roth yelled to his team. They didn't need his coercion. Both of them were hurling mortar rounds at the Blood Gorgon with a reckless desperation. A chain of explosions crackled in the wake of the Centaur, blowing fragments of stone from the road. They aimed the mortars low, banging them against the vehicle plating and skipping them at the Blood Gorgon's legs.

By the time Vandus careened the vehicle down Angkhora's gate causeway, the pillars of the Blood Gorgon's legs were blackened and scorched. Fluid sprayed from fissures in the ceramite with each thundering step, either blood or machine fluid.

'Keep him off us, this is going to be a tight stretch!' Barq shouted from up front. Roth turned to see for himself and swore. The causeway was a broad and unbroken ribbon that snaked down two kilometres. There was nowhere to turn.

The Blood Gorgon caught them. He closed the distance with one last sprint and then leapt into the air with monumental effort. He swung the double-handed chainsword down in an executioner's arc and took the entire rear plating off the Centaur in one crumpled sheet. Without pause, his next strike, a horizontal backhand, sheared the roll-cage off the Centaur with a rending shriek of metal and buzzing chain teeth, throwing out a fan of orange sparks.

Roth rolled backwards and kicked away lamely. The Blood Gorgon punched at Roth, a downwards hammer-fist. Roth managed to shrimp away from the ceramite fist as it bashed a crater into cab decking.

Roth would never forget what happened next. He would owe his life to it.

Captain Pradal rose before the Traitor Marine. He stood between Roth and the towering, armoured giant. The junior officer drew the bolt pistol and fired, two shots, point-blank into the Blood Gorgon's helmet. The grille dented and warped under the impact of the shots. The force was enough to whip the Marine's head backwards.

The staggering giant lurched, turning his head away. A gauntlet swung out, seizing the captain's head between the vice of his segmented digits. Pradal didn't even scream as the Blood Gorgon squeezed with iron-grinding strength. The good captain died without a word.

Pradal's blood washed over Roth in a blinding mist of red.

Roth knew he had perhaps one heartbeat, perhaps two, before the opening was gone. The inquisitor stopped thinking – thinking would slow him down. He drove himself forwards and threw the single most important punch of his life, a lunging, overhand right. His Tang War power fist impacted into the Blood Gorgon's sternum, at the point where the buttressing cables of his abdomen met the ceramite of his lower pectoral slabs.

There was a snap of negatively charged atoms colliding as Roth drove his fist into the giant's chest. The Blood Gorgon roared. The decibels actually blew out his chest speakers. Roth doubted he would ever have full hearing in his right ear again. The power fist splintered the fused calcium growth of the giant's ribcage and parted dense cables of muscle. It wouldn't be enough to kill him.

Roth drove his glove upwards, sharply and to the right. He ruptured the Blood Gorgon's secondary heart before spearing for the primary.

Finally, with a tectonic shudder, the Blood Gorgon died. He slid like an avalanche off the gaping rear of the Centaur.

Roth sagged to his knees, blinking the blood back from his eyes. It was getting into his nose, his mouth, sinking into his teeth. None of it was his own. As the V-8 Centaur pulled out of the final stretch of causeway from Angkhora, Roth keeled over onto his side, completely and utterly spent.

CHAPTER TWENTY-FOUR

'The Archenemy knew. They knew all along. They were just waiting for their time,' Inquisitor Barq murmured listlessly.

'They tricked us then. They outplayed us,' Roth agreed, staring vacantly into the distance.

They sat on a mesa, sixty kilometres north of Aridun Civic. Far enough from the savannah and deep enough into the wasteland to be surrounded on all sides by undulating dust plains. It was early dawn, and the sands gleamed a bone-polished ivory, the ridgelines ribbed by morning shadow. The V-8 Centaur, or rather the mangled remains of it, was parked some metres away, empty of fuel. They had ridden the vehicle as far it would go, as far as it would carry them from the southern belt. The body of Captain Pradal lay close by covered in a plastek sheet, his arms folded over his chest and rifle.

'Tell me,' Roth began. 'Tell me again, how this came to be.'

Barq flexed his fists and closed his eyes, as if shutting out memories he didn't want to relive. 'Five days. Five days ago, they hit Aridun. Damn, were they good. They took out the communications first, took out the listening stations, comms towers, broadcast ports. Everything. Completely shut this place down.'

Roth scooped up another handful of sand and rubbed it into the dried blood on his armour, scouring away the red-tinged flecks. 'Then the Guard?'

'Yes. Without communications, isolated garrisons can't muster much defence.'

'Then the southern belt?'

'Yes. Before cleaning up what isolated settlements lay outside the savannah region,' Barq said, irritably. They were all feeling volatile. Roth felt the same way, the urge to curl up and sleep, and never to wake up, was overwhelming.

'One company of Traitor Legionaries, you say?' Roth pressed again.

'In my opinion, at least one company, no more than two. Any more than two hundred Space Marines and there wouldn't have been much of Aridun left.'

It was evident in retrospect. It was always evident in retrospect. The Archenemy had been meticulous in planning. They had seized Medina, one planet after another, preparing to wake the Old Kings, staying one step ahead of the Imperial resistance. Meanwhile, they had gathered mounting forces on Aridun, beyond the demarcation line, waiting. Lulling High Command, drawing resources away from Aridun onto other war fronts. Waiting until the alignments of the planets were true and proper before dispensing the Traitors to cleanse the entire inhabitable stretch of Aridun.

'Is everyone dead?' Roth hazarded to ask.

'Some fled into the wastelands, but without water, I doubt they would have lasted long. For those who do, I have no doubt that they'll run into Ironclad land forces coming across the subcontinent.'

'That's very bad indeed,' Roth said. It was quite the understatement.

Barq opened his eyes and levelled his gaze at Roth. 'It was nice of you to come back for me. It's good to know that my friends do not think I'm trying to kill them any more.'

Roth looked away, suddenly aware of his friend's inference. 'I'm sorry, Vandus. I had no choice.'

'I'll beat you thoroughly when this is all over,' Barq said, breaking into a slight smile.

Roth opened his arms and chortled softly. 'Vandus, if this is ever over, I'll gladly give you a free shot. You'll need the handicap if we spar again.'

'What do we do now?' Madeline said suddenly. They were the first words she had spoken for several hours. Since she had seen Pradal killed.

'As strange as it may sound, by the God-Emperor's providence, we are fortunate,' Roth announced confidently.

Madeline and Barq both looked at him as if he had gone entirely insane.

'I will contact Gurion by vox, and request the immediate deployment of standby forces from the Ninth Route Fleet. Our first priority is to reclaim Angkhora from the Blood Gorgons, before the Ironclad can consolidate their grip on the region.'

'How do you know the Archenemy do not have the Old Kings in their possession already?' Madeline asked.

'My dear,' Roth began, 'do you think any of us would still be alive if they did?'

The Ironclad on Aridun were mobilising. Across the Punic subcontinent, two thousand kilometres across the fossil plains, the armoured and motorised columns of the Archenemy trawled across the desert. Beyond the Cage Isles, a fleet of iron submersibles and propeller-driven barges set sail across the saline channels. From the furthest salt flats of west Aridun, to the endorheic basins in the continental tip, the Ironclad emerged from hiding, converging on the Fortress Chains.

Four figures, small and inconsequential, watched the mobilisation from the crest of a sand dune. The bone dust clung to their shaggy reed camouflage in powdery white. They looked to be nothing more than a bank of mossy taproot.

'We're moving out with them,' Silverstein declared.

'What, with them?' Temughan asked, pointing into the horizon with a dirty finger. Before them, the Ironclad were deploying in force. There was no need for camouflage netting or concealment any more. Even if they did, it would not have concealed the thousands of vehicles amassing on the continental sand sheets. Bone dust rose in solid, expanding walls.

'Surely not,' Asingh-nu echoed.

'It would not be possible, we'd all be killed,' Apartan argued. 'How would we even follow their advance across the salt pans?'

'Come on, men, where is your sense of adventure? The calling of Imperial endeavour? Plains to be conquered, worlds to be liberated,' grinned Silverstein half-jokingly.

The huntsman shimmied back on his stomach, away from the ridgeline, before rising to his feet. He noticed his boots were dirty, and he remembered he had not taken them off since leaving the *Carthage* for Cantica, all those months ago. How long had it been? Silverstein couldn't remember.

He crossed over to his quad-bike. The bare metal had been baking under the suns and was hot to the touch. Silverstein secured the jerry cans of fuel and water on the saddle-pouches, checking the locking straps for friction. The bullpup autogun he had liberated from the Ironclad Naik was buttoned down, running parallel to the bike's rear chain and sprocket for quick access. Silverstein hadn't stolen the bullpup at all; the weapon still bore the Munitorum script and serial of a Bastion Ward regiment weapon. Silverstein was simply returning the weapon to the Imperium.

Silverstein smoothed out his cloak of desert taproots and tied it over his head. 'In all seriousness, gentlemen, the Ironclad are on the move.

We can hide, but there will soon be nowhere to go. Have you thought about that?'

Apartan plodded through the bone dust and tugged the netting of xerophyte moss and tangle root from his bike. He too secured the camo shawl over his shoulders. 'If the Archenemy are getting ready for a fight, I don't want to miss it.'

Temughan and Asingh-nu crossed over to join them with some trepidation.

'If we must,' they chorused.

Silverstein laughed. 'Follow my lead. We'll make it fun, like tracking big game. Really big game.'

The call to deployment reached Gurion by long-range vox just minutes before his arrest.

Lord Gurion placed down the vox horn as the door to his stateroom was breached by provost marshals. Six provosts stormed into Gurion's room, racking shotguns and barking at him. Following them at an unhurried pace was Lord Marshal Khmer, a cape thrown casually over one shoulder. At his heels came a trio of black-coated political commissars, clutching sheaves of edict warrants.

Gurion simply raised his hands.

'Lord marshal, you've come for me, I see?' Gurion said.

'We'll be asking the questions now, inquisitor,' Khmer sniffed haughtily.

'Oh I see. Can we do this after we deploy the forces onto Aridun? I have just received word from my Task Force that the situation has become most dire.'

'No. Gurion, never. You are under arrest by power of military law,' Khmer said. He clicked his fingers at a waiting commissar. The political officer clopped one step forwards with his polished jackboots and read from the warrant in his hands.

'Inquisitor Forde Gurion. You are hereby charged with conspiracy to impede sound military strategy. Until your date of hearing, you are to be confined to the brig with temporary suspension of any and all powers. By written rule of Section 22 of the 599 Military Charter.'

'I'm an inquisitor,' laughed Gurion. 'Your military laws do not apply to me.'

Khmer smiled. 'That may or may not be true. It will be up to a council of sufficient authority to decide. Until then, you are to be confined for your own good, and the good of the Medina Campaign. I'm terribly sorry, but you will not be able to use your Imperial authority to deploy any of my troops until this matter is cleared.'

'Well played, Khmer,' said Gurion, nodding slowly.

The lord marshal dipped his head. 'I am mobilising all resources to transit for the Bastion Stars as we speak. When and *if* this matter is decided by council, then you can feel free to pull my troops back from the Bastion and return here to Medina, in your own time.'

Gurion drummed his mechanical hand on his desk impatiently. 'Are you finished, lord marshal?'

Khmer narrowed his eyes warily. The change in Gurion's tone foreshadowed something else. Suddenly, the half-dozen provosts he had brought with him didn't seem quite enough.

Gurion rose from his seat. 'You don't challenge me, Khmer. That is your flaw. I had long predicted you would try something like this. But it doesn't really matter.'

In the corridor outside the stateroom, there was the sound of a scuffle – harsh, angry voices followed by the muffled grunts of men. There was a smacking sound and the thump of something hitting the carpet.

Khmer suddenly looked uncomfortable. He wasn't sneering any more.

'Don't mind them. Those are just Inquisitorial stormtroopers overpowering the provost marshals you posted outside. Don't worry, my men are very well trained and wouldn't hurt yours unnecessarily.'

'Is this a mutiny?' Khmer snorted.

'Of course not. It's a denouement.' Gurion pointed at the lord marshal with his mechanical hand. 'Varuda Khmer. I have evidence beyond doubt that you have used your rank and authority in the perversion of Inquisitorial duties.'

The provosts and commissars in the stateroom edged away from the lord marshal. The uncertainty slackened their faces. Shotguns aimed at Gurion listed slowly towards the floor.

'You infiltrated my Conclave with a compromised inquisitor. Whether you blackmailed her or what you offered her is beyond my care. You have tried several times to murder my staff. I've had enough, Khmer. The campaign will be better off without you.'

The lord marshal began to back towards the door. 'We will see what the council has to say after they've heard your evidence.'

'I don't need anyone to hear my evidence. I am the Inquisition. The only reason I kept you alive was because I did not want to needlessly kill a veteran officer in the middle of war. I kept you alive, Khmer, remember that.'

The lord marshal snatched for the Lugos autopistol at his belt.

But Gurion was already armed. The brass tip of his index finger – the finger pointed squarely at Khmer the whole time – hinged upwards. A monofilament thread shot out and penetrated his chest, barely disturbing the fibres of Khmer's jacket. The monofilament uncoiled inside the lord marshal's ribcage. Massive internal bleeding and trauma to his internal organs sent him down immediately. Lord Marshal Khmer fell onto his face and never moved again. With a flick, the monofilament fibre retracted, leaving a pin-prick wound that resealed airtight. Not a drop of blood was spilled.

'Put down your guns,' Gurion said to the provosts. The men hurled their shotguns down obediently.

'Khmer is done. Temporary authority of the 9th Route fleet is ceded to me. Does that conflict with military law, commissars?'

The political officers shook their heads. 'No, sir, it does not.'

'Good. In that case, give order for the chief of staff to mobilise and deploy to Aridun, according to the contingency plan. Don't stand there nodding, go!' shouted Gurion.

The commissars clicked their heels sharply, saluted and ushered each other from Gurion's stateroom.

CHAPTER TWENTY-FIVE

The Last War began six days after the helical-lunar cycle. When the fringe world of Naga aligned precisely with the equator of Baybel, and the helio-lines of the core worlds drew a straight plane across the Medina Corridor.

All Imperial military power in the system was committed. Every last fighting man.

A quick-reaction force of one hundred and twenty thousand Cantican Colonials on standby in orbit above Aridun was immediately deployed. Lord General Faisal, operations commander, wrote, 'In the event of a full-scale defensive, Angkhora would be the target for this war of attrition but holding the Fortress Chain would be the key to victory.'

In the days preceding the reactional deployment, a further sixteen divisions of CantiCol Guardsmen hurtled down from the sky in a storm of troop carriers, braving the lashing storm of aerial defence across the Fortress Chains. Artillery, cavalry and, above all, infantry landed in masses. The Hasdrubel Fifth, heavy infantry from the neighbouring Seleucid subsector and elements of the famed Aegina Prestige regiment were committed to the Last War. Four hundred and sixty thousand men, all told.

The company of Traitor Marines holding Angkhora was dislodged only after a relentless campaign of aerial superiority. Imperial Marauder bombers of the Ninth Route Fleet strafed the dead city, pounding the prehistoric structures with kilotonnes of incendiary explosives. Even then, it took the combined strength of the standby reaction force to besiege and

257

reclaim Angkhora and the site of the Old Kings. Casualties, even during the formative stages of the war, were very high.

Imperial scholars would later attribute the initial deployment of the Last War to air superiority; air superiority provided by the Ninth Route Fleet that the Archenemy did not have. Without it, the landing forces could not have been inserted directly onto the Fortress Chain. They could not have threatened the Traitor Marines with ground forces alone. Certainly, they could not have consolidated their position in the face of Ironclad deca-legions advancing across the subcontinent.

It was the greatest providence of the God-Emperor. Lord General Faisal highly commended the work of Inquisitor Obodiah Roth, Inquisitor Vandus Barq and Professor Madeline de Medici for the intelligence, which facilitated the Imperial deployment to Aridun before the Fortress Chains could be consolidated by Ironclad forces manoeuvring inland. Inquisitor Felyce Celeminé was posthumously awarded the High Lords' Order of Gallantry for her work and remembered for her death at the hands of the Archenemy, so that others could live.

Orbital reconnaissance from above Aridun revealed the advancing thrust of the Ironclad legions. Scouting elements sent to probe against the advancing enemy returned in terrified states. The Archenemy numbered, even by conservative estimates, in the region of perhaps seven million tanks, fighting vehicles and marching legions. Imperial Marauders sallied forth to harass their advance. Pilots remarked it was like dropping stones into water. There was no effect on the tide.

It took High Command some time to realise that the Archenemy was in no hurry to consolidate the Fortress Chains or the Old Kings. It made no difference to them whether the Imperial armies dislodged the Blood Gorgons to claim the city of the dead... They had no strategic need for time. The Archenemy, since the Medina Campaign, had fought a slow, methodical war, preparing the trap and closing it like a steady vice. Seven million Archenemy did not hasten.

General, commander of Fifth Division made the most resounding quote of the war. He remarked that, 'They were dead men, dead men defending dead things.'

At 04:57, three days after the Imperial deployment and nine days of the lunar cycle, the Ironclad rose within view of the southern savannah. The banners of Chaos thrashed in the hot wind, the legions marched, the crash of their boots like a sonorous, continuous scarp of thunder. They pounded war drums, sounded braying, plaintive war horns. Columns of armour advanced in the fore, winding like rivers of glistening steel.

The Guard had known the numbers of the enemy, but they had not been prepared for the sight of them. They flooded the open plains. Artillery observers from the upper tiers of the cities reported that the thousand kilometre reefs surrounding the chain had been churned into a marsh of smeared mud in their wake. On the ramparts, Guardsmen penned their last thoughts to paper and cast them into the wind. They hoped the Emperor's cherubs would deliver their prayers to their loved ones. It was even reported, though unconfirmed, that there were incidences of Guardsmen throwing themselves off the city walls at the sight of the advancing Chaos legions.

Thirteen minutes past the hour of five, batteries of the 11th Colonial Artillery fired the first shell. The Ironclad exchanged siege fire from advancing tank columns. Sabot shells pounded the city-chains with colossal plumes of dust.

These shots heralded the Last War.

'Sir, the Old Kings are interred deeply, of that there is no doubt.'

The man who spoke was a Cantican corporal, his brown felt jacket matted with salt and grit dust. He leaned heavily on a shovel, panting, sweat plastering his hair in greasy whorls across his forehead. The pale blue rank sash denoted him as a corporal of the Cantican First Combat Engineers, but until the excavations were complete, he was relegated to shovel digger.

'I propose that we utilise the explosives, at least until we break the silt layers,' Roth said. He shielded his eyes from the sun with his hand and cast an appraising eye over the excavation site.

'Heavens no! No more demolitions,' Madeline called as she climbed over a loose mound of dug-up shale. 'It's too much to risk triggering something unexpected. From now on, manual digging only.'

Roth shrugged reluctantly. 'You heard the lady. No demo, corporal.'

The Guardsman breathed heavily, shouldered his shovel and ran back down the excavation slope, barking out commands.

The dormant site of the Old Kings, as calculated, rested in the centre of Angkhora, exactly ninety degrees from either hemisphere and at balanced angles with the three suns, and with the Medinian moon at the zenith of the lunar cycle.

Unfortunately, that had placed the site directly underneath a tomb stack in the eastern quarter of the city. It was a vaulted, multi-segmented mausoleum of carved stone sixty metres high, its slightly sloping walls resembling a lotus bud with six hundred thousand tightly coiled petals. Each petal was an individual tomb wreathed with bas-reliefs depicting the character and deed of the deceased within.

In the words of Madeline, it made for a 'delicate endeavour'. Military engineers cratered an opening at the base of the tomb stack, a dry, jagged wound in the ground that led into a steep artificial canyon. Controlled demolitions and pneumatic drills had shattered through eight stratum of sediment, limestone, shale and mineral.

'We just need more time to extract the ironstone layers,' Madeline said.

'If it were so simple to excavate, then even the Traitor Marines would have completed the task already.'

The layers she referred to were the hard seams of clay and iron ore deposit that had collected during many tumultuous climatic changes. The ironstone formed a porous lattice of dense, rust-red stone. Iron ore was not easily broken by pneumatic drills.

'Time is something we do not have at the moment,' Roth replied. To punctuate his words, the sky throbbed with the pyrotechnic light of nearby explosions. The crump of shelling could be heard seconds later, low and ominous.

'The Archenemy are pounding at the gates of Angkhora,' Roth said. 'Thirty minutes ago, the eastern wall district was lost. The 22nd Battalion were routed, and the 9th suffered forty per cent casualties by last report. The enemy are no more than sixteen kilometres from this very point.'

Madeline rubbed her temples. 'I know what I'm doing, Roth. Four or five days. Give me that and I'll have reached the Old Kings.' She paused as another crackle of shelling flooded out all sound before resuming. 'I've never been wrong in all my academic career.'

Just then, an aide wearing the rank sash of lieutenant appeared at the rim of the crater. He had come by horse. Judging by the grit on his cheeks and the scorched, blackened muzzle of his lasrifle, he had just ridden from the front lines.

'Inquisitor, sir, your counsel is requested by the lord general,' the junior officer gasped, struggling to rein in his horse as it pawed at the flak board laid out around the excavation site. In his other hand, the officer led a riderless steed, saddled and ready for Roth.

Roth nodded and turned, his obsidian tabard winking with a sharp snap of his heels. Before climbing up the shale slope, Roth turned back to Madeline.

'I don't know if you have four or five days. The Archenemy is already in amongst us, street to street, house to house.'

'Five days or nothing, Roth,' Madeline called after him.

The first eight hours of fighting were the worst. The white, searing sky of morning could not be seen under the pall of smoke that hung like swollen storm clouds over the southern belt. Throbbing outbursts of fire raged along the Fortress Chains. Manes of flame licked along the connective ramparts and swirled into the urban strongholds. The shockwave of shells that shook the ground became incessant.

Most of the cities along the chain lacked truly defensive walls. The fortifications had been built for an era when war was made with lance and mace, and the walls had since then crumbled into worn stubs of bas-relief and historic friezes. The vast ocean of Archenemy hit them like a tide, crashing into the boundary walls, spilling onto the causeways, saturating the arterial streets. The Ironclad foot-soldiers did not, at first, use their firearms. They came in a seething horde brandishing the brutally pugnacious instruments of close combat, the implements of the raider. They clambered over the low walls, face first into the firepower of CantiCol defence lines, seven million voices thrumming as one.

Within minutes, the frontline battalions were pushed back by the sheer magnitude of the Archenemy offensive. The CantiCol's close order drill collapsed as punctures opened up across the lines defending the major causeways and connective ramparts. Cantican field officers withdrew from the outlying districts, turtling their forces into civilian housing or anywhere with cover.

The initial trauma of assault was demoralising for the Guard. Despite the tactical firing lanes set up along the causeways, the defensive bottlenecks along the outer perimeters, the overlapping firing arcs, gun nests and wire cordons, despite every tactical advantage, they were swept aside. Across the Fortress Chain, entire brigade positions were perforated and dismantled by the spearing advance of Ironclad. Companies and platoons became isolated and encircled. H Company of the 46th CantiCol Battalion took shelter in a textiles mill on the outer districts of Chindar City. Cut off and besieged, the company held out for almost an hour before they ran dry of ammunition. Their bodies were chained and dragged through the streets by Ironclad FPVs. Several kilometres east, in the chain city of Barcid, a platoon of CantiCol led by an inexperienced lieutenant actually tried to surrender as their temple was overrun. The captive platoon was marched within view of the 19th Battalion, holding a static defence across the eastern Barcid viaduct. In view of their comrades, each man in the platoon was strangled by an Ironclad Elteber, by hand, until dead. Their bodies were rolled unceremoniously into the canal.

By the sixth hour of fighting, there was very little semblance of a war front. The Archenemy were out-manoeuvring the beleaguered Imperial positions. Units were constantly ordered to withdraw in order to protect their rear-line artillery and command positions.

In the roiling mass of street fighting, Imperial Navy aircraft were unable to pin-point enemy targets. The Archenemy pressed hard, fighting in and around the Imperial defences. It was a tactic that the Imperial High Command coined 'hugging' and it robbed them of their one advantage in air superiority. Marauder bombers were relegated to strafing runs of the rear Archenemy lines, bridging the role of mobile artillery.

Angkhora, the resting place of the Old Kings and the concentration of the heaviest fighting, was the most firmly held. The plazial causeway from Angkhora's monument gates was heavily contested; its stone-slabbed thoroughfare would allow the conveyance of Ironclad heavy-tracked vehicles into the city, five abreast. The Imperial Command could not allow that.

Colonel Isa Batam had been given charge of holding the central causeway, an assignment he considered a forlorn hope. He nestled his men down behind the animal statues that flanked the overpass, creating a firing lane bristling with cannons, rockets and serried ranks of las. They had waited as the constant stream of vox reports crackled over their comms channel, relaying the enemy advance as they broke through the struggling defences of the outlying Angkhora region. The muffled screams and stilted report of gunfire washed with static unnerved his men. They chewed tabac to relieve the tension – jaws set, eyes wide, breathing hard through their nostrils.

The advance of the Ironclad was pre-announced by the vox-broadcast death screams of the commanding officer assigned to the defences of a neighbouring district to Batam's direct east. The Ironclad burst through the ceremonial gates, a full deca-legion of foot-soldiers in a sweeping phalanx of ten thousand. Batam had exactly six hundred and ninety men under his command.

Although the approach was heavily mined, the advance of the Ironclad was undeterred, unhurried, marching to the rhythm of a sonorous war drum. At the front of the column, an Ironclad Naik brandished the paper lanterns of Khorsabad Maw.

His men fired shots. Batam almost wondered if the Archenemy realised they were there, and if they did, whether they even cared.

But care they did. The Archenemy broke ranks, surging apart to assail Batam's flanking positions. Threads of las-fire connected his thin lines of Guardsmen to the swell of Archenemy fighters. They managed three seconds of unopposed fire before the Ironclad swarmed over their positions.

An Ironclad trooper wearing a wedged breastplate leapt over the hippocampus statue that Batam had crouched behind, slashing the air with a palm razor. Batam plunged his spike bayonet into the Ironclad's hip, at the seam where his breastplate met the fauld petals. The spearing strike arrested the Ironclad's airborne momentum, jarring Batam's shoulder sockets. Batam fired a burst of las into the Archenemy, point-blank, and stomped him off the end of his rifle.

'Hold now, die where you stand!' the colonel shouted. He looked around at the heaving scrum of flashing blades and desperate bodies. One of his company captains, Siem, appeared by his shoulder, draining his clip on auto.

'Sir, I think it's time. We're doing less than we expected,' Siem shouted above the clash.

It was indeed time. Colonel Batam could see the twin pylons of the Angkhora gate, about a kilometre down the causeway. The monolithic tines were wreathed in gunsmoke, solid and unaffected by the carnage below. Captain Siem was right. They could not hope to hold the causeway. As a pillar of Guard doctrine, when position becomes untenable, deny all strategic utility for the enemy.

'Trigger the charges, captain. Damn it, man!' Batam called. The colonel turned and realised the captain was already dead, his jostling corpse held upright by the press of bodies. A razor slashed at Batam's head and the colonel ducked under. The blade took his right ear and part of his scalp clean off. Batam, clutching the bleeding ruin of his head, fumbled for the wired detonator around his belt webbing. He grabbed it and frantically scrunched the charge receiver with his palm.

Demolition charges secured around the base of the gates blew out in an expanding ring of smoke and fragments. The three hundred metre tall pylons buckled and began to topple with ponderous speed. Thousands of tonnes of carved stone – with the cavorting animals that revered the dead – came crashing down onto the causeway. The avalanche tremors could be felt by the men fighting at the furthest chain cities, even above the shock of shelling. Six thousand tonnes of limestone falling from a height of several hundred metres was a sound one did not hear often.

Colonel Batam and all his men died instantly. The central Angkhoran causeway was reduced to a broke back ridge of rubble. Dust debris thrown up by the force of collision continued to rain back down in a deluge for many minutes after. Across the Fortress Chain, the fighting resumed unabated as if nothing of great significance had occurred at all.

Inquisitor Roth rode to Joint Command as fast as he dared to press his horse.

In an unassuming crypt, vaulted in one of the oldest burial districts of central Angkhora, Lord General Murat Faisal presided over the Last War. Incidentally, the crypt was also the family tomb of Aridun's first post-Reclamation Governor. Roth thought it was a poetically fitting place to orchestrate the Last War.

The war room was much more orderly than Roth had expected. General Faisal had dismissed most of the staff aides, junior officers and non-essential personnel from clogging the dark confines of the crypt. Bays of vox and communications equipment surrounded the circular, vaulted chamber. In the centre of the tomb, the stone coffin of First Governor Faribault had been converted into a makeshift chart table. Amid a hunched ring of staff chiefs, General Faisal received incoming reports of the collapsing front with a level stoicism.

Faisal was a native Cantican by birth, with fierce angular features mantled by dark wing-like eyebrows and skin the colour of sand-blasted wood. He wore a lengthy ceremonial coat of brown Cantican felt with simple, hand-painted shoes of cerulean silk that gave way to leather bindings up his calves. His ivory rank sash, wound around his waist and diagonally across his shoulder, denoted the deeds of his ancestors, and his long martial bloodline. Roth knew little of his reputation except that he was a fastidious, efficient yet altogether uninspiring commander.

Having known that, anything was better than his predecessor Khmer.

'I was requested, lord general,' Roth said, bowing slightly but making no military salute. Although he had not meant to, Roth's mind could read Faisal's red-hot panic beneath his facial wall of weary calm. He noticed that Faisal's top collar buttons were popped open, and his laspistol sat loosely in an unbuttoned holster.

'Inquisitor, what news of the Old Kings?' Faisal asked. The terminology, or rather the acknowledgement of the relics, coming from the mouth of a high-ranking commander seemed awkward, like his tongue was reluctant.

'We have located them but it will be some time before we can excavate to the required depths.'

'The entire western flank of the Fortress Chain is collapsing. We lost contact with Fifth Division Command in the city of Argentum. Gone. Overall casualty reports estimate anywhere between sixty thousand to one hundred thousand in losses.'

Faisal let his report hang in the stale tomb air.

'Sir, are you… attributing such losses to the Conclave?' Roth tested.

'Should I be?' Faisal asked wearily. 'I don't truly blame you inquisitor, rationally I shouldn't. But it's hard to send these men to their deaths. Show me something of substance, inquisitor.'

'Angkhora is of substance. We need five days, lord general.'

'And what of the Old Kings? What will you do once you have them?'

'If circumstances allow, we will ferry them off-world. Hell, sir, I'll eat them with a knife and fork if I have to, as long as the Archenemy does not reach them.'

Faisal nodded sagely, concentrating on the map before him. 'How do you propose my armies bide the time required?'

Roth crossed over to the map of southern Aridun. It was a good map, military-grade, with precise grid referencing and good aerial outlay. Tapping the eastern-most tip of the Fortress Chain, Roth indicated to the city of Bacaw. 'Start a fighting withdrawal from here, contract our defensive lines,' Roth traced the Fortress Chain down with his finger towards the middle, 'and concentrate our defences on Angkhora.'

'I agree, sir,' said Major General Ashwan. 'Our only hope of defending Angkhora is if we initiate a fighting withdrawal. We can't hold a four-hundred kilometre stretch of city. Ours lines are too thin. We have some sectors where one or two kilometre stretches are being held by a single platoon and one support weapon.'

'If we withdraw ourselves to Angkhora,' Faisal mused, 'then we have nowhere left to turn. We will have conceded ground to the enemy and run ourselves into a grave.'

'It won't do, sir, the Ironclad are raiders first and foremost. We need to weather their initial storm, and storm they will,' Roth said.

General Faisal shook his head bitterly. 'I agree but this just seems to go against all my military logic. We are the Guard, we hold ground, we seize ground and we fight for position. I agree with you, Roth, I really do, but it's hard when this is all so abstract.'

'Let me put this in a more sequential manner. The Archenemy need Angkhora. Deny them,' Roth said, plucking up the force counters representing Imperial battalions, and placing them in a ring around the cartographer's sketch of Angkhora.

The lord general loosened his collar. 'Let me tell you a story, inquisitor. I fought during the Petro-Wars of 836, very long ago. I was a captain of infantry then. I still remember, on the cotton fields of Baybel I lost my entire company to an ambush. We were shot to pieces by an unruly mob of agri-combine workers. Why? Because I deviated from my patrol route. Do you know what a Baybelite cotton field looks like when it is covered with the blood of your men? It weighs heavily on your conscience, inquisitor. As an officer, you do not forgive yourself for something like that. Forty years later, and it still keeps me up at night.'

'Do you know what would happen to the Bastion Stars, what would happen to holy Terra if the Archenemy had the capability to unleash an embryonic star into the system?'

Faisal shook his head. In truth, Roth did not either. But the tactical implications of such a weapon would be convincing enough to any military man.

'We can do this,' General Ashwan concluded, jabbing at the map with an index. 'Collapse the ramparts, causeways and arterial routes as we withdraw. Leapfrog the battalions towards the centre. If we keep moving, we can dull their numerical superiority.'

Roth looked to Faisal. 'They're your men, lord general. What say you?'

'I think this operation speaks for itself,' Faisal said. 'We'll fight from house to house and make them bleed for every inch of ground they take.'

CHAPTER TWENTY-SIX

Down below, in the narrow defile of a laneway, a platoon of metal-shod troops picked their way through the skeleton of a commercial bazaar. Behind them, a Scavenger-pattern light tank idled at a walking pace, its eight wheels grinding over the brittle remains of canvas tents.

The light tank was an ominous beast, the sloped, hard angles of its hog-faced hull painted in chipped white. A flat turret mounting a 55mm autocannon traversed slowly, like an animal snout sniffing for scents.

Barq waited in the upper-storey miradors, watching the tanks intently. The Last War required the efforts of every available man, and Barq did not think an inquisitor was any exception. Much to the chagrin of the Conclave, Barq had volunteered as an attachment officer to the 76th Battalion. Gurion had reckoned the battlefield no place for an inquisitor, but Roth was on the front and Barq could not let his old friend do it alone. Besides, he did not wish to be outdone.

From his ambush point, Barq allowed the Ironclad below him to prowl their way down the laneway. Behind the advancing platoon, a column of heavier-armoured vehicles brought up the advance. Some of the tanks, mostly squat heavy-weapon platforms, barely manoeuvred down the thoroughfare, their sponsons gouging against the crumbling brickwork on either side. Barq waited until the last battle tank had edged its bulk into the throat of the alley before he tapped three pips on his vox headset.

A domino-ripple of explosions tore down the lane. The light tank directly below Barq's position seemed to unfurl as if the bolts that held the tightly hammered plating had sprung loose. Sheets of metal blistered and peeled away as the Scavenger's chassis caught fire.

From high up, along the miradors and rooftops, CantiCol Guardsmen volleyed down stabbing beams of las-fire and pelted grenades. The backwash of heat was furious enough that Barq could see it – a warped, shimmering curtain of steam, smoke and tangible high temperature.

Barq leaned over the galleried balcony and unracked his plated gloves. The multi-barrelled systems – fed by two belts of .50 cal winding around to an ammunition cache on Barq's back – kicked into gear. Barq swung his fists in wide arcs, an almost liquid coil of tracer unwinding from his rig. Ejection ports set near his thumbs bubbled forth with spent cartridges like copper foam, hundreds of steaming casings cascading onto the streets below.

The sustained fire from Barq's glove-guns raked into the reeling platoon of Ironclad. If it were not for the piston banks and stabiliser cables of Barq's plated arms, the recoil alone would have detached muscle from bone. Five hundred rounds of .50 cal gouged deep punctures. Five hundred rounds in five seconds, and then the feeder belts clicked empty.

'Inquisitor, division command has ordered a regional withdrawal, effective immediately.'

Barq turned to see Private Haunen, the vox-operator of Alpha Company, 76th Battalion, stepping into the plasterboard ruin of the upper gallery. The private proffered the vox-speaker in one hand, and in the other held his smoking lasrifle upright.

Barq waved the handset away. 'Withdraw to where?'

'High Command is retracting our battle lines and pulling our forces towards Angkhora and redrawing the fronts to Iopiea and Sumerabi, both three links along the chain from Angkhora, east and west. The further links of the chain, Chult and Methual have, already been abandoned with more to follow.'

The withdrawal had certainly been overdue, thought Barq. Since the initial battle, the Imperial army had been pummelled into disarray. Barq barely knew which way was forwards and which way was back any more. Twice in the last eight hours they had almost triggered ambushes upon their own retreating forces.

'Echo Company of 76th will be falling back behind our positions now, directly to our rear. We are to pull back immediately under cover of their fire.'

'Let's get moving then,' Barq agreed.

Further down the laneway, CantiCol began to retreat from their firing posts. Flitting figures in white kepi hats darted along the rooftops and disappeared. Their withering blitz of fire softened to sporadic parting shots.

'Go on then! Move!' Barq ushered Private Haunen across the room and down the stairs. Behind him, the mirador he had occupied was obliterated by a tank shell in a blossoming cloud of sandstone. The Archenemy were staggering back from the shock of their trap.

Barq's company melted down into the winding stair-streets and circulatory laneways, weaving into the old city where vehicles could not.

'Fifteen degrees east, adjust one mil vertical,' Silverstein instructed as he peered into the distance.

Apartan, nestled down behind the length of his autogun, adjusted his aim and fired. The round cracked down from his position at the embrasure of a prayer tower, disappearing amongst the fire and smoke of battle below.

'Hit,' Silverstein reported.

The huntsman clambered up the ziggurat to Asingh-nu. Like Apartan, the Cantican was crouched over an autogun, the foregrip of the rifle resting on the statue of a six-limbed dancer. From here, Silverstein was afforded a different vantage point of the battle, a different target. Since the Ironclad had besieged the Fortress Chains, the guerrillas had stolen amongst the confusion, shooting and running. It was not much, but every Archenemy downed gave them a certain measure of victory.

'Six hundred metres to your eleven o'clock,' the huntsman said, reaching out a hand to correct Asingh-nu's aim. 'Adjust minus two mils vertical, steady the breathing now, your aim is terrible, shaking all over the place.'

Asingh-nu fired, without even looking.

'Hit,' Silverstein said. He clapped Asingh-nu on the back.

From behind the Archenemy advance in the fallen city of Chult, Silverstein's guerrillas could see the battle that was heaving out to their front. The Imperium had withdrawn in ragged, wounded swathes and the Ironclad had pressed forwards, leaving a trail of corpses and fire in the suddenly empty city of Chult. Several kilometres away they could see the muzzle flares of distant artillery duels, the luminous pulse of explosions they could barely hear.

It gave Silverstein the perfect opportunity to stalk his quarry. They had ghosted at the tail of the Ironclad war front, harassing them. By Silverstein's count they had killed thirty-nine Ironclad Eltebers, Naiks and other field-grade commanders, as well as a handful of regular troops, although those were less valuable as targets. Given that they had tailed on the dust plumes of the Ironclad advance for days, thirty-nine was a fair number.

Dancing precariously close to the edge of the gopuram stair-tower, Silverstein edged along the painted steps to where Asingh-nu's rifle was facing towards the connective ramparts of the chain. Settling into a comfortable crouch, Silverstein began to scope for targets with his eyes.

'Let's see if we can get our fortieth kill,' he said to himself.

The legions of the Archenemy pressed their advance relentlessly throughout the coming night.

As Aridun slipped into evening, they split their advance into several concentrated spearheads aimed at breaching fractures in the Imperial cordon. At Iopiea, the newly drawn-up defensive front, a column of fast-moving fighters – mostly fighting patrol vehicles and outriders – rolled in fast to hit the Iopiean central causeway. The CantiCol 112th Battalion and Fifth Lancers were fighting with their backs against the wall, drummed into flat-footed submission by the sudden speed of the assault. It took twelve minutes of heavy fighting before they were relieved by elements of the Hasdrubel Fifth Founding.

The second attack pressed in along the western front of Sumerabi, hooking in like horned pincers. Motorised bikes and single-engine quads shrieked through the tightly wound streets of the Sumerab manufactory district, penetrating into and amongst the company-strength forces there. They forced the Imperial forces to scramble for cover, scattering into the many blockhouses and production mills. For a long while, the mounted raiders of the Archenemy ruled the night. They gunned their bikes in circles around the cowering CantiCol, firing machine pistols into the sky, hooting and screaming in the dark tongue.

These were all diversionary attacks to preoccupy Faisal's senior commanders. The main thrust of the attack occurred in Angkhora. Unable to utilise the central causeway, an armoured formation of seven hundred tanks rolled through the outlying cemetery districts that ringed the upper tiers of Angkhora. Their tracks crushed thousands of headstones. In regions of thin topsoil the tanks even churned up shrouded corpses and stiff, buried limbs.

Brigadier General Matani Gaul mustered a staunch defence along the threatened regions with a combined brigade-level counter-attack of artillery and well-placed infantry positioning. Unfortunately, General Gaul himself was dispatched by a stray shot from a Vanquisher cannon in the first ten minutes of fighting. His second, Colonel Shedu, could not regain the general's momentum.

Hesitant and indecisive, Shedu adopted a raggedly ad hoc approach, committing piece-meal companies to the offensive, splitting his forces and feeding them part by part to the advancing tanks. Within six minutes, Shedu had lost the equivalent of two thousand men.

It took the arrival of the Aegina Prestige regiments to prevent total collapse along a three-kilometre stretch of the cemetery district. Resplendent in their armour of wire and carbon-diamond plate, the Aegina heavy infantry hit the flank column of the Ironclad armour. Mortar and lascannon lit up the night as the Aegina moved in to insulate the defences. Ironclad tanks were reduced to ruptured ruin as the Aegina moved in close, their heavy weapon fire-teams funnelling 'murder lanes' with their mortars and laying down a fan of lascannon into the channelled groups.

So fiercely methodical was the Aegina counter-offensive that the inevitable infantry advance never came. Four deca-legions of Ironclad faltered at the rubble-strewn plains of the cemetery district, milling into a confused halt. In the darkness, the four hundred Aegina troops lay down enough sustained fire to convince the enemy there were at least ten thousand Imperial troops holding the lines there.

CHAPTER TWENTY-SEVEN

There were rumours, all across the front, that Khorsabad Maw himself was leading the Archenemy on this final offensive.

Vox relays from the field officers and brief reports from divisional command eventually filtered their way up to the Joint Command at Angkhora. These reports all adhered to a certain theme – Khorsabad Maw or someone believed to be him had been sighted leading the Archenemy invasion.

As the first night drew to a close, both sides withdrew to lick their wounds. Although the fighting didn't stop, the murderous storm ebbed into sporadic exchanges of fire from buildings and street corners.

The toll, according to Imperial intelligence, was severe. Of the four hundred and sixty thousand men who had manned the defences of the Fortress Chain that day, ninety thousand were dead and twenty thousand lay within the infirmaries that had been established in the green zones. A further sixteen thousand men were unaccounted for, swallowed up in the confusion of fighting.

The Imperial Guard had, in the span of twenty-one hours, abandoned thirteen of the Fortress Chain cities, thickening and bolstering their warfront around Angkhora and six cities on both western and eastern flanks. Already, they had lost two-thirds of their defensive position, an inordinate amount by anyone's standards. In the wake of the fighting, those desolate strongholds barely resembled the great tiered cities of Aridun. Artillery had eroded them into molars and stumps of foundation, the tracks of heavy vehicles grinding the rubble into dust.

As dawn prepared to break on the second day of fighting, the Guardsmen were roused into activity by tin whistles. They smoked tabac vacantly, trying to shake some feeling back into trigger-numbed fingers. Others broke open ration tins, scooping the contents out with their hands and into their mouths hungrily. Ash blackened the faces of the men and dulled the light of their eyes. They were resigned to the knowledge that the second day of fighting would be worse than the first. Fatigue had already set in, and the killing had become rhythmic.

Lord General Faisal and Inquisitor Roth toured the frontlines on horseback. The war, Faisal decided, could no longer be waged from behind tactical spreadsheets and sheltered bunkers. The Archenemy were at the gates and it was time for even the senior officers to commit themselves to fighting. The troops would need the morale if they were to see out the day.

Roth attached himself to the Tenth Brigade, holding a strategic point across the eastern face of the Angkhoran canal, a boundary moat on which funeral pyres had once been set adrift. Brigadier Sasanian of the Tenth and most of his staff had been killed in the early hours of the day before. The Tenth would need leadership if they were to prevent the Archenemy from using the canal. It was now a strategic crossing, a bridge into the central heart of Angkhora. Roth decided, with his usual clarity, that this was very much like Tamburlaine's theatrical *Crossing of the Medes*. It would be a place to die a good Imperial death, if the Emperor willed it.

Fighting re-erupted before the suns had even cleared the horizon. At 02:58, Inquisitor Barq, leading a forward patrol company on the ramparts of Iopiea, voxed a frantic request for reinforcement. Archenemy troops, of a disposition not yet encountered before, had engaged them with brutal efficiency. The distress was soon echoed by commanders across the first-line fronts. A new troop-type was leading the advance, running roughshod over the CantiCol. A company commander of Alpha Company, 66th Battalion at the Iopiean defence voxed in that it was, 'too damn early in the morning for this,' before his vox-line went dead.

The Archenemy were bringing their most potent weapons to bear.

'The 101st and 104th Battalions are being pushed back across the canal. The 99th Battalion, as far as I'm aware, are all routed,' reported Major Cymil. He hunched down next to Roth, one hand holding his kepi in place as if he were trying to push his own head as low behind the broken wall as he could.

'And what of the 102nd?' Roth said, naming the fourth and last battalion in his command.

'Advancing across the canal bridge to cover the 101st and 104th from pursuit,' Major Cymil shouted back above the percussive thrum of shelling.

'Dammit no! Vox the 102nd to hold the line at the bridge, I don't want battalions advancing to support retreating units, we don't have the damn numbers!' Roth bellowed. The brigade major scrambled away, holding his hat the entire time.

Roth turned his attention back on the scene before him. The boundary canal was a wide irrigation ditch that was more dam than canal, running from Angkhora into the mangrove wetlands of the surrounding region. It stretched five hundred metres across, from bank to bank, as old superstition believed that would be too far for restless ghosts to cross from the burial city and escape into the Fortress Chains. The ribbons of two pontoon bridges had once provided pedestrian thoroughfare for the living. These very bridges were now the source of Roth's despair.

The four battalions in his command were bunkered down on the Angkhoran side of the canal – almost four thousand men, foraging for cover in the broken teeth ruins of rubble, trading shots with the Archenemy on the opposing bank. Many of the shots landed short of target, drumming into the water and walking frothy plumes across its entire surface.

Across the algae-rich water, a line of Ironclad were drawn in a two-kilometre battle line on the bank, at least one hundred men deep – judging by the sheer volume of enemy fire that was tearing the brigade into constituent companies, it was a conservative estimate.

'The enemy are advancing!' came the relaying cry across the banks of the canal.

Roth peered over the wedge of masonry and saw the Ironclad legions navigate onto the bridges. The war-drums were sounding their inevitable beat, the enemy marching in an extended column with banners fluttering like the primitive spearman.

Roth darted from cover. He was sprinting towards a depressed ridge of scree where fifty or more CantiCol Guardsmen were taking cover. He hurled himself across the open stretch of ground as plumes of enemy shot chased his heels. Roth landed amongst the huddled press of Guardsmen.

'Major Cymil, where are you?' Roth called.

'Sir!' came the resounding reply. Cymil rose into a half-crouch and hurried over to the inquisitor.

'We don't have long, so make sure this message is voxed to all battalion commanders in the brigade. I want them to allow the enemy to cross the bridge–'

Cymil cut the inquisitor off mid-sentence. 'Sir? Allow the Archenemy to cross the canal?'

'Yes!' Roth shouted, juicing some extra clarity into his words with a touch of psychic resonance. 'I want half of the march column to be allowed to penetrate our lines here.'

The look that Major Cymil afforded Roth implied he was clearly, and beyond all doubt – mad.

Roth continued, 'Once the Archenemy have formed more than half of their numbers on our side of the canal, I want the battalions to bring down the pontoon bridges and split the enemy forces from mutual support. Once we've cut them in half, I need the Seventh Artillery to be on standby to flatten those bastards on our side of the canal. Understood?'

Major Cymil swallowed. 'This could become a right mess, sir.'

Roth gripped the major's lapel and pointed to the marching enemy. 'That is a right mess. Once they get to grips with us, that will become a right mess.'

The brigade major saluted and scrambled away, howling for the primary vox.

Barq saw the vibro-pike slash in and shoulder-rolled away, the blade humming over his head. The Archenemy trooper retracted his lunge and squatted down into a flare-legged fighting stance. The enemy trooper didn't move, daring Barq to come forwards.

'Vox to Bravo Company, tell them we're falling back and have them cover our tails!' Barq shouted to his adjutant. But the assault had been so fast, his adjutant was in all likelihood dead.

The Archenemy warrior shuffled one step forwards, prescribing a slow circle in the air with his vibro-pike. He was one of those in the Archenemy formation who had led the assault since morning, rolling over the forward CantiCol formations. Having been privy to intelligence documents that the line Guardsmen obviously did not, Barq recognised them as the Iron Ghasts. These 'Ghasts' were the elite ship-boarding raiders of Khorsabad's armies, and also his personal retinue. Wherever they went, Khorsabad was sure to be. Already the CantiCol were referring to them as 'Guard-fraggers' in vox reports. It was an appropriate name given the ease with which these troopers dispatched other fighting men, making the post-mortem look more like a homicide than a fight.

The Iron Ghast before him was insulated in steel, sets of small iron plates laced together by cord. It had a box-like appearance, with large oblong shoulder guards. He was broad, excessively armoured and monstrously imposing. The iron cuirass that gave them their name resembled a belly-wrap of thick girded metal that fell into a plated apron. The antlered helm and iron mask were forged as one. The iron that shod the wearer's face resembled a burial mask with long, smiling, stylised teeth. Unlike the scrap-heap arsenal of the Ironclad raiders, there was a disciplined and therefore dangerous uniformity to their battledress.

Barq back-pedalled, almost losing his balance on the rubble spill. His glove-guns were dry of munitions and he had only the plated fists. Those, and the autopistol at his hip. Around him, his company was in disarray. Lieutenant Pencak's platoon was cut off, presumed lost during their retreat. Barq's other three platoons were engaged in a fight that spilled out between the ruins of a tenement block and the surrounding streets around it. His men were everywhere. They were running, not retreating, running in all directions.

The flood of vox from the first-line defences was much of the same. The loose array of infantry companies sent into the bombed-out ruins ahead of the Imperial battle lines as spotters and forward observation teams were being butchered. They had all been hit hard since the early hours of morning. Guard-fraggers, these devils truly were. The dismembered remains of Guardsmen littered the streets, their flesh, pulverised by vibro-pikes, attested to that fact.

The Ironclad shot forwards with his pike again, two metres of violently oscillating steel spearing for Barq's sternum. The strike was so fluid that Barq had no time to react. He simply watched the pike plunge. It was a killing strike, of that there was no doubt; the sonic tremors would likely separate the fibres of his upper chest and overload his heart. But the strike never impacted.

Barq's force generators kicked in, throwing up a minor bubble of anti-gravitational force. It blunted the pike's force with a syrupy envelope of friction. The force generators were not strong enough to stop the pike completely, but it was enough to slow it down before impact. Barq seized the chance to swim around and under the polearm with his upper body. He weaved upwards with a short, snapping uppercut inside the Ironclad's guard. The bank of pistons powering his arms provided Barq the mechanical leverage he needed to pound a concave into the Ironclad's face plate. The chin dented, warping the long, smiling teeth. Three months training with the Cadian Kasrkin had taught Barq to chain his strikes, and chain them he did. He stomped his heel down onto his opponent's knee. As the armoured form began to buckle, Barq slammed a forearm down in the gap between the Ironclad's cuirass and the semi-circular lamé of the helmet's neckguard. The piston-driven strike shattered the vertebrae.

Barq did not pause to savour victory over his fallen foe. A squad of the Ghasts, a bristling wall of vibro-pikes and lasguns, were storming down a narrow stair-street to his front. More were emerging from the surrounding streets and tenements, the blood of Barq's company skidding off their humming weapons like water off a hot surface. A beam of las punched into the force field, pushing it to its limits, sending kinetic ripples across the air. Residual heat scorched a neat little hole in the enamel of his armour. Tau-tech was good, but it was not indestructible. The adrenaline and temple-hammering panic of closing death impelled him into action.

'Company withdraw. On me!' Barq turned and slipped behind the blasted stump of a public fountain as las-shots drilled smoking holes where he stood. The scattered parts of the company, in limping, scrambling handfuls, fled down the street.

Barq, drawing his autopistol, crouched behind the fountain waving his men down the street, hoping that Bravo Company were still holding the east quadrant and that he was not shepherding his men into the enemy. It had gone to the point where he was not sure any more.

'Sir, you have to move,' a Guardsman said as he staggered by. Corporal Tumas was perhaps his name, Barq thought, but he could barely recognise him. Ash turned the corporal's face into nothing more visible than a set of teeth and eyes.

'Is that all of us?' Barq asked.

'The ones we could carry, sir,' the corporal admitted painfully.

The inquisitor fired several pitiful, defiant shots down the street, in the direction of the enemy. The dull cracking report told him he did not hit anything. Keeping his head low, Barq joined the remains of Alpha Company of the 76th Battalion in full, panicked retreat.

Madeline was losing her excavation team.

In the first morning, an enemy shell had landed amongst the mountain of loose earth adjacent to the excavation basin, the shower of grit getting into their eyes, mouth, nose and clothing. Madeline had thought that was bad enough.

On the second day however, the shells were beginning to find their mark. Two had landed into the quarried basin itself, killing thirteen Guardsmen who had been hauling wagons of rock from the shafts below. Within four hours, she lost another twenty men, all to shelling above ground.

It was deemed too dangerous for her, and Captain Silat, operations commander of the 1st Combat Engineers, had confined Madeline to the digging shaft that had burrowed six hundred metres below ground.

At first Madeline had been thoroughly displeased. She had wanted to oversee the excavations from above ground. That and the fact she had always been horribly claustrophobic. But now she was sure her aggravations were unfounded. It was amazing to see the Guardsmen unearth the chamber seal of the Old Kings, scraping the dirt and earth away from the ancient structure with careful reverence. It was still half-obscured by ironstone and loose earth but already it was the most wonderful thing Madeline had ever seen in all her academic endeavours.

It was the sealed entrance. She was sure of it. She could read the curving script, or at least bits of it. Some of it was written in stylised Ancient Terran Anglo, one of the root linguistics of High Gothic. The rest was finely engraved lines of script in Oceanic Terran, a pre-Imperial language she had dealt with but never specialised in. The language was thirty-nine thousand years old and originated from the south-eastern archipelagos of very early Terra.

It proclaimed, in rough translation, of the dormant star that slept within, and of the alignment of the constellation that would awaken it.

There was more, but Madeline could not translate it.

The seal itself, although still largely buried, was undeniably disc-shaped, with a radius of around sixty metres. Blocks of script and engravings depicting the flora and fauna of Aridun in relation to the constellations and galaxy covered millimetres of its exposed surface. Madeline could only see the carvings when viewed under the lens of a jeweller's scope – the birds, flowers, insects and traipsing mammalians were only millimetres big, and the largest carvings of a trunked mammoth was no bigger than her pinky nail. She could not imagine the tools required to create artwork of such a scale to such finite precision. As a rough estimate, there must have been tens of millions of figurines on the seal.

'Ma'am, one of my men has found something you have to see,' said Captain Silat.

'What is it, captain?'

'I have no idea, that was the question I wanted to ask you.'

They picked their way up a steep scarp of ironstone that encrusted the lower half of the seal. Silat led her past a long section of narrative depicting thousands of dancing humans worshipping constellations until he found a slab of inscription. The carvings there seemed out of place. They were crude, with chipped chisel markings where none existed on the rest of the seal. Most importantly, however, it was written in Low Gothic.

'It's right here,' Captain Silat said, pointing to the patch of ironstone that Madeline was almost standing directly over.

She startled, almost slipping on the scarp. Half-exposed by pick and shovel, the mummified remains of a man gazed up at her, its jawbone gaping open. Much of the skin was immaculately preserved, the waxy brown rind sagging over a skeletal structure that had been flattened by the rock deposits.

'It's holding a chisel and flint,' said Captain Silat.

Madeline crouched down to examine the body. Indeed, gripped by the leathery fingers was a head of flint and a chisel. The man, or woman, had obviously been drowned by the avalanche of clay and silt in the act of adding the cruder inscriptions to the seal.

'May I point out that he is wearing the period dress of a pre-Imperial Medinian warrior?' she said.

'You can tell?'

Madeline nodded. Although the cloth on the body was stiff and soiled, like the body it was well preserved by the mixture of clay and ore. The corpse wore a hauberk of knotted rope, armour of finely woven hemp designed to turn the point of a blade. On its skull, a layered headscarf was embroidered with the Oceania Terran word for 'resistance'.

'The helmet is a giveaway. It is from the Reclamation Wars. This is one of the insurrectionists who fought Governor-General Fulton and his campaign to bring Medina back into the Imperium, six thousand years ago.'

'And of the inscription, does it mean what I think it means?' Captain Silat said, catching the block of text under the beam of his phosphor lamp.

Madeline squinted at the writing and began to read aloud. 'So ends the chapter of freedom. We tried to awaken our Lord, our Star, but the constellations were not aligned for his coming. Our Lord awoke, yawned and returned to slumber but with his brief release, he took this world from us. The floods and storms are our doing, let the Imperials know this.'

Madeline stopped reading. She heard Captain Silat's exhalation, sharp and breathless. In all likelihood Silat had little concept of what that meant, but Madeline knew all too well. According to the inscription, the insurrectionists had attempted to release their embryonic star during the War of Reclamation, that much she could gather. But the helio-lines had been undrawn, and their planet's alignments had been incorrect. The star had been released, but the incorrect schematics had led the star to 'yawn and return to slumber'. Astronomy and cosmology had never held her interest, she had preferred to study humanity and history's place within the universe rather than the universe itself. In retrospect, those dreary cosmology lectures were coming to fruition now. In her opinion, it could only mean the star had flared, but likely collapsed back into a stable proto-state.

The flare. The flare would have been enough to release enough radiation to deplete Aridun's ozone and atmosphere, bringing with it flood, drought and mass extinction. The Old King had been the reason that Aridun died the first time.

If the embryonic star was to be released at the height of its power, Madeline had no doubt that it would consume the entire Medina Corridor and project enough radiation to reach the nearby Tetrapylon and Manticore subsectors. The energy released from an expanding star would be enormous. The dense molecular expansion of a formative star would destroy entire worlds, star systems, subsectors.

'What this means,' said Madeline slowly, 'is that beyond this seal exists an entity which can consume everything. It means that we cannot allow the Archenemy to reach it.'

High above them, the quaking of shells reminded her of the war that raged above the surface. 'Captain, hurry please, we have to double-shift the work teams. We don't have time to squander,' she implored him.

CHAPTER TWENTY-EIGHT

'Form a line!' Roth cried, and his orders were relayed along the bank of the eastern canal with shrill blasts of the drill whistle.

The 102nd Battalion were to hold their position at the mouth of the bridge. The 101st and 104th Battalions were to fall back, goading the Ironclad to press forwards. In any event, that was Roth's plan.

The 102nd were veteran soldiers, hardened by over a decade of bandit insurgency in the Sumlayit mountains of Cantica. If any battalion had the mettle to hold their front against a tidal assault of the Archenemy, it would be them. On the other hand, the 101st and 104th were garrison battalions, unblooded troops who had never experienced anything more taxing than border patrol. Roth only hoped they would make an orderly withdrawal and steer the enemy into the proper artillery zones. The 99th and 105th of 10th Brigade had already been decimated in the first day of fighting, their remnants attached to the surviving battalions.

As the Archenemy column marched past the middle of the bridge, they broke into a shuffling jog. The porous stone and rope of the pontoon began to sag under the weight of so many troops. Their war-drums began to pound faster, louder. The Archenemy broke into a stampede.

Along the bank, the Tenth Brigade unleashed a volley of las in staggered firing lines, the second rank firing over the crouching heads of the Guardsmen in front. Although the enemy possessed long-barrelled firearms, they fired back with pistols and carbines and brandished melee weapons. The choice of armament was largely important in an urban context, and mated an aggressive mobility with tactical organisation. Roth did not have much faith in static bayonet defences against the devastating impact of mauls, hammers, flanged maces and machetes.

'Guardsmen of Cantica! These are the men who burnt the houses of your ancestors! To arms! To arms!' Roth bellowed.

The 101st and 104th were strung out in a thin line, anchored at the bridge by a defensive wedge of the veteran 102nd. As the Ironclad closed on the bank, the raiders began to surge off the narrow pontoon into the waist-deep water. The enemy spread into frothing waters like scuds of piranhas, kicking the water into foam. Roth did not doubt that hundreds of them drowned in the stampede, but thousands more charged up onto the bank within seconds, shrieking and baying in their dark tongue.

Roth stood at the fore of the 102nd, the battalion holding a wedge adjacent to the bridge. He walked purposely upright against the unnerving whine of incoming fire. It would do no good for his battalion to see him cowering for cover. He blew on a tin whistle at one-second intervals, directing a steady volley of fire. Support weapons pounded larger, heavier rounds into the water, spewing up geysers that were ten metres high. They kept firing even as the Ironclad were an arm's length away, close enough for them to see the intent in their enemy's posture, the lowered heads, the raised weapons. Some of the Ironclad reached out for them as they scaled the bank, grasping with their dirty fingers.

When the Ironclad charge hit them, it hit them with all the force of seventy thousand troops behind the surging scrum. The first wave of Ironclad did not even have room to fight; they simply crashed into the line of bayonets, going under as the next wave of Ironclad trampled over the top of them. It was hell. Everywhere Roth looked was killing, terrible and bizarre in its reality.

He saw a Cantican Guardsman spear an Ironclad with his bayonet. The Ironclad slid down the length of the spike and began to gouge the Guardsman's eyes with both hands. He saw a monstrously thick-necked Cantican cave in the face-binding of an Ironclad with the butt of his rifle, and stab a second and a third. The next time Roth looked back, the same Guardsmen was strangling an Ironclad by the neck even though he was bleeding out from a dozen gunshot wounds. The true mettle of a man was laid bare, often in the minutes preceding his death. It was a horrible revelation.

Roth beat his power fist as if he was threshing wheat. There was simply no room for footwork, for slipping his hips into the punch, for pivoting on the balls of his feet. He lashed back and forth, left, right, forwards – left, right, forwards, as fast as he could drive his arm. His shoulder ached with the act of killing. Something glanced off his head and Roth felt his skin split. Blood pressed down on his eyelashes and blinked into his eyes. He laughed. He laughed at the mess he had got himself into as blood streamed down his face. His nose was broken too; he could see the bridge of it, on the edge of his vision. Laughing hurt his nose, but he couldn't stop.

As expected the 101st and 104th began to collapse, falling away from the bank. The Archenemy pushed after them, swarming onto dry land. To their credit, the battalions peeled away with some semblance of a line, segmenting into companies and drawing the Archenemy in their thousands across the rubble-strewn district beyond.

'Advance, in formation, advance!' Roth bellowed, amplifying his voice with psychic resonance to be heard above the caustic crash of weaponry.

The 102nd, in their V-formation, drove a wedge into the horde of Archenemy, pushing closer towards the bridge. CantiCol Guardsmen waded into the water, fighting their way towards the pontoon bridge.

Roth blew his whistle and, as he had instructed, any Guardsmen within throwing distance began to hurl krak grenades and demo charges at the bridge. The water exploded in shattering columns of steam, rocking the pontoon. The tension cables holding the bridge snapped under a barrage of explosives. Section by section, like a drowning serpent the bridge rolled and submerged. Freed of support, sections of the pontoon twisted and flipped, shedding hundreds of Ironclad into the water. The winding column of Ironclad was swallowed in the aquatic murk, thirty metres deep at the canal's centre. Armoured as they were, Roth imagined they would sink quite quickly.

Suddenly cut off, the Ironclad on the rubbled plains of the bank stopped engaging the 101st and 104th. Perhaps they even realised it was a trap as some of the Archenemy troops turned around, heading back towards the water. It did not save them from the pre-designated ordnance zones as artillery began to fall amongst them. Those that escaped the artillery were rooted out of hiding and mopped up by the remainders of Tenth Brigade.

Bitter fighting raged in every street, every temple, every house, every basement and every staircase. Fire-fights even trickled down to the underground burial systems.

However, as a pale, hollow dusk began to settle on the second day of the Last War, the fighting began to fade with the light. The suns sunk, the haze of twilight quickly diluted by the ink of purple. The darkness was too treacherous for the conduct of fighting.

As night fell, shelling on both sides intensified and the CantiCol withdrew from the wingward cities of Iopiea and Sumerabi. Swathes of the city, entire acres were nothing more than an undulating desert of rubble. In some narrow streets and connective stairwells the corpses piled so high that the retreating Guardsmen had to kick them down in order to go over them. Iopiea and Sumerabi had become untenable. Quite simply, there was little left of the cities to defend.

Intelligence reports at dusk estimated there were less than one hundred thousand fighting men defending Aridun. The trauma of such high casualties on the psyche of the troops would be a telling factor in their disposition in the final efforts to come.

Against the backdrop of pulsating shell explosions in the night horizon, the frontline receded to reinforce the defenders at the central-axis cities of the Fortress Chain – the cities of Phthia and Archeh. Broken remains of retreating brigades were merged with the beleaguered forces at the new front. Where the officers had all been killed, command was given to the most senior ranking Guardsman. It was rumoured that the nine thousand men amalgamated into the 5th/8th Brigade was led by a junior lieutenant newly graduated from staff academy.

There was now no place left to retreat. A collapse at either Phthia or Archeh would allow Archenemy legions to launch unopposed offensives against the exposed eastern and western flanks of Angkhora. During the retreat, someone had scraped onto a passing wall, 'There is no ground for us, not beyond here.' Regardless of who had written it, the wry scrawl was picked up and relayed across the Imperial vox-networks as a catch-cry of the last efforts.

At the newly established Imperial front, in the late hours of evening, Lord General Faisal himself toured the dug-in CantiCol lines, at the fringe districts of Phthia. Against the advice of his chief of staff, he was still dressed in his ceremonial coat of brown Cantican felt, complete with neat rows of medals that began at the chest and ended well below his thighs. Crossed over his belt were a pair of Cantican cavalry sabres, and over these, a twin pair of curved daggers, the quartet of blades sweeping from his waist like an impressive set of tusks. Unarmoured, and almost unarmed, Faisal was determined to tour the lines in traditional regalia. It was a subtle message to his troops – that everything was as it should be.

The lord general was genuinely impressed with the way his men had fortified the district. They were strung out in mutually supporting companies, holding positions in the tenement halls and storage-houses which faced the bombed-out ruins of the eastern approach. The barrels of guns bristled from the broken windows and rooftops of almost every building he saw. The line stretched for thirty kilometres around the city limits, interposed by strong-points of support weapon batteries. Beyond them, along the rampart walls that connected the cities of Phthia and Iopiea, the 22nd/12th Brigade held the winding stretch of brickwork. Mortars and bombast platforms trundled on rail tracks along the battlements. In some parts, enemy artillery had collapsed the rampart into a sagging slope of rubble spill, scorching the limestone a dense, streaky black, but the troops still held the position.

The lord general dismissed his cadre guard of Lancers and walked, unescorted, to the frame of what had once been a chariot shed. The stables were now fire-blackened columns of stone, and the clay tile roofs had shed broken-teeth gaps to reveal the support structure beneath.

Inside the chariot shed was a sentry team of Cantican Colonials. Three Guardsmen huddled around the embers of a hexi-block ration fire. Two more had set up bipod lasguns on the low stable walls overlooking the rubble plains of the east, observing the direction of the Archenemy approach.

As Faisal stepped into the chariot shed, the Guardsmen abruptly stood to attention. Their senior, a sergeant with a curling beard, snapped him a quick salute.

'Sergeant Sulas – sentry post 11/A, 55th Battalion of the 7/15th Brigade, sir,' bellowed the sergeant in his loudest marching voice.

'At ease soldiers, at ease,' Faisal said, waving them down. The lord general looked at the Guardsmen of sentry post 11/A. They were haggard-looking men, badly bandaged and languishing. Most of the sentry posters, Faisal knew, were wounded men who the medics simply did not have the supplies to treat. Knowing that the injured would hamper the fighting efficiency of a platoon, these men were left as sentry posts along the front lines as forward observation teams. In all likelihood, these men would be dead by morning.

Faisal crouched down next to the sergeant by the glowing fire and warmed his hands a little. 'What is the order of the day?' Faisal asked.

'Grabbing some tiff, sir,' replied Sergeant Sulas.

The sergeant was stoking a tin of ubiquitous 'Meat C-Grade' that he had thrown into the ashy embers. He jabbed at the little canister with the tip of his bayonet, warming it up whole.

'You could join us, sir, that is, if you'd like to, sir,' a young private offered.

Faisal realised he had not eaten properly since landfall, and he was ravenously hungry. 'Of course, I would love to, that is if you have the rations to spare,' said the lord general.

With expert hands, Sergeant Sulas snatched the Meat C-Grade from the fire and doused the tin into a pot of cold water and ration tea leaves. The hot tin heated the water, drawing a cloud of steepage from the tea leaves. Without pause, the sergeant pinch-gripped the tin out of the hot water and peeled it open with the flat of an eating knife. The opened can revealed a surprisingly wholesome-looking round of marbled meat.

'The trick is, sir, to eat this meat without tasting too much of it,' Sergeant Sulas said. He scraped the meat out into the sheet of rehydrated rice and began to douse it with condiments, his fingers darting from ration packs like some sleight of hand.

'Pepper and pickled bell chilli are the key to good tiff. Masks the chems they use to preserve this meat,' said the sergeant as he scooped some of the rations into a cup canteen and offered it to the lord general.

The tin of gelatinous meat melted into the dehyd rice. Small pods of angry-looking chilli bells were mixed into the steaming container. Tugging off his gloves and using his hands, the lord general unceremoniously pushed the rice into his mouth, making muffled, appreciative sounds. It was salty and oily without being greasy. The spicy sourness of the pickled chilli made him inhale the meal. Within seconds, Faisal was teasing the last scraps of chilli and rice from his cup canteen.

Faisal waited for the Guardsmen to finish eating in contemplative silence. Once the meal was done and tea was shared, Faisal gestured to the sergeant. 'What is it that has confined you to sentry duty, sergeant?'

Without a word, Sulas unbuckled the gaiter around his calf and slid his boot off, slowly and smoothly. His sock, sticky with blood, was plastered to the boot and peeled off, along with several strips of skin. It was a laswound, partially cauterised and seeping tears of blood and pus. Faisal was shocked to see a hole in the top of the sergeant's foot, moist with infection and blistering with white skin cells.

'Doesn't hurt, sir. Can't feel a thing but I sure as frag can't run like I used to,' Sulas shrugged.

'And you, private, what is your name and why are you here?' Faisal said to the young man squatting next to Sulas.

'Private Kabau, sir. Las-shot to the upper arm. Tore away my upper bicep down to the bone,' said the young man. He wormed a finger into the loose, yellowing bandages around his arm to reveal the top of his wound. Faisal could see the puckered mass of melted skin and even the whiteness of bone. Las-wounds were a horrible thing to behold. They cauterised the wound, deadened the nerves and were crippling. Men didn't die immediately from blood loss, instead, they lingered for days in agony until infection set in. It would drain the platoon of resources and limit the unit's field effectiveness. One wounded soldier could be expected to take a further three or four men to carry and care for him. It was, in effect, the perfect weapon of mass war.

'Have they given you fentanyl for it?' Faisal asked.

Private Kabau with the sheared arm shook his head mutely.

Faisal popped the gold buttons of his coat and drew out a foiled sleeve of tablets. It was the plus-grade chems that all high-ranking officers were issued with – pure opiate analgesic. Faisal handed the packet to Sergeant Sulas, who took them with a mixture of relief and dismay.

'Distribute them accordingly, sergeant.'

Dawn came, but the suns did not. Intensified shelling had diffused the sky to a husky graphite-grey. The suns did not penetrate the pall of smoke and everywhere Guardsmen whispered of dark Chaos magic.

In the twisted remains of Iopiea, the streets were empty. The Imperium had vacated the city during the night and now the Archenemy marched in unopposed. All of the Imperial Guard had retreated, all but Watcher Platoon of Bravo Company, 45th Battalion. Somehow, somewhere during the hurried mess of mass withdrawal, the Watchers had been left behind and cut off by the sweeping Ironclad advance.

As the pale deepwater-blue of dawn began to light the courtyard of a grain mill, Watcher Platoon spread out to cover the main avenues of approach. Lieutenant Almyra pulled security at the gates of the courtyard with half a dozen able-bodied Guardsmen. On the north side of the courtyard, where the terracotta walls had been demolished, Sergeant Cepat curled up behind the rubble line with six or seven men, pointing their weapons into the maze of staircase-streets and sloping laneways that bordered the mill.

The enemy, they knew, were fast approaching. They could follow the movements by the flutter of distant war drums. But try as he might, Sergeant Cepat could not focus on the danger of their circumstances. His mind kept wandering to stupid, inconsequential things. He remembered that tomorrow, the date would fall on his annual medical examination. As a fifty-year-old infantry dog, Cepat was required to pass an annual clearance run on brigade orders or else be retired to administrative duties. Cepat wanted to know if the exam would still be required. He shouted to Almyra.

'Sir! Am I still scheduled for that damn yearly medical?'

The lieutenant turned to regard his sergeant with a confused look. He shrugged, motioning for the sergeant to stay quiet.

Cepat was still thinking about the cold, intrusive medical instruments they used when the first round sent up a clod of dust in front of him. The first shot was followed by a sharp brittle volley. In under a second, the courtyard was deafened with the popping of rounds, grenade bangs and the urgent shouts of Guardsmen calling out targeting sectors.

Ironclad troops began to clatter down the stairs, firing as they came. Cepat put six rounds downwind, then another two for good measure before weaving back behind cover.

Cursing, the sergeant hunched down behind the wooden stock of his lasrifle and began to pick steady shots. He was angry because the damn lieutenant never did tell him whether he needed to take that damn examination.

Under the ruddy half-dark of dawn, Silverstein led his guerrillas on foot through the unmapped maze of Phthia. They moved slowly, feeling their way through heaps of rubble some eight metres high.

They were no longer simply following in the wake of the Ironclad advance, now they were amongst them. The guerrillas and their huntsman picked their way carefully along through city blocks. In the streets they found nothing but corpses, broken vox-sets, torn bits of clothing, stains of blood. Over all of this was a blanketing deluge of spent ammunition, millions upon millions of brass cartridges, las-cells and discarded magazines. Silverstein could not put his foot down without stepping on one of them.

They avoided the main columns of advance, but occasionally, they would come across a roaming murder squad, or some other flanking company-sized formation. During these times, Silverstein's expertise in camouflage and concealment saved their lives. Shadow reflection, seam blending and natural curvatures were all part of the huntsman instinct. They navigated the shadows well.

'This is the spot,' Silverstein proclaimed. He was looking up at the collapsed shell of a tenement building. It was a recent addition to the city, judging by its rockcrete support and probably only centuries old compared to the crumbling millennial sandstone around it. All the windows had been blown out and a good third of it had caved inwards like a rotting shipwreck.

The guerrillas scraped up the scorch-blackened hole in the tenement's side and moved to the upper galleries overlooking an uneven tier of ground-down city.

'What I'd give for a wedge of smoked cheese and a snifter of wine,' Silverstein said as he stabilised his bullpup autogun on its bipod.

Asingh-nu sniffed. 'I was never an appreciator of cheese myself.'

'That's because Asingh is a rural plebe. He wouldn't tell cheese from cattle groin,' Temughan taunted. Apartan laughed his harsh, barking military laugh.

Silverstein shook his head. 'That's because you've never had a good cheese. Balance of sharp saltiness and mellow sweet, well aged and earthy, cured from Odessian goat's milk. Have you ever imported a Stilt-On-Haystack smoked from the Narbound Subsector, smoked with hay-twig? Gorgeous, I have a round sitting in my cellar… back home on one of my estates…'

He trailed off, suddenly weary. It became clear to him that he was very far from the comforts of home. It occurred to him that if he made it out of this mess alive, he would discharge from the service of the Inquisition. Then, pondering more, he remembered the forty-three kills he had amassed, and reconsidered. Where else would he be able to hunt game like this?

'Fire as many good shots as you can get off in under one minute, then we move. Clear?' Silverstein said.

The others nodded. They were working in teams of two now, each shooter with a spotter. Temughan, with his artisan's hands, lay behind the wooden stock of a Garlans-pattern autogun. Its slender, bottle-nosed profile was of fine-grained wood and the straight-grip stock fitted smoothly in the his hands. Apartan the ex-Guardsmen hunched next to him with a pair of magnoculars, not seeming to mind that the diminutive clocksmith was making the shots.

Silverstein allowed Asingh-nu to fire the bullpup. Although the huntsman was an immaculate shooter, his optic augmentations made him an even better spotter. Asingh-nu simply had to squeeze the trigger and breathe when Silverstein told him to.

Even with the poor visibility, they could see a defiant line of tall chimney mills intact despite being surrounded by broken lumps of rubble. Several hundred metres away, Ironclad scouting parties would be picking their way through the city in preparation for another mass offensive by morning. Silverstein would make sure the way was not clear for them.

Suddenly, the smooth dome of a steel head bobbed into view less than two hundred metres away.

'Sighted,' Apartan called from their position.

'Be my guest, gentlemen,' Silverstein said as he watched the top of the head move along a crest of jagged sandstone. The target moved unevenly, almost staggering. Something about it made Silverstein nervous. It dawned on him.

'No! Cease fire!' he hissed urgently.

It was too late. Temughan's shot rang out. The round struck the top of the bobbing head and it went flying. The target had been nothing more than a shaped hub of metal propped up on a rifle.

'Damn it,' Silverstein managed as he threw himself flat.

Return shots flashed from the crest line. Out there, someone opened up with a heavy support weapon, hammering the tenement shell with fat-calibre rounds. Temughan rolled violently off his rifle, blasted into three distinct parts. Apartan jerked backwards, shuddering as a round exited out of his back. The support weapon stopped firing and just like that, the dawn was quiet again.

Silverstein, swearing repeatedly under his breath, rolled onto his knees in a cloud of brick dust. 'Are you fine?' he asked Asingh-nu.

The guerrilla patted himself down. He nodded with wide, terrified eyes. The huntsman, still swearing, pointed to Temughan's rifle.

'Take that, fire once from the fifth window when I tell you to, then get away from there. Perfectly clear?'

Asingh-nu shot him a puzzled look but nonetheless nodded and timidly crawled over to the blood-burst stains of Temughan and Apartan.

The huntsman seized his bullpup and crept to the edge of the tenement, where the wall ended like the broken pieces of a jigsaw. He leaned out and scanned the area with his bioptics. By eye, he gauged wind current, temperature and visibility. Satisfied, Silverstein gave Asingh-nu the thumbs-up.

The guerrilla fired and threw himself away from the window. Out on the crestline, the muzzle of a heavy bolter was lifted into position and the silhouettes of three Ironclad – appearing as grainy monochrome shapes to Silverstein's eyes – raised themselves.

Silverstein snapped off a trio of fluid shots, dropping two of them. The third round missed, fragmenting off the heavy gun's hand rail. Re-aligning without pause, Silverstein banged off a fourth shot that might have clipped the Ironclad as he disappeared behind the crest.

'I think it's time to move, we've been here too long.' Silverstein gestured for Asingh-nu to follow him. The huntsman turned towards the remains of his comrades sprayed out across the apartment floor. He spared them one last glance and headed down the staircase.

Sometime during the night, the remains of Barq's company, just nineteen men, staggered upon the outpost of Zulu Company, patrolling the city grid beyond the ramparts of Phthia.

Zulu Company had bunked down in a gatehouse overlooking the main western causeway that linked the outskirts of Iopiea. It was a solidly strategic post. The gatehouse itself was a squat tower of ancient stone blocks. Barq was sure that beautiful carvings must have once run up the gate-tower, but the stones had gathered several thousand years of moss, clumping together in thick, rotting beards of green.

Captain Bahasa was the leader of Zulu Company. His men did not call him sir, they called him boss because that was the kind of officer he was. Dour, stern and as broad as he was tall, Bahasa stalked the battlements with a T20 Stem autogun looped across his chest and a stub of tabac winking out of his mouth. It was common knowledge that Bahasa had nothing left to lose, like most; none of his family had managed to board a refugee barge during the opening months of the campaign. He went about the defence of the gatehouse with a reckless abandon borne of vengeance. He laughed, he barked and he joked in the face of death.

As morning came, Zulu Company dug in. The railed bombast platforms were wheeled into position to face the east, thick-rimmed bronze barrels turned skywards. Industrial trolleys of ammunition were sent along the rampart rail-line to the gatehouse, re-supplying the heavy stubbers that lurked in the murder-holes and gun loops. The grated portcullis was welded shut and the stone gates were barred.

On the battlements, Inquisitor Barq surveyed the teams of mortar-men. He walked between them, offering words of encouragement and envelopes of opiate pain-killers. It was little more than a gesture of assurance. For the company of over one hundred men, they had only been spared one combat medic – Corporal Rwal. He was young, inexperienced as far as Barq knew, and had been promoted in rank yesterday after their medic sergeant had been hit by a stray round.

'Corporal, do we have the supplies on hand to tend to these men?' Barq asked.

Corporal Rwal was standing at the edge of the parapet. He was nervous. Barq could tell by the whites of his eyes, and the way he chewed his tabac, clenching his jaws.

'Corporal, supplies?' Barq repeated.

Rwal turned suddenly from his thoughts. 'I have the supplies. But I don't have enough hands, sir.'

'I'll stay with you during this fight. Tell me what needs doing, corporal, yes?' Barq said, moving to join him by the parapets.

Corporal Rwal didn't answer. He was off again, chewing and gazing into the distance. Plumes of smoke rose like bubbling black pillars across the ancient city. Even now, in the early quiet of dawn, Barq knew that the foot spotters and Ironclad scouts were prowling through those streets. The attack, he knew, would not be long in coming.

He was right. At 03:55, as the suns rose against their eyes, the Archenemy attacked. They kept the glinting glare of sunrise behind them. Against the suns, the Ironclad rose like haloed silhouettes – dark figures, horned and plated against a liquid orange horizon.

Small-arms fire trotted along the brick embrasures. The Ironclad broke across the band of wetland bordering the gatehouse, sloshing across the soupy reed paddies. Packs of fast-moving outriders and treaded FPVs preceded the main assault, blasting up at the gatehouse with automatic fire. Behind them, a battle line of Ironclad foot-soldiers almost a kilometre wide closed in on the gatehouse in a flanking sweep.

Barq and Corporal Rwal rushed to the top of the battlements where two platoons of Zulu Company were manning the mortars and unleashing las-volleys over the walls. There was so much activity happening in such a confined space. Company Captain Bahasa was standing upright over the battlements, changing magazines from a T20 Stem autogun. Barq screamed for him to get down, but the captain didn't hear, working the mag into his weapon. A round hit Bahasa in the chest and the captain collapsed. Barq thought he was dead for sure but the captain picked himself up, laughing. The bullet had pierced the compass he clipped to his webbing strap, lodging itself in the metal dial face.

To their front, a stub gunner slumped over his weapon and slid limply down. Barq and Rwal rushed over to the gunner but were stopped short by a cry for help across the other side of the battlements.

'Medic! Medic!'

The cry echoed from various points across the battlement, plaintive and loud even above the roar of gunfire. It came from all directions as casualties mounted.

Corporal Rwal did what he could. Those mortally wounded, such as a mortar loader who had taken shrapnel underneath the chin, were jabbed with the painkillers Barq had distributed earlier. There was no saving those ones, especially when their skin was greying and their eyes were rolling back to white. Those who could fight again – injured limbs, bleeding wounds – Rwal would work on frantically, holding a drip-bag high in one hand. Barq followed the young corporal with a leather case, handing him the surgical instruments as the corporal shouted himself hoarse.

Below, the enemy were banging on the gates. Rockets and heavy support weapons pummelled the walls relentlessly. A private on his knee, firing over the lip of an embrasure, was hit. The shot snapped his head back and sent him straight down. Another Guardsman of Zulu Company sprinted forwards, dragging him by the webbing straps away from the wall and swung his body towards a pile of dead and wounded, collecting in the centre of the turreted rooftop. Another Guardsman would take his place. The scene was repeated again and again like a maddening loop. Dying, firing, reloading and dying again.

Blood covered Barq's gauntlets in a red sheen, trailing fine threads up his forearms. He stopped thinking and let his hands do the work, pinching down on sutures or administering chems as Rwal directed. The faces of the Guardsmen, sometimes mouths open in mute pain, would stay with Barq for the rest of his life. These were fighting men, the warriors of the Imperium, screaming violently, their muscles hanging open in bloody flaps. Barq vomited twice, and the third time was retching bile as he worked. He dared not vomit onto the wounded, so he vomited onto the wall merlons, ducking his head below the crenels.

Sickness threatened to overwhelm him for the fourth time while powdering the shredded thigh of a Guard sergeant. The inquisitor leaned towards the parapet and heard a hollow pop. He opened his eyes and saw a grenade hit the edge of an embrasure. It bounced up off the edge and rolled off the block of stone. Then it went off.

The embrasure absorbed the flak and explosion of the blast but disintegrated. It threw out a disc of gravel, tight and compact. The storm of grit hit Barq full in the face. Barq went to his knees, his face transformed into a raw, bleeding graze. He had never even had time to activate his force generators.

'I can't see a damn thing,' Barq spat, teetering along the parapet, his hands groping blindly. 'Can't see a damn thing!' he said again, this time tinged with a wail of urgency.

Captain Bahasa, firing from the wall, ran to the inquisitor's aide. Corporal Rwal rushed over as well. Barq was screaming.

The medic took one look at Barq's face and shook his head at Captain Bahasa. It wasn't good. Grit and rock filled Barq's open eyes, like a lens of densely packed sand.

'My eyes?' Barq said, pawing at the corporal.

'You'll be fine. A temporary side effect,' he lied.

The inquisitor brushed him away, suddenly wailing. 'Don't lie to me. Am I blind?'

'Yes,' said Bahasa.

'Holy Throne, not now,' Barq hissed through gritted teeth. He staggered along the parapet, driving his plated fists into the crenels. Ageing limestone crumbled like chalk beneath his frustration.

Bahasa and Rwal both urged the inquisitor to get down. Barq did not wish to hear them. The enemy below fired up at his exposed upper body.

A solid slug punched into Barq's shoulder, spinning him around. Another shot entered upwards through his lower back, where the upper-body rig offered no protection. The round pierced his heart and exited through his upper chest. A small convex puckered outwards on the plate there.

Inquisitor Barq was dead before he hit the ground. Rwal hoped the wound, through his heart, had caused him very little pain.

CHAPTER TWENTY-NINE

The Ironclad were wrestling the Fortress Chains out of Imperial control. By the third day of the Last War, seams were fracturing along the encircled Imperial front.

The locomotive railheads at Phthia across the central-eastern canal changed hands twelve times in five hours. At some places, the firing was so dense and constant that troops were reduced to raking blindly around corners and over ledges with the barrels of their weapons.

Facing the enemy assault towards the west at Archeh, the Canticans could not hold any longer. For many of the Guardsmen, there was simply nothing left to give. After the adrenaline, after the terror, after fifty-six hours of close-quarter combat, there were erratic reports of men dying from exhaustion.

Throughout the day, Imperial Vulture gunships and snarling, fat-bellied bombers made low strafing runs over Archenemy positions. They flew against snagging flak curtains thrown up by tracked, super-heavy anti-aircraft decks and even the vectoring fire of portable rocket tubes. Despite the high casualties, pilots flew sorties throughout the daylight hours, pausing only to refuel their craft.

The chief of staff predicted that total, absolute collapse would occur within twenty-four hours, perhaps forty-eight at the greatest. At the excavation site of the Old Kings, engineers wired thermal charges along the basin and shaft tunnel. If the Archenemy came upon them before the Old Kings could be unearthed, they would bring down the site. It would not deter the enemy, but it would be a last act of defiance. Captain Silat of the 1st Combat Engineers vowed that the Archenemy would not finish the work he started.

The defeat began at exactly high noon on the third day. At the cargo station district of Archeh, the combined 2/15th Brigade under the command of Brigadier General Dreas Dershwan were broken. Their dead littered the cargo bays amid rotting boxes of vegetation and spoiled meat. Brigadier Dershwan was hung from the highest temple spire, suspended by a thread of spool wire. It was rumoured, although unconfirmed, that the remaining elements of Blood Gorgon Traitor Marines punched their way through the turtled Guardsmen. In this way, the 2/15th were soundly defeated, leaving a wide puncture wound to the heart of the held Imperial positions.

The end, as predicted by High Command, came much sooner than they expected.

'Keep in formation! Advance in platoon order!' Roth barked at the men around him. They were struggling. He could tell. Nearby, a Guardsmen fell to his knees and slid against a slope of jagged wall. The soldier leaned on his rifle, with his head down. He would not be getting up again.

Discipline, the foundation of military efficiency, was eroding.

Roth stomped about the formation, dressing the ranks of his men. Behind their ragged line of advance, the cardinal tomb-towers of Angkhora rose up, their sloping apexes swathed in a swirl of smoke.

Roth no longer commanded the Tenth Brigade. He was not sure who he commanded. Throughout the night, the remnants of withdrawing CantiCol had filtered through his position without any semblance of command structure. Companies, platoons and even lone, wounded soldiers trickled towards the Tenth.

Within an hour of daybreak, Roth was despairing. He estimated he had at least six thousand men, ten thousand at the most, under his faltering command. Infantry, Lancers, gun crewmen, even transport and ordnance had gravitated under his jurisdiction. Many had no idea who their immediate seniors were, or who had overall command of a platoon or company, let alone the battalions.

As they advanced, the Lancers consistently moved ahead of the brigade, deftly picking their way through the rubble landscape. With their distinct grenadier belts and drawn sabres, the elite Guardsmen almost showed an abject contempt for their lagging comrades. They communicated with deft hand signals while the officers and NCOs had to shout orders at the non-Lancer troops around them. The younger and more inexperienced Guardsmen drifted away from their platoons and followed the Lancers, huddling close. There was no sense of order to the advance. It seemed with the impending final days of war, the Guard had no fear of military punishment. They were in hell already.

When the fighting began in early morning, it came as no surprise to Roth when the diluted Tenth Brigade dissolved into disarray.

The fire-fight started abruptly. Ironclad tanks – heavy-tracked weapon platforms with splayed hulls – crunched through the remaining partitions of upright masonry. Ironclad foot-soldiers moved amongst them, their muzzles flashing from wall-less door frames, roofless windows and scattered foundation blocks. The result was panic.

The Lancers charged ahead, brandishing their cavalry sabres. The rest of Roth's brigade lingered, headless and without a functioning command system. Some units made no attempt to advance, they simply sank down and returned weak, uncoordinated fire. Officers stormed about in an attempt to rouse their men but the men had no fight left in them. Others units routed, fleeing deeper into the Imperial lines.

'Major! Major! Rally the men with me, we are to withdraw and regroup!' Roth shouted at the closest ranking officer. The major was standing in the open, with his back to the enemy. Serene, almost complacent, he was readjusting the straps of his webbing as small-arms fire kicked up clods of dirt around him.

Roth had seen it before. Neural overload. There was too much noise, too much fear to the point where the brain was ignoring it. The major stood in the open as tracer zipped around him. A round thudded into the back of his head. He went down face-first and didn't move any more.

Roth shimmied behind a stone coffin. The heavy casket had been thrown from a bombed-out mausoleum some thirty metres away. Evidently the force of the blast had deposited the coffin neatly in the middle of the road, upended but intact.

'Excuse me, I can't see anything. Would you point me in the right direction?'

Roth spun about to see a Cantican trooper pawing at his shoulder. The man's eyes were bandaged and he was crawling amongst the sharp stones on his hands and knees.

'Towards the enemy, or towards our main lines?' Roth said, easing the man behind cover with him.

'Whichever one will give me a quicker death,' answered the blinded private.

'I remember the grand poet Huerta once wrote the only thing that matters in death is permanency. We're all as good as done – today, tomorrow or the day after. Die with a rifle in your hand,' Roth said.

As if to reiterate his point, the husk of a chariot shed under which a platoon of CantiCol were taking cover went up in a vertical cloud of fire and grit. The building had been close by, and rained ashy detritus down on Roth and the blind Guardsmen. The tank that flattened the building rolled over its remains, the snouted turret traversing slowly from left to right, no more than twenty metres to Roth's left.

'Can you hear tanks?' said the Guardsman, sitting with his back to the wall.

'Oh yes. I can definitely hear tanks,' Roth agreed. The sprawl-hulled tank trundled past him.

'No, not the enemy tanks. I can hear Imperial tanks,' the blind Guardsman said.

'You can tell?'

'Yes, because I hear horses too. I can hear their hooves trembling the stones.'

Roth tried to focus yet he heard nothing. Nothing other than the deafening fury of a short-range firefight. Perhaps the Guardsman's loss of vision allowed him to focus his sensory faculties on things he otherwise would not.

And indeed the Guardsman was right. The Archenemy tank that had creaked past exploded as a shell erupted against the flank of its armour.

'Yes, I definitely hear horses,' the Guardsman agreed. He stood up, craning his head as if he could still see.

Tanks in the reverent brown of the Canticans were cutting across the enemy flank. Between their thickly armoured bulks, mounted CantiCol Guardsmen fired upright from the stirrups of charging horses. Their angle of approach allowed them to spear at the softer flank of the Ironclad armour. Detonations erupted everywhere. Turrets began smoking.

'It's our cavalry,' muttered the Guardsman.

The squadrons powering across the rubble were mostly ancient, obsolete tanks. Siegfried siege-tanks, Centaurs, several Leman Russes. The Canticans did not possess many armoured vehicles at the beginning of the war and they did not now. What cavalry, motorised or organic, they had, they assembled it into a motley armoured regiment. Roth saw before him now – the Cantican First Mech-Cavalry Regiment.

Ancient engines of war, their plates held together with bolts and reverence rumbled alongside the thunderous hooves of Lancer cavalry. Yet as they blazed through the enemy attack, clashing steel on steel, it was the most beautiful sight Roth had ever seen.

'Be advised, command element is dead. Be advised, command element is dead. Over.'

The same message was relayed a thousand times over the Imperial vox-net. The channels buzzed with the frantic chatter of news. Lord General Faisal was dead.

Doctrine should have warranted a restriction of information. No one, especially not demoralised rank-and-file, should have learnt of their general's death. Yet a corporal who had witnessed the event had released the word and now it spread like an incendiary bomb.

Corporal Bacinda had been the closest one when it happened. He was also the vox-operator of Echo Company of the 46th. The lord general had been touring the lines, resplendent on his horse and his traditional dress, and standing high in the stirrup on his painted shoes.

The troops had been dug in behind a breastwork of rubble and furniture, their rifles pointed towards the smoking western front. The morning's engagement had been predictably brutal and Bacinda's platoon had been cycled back to the secondary lines in order to rest briefly. The men had been eating what food they could forage and slumping asleep while leaning on rifles. Then Faisal had come and they had all staggered to attention. Bacinda remembered seeing the throbbing glow of explosives in the horizon and the lord general ride against it, administering words and stern, knowing looks to his men. It almost made Bacinda forget his hunger as he watched.

No one saw it coming. The artillery shell landed thirty metres away, exploding in a mushroom of dust.

Faisal was killed by a small piece of shrapnel that entered his ear. The shrapnel exited the forehead and Bacinda remembered looking up at the general's face. It was serene. Faisal never knew what killed him. Perhaps he never knew he had died.

The general's blood, hot and arterial, spurted into Bacinda's face. It fell into the mess tin he was cradling in his hands. His meal of boiled grains was ruined. It came as a great surprise to him that the sudden shower of blood into his meal upset the corporal so much more. He tried to cover the tin with his hands. It had been his first meal in three days. Ludicrously, Bacinda even considered whether the meal was still edible.

Faisal's horse panicked, carrying the general's body away down the breastwork. In a final show of the macabre, the general's body stayed upright in its saddle. The platoon line didn't react. They didn't know how. Even old Sergeant Habuel looked shockingly still. Of all Echo Company, it was Bacinda who put down his tin of bloodied grains with weary resignation. He sighed, lamenting the loss of his rations, then picked up the handset of his vox-caster.

The towers of Angkhora. Or so Asingh-nu told Silverstein.

The burial-centre of Aridun, placed at the axial centre of the Fortress Chain. From their vantage point on the scorched tin of a production mill roof, they could see the skyline of Angkhora. It was hazed by a shimmering screen of heat – heat emanating from the embers and hot, molten rubble of shattered cities.

Although the rural labourer had never been there, he had heard stories of the Fortress Chain from a wealthy cousin. The man had coveted a finely woven rug that depicted the lotus-bud towers where the ancestors of Aridun rested forever. It had made Asingh-nu very jealous.

'The enemy have been pressing towards that central stronghold ever since the first shot. Why?' Silverstein asked as his bioptics clicked and whirred, capturing still images for photo-analysis.

'A man of my education is not meant to know these things. But anyone can tell you it's bad luck. Places where the dead go are not places for the living,' Asingh-nu said, tightening the grip on his autogun.

'Do you hunt, Asingh-nu?' Silverstein said, changing the subject smoothly. He turned to regard the guerrilla with his sutured yellow eyes.

'I was a rural. Of course we did. My sons and I did often. At night we'd walk through our lagoon paddies with a good blunderbuss and track swamp pigs. They were small, but very fat and very delicious with good vinegar.'

'Did you ever lure them, bait them to ensure the fattest, largest bull-swine would appear for the show?'

'Small clumps of stale grain would do the trick. The staler, the yeastier, the better. Sometimes we'd lure three or four of them together at once, fighting over the bait.'

'Well, look at it this way, Asingh-nu. Angkhora is the bait for the Archenemy. It's something they want. That usually means the big game is there, the bull-swine, if you will, of the den.'

'You mean their leader? I'm rural, not stupid,' Asingh-nu shrugged.

Silverstein laughed. 'Of course. But we can really hurt them there. Maybe tag ourselves a few Chaos generals. Would that not be grand?'

Asingh-nu surreptitiously made the sign of the aquila at Silverstein's mention of Chaos. He tapped the mapwood stock of his Garlan auto for good measure.

'I'll go,' he said. 'Maybe I'll find the one who killed my sons.'

The fighting was so close that if Madeline was at certain points of ampli-fication in the cavity tunnel, she swore she could hear the individual gunshots from the city above.

'Captain Silat, have your men prepare the thermal charges. If we – if I – am unable to decipher the text on this entrance seal–'

The captain snapped his heels in salute. 'Already executed, ma'am. I've posted a section of my men around the excavation perimeter. We'll be ready to do it if the Archenemy comes.'

'Thank you, captain, your aid has been invaluable.'

Satisfied, Madeline turned back to trawling the disc-seal with her jewel-ler's lens. It was a monumental effort as the inscriptions were minuscule and her lens, which fitted over one eye, was no larger than the circle formed by her thumb and forefinger. She had not slept or eaten since the Last War had begun. Climbing the scaffolding to study the disc was all she had done.

The disc itself, once unearthed, was exactly seventy seven point seven metres in diameter, and geometrically perfect. The surveyance laser, when it measured the size of the disc, had displayed a mathematical constant. What was more alarming was that the disc was formed entirely out of one solid medallion of bone. In her years of archeotech knowledge, Madeline knew when to recognise bone when she saw it. A well-aged bone was neither dense nor brittle. Soaking up the terroir of its surrounding earth, bone tended to become a waxy, matured ivory that deepened in colour with age. The colour of this bone was tarred brown. She couldn't fathom what kind of creature had bones of such gargantuan width.

'One more thing, ma'am.'

Madeline turned reluctantly from her work and looked down the scaffolding to see Captain Silat standing to attention below.

Madeline rubbed the bridge of her nose. 'Yes, captain?' She said wearily.

'My company. We've been working on this excavation for days and now – well now I've sent most of them upside to defend it. They'll probably die doing so. What I'm trying to say is, ma'am, could you tell us what this is? My boys want to know what they're dying for.'

'Of course, captain,' Madeline said softly. She began to edge her way down the scaffolding.

'What the inscriptions say, and there are many, is that the Old King sleeps within. He will only be awakened at the proper alignment of the ancient planetary schematics and their relation to the stars. It's all very ritualistic. They worshipped the stars here, before Him on Earth, these people worshipped stars like the very old tribes of Terra.'

'Are the stars aligned?'

Madeline bit her lip. She was not sure how much intelligence she should share with a field officer. As she debated with herself, she heard the clatter of bombs through the thick stone overhead. It sounded like a truck had dumped a cargo of anvils onto rockcrete. She concluded that they would not have long anyway. The captain and his men had a right to know.

'Yes. They are. It's what the Archenemy have been planning since the beginning of their invasion. They were marking out the lines of ritual on each conquered planet and waiting for the proper orbits. They were fighting this war on a schedule.'

Silat was stunned. His face was evidently trying to understand. 'They knew?'

Madeline nodded.

'So, if we break the seal, will we wake him – it?' the captain asked.

'That's what I've been trying to decipher. Much of this is written in an old Terran language I have not been properly schooled in. It seems to be recurring that the Old King is captured within some sort of containment vessel beyond this disc. If my translations are accurate, some kind of a "bell" within this tomb.'

'So we should set demo charges to it then?'

'Gosh no!' Madeline said. 'We do not know what is on the other side. We could damage, or worse, somehow wake the Old King. No, no demo!'

'Well what then, ma'am?'

'Give me one or two hours, there is some more text I would like to examine before we attempt to open this seal.'

'What should I prepare then?'

'Prepare a drill. An orthodontic bone drill would be perfect,' Madeline said.

'We're engineers. We have a powered drill-tractor,' the captain offered.

'That'll do, captain. And also, if you could spare at least twenty of your best men. I want them to be here when this disc is breached. Just to be sure…'

The captain saluted with a renewed sense of purpose. 'Of course, ma'am. I'll bring forty.'

CHAPTER THIRTY

The final offensive was mustered at the crematorium district. It was the only sizeable tract of land on which Imperial forces could consolidate without the presence of heavy enemy fire and the threat of repeated ground assault. The intense heat and clamour of war raged in the surrounding districts, but this area was still and quiet.

It was a square plaza, dotted with funereal kilns, arrayed in a pattern that mathematically matched the major constellations overhead. Most of the kilns had been rendered to dust by shelling, and those which had been unscathed were crushed by the heavy tracks of the assembled vehicles.

The assault of the First Mech-Cav had broken the main spear of the enemy advance not ninety minutes past, allowing the infantry battalions enough respite to regroup. Now, as the street-to-street fighting renewed, Cantica's only armoured division ranked together for one final assault. It would be all they'd have left.

The soldiers of the First Mech-Cav sat on the hulls of their tanks, the Lancers nursed their steeds. All stood to attention as Inquisitor Obodiah Roth clambered atop the turret of a Siegfried siege-tank. Standing up there, Roth looked as hardened and tattered as any of those Canticans before him. The inquisitor, they all knew, had bled and fought hard to save their home. He had given them the chance to use all of their training to inflict as much punishment on the Archenemy as possible. As far as the Guardsmen were concerned, the inquisitor was one of theirs now.

303

Roth still wore his fighting-plate and his black scale tabard. The plate was battered, scorched and rashed with pock-marks, and the obsidian was broken-toothed. Over that, he wore the ceremonial longcoat of a Cantican officer. Intelligence staff had instructed him to wear it unbuttoned, so it streamed in the wind like a ragged cape of brown felt. His right hand was loosely viced under the segments of his Tang War power fist and the Sunfury MKIII in a shoulder rig under his coat. To everyone else, he appeared unarmed, utterly in command of himself. It was a time when these men needed the morale, and the intelligence staff had executed their job perfectly.

Roth pulled his long, lupine frame up to full height, standing atop the turret. The suns glinted off his wiry shoulders and made his armour gleam silver. He surveyed the mustered regiment before him. All of the machine-powered war engines that the CantiCol ever had at their disposal, even before the Medina Campaign, had been assigned to the 1st Mech-Cavalry Regiment. The tanks were exceedingly rare and the months of fighting had drained them to their limits. Every tank showed the scars of on-the-run repairs. In all, there were over six hundred tanks – a majority of Leman Russes, a solid lance of Siegfrieds, a scattering of ageing Salamanders, Kurtis tanks and even Centaurs. Escorting them were two battalions of mounted Lancers. Roth knew not all of those were true Lancers; some were Guardsmen who had adopted a spare horse in the heat of battle. But they would suffice, thought Roth. If the last several days of fighting were anything to go by, Roth was sure they would not fail him.

In view of the assembled Guardsmen, an officer of the Aegina Prestige hoisted himself onto the frontal hull of the Siegfried. He snapped up his face visor of diamond polyfibre, in the way of an Aegina salute.

'Major Sebastion Glass of the Seventh Muster, Aegina Prestige, sir.'

'Inquisitor Roth of the Ordo Hereticus.' Roth shook the major's hand and bowed low.

Major Glass, like others of the Prestige, was clad in the bulky accoutrement of urban combat. Grey fatigues, flame retardant boots, thigh holsters, dump pouches, chest harnesses, all made the standard-issue CantiCol canvas satchel look positively spartan. Over this, he wore an outer tactical vest of hand-sewn diamond inserts, complete with throat and groin plates. The vest of diamond sheets had a frosty sheen that showed a subtle contempt for enemy fire.

'Inquisitor Roth. With the fatal wounding of Lord General Faisal, command is granted to you on request of Inquisitorial authority. The Aegina accepts this, and I pledge all the men and arms I have remaining under your command structure.'

Roth bowed formally. 'Thank you, major. How many men do you have?'

'Only two platoons, sir.'

The major gestured to four slate-grey Chimeras. The Aegina Guardsmen were making final weapons checks in two neat rows. Even their standard-issue lasguns were complicated pieces with additional scopes, bipods, folding stocks and even underslung grenade launchers. Others were cleaning and greasing mortars and lascannons. The Aegina were motorised heavy infantry who worked in organic fire-teams. Their platoon-level support weapons and their combination of precision ordnance and lascannon had been invaluable during the last three days of urban fighting. Despite their techno-finery, Roth knew they were good soldiers who had suffered badly. Two full battalions of them had made landfall on Aridun, just four days past.

'You must have suffered heavy casualties in this war, major. The Emperor appreciates the sacrifice the mothers and wives of Aegina have made.'

Major Glass nodded and snapped the clear visor down. As he descended from the tank, Roth turned to address his men.

'Gentlemen. I am not of worth to address you for this coming battle. You have all been soldiers far longer than I ever will. There is nothing I can tell you that you will not already know. Rather, I will tell you intelligence has pin-pointed the location of the Chaos commander, by the preceding movement of his elite retinue. It is a chance to clash our iron against theirs. That is all. Go to your vehicles, gentlemen, and grace be with you.'

Roth hopped down into the turret of the Siegfried as the crew of 1st Mech-Cav scrambled to their stations. The plaza flooded with the harsh, throaty burble of gunning engines. The air was cut by the sweetly toxic stink of petrol. As one, the entire fleet of Cantican armour rolled out to the fighting in a three-pronged column.

The advance rumbled through the streets at full power, hurtling over rubble and pounding through walls. Their tracks churned through the ruins of mausoleums, throwing up a cloying storm of corpse dust and limestone. The Siegfrieds – a hybrid armoured bulldozer and light tank – forged a path at the front of the column, their dozer blades ploughing through the rubble.

In some sectors they encountered unorganised resistance, but speed and combined firepower pushed the Ironclad infantry on the back foot. Their battle cannons, pintle-mounted weapons and auxiliary support guns threw out a wide, branching chain of fire before them. Their advance could be tracked by the streams of tracer, las and shell smoke that latticed the air as the column weaved through the old city.

'Command, this is call-sign Starlight. Repeat Big Game's location. Over,' Roth shouted into the radio speaker over the creaking and thrumming in the tank's confines. 'Big Game' was the code for the Chaos commander, a code Roth was sure that Silverstein would have used had he been with him.

'Starlight, this is command. Our trackers show you are on course, keep moving north, about half a kilometre out. Expect thickening resistance as you near designated zone,' crackled the anonymous intelligence officer over the vox-net.

Roth thought he heard gunfire in the background of the vox, but he could not be sure over the roar of his tank. 'Loud and clear. Can you give us a vox warning as we move within one city block of Big Game? Over,' Roth shouted with one hand to his ear.

There was a tinny but audible sigh on the other end.

'That's a no, sir. Command base is being overrun as we speak. I'll stay on the line for as long as I can.'

Roth dropped the handset from his mouth and swore softly. 'Command, save yourself. I'll keep sharp for Big Game. Keep one round for yourself, soldier. Good luck.'

'Thank you, sir. Out.' The message was said with great finality. The command vox-net clicked out for the last time.

The huntsman stole amongst them. Up until that point he had laid low during the day and shadowed them during the night. Now he scampered above the eaves and rooftops, penetrating deep into the ten kilometre long marching column of Ironclad troopers.

Like any good hunter, Silverstein had learnt by watching the behaviour of his quarry.

Silverstein slid over the ridged guttering of a mausoleum roof. He made sure the stair-street was clear before dropping down and slipping deeper into the warren of lanes. Asingh-nu dropped down and followed him.

No more than one city block away, perhaps closer, they could hear the marching orders of the Ironclad and the brief fire-fights that would erupt as Imperial elements harassed them.

Silverstein halted at a corner, peered around the bend and nodded to Asingh-nu. 'He is close. I can see banners, I see his own men.'

Asingh-nu breathed deeply. 'Back when I was tilling my paddies, I never had to kill a Chaos warlord,' he pronounced insightfully.

'This can be your first,' said Silverstein, and with that the huntsman disappeared around the corner.

'Enemy blockade at intersection ahead. Sight confirmed?'

'Confirmed.'

The backwash chatter of Roth's vox headset was drowned out by the echoing thump of weapons on cyclical fire. Leaning waist up from the Siegfried's turret, Roth sighted the Ironclad blockade from his magnoculars.

There was perhaps a company-sized formation of enemy infantry at the intersection. They were still uncoiling razor wire and attempting to forge together a hasty defence as the front of the First Mech-Cav column closed within firing distance. The enemy fired at them from rooftops, windows and side-alleys. A rocket streaked in front of Roth's tank on a plume of unwinding smoke. As Ironclad troopers appeared in the mouth of laneways, pintle-mounted stubbers from the column spat tracer at them until they disappeared from view. Roth saw the turret gunner from the Leman Russ in front kneecap an Ironclad with a sustained drag of his stubber. As the Chaos raider buckled in two, the gunner yelped in triumph. A shot from an adjacent balcony took his head off and he slid lifelessly back down the turret. The drumming of small-arms fire on armour plate became a deafening rain.

'Spear Three, this is Spear Two. Enemy blockade sighted at right of advance, engaging – over.'

'Received. Out,' Roth shouted into his wraparound vox-mic.

As promised, Spear Two, the second prong of the advance, cut through the Ironclad blockade in a perpendicular direction. They lit up the enemy to their front with a salvo of flanking fire. There was a shattering report and the explosive bark of cannons. One second Roth saw through his magnoculars the running shapes of Ironclad, scarpering behind a makeshift roadblock of rubble and tin sheets. The next he saw the blockade shred in all directions and the running shapes break and bounce into chunks of meat.

'Two to all spears, the intersection is clear of hostiles.'

'Loud and clear, Two, good job,' Roth voxed.

The two prongs merged at the intersection before splitting into opposing pincers around a cemetery block. Paralleling their route, the third column rumbled their way alongside the viaduct, throwing tracer and shell out across the canal. They continued, trading shots with heavy resistance, towards their objective.

The bandit insurgency had never been this bad. Bombardier Krusa had been stationed for eight years at Mon Sumlayit in Cantica, fighting the bandit kings. It had been bad then, patrolling those harsh, windy hinterlands. It was not uncommon for bandits to trap lone patrols of Cantican Guardsmen, surrounding them during the night and butchering them with stick bombs and machete. The war had raged there for thirty years and was as bitter the whole time Krusa served there. Roadside bombs, night raids, close-quarter skirmishes – taking the mountains had been hell. For every one and a half bandits killed, they lost the life of one Guardsman and still the insurgency swelled with the influx of rural, poverty-stricken men. It had been a mean fight and Krusa had lost many friends there, yet this war made the insurgency feel like a comfort tour.

Bombardier Salai Krusa served with the 5th Cantican Colonial Artillery, and they held position on a demolished plateau of an upper-tier burial stack. Up until eight hours previously, their front had been defended by several battalions of CantiCol infantry, allowing the battery to work their Griffons, Basilisks and field guns against the Archenemy. But now the Archenemy had penetrated to the rear lines. The soft belly of field hospitals and comm stations behind the fighting front were the first to go. It was heard over the vox that the Ironclad were running their heavy tanks over surgical tents along with the occupant wounded.

It had been traumatising to listen to the voices of infantry officers he recognised, broadcasting last goodbyes over the vox-net as their positions were overrun, one by one. First it had been the frantic voice of Sergeant Samir of 40th Battalion radioing enemy positions, then it had been Captain Ghilantra, commander of Zulu Company of the 55th screaming sit-reps before his link went dead. They were all men that Krusa had worked with at one point. One after another, and now the Archenemy were on them.

'Load the case-shots! Case-shots in the line!' yelled an artillery officer. The call was echoed along the batteries and Bombardier Krusa took the command to his loaders.

His loaders moved quickly despite the ceaseless days of toil. Their cotton shirts were stiff with salt and their braces sagged by their breeches. Sweat rolled in beads along their grimy necks.

'Case-shot loaded,' announced Private Surat. A shell of close-range ordnance was loaded into the breech of the sixty-pounder.

Ironclad troopers appeared over the crest of their plateau – thousands of them at once with no semblance of spacing or tactical manoeuvre.

'Hold! Hold!' shouted the artillery officers.

The Ironclad charged across the open field of broken rock towards them. There was less than fifty paces of open ground between them. Krusa took hold of the firing chain with both hands.

'Fire!'

There was a jagged crack of guns. Jets of smoke and muzzle flash rocked the massive field guns. They jerked back on recoil pistons. Eight guns fired in unison, vomiting a dense cloud of hyper-velocity ball bearings. It blackened the open space between them like a swarm of insects. The bandits on Mon Sumlayit had always baulked at a whiff of canister-shot. No matter how hungry or desperate the bandits got during the arid seasons, canister shot had always been enough to scatter, force them into trading shots with poorly maintained autorifles. Never in his service had Krusa seen the enemy run headlong into a wall of shrapnel. Like crumpled puppets the first rank of Ironclad shed away onto the ground.

Unabated, the ranks behind them kicked and stomped their way over the wounded. One volley was all they had time for before the Ironclad were swarming over the sandbags.

Bombardier Krusa was amongst the first killed. A beaked warhammer punched through his thin orbital bone and spiked into his brain. His last thoughts, even as the warhammer was protruding from his eye, was that it would have been better to have died like his friends on Sumlayit. Bombardier Susilo had been shot by a machine pistol while on night sentry. Even Private Riau who was shot by a sniper while on border patrol had been killed cleanly by headshot. It took Bombardier Krusa some time to die. He was still very much struggling to live, spasming in shock and bleeding out from his face as the Archenemy stomped over him. This war was much worse than any he had seen.

CHAPTER THIRTY-ONE

Khorsabad Maw was in his gunsights.

Khorsabad Maw, the King of Corsairs. Arch-heretic of the Rimward East. Sworn servant of the Apostles Martial.

Silverstein had the Chaos warlord wavering under the targeting reticule of his autorifle. With each steadily drawn breath, the reticule rose and fell.

Down from his minaret balcony, three hundred metres down on the streets below, Khorsabad was marching with his garish procession, singing, chanting, the column macabre in its harlequin manner. Spilling out to either side of the Chaos lord were his Iron Ghasts, surrounding him with no semblance of rank or order to their unruly mob. They brandished ornamental paper banners and papier-mâché scenes detailing four thousand years of misdeed. Amongst the forest of vibro-pikes, Ironclad were rattling hand drums, warbling discordant horns and dancing in a stiff-limbed frenzy. As their warlord's procession ebbed past, Ironclad troopers pushed towards their Arch-heretic in a show of adoration. The Iron Ghasts kept them at bay with their pikes, fighting on the verge of rioting. To the untrained eye it resembled more of a carnival than a military motorcade. Silverstein even spotted an Ironclad trooper, starkly naked but for his face-bindings, dancing about, swinging a smoking censer and cutting himself with a razor in the other hand.

Once a long time ago, Silverstein had visited Murahaba during their festival of love lost. The people there had paraded, some dancing in a possessed frenzy that was eerie to behold. The crowd toted papier-mâché masks of monstrous proportions and chanted in tongues. Paper effigies were burned and discordant instruments were drummed ceaselessly. The Chaos lord's procession had a similar taint of the mystic macabre.

'Frightening, isn't it? Do you see him?' said Asingh-nu, peering down at the dizzying drop below.

'Yes. I see him.'

Silverstein made sure to see the warlord through the filtered lenses of augmetics. He dared not study the warlord in such clarity with his naked eyes. Silverstein was sure that only bad would come of it. Under the intensified spectrum of his bioptics, Silverstein could measure every detail of Khorsabad Maw.

He was still a man. Or rather, he still held the shape of one.

Khorsabad was not at all the brutal monstrosity Silverstein had expected. Maw was slim, and well articulated to the point of being doll-like. The litheness of his limbs could not be hidden by the overlapping warren of silk, splintmail and chain that wadded him. His face was of elaborately woven iron, slightly reminiscent of a porcelain doll. It was smooth and featureless except for a small, up-turned pinch of the nose. At one and a half metres tall, Khorsabad would have looked like a finely costumed iron toy had it not been for the mantle of quills running along his shoulders and back.

He was borne aloft on a gaudy litter of painted paper and textured fabric, by a solid phalanx of Iron Ghasts. The Ghasts stood upright on a crab-shelled super-heavy tractor, as if forming some unholy ziggurat. Escort FPVs and mounted outriders rolled alongside the pedestrian traffic. Parting the crowds like oceanic leviathans were the hulls of broad, super-heavy flamer tanks, their trawl turrets snorting wisps of fire.

'Asingh-nu,' Silverstein began, 'I only have one shot at this. This is the only shot, of all my shots so far, which matters. I need you to sit here and not say a word. Do not move. Do not sigh. Do not tremor. You have been a good friend up until now and I expect you will not let me down.'

The guerrilla nodded warily and settled down into a hunch, hugging his autogun. Silverstein adjusted his scope bracket and snuggled down behind it.

He began by tracking for a weakness on Khorsabad. His entire spine was exposed and pitted like raw ore and sutured with his silks. The iron quills formed clusters of scaly scuttles at his lower back and lengthened gradually into the fifty-centimetre long pikes that branched out like floral growth along the top of his back. Silverstein decided that shooting the natural armour of any creature would not be a killing shot. He tracked his scope to the Chaos lord's head. It was dainty and perfectly formed with a complex braid of iron lattices. There were no vision slits or mouth pieces. It was more than likely the Chaos lord's head, and that was where Silverstein hovered his target reticule.

Silverstein closed his eyes, loosening the muscles of his shoulder and neck. He took two breaths and then adjusted his aim to be several centimetres in front of his target's expected path. The ambush method was the basic method for hitting moving targets, and Silverstein's favourite. He settled himself, slowed his breathing and his body's intake of oxygen.

The huntsman thought back to his days as a scout for the senior hunters of the lodge. Back to his youth in the conifer woods of Veskipine, when the northern lights would shine at dusk and air was crisp with cold. He had tracked exotic off-world game on the estates for days at a time. His favourite had been hunting the sentient primates. Those animals fought back, organised and used tools; sometimes the primates even hunted them. Those had been the best hunts and Silverstein had spent much of his formative years shouldering his brother's autorifle and mimicking the mating dirges of the meso-ape.

Silverstein opened his eyes. Khorsabad Maw was ghosting towards his centre of aim. Silverstein exhaled, allowing the scope to sink. His gradual inhalation buoyed the reticule back on target. Khorsabad Maw's polished cranium slid perfectly and precisely within the target's sights. The huntsman allowed the target a nanosecond shift to the left, allowing for wind direction and the natural curve of trajectory.

Silverstein fired.

The trigger pull was smooth despite the speed with which his nerves had wired the command to the muscles of his hand. The trajectory, the fall of mark, the wind current. Everything was as Silverstein knew it would be.

But the round never made its mark. Khorsabad Maw's force shields crackled with static film as the round impacted with it. The sudden discharge showed a perfect semi-sphere of iridescent force where it had been invisible before.

Silverstein jumped up from his post, his eyes wide. Suddenly, up on that minaret balcony he felt utterly vulnerable. The eyes of all those Archenemy soldiers below looked up at him, as one.

'Get down, Asingh!' shouted Silverstein. He threw himself backwards as the entire balcony erupted and literally shook apart. The assembled masses below opened up on the tower with all their combined arms. The stone balcony became a rapidly deteriorating sponge as chips of rock disintegrated under the storm of fire. Asingh-nu took a round in the stomach. Silverstein dragged the guerrilla into the tower proper. Heavy-calibre rounds punched holes through the walls and shattered the windows. Smoke and brick-dust was making him gag.

As the dust settled, the balcony was no longer there. There was just a scorched hole in the wall and empty space beyond.

'I'm hit,' Asingh-nu groaned. He shrimped up into the foetal position, clutching at his abdomen. Blood seeped out from between his folded arms.

The fire died down as quickly as it had started, but the huntsman still heard the frantic pounding of weapons. Only now, he was no longer the sole target of their ferocity. He expected to hear the sounds of forced entry at the tower below, but when none came, he decided to hazard a peek from the holes in the wall. The sounds of fighting below were too enticing.

Fifty storeys down, he saw Khorsabad's procession engaging with targets to their front and flanks. Further up the road and along a side junction, Silverstein saw an approaching column of armour. Imperial armour. They were charging at full power, turret weapons flashing.

Leman Russes rammed into the procession, pintle mounts throbbing and battle cannons seeking out Maw's motorcade escorts. The Ironclad replied when the flamer platforms began belching horizontal tornados of fire. They fired indiscriminately, at Ironclad and Imperial alike, spewing masses of flame that consumed oxygen with audible roars.

Amongst them, Silverstein picked up the distinct profile of a Siegfried siege-tank, with a pugnacious snout of its dozer blades and its swivelling tower turrets. There, leaning out of the cylindrical turret and firing the tank's pintle-bolter, Silverstein saw Inquisitor Obodiah Roth.

Khorsabad's victory procession was moving down the central high road of Angkhora, a broad access-way that was wide enough to accommodate the legions of Ironclad streaming out behind the advance of the Chaos lord.

As the Imperial column hooked in at a mid-route intersection, Khorsabad's procession lurched into view. Immediately, hundreds of Ironclad troopers greeted them with small-arms fire. Some took a knee, their shots spanking off the metal tank hulls. Others threw themselves before the tank treads, laying prostrate in sacrifice to their Khorsabad.

Lancer cavalry burst in ahead of the tank charge, their sabres flashing. There was an audible crunch as the Lancers rushed amongst the Archenemy in a wall of lashing hooves and slashing swords. Men flew off horses, or were trampled in the press. Khorsabad Maw's Iron Ghasts braced themselves around him, standing back to back and shoulder to shoulder in a semi-sphere of bristling vibro-pikes.

The firing became frantic. The statues that lined the street began to explode, one by one. The walls along the streets looked as if they were being sand-blasted.

Roth didn't even bother hunching down behind his turret. There were too many rounds in the air and he'd just as likely get hit standing up or squatting down. A frag missile reared up and shot out at Roth's tank from the jolting mass of Ironclad. The warhead punched through the plating of the turret, the tip of the missile emerging around a flower of ragged tank metal at waist-level. It was suspended there, quivering but dormant.

Looking at the unexploded missile, Roth began to laugh. The laughter was solace. It held him together and came easily.

In the pandemonium of shooting, Roth's Siegfried bulldozed into the line of Ironclad. Vibro-pikes snapped holes into dozerblades and reached up alongside the hull, jabbing at his turret. Someone was blasting a machine-pistol at him at point-blank range, the fat-calibre rounds ricocheting off the tank with angry sparks. The surprise of being shot at overrode the compulsion of fear. Rather than ducking, Roth gripped the pintle-mounted bolter and shot off a few loud, booming spurts.

'I'm taking fire to our flanks and front!' Roth shouted down the turret at his crew. It wasn't necessary. The crew knew it was all close quarters from here. The Siegfried's multi-laser swivelled and unleashed a short cyclical pulse, hosing the enemy from left to right. Ironclad toppled and the rest scattered, trying to put some distance and other bodies between themselves and the spitting turret.

'Everyone is taking fire everywhere!' an anonymous crewman shouted back up at Roth from the interior.

By the time the fight had boiled into a close-quarter street fight, the column had already taken some heavy damage. Every vehicle was low on ammo; they had expended thousands of rounds just fighting their way through the city towards the objective.

The siege-tank to Roth's immediate left had its turret disabled and could only fire along its axis of advance. The Siegfried to his right had blown both tracks and was being pushed along by the Leman Russ behind it. All of the Imperial tanks Roth could see were punched through with holes, so badly in places that the hulls looked like perforated mesh. A Kurtis tank several metres in front was smoking, a gaping rocket wound in its front. Ironclad were swarming over the vehicle, dragging the crew from the hatch.

Through the seething press, Roth could make out the throne of Khorsabad Maw. The Chaos lord looked child-like in his swaddling mantle of silks, plate and chain, his porcelain hands folded neatly atop each other. He did not seem at all fazed by the fight that raged around him. If it were not for the spinal quills that rose in majestic wreaths from his shoulders, Roth might not have recognised Khorsabad Maw at all. The guards who carried him took care not to jostle his throne, even as they lashed out with their pikes. The Chaos tank on which the warlord's sedan was mounted rolled along at a lumbering pace, gouting sheets of flame at everything before it.

The sight of the Chaos lord made Roth's breathing sharp and shaky. He had the architect of this entire hell-fight before him. Adrenaline coiled like a spring in his belly, pressurised and loaded. It compelled him to jump up and down, fury and anticipation thrumming from his fingertips. It was like a fist-fencing prizefight. Roth's focus became singular. His vision tunnelled in on Khorsabad Maw; everything else became distant, detached and utterly incomprehensible.

Roth sharpened his words into a psychic spear: +Minion of the Apostles Martial. I have come for you!+

The words did not seem to startle the warlord. Instead Khorsabad Maw looked at him. Even without vision slits, Roth felt the Chaos lord actually look at him. Roth couldn't shake the feeling he had incurred the attention of the Ruinous Powers at that very moment.

Roth lifted his Inquisitorial rosette in challenge.

Khorsabad Maw leapt from his litter with a tremendous jump. He went up high like an ordnance shell before coming down sharply, bouncing from tank hull to tank hull. He was moving at speed, clearing a distance of fifty metres before Roth could draw his pistol. As Khorsabad leapt, the multiple capes of his regalia flew out behind him. The carapace armour beneath could not hide the lithe, powerful body, fine-jointed and perfectly proportioned like a dancer's.

He landed on an FPV, blowing out its windows and crumpling it flat like an anvil.

He must weigh at least half a tonne, thought Roth. He hit like a little wrecking ball.

The Siegfried opened up all its support weapons on the Chaos lord at a distance of less than ten metres: turret multilaser, hull-mounted heavy stubber and pintle-mounted storm bolter. The deluge of tracer had drummed Khorsabad's force field like a deluge of molten orange rain. It was so bright that Roth had to shield his eyes away from the point of contact. Despite the slight twitch of electrical static, the ammunition cycled dry before the force field could short. Immediately the Chaos lord was on them, jumping onto the front hull with enough force to rock the tank.

The Chaos lord moved with such liquid speed that Roth barely had time to throw out a timid jab with his power fist. Restricted in his turret, the punch had no weight or vinegar behind it. It agitated the force bubble and staggered Khorsabad Maw. Suddenly wary, the Chaos lord circled the turret, stomping fracture dents into the top of the tank as he moved.

'Are you done reloading this bloody thing?' Roth screamed at his crew as Khorsabad stalked him in circles like a hungry predator. Those dainty hands – Roth was sure – could dismantle him like boiled poultry.

He had never seen such raw power before. The Blood Gorgon who had claimed Pradal had been a behemoth of strength and towering rage. But Khorsabad Maw did not possess the visual size and power of an Astartes. Khorsabad Maw was a full head and shoulders shorter than Roth and he was not in power armour, yet there he was, about to shred the tank with his bare, delicate hands.

The multilaser suddenly popped into life, juddering a spray of incandescence at Khorsabad. The Chaos lord bounded backwards off the tank and out of sight.

Roth slapped the side of the turret with his hands. 'Reverse the engine!'

The Siegfried lurched backwards sharply before jolting forwards again.

The siege-tank ran into and over the Chaos lord. With a dull thump, the tank went over, heavy treads grinding. Roth could hear the squeal of mangled metal, yet when Roth turned to inspect the damage, the Chaos lord was standing. Roth fumbled to reload his plasma pistol.

Faster than Roth could react, Khorsabad Maw snatched the rear of the Siegfried in his hands, fingers denting buttery holes into the metal. The Siegfried's gas turbine engines were pushed to their limit, grunting like a wounded bull. Khorsabad fought the tank, digging his heels into the rubble. Then with an explosive cleaning motion, Khorsabad Maw launched the entire vehicle over his head and into the air.

The Siegfried came down, bottom side up, after flipping cleanly in the air. The weight of the tank virtually destroyed itself. Armour plating flew, the engine block compressed the crew compartment. Tracks flipped high into the air. If the initial shock of crash-landing had not killed the crew, the physical trauma of six tonnes of steel imploding and exploding surely would have. Roth lay prone some metres away, having been thrown out of the open turret during the tank's spiralling descent. He had landed badly.

When Roth came to, he was sure his leg was broken. It was the pain that roused him from unconsciousness. He felt the edges of his femur grate against muscle and test his sinew.

Khorsabad Maw stalked towards him. The Chaos lord's force field was flickering in and out, but he was otherwise unscathed. The tank had done little to hurt him.

Khorsabad Maw spoke to him. The words had a soft metallic hum to them, like a wind being blown through the tubes of an iron organ. 'You are a dead man. I am going to kill you, I am going to break you and I am going to pour molten silver in your ears.'

With a wild cry, two Cantican Lancers wielding their sabres overhead charged at the warlord. Khorsabad Maw dealt them one soft tap to the neck each. The movement was so casual that it was barely perceptible. Both Guardsmen fell sideways, their necks so utterly shattered that their chins rested in their chests. More Cantican Colonials rushed the Chaos lord. Horse cavalry ringed a rough box around them, pushing against the Iron Ghasts who formed a mauling scrum towards their lord. Sabres clattered against vibro-pikes. Guardsmen were fighting to form a desperate ring around the wreckage of Roth's tank. They knew full well the outcome of engaging the Chaos lord but they did it anyway. Five or six Lancers rushed at the Chaos lord. Roth didn't want to see. He closed his eyes, propped himself up on his elbows and reloaded his pistol.

As Khorsabad turned his attention back to Roth, the inquisitor shot him. The force shield blinked but held. The Chaos lord sprinted towards him, his acceleration inhumanly fast.

Roth braced himself. Khorsabad closed the distance. Roth shot with his plasma pistol. The spheres of energy warped as they made contact with Khorsabad's force field, dissipating with bright flashes. Blue static convulsed across the shield's surface.

A fraction away from striking distance, the Chaos lord's head snapped up. At first Roth thought Khorsabad Maw had tripped. Khorsabad Maw, Arch-heretic of the Rimward East, did not trip.

Someone shot him. Twice.

The two bullets had passed the flickering shield as Roth's plasma rounds tested the generators. A neat entry hole opened up on Khorsabad Maw's left temple and exited in a fist-sized crater out his opposite cheek. Another went through his neck. At first there was no blood. Then there was lots of blood. It burst in great arterial spurts, filming the inside of Khorsabad Maw's force bubble. Someone had shot the great Khorsabad Maw.

Roth was lying at the Chaos lord's feet. The inquisitor watched the four-thousand-year-old Arch-heretic fall to his knees, batting his hands weakly against his ruptured head. It was all that mattered. The rest was in the Emperor's hands now. CantiCol and Ironclad swarmed around them in a surging mess, but Roth lay down with his broken leg. He had already done all that he could for this war and no one could ask any more of him. He lay down and watched Khorsabad Maw die.

Tap-tap.

It was an instinctive double shot. Silverstein had pre-empted his shots between the electrical convulsions of the Chaos lord's force generators.

The huntsman had just claimed his one perfect shot. Twice. But that did not matter to Silverstein. He was already tracking with his scope. An Ironclad rushed towards Roth. Silverstein put a round through his sternum. The scope moved again, floating over an Ironclad charging at Roth with a maul. The huntsman shot him down too. The shots sounded with clarity from the minaret, putting down the Ironclad around Roth's prone form.

'Damn!' hissed Silverstein.

The fight condensed into a roiling, heaving mass of bodies. CantiCol and Ironclad obscured Roth from Silverstein. He tried to pan in with his bioptics, zooming his vision into grainy pixels, but he could not see Roth. The Canticans were pushing forwards, the Ironclad momentum disintegrating with the demise of their Corsair King. Further back from the fighting, the empty paper throne toppled, its fluttering pennants crushed beneath the retreating tracks of an Ironclad super-heavy. The

Ironclad were flooding back down the way they came.

Silverstein tossed a crumb of rubble in frustration. There was no way he could get to Roth through the killing down there. Reluctantly, the huntsman backed away from the stumps of the balcony. There would be no following Roth. Not through the dense lines of Ironclad. And he could not leave Asingh-nu to die by himself. Silverstein had grown rather fond of him. The huntsman stole one last look at the area where Roth had been.

'Good luck,' he whispered. With that, Silverstein returned to Asingh-nu to wait out the end.

The remnants of the 1st Mech-Cav and their Lancer escort withdrew hurriedly once the damage had been inflicted. The armoured columns, now substantially reduced in size and leaving a wake of burning wreckages, fought their way back to the last Imperial-held district in Angkhora – the excavation site.

A squad of infantry dragged Roth into the back of a Chimera. The ride back to the green zone was crowded and bumping. He could hear the enemy weapons bashing at the outside of the vehicle and wondered if a heavy weapon might score a lucky shot and smoke them all. Every bump in the road jostled his broken leg. He blacked out several times, and the journey back was lost.

Roth came to in a darkened tunnel, with a field medic shining a torch into his eyes and applying smelling salts beneath his nose.

'Get that away from me!' Roth said, a tad snappier than he had meant to.

He tried to rise and realised that his left thigh had been stripped and given a field splint. His leg throbbed, but he had stimmed enough painkillers to settle the pain into a dull glow. The acrid ammonia of the smelling salts were still fuming his sinuses, rousing his pain-addled mind.

'Why am I down here? Where are my men?' Roth started.

'The lady, Madame Madeline, requested you be brought down here, away from the fighting,' the medic said, stepping away. Roth realised he was startling the young Guardsman.

'My apologies–' Roth began.

'Stow it, Roth. I don't mean to be terse but I wanted you to be here when I open the seal.'

Roth craned his neck to look behind him, squinting at the sodium lamps that lit the subterranean darkness. Madeline de Medici was standing behind him. She was wearing a curious outfit that resembled a diving suit. Roth could see her face through the porthole window of her bulbous helmet. Hazard work-suits – he had seen Guard engineers working with them in chemically treated environments. The rubbery leather overalls were lined with lead, and the wrist and ankle cuffs were seamed to the gloves and boots.

'You look good,' Roth said.

'You look a mess as usual,' Madeline said. She crossed over to him and helped him up with thickly mittened hands. Roth wobbled slightly as he adjusted to his crutches.

'Tell me that it's opened,' Roth said.

'We're about to open it. Once Medic Subah here helps you into one of these hazard suits.'

Roth raised a questioning eyebrow as the medic began to scoop the thick overalls and boots over Roth's leg. 'What is this for?'

'It's an embryonic star we are dealing with, Roth. Elementary knowledge of the galaxy would mean that there will be radiation if the star breaks free.'

'Elementary knowledge would also suggest that a star is likely not going to be standing behind that rock-door waiting to greet us. It *should* be contained, remember?'

'We don't know that for sure. It pays to be careful, Roth,' she said in a serious tone that concluded all argument.

The city-fight was so close to the excavation site that they could hear the echo of guns coming down the tunnel shaft.

'You better hurry, we have enemies at the gate,' Roth said, screwing the porthole of his helmet tight.

The industrial tunnel-boring machine was Guard-issue and no larger than a tractor. The driver gave a thumbs-up with his hazard mitten and the nose-coned drill started. With a monotone shriek it ground into the ancient bone disc. The drill spat a spray of sparks when molten bone shavings fizzed into the air.

There was no explosion, or sudden release of cataclysmic energy as Madeline had feared. The drill punched a wide hole into the thick disc and reversed its cycle as the tractor backed away. It revealed a circular cavity in the bone, rough and smoking where the polished bone had been drilled away. There was darkness beyond, and a hole big enough for a man to fit through.

The Guard platoon in their bulky suits all aimed lasguns at the smoking darkness. Madeline, aiding Roth on his crutches, hurried over to the break in the seal.

'There is a whole other chamber in here,' she said, shining a phosphor torch into the entrance.

'I'll go first,' Captain Silat volunteered. Madeline stepped aside to let the captain shimmy through on his belly, rifle-first. They aided Roth through, passing the crutches over and then easing him through legs-first. Madeline and several other Guardsmen followed.

Inside, the chamber was immense. A perfectly cut cube inside the crust of Aridun's rock mantle. There was a sense of perfect symmetry to it. Roth perceived it because he had never been surrounded by an artificial structure so precise in its execution. It gave him a strange sensation of humbling vertigo.

'The carvings, look at the carvings,' gasped Madeline in awe as she played her torch beam along the walls and ceiling.

There on the smooth stone were the constellations of Medina and its surrounding systems. Like a cartographer's chart, lunar trajectories, planar cycles and heliocentric orbits were mapped out in sweeping lines and curves. Roth could see carvings of the Shoal Clusters, the Kingfisher's Belt and even constellations in regions that the Imperium had not yet explored.

'Are these carvings accurate?' whispered Captain Silat.

'Do you doubt them?' Roth asked. The captain had no answer for him.

The smooth floors were marked with carvings, too. They were standing on a map of the Medina Corridor, its planets all in proper alignment, the ley-lines across every planet's surface forming a conduit – according to Madeline's notes – of polar energy.

At the centre of the map, where Aridun should have been, was a bell-shaped silo. It was planted squarely in the otherwise empty chamber. The silo was about the height of a man, not particularly large by any means. Formed from verdigrised copper, its bas-relief surface was coarse with rust and mineral deposit.

'Is that it?' Madeline asked.

Roth limped towards the bell for a closer inspection. Slowly, he edged his hand out to touch it. The surface of it was cold. In a patch of green copper, Roth could make out carvings of crude straight-lined men dancing beneath depictions of flying ships. There were also inscriptions, written in a flowing cursive script that Roth could not understand.

'Madeline, this is ancient.' Roth beckoned her closer. 'Can you read it?'

The archaeologist pondered over the bell, examining it closely. 'Some parts. It's written in a very poetic form of Oceanic Terran language. It describes the correlation of the dormancy of this star-ancient, to the orbit of the star system and the helio-markings of each planet.'

'Time, Madeline, time. Please hurry,' Roth said, reminding her of the battle that threatened to overrun them.

'These are not the exact words. But it seems to suggest that when the planets are not in alignment, the embryonic star is in a stasis state of condensation, shrinking towards itself. It becomes dense matter. They describe it as coiling slumber.'

'Please, for us laymen?' Captain Silat asked.

'Dense space matter becomes immeasurably heavy. You would not be able to budge this silo anywhere with all your industrial machines. It would also be in a stasis-state of reduction.'

'I see. So what does it say about when the Medina Corridor is in the correct alignment?' Roth asked.

Madeline shrugged her suit. 'I can only gather from what I read here. When the polar lines are in alignment, it changes the polar alignment of planets. The embryonic star contained within goes into a state of expansion, and its mass becomes less dense. Light enough to be transported in its state of stasis.'

'Transported and perhaps released from stasis?' Roth said. He flexed the lead-lined leather across his neck to smear the sweat away. It was cold in the chamber but he was sweating profusely. A by-product of too much adrenaline.

'Correct. Once the stasis state of this star is broken, it will continue to expand and expand and expand.'

'The Archenemy do not need this star to destroy the Medina Worlds. That would bring them nothing. But once the stasis is broken, they can transport this star anywhere, even to Terra, or the Cadian Gate. Better it here, than anywhere else.' Captain Silat was thinking strategically, as he had been taught to.

Madeline left that statement unchallenged. For a while nobody said anything. Within that silo, captured in stasis, was an embryonic star. This was just one of the Old Kings that pre-Imperial Medinians had worshipped. But this one they had plucked from the sky with the help of the Early Sentients. This was the angry god they would unleash if ever their civilisations were threatened.

The very same angry god who had been unleashed in the Reclamation Wars. The star hadn't been in expansion then, the polar conduits had not been carved to the precise schematics ordained by the Early Sentients. Instead the gamma flare as the star sparked and returned to stasis had eroded Aridun's ozone and caused the mass extinction. This thing was a destroyer of worlds.

'I'll break it.'

Everyone turned to look at Roth.

'I'll break it from stasis right now,' Roth declared again.

Madeline opened her mouth to speak but Roth silenced her with a wave of his hand.

'There's no time to think about it. The Archenemy will take this and they will use it on the Bastion Stars. I cannot allow that. Better I release it from its sleep here. How big can a star get?'

'Big enough, probably, to consume the entire Medina Corridor. It's impossible to tell,' Madeline suggested.

'Medina is gone. Chaos has subjugated the whole damn system.'

Roth turned to face the silo, patting it gently with his Tang War gauntlet. With one swift motion he pushed the silo over. It yielded like a ripe fruit and toppled from its base with a clang that echoed around the perfect amplification of the cubic chamber.

'Go now. Or stay if you must. I'm going to open this here.'

Madeline moved towards Roth, but Captain Silat stopped her and tried to usher her away by the elbow.

'Professor de Medici. Your service has been invaluable to me,' Roth said.

The inquisitor stood over the bell silo. He tugged the mitten off his Tang War gauntlet and allowed his weapon to charge. He took one last look at the artefact that had cost him so much. The Old King, the Star Ancient, the astronomical body worshipped as something it had no right to be. Roth lifted his power fist and fractured the silo in one clean strike.

The tomb bell was split, opening a chasm down its centreline. Inside was the star, now released. At first it was subatomic, an infinitesimal particle invisible to the naked eye. Yet its existence was undeniable as it bathed the entire chamber in an ambient green glow. It was like a microbial sun casting its light for an interior universe, colouring the sweeping map of the Medina Corridor, illuminating the mathematical lines.

Roth could feel its energy, thrumming harmonics in the air, prickling heat upon his skin. He waited in reverent silence as the star continued to grow. Soon it was as large as a fist, a boiling sphere of emerald gas. The interior casing of the broken tomb bell began to scorch and bubble into molten slag. The temperature and radiation accelerated so quickly that Roth could wait no longer. Without a word, the Task Group scrambled for cover as the star began to awaken.

EPILOGUE

During the sixty-eighth hour of the Last War, the embryonic star was roused from its dormant state.

At the centre of the four hundred-kilometre wall of Fortress Chain, a swirling disc of light could be seen, even from orbit by the Ninth Route Fleet. It appeared as a whirling nexus, the energies of thermonuclear fusion spearing outwards with solar flares. The pulses even disrupted communications equipment on board the *Carthage* at high anchor.

The last Naval craft to leave Aridun tried to evacuate as many personnel as it could carry from the excavation site. Brigade commanders and staff generals were crammed alongside shell-shocked privates and NCOs. The Naval pilots simply tried to get as many bodies into their hangars before the Ironclad overran the perimeter.

Inquisitor Roth – all that remained of the Conclavial Task Group – along with a Professor Madeline Rebequin Louise de Medici boarded the last flight out of Aridun. A Marauder fighter-bomber was risking one last sortie to evacuate Roth. They carried him up on a stretcher, the Guardsmen parting the crowd for Inquisitor Roth as he was rushed up the landing ramp. Already some of the NCOs nearby were barking at the younger soldiers to make way for 'their general'.

The CantiCol still fought, up until the last hour of the planet's existence. The resistance, however, was largely pyrrhic. Pockets of CantiCol Guardsmen who had been scattered during the Archenemy siege continued to resist. Wallowing through the smoke, Guardsmen sniped at

Ironclad formations. For the many who had run out of ammunition, they took themselves out into the middle of the streets, clutching unpinned grenades to their chest. They walked out into the night to find a suitable patch of rubble and lay down to die. It was in the hope that they would fall asleep and release the grenade, or the Archenemy would disturb them. Either way it was as quick and dignified a death as they could manage.

Before the fourth dawn of the Last War, the CantiCol no longer existed as a fighting regiment of the Imperial Guard. But by then, the entire Medina Corridor was well on its way to extinction. The embryonic star had convulsed into a rapidly expanding swirl of dust and dark matter. It glowed and flashed like the heart of a scarlet hurricane. Cones of contrasting green gamma flashed from its pressure gradient as expanding gas clouds boiled around it in smoky wreaths. The incalculable heat and pressure entirely consumed the planet of Aridun, and as it gradually gyrated into an expanding sphere, it consumed Cantica, Orphrates and Kholpesh. Within the end of the lunar cycle, the star had expanded into a fully-fledged white sun.

As of 999.M41, the Old King star is one of the largest celestial bodies in the Eastern Fringe and a navigational marking for the rimward shipping lanes. It resides where the Medina Corridor had once been, having consumed the majority of planets and rendering the frontier planets of Naga and Sinope inhabitable by proximity.

Not much further is mentioned in the annals of Imperial history regarding Inquisitor Obodiah Roth, at least not in the chronicles of the Medina Campaign. He was transported back onto the *Carthage* and monitored for signs of radioactive exposure in the presence of the embryonic star. It is said that he recovered quickly, and spent most of the proceeding days viewing the demise of the Medina Worlds from the starboard ports until the star grew too bright to be directly gazed upon. It would have blinded him, had he tried. Roth would later write in his memoirs, that the fate of the Medina Corridor rested heavily on his shoulders and followed him to his deathbed.

Of his final decision, he wrote: 'To no great surprise of my own, I was never the general in shining armour or apostle of the martial virtues. History has a place for those but I was just a young man incumbent with duty. Everything I had ever accomplished, up until that point, had led to this... [The Medina Extinction] The consumption of an entire star system was entirely my doing. I often wondered what Gurion, back on board the *Carthage*, truly thought of me. He had not been there. And if he had, would he have done the same? It is a point I regret never having discussed with him until his passing. To this day, I am not sure whether this had been my ultimate victory or most infamous failure. The Archenemy had been denied their objective. In military terms, that should rightly be considered a victory. Yet it is a difficult view to reconcile. In achieving it, I had lost the entire Medina Corridor, billions of lives, vanquished history and lost many, many friends.'

Bastiel Silverstein sprinted up the ramp of a docked troop carrier. Archenemy soldiers surged around him, fighting for position onto the frigate. There was no order to their retreat. The raiders pushed and elbowed, some were even stabbing or hacking their way onto the vessel. To his front, an Ironclad Elteber raised a flak pistol and fired into the air in an attempt to restore order. Someone shanked him with a blade to the ribs and the underlord disappeared beneath the tidal crowd.

Silverstein kept his head down low, pushing a stinking metal mask over his face. The inside smelled of coppery blood. A chainmail tabard hung loosely from his wiry shoulders and greasy scraps of metal dangled like bead strings from his ill-fitting rags. He had never thought he would strip an Archenemy corpse for its attire. Perhaps several months ago, a different Silverstein would have scoffed at the idea. But now, anything was better than the alternative.

Behind him, rising like a hemisphere on the horizon, a star was expanding. The atmosphere was burning in searing flashes of red and black. It was melting like a photo-lith exposed to acid, black holes popping and yawning across its surface. The very ground shook as the planet began to lose atomic integrity. For the first time in as long as he could remember, Silverstein became really frightened. Ironclad vessels filled the darkening skies in a mass exodus. His would be one of the last flights off Aridun.

The docking ramp began to shut with a hydraulic squeal. The huntsman, along with the Archenemy troops jostling on the ramp, spilled into the belly of the carrier. They tumbled into the dim, cavernous belly. Dozens more Ironclad spilled off the sides as the ramp receded upwards. Some hung on by their fingers, until the ramp snapped shut. Silverstein could hear the muffled shrieks from outside. Outside, Ironclad hammered away at the hull in a maddening metallic cacophony. –

It was pitch-black inside the carrier. Silverstein chose not to use his augmetics to see. He didn't want to. He could feel the sour, tainted warmth of Archenemy soldiers around him. The vessel shuddered as its thrusters propelled it away from the surface, the air pressure in the cabin becoming heavy and oppressive. Pressing the broken fragment of iron over his face, Silverstein began to pray to the Emperor, repeating the same prayer again and again.

FLESH AND IRON

PROLOGUE

'Tell me, lieutenant,' the old woman said, 'did my son fight well?'

'Mamsel,' said the lieutenant, taking off his khaki cap and mopping his brow. 'I've never seen a man fight like he did.'

'I know this,' the lieutenant continued slowly. 'From the time that your son was assigned to my platoon, even though he was native, he was one of us. If it were not for his bravery and his knowledge of this land, my men and I might not be here now.'

The tall lieutenant sat down, folding his long limbs on the steps of the stilt-hut next to the old woman. He looked awkward in that village, clad in his sweaty fatigues of tan, khaki and pale creamy green. They sat together for a while, on those rickety wooden steps, watching the river ebb beneath their feet through the gaps in the planks.

'We were the same in many ways, he and I. I would tell him of my native Ouisivia, of the bayous and the steaming swamps. How the men of the 31st Riverine and I would ride through those waters on motored boats fighting swamp orks. He would tell me about Solo-Bastón, and how he would spear-hunt with his father along the riverbanks here. We were not so different.'

The old woman seemed to be half listening. As she stared vacantly into the river, there was something on her mind that she could not bear to think about. Finally she relented.

'Tell me how he died,' she said. She locked eyes with the lieutenant for the first time, eyes buried within a nest of weathered wrinkles and hardened from a life in the wilderness. 'I need to know.'

'Guiding my men through the rainforests of Bastón. He died in the service of the loyalist cause.'

'But how?' she persisted. 'If you do not tell me, I will never sleep again.'

And so Lieutenant Eden Barcham of the 31st Riverine Amphibious told the old woman a story of the Solo-Bastón insurgency and the part her son had played.

Lieutenant Barcham, a swift boat commander, had been one of the first officers in his regiment to be selected for deployment to Solo-Bastón. They had mobilised a force of eight thousand Guardsmen to quell an insurgency so far from their homes they had never heard the name of the place before. Although founded on the world of Ouisivia, the Guardsmen of the 31st Riverine had been especially requested by the Ecclesiarchy for their specialisation in jungle and semi-aquatic warfare. But deployment had been four months earlier and, since then, the insurgent heretics of Bastón had proven to be far more tenacious than the Imperial forces had estimated. They called themselves the *Carnibalès,* a phrase meaning 'martyrs who eat meat' in the local dialect. The enemy used the terrain well when they fought and melted into the civilian population when they chose not to.

Since Barcham first set boot in the dense rainforests of Bastón, Inawan had been assigned to Barcham's platoon as a guide. A young warrior from one of the few remaining loyalist tribes who had not joined the insurgency, Inawan had spoken to Barcham in fluent Low Gothic and, in turn, Barcham referred to Inawan as *Kalisador* Inawan – the native word for a practitioner of weaponry. The mutual respect would serve them well for the hellish months to come.

The first months had been far worse than Barcham had expected. The Ecclesiarchy, the ruling authority on Solo-Bastón, had dismissed the insurgency as a minor revolt against Imperial agricultural settlements. The reality was far more severe. Within the first week, Barcham had seen combat three times. In the worst of these engagements, he lost two of his four amphibious Chimeras to ambush in the muddy estuaries. The insurgent heretics had surged out of the rainforests and into the river, armed not with javelins and machetes, but with lasguns and bolters. The slow-moving Chimeras languished in the river, taking pot shots from the riverbanks.

The battle had drawn on for forty minutes until the enemy was chased into the wilderness by the swooping Vulture gunships. In the aftermath, two of the armoured carriers were ablaze in the water, cast along the stream like funeral pyres. Barcham lost eleven of his forty-man platoon and swore never again to use amphibious Chimeras in a river patrol. Such ponderous machines died slowly in the water.

In the days after the attack, the local insurgents began distributing hand-drawn leaflets to the villages in the region claiming that the Imperial soldiers had been massacred. They challenged Imperial forces for control of the province and began to recruit loyalist tribes into their insurgency.

Lieutenant Barcham did not let this slight go unnoticed. He requisitioned inflatable Riverine assault landers for his platoon and, with Inawan leading the way, they propelled themselves deep into regions that had been lost to Imperial control. Again the enemy fought a game of hit and run but, this time, the 31st Riverine took the fight to them, strafing the enemy in their motored boats with guns blazing. The insurgents melted into the wilderness and issued no more leaflets.

Barcham's platoon equipped all subsequent patrols with either inflatable landers or swift boats – ten-metre-long shallow draft vessels that housed a crew of six and one precious pintle-mounted bolter. They made many forays into the heartland with their flotilla of swifts. At night, they drew their vessels into a protective circle, like the frontiersmen of Old Terra with their steed-drawn wagons. They slept in cramped bunks in the vessels' bellies, and ate their rations cold so as not to light fires and draw the attention of insurgents. When it rained, and it often did, the troops had to deal with sleeping in the downpour and tramping about the boat in ankle-deep water.

'It was miserable,' said Lieutenant Barcham to the old woman, 'but Inawan helped to pull us through it. He could brew hot tea from foraged water roots and tell vivid stories of folklore. Little things like that helped keep our minds intact.'

'When it wasn't miserable it was sometimes exciting,' the lieutenant continued with a wry smile. 'The enemy learnt to fear us. We'd come upon their secret hideaways, rafts tethered on the water bearing caches of arms and ammunition. At first they would run inland and we would chase them with firepower, unleashing volley after volley into the undergrowth until we had flattened the area.'

In the fourth month Lieutenant Barcham was called away from clearing operations and ordered to mount an inland patrol on Chimeras. The platoon was to carve a path into the central rainforests in order to exert their influence on isolated inland tribes. They were to ride into the sloping hills along a winding dirt road, flanked on both sides by a strangling mass of gum-sap trees and clusters of epiphytes.

The lieutenant did not see the merit in such an exercise and Inawan agreed that it was unnecessarily dangerous. It had become common knowledge by then that the insurgents were using lasguns and even missile tubes that came from unknown sources. The sloping rainforest would be a perfect ambush point for the entire duration of the patrol.

But a Guardsman's first objective is to obey orders. So it came to pass that Barcham's platoon set forth in four separate Chimeras, each carrier housing a squad of ten Riverine Amphibious. When they arrived at each village, the Chimeras went through one at a time, training their turreted multilasers on the stilt-huts for protection.

As they came to the fifth and last village on their route, Lieutenant Barcham began to instinctively feel 'the churns'. It was something a veteran Guardsman picked up the longer he was deployed: a finely honed instinct that warned him something was amiss, a cold dreadful nausea at the bottom of their bowels. All Guardsmen knew of the churns and, in the past four months, Barcham was more than familiar with the feeling. He could not exactly express his concern but something was wrong about the village. Inawan was similarly grave and he vigilantly trained a vintage autorifle on each thatched window and door they passed. To their relief, the platoon passed the village without event and reached their designated checkpoint.

Although they had not spotted any signs of enemy activity, Barcham and Inawan agreed that their presence was certainly known to the insurgents by now. Deciding not to make camp in unfamiliar territory, the lieutenant hoped to race the dusk and return to base camp before nightfall. As they came down the mountain, the sinister fifth village was the first settlement they reached on the return path. Here the dirt road funnelled into a ravine that led a winding path through the hamlet. It was late afternoon and the monsoonal skies were swollen rain clouds, cradling the village in deep shadow.

Tribesmen lingered along the dirt road but fled at the sight of the platoon. They faded into their stilt-huts, some sprinting away to shutter their windows and bar their doors. Barcham ordered the four Chimeras to advance in single file, cautiously nursing their engines down the slope. Once again they rumbled through the village unmolested, coming around a bend in the path. The first carrier in line negotiated the steep twist.

That was the signal for the ambush.

Las-fire, rockets and heavy calibre rounds drummed down on the armoured carriers. The Chimeras rocked on their suspensions, hammered from all directions by enemy fire. Guardsmen scrambled towards the vision slits of the Chimeras, firing blindly out with their lasguns.

'Get going! Don't stop moving!' Barcham barked into the vox-unit. It would be their only chance to survive the ambush.

Insurgent heretics swarmed out from hiding, rushing in to mob the Chimeras. Some of them were not even armed, pelting the carriers with rocks and debris. Others were Kalisadors, armed tribal warriors who, according to Imperial intelligence, were ferociously cruel in combat.

Lieutenant Barcham socketed his bayonet onto his lasrifle just as the top hatch of his carrier was pried open. An insurgent Kalisador slithered into the compartment, brandishing a machete and machine pistol. The

Bastón warrior was garbed in traditional battledress, a loose cotton tunic and breeches with calf-length sandals bound by intricate hemp cord. Around his shoulders, torso and headdress was the chitinous plate of a cauldron crab, heavy and dark grey. Fluttering paper litanies and shells woven into coloured string clattered against his armour. Around his legs and hips, beards of knotted string interwoven with coloured glass proclaimed, in their way, the great reflexes and stamina of the warrior and the great length of his sword arm. This was the ritualistic battledress of a heretic; the lieutenant recognised this, as Inawan spoke often of the superstitions of his people.

The lieutenant fired once from the hip at point-blank range. The shot flashed white in the confined compartment, hot and brilliant. In the sizzling haze the insurgent bounced off the metal decking and lay there unmoving. The lieutenant stepped forwards to inspect the body.

That was when the hatchway swung open again. A hand appeared, tossed in a grenade, and slammed the hatch shut. Lieutenant Barcham dropped into a crouch and turned his back to the grenade. It went off with a stiffly concussive report. Something stung his back. 'Direct hit!' he shouted at his men, turning to inspect the damage.

That was when he saw Inawan curled up on the floor. His insides were spilling out from the middle of his torso. Inawan wore no chitinous plate, or the trinkets and fetishes of heretic Kalisadors. He simply wore loose cotton garments bound at his calves and forearms by intricate rope work, eschewing the heretical magicks of the insurgents. Inawan had professed a strong faith in the Emperor and that was all he had needed to protect him from the guns and bullets of his enemies. Barcham had never met a man more stoic in his belief.

But there was no time to mourn. 'Don't stop to fight back! Just keep moving,' the lieutenant shouted at his driver. The remaining Chimeras fell into line, following their lead.

'We were shooting as much as we could, in any direction,' Barcham recalled to the old woman. 'The men were hosing guns out from their vision slits, lobbing grenades out from the hatches. The enemy chased us, hugging the tree line and firing as they came.'

Of the four carriers, two remained, but in weary condition. Black smoke plumed from their engines, small fires fluttering from the treads. Snipers popped shots off their battered hulls and mortars burst before them, sending shrapnel hissing through the jungle canopy. But the platoon moved on, down another narrow gulley and up a sharp cleft in the terrain.

'Once we crest this gorge, we'll be in open ground and they won't follow,' Barcham urged his men over the vox systems.

Gunning the last dying splutters from their engines, they cleared the final crest. The enemy fire waned as the Chimeras surged on and left them behind. But the platoon did not stop for another five kilometres, until one of the carriers finally rolled to a halt, its engine dead and its armoured compartment filled with oily black smoke. By now, Vulture gunships were making low attack runs on the village and its surrounding region. The Imperial retribution was furious and coils of orange tracer lit up the sky long into the evening.

Back at the base camp, Lieutenant Barcham waited to gather his dead. Throughout the night Vultures touched down to refuel, bringing back with them the plastek body bags of his broken platoon. They would unload the remains of his men before whooping away on their turbine engines, back into the night. The dead – fifteen men in all – were laid out on the parade ground. The injured – twenty-two including Barcham himself – were taken to the infirmary. Three Guardsmen remained unaccounted for. The insurgents had cut out the livers of those who had been left in the field for several hours, but Barcham did not tell the old woman this. The practice of ritual mutilation was *bating bating*, a grave insult to the dead and strictly forbidden.

'My platoon was no more,' the lieutenant concluded. 'Not one man emerged unharmed.'

Within a week, those of his platoon with minor injuries were dispersed into other fighting units. Lieutenant Barcham, limping with shrapnel in his left leg and lower back, was placed on temporary administrative duties until recovery. He was a grade three – wounded with grievous bodily harm – and given two weeks' recuperation.

But before they were disassembled, the men who survived held a service for the fallen. Kalisador Inawan was included in the platoon's registry and buried with full honours, as befitted a Guardsman of the 31st Riverine. Back home on Ouisivia, fallen soldiers were set adrift in the bayous. Here their bodies were cast on rafts down the waters of the Serrado Delta.

'That is how your son died. If there were more loyalist men on Solo-Bastón like him, this war would already be over.'

CHAPTER ONE

Out across the oceans of Solo-Bastón, far beyond where the muddy inlets gave way to thrumming tides, the water became a foamy jade. From those frothing waves rose the towering might of an Imperial Argo-Nautical, a warship of distant Persepia. From its forward-jutting ram prow to its stern, the Nautical was a vast floating gun battery. The solid, blue-grey sheets of its hull towered over the water like a fortress, sloping up on an incline towards the deck. The Argo-Nautical dominated the ocean, eclipsing the horizon as it drew astern with an offshore platform. Its sheer bulk made the support girders of the platform appear frail and dwarfed even the Vulture gunships roosting on the landing pad.

Upon the platform, the high officers of the Bastón campaign were assembled with their accompanying ceremonial guard. They had been summoned by Cardinal Lior Avanti, head of the diocese on Solo-Bastón, acting governor-general and, without a doubt, the most powerful Imperial authority on the planet. Rarely was such a meeting requested of them; the staff officers shifted uncomfortably as they stood to attention.

Also present was Major General Gaspar Montalvo of the Caliguan Motor Rifles. He sweated in the sun underneath a furred mantle and a full suit of burnished copper. Accompanying him were two of the tallest, most imposing men in his regiment. The soldiers were men of the 105th Motor Rifles, a mechanised formation from the oil-rich world of Caligua in the Bastion Stars. They wore loose-fitting jumpsuits of dusty brown with pads of ballistic mesh sewn into the thighs, chest and shoulders of their utility uniforms.

Henry Zou

Standing opposite was Admiral Victor de Ruger of the Persepia Nautical Fleet. He stood smartly in his sky-blue dress coat, with silks arranged in layers across his left shoulder and a feather-crested helm curled under one arm. A coterie of attendants and officers flanked him, bearing his personal shield, standard and refreshment towels on platters. Persepian Nautical Infantry were arrayed in ordered ranks behind him in their chalk-blue frock coats and polished chrome rebreathers. Lasguns fixed with boarding pikes were held vertically in salute, a bristling forest of steel that glinted with oceanic reflection.

Almost unnoticed, Brigadier Kaplain stood off to the side. He hated ceremony, like all men of the Riverine Amphibious. Regardless, Kaplain had shaved and even pressed his uniform that very morning. A tall, thin man of late middle years, the brigadier looked more like an administrative clerk than the commanding officer of the wild Ouisivians. He wore fatigues of muted swamp camouflage, standard issue amongst all Guardsmen of the 31st Riverine. Even as the docking ramp of the Nautical was lowered towards the rig platform, Kaplain continued to smoke his tabac. There was no way that he was going to salute a man who had never earned his right to be saluted.

Overhead the Nautical sounded its boarding horns, braying with tremulous urgency. Air sirens whooped as the boarding ramp locked into position. Below, the assembled soldiery snapped their heels and stood to attention in unison. Kaplain sighed wearily and stubbed out his tabac with the heel of his boot.

Slowly, with measured strides, Cardinal Lior Avanti descended the ramp. Avanti was overwhelmingly tall and upright for a man of so many centuries. Although the skin of his face was like veined parchment, his features were heavily boned and well proportioned. A web of metal tubes sutured to his nostrils trailed into his voluminous robes, connecting him to a life-support system deep within his attire.

His every movement was deliberate and sure, exuding a great conviction that he could do no wrong. His holy vestments of embroidered tapestry, rich with midnight blue and purple, cascaded in perfectly measured lines, strangely unmoving despite the whipping ocean wind. Over this he was draped in a cope of needled gold and a lace train of tremendous length. Behind him, walking two abreast, sisters of the Adepta Sororitas in white power armour carried his lace train for a length of eight bearers.

The cardinal finally reached the ramp's landing and levelled his gaze on the Imperial officers. He drew an imperious breath.

'Gentlemen. Every morning I pray for victory. Do you?' Avanti asked.

Major General Montalvo risked a sidelong glance at Admiral de Ruger, syllables stuttering behind their teeth but not forming any words. Kaplain, however, kept to the old regimental adage – 'Keep your chin down, your eyes high and your mouth shut.' He did exactly that, keeping himself towards the rear of the assembly. For Kaplain, this entire meeting was a farce. He would have much preferred to be back on base camp where he was needed. In the past few days they had experienced a spike in insurgent activity and there were even rumours that they had lost favour with the local loyalists in the surrounding provinces. In his opinion, he had much better things to do than curry favour with the Ecclesiarchy, but orders were orders.

The cardinal approached Major General Montalvo and placed a hand on the officer's shoulder. The squat, pugnacious officer shuffled uncomfortably from foot to foot for a brief second. Kaplain almost pitied the man. He was already sweating profusely underneath his fur mantle and copper plate and doubtless the cardinal's attention did little to abate his condition.

'It hurts my heart,' the cardinal proclaimed. He turned to address the entire assembly before continuing. 'It hurts my heart to think that men of the Imperium are not fighting hard enough or faithfully enough to have ended this war already.'

Montalvo looked to Admiral de Ruger for support. De Ruger simply stared straight ahead to attention, evidently glad that he was not the object of the cardinal's ire. When no help was forthcoming, Montalvo gritted his teeth. 'We are operating at maximum capacity considering the situation. Strategically, the enemy hold the mainland and its super-heavy siege-batteries,' he conceded.

'Yes, I've already heard enough about the curtain guns that it hurts my head at their mentioning. I've known about these siege-batteries since you landed. I can't figure out why, with so many troops at your disposal, you cannot wrest control of these defence silos from the enemy?' At this, Avanti directed his gaze on Admiral de Ruger, expecting an answer.

Kaplain was now more amused than before. Admiral de Ruger, a thin man with avian features, long of face and long of neck, began to fumble for an explanation. For a moment, the wide-eyed look on the admiral's face threatened to dislodge the monocle he wore over his left eye. It amazed Kaplain that two of the most dominant military officers in the subsector were being terrorised by an old man with barely functioning joints.

'We've performed numerous bombing runs but the canopy is dense and the super-heavy batteries are well fortified due to terrain. But we will send more, increase bombing runs twofold, supplies allowing.'

Avanti leaned in close, a smile curling the corners of his mouth, but there was no mirth in his slitted grey eyes. 'Then why can we not dissuade these indigenous savages from undoing the good work of the God-Emperor here? What is it about these savages that His armies cannot overcome?'

Now it was Admiral de Ruger who looked to Montalvo for support. Neither officer spoke a word.

'Because they're holding the super-heavy battery on the mainland and blasting the snot out of our transport craft every time we attempt to deploy anything,' Kaplain called from the rear.

The brigadier could not help himself. He would bring an end to this farce. He had little regard for the Ecclesiarchy. As far as he was concerned, the military and theology were distinctly separate entities and he did not answer to the cardinal. Pushing his way through the ceremonial troops, jostling aside platter bearers and junior attendants, Kaplain emerged at the front of the assembly.

'What my comrades here are trying to say, in the simplest terms, is that the insurgents have captured the island's big gun. This big gun blows up big boats. But we need big boats to deploy troops onto the mainland, and we need big boats to run supply lanes in order to sustain any mass mobilisation. But as long as this big gun remains in enemy hands, we have to skulk beyond their range.'

Although Kaplain's fellow officers were glowering at him with unrestrained anger, the brigadier continued. 'So, for the past four months, we've been sending piecemeal patrols into the wilderness and getting thoroughly licked. I would send in an expedition, but my esteemed comrades here,' Kaplain gestured at his fellow high officers, 'outrank me, and refuse to do anything but send high-altitude bombing to disable the guns. They don't seem to understand that the heavy canopy cover and terrain protect the battery and renders it almost impervious to bombardment, and I can't send my boys out there without support. And that, my surly friend, is why these savages are tying your hosieries into a knot.'

There came a collective gasp from the audience. Several members of the Adepta Sororitas took a step towards the brigadier, their plated boots thudding with intention. For a moment, Kaplain wondered whether his Ouisivian manners had pushed the cardinal too far. But the cardinal began to chortle. His laughter wheezed through bundles of tubing that connected his nostrils to pressure filters hidden beneath his voluminous robes, sounding like a discordant metal organ.

'Well said, brigadier. I appreciate your candour,' commented Avanti with his eyes twinkling. He turned back to Montalvo and de Ruger. 'You could learn much from this man. You propose a different method, brigadier?'

The generals began to trip verbally and wring out excuses. They listed a lack of sufficient logistics, supplies and even blamed the monsoonal weather. But the cardinal had ceased to pay them attention.

'It's hot and I don't like this weather. I need to retire to my chambers,' the cardinal decided. 'Brigadier, if I give you authority to commit to an inland operation, can you break this stalemate?'

Kaplain nodded. 'Yes. But my men will need low altitude overhead support. I won't send my soldiers out there into enemy territory without any lifelines. I expect Vulture gunships and Persepian aviators to ghost them.'

'Pure folly,' the admiral interjected. 'The enemy have access to anti-air weaponry. I will not expose my fliers on low altitude runs.'

'Stop saying words,' the cardinal ordered. 'You will give the 31st Riverine all the support they need to conduct this operation. I want those guns silenced with all possible haste.'

The officers knew that all discussion was over. The admiral saluted crisply, and Montalvo slapped the breast of his armour with the flat of his palm in respect.

The cardinal turned his back on them. 'Excellent! Dismissed.'

The assembly dispersed swiftly as the generals stalked away towards their waiting Valkyries. Already the engines were whirling to life and ready to airlift them back to their mainland provinces.

Kaplain watched his fellow officers leave, growling angrily and snapping at their attendants. Chortling, the brigadier reached into his breast pocket and slid out a tabac stick.

'Are you an intelligent man, brigadier?'

Kaplain looked up, the tabac hanging unlit between his fingers. Cardinal Avanti stood before him, smiling with only his mouth. Despite Kaplain's considerable height, the cardinal was far taller and thinner, towering over the brigadier with his spectral shadow.

'That can be subjective,' Kaplain said, staring up at the cardinal. He was not intimidated by Avanti, if that was what the cardinal was trying to achieve. The old man moved in closer, far closer than would be considered a polite distance.

'I'd like to think you are. So I'll tell you this, brigadier.' The cardinal leaned in towards Kaplain, smelling strongly of ointment and rose powder. 'If you ever patronise me like that again, I will have you executed for contempt of the Emperor's servants. That's just how it works, my boy. Dismissed.'

Kaplain said nothing as Cardinal Avanti and his lace bearers slid up the docking ramp. Cardinal or not, the next time Avanti threatened him like that, Kaplain swore he would shoot the man himself. That was the way the 31st Riverine worked on Ouisivia.

CHAPTER TWO

At the centre of the Bastón mainland, at equal distance from the western seaboard and eastern peninsula, the Earthwrecker was a conduit of maritime dominance. A rail-mounted artillery piece based on the Earthshaker design, the super-heavy Earthwrecker was an immense artefact of war. It lay dormant in a subterranean rail network built specifically for its containment, a military installation situated in the Kalinga Curtain and stationed with six thousand servicemen. Unstoppable, undefeatable, its machine pulse could be felt across the archipelagos. Girdled by hills and powered by iron-hulled engines, it was manoeuvred ponderously by way of rail-track to any number of firing vents carved into the hillside.

The Kalinga Curtain covered an area of thirty-five square kilometres and contained an entire underground rail system and hundreds of anti-air raid structures. The subterranean complex was said to have been mostly hand-dug by eighty thousand local residents during the first stages of Imperial rule.

Inevitably, it was the first target of the Carnibalès and fell into insurgent hands in the early stages of the war. With its eight-tonne rocket-propelled warheads, the Carnibalès had managed to thwart every Imperial attempt to land troops or supplies onto the mainland. Insurgent forward observers, usually no more than rebel peasants with hand-held vox-units, kept a vigilant watch for Imperial movement. When such movement was spied, the inevitable warheads would roar. The Imperial Guard lost thousands to the Earthwrecker in those early stages of conflict.

The Persepian Nautical Fleet wasted thousands of tonnes of munitions in relentless bombing sorties in an effort to neutralise the threat but to no result. The gun's very presence emboldened the insurgency. It allowed a dissident force of ill-equipped agriculturalists to stalemate many times their number of disciplined, well-trained Imperial Guard.

Every few days, the shores of mainland Bastón would light up with the rolling thunder of detonations. For several hundred metres along the eastern coastline, amphibious transport vessels would disgorge waves of Guardsmen who waded through the sand, lancing the air with las-fire. The Guardsmen of the 31st Riverine Amphibious practised their live fire drills here. In between the monotony and terror of river patrols, the men of the 31st worked on their land assault tactics in the hope that soon, maybe in the coming weeks, the Serrado siege-batteries would be silenced. When that day came, the Imperial armies would deploy en masse and come to grips with the enemy. Until then, they trained.

Against the backdrop of ocean and jungle, these Guardsmen were quite a sight. Bronzed and tall, they wore fatigues of swampland camouflage: a splinter pattern of pale, milky green and dusty tan that had been produced for the jade swamps and sandy riverbanks from whence they came. Sweating in the subtropical heat, many of the troopers cut the sleeves and legs off their standard-issue fatigues. It was entirely against regulation, but Riverine officers understood the men under their command and, by their nature, draconian discipline would likely have an adverse affect.

They committed many other offences that were against regulation too. Bandoleers of ammunitions were slung across their chests exposed to dust. Autoguns were shortened, the webbing around their hips was loosened, magazines were taped and blades hidden. Above all, the threat of infection in sweltering climates prevented shaving and every man was thickly bearded. Each a minor infraction within itself, their accumulated discrepancies earned them quite a reputation amongst the other Imperial regiments they served with.

On this day it was the men of the 88th Battalion of the 31st Riverine Regiment that came ashore for their assault drills. They were five hundred and fifty men in all, transported by a flotilla that lined up for the race to shore. The forty swift boats got a head start, for they had to arrive first. Their lean-bladed profiles painted in the cream green and tan of the Riverine colours bounced atop the tidal waves as their gunners swept the beach with their mounted bolters. Next came the inflatable assault landers, black rubber and U-shaped. Each carried a twelve-man squad of Riverine troops. Behind them came a support squadron of fifteen gunboats, flat hulled and fifteen metres in length. These were robust vessels resembling squat river barges, each housing a single autocannon or heavy flamer. Oversized flags of the 31st Riverine, displaying the sword and dragonfly, flew proudly from most boats; a glorious touch.

The waters of Solo-Bastón were clear, far too clear when compared to the silty bog that the Riverine were accustomed to on Ouisivia. The vessels beached themselves too far out from the shore and the men in the rubber landers splashed into the water, dragging their inflatables behind them. The sand was loose too – not like the sucking mud of home, which was firm and slippery. Here and there a Guardsman tripped and fell into the waist-high water, resurfacing with laboured gasps.

'Secure positions at the sandbanks. I don't want any piecemeal formation like last time,' barked Colonel Fyodor Baeder of the 88th Battalion.

The colonel ran at the front of his men, taking care to lead the pack. At thirty-three years standard, he exerted himself more than any of the younger men. He took care to lead by exemplary performance, as respect between the soldiers of the 31st and their officers was difficult to earn and easy to lose. These were resilient men, and Baeder knew that they did not respect him. He was a new officer amongst their ranks, transferred to the 88th Battalion after their last commanding officer 'disappeared' during a cleanse operation.

It did not help that theirs was a lawless world. On Ouisivia, the steaming semi-habitable swamplands created rugged men who eked out a living netting for shrimp or hunting for gator or swamp rat. It was either that, or join the Guard. Colonel Baeder himself had been born and educated within the sheltered administrative parishes and, like many of his fellow officers, had attended military academy in the urban heartland of Norlens. He was not welcome amongst these swampmen and he knew it.

'Hold this line steady,' Baeder yelled as he crashed belly-first into the sand dune. He dragged the last ounces of strength from his lactic-burnt limbs and made sure to edge himself ahead of his men. They leopard-crawled through the sand, heaving and grunting. Something popped in the colonel's lower chest, but he could not stop or his men would make their disdain well known to him. 'You move like old people dance! On! On!' Baeder urged, with a confidence his body did not feel. Over their heads, the gunboats and swift boats shredded the rainforest ahead with heavy support fire. The noise and exertion was physically deadening.

Finally, they reached a long sandbar before the tree line. The Riverine lay prone behind their lasrifles and snapped sheeting volleys into the vegetation, chopping down trees and brush. Under the combined firepower of the battalion, even the thick-limbed gum-saps leaned and fell over.

'Cease fire! Cease fire!' Colonel Baeder yelled hoarsely into the battalion vox-unit. The firing withered and died away. Exhausted, his men rolled over onto their backs, staring at the sky. Others tugged their canteens from their hip webbing, taking long, throat-bobbing gulps. Baeder had no doubt that it was not purely water his men were drinking.

'Well done, ramrods. Seven minutes and eighteen seconds. Best time this week.' Despite his weariness, Baeder did not wish to show fatigue or thirst in front of his new battalion. Instead he hauled himself up and began to move down the line on shaking legs, making ammunition and weapon checks.

After the battalion was settled, Colonel Baeder stood before his line of soldiers. They lounged on the sand before him, canteen bottles uncapped, looking up at him while shielding their eyes from the early morning sun. Baeder liked to think he was what an Imperial officer should look like but he knew that was likely not to be the case. He was not tall compared to most of his men, and certainly not as thickly shouldered. Rather, he was slight of build, with a young boyish face and, unlike the other men of the 31st, Baeder could not summon more than patchy stubble on his chin and neck. He knew it would be a long while, if ever, before the battalion would be used to him. But despite his appearance, Baeder had a fine martial record, and his neck bore the scar of a swamp ork's teeth. The bite formed a ridged scar two fingers from his jugular as testament to his experience. Baeder knew how to run a battalion and he would make these men understand.

'Today was an acceptable time. It has been our best all week. Incidentally, this week has been by far the worst since I joined this battalion. I don't know if it is boredom, or the lack of a tangible fight, but we are getting lax. We cannot allow the 88th to become the worst battalion in the 31st Riverine.'

The men began to murmur. They knew what was coming and some even cursed openly and loudly.

Baeder nodded. 'Reorg. We're running the drill again until we can hit under six flat. Be up and ready to move in five minutes.'

By mid-afternoon, the battalion had run the drill another five times over. Their clothes were crusted with a fine evaporation of sweat and seawater. At the end of the sixth landing drill, most of the men lay face down in the sand with their eyes closed. Some, less fortunate, were dry retching into the sand. Colonel Baeder moved briskly down the line, hiding his weariness well. He worked relentlessly, first moving to each and every man, praising him for his efforts and offering him water. Next, he gathered his captains and sergeants together for an analysis of their performance. Not once did he sit or slake his thirst. Finally, after his duties were fulfilled, Colonel Baeder left his battalion strewn across the sand at rest, and slipped into the tree line on his own.

Staggering into the humid darkness of vegetation, out of sight, the colonel braced his arms against the trunk of a gum-sap and bent over double. He vomited. He emptied his stomach until he tasted the acidic burn of bile and his lungs locked up with exertion. Completely and utterly drained, Baeder collapsed as the straining ligaments of his hamstrings went out underneath him.

'I knew I would find you here.'

Colonel Baeder craned his head and saw a tall, thin figure standing before him in crisp fatigues. The man stood with his hands on his hips, shaking his head.

'Brigadier Kaplain, sir.' Baeder struggled to push his back against the tree and rise to salute.

The brigadier waved him down. 'At ease, at ease. You've done enough for today.' Crouching down next to the sprawled out colonel, Kaplain proffered him a canteen of water.

'How are you settling in with the 88th?'

With a heave of effort, Baeder wedged his back against the tree into a slumped sitting position. 'They are a hard bunch. It takes more than some dog-pissed inspirational speech to get them moving. Constant action is what they need.'

Kaplain laughed. 'Speeches? This isn't some war hero story. Leave the talking to the Commissariat.'

'True as that may be, I'd like to instil some sense of trust between the men and me before we may have to mobilise as a battalion. So far I've had the platoon on rotational patrols, fragmented puissant business.'

Kaplain smiled. 'Let me guess – the closest you've got to combat so far has been reading patrol reports from your platoon commanders?'

'I need a cure for the itch, sir,' Baeder shrugged.

The brigadier clapped the colonel on the back knowingly. 'If your legs can still move, take a walk with me, the Persepian Nautical Fleet are bombing the hills again. It's a glorious if wasteful sight.'

The two staff officers meandered back out onto the beach as squadrons of winged craft climbed to high altitude overhead. As they scaled the slippery tusks of igneous rock that littered the coastal slopes, bombs were already spilling out over the high hills of the mainland.

Kaplain gestured at the undulating horizon, carpeted in green. Explosions were swelling up in the distance, tiny bubbles of orange that burst into rolling black smoke and flame. The hills were trembling as the chain of explosions popped and expanded. 'Those damned siege-batteries. Who would have thought that a handful of insurgents could stalemate twenty divisions of Imperial fighting men.'

'I understand that the Persepian Aviation boys have been flying sorties to the mainland night and day. We've barely had any sleep from the constant noise,' Baeder replied. Although they were too far off to be seen, Baeder could imagine the Marauder bombers of Persepia, painted chalk blue, devastating the landscape on wide banking runs.

'The Earthwrecker sunk another one this week, you know. High Command have kept the sinking classified, but word will be out sooner or later,' said Kaplain.

'Sir?'

'A Persepian Argo-Nautical. The warship *Thrice Avenged* attempted to land fourteen thousand Motor Rifles onto the mainland just two days ago. It managed to sail within visual distance of the island before the super-heavies began firing ordnance on it. One shell went clear through the hull and the whole mess went down within minutes. We lost about ten thousand Caliguans and almost the entire crew. What a disaster.'

Baeder was not sure how to accept the news. In a way he was angered by the High Command's relentless stupidity. It was not the first time the Nautical Fleet had lost one of its precious warships to the siege-batteries. If the two warships sunk in the early days of the war did not teach them to stop deploying the vessels, then the subsequent three sunk in the following months should have. Yet they persisted, sending one after another of the great warships towards the mainland loaded with supplies, fuel and men, hoping that this one would make it through unnoticed by the siege-batteries and their distant spotters.

Rudimentary logic would have concluded that, where one tactic has failed, trying it repeatedly would not increase the success rate. But that was exactly what High Command had continued to do. The war had begun with a full complement of twelve great Nautical warships, a dozen floating fortresses that should have stopped the war within days. Now, four months later, they were left with seven and were no closer to finishing the war than when they had started.

'That's a mess, sir. Are the pilots homing in on the exact coordinates of these super-heavy pieces? My men are getting testy. We're burning out from the waiting, sir.'

Faraway, the explosions began to calm. Fire, like an emergent sun, glared on the horizon, burning thousands of acres. Kaplain watched the pyrotechnics for some time before replying. 'A deeply fortified gun piece. We know it's dug-in on a range of hills known as the Kalinga Curtain with a cannon large enough to compensate for the cardinal's glaring insecurities. We have approximate locations from old militia schematics, but the gun is embedded in an underground system and the Persepians are too scared to fly any lower. We probably haven't even scratched its paint job.'

Judging by the crease of Kaplain's brow, Baeder knew there was something the brigadier wanted to say. Finally, Baeder could wait no longer. 'What will High Command do now then, sir?'

'High Command wants me to send troops into the heart of Bastón. I'm going to send you.'

'Sir?'

Kaplain nodded. 'The siege-batteries are preventing us from launching any sustained assault on the mainland; you know this. The Motor Rifles need fuel and transport for their vehicles and it's obvious the Persepians are trapped out at high anchor. The Riverine are the only regiment who have a foothold on the mainland. We can't take this island ourselves, but we can send in a smaller probing force to find and disable this gun. I'm sending the 88th to fix this mess.'

'Sir. We're not ready. The 88th Battalion is not cohesive yet. I've been with my men for four months! We have not even operated at a company level. Any of the other battalions are more tightly knit, even the 76th, frag it, even the 123rd would do a better job.'

'Don't make this harder than it has to be, Baeder.' Kaplain suddenly looked very weary. 'It doesn't get any easier for me to send men to their deaths. This will be a dangerous operation. You will lose men, colonel. But we need this done, and I can't entrust a lesser battalion with the job.'

Before the insurgency, the Serrado Delta had been the major artery of trade for mainland Bastón and its infant islands. Ramshackle fishing trawlers from upriver would ply their daily catches amongst the coastal villages. Along the banks, makeshift markets sprang up here and there, motor-canoes and rafts laden to the tipping point and tethered by the rushes. There they sold all manner of fruits and vegetables from local water gardens, pungent spices or urns of fermented fish.

For the past few months, the Serrado Delta had become hauntingly empty during the day. Insurgent attacks had concentrated on razing agricultural settlements, leaving burnt scars of earth where production had once been abundant. The only trade barges that traversed the delta during daylight hours were the coffin makers, who had more business than they could supply.

At night, refugees meandered downstream in sad, sodden convoys. They were mostly tribes fleeing the turmoil of the inland wilderness, hoping to reach Imperial-controlled territory without being spotted by insurgent heretics. Since the early days of war, Persepian aviation had dropped leaflets on isolated settlements promising them safety under the bulwark of Imperial military presence. For most tribes, fleeing was a far better option than staying on their ancestral lands. At best, tribes considered neutral were harassed constantly by insurgent propagandists, rounding up their young men for recruitment or demanding exorbitant taxes. At worst, tribes who were heavily vested in agriculture or revealed to be Imperial loyalists were considered lost to the old ways, often becoming the target for raid or massacre by insurgent warbands.

One such tribe were the people of the Taboon. Like all tribes of Bastón, they were a loosely-related kin group of extended family forming a network of elaborate social hierarchies. Together they had travelled for eight days down the delta, sailing only under the cover of night. There were eighty in all, crammed onto all manner of propeller canoes, junks and tow barges.

Like most tribes, they revered the strength of their warriors. The people of Taboon had two such men, also known as Kalisadors. The indigenous people of Bastón had never been a warlike culture and it was not uncommon for tribes of two or three hundred people to be represented by a single Kalisador warrior. As such, the entire pride, history and prestige of the tribe was vested in a single man. These Kalisadors were of special status. In times of inter-tribal conflict, Kalisadors would engage in one-on-one combat in a ritual mired in ceremony and etiquette under the audience of both tribes. There was an air of festivity during these bouts, with much dancing and drinking. Fights were often only to first blood, and upon the completion of the duel the inter-tribal conflict would be resolved, forever and indisputably so. The Bastón tribes had a great fondness for festivity and any excuse was made to duel their tribal champions, anything from territorial disputes, to the loss of rural produce. This method of conflict, of course, had been before the insurgency.

Times were much harder now and the Taboon looked to their two Kalisadors for guidance. Luis Taboon was a Kalisador of old, a man of greying years. He had settled many illustrious victories for the Taboon and, although he was old, his wiry frame was known for his fast knife disarm, a specialty of his, as well as his elaborate pre-duel dance ritual which none could match. There was also Mautista Taboon, a very young man, third cousin of Luis, with narrow shoulders but long limbs and a fierce mane of hair. Although Mautista was young, he showed much promise, having already mastered the Kalisador art of stick and dagger.

During their exodus, the two Kalisadors had led the way. Although they knew their unarmed expertise and tribal weapons were no match for the insurgent firearms, the pair had kept a sleepless watch over the convoy. Remaining vigilant, they navigated ahead of their tribe in a single-motored sampan, singing loudly to frighten away bad luck and evil spirits that lurked in the treetops. When the tribe broke camp during the day, the pair gathered volunteers to spear for cauldron crab in the shallow mud. Although they had not slept or rested, the Kalisadors always gathered more food than the others of their tribe.

Now, eight days into their trek, the pair were haggard. The past days had chipped away steadily at their constitution, grinding down their resolve and their stamina until they were sore and short of breath. But they were close to safety now. The pair knew this and probed their sampan far ahead of the column. It was dark and the trees extended their branches far over the river in an arch overhead. Vines fell around them at head level, while the nocturnal animals watched them from the murky darkness with glazed, glowing eyes. Mautista clapped a machete against a straight stick in timpani that warned away ghosts while Luis sang, for his voice carried well whereas Mautista's did not. Night was a frightening place in the rainforest but they pressed on. Ahead, they could see the lights of an Imperial camp. It meant safety and they would not stop now.

'Praise the Lord-Emperor. We're finally close,' said Luis in his trembling baritone. Although age had shrunken his frame it had not robbed him of his voice and Mautista was comforted by that same calmness which warded away evil. Beyond them, the winking lights and search probes of the Imperial blockade played across the water.

'These Imperial soldiers, are they good men?' asked Mautista. Although he had seen some of the Planetary Defence soldiers at trade markets, Mautista had never spoken to off-world Guardsmen before. He took out his straight dagger and laid it anxiously across his lap. The sight of the naked steel helped to calm his trembling hands. He was nervous, but he could not work out why.

Luis nodded enthusiastically. 'They are good men. I met a sergeant from a distant land once in my younger days. They have strong faith in the Emperor.'

Suddenly the older Kalisador began to smooth out his balding pate. 'How do I look? We must show our ceremonial best, warrior to warrior as we meet these men.'

'You look fine,' Mautista replied.

In reality, the older Kalisador looked more than weathered. He wore a tunic and loose shorts of grey hemp, plastered to his gaunt limbs with days of accumulated mud. The ceremonial rope bindings on his forearms and calves were dry and fraying.

Mautista imagined his presentation to be remarkably similar. The breastplate of cauldron crab shell had chafed his underarms raw, bleeding into his shirt and drying in trickles down his arms. The many pennants and bead strings that adorned his attire had been lost in their trek. In particular, Mautista had lost a hoop of beaten copper he had worn against his right hip. The copper crescent had been a gift for tracking down a gang of cattle rustlers deep in the Byan Valley and beating all five of the men with a binding club until they were dark with bruises. In gratitude his village had gathered their harvest money and commissioned a local artisan to shape a tiny sliver of precious copper into a crescent symbolising the return of cattle horns for their brave Kalisador. Mautista would have very much liked to show these off-world warriors his medal, and perhaps compare their deeds.

'Look at their lights and guns,' marvelled Luis in awe.

They were very close to the blockade now. At the narrowest point of the channel ahead, the Imperial Guard had erected a series of pontoons and sandbags into a floating blockade. A flashing siren light marked the military checkpoint, spinning in fast, pulsating circles. Behind the wall of sandbags, Guardsmen played drum-like searchlights across the black water. Despite the evening darkness, Mautista could see the silhouettes of men with guns prowling along the blockade wall.

Luis leapt to his feet, waving his arms frantically. 'Friends! Friends!'

he cried, rocking the boat with his jumping. Immediately, a searchlight swung to bear on them, its harsh white beam cupping their entire vessel. Mautista threw up his hands to shield his eyes.

A deep voice, crackling from vox speakers, barked out of the white void. 'Halt. You are entering the Imperial safe zone. State your business.'

Giddy with excitement, Luis reached into leather pouches sewn into his tunic and began to pull out the leaflets that Imperial craft had dropped for them. Many were crumpled, others were melted into furry wads by river water, but they were all the same. Luis tore them out of his pouches and thrust handfuls of them before him like an offering. 'We are loyalists seeking safety within the military zones!' he replied.

There was a long pause before the vox speakers clicked again. 'Come closer but stay a distance of five metres from the checkpoint, then switch off your engines and keep your hands above your heads.'

Hands shaking, Mautista nursed their keel motor towards the blockade. Up close he could see almost half a dozen soldiers in thickly-padded jumpsuits, each training a lasrifle at their vessel. Directly to their front, another soldier took the cap off his head and waved them in like a flag.

'Switch off the engine,' Luis hissed to him. Careful not to make any mistakes or sudden movements, Mautista shut off the propellers and let the sampan glide in to close the gap. Then with slow, exaggerated movements, Mautista and Luis laced their fingers behind their heads.

Leaping over the sandbags, the soldier with the cap waved at them. 'Welcome to Checkpoint Watchdog. I'm Sergeant Descont of the Caliguan Motor Rifles. Sweet merciful frag, do you boys look like you need a drink.'

Mautista almost sagged with relief. After spending eight days constantly looking over their backs and fearing discovery, the notion that they had found safety was enough to drain all the adrenaline that was left from his body.

'Where are you from?' the sergeant asked.

Luis began to speak, exposing his wrists to the soldiers as a gesture of peace. 'We are the Taboon people, from the inland Byan Valley. There are more of us, eighty more, further back upriver. We are fleeing–'

The sergeant cut him off with a lazy wave of his hand. 'Sure. Sure. Eighty, got it. I'm going to let you boys come through the checkpoint while I vox my superiors. Then we can see about bringing up the rest of you.' With that, Sergeant Descont flashed the thumbs up to his men and turned to go. Another soldier, still aiming his firearm on them, motioned with his head towards a chained docking picket behind the barricade.

By the time Luis and Mautista had tethered their boat to the floating checkpoint, a group of soldiers were waiting for them. Luis and Mautista hopped off the vessel onto the gently shifting surface and immediately reached out to thank the Guardsmen with grateful handclasps.

The soldiers shrank back, chuckling and shaking their heads. 'You're not touching me with those filthy paws, indig,' laughed the closest soldier.

Mautista exchanged an uncertain look with Luis. The young Kalisador had expected men of good Imperial faith to be kinder, but these soldiers simply stared at him from a curious distance. He noticed these were tall, powerfully-built men. Well-nourished and well-trained, more power-fully built perhaps than even the Northern Island Kalisadors who lifted heavy stones and hand-wrestled. They all wore glare-shades and chewed constantly.

'You're one of those fragging indig warriors, uh?' drawled one of the soldiers as he spat his dip. 'I hear you boys do all sorts of slap-happy unarmed fighting, uh?'

Mautista saw Luis bristle with indignation. The soldier swaggered forwards with a pugnacious smirk until he was face-on with the old Kalisador. The old man levelled his gaze on the soldier, the wiry muscles of his jaw twitching slightly. 'We know how to duel with bare hands. But we also duel with twin sticks, war clubs, daggers and machetes.'

'Is that so, indig?' cawed the soldier, as he turned to his friends. Turn-ing around, he thrust his lasrifle before Luis. 'How does that compare with one of these?'

The soldiers burst out laughing, but Luis said nothing. Mautista had to admit that the lasrifle was impressive indeed. Sleek and matt black, with a long silver snout and a leather strap that the soldier wound loosely around his forearm, the lasgun was quite frightening. It had a lean, uncomplicated design that did not hide its purpose to harm. Mautista was startled to think that all their years of devotion to the Kalisador arts could be undone by any man with basic knowledge of these firearms.

'Trooper Nesben, stow it for later,' barked Sergeant Descont as he emerged from the command tent. Strangely enough, the sergeant wore glare-shades now too, and spoke to the Kalisadors with a detached ano-nymity. 'You've got clearance. Bring up the convoy,' he said, pointing at Mautista.

Unwilling to compromise safe passage for their tribe, the Kalisadors avoided eye contact with Trooper Nesben and his jeering cohort as they turned to retrieve their sampan.

'Not you. You stay here,' Sergeant Descont said, aiming his index finger on Luis.

Mautista felt a surge of sudden uncertainty, but Luis simply nodded. 'Go and get the others. I'll be here when you get back. I'm sure they just need me to answer some questions.'

The young Kalisador was not so certain, but he clasped hands with the old man and slipped away. Later, as he loosened the moorings of his sampan, Mautista realised his earlier elation had long since washed away and he only yearned to be away from this checkpoint. These soldiers, he knew, were not good men and he only hoped the Imperial authorities in the safety zones were kinder. Suppressing his instinctive fear, Mautista was only glad that he had slipped Luis a butterfly blade in his palm before they parted.

The people of the Taboon were huddled in their vessels just beyond a natural bend in the river. As Mautista rounded the turn in his sampan, pinched and malnourished faces looked at him anxiously. His family, for they were all related in some way, peered at him from their overcrowded boats. He saw Fernan and her four girls; she had not eaten for a week so her children would not go hungry. There was Cardosa the village carpenter, Mautista's second cousin, and Lavio the net-mender, both strong men who were now weak with fever. Even Bustaman the village elder was jaundiced from starvation. In all, eighty desperate faces looked to Mautista for hope.

'We are here. The Imperial armies are up ahead and we are free to go through. We will be safe then,' Mautista called out to them as he steered his sampan close.

Word spread quickly along the cluster of vessels. An excited babble of voices filled the humid evening air. For the first time in eight days, the hushed and fearful silence was lifted and the Taboon spoke loudly and freely amongst themselves. Motors were gunned loudly and vessels throbbed ahead, eager to meet the checkpoint.

'We have done it, Bustaman,' said Mautista as he drew his sampan alongside the elder's trawling vessel. 'We've led everyone to safety.'

The village chief, leaning over his trawler, sighed. The folded creases and wrinkles that webbed his face appeared deeper than they ever had before and Mautista immediately knew something was wrong.

'We did not guide all of them. One of our youngest members, Tadeu, died tonight. Hunger and fever took him. We must bury him together, chief and Kalisador,' the old man wheezed weakly. He spoke softly, so as not to alarm the other people on the trawler, and it was evident that not all of the tribe knew yet.

'Tadeu? Tagiao's newborn son?' Mautista hissed with a mixture of frustration and disbelief.

Bustaman nodded. 'Yes, we must bury him now, so as to not bring the dark spirits with us when we journey into our new home.' Weakly, with arms not thicker than bone, the village elder held a small bundle to his chest and prepared to climb over the trawler and into Mautista's sampan.

'Wait, Bustaman,' Mautista said. 'You are sick. I can bury Tadeu myself, I can perform that rite as Kalisador. You go on ahead with the others and receive water and food.'

The old man hesitated, halfway over the trawler. 'I am the elder, it should be me.'

'You cannot help anyone in your state, elder. I am Kalisador and I have a duty to protect my tribe, including you. Please go,' Mautista said as he reached out to take the bundle from the old man's arms.

Bustaman had no strength to argue. He sagged back onto the deck of the trawler, his shorts and tunic flapping loosely around his skeletal frame. As the trawler steered away on the steady chopping of its engines, Bustaman and the others waved at Mautista. The Kalisador waved them away, and found himself drifting alone on the delta as the throb of their engines faded.

'The Emperor protects,' Mautista murmured to himself as he drew the points of the aquila swiftly across his chest. Peering into the depths of the riverbank, the spaces between the trees created yawning pits. Even though Mautista had grown up in the rainforests, the night had always been a time of ghosts and daemons in Bastón folklore. Gripping his striking stick in one hand and a machete in the other, Mautista prepared to find a place in that forest to rest little Tadeu.

The soldiers said nothing to Luis Taboon as they waited for his tribe. The only sounds were the chirping of insects and the occasional ring of the spittoon as a soldier spat his dip, so it was a welcome relief to Luis when he spotted the flotilla of river craft approaching the checkpoint.

'My people!' said Luis, beaming proudly at the men around him. Sergeant Descont nodded, almost in blank-faced affirmation.

Searchlights raked across the flotilla as it meandered closer on the steady *chut chut chut* of ageing motors. This time, however, Luis was glad the soldiers did not point their rifles as it would have frightened the children, many of whom had never seen an off-world soldier before.

Sergeant Descont raised a loudspeaker to his lips and issued a static-laden command. 'Welcome to Checkpoint Watchdog. Please moor your vessels to the right side of the bank and disembark. We have fresh water and rations waiting.'

By now Luis noticed torch beams criss-crossing the riverbank to his left, just before the checkpoint. Soldiers waded out into the water to pull the smaller boats in to the shore and help his people onto the land. Luis was surprised at the swift efficiency and preparation of these Imperial soldiers.

Sergeant Descont escorted Luis onto the riverbank where the Taboon were sitting around on the loamy soil, hungrily digging into ration parcels. Soldiers moved amongst them with jerry cans of water, issuing tin cups. The soft, muddy earth had never felt so secure beneath Luis's toes. The Kalisador sat down in weary gratitude and was content to just fall asleep.

'Have some grub,' Sergeant Descont said, handing Luis a parcel in brown plastek foil. 'Standard-issue ration. It's good eating,' he promised.

Luis tore open the package with his bare hands, spilling the contents onto the ground. Tubes of sugared fruits, tins and packets fell out like a new harvest and Luis ate with the enthusiasm of a man who had not eaten properly for eight days. There were tinned curds, cereal crackers and tubs of meaty paste. The tribe marvelled at the foreign food and packaging, trading and taste-testing everything with childish awe. A village fisherman held up a tube of fruit-paste triumphantly, declaring, 'This must be what the wealthiest lords and cardinals eat every day!'

Luis plucked up a tin labelled *lactose syrup, sugared* and placed it into a pouch for safekeeping. The bits of torn packaging and foil he lovingly folded into squares and placed into pouches too, as souvenirs he could one day show the younger generations of the tribe. He would tell them of the time that Imperial soldiers saved the Taboon people.

'All right, people, enough time for eating. Up! Up!' shouted a newcomer. He moved amongst the tribe, ushering them to stand; a rake-thin man, with glare shades perched on a hatchet nose. Like the other soldiers, he wore a jumpsuit of light brown, layered with mesh in some parts but, unlike the others, he wore a series of stars and badges on his sleeves. It was obvious, even to the tribe, that this was a higher-ranking soldier simply by the way he walked and spoke if not by his uniform.

'All right, indigs! I am Captain Feldis of the Caliguan Motor Rifles, 10th Logistics Brigade. I'll be taking you to your new settlement where you can get sorted for registration and camp details. Get up, put away what you are doing and get moving. Go!' he shouted, kicking the dirt for emphasis.

The atmosphere changed very quickly. Soldiers began to haul people up by their arms, trampling or knocking over their food and water. The Taboon looked confused and suddenly hurt, and Luis shared those feelings. The Kalisador turned to find Sergeant Descont and ask what was happening but instead he found Trooper Nesben leering in his face.

'Come on, indig. It's time to get settled,' he smirked, jabbing Luis in the ribs with the butt of his lasrifle. The soldier tugged the knives and warclub from Luis's harness, throwing them into the dirt. The Kalisador had never felt so helpless. One by one, the Taboon were herded by soldiers into a marching line. Widow Renao tried to leave the marching column and head back to her canoe, but soldiers gently yet persistently escorted her back into the line. She pleaded that she had to retrieve her possessions from her boat first but the soldiers were not listening.

'Get these dirty indigs out of here for processing,' the captain whispered to Sergeant Descont. Luis overheard their exchange and wished Mautista was with him, but of the young Kalisador there was no sign.

Mautista covered the makeshift grave with handfuls of peat. Wiping his damp hands on his trousers, the young man slid a volume of Imperial scriptures from his hip pouch – *The Scriptures of Concordance*. Unwrapping the muslin cloth, he opened the book on his lap, careful not to smear the pages with his soiled hands. Dirtying the sacred text would be blasphemous. When he was a child of ten, Mautista had accidentally dropped his scripture book into the swine pen. The village preacher found out and lashed him a dozen times with a switch stick. It had left a lasting impression on him.

Kneeling before the tiny cairn of heaped soil, Mautista began to read aloud the 'Resting of Saint Carlamine'. Despite Imperial teaching, superstition was bound to the Bastón psyche. By reading the prayer, Mautista would quell the angry, tragic soul of the child. He hoped the words would placate Tadeu, so the child's ghost would not follow him, clinging to his back and bringing him misfortune.

As he read, a chill spread through his limbs. The words tripped in his mouth and Mautista rose suddenly to his feet. He looked around him, peering into the gloom. Something had spooked him. A feeling of foreboding had yoked down on his shoulders. Looking at the grave, Mautista shook his head at how unnerved he had become. He reasoned that the past few days of starvation had diminished his rationality.

Regardless, the rainforest lingered in the strange hours between dawn and night. The nocturnal animals had receded to their dens and the birds of morning were still asleep. It was dark and silent and Mautista did not wish to stay for any longer than he had to. He finished the last prayer and scurried back to his canoe, as fast as his legs could slosh through the water. The feeling of foreboding did not leave him.

By the time the Taboon marched to their destination, the sky was indigo with predawn morning. The tribe had threaded their way along a dirt path carved out of the cloying undergrowth until they reached a wide clearing. Here the ground was ugly and barren, stripped bare of any vegetation. An abrasive chemical stink hung in the air, no doubt the solvent used to disintegrate this swathe of nature.

An Ecclesiarchal preacher waited for them in the clearing. Dressed in sombre robes of black, edged with gold, the preacher cut a stoic, solitary figure. As the tribe was led into the clearing, Luis tried to wave towards the preacher. To the tribes of Bastón, the Ecclesiarchy had always occupied a role of guidance and faith and their preachers were considered family by many. Luis tried to flag his attention, but the preacher avoided eye contact.

'Stop waving and get into line with the others,' Captain Feldis snapped at him. The Taboon were forced into a rough line, flanked on all sides by upwards of thirty soldiers. The tribe were uneasy; Luis could feel it. After their ordeal, most did not have the mental faculties to process what was happening. Luis himself was confused. He could not grasp how or why they were being treated in such a way. Surely, once the soldiers handed them over to the care of the preacher, they would be allowed to go free?

The captain approached the preacher and saluted stiffly. 'Where do you want the children?'

'Set them aside first, I don't want them causing a fuss like last time. We need them in a good state for the plantations,' the preacher said flatly. He paused and laughed, 'Assimilation is what's needed for these filthy indigs. Inter-breed them with pure Imperial blood when they are of good breeding age.' These were the first words to come out of his mouth and in an instant Luis knew their ordeals were not yet over.

Soldiers waded into the crowd of refugees with their rifle butts, dragging the youngest children away. The tribe erupted hysterically, pleading and plaintive. Fernan drew her four girls into her arms like a protective mother bird. Strong hands wrenched her children away and Fernan collapsed to her knees, pulling at her hair, but silent. She simply had nothing left, not even to make a sound.

'Do not fear. Your children will be well treated and given Imperial education in our institutions. We are simply protecting them from ignorance, so they may have a better life,' the preacher announced.

The tribe was not calmed by his words: many continued to struggle and the soldiers began to use their rifle butts with rigorous force. Strangely enough, some of the soldiers seemed uncomfortable, even ashamed at what was occurring and many, including Sergeant Descont, stood to the side and looked away. Briefly, Luis considered the butterfly blade that Mautista had slipped him, tucked away beneath his wrist braces. His hands tingled at the thought of driving the leaf-shaped shard up into Trooper Nesben's chin, but he did not. To do so would not bode well for his people.

After a brief struggle, the children were loaded onto a waiting military truck, parked at the edge of the clearing. It had all been prepared, Luis realised. The soldiers had obviously done this before. Some of the Guardsmen wandered about casually, chatting amongst themselves and lighting tabac. For Luis, it was like a surreal dream. He kept waiting for something to happen to make his semi-lucid reality normal again. He wanted the preacher to tell them that it was simply a test of their faith in the God-Emperor, that they had passed and that another truck would be arriving shortly to take them all to their new settlement grounds.

'Line them up!' Captain Feldis barked.

'I can't watch this,' Luis heard a soldier say to Sergeant Descont. The sergeant shook his head. 'I can't do this either. That's why I wear these,' he said, tapping his glare shades. 'I don't have to look them in the eyes this way.' With that the sergeant padded away.

They spoke as if Luis were not even there. Several other soldiers, shaking their heads sadly, filed out of the clearing. Not one soldier acknowledged them or looked at them. Only a dozen Guardsmen remained in the clearing, Trooper Nesben and Captain Feldis amongst them.

'Have they been given their last meals?' the preacher inquired of the Captain. Feldis smiled tight-lipped and nodded, before leading the preacher away from them.

Luis's head was reeling. For the first time, in the dawn light, he noticed the barren earth was rugged with trenches. Shallow pits that were eight or ten metres long and two metres wide, lining the earth like tilled soil. He looked at his people, and his people all looked at him. Everyone Luis had known in his lifetime looked to him, their Kalisador, for an answer and he had none to give them. In the background the officer and preacher continued to chat as if nothing out of the ordinary were occurring. It was not real, Luis told himself.

'–but it turns out I could buy it cheaper if I purchased three at once,' the preacher said to the captain as they passed by. The Kalisador caught the tail end of their very ordinary conversation and he snapped back into reality.

'Kneel! Get those rural knees onto the rural soil now!' shouted a soldier. 'Don't turn around,' barked another as they moved behind the tribe. 'Eyes straight ahead,' they shouted from behind.

Luis felt his throat turn dry. His shoulders began to tremble. Off to the side, lounging against the side of the truck, the captain and the preacher continued their conversation about local poultry prices.

'Find marks. Set to rapid. Ready!' The Guardsmen shouted in unison from behind. The old Kalisador suddenly felt no reason to turn around and see what they were doing. There was no point or hope in doing so. With regret, he slid the butterfly blade from its concealment and wished that he had died fighting. But the time for that had long passed. Without further warning, the Guardsmen began to fire their rifles.

CHAPTER THREE

The sound of gunfire travels wide in the wilderness. Its distinct report reverberates amongst the trees, sending animals scarpering up the trunks and startling flocks of birds into flight. The echo lingers for long after, interrupting the flow of nature with its rude, artificial presence.

Although Mautista knew little of firearms, he knew enough to recognise its sound in the still air of dawn. Especially the sound of multiple shots, crackling with a constant rhythm. The Kalisador knew instantly that something had happened to his people. If he closed his eyes and steadied his breathing, he could almost hear the screams, distorted behind the threshing blasts of weaponry.

Warily, Mautista guided his sampan close to the checkpoint once again. He steered the outboard motor by the tiller, the engine throbbing gently while his other hand gripped a machete. Before him, the checkpoint was strangely empty. The searchlights tilted down limply in their mounting brackets and no soldiers were in sight.

It was only then that Mautista saw the empty boats. All along the right side of his approach, the ramshackle assortment of his tribe's transport bobbed and bumped against each other in the morning swell. They were tethered like despondent beasts, the tribe's possessions bundled and roped, lying unclaimed upon their backs.

'You there! Come closer!'

Looking back to the checkpoint, now less than fifty metres away, Mautista saw the outline of a Guardsman appear on the pontoon. The soldier stood there, staring at him. Mautista froze, staring back. There was a long, awkward period of indecision as both men simply stared at one another. Then another figure appeared on the pontoon, shouting something at his fellow soldier. The lasrifle in the second soldier's hands forced Mautista into action. Groping for a cloth bundle containing foodstuff and medicine, Mautista propelled himself off the sampan and into the water with one fluid motion.

A las-shot sparked into the side of the sampan. It was the first time Mautista had been shot at and the proximity of death ignited his body with twitching movement. Another las-shot sizzled into the water sending up a geyser of steam, forcing him to plunge underneath the surface. Brown water gurgled around him as river debris darkened his vision in thick, blackened clots. The Kalisador swam, his limbs carving the water with desperate, life-saving strokes. By the time he resurfaced, Mautista emerged just in time to see the sampan he had left behind erupt into a shower of splinters. The boat was blown upwards and out of the water, spinning in mid-air as pieces of wood and tin peeled away. Up on the pontoon, a soldier was raking the water with a mounted weapon, something Mautista recognised from Ecclesiarchal teachings as a heavy bolter, a weapon used by the Emperor's crusaders in the early wars of scripture. A rapid succession of what resembled burning hot embers erupted across the water as the heavy bolter swung back and forth. Not waiting another moment, he cleared the short distance to shore with practised strokes and surged out of the water headfirst. The shallow riverbank pulled at his ankles as he sprinted towards the tree line, acutely aware that the bolter would no doubt be tracking his back.

For a brief, absurd moment Mautista considered allowing himself to be shot. His tribe were probably gone, and he had failed them as a custodian of his people. There was nothing left for him in this world. But it was a passing moment and his warrior's instincts pushed him onwards. All around him, thick gum-saps fell, throwing up a solid wall of splinters and mulched vegetation. Mautista hurdled a log as bolt-shots stitched the ground to his front. He continued to run, deeper and deeper into the rainforest even as the bolter stopped firing. He ran and ran and did not stop until his lungs were seized from exertion and he could no longer tell where he was.

Colonel Fyodor Baeder, stripped to the waist in the afternoon sun, made his way around Riverine Base Camp Echo with a purpose to his stride. The men of his battalion were 'bombing up' on the parade ground, prepping their kit for their first true taste of conflict on Bastón. There was a general air of excitement on camp and even detachments not assigned to the 88th were lending a hand with the preparations. Soldiers laid out all their equipment neatly on plastek groundsheets, cleaning and repairing.

He darted around them, and stopped to allow a forked lifter delivering pallets of rations from the storage sheds to pass.

Riverine Guardsmen from other battalions passed by, carrying stamped boxes of ammunition and strongboxes of rifles. They were sweating under the relentless heat but everyone on base worked tirelessly to get the 88th Battalion ready for their operation. It may have been his battalion preparing for operation, but it would be the entire 31st Riverine that was preparing for war.

'Fyodor, you lucky bastard. Enjoying the attention?' Colonel Tate called out to him from the open entrance of a vehicle hangar.

'Enjoying doing something for once,' Baeder replied, grateful for an excuse to wander underneath the shaded hangar roof.

Colonel Tate and a handful of his men were smeared in machine grease. The hangar was sour with the smell of polish, promethium and burnt rubber. Behind them, a line of swift boats secured in tow racks was being worked on by the Guardsmen – hammering, tinkering and mending. Sirens sounded as an engine block was winched up towards the ceiling by a clanking pulley system.

'Leave some of them for us. I don't want you doing too thorough a job and leaving us squatting in ditches,' Tate joked.

'I think there will be plenty of insurgents left by the look of things,' Baeder responded. 'But if it'll make you sleep better, I can try to go easy on the ones we do find.'

Tate laughed and his men laughed with him. Baeder had known Ando Tate since they were both junior officers serving in Snake Company back in their early days. Ando Tate, with his broad grin, had been a natural amongst his men, rough and hardy despite his privileged upbringing. Baeder had always admired his ability to lead so effortlessly; it was something he never believed he could do.

'So what's the word, Fyodor? When are you lot moving out?'

'06.00 tomorrow. I'll be making last inspections at 04.00. It's really happening this time.'

Colonel Tate whistled appreciatively. 'Wish I could be there with you, brother.'

'I do too. But I'll see you out there soon,' Baeder said, clasping forearms with his old friend. As he turned to go, Baeder called over his shoulder mockingly, 'Don't mess up my boats either, Ando!'

Hurrying against the flow of traffic, Baeder passed beneath the girders of a guard tower. Despite being situated in a designated safe zone, soldiers manned the defence turrets constantly against insurgent mortars far out in the wilderness. Rows of green canvas tents were erected underneath its protective shadow. It was there that Baeder found the H-block administrative quarters, a rectangular green tent with spray-stencilled writing on the entrance flap. A corporal saluted and escorted him inside to meet the bored-looking admin clerk at the front desk.

The clerk, a red-faced captain sweltering in the heat, flicked the colonel a lazy salute as he entered. Judging by the spreading patches of sweat darkening his uniform, and the red rash on his neckline, it was evident to Baeder that the captain did not want to be stuck in administrative duties.

'Captain Brevet, sir. What brings you here?'

Baeder saluted sharply. 'A request came in that Brigadier Kaplain required me for a matter of great urgency. Any idea what that's about?'

Displaying no sense of urgency, Captain Brevet began to rifle through a sheaf of papers. He mumbled to himself as he worked until finally he triumphantly produced a slip of paper. 'Ah!' he announced, 'it says here, that an insurgent has been captured while on patrol. Brigadier Kaplain requests that you be present during interrogation, before you leave for the operation.'

'Very well. I will find him at the command post, I gather?'

The captain nodded. 'Yes, but do you need transport? It's a ten-minute walk,' he said, smearing his brow with his cap.

'No. I'll be fine, thank you, captain,' said Baeder turning to go.

'Wait, sir. Is it true? Your battalion is moving out to clear the siege-batteries so we can break this stalemate and finish this war?' the captain asked.

'We'll try,' Baeder responded.

Before he could say anything else, Captain Brevet swivelled on his seat and shouted at the only other man in the tent, a lieutenant standing only an arm's length away. 'See to it that the colonel gets a ride to the command post! Immediately!'

The lieutenant led Baeder out the back of the admin tent and down a narrow lane of storage sheds, until he found a sergeant smoking tabac underneath the shade of a signpost. 'Take the colonel to the motor pool, immediately,' he ordered the sergeant.

After threading through the base for some time, Baeder found himself outside a docking hangar marked *Motor pool – H Block*. Here, the sergeant deposited the colonel with a corporal who was unfortunate enough to be caught lounging on the bonnet of an all-terrain four wheeler. 'The colonel here needs to get to command post. I have important things to attend to so you'll have to take him.'

The corporal looked around desperately but there was no one else in the hangar. Reluctantly tugging his flak vest on, he saluted Baeder. 'All right, sir. Command post it is.'

As the pair strolled out towards a parked four-wheeler, a young trooper carrying two buckets hurried past. 'Timmons!' shouted the corporal. 'Come here for a second. Where are those damn buckets going?'

The trooper wandered over. 'The boys over at boat shed F have oil leaks on one of the swifties. They need buckets.'

'Give me those. I'll take them, it's just a short walk. You drive Colonel Baeder over to the command post right now!' snapped the corporal as he snatched the buckets from Trooper Timmons.

Trooper Timmons scrambled into the vehicle. He gunned the ignition then stared blankly at the fuel gauge. 'Sir,' he began, 'there's not enough fuel in the tank. If you don't mind waiting I can send one of the other troopers to go requisition some from the fuel depot.'

Baeder could not help but laugh. The Guardsmen of Ouisivia were terrifying soldiers in a firefight, but the majority were swamp dwellers at heart. If they did not have their lasguns in hand, they preferred to be boozing, sleeping or smoking in any combination. 'Emperor bless the Ouisivian way,' Baeder chortled, 'but I think I'll walk instead.'

Inside the command post, it was dark and unlit. A single lume-globe hung, suspended from the canvas tent by a black cable.

Around the lonely pool of light stood three men of the 31st Riverine, all of whom Baeder knew well. Present was Brigadier Kaplain, as well as the two most senior men in Baeder's battalion. Evidently, Kaplain had summoned the key commanders of the 88th to be present at the interrogation.

'Baeder, sir,' nodded the closest officer, a man with an ork skull tattoo scarring his face from forehead to chin tip. Like Baeder, the officer was clean-shaven. The finely-inked bones of a greenskin hid his entire face beneath a mask of black and ivory.

'Major Mortlock,' Baeder responded. As Baeder's second, Cal Mortlock was one of the most feared men in the battalion. His brutal look commanded a hushed reverence among the rank and file and the men simply referred to him as a monster, but never to his face. Despite outward appearances, like Baeder, the officer was born and raised in the relatively sheltered provincial parishes of Ouisivia and was thus remarkably soft-spoken for a man with ork teeth etched into his lips.

Standing off to the side in silence, Baeder noticed Sergeant Major Giles Pulver staring at him while picking his teeth with a huntsman knife. The sergeant was the most senior non-officer in the battalion, a rough-shed of pure Ouisivian frontier stock and a swamp rat through and through. He wore non-issue snakeskin boots and a flak vest over his bare torso in total disregard for regulation. His beard was longer than any other soldier's, his uniform more faded and his hands more calloused. In short, he was everything that Baeder was not. The contempt that Sergeant Pulver held for the slim, unassuming colonel was palpable.

'Sergeant Pulver, how do you do?' said Baeder.

The sergeant took his time to answer, working the blade between his front teeth with a surgeon's precision. 'Fine,' he replied finally in his thick, Ouisivian drawl.

If Brigadier Kaplain noticed the terse exchange between officer and soldier, he chose to ignore it. 'Fyodor Baeder, we've been waiting for you. How are the preparations?'

'Excellent, sir. Prowler and Serpent Company are both prepping to schedule. Seeker Company is a little late as usual. They have engine problems with several boats but Captain Fuller will have them sharp in time, I'm sure. As for Ghost Company, well they've been ready since morning and are chomping at the bit to deploy.'

Kaplain mulled over the news like fine wine. 'Good to hear. I have something to show you, colonel, it's quite different from what we've encountered previously.' The brigadier beckoned into the unlit depths of the command tent and two Riverine troopers stepped forwards and hurled the bound captive unceremoniously beneath the pool of light.

'Lord of Terra...' Baeder gasped.

Lying there, at his feet, was an insurgent. He was a native Bastón man and, like most of his people, slender and light of frame from poor nutrition. At first glance he looked just like any other insurgent, a rural villager in mud-stained sandals, his joints bulging with sinew from a lifetime of farming. But there was one startling difference – the man had no eyes, just a smooth sheath of skin where eyes should be.

'Can he see?' Baeder asked.

'Oh yes, quite well by all accounts,' Kaplain replied. 'He was caught taking potshots at passing river patrols with an autogun just six hours ago. Apparently led our platoon on a merry chase through the wetlands too so yes, I would say he has no problem with eyesight.'

Baeder knelt down to inspect the captive, taking care to keep a hand over the autopistol at his hip. The captive turned his eyeless face towards him in a parody of a stare. Baeder backed away, thoroughly unnerved. 'What do you know about him, sir?'

'He first claimed to be a local fisherman. Don't they all? After initial questioning he admits he is an insurgent, a *Carnibalès* by night and local river bargeman by day. He says his name is Orono of the Musan people. That's all we've gathered from him so far,' said Kaplain.

Baeder noticed the brigadier used the term Carnibalès, a native word for the insurgent fighters. As far as he was aware, *Carni* was indigenous for meat-eater, virile symbolism of the warrior, while *Balès* meant cabal. In essence the insurgency referred to themselves as the carnivorous cabal, a theatrical name if any.

'Let me at this meatball. I'll knock the corn out of him,' growled Sergeant Pulver.

'Not now, sergeant. Civility for our guest, please,' Major Mortlock interjected. He grinned monstrously at the captive, the tattooed incisors on his lips pulling back to reveal his natural teeth. If the captive was frightened, he hid it well beneath a show of jaw-clenched defiance.

'Are those mutations?' Baeder asked Kaplain.

The brigadier shrugged. 'He claims he was born with them. But I'm not convinced – you can see fresh scar tissue around his eyes and some scabbing on his upper brow. He's the first captive to show signs of mutation but you should see the weapons we've been taking from his friends.' The brigadier led them towards a folding table at the edge of the tent and flicked on the desk lamp. Upon the steel surface autoguns, a lasgun and several sidearms were arranged in neat rows.

'Look at this,' Kaplain said, picking up an autogun. 'It's not Imperial issue, it looks home-brewed, but the working mechanisms are too precise for them to be producing indigenously. Imperial intelligence suspects that advanced working mechanisms are smuggled onto the planet before being batch-assembled with native components.'

Baeder inspected it carefully, testing the weight in his hands and cocking the weapon. The brigadier was right, the autogun was roughly manufactured with a stock and body carved from soft gum-sap wood. While the wood was shaped roughly, showing uneven chisel marks in most places, the metal firing mechanisms were of advanced Imperial design. It was likely that the finer working mechanisms were sourced externally and then mass-produced on Bastón. The same could be seen of the lasgun, its body and stock constructed of cheaply-stamped metal.

Passing the autogun to Major Mortlock for inspection, Baeder blew a breath of disbelief. 'External sources then? The Carnibalès are getting off-world aid?'

Kaplain nodded. 'Every patrol into insurgent country turns up at least one crude weapons factory.'

'The ramrods from Sergeant Traiver's company turned in a seventy-year-old grandmother last week. She had her grandchildren mass-producing gun stocks in the smoking shed,' Pulver added with a dry laugh.

'Underground workshops, house-factories, canoe-borne bomb makers. Fragging everywhere nowadays. We intercepted a poultry truck this month. Every bird carcass had a plastek wrapped lasgun firing-mech sewn into its arse. Four hundred and eighteen poultry birds. Four hundred and eighteen lasgun mechs which were undoubtedly off-world and smuggled,' Mortlock reported. 'Creative little bastards, aren't they?'

A frown creased Kaplain's face. 'The guns have always had us scratching our heads for months, but now the mutation sends alarm bells ringing. Although this is the first sign of mutation we have encountered, I'm beginning to suspect that something is influencing the course of events here.'

'What?' Baeder asked.

'The Dos Pares,' Kaplain said. 'It means "Two Pairs" in the native tongue.'

'Dos Pares!' echoed the captive from the centre of the tent. 'Dos Pares!'

He was swiftly silenced by the kicking boots of the troopers standing over him.

'What the frag does that mean?' said Sergeant Pulver.

'Intel is unsure at present. But we believe it's the name of whatever cause, faction or leadership the insurgents are rallying under. Most captured insurgents mention the title in some way,' Kaplain replied.

'Or arms suppliers,' Baeder mused. He had indeed heard of the 'Two Pairs' before. He had filed enough patrol reports from the past few weeks alone to notice that the Dos Pares were a recurrent theme in the insurgency.

'Either way, they are keeping them well-armed and organised,' Kaplain said. He selected another autorifle from the desk, this one even cruder than the last, with a chipped wooden stock and a blunt-nosed barrel of sheet metal all held together in places by rubber banding. Despite its poor craftsmanship, there was no mistaking the 6.65mm hollow point ammunition in its drum magazine.

'Men, we have suspected for some time that this is no indigenous revolt. There are outside influences at work here. I wanted you all to see today that this insurgency has escalated beyond disenchanted natives causing mischief. Neutralise those siege-batteries quickly, so we can put an end to this mess.'

At 06.00, the five hundred and fifty men, four companies in all, slipped out onto the waters of the Serrado Delta before the moon had peeled away from the sky. Although the delta was not the longest river of Bastón it was certainly the largest, connecting a series of major river systems, some of which fragmented the landmass into a series of jig-sawed islands. In parts, the delta became so narrow that the trees above met in an arch, forming a net of dappled greenery above. Its variable width, combined with seasonal variations in flow and the presence of rapids and waterfalls, made navigation extremely difficult. Although pre-operational maps and navigational data sheets had been meticulously researched by Imperial intelligence, pre-planned routes would require a large measure of luck and guess work. The wilderness had always been the insurgency's one greatest ally.

Once on the narrow delta channel, they were forced to navigate as a trailing convoy, the swift boats leading the tip of advance. Behind them came the tubby gun-barges, flanked on all sides by inflatable landers ready to engage any threats along the riverbank. Each man carried one month's worth of provisions, a full combat load of ammunition and spare canisters of fuel.

Overhead, a single Imperial Lightning flew overwatch. Admiral de Ruger had, with great reluctance, spared the Riverine a single piloted aircraft to provide scout and reconnaissance. Baeder suspected de Ruger had not wanted the Riverine swamp rats to steal his glory and the admiral had made it clear, under no uncertain terms, that his pilot would only provide cover for eight hours of the day, and even then, no further than eight hundred kilometres from the green zone. Beyond that range the convoy would be left without support of any kind. Despite this, the combat aviator was an enormous boost to battalion morale. Although unseen in the deep-water wash of dawn, the Lightning's tail-lights were clearly visible, winking like a guardian star that ghosted the battalion. It was a benevolent presence that reminded the Riverine Guardsmen below that they were not quite alone. His call sign, appropriately, was Angel One.

It was a common saying amongst the troops that, although the Imperium still ruled Solo-Bastón, the wilderness belonged to the insurgency. Unfortunately, the wilderness was also four-fifths of the Solo-Bastón landmass, with the Imperium holding the remaining rural provinces and seats of government. As a result, the 88th Battalion would venture deeper into the Bastón rainforest than any cleanse operation or patrol, well beyond the range of timely Vulture gunship support and certainly beyond the range of standard artillery.

As the battalion flotilla left the docking piers of Base Camp Echo that morning, the officers and men lined the shores, standing in stoic silence. The 'Ferryman's Post' was played on a bugle, accompanied by the steady crump of artillery in salute. It was an honour usually reserved for fallen Riverine Guard as their funeral barges carried them away on the bayou.

Lieutenant Tomas Duponti was a real Persepian officer. When he did something he did it right and he did it with flair. He was a combat aviator of the 245th Nautical Squadron, and he fought the Imperium's wars from a cockpit at supersonic speeds and prided himself on four dogfight victories.

For the past four months he had been flying his Lightning interceptor over Bastón. The enemy here could not summon any aerial threat to challenge him and Duponti had suffered the tedium of high altitude reconnaissance mapping with nary a skirmish in sight. When he heard that he had been the only pilot selected for a low-altitude escort mission in cooperation with advancing ground troops, Duponti had never been happier. Finally, with the wind at his back and the canopy at his wing tips, he felt like a combat pilot again.

Lieutenant Duponti was one of many Nautical aviators who scrambled Lightning interceptors from the flight decks of a Persepian fleet. The planes, painted a powdery blue, were a workhorse of the Persepian Nauticals. They were light and clean to handle, unlike larger, more cumbersome craft, and their fuel efficiency meant they could probe further inland than any other Imperial flier on Bastón. In that time, Duponti had become quite adept at high-altitude surveillance, boring though the task might be, and had been recommended for this combat mission by Admiral de Ruger himself.

Of course, reconnaissance flights were by no means risk-free. Only two weeks ago, Duponti had been forced to fly at a significantly lower altitude due to monsoonal storm clouds. The gale had buffeted his little craft with sledgehammer force and, during the entire flight, his Lightning had rattled with the force of wind and rain. Descending low for his homeward flight, an unseen insurgent gunman put a heavy bolter round through his engine. Bleeding smoke and fire, Duponti put his plane down on an emergency strip in the rainforest, forty kilometres out from the closest Riverine outpost. The lieutenant abandoned his burning craft on the strip, escaping into the underbrush with his hand vox and service laspistol. There he hid, neck deep in mud, watching insurgents converge on his position. He was paralysed with fear for almost an hour as heretics swarmed over his wreck, tearing off pieces of fuselage as trophies. It took that long before a platoon of Riverine Chimeras reached his position and scattered the insurgents back into the sodden jungle. Duponti had struggled out of his hiding place, his grey flight suit slathered in mud while waving his white undershirt above his head. He had come so close to dying that day.

Still, it was nothing compared to a combat flight. By 06.00, when the 88th were scheduled to deploy, Duponti had already been in his cockpit for a good two hours, wired in anticipation. He soared north over the Calista Hinterlands, going as low as he dared to, slightly beyond the range of ground fire but close enough to watch the canopy streak beneath his wings. The exhilaration, combined with the G-force on his circulatory system, made his entire body throb with intoxicating energy.

De Ruger had outlined his task as overwatch – a simple support role. For an eight hour shift, Duponti would be on standby aboard the warship *Iron Ishmael* waiting for an emergency call from the 88th while occasionally flying out as reconnaissance for the battalion. Importantly, it was a low altitude mission and Duponti would be in range of enemy ground forces, and they within range of his autocannon. In a way, the lieutenant saw it as a duel.

'Angel One, this is Colonel Baeder from Eight Eight. We are on the move, over,' a voice crackled over Duponti's headset. The message was like a jolt after hours of static wash and Duponti swallowed his stimms.

Clicking his vox piece, Duponti took a deep breath. 'Eight Eight this is Angel One. Lieutenant Tomas Duponti reading you loud and clear. I'm fuelled and ready to scramble, over.'

'Good to hear, lieutenant. How many squadrons do we have as support? Over.'

'Just me, sir. Over,' Duponti admitted.

There was a hesitant pause at the other end. 'Lieutenant, say again. Just your squadron? Over.'

Duponti chewed his lip beneath his flight mask. 'No sir, no squadron. Just me and my bird. Over.'

The aviator thought he heard some cursing in the background before the colonel spoke again. 'One flier? Admiral de Ruger must have been feeling generous.'

Duponti understood the colonel's concern but there was little he could do about it. Orders were orders. 'Sir, I'm just one man,' Duponti began. 'But I fly damn hard and I'll do what I can. We can both forget about the admiral's eight hours per day. I'll be on call twenty-four hours and fly recon as much as I can take. I'll sleep in my flier if I have to, it's the best I can do sir. Over.'

'Thank you, lieutenant. I appreciate that,' crackled the headset. 'Look, we won't need you right now so get some sleep while you can. I have a feeling that over the coming weeks you'll become my favourite person, Duponti. Expect to hear from me plenty, over.'

'I'll catch a nap when I can, sir. Nothing further? Over.'

'Nothing further. Out.' The vox-channel went dead.

With that Duponti tilted his Lightning into a tight ascent. His pupils were dilated and his breath was coming sharp and fast from the stimms. There was no way he could get to sleep now. The dawn sun bathed his cockpit in a hard orange glow and Duponti continued to chase it, engines burning as he climbed the sky.

CHAPTER FOUR

Mautista wandered into the village in a daze.

He had no idea how long he had been walking, or how far he had walked. He only knew that his bleeding feet had carried him into a rural hamlet, deep inland.

It was a village that Mautista did not recognise. Rows of huts with roofs of rusting corrugated metal lined a dirt road. Poultry pecked aimlessly on the ground, fish dried on racks in the sun and old men squatted on the stoops of their huts. Behind both rows of homes, a grid of paddy fields provided much of the village's sustenance and trade during the dry season. It was a familiar sight, like most Bastón villages, but Mautista had never been here before.

'Where are the Dos Pares?' Mautista began to howl. 'Where? If they defend Bastón, where are they when it matters?'

The villagers shrank away from the newcomer who had wandered into their town. Most walked briskly in the opposite direction, darting frightened glances in his direction, and even the wandering poultry were startled by his outburst.

'Where are you? Show yourselves!' Mautista screamed. Mad with grief, he stumbled towards the closest hut. A middle-aged woman shushed her curious children into the house and slammed the tin sheet door, just as Mautista reached it. Delirious, he began clawing at the door. He knew that every village in Bastón had a contact with the insurgency in some way, whether it be child-spy or fisherman but, either way, the Dos Pares had eyes and ears in all places.

A handful of stout village men encircled him warily – the mad man in Kalisador garb, dishevelled though he was, was no less a frightening sight. They surrounded him but kept a hesitant berth. 'Fetch help,' one of them decided, and with that they left Mautista well alone to howl at the sky. Soon, most of the village had shuttered their windows and barred their ramshackle doors, leaving Mautista to vent his anger alone.

Mautista collapsed on the ground and fell asleep. When he awoke, he was roused by the rumble of engines. He felt as if he had slept for hours, but it could not have been for long as the villagers had yet to re-emerge. Bleary eyed, Mautista pulled himself up and looked down the single dirt-track that led out of the village. Shielding his eyes from the sun, he saw approaching vehicles in the distance. As they rumbled down the winding dirt road from the hills, he could make out an agri-truck and a rural autobus. By the time the vehicles applied their squealing brakes, Mautista was waiting for them alone in the middle of the dirt-track. He already knew who these people were – they were insurgents of the Dos Pares, they were Carnibalès. The truck and autobus ground to a halt just metres before him, wheels throwing up a fan of dust.

Almost twenty Carnibalès fighters piled off the vehicles – an entire insurgent warband. At first glance they looked like any other villagers, clad in rural canvas garb and salvaged scraps of PDF leather armour. But there was a ferocity to their demeanour. Mautista had seen livestock bandits before and these men had the same ruthless look about them. Some were shaven-headed while others styled their hair into oiled topknots. Many others hid their faces beneath wound strips of leather so only their eyes could be seen. One brute even had traditional protective scripts tattooed into his shaven scalp: text and diagrammatic shapes criss-crossing his entire head and neck.

'I want to join the Dos Pares cause,' Mautista began. 'I want to kill Imperial men–'

The brute with the tattooed scalp punched him in the jaw before he could finish speaking. Before he realised what had happened, Mautista was on his back looking up at the sky.

'Balls of a great ape,' spat the insurgent. 'Who do you think you are? Coming into our region and causing enough trouble for these folk to send for us.' The insurgent stamped down on his ribs with the flat of his hemp sandal. 'Well we are here now. Is this what you wanted?'

Mautista did not have a chance to reply. The other Carnibalès swarmed over him, beating his prone form. The Kalisador fought back even as the warband laid into him, groping out and catching someone's hand in the kicking, stamping mess. Immediately, Mautista began to apply a wristlock, one of the basic principles of Kalisador duelling known as 'defanging the snake'. He applied pressure by bending the victim's hand even as someone stepped hard on his ankle. A kick broke his nose with a wet snap. Someone else began to pull at his mane of hair but Mautista would not relinquish the wristlock. The Kalisador swore to himself, even as fists pounded the back of his head, that he would break that hand if it cost him his life. Finally, as his vision hazed from concussion, he wrestled the hand into an unnatural angle and snapped it. There was a popping crunch, but Mautista had no time to savour his victory. The beating continued as the village crowd gathered around, watching.

Eventually, the blows wilted and slowed. With one last kick, the Carnibalès warband parted away and towered over the Kalisador. Mautista did not know what he looked like, but judging by the blood rolling in oily sheets down his forehead, he must have been a mess. He breathed heavily and bubbles of blood frothed at the corners of his mouth. He staggered onto his feet, wincing as bruised joints clicked into place.

One of the insurgents in the mob began wailing. 'He broke my hand!' he shouted, nursing his shattered wrist. 'Frag! He broke it!'

The insurgents glared at Mautista as one. Twenty wild, ferocious men staring at him with murderous rage.

'He fragging deserved it,' Mautista managed to say. When he smiled, blood drooled out of his numb lips.

The insurgents immediately surged forwards, a swarm of flailing fists. The Kalisador turtled up, shielding his head from the worst of the blows. Rough hands seized his clothing, pulling and tearing at him. For each hand that lingered too long, Mautista reached out and snapped fingers. Disarming an opponent's weapons or neutralising his ability to fight was one of the primary methods of Kalisador unarmed fighting and, although Mautista had never excelled in that area, he was more than capable against untrained combatants. Mautista continued to break fingers and he counted seven digits. It was the only thing that kept his mind off the pain.

When the insurgents had finished with him, Mautista was wedged against the wooden fence palings of a poultry coop. His left eye had swollen shut and his right eye was almost the same. Hazily he could see villagers forming a curious ring around the Carnibalès who encircled him. In a way, Mautista was glad he could not see them properly, if he had perhaps he would not have been so brave.

'I broke seven of your fingers, something to remember me by,' the Kalisador croaked. He tried to laugh, but it hurt to breathe and he trembled instead. He was sure they were going to kill him. He wanted them to kill him. He wanted to die so he could see his tribe again. The insurgents edged in closer, several of them nursing mangled hands. Then tattoo-neck slid a knife from his rope belt with slow deliberation. Mautista tried to get up.

'Tacion, enough. That one is a tough and very stupid boy,' called a man as he stepped from the autobus's accordion doors. The Carnibalès parted to let him through and Mautista almost thought he was not a man at all. He was one of the tallest men Mautista could ever remember seeing, taller even than the off-worlders. The man's entire bone structure seemed elongated, with shank-boned forearms and tall blades for shins. This unusual appearance was enhanced by white chalk daubed all over his skin and black paint smeared on his mouth and around his eyes. With slow, unfolding strides, the man approached Mautista, his ex-militia leather armour creaking.

'I want to become a Carnibalès,' Mautista wheezed.

'Yes, you do,' agreed the ghost face. 'I can see that you do.' He crouched down next to the Kalisador and cupped Mautista's head in his hands. His fingers were cold and strong, pinning Mautista's head against the fence. With thumb and forefinger, he stretched the skin around Mautista's eyes, while peering into them.

'Are you looking to see if I lie?' said Mautista without flinching.

Ghost-face smiled in reply. 'No. I'm checking for concussion.' Finally satisfied, ghost-face gripped the backplate of Mautista's crab shell, levering him upright with surprising ease. As he patted dust and blood off the Kalisador's breastplate, Mautista realised that he was a full head and shoulders taller.

'Are you of the Dos Pares?' Mautista dared to ask.

'I am a Disciple. One of many direct students of the Dos Pares. I will tell you my name once you tell me yours.'

'Mautista of the Taboon people,' Mautista began, and then haltingly corrected himself. 'I was of the Taboon people.'

'I am Tabinsay. I have the authority to recruit you to become a Carnibalès. Is that really what you want?'

'I'm bleeding all over the dirt, am I not?'

Tabinsay clapped his hands in soft amusement. 'Very true.' Standing up, the Disciple beckoned towards his men. 'Blindfold our guest. We'll take him with us.'

Mautista did not even have time to say his thanks before the mob was on him again, binding his hands with cord and lashing a cloth around his eyes with a brusqueness that was all too familiar. Soon they were frog-marching him up onto the agri-truck, ready to take him to the inland hills.

Mautista began to count in his head, slowly, one by one, focusing his mind on the rhythm of one number following another. The road up the hills was rough and nauseous. Blindfolded as he was, Mautista felt every bounce along the dirt-track as the truck's wheels sought purchase along the steep climb. So it was of great relief when the truck finally lurched to a halt. Mautista had lost count by then and he had no idea how long it had been.

As the blindfold was wrenched off his head, Mautista squinted out of the truck's flatbed and took in his surroundings. They were in an isolated village, so deep inland that the air seemed thick with leaves. Everywhere he looked, vines and creepers criss-crossed his vision, while drooping beards of curtain figs touched his head from an eighty-metre high canopy. Amongst the deeply ridged trunks of moss pillars, rings of lean-tos crouched beneath their girth. Mautista had expected some kind of military base like the militia installations from before the war, or perhaps a fortress of some kind. This settlement, with its scattering of lean-tos, was not where the proud resistance was based. Or, at least, that was what Mautista had envisaged.

'Is this the Dos Pares camp?' Mautista asked the insurgent seated next to him. The insurgent shot him a knowing smile.

'You'll see.'

And see he did. The insurgents concealed their vehicles with tarpaulins before stooping into a nearby lean-to. The sheet of tin, propped against sprawling taproots, concealed a trapdoor below it. Mautista slid down feet first, followed by the insurgents one after another. The opening was barely wide enough for his shoulders and once inside it was little better. They moved along at a semi-crouch, scraping their heads against the low wooden rafters above. Luminite strips glowed dull blue along the tunnel, sometimes branching off in forks, leading them deeper and deeper into the subterranean depths. At certain intervals, Mautista had to avoid knocking over caches of arms: strongboxes of ammunition and lasguns propped upright against the walls.

'Who built these?' Mautista asked.

'We did,' replied Tabinsay from behind him. 'The Dos Pares planned this, and our people dig. Sometimes I don't see the sun for weeks,' he said, his white pallor almost luminescent in the dim lighting. 'We come out only in the night.'

In some parts the tunnels dipped into wider, larger bunkers, their walls supported by interlocking logs and hard-packed clay. Some of these bunkers were lined with rows of sleeping cots, while others were storage sheds. One in particular was some sort of crude weapons factory, scattered with workbenches and tools of a metal smith. The insurgent labourers looked up from their work to glare warily as Mautista crept past them.

'Through here,' Tabinsay instructed, pointing at a small, square opening in the wall no more than fifty centimetres in height and width. It would no doubt require Mautista to crawl on his hands and knees, an agonising task considering the injuries he had sustained. But on he crawled through the serpentine stretch, as his bruised ribs rubbed against the ground the entire way.

Mautista shimmied out into a bunker, Canceo following close behind.

He found himself in another underground chamber girded by logs and lit by vapour lanterns. The sodium glare illuminated overlapping maps and charts on the walls. More paper spillage lined the floors, printed leaflets of propaganda showing crude pictures of happy, smiling villagers standing over a trampled Imperial aquila.

'Simple, but fine illustrations, aren't they?'

Mautista was surprised to see a trio of tall, white-painted men squatting around the bunker where he didn't see them before. Like Tabinsay they too were raw-boned and lean – somehow stretched – yet there were subtle differences. One of them, the closest to Mautista, had long tendrils of hair, like white tentacles that seemed to merge seamlessly with the flesh of his scalp. Another Disciple seemed even more distorted, the bones of his shoulders and knuckles distended to thick, rock-like proportions. The abnormal changes fascinated Mautista and the Kalisador instantly knew that these men were somehow different from the regular Carnibalès.

'Yes. Quite beautiful,' Mautista replied, picking up a leaflet. While looking at the sketched renderings of the joyous villagers and the Imperial defeat, the Kalisador thought about the Taboon people and felt a strong yearning. There was something to the strokes of ink on that paper which stoked a surge of pride in him. For the first time since the massacre of his people, Mautista's anguish was replaced by a hot spike of purpose.

'You no doubt wish to join our cause? Otherwise you wouldn't be here alive,' said the Disciple with the flesh-ridged scalp. He spoke to Mautista while barely acknowledging him, working a guillotine rack with deft, practised fingers, chopping wide sheaves of papers into smaller blank leaflets.

'More than anything,' Mautista proclaimed.

'I'm curious, Kalisador,' said the one with distorted shoulders. When he spoke, his voice was low and garbled, as if his jawbones were too wide for his skull. 'You look a frightful, bleeding mess. Why?'

'I can explain that,' said Tabinsay. 'We beat him. Hard. But he wouldn't stay down, kept fighting back and even broke the hands of several of my best shooters.'

Suddenly, all three Disciples in the bunker looked up and regarded him with raised eyebrows of respect. 'A true Kalisador,' said one.

'We can find a place for you in the insurgency, if you are willing to learn amongst normal Bastón-born men – farmers, boatsmen and beggars alike.'

Mautista nodded. 'Of course.'

'Good,' grunted blunt-jaw. 'Blood-brother Tabinsay will take you to the barracks. You should clean up, rest. Tend to your injuries. We'll call for you before dawn tomorrow and assign you to a training mob.'

'When do I get a gun?' Mautista asked.

'Soon. Now go,' said the Disciple, waving him away.

For the first several days, the 88th Battalion slid along the Serrado Delta. They travelled slowly, particularly along the narrow winding inlets. There amongst the needle rushes and overhanging bowers, insurgents liked to take potshots at passing river patrols and, in such confined areas, the snipers often picked off two or three soldiers before melting into the wilderness. As a consequence, the convoy crept with their engines humming quietly, guns facing all directions, all eyes scrutinising the dense undergrowth for any signs of irregularity, perhaps the curve of a hat, or a patch of cloth amongst the green.

However, the battalion received no fire in those few days of the operation. They were still close to the green zone and it was well known that the insurgents were terrified of straying too far along the coastal regions. They were too frightened to come within range of Imperial support weapons to engage troops so close to Imperial-controlled provinces.

They were far too frightened of the Vultures.

This close to the seaboard base camps, a Vulture gunship could be voxed and en route within minutes. With an operative distance of five hundred kilometres, the gunships threatened a wide radius of wilderness that the Carnibalès insurgents had taken to calling the 'death circle'. Only the hardiest or bravest insurgents dared to operate within the death circle. At any moment, a Vulture could rise above the canopy, its presence heralded by the ominous *whup whup whup* of turbine engines. The sound itself was enough to send insurgents scrambling into hiding. There the Vultures would hover above the canopy, pivoting on the spot while hunting for movement. Once sighted, the Vulture would sound its guns, thunderous and clapping like a locomotive chattering through a tunnel.

Vultures were heavily favoured by the 31st Riverine. Back home on Ouisivia, the swamp orks were so wary of these war machines that they considered them an incarnation of Gork's wrath. And indeed, there was a crude resemblance; painted in the jade green and tan of the Riverine with its sloping, pugnacious profile, the Vulture was a predator in the field of war. A chin-mounted heavy bolter was housed below the cockpit, while two autocannons were cradled in hard points beneath its wings. These weapons discharged in rotation so that while one fired, the others would load, generating enough firepower to flatten a hectare of mangrove into quagmire within a minute.

But the Riverine pilots preferred to hit and run, strafing the enemy with conservative bursts of fire. In one swooping charge, the tracer trials from its combined arms seemed to merge into one puff of orange flame. With such air dominance at their disposal it was little wonder that the insurgency resisted attacking the 88th Battalion during the early stages.

But a flotilla of such size is hard to miss and Colonel Baeder made no attempt to hide their presence. Either way, the insurgency had operatives in most villages. Most settlements clustered along the waterways, and the flotilla passed them often. The grey-brown water from the sea served as highway, laundry, sewer and bathtub, and curious villagers watched them with trepidation. Soon, when they travelled out of range of Vulture support, the enemy would be waiting for them. Colonel Baeder knew this. His men knew this also and it was only a waiting game.

CHAPTER FIVE

The 88th Battalion headed south, threading along the river towards the deep subtropical depths of Bastón. According to Baeder's maps, the super-heavy battery would be a hard three weeks of sailing, weather permitting. But out in the wilderness, the maps and calculations amounted to nothing. The swell of monsoon season varied the channels, flooding new inlets into the delta's arterial spread and creating dangerous rapids where the water had been calm. The foliage spread in the wet season with roots snaking out into the water, clogging propellers and beaching vessels atop nests of mangrove. Slowed, frustrated and snagged by terrain, the flotilla became spread thinly, losing formation as vessels lagged behind.

Although the Riverine Amphibious were expert boatsmen, their home world of Ouisivia had not prepared them for the conditions of jungle fighting. There, their chosen terrain had been flat, low lying wetlands; saline fens where the climate was humid but tolerable. On Bastón, the rainforest seemed to exist as a single, seething entity that attempted to thwart the off-worlders in any way organic. The air was steaming, a shimmering pall of fetid heat that sat heavily on the lungs. Sweat glued their fatigues to them in wet, peeling swathes, so much so that most of the men went bare-chested.

Worst of all were the insects, constantly biting and darting like dog-fighters. The buzzing sand-biters had a sting that could penetrate even the flak vests, leaving an itching welt that swelled to the size of a thumb. Drenched in constant sweat, the bites became puffy and raw. The

Guardsmen scratched themselves constantly. It amazed Colonel Baeder how a simple insect could deteriorate morale so dramatically.

Baeder tried to instil confidence in his men by not allowing the climate to defeat him. He steamed under his full-length fatigues and boots, sweating so badly that his spare uniforms became stiff and board-like. He refused to scratch his bites although they burned like throbbing embers beneath his sticky uniform. Above all, he displayed a calm he certainly did not feel inside, navigating as best he could by the maps he had been given. One wrong turn and his men would forever see him as the weak, pallid high-born officer who would become the target for all their collective torment. It was a fine line he walked between focus and boredom.

Baeder was still lost in thought when his vox headset crackled. 'Sir, this is forward scouts, reporting,' came the soft, metallic voice on the other end. Roughly half a kilometre upriver, three swift boats maintained a constant lead on the flotilla as forward scouts and it was their job to stay in constant vox contact, updating the battalion on terrain changes ahead.

'Go ahead. Report,' the colonel said, dismissing vox protocol altogether. Judging by the urgent whisper, Baeder knew something was wrong; he could not account for it, but he could hear it in their voices.

'Sir, there are bodies floating in the river and some piled up on the riverbank. I think I see more tangled up inland, but I can't be sure.'

Baeder's entire back tingled when he heard this. 'Understood. Hold position where you are and stay edged. We will be up to meet you shortly.'

The colonel was riding in an up-armoured swift boat at the front of the column. Acting fast, he ordered his crew of five to vox for a reinforcement section. He required three assault landers, and one extra swift boat to join him. A gunboat equipped with a heavy flamer was also requested to lend onsite supporting fire. The rest of the battalion was to maintain a defensive formation and power down their motors until further command.

Major 'Ork Skull' Mortlock, standing at the prow of his swift boat, answered him. Mortlock had been with the battalion for two foreign campaigns and by all rights should have been promoted to colonel when their previous battalion commander had perished. But elements of brigade leadership had deemed the major too much like the wild men under his command and assigned Baeder, a staff officer from Operations Command, to the 88th instead. Watching him standing on his swift boat with the sleeves torn off his fatigues and a helmet sitting askew atop his death's head, chin straps hanging loose, Baeder realised why the command feared Mortlock. They feared him because he was everything that most Riverine officers tried to be, but could not be.

'Ready to go?' Baeder called out as his swift boat drew astern.

'That depends, sir,' Mortlock began. 'What's in store?'

'The scouts have reported some suspicious activity ahead. We're going inland to investigate.'

'A fight, sir?' Mortlock asked eagerly.

It was an act, Baeder knew, and a good one. Mortlock was not the pugnacious thug that he portrayed himself to be, but it was good for morale. A timid leader did not lend his soldiers much confidence.

'I can't say,' Baeder replied, then paused. 'But they've found something we should look at.'

Mortlock raised his lasrifle, addressing the three squads of Guardsmen in assault landers that had drifted alongside. 'Did you hear that? Let's see if we can get ourselves a good fight!'

The men in the landers roared, clattering their rifle butts in approval. Baeder smiled. The major certainly had a way with the rank and file.

The village of Basilan had recently been rebuilt. A long-range patrol from the 31st Riverine, Snake Company of 506th Battalion, had reached the village at the limits of their patrol route. Upon witnessing the state of disrepair that the village had suffered during the war, the company had offered to rebuild the local chapel and schoolhouse. A mortar fired into the village had blown the roofs off both buildings and inflicted considerable damage to its structure.

Snake Company had stayed for three days, foraging corrugated metal and forest wood for the repairs. On the third morning, Vultures chutedropped medical supplies onto an old militia landing strip and Snake Company Chimeras had ferried the supplies back to the village. The villagers had sorely required anti-bacterial soap as the jungle heat bred infection and soap was a precious commodity in Bastón, even long before the war. For the first time in months the people of Basilan tried to re-establish their fishing trade along their little strip of the Serrado Delta.

By the time Colonel Baeder came across their little strip of the delta, all the Imperial aid had become undone.

A dozen bodies bloated with gas remained buoyant in the water. Bodies of more villagers were scattered on the wooden pier overlooking the river. Some had even managed to reach their boats but had died there before they could cast off. There was even what appeared to be the remains of a woman tangled high up in the branches of a riverside gumsap. Baeder had seen killing before, but there was something about the still, secretive nature of the rainforest that disquieted him.

Quietly, the inflatable slid into the reeds of the riverbank. Baeder and Mortlock had joined the assault landers and they splashed into the knee-deep water with the platoon. Baeder noticed half a human hand nodding softly amongst the tall needle grass. He signalled for his men to thumb lasguns off safety as he unholstered his autopistol. Behind them, the remaining crews of the swift boats and scouts waited under the protective gaze of a heavy flamer barge.

Sergeant Luster sloshed next to Baeder with a worried look. Like all swamp-born Ouisivians, he was a big man with a thick neck and shoulders broadened by a childhood of swimming and dragging trawl nets. It was disconcerting to see a man like Luster so spooked. 'Sir, should we call another platoon?'

Baeder weighed up his chances. Once inland, he would have only his platoon to rely on. The battalion was another half a kilometre downriver. Then again, if he called up a company-strength formation to sweep the area only to find nothing, he would cause undue tension on already combat-stressed soldiers. He decided against it. He would do the job with the men he had at hand.

'No, sergeant. We'll go in as is.'

Sergeant Luster did not look pleased and neither did the troopers as they waded up the riverbed and secured the perimeter of the bank. All along the tree line, there was no movement nor sound. Birds did not like the stench of rotting death and the area was eerily quiet except for the soft lapping of water. A dirt path carved into the dense net of greenery wound its way deep towards the village.

'Mortlock, split the squads into two. I'll take the main path with squads one and two. You take squad three and ghost alongside the path well hidden. If we get hit, hook around and flank them. Got it?'

Mortlock gave him the thumbs up and promptly melted into the undergrowth with his section in tow. Splitting their advance would not only leave them less vulnerable to ambush, it also split the command elements of his battalion, so that both commanders would not become casualties if misfortune befell them. But it also divided their already meagre firepower and some of the Riverine growled and muttered visibly. Baeder did not blame them: the unfortunate female victim, dangling stiffly from the high branches above, cast an ominous pall on the entire task.

They set off up the path cautiously, taking care to walk on the edge of their boots and roll onto the balls of their feet to minimise noise. As they moved out of the dappled sunlight into the shadows of mossy trunks, Baeder felt a chill that overwhelmed even the maddening heat.

The devastation was all encompassing. Human remains were scattered in deliberate hiding places, stuffed between branches, noosed up in vines or loosely buried in soil. The act of killing was outstripped by the morbid cruelty and unspeakable acts performed on the victims afterwards. With one curt hand signal, Baeder brought Trooper Castigan and his squad flamer to the front. Tactically, it was a sound decision, but mentally, Baeder liked to have the tongue of ignition flame by his side.

'If we were back home, I'd say this the craft of swamp orks,' Mortlock said over the vox headset.

'I don't think the ferals were ever this brutal. Cover us and stay put, I'm moving my squad into the village proper,' Baeder instructed.

Mortlock and his section lurked at the tree line just beyond the paddy fields as Baeder and his men fanned out into the village. The hamlet had been built at the centre of a large square field of cleared rainforest and buffered by agrarian fields. The people here had grown cassam tubers and the paddies were chest high in water during the monsoon season with broad hand-shaped leaves skimming the water surface. The huts were built on stilts overlooking the agrarian plots, their sagging roofs giving them the look of tall, tired old men.

Holding their lasguns at neck level, above the waterline, Baeder and his squad waded into the paddies. The soil was unexpectedly mushy and Baeder's first step plunged his chin below water, his mouth gulping mud. With the ground yielding to the ankles with every step, their progress was slow and vulnerable. Behind every leaf frond Baeder expected something to be lurking and waiting but nothing moved. Here and there, the body of a villager could be seen floating face down, shot from behind as they fled across the paddies. The team cleared each hut in turn, Trooper Castigan moving in first with his flamer and Baeder following with pistol in hand as the rest of the squad surrounded the structure. Inside, the remains of half-eaten meals could be found on the rush mats, evidence that the attackers had come quickly. Baeder envied the simple life that these people had lived before the war. The villagers must have formed family circles on the hut floors, sharing roasted cassam tubers, fermented fish and the boiled leaves.

A wail from outside brought Baeder around sharply. The colonel darted out of the hut, forgoing the short ladder and jumping straight into the paddy water with an ungainly splash. His soldiers were already ploughing through the water towards the source of the scream. One hundred metres away, a woman stood in the middle of a distant paddy, her head and shoulders visible but shaded by cassam fronds. She was Bastón-born, judging by her loose linen shift and large shell earrings, traditional garb amongst indigenous women. She wailed again and once she saw the soldiers she would not stop wailing. Troopers surrounded her, aiming their lasguns as Baeder waded closer.

'Hush, hush,' Baeder hissed pleadingly, unsure of what to say. He held up his hands and lifted his finger off the trigger of his pistol to show he meant her no harm.

She was young, her face unmarked by the traditional dotted tattoos around her eyes that would show she was a married woman. Her hair was wild from where she had pulled at it and her eyes were rheumy from weeping. As Baeder moved closer, she continued to garble and wail unintelligibly.

'Slow down, speak to me,' Baeder called to her. 'Speak to me,' he said again, holding his hands out in front of him.

'I'm standing on a mine!' she wailed.

Baeder's gut lurched at her words, but he fought down the panic. 'Get back,' he said to his men. Whether it was their pride or the culpability of placing their commander in danger, the Riverine hesitated. 'Stop horsing around! Get back!' Baeder shouted. As his troops retreated to a safer distance, Baeder edged closer towards the woman. 'How did you come to be standing on a mine?'

'They forced me to...' she managed to say before trailing off into sobbing murmurs.

'I need you to tell me everything that happened, or we can't help you.'

The woman took a breath but was well beyond composure. 'Two nights ago, monsters came during dusk. They killed and killed; they killed everyone. They made me do this so I could warn everyone who found us about what happens when we support Imperial bastards.'

'Monsters? Do you mean insurgents?' Baeder asked.

'No! Monsters!' she insisted. 'Our Kalisador killed one and left it in the trees, over there,' she said, pointing to the eastern paddy. Baeder motioned for four of his troopers to investigate without looking away from the girl.

'Can you promise me you won't let the monsters eat my liver when I die?' she asked suddenly. Baeder understood vaguely what she meant. The Bastón-born had a superstitious fear of mutilation after death, as they believed they would suffer the pain in the afterlife. Despite the best efforts of the Ecclesiarchy to neuter the old beliefs, elements of them persisted and had experienced a resurgence since the war. By all reports, the Carnibalès had a habit of eating the livers of their victims. Many of the Guardsmen bodies that Baeder had seen at the base camp morgues had been mutilated.

'Yes. We can protect you and take you to the next village we pass.'

'No. I can die here, at home. I can die now, now that you'll protect me. Stand back,' she said softly.

Baeder's eyes widened in shock. He opened his mouth but before he could say anything, the girl took a step. He was only five metres away when it happened. The mine expanded in a blistering bubble of white water. With a fractional second to act, the colonel hurled himself backwards and was submerged. Underwater he heard a loud, wet burp and then his ears were ringing. He hoped the water would be enough to slow the ballistic properties of shrapnel as the force of the detonation spun him around. He felt as if he were caught in a whirlpool. His vision became clouded by a frothing mass of churned mud.

As he surfaced, the first thing Baeder did was to scream for his men to report injuries, but he could no longer hear the sound of his own voice. He'd been deafened. His men rushed towards him, asking for orders or checking his condition, but he could only hear the gurgle of his own ears. Baeder struggled in a daze, feeling as if he had taken a sledgehammer blow to the skull. Troopers stood around him. He saw flickers of a man screaming into the vox, presumably to Mortlock, but he could not hear a word of it. Further away, he caught a glimpse of the four troopers he had sent away, dragging something between them. Blinking rapidly, Baeder lost his footing and slid back into the murk, his lungs filling rapidly with water as the world spun in directionless circles.

Mortlock knew the sound of explosions on water. He had become accustomed to the dull, resonant clap and the gusty roar of liquid. In the distant agri-ponds, he saw a spear of water shoot into the air, white and vertical.

'Move and engage!' Mortlock shouted into his headset.

The Riverine dispersed into an open file advance, sweeping out of the tree line with lasguns levelled. Mortlock hacked at the cassam fronds with a machete. As he slogged his legs through the mire, he could hear the muffled shouts of men in the distance.

'Burn these huts as we go!' Mortlock instructed his squad flamer. The major had not liked the eerie quiet of the village from the start and he wanted to take no chances with enemy hiding places. The trooper juiced his flamer with a short, liquid burst and began belching a curved line of flame at the walls of each structure. He triggered on the move, raking the flames back and forth along the buildings. Each hut, cobbled together with irregular wooden planks and scrap metal, caught easily, the flames whirling some twelve metres into the air.

As the fire-team pressed on, the squad vox-unit began to receive from Baeder's squad. Connected to a bulkier vox array on Trooper Colham's back, the vox receiver piece transmitted the confusion directly from Baeder's position for Mortlock to hear.

'Mortlock, this is One. The colonel is down but uninjured, no casualties to report. We had a fraggin' native set off a booby trap. Dumb indig scared the hell out of us. Request cover, over.'

'This is Mortlock's escort. We're on our way. Stay calm and hold position. Out,' relayed Colham on the run.

By the time Mortlock reached them the colonel was waiting for him, his silver hair matted across his forehead, his chest swelling in great heaves. 'Major–' he began imperiously.

'Are you good, sir?' Mortlock asked.

'I'm fine. A little headache and some bruised eardrums. That's not so important right now.'

'Sir–' Mortlock began.

'Not now, major. Look at this,' Baeder said. Mortlock followed the direction of Baeder's pointing index finger and saw there, held afloat by four troopers, the body of a subhuman monster.

* * *

'This does not bode well,' Mortlock said, scratching his chin as he was wont to do when in contemplation.

The 'monster' was spread-eagled on the ground at their feet. It appeared human but beyond the continuation of two legs, two arms and something resembling a head, the similarities ended. Sergeant Luster cut away the insurgent's leather face bindings with his bayonet, peeling them away like loose skin. Beneath its flat, almost inverted face was more mouth than anything else, with a wide, slack maw so deep that its gaping throat was lost to shadow. The skin that covered its body was thickly wrinkled, forming a hard rind that resembled the peel of dried fruit. When Baeder touched it, it felt rubbery and slightly yielding, causing him to rub his hands on his trousers gingerly.

Most tellingly, it wore calf length trousers of white canvas and a leather jacket with one shoulder plate. The leather was a shade lighter where the insignia had been stitched off. There was no mistaking the scavenged apparel of an insurgent. Parts of uniforms foraged from dead local militia troops, mismatched with traditional garb, had in a way become a uniform of sorts for the insurgency.

Baeder sucked his teeth. 'The taint. Guns. These insurgent warbands aren't fraggin' around with us are they? This is serious.'

'You reckon this is a mutant? Not just some awry genetic accident in the womb?' Mortlock asked.

'Let's be pragmatic, major,' Baeder said. 'This is extensive mutation. The thing barely looks human. It's just too much to be natural.'

Mortlock nodded, his brows knitted in deep concern.

'What do you want to do with it?'

'Burn it,' Baeder said. 'I'll log the report to the Ecclesiarchy. They should be intrigued to learn about ruinous mutations among the insurgency.'

Cardinal Avanti strolled out onto the flight deck of the *Emperor's Anvil* and into the hard sun glare of the open sea. His bodyguard of battle-sisters in their alabaster armour trailed behind him, keeping even the Persepian armsmen at a respectful distance.

Avanti had a fondness for morning strolls along the flight deck. He walked the full length of the great Argo-Nautical, inspecting the string of parked fighters and bombers. Often, he ran a white-gloved finger along the painted metal and if it came away with dust the flight crew would be flogged. Sometimes, depending on Avanti's mood, he would be merciful or he would not. It was, he believed, good for discipline and the upkeep of faith. It reminded these soldiers that, despite their guns and training, the ultimate power lay within the Emperor and his highest servants – the Ecclesiarchy.

As Avanti circled the fuselage of a Marauder bomber, peering at the waiting aircraft with cold scrutiny, a young Ecclesiarchal page clattered down the steps of the bridge tower. He appeared to be in a rush, his face red from exertion.

The boy halted just short of Avanti's bodyguard and bowed, gasping hard to restrain his breathing in the presence of the cardinal. 'My lordship, there is an urgent vox transmission that requires your attention. It is a Captain Brevet from Riverine Base Camp Alpha.'

At this, the flight crew who had been standing next to their bomber in an apprehensive huddle, relaxed visibly. Some still bore the flog-marks of Avanti's discipline from several days past.

'You have been excused today,' said Avanti, addressing the crew chief directly. 'But consider this, anything shy of the perfection of duty is negligence towards the Emperor. To neglect the will of the Emperor is to invite slothfulness into your soul. It is the first step towards damnation,' Avanti said, wagging his finger with a mirthful gleam in his eye.

The crew chief stiffened visibly. Although he was a lifer with combat honours and thirty years of service to the Guard, he could do naught but nod. 'Yes, your lordship.'

It gave Avanti little pleasure to cut short his morning stroll, but he considered himself a pragmatic man. He soon found himself in the command tower of the Argo-Nautical. The vessel was at high anchor and the command bridge, usually thrumming with activity, was largely empty but for a handful of junior officers on standby. Avanti dismissed them. He preferred to handle intelligence personally and decide what it was that the military seniors could and could not know. It simply made things so much easier.

'My lordship, may I speak?'

It was Palatine Morgan Fure, a sister-soldier from the Order of the Steepled Keep. She was a short, well-muscled woman with a stern, broad jaw and heavy cheeks set like chapel stones. She wore power armour of form-fitting ivory plates, a bolter mag-clamped to her cuirass.

'Yes, child, you may,' said Avanti.

'I can take this vox message in your stead. Your lordship should not have to negotiate the petty foibles of a field officer.'

Avanti nodded. Palatine Fure was, in his opinion, one of the most loyal individuals he had ever encountered. She was intense, not only in her physical demeanour but in all manner of focus and piety. She and her company of sisters had been assigned to him for the better part of a decade since his ascension to cardinal and Fure had taken upon herself the task of his safety with a vigilance that bordered on the obsessive. She slept four hours a day, devoting the rest of her time to her training as a monastic militant. In her supervision of Avanti's guard detail, the cardinal had never feared for his safety, no matter where he travelled. Avanti enjoyed the rightful obedience he wielded over her and allowed her to display her devotion whenever it pleased him.

Fure snatched the vox receiver from a towering command bay and keyed the frequency.

'Speak,' she commanded, with total disdain for Imperial Guard protocol.

'Halo,' crackled the other end, using the call sign for high-ranking Ecclesiarchal members. 'Halo, this is Riverine Base Camp Alpha. I am Staff Liaison Captain Brevet. Who am I speaking to?'

'You are speaking to Palatine Morgan Fure. What message do you have?'

'I must speak with either Cardinal Avanti, or any staff officer of high command.'

'I am his aide. You may speak to me.'

'As you wish,' said Brevet with an electronic sigh. 'This morning our base camp received intelligence from the 88th Battalion gathered during the course of Operation Curtain.'

'Yes. And?' Fure snapped.

'Well, they retrieved the corpse of a slain insurgent. The corpse bears extensive signs of mutation.'

Palatine Fure looked to Cardinal Avanti. The cardinal waved his knurled hand once, in dismissal. 'Is that all?' she said in a flat tone that revealed no emotion. Before Captain Brevet could summon a reply she released her finger over the transmit button and hung the handset back in its bracket.

Avanti tutted to himself, drumming his fingers as he thought. 'This is a good thing,' he decided finally.

'A good thing, my worship? I thought we were to allow the Imperial Guard to know only what we needed them to know,' Fure asked.

'It was only a matter of time before they realised this is no simple peasant uprising. At least now we can use the influence of Chaos as legitimacy for waging this war,' Avanti cawed.

'But, my worship,' Fure said with a dull look, 'these mutations only began to occur many months after we began repossessing the land from the natives.'

Avanti sighed. Palatine Fure was a stoic servant, but she was frustratingly simple at times. Some people were just not set up to think politically. It was indeed true that the Imperial authorities had begun to uncover the beginnings of otherworldly influence many months after the Ecclesiarchy had begun to claim indigenous land for agricultural use, but that was no longer relevant.

For the past two years Avanti had implemented a policy to reclaim the land for Imperial use from the indigenous tribes. The local militia had been given Ecclesiarchal clearance to forcefully evict the indigenes from their lands. The parameters for 'force' were open to interpretation. It had been a glorious time of productivity for the Ecclesiarchal coffers.

Convoys of local militia trucks rumbled into the heartlands to claim regional provinces for direct use of the Ecclesiarchy. Those very same trucks would return, their cargo holds swollen with Bastón tribals ready for placement into work camps.

To Avanti's concern, the natives had begun to fight back, in small resisting mobs at first. Trucks began to disappear. Then isolated outposts both civilian and military were burned and razed. The Imperial authorities had not suspected those primitives capable of such a thing. Then the resistance became organised. Roving mobs became warbands; random acts of violence became planned raids. Rumours began to surface of a faction known as the Two Pairs. That was when the Imperial Guard from distant worlds began to deploy. For a moment, things hung in the balance for Avanti. The involvement of Guard forces meant the cardinal did not have the autonomy to pursue Ecclesiarchal interests at a whim. It frustrated him that officers would be so daring as to question why he was ordering both the killing of insurgents and civilians. Now things were falling into place quite nicely. If Chaos were indeed exerting influence on the insurgency then it was a good sign as far as Avanti was concerned. Now he had legitimacy to cleanse the mainland of its inhabitants and he would be right in doing so.

'Palatine, if the inland is corrupted, then we will scour it clean,' Avanti declared, using the impassioned tone that he reserved usually for sermons. 'We will have to sanctify the land of Bastón so that further generations of good Imperial citizens may make use of its soil.'

CHAPTER SIX

At exactly 16.00 on the one hundred and twenty-second day since deployment, the Persepian fleet steamed one of its grand Argo-Nauticals – the *Manifest Destiny* – to within sighting distance of the mainland. Their intent was to sail the vessel, by cover of darkness, into the placid Torre Gulf. From there, fourteen thousand Guardsmen would be deployed with supplies and motor fuel to establish an Imperial foothold on the island and reinforce the Riverine Amphibious already on the mainland.

It was a brave effort. Eight kilometres out from the coastline, Carnibalès spies planted in the coastal villages alerted the enemy of the Imperial movement. Three minutes later, the first Earthwrecker shell landed in the water just shy of the *Manifest Destiny*. Despite its gargantuan bulk, the Argo-Nautical was rocked by tsunami-level tidals created by the warhead. The second warhead, howling on contrails across the sky, did not miss. The hyper-velocity round – more missile than ordnance shell – split the Nautical's deck and released its charge inside the ship's hold. The resulting explosion whitened the night sky. Within the Imperial administrative cities occupying the coast, thousands of loyalists were awakened from their sleep by light streaming through their windows. Upon waking, their first sight was of a mushrooming cloud out on the horizon. They knew, one and all, that the Earthwrecker had spoken and Imperial salvation had been denied again.

* * *

Mautista's early days of training were hazy and fragmented. It did not seem so long ago that he had lived an enviably simple life as the warrior custodian of his people. Now he shared an underground bunker with fifty other recruits, their living spaces confined to narrow cots three shelves high. His days became a blurred routine of training, eating and negligible amounts of sleep. He was no longer subject to the troubles or joys of common life. Mautista no longer worried about the dry season harvest. There were no village festivals to look forward to, nor the courting of village girls. He knew exactly what his training day consisted of, from the moment the instructor roused them from sleep to the time he collapsed exhausted in the early morning. Mautista felt like his life had already ended.

The absence of any distraction allowed his mind to focus only on the task at hand. Upon receiving his standard-issue kit – a press-stamped lasgun and canvas bandoleer – Mautista began his indoctrination. He learnt the basic use of a firearm and its maintenance. He learnt how to shoot and, at night, their instructors would take them above ground to practise their shooting at nocturnal game. Mautista came to enjoy the firing, especially the reassuring recoil against his shoulder. He remembered the mix of awe and frustration he had felt when he had seen those soldiers brandishing their brutal las weapons at Luis. That same fear drove him on to master the rudiments of insurgent warfare.

The days were long and they trained hard for eighteen hours of the day, with short breaks in between. Recruits were expected to volunteer for an insurgent warband within two weeks of training, but they were also expected to be ardent supporters of the Dos Pares philosophy, known as the *Primal State*. When they did rest, the insurgent recruits would be lectured on the insurgent cause, philosophy and their many grievances towards the Imperial cult. In essence, the Primal State was a renaissance of the old religion and culture of pre-Imperial Bastón, yet at the same time there were distinct elements of anarchy, of revolution and of a strange, foreign theology known as *Kaos* in the native tongue. Here too, the Kalisador's keenly-focused mind excelled, and he engaged his instructors in lively theological debate. The destruction of the Taboon had deteriorated his faith in the guidance of his Emperor and the philosophy of Mautista's instructors suddenly made so much sense to him.

So great was his advancement, that Mautista was soon singled out amongst the recruits. There were hushed whispers that the insurgent leaders were watching him, that he would be a candidate for becoming one of the Dos Pares Disciples. So it came as no great surprise that, on the fifteenth day of Mautista's indoctrination, an instructor came to visit him.

'They're here for you,' said his instructor just as he had returned exhausted from a night training march. Mautista had just collapsed into his cot when he realised his instructor was standing over his bunk. 'Get up and pack your belongings.'

'Who is here for me?' Mautista groaned wearily.

'I am,' said a tall man, standing outside the underground barracks. His face was daubed in chalk and ink, his forehead deeply knotted with bony growth. Dressed in leather armour, with a lasrifle slung across his back, it was obvious that he was a Disciple of the Dos Pares.

Mautista immediately sprang to his feet. 'Why?'

The Disciple said, 'The Dos Pares have granted an audience with you.' It was the phrase every recruit wished to hear. It meant that he was selected to become a Disciple, a leader of the insurgency. Or at least have the chance to be deemed worthy. Whether successful or not, no recruits ever returned to their warband again.

'Pack your belongings,' the instructor said. Mautista was not sure, but he thought he saw a taint of envy sour his instructor's expression.

Mautista reached beneath his bunk and pulled out a roped bundle. Since his recruitment he had eschewed his Kalisador garb. His possessions were meagre – a lasgun, a canvas bandoleer, a canteen and a scavenged militiaman's leather jacket with one metal pauldron on the left shoulder. This was all he owned beside the canvas rural garb upon his back.

'I'm ready,' he told the Disciple. With that Mautista left with the tall man to meet the Two Pairs.

The Dos Pares, to most, was a standard bearer of rebellion. In the old language it translated to 'Two Pairs'. It became a synonym of unity steeped in an even older culture. To most, even to the common insurgent who was farmer by day and guerrilla by night, the Dos Pares was nothing more than a spiritual motif. The words were inked in the propaganda posters distributed by the guerrilla network, or whispered amongst old men in drinking dens.

Most Bastón-born did not truly know who or what the Two Pairs or the Dos Pares were. There were many who believed it was simply a term that encompassed the insurgency as a whole. Others still, believed the Dos Pares to be nothing more tangible than a philosophy, a rebel ideal that had spread from the jungle interior to the outer provinces.

The Disciples, however, knew the truth. These select few saw the Dos Pares as flesh and blood. To them, the Dos Pares was the physical, driving force of the entire insurgency. They were the masterminds of strategy, the leaders who trained natives in modern forms of combat and the entire reason that the Bastón-born insurgency had not already collapsed under the Imperial war effort.

Since the early days of Imperial aggression, the natives were rallied by the Two Pairs. These mighty beings taught all they knew to their Disciples, nurturing both their minds through instruction and their bodies through chemical treatment. This cadre of Disciples in turn marshalled a crude yet determined force of heretic rebels against the Imperium. Although many thought of the Dos Pares as a product of vivid propaganda, very few knew them to be real.

Mautista however, would be one of those privileged few.

A Disciple by the name of Phelix took him through the tunnel complex, through the tracts of freshly excavated tunnels. Mautista was led down passages he had never known existed. Only while lost in those claustrophobic depths did Mautista realise the enormous scale of the underground earthworks. The tunnels resembled bowels of freshly uprooted soil, coiling and uneven. Finally, Phelix and Mautista emerged in one of the many gun production facilities hidden underground. There amongst the workbenches, milling machines, lathes and grinders, Mautista met the Two Pairs.

The Dos Pares were four men. Four identical men.

That is, Mautista could not think of any other way to describe them. They looked like men in all aspects of physical semblance, that much he was sure of. But there was a solid presence to their power, an aura of overwhelming control that was beyond their physical appearance. They were men who seemed to make no mistake. There was a perfection to them that seemed to defy mortality of men. In that sense, they seemed inhuman.

The Two Pairs were tall. Taller than even the lithe Disciples, so tall that Mautista's head barely reached the middle of their torso. And how big those torsos were! An expansive ribcage and solid abdominal wall that rose like that of a fortress, matched in proportion by the rest of their body. Next to these giants, the Disciples looked like children suffering malnutrition. The Two Pairs wore simple loincloths of hemp, their bare muscles daubed with white from their shaven heads to the bulges of their calves. Like their Disciples, black kohl was smeared into their eye sockets and around their mouths so that they appeared as white, ghostly spectres. That's what they looked like, Mautista decided – like ghosts from another world.

'Come here and let me look at you,' commanded one of the four. There was a certainty to his voice, as sure as the sun would rise.

Mautista stepped before the quartet of white titans. The back of his neck knotted with anxiety. The simple act of the Two Pairs looking at him caused his nerves to seize up in awe. With men such as these leading the insurgency, there was no way they would fail. Mautista was sure the insurgency would succeed simply because these men said so.

'Tell me, Mautista Taboon,' began one of the Two Pairs, 'what is the role of a Disciple?'

'A Disciple leads warbands into battle against Imperial forces. He uses his men as a force multiplier against numerically superior forces by disrupting supply lines, raids, ambushes and harassing their area of operation,' Mautista answered automatically, as if from rote.

'A Disciple is a teacher. He takes that which he learns from us and he disseminates it amongst all people,' said the first giant. 'The Disciple is an embodiment of the primal state of Kaos, and he empowers others with this same conviction.'

'A Disciple is our mouthpiece. He goes where we cannot, spreading the insurgent cause while imparting his militant methods upon everyone, from child to grandmother,' rumbled the second.

Mautista nodded once, timidly.

'He is not just a soldier, but an operative. The operation being the expulsion of Imperial influence from his birth land. You must learn from us, and what you learn you teach to others,' said another.

By now Mautista could no longer discern where the voices were coming from. The Four seemed to speak as one.

'I understand.'

'Good. Come closer.'

One of the giants took a syringe from the steel worktable. Mautista had seen such things before. A local militia medic had often visited his village before the war, once every two months to inoculate the children against tropical infections. The needle looked much the same, but this one was much larger and filled with a dark red liquid. Mautista did not dare ask what it was for. Instead he simply proffered his arm towards the waiting giant.

'This will change you,' the giant said. 'But it is the only way you can learn from us within such a short amount of time. Time is not on our side and every day the Imperial forces grow stronger. We must accelerate the process: expand your mind and your body.'

Mautista did not understand, but the giant was so soothing in his tone that Mautista was no longer listening. He felt the needle slide into his bicep vein, intensely cold and intrusive. For a moment he was overcome by a surge of euphoria. And then the pain came.

It travelled up his arm, into his shoulder and then speared into his heart. It was a deep pain. He felt it in his marrow. It felt as if his entire body was being crushed together from all directions. Once, as a child, Mautista had a molar extracted by the village ironsmith. The pain was comparable, except this time it penetrated every bone and organ in his body. Mautista opened his mouth but could not scream, the pressure on his lungs was too great. Locked up and seizing, the pain intensified. Dark spots feathered his vision.

The Two Pairs made soothing sounds at him. 'An inevitable side-effect,' said one.

'It will pass,' said another.

'But if you die, then the warp wills it. What will be, will be.'

The Two Pairs continued to stand there, watching Mautista, doing nothing as he spasmed unceremoniously on the ground.

One of the giants knelt down next to Mautista. 'This will continue for several hours. Perhaps most of the night and tomorrow. You will live if you choose to live but it is easier to let go,' he whispered.

High above the tunnel complex, above the topsoil and undergrowth, it was raining again. Misting the air silvery grey, the monsoon washed down in sheets, shivering the canopy.

The 88th Battalion flotilla travelled at its slow, constant pace unperturbed. Hoping to avoid the worst of the torrential flooding along the main channel, the convoy snaked north-east along an inlet parallel to the major delta. They had made good progress in the past few days and, according to their charts, the first of the super-heavy batteries was no more than four days' travel to the east, five if the weather was poor.

Baeder's intention was to reach the large rural settlement of the Lauzon people by the end of the day. It would be a steady forty-kilometre stretch if the flood tides did not hamper their progress. By all accounts, Imperial intelligence had marked the Lauzon community as loyalists and there they could resupply their provisions and prepare themselves for the assault on battery one. From that point on, they would be less than one hundred and fifty kilometres from the super-heavy and enemy presence would undoubtedly become dense. The siege-batteries were the lifeline of the insurgency and the region would be fiercely defended.

Sergeant Major Pulver rode at the rear of the column, his swift boat bringing up the rear guard. Pulver considered himself an infantryman at heart, always preferring short stints on an inflatable assault lander that could get him close to the enemy, quickly. He had been born and bred on the feral marshes of Ouisivia and the cramped, claustrophobic confines of the swift boat's hab quarters did not suit his temperament. It made him irritable.

'Frag this, sergeant, I can't even get a decent meal in,' Trooper Sceri shouted from under the cover of the pilothouse awning. The torrential downpour sleeted sideways and, although the trooper huddled beneath the pilothouse eating his rations, rainwater was filling his mess tin.

'Suck it up, Sceri,' Sergeant Pulver called from the rear deck. He made no effort to even look at the young trooper.

'Did you hear?' said Sceri, trying to change the topic. 'The colonel apparently saved some boys the other day when they made that landing. Word is he walked face-first into a landmine so the others wouldn't have to. That's some heroic business. He's a true ramrod.'

That got Sergeant Pulver's attention.

'The colonel is a fragging meatball is what he is,' Sergeant Pulver said, stamping sodden serpent skin boots through the puddles towards the pilothouse. 'Who is he trying to impress with that idiotic gesture?'

Trooper Sceri shrugged sheepishly. He looked down, trying unsuccess-fully to tip rainwater from his mess tin without losing any of his dehyd gruel.

'He could have gotten himself killed. That would have landed us in a cluster-frag, I guaran-fragging-tee it. I don't have faith in this colonel more than I can throw him, but this early into the mission, losing our commanding officer would be death for morale,' Pulver concluded.

Sceri said nothing. He continued to pick gingerly at his steadily dilut-ing food.

'High-born overachievers always have something to prove.'

'Suppose we frag him later.'

The door to the pilothouse slid open and Corporal Schilt sauntered out onto the deck.

Pulver was not surprised. 'Plotting again, Sendo. Your mother was a snake,' he said dryly.

Corporal Sendo Schilt was a wiry little man, with a face like a snub-nosed swamp bat. His irises were a slit-eyed blue and, when he smiled, he showed pointy canines. Schilt was a man the sergeant would not turn his back on. As a sergeant major, Pulver had seen Guardsmen come and go, but Schilt was one of those rare few who were survivors. It did not surprise Pulver at all that Schilt would kill any officer who put him in unnecessary danger. In a way, a man like Schilt was a liability.

'Of course. I'd wager that our colonel volunteered us for this suicide mission to pad his career record,' Schilt hissed.

'It's too early to be talking about fragging him, corporal,' Pulver said. 'But if he pulls any more chivalrous rubbish that endangers both the mission and our boys, I'm going to put him out.'

'Yeh, well this mission is suicide. A lot of us have come to that conclu-sion. We're not happy either. If it comes down to our skin, well then we're acting. I know boys within the battalion who'd be willing to get the job done, sergeant, if you get my drift.'

'Keep your sights on the objective, corporal. Until then, I'll decide how best to keep this battalion intact, with or without the colonel,' Pulver said darkly.

Just seventeen kilometres out from Lauzon province, the scouting lance of three patrol craft stopped. Their motors idled as their guns panned the area around them. It was still raining and visibility was reduced to a grey curtain no more than ten metres in each direction. The downpour threw up a mist as it pounded the river surface, swirling like a landlocked cloud.

The way ahead was blocked by a dam. Crudely constructed of logs piled one over another, it stretched the entire fifteen-metre width from riverbank to riverbank. Despite the rising water levels, it rose just high enough to prevent the shallow-draft vessels from crossing.

Lieutenant Riddle, commander of the scout lance, voxed immediately to the main line of advance. 'Sir, we have solid obstruction here. The locals have decided to dam up for the wet season and it's a bloody no go.'

'How big is this dam, lieutenant?' Baeder voxed back.

'Nothing my men and I can't handle, sir. Do you want me to remove it? It might take a while.'

'Only remove as much as we need to get past. I don't want us to be held accountable for fragging up the livelihood of local farmers, understood?'

'Yes, sir.'

With an unspoken efficiency, two of the swift boats went to shore while one remained in the channel to provide overwatch. Riverine Guardsmen fanned out to secure the clusters of tendril beards overlooking the water as a work team waded out to clear the obstruction.

In the flash tides, the footing was treacherous. Riddle and his volunteers clung on to clumps of needle rushes as the water pushed up against their thighs. Each man held an entrenching tool, a small fold-out shovel issued for digging gun pits and shell scrapes. They were the only tools at hand for dislodging the logs from their foundations. The Riverine worked quickly, unearthing clumps of soil holding the dam in place. The rain drummed off Lieutenant Riddle's head and, clad in shorts, his joints were soon numb from the cold.

'Sir! There's no foundation to this dam!' shouted Trooper Wiman.

Curious, Riddle picked up a mossy branch that had shed from a nearby tendril beard and plunged it underwater, jabbing for the part of the dam that was obscured by water. The strong current tore the branch from his grasp. Riddle watched as the branch resurfaced on the other side of the dam and was carried away on the tide. Wiman was right, the dam had no middle nor bottom. It was simply a skirting of logs that obstructed the surface of the river and roughly half a metre below it. Dams were meant to stop water, not allow it to pass underneath.

This was not a dam. This was a boat trap.

Panic began to set in. 'Clear it!' Riddle shouted, kicking at the logs. 'Clear this quickly!'

As his men began to set to at a frantic pace, Riddle sprinted back towards his swift boat. He scrambled aboard, ploughed into the pilothouse and tuned his vox.

'Calling all formations! Obstruction is not a dam, prepare for insurgent activity. Calling all–'

Riddle let the vox speaker fall away from his mouth. In the distance he could hear the distinct popping and cracking of small-arms fire. As he peered out from the rain-streaked windows of his pilothouse, he caught glimpses of movement amongst the deep trees.

They lost all sense of order. The vox-channel was suddenly alive with the shouts and screams. But Riddle did not pay attention to the vox. He had more pressing matters at hand. Outside, he could already see muzzle flashes and hear the reports of loud, point-blank gunfire. Streaks of pale las-light lit up the rain curtain. Grabbing a lasrifle from the gun rack, the lieutenant threw open the cabin door, firing as he went.

Flashes of light, rotating, sparking, lancing, rippled along the left side of the riverbank. Insurgent skirmishers scurried in between the trees, their shapes barely visible in the sleeting rain.

Standing on the bow, Baeder saw a skirmisher make a dash between two gum-saps. Tracking his movement with the scope of his lasrifle, Baeder put him down with a clean shot. The man dropped hard, disappearing from view.

'Ambush on portside! Enemy infantry sighted!'

The swift boats and gun-barges opened fire. Autocannons, heavy bolters and belt-fed heavy stubbers poured fire into the wilderness. Above the gunshots, Baeder heard the crackle of wood as trees were felled and shorn branches crashed.

Enemy shots stitched the portside of Baeder's vessel. Sergeant Volcom threw back a tarpaulin that had diverted rain off their bow-mounted heavy bolter, stood up and began to fire. But a Carnibalès sniper was already in waiting. The insurgent, unseen, fired two shots. The first spanked off the bolter's mantlet but the second entered the sergeant's sternum, throwing him back with an upward spray of blood. He fell, dead, onto the deck. Then someone ran a row of las-shots along the swift boat's deck railing, forcing Baeder into cover.

'Frag!' Baeder bellowed. He sprinted into the swift boat's pilothouse as another las-round hissed over his head. Inside, Corporal Bellinger had knocked out one of the windows with the butt of his lasrifle and was picking shots with his gun against the windowsill. Rainwater was spraying onto the vox array and delicate navigational banks inside the boat but now was not the time to be fussy. Baeder popped out the plexi-pane of another window panel and squeezed his trigger on full auto. White las-shots beamed out from the Imperial positions, criss-crossing with the pink of insurgent las. A trio of insurgents began to set up a mortar plate beneath a stand of tendril beards and Baeder juiced his entire clip in their direction. The rain made it hard to see what he was doing, but by the time his muzzle stopped flashing, all that could be seen was a toppled mortar and no more insurgents.

An inflatable lander exploded nearby, struck by a missile. Baeder saw the smaller craft cartwheel in the air, its black rubber flaming and shredded. It landed, belly up, the entire squad of Riverine lost to the explosion. The insurgents were targeting the troop-laden landers now with support weapons; portable missile launchers and even mortars aimed point-blank at a horizontal axis. The landers ripped across the river on outboard thrusters, disgorging Riverine Guardsmen into the shallows, ready to assault up the steep embankment.

Baeder knew the Guardsmen rushing up towards the tree line would be scythed down by hidden gunmen unless the battalion provided accurate covering fire. The gun-barges which had, up until that point, not fired their main weapons for fear of fratricide would have to be brought into play. Risk be damned, thought Baeder.

'Bellinger!'

'Sir!'

'Vox air-support then ground support. Tell him there are friendlies, danger-close, assaulting the tree line. Pick his shots and be clean about it!'

'Sir!' said Corporal Bellinger, picking up the waterlogged vox receiver.

Baeder turned his attention back to the men scaling the slope towards the gunmen amongst the trees. Their bayonets were fixed and they fired as they ran. Guns barked from the foliage, dropping Guardsmen back into the frothing delta. Baeder continued to shoot into the silver haze, picking out targets when he could see them, firing blind when he could not.

The main thrust of the ambush came up behind the 88th Battalion, jamming them from retreat. From out of the rain, motored sampans, cutters and keel-hulled trawlers carved a direct path towards the rearguard. These were a motley collection of vessels, up-armoured with sheets of hammered metal, but there were lots of them. Collectively dubbed 'spikers', these boats had been prevalent since before the war as the chosen transport of estuarine bandits. Now they were the mainstay of insurgent raiders, crude yet simple to produce in great numbers.

Sergeant Pulver found himself firing the stern-mounted heavy stubber as Trooper Sceri fed the belt ammunition. Both enemy and Imperial vessels manoeuvred tightly in the river confines. The constant swerving and jinking of the motored vessels caused las-fire and gunshots to lacerate the air wildly.

'Keep this thing moving! They're all over us!' Pulver bellowed at his coxswain.

A motored sampan laden with insurgents firing autoguns streaked past them, stitching the hull of the swift boat as they passed. Pulver tried to track them with the mounted stubber but the sampan was much lower, and the swift boat was moving at great speed. As they passed each other, the stream of tracer went wide, streaking over the insurgents.

'Damnit,' Pulver swore as he corrected his aim.

The insurgents were using the speed of their smaller vessels well. They never stopped moving, churning the water white as they twisted and turned around the swift boats, hitting and running. Pulver's coxswain pivoted their boat as another sampan ripped past, spraying ammunition. As the boat settled, they found themselves face on with another spiker.

'Ram the fragger!' Pulver shouted.

Their target was a fat-hulled trawler, its prow augmented with a beak of cold-rolled iron so that it resembled a broad, frilled fish. Pulver's swift boat cut a sharp angle and sped straight forwards. The bladed profile of a swift boat was streamlined for ramming and all fifteen metres of hull cut into and over the spiker. The trawler was shaken apart under the impact of the larger vessel and forced underwater. Insurgents, many of them broken by the collision, were swept up by the rushing waters.

Pulver slid on the slick deck and fell as the swift boat jammed hard in another evasive manoeuvre. A missile missed them, skimming across the foredeck to explode far out in the trees beyond. The river fighting had become so dense that it was hard to tell whether the missile had been friendly or insurgent.

Nearby, close enough for Pulver to reach out and touch, a swift boat met an incoming spiker head on. They missed each other by a matter of centimetres, both vessels moving at full throttle. They passed each other firing, but the Imperial bow-gunner was better. He laced a cord of fire perpendicular to his boat so that the insurgents sped face first into it. At eight hundred and fifty rounds a minute, the heavy bolter emptied the canoe of all enemy life in seconds.

Twenty metres out, Pulver saw an assault lander collide with a keel-hull. Riverine Guardsmen immediately boarded the enemy vessel, piling on with bayonets fixed. The insurgents could not match the aggression of soldiers who had trained for years if not decades. They were Guard, damn it! Pulver couldn't help but laugh at the absolute chaos of the engagement. Regaining his footing, he dragged himself up behind the heavy stubber and rattled off a short burst. It was only then that he realised his ammo-feeder, Trooper Sceri, was no longer in sight. The trooper must have been thrown overboard at some point, inbetween the weaving and ramming. Cursing as only a sergeant knew how, Pulver continued to blast tracer into the fray. He would avenge Sceri by punishing the insurgents. He would make them regret their decision to ambush the 88th Battalion. He wanted to know that, when the survivors returned to their camps, they would have lost more than they gained – that was the Ouisivian way.

Up on the embankment, amongst the shuddering rushes, Major Mortlock fell off the bow of his swift boat and onto the soil. His was the only swift boat that had joined the assault landers in charging inland, but there was no way he would miss this.

Immediately, las-shots drilled into the ground around him. The hard rain blurred his vision and he could see shapes flitting amongst the trees, snapping shots at them. The enemy were well dug-in, hidden amongst shallow ditches and even up in the trees. Coordinated gun nests were chopping down his advancing men, tumbling them back down the sloping riverbank as they appeared over the top. They were killing his boys and that made Mortlock irrationally mad.

'Come on, Riverine,' Mortlock roared. 'Are we soldiers? These are dirt farmers! Show them how it's done!'

A grenade went off in the trees nearby. For a moment his world blurred and spun. Clods of dirt filled his vision. Mortlock tumbled, fell, staggered back up and lifted his weapon of choice – a fen-hammer. In reality it was a small four-kilogram carburettor, stripped from a boat motor and hot-welded onto a metre of solid steel piping. The weapon was crude, weighty, and common on Ouisivia for crushing ork skulls. Swamp orks were known to survive multiple bayonet stabs, but a blow from a fen-hammer could lay down even the toughest greenskin.

Mortlock crashed into the undergrowth, half-blinded by rain and bomb shock. He lashed his hammer in wide arcs, the valves and ridges of the hammerhead tearing chunks of wood from a gum-sap. Insurgent gunmen, surprised by the Guardsmen in their midst, began to flee. Mortlock brought his hammer down on the back of a sprinting insurgent, bringing him down heavily. He swung again, mangling the barrel of a lasgun that had swung up to aim at him. Wielding the weapon two-handed, Mortlock chopped like a lumberjack, his shoulders and forearms rippling with hard muscle. Insurgents scurried in his wake, screaming of a skull-faced ghost that could not be killed. Mortlock chased them, splintering, breaking and pounding.

Riverine Guardsmen followed Mortlock through the break he had carved in the insurgent position. They fell amongst the slit-trenches of their enemies, engaging in close-quarter fighting. The rain reduced visibility and churned the ground slippery with mud. It was a savage tussle, the conditions and terrain negating all skill. Grenades exploded, point-blank. Bayonets and knives glinted in the grey.

Something bumped Mortlock from behind and he reeled, instinctively lashing out with a backfist. The punch narrowly missed Colonel Baeder.

'Sir?' Mortlock yelled above the clashing.

Baeder was already bleeding from a cut above his brow and his lower body was grey with mud. 'I came as quick as I could. Didn't think I'd let you do all the work, did you?' Baeder said, flexing the fingers of his power fist. It was a standard design issued to staff-officers, with an external power pack that limited its battery life. Baeder kept one in the vessel's stow trunk and only unpacked it when the situation was bad. It was now very bad.

There was no time for further talk. An insurgent splashed out from a nearby slit trench with an outthrust bayonet. Baeder swatted at the weapon with the palm of his power fist, tearing the weapon away from the insurgent and breaking his wrists with the kinetic force. With his free hand, Baeder fired two shots into the insurgent's chest, dropping him down onto his rear. The battalion had already lost too many men that day and Baeder was determined to inflict heavy casualties on the insurgent force, deterring them for the weeks to come.

Together, Baeder fought back-to-back with Mortlock as insurgents melted out from the smoke and downpour. Although he could not match Mortlock's strength or ferocity, Baeder considered himself an infantryman first, and an officer second. He fought until his limbs felt loose and hollow. He slid in the mud, fell to his knees and even took a stinging war club in the thigh, but he kept a constant pace of attack with fist and pistol.

'Is this what you wanted when you woke up this morning?' Baeder bellowed at the enemy. His troopers joined their voices in an enormous roar. Baeder fired his autopistol into the trees, banging out six or seven shots for emphasis. Mortlock continued to press on with his rhythmic striking. Slowly, step by grinding step, the Imperial Guardsmen dislodged the enemy from their positions.

'Eight eight, this is Angel One. Report status, over.'

'Angel One. Holy frag! We are taking some heavy fire. Insurgents all over us along the east bank and up our arses.'

Lieutenant Duponti's fighter was hovering some eight hundred metres over the canopy below. He had ghosted the region flying back and forth in the rain, watching his fuel gauge with anxious attention. The weather conditions were bad and high winds hammered his craft, rattling the cockpit. After what had seemed like hours of inaction, it was finally happening. Below him, amongst the sprawling greenery, he could see strobes of light dancing along the Serrado Delta. Ambush.

Yet there was little he could do. With nervous frustration, Duponti tuned his vox frequency to the battalion channel and listened to the wash of screams and gunfire down below. The insurgents were too close to the flotilla for him to use his arsenal, so he paced across the sky, describing impatient circles amongst the storm clouds.

Finally, unable to handle the wait, Duponti nursed his Lightning through the slamming gale and horizontal rain to a lower altitude. There, he could make out distinct explosions, the firepoints of gun barrels and even the flaming wreckages on the delta. Just being so close to the fighting made his fingers itch over the firing stud of his flight-stick. His practised eyes could spot the Imperial battalion making a counter-assault along the riverbank. White las-beams like flickering spider webs crisscrossed the enemy positions. Pink beams of enemy fire stung back. The fighting went on like that for some time until the pink las-fire began to wither and die away. On the Imperial vox-channels, he could hear that the insurgents were breaking away.

'Angel One. This is eight eight.'

Duponti started in his seat. This was it. 'I read you, eight eight. What can I do?'

'We've got them reeling. They're peeling off. Can you chase them down and clear them out? We can't afford to have any stragglers coming back later for more when they feel brave again.'

'Sir, I'll scare them so much they'll turn themselves in.'

'Loud and clear. Make them hurt.'

With that, Duponti threw his Lightning down towards the rainforest. It came down fast with his machmetre needle hovering at close to four hundred metres a second and the view outside the cockpit a blur of melted greys and greens. He clipped up and banked at the last fraction of a second, skimming up across the canopy before slowing and announcing his presence with a volley of hellstrike missiles. Explosions rolled away underneath him. He was going too fast to make out targets, but he knew where to hit so he dived back and forth over the trees. He heard enemy fire snap past. Ground gunners blazed up at him. In reply, Duponti spread lascannon fire through the canopy.

'Angel One is dry,' Duponti voxed. He spat out the last of his hellstrike missiles and began to gain altitude. The ground forces voxed something in reply but Duponti could only hear the howl of blood in his ears as the speed of his attack runs crazed his circulation. Looking down, a swathe of rainforest was burning bright and hot. As a veteran pilot, Duponti never ceased to be awed by the destruction he was capable of inflicting. He banked his strike fighter around and checked his fuel gauge again.

'Eight eight, this is Angel One. I'm all out of shots and low on fuel. Anything further?'

'No, Angel One, we've got them running. Thank you. Out.'

With that, the vox-link clicked dead. Although it was unspoken, Duponti knew the gratitude of infantry when he heard it. Still running on the residual adrenaline, Duponti crested his plane high, tore off his flight mask and whooped loud. He promised himself one hot brew when he returned to the Argo-Nautical. He deserved that at least before he refuelled and flew out once again.

The insurgents fled, chased by fire into the hills.

Dead men were scattered alongside broken trees. An entire section of the rainforest, mostly along the waterline, had been deforested by intense gunfire. On the delta, three swift boats and five assault landers were now flaming rubber carcasses reflecting orange onto the river surface. Of the men, nineteen had been killed in action with a further five injured.

Slighter injuries were common amongst almost all the Guardsmen who had assaulted the riverbank.

Colonel Baeder moved along the shore, crouching by each dead Riverine laid out in neat rows. He made sure to find out which of the men in his battalion were killed. He had gone to great lengths to remember each and every man in his battalion by name, even though most did not know that, and he would at least make the same effort to know who had died.

Through the billowing smoke, medics rushed back and forth bearing drip bags and field dressings. Most of the flotilla was moored by the riverbank as injured men were ferried off their vessels. Many Riverine sat in a daze along the sloping embankment as the adrenaline of combat was replaced by exhaustion.

Baeder found himself standing before the body of a trooper called Beldia. Baeder remembered him as a support gunner of Three Platoon, Serpent Company. He had even listened to Beldia's story about blowing up an ork swamp hovercraft with a heavy stubber just weeks ago in the company mess hall. Although Baeder had never known Beldia personally, he knew the man had been a boastful soldier but an accurate shot. The body before him had a laswound in his throat and a filmy glaze in his eyes.

'Beldia. He was a stout one,' said Sergeant Pulver, picking his way through the broken undergrowth.

'Yes, I knew of him.'

'You didn't know him,' Pulver said flatly. In his fist, the sergeant gripped a clutch of ident-tags, red and gory. He held the metal tags in front of Baeder and threw them on the ground at his feet. 'These are all the men who died today because you did not stick to the main route.'

The sergeant's lacerating words stung Baeder into shock. 'Sergeant. This was an ambush. The enemy were well dug-in and waiting.'

'And you fed us straight to them. What the frag were you thinking? Were you thinking at all?' Pulver spat.

Baeder curled his power fist in anger. Baeder knew Pulver was a veteran soldier – a lifer – there was no way he could honestly believe Baeder was responsible for the ambush. He knew it and Pulver knew it. There was something else that had ignited the sergeant.

A handful of Riverine squatting in ditches turned their heads curiously. It would not be long before the entire battalion knew of this exchange. 'Sergeant Pulver,' Baeder began, choosing his words carefully. 'If you have something to say to me, then say it directly. But no soldier in his right mind would believe I was the cause of this engagement.'

'You are a glory hound, sir. This entire engagement, this entire mission is a result of your hunt for rank,' Pulver said accusingly.

Baeder gritted his teeth. 'Sergeant, this mission was not of my choosing. It was simply a task assigned to me and one that I intend to complete.

Your job is to liaise between myself and the soldiers under my command. You are a senior soldier, act like it.'

Pulver spat his dip into the river, a wild hateful look in his eyes. 'You have not earned your right to be my commanding officer.'

In any other regiment, Baeder would have had his sergeant major executed by a commissar. Hell, Baeder had every military right to shoot Pulver himself then and there. But this was not any other regiment. It was, time and time again, not the way things were done on Ouisivia. Besides, his men adored the sergeant major and such an act would damage morale if not incite outright mutiny.

'This is not finished, sergeant,' Baeder said, 'but you should know this is not the time. We are deep in enemy territory, cut off from support of substance and responsible for the most crucial undertaking of this entire campaign to date. You will not turn the battalion with infighting. Is this clear, sergeant?'

'It's clear enough. I won't, but I can't guarantee that some of the boys won't air their grievances in some way.' And with that dark threat Pulver stalked away.

Baeder shook his head. No matter how hard he fought, or how hard he tried, the sergeant major would always view him as the 'other'. Their backgrounds were too different and their leadership styles were mutually antagonistic. Yet the ultimate responsibility of command fell on him as a colonel and, in the end, he was indeed accountable for every death in his battalion. The only thing he could do in a time of war was to mitigate the casualties while getting the job done. He just wished that Kaplain had not thrust this monumental task upon his shoulders so early in his command of the 88th.

'Bury the dead,' Baeder said to a passing junior officer. 'We need to press onto Lauzon province to treat our wounded. Have our men bombed up and ready to go in thirty.'

The subaltern nodded, saluted and sprinted away. Left alone again, Baeder took his bush cap off his head and rubbed his face. There would be a long way to go yet before they could silence the siege-batteries, and most likely many more casualties to tally. He only hoped he could hold the battalion together for long enough to get there.

CHAPTER SEVEN

In the days following the chem-injection, Mautista noticed changes. Changes in his body, but changes deep in his thought processes too. It occurred to him that he no longer missed his Kalisador armour. Since the day that he had lost his people, Mautista had clung to his armour as the last reminder of his old life. But his cognitive process was sharper now: logical and uninhibited by sentiment. He discarded the old breastplate of hardened shell because there was no need for it any more; it was a rational conclusion. He felt, for lack of a better word, enlightened. As if his mind had been placed in a higher place, a place where petty things like ego did not trouble him. It made him sure of himself, surer than he had ever been.

His body changed painfully. Every day his joints ached and at night it was worse, especially his shins, his shoulders and deep in his liver. He grew rapidly from a height of one seventy centimetres to almost one ninety in a matter of days. The chemical injections continued, administered daily by the Dos Pares. Although they hurt less with each successive treatment, the pain never went away. Mautista became spider-thin, almost distended. The Two Pairs assured him it was a necessary side-effect of his treatments. In turn, Mautista asked no further questions.

The Four became Mautista's teachers, alongside twenty-two other prospective Disciples. Mautista even dared to call them by their names, although he knew he could never consider them friends. These were not men or comrades; they were, in a way, guardians of a cause greater than any single individual.

During this time, Mautista came to know the Four personally. There was Jormeshu, there was Atachron and there was Gabre and Sau. They came from a distant star, although where, they would not tell. They knew things that no Bastón-born could know and their physiology seemed superhuman. During a particular training exercise in ambush methods, a fledgling Disciple was crushed by his own poorly-rigged log trap. One of the four – Gabre – simply levered the half-tonne log off the dead man and Mautista saw with his own eyes the way Gabre barely strained to lift it.

To his great astonishment, Mautista learned that it was not the first time beings like the Four had set foot on Solo-Bastón. They told them that for thousands of years, others like the Four had come down on Bastón and selected the healthiest young boys from various tribes and taken them away into the stars. It coincided with the folklore that Mautista had known since childhood, of eerie white titans descending from the rain clouds to steal children away forever. These four were like those very same star visitors.

The Two Pairs even revealed that their kind had a name. Although Mautista did not know what the name meant, each of the Four carried an emblem on their loincloths, a female face fanged and serpentine, painted in bruised red. They called themselves Legionnaires of the Undivided; they called themselves the Blood Gorgons.

The Lauzon community appeared in the dusk of post-storm, as the waning orange of day glowed on the edge of an otherwise grey horizon.

As the 88th Battalion flotilla rounded a bend in the river, they saw tall houses of beaten sheet metal made taller by the stilts that held them. Between the trees and houses on either side of the channel, strings of multi-coloured glow-globes laced the open air with a gaudy yet welcoming fluorescence.

Baeder voxed ahead, reaching the village chief on an open channel, and brought the convoy to a halt just shy of the village watchtower. There the battalion disembarked and waited in the soft glow of twilight. They waited with their weapons stowed, for entering a village while armed was against Bastón custom. But although the Lauzon were marked as loyalist on the map, Baeder had learnt not to trust his maps and would not let down his guard. A skeleton crew working on rotating shifts would man the vessels at all times. The flotilla drew up a defensive rectangle on the water, their guns covering all arcs of fire.

As Baeder waited for the welcoming party to arrive he began to make a mental map of the area. Like many riverside villages, the Lauzon community was built up in tiers along the Serrado Delta overlooking the river as its main source of trade, commerce and thoroughfare. The town was one of the largest Baeder had encountered outside of the Imperial-controlled provinces, with houses three or four ranks deep on the sloped banks. Defensively, the town spaced watchtowers at both ends of the river and a low fence that separated the cassam paddies from the township further inland. Baeder estimated, by the sheer amount of homes and the large extended families usually housed in each, that the Lauzon had a population of at least a thousand if not more. It was a bustling town by rural standards and the war did not seem to have diminished that.

When the welcoming party trailed its way along the waterline, it did so with customary flair and festivity. The Lauzon chief, a portly man in his late middle years, led the procession looking slightly ridiculous in his oversized headdress of tightly-wound cloth, layered with painted fish scales. Behind him wound a ribbon of local girls carrying urns of water. The village Kalisadors, all five of them, a sizeable amount for any one tribe, walked behind the procession looking very serious. Baeder was interested in these men the most, as they each wore a suit of shell armour handed down through the generations and heavily customised according to tradition, deeds and history. They walked like trained fighters, their hips steady as they strode with each step.

As they neared, Baeder offered his hand for the chief to shake, but the man smiled broadly and shook his head. 'None of that, good colonel!' he laughed, latching onto Baeder with a wide embrace. Adapting quickly, Baeder hugged the chieftain before accepting the water jug from a Lauzon girl. The chieftain moved on to hug Sergeant Pulver and Baeder chortled softly as the sergeant major stiffened involuntarily, before patting the chief on the back.

'I am Tusano Lauzon. Come, come, you are welcome to make camp under our protection,' Tusano said, beckoning them all to follow him. 'We will get very drunk tonight!' He laughed as he led the weary string of Guardsmen towards his town.

The men made camp around the cassam paddies, pitching two-man bivouac tents on the higher dry ground that girt the watery pastures. It was the first time in almost nine days that the battalion had a chance to stretch out cramped limbs on dry land and Baeder used it as a chance to refresh his men.

Soldiers dispersed out onto the river to swim or cooked a hot meal over a proper gas flame. Some of the more dedicated boatsmen took the opportunity to tighten up the creaks and stutters of their boats. Baeder himself relished the chance to wade out into the delta and scrub the grime from his body and beat his uniform against flat river stones. It was night by then, the delta lit by the pink, blue and yellow glow-globes strung up overhead. After he was thoroughly refreshed, Baeder took it upon himself to make a camp inspection before turning in for the evening.

Many of the soldiers huddled around portable gas burners boiling ration packs. Light wounds were attended to with the deliberate care afforded by a break in operations; ammunition and supplies were redistributed. Baeder crouched with each group he came across, doling out small quips and thanks for their efforts. There was no mention of Pulver's insubordination and overall the men were excited and still riding on the high of a successful combat engagement. Stories of gun fighting, some embellished, most much funnier in retrospect than at the time, drifted merrily from camp to camp. It was a way to deal with the otherwise stifling trauma of post-combat and Major Mortlock was the worst of them all, bellowing uproariously as he strode about camp, inciting laughter wherever he went.

Around the perimeter of the paddies facing the dark edges of the rainforest, a small picket had been set up on two-hour shifts throughout the night. The fire-team on first shift had no chance to clean or recuperate and knelt amongst the mud with their guns aimed vigilantly into the depths of the wilderness. Baeder brought them hot tea and cereal biscuits from the officer's stores. It was a small token, but the Guardsmen were appreciative of the gesture.

As he returned wearily to his own tent, Tusano Lauzon strolled down from the township. 'Colonel, you must join me for a meal,' he cried out. 'You must share your stories with me.'

Baeder was in no mood to humour the chieftain. He was exhausted, he was sore and his eyes were stinging from lack of sleep. But custom was custom and it would do the Imperial cause no favours to offend the few remaining loyalist tribes. He hung his head and sighed bitterly into his chest. By the time he looked up, Baeder had forced up a weary smile.

'Tusano, hospitality in such trying times can't be refused,' Baeder said, following the chief.

He was led up some wooden beams embedded into the dirt hill as crude steps, winding his way through the cramped jumble of houses. They came to a long shed-like structure with a warm orange glow shining from the windows. A chalkboard outside the entrance with last month's fishing quotas and lost property marked the shed as the community hall. As Baeder stepped inside the rush-mat interior, he was immediately taken by the earthy smell of rural cooking. Two village fishermen were laying out steaming clay platters on the rush mats around which sat thirty-odd family members of the chief: aunts and uncles, nephews, nieces and many grandchildren. On Bastón, the fishermen were customarily appointed the village cooks, as their knowledge of their product and how to best cook it became a source of pride for every trawler, netter or angler. Baeder was suddenly very hungry indeed.

They began to eat with no great ritual, as was the way on Bastón. The indigenous people had a fondness for good honest eating and no fanfare was made of the matter. For a time, nothing was heard in the hall but appreciative murmurs in between chewing and clinking of spoons. Baeder dipped roasted cassam tubers into a salty paste of fermented shrimp and ate heaping spoonfuls of cassam leaves sautéed in lard. The villagers piled salads of minty leaves and crunchy water sprouts onto his bowl accompanied by fish steamed in its leathery skin. Strangely enough, Baeder even developed a liking for a clear sour broth made from the bones of an aquatic reptile and bitter greens. The meal was light, savoury and extremely sharp on the tongue and soon Baeder found he had eaten far more than he was comfortable with. At the conclusion of the meal, urns of indigenous alcohol were brought to the fore, a salted elixir that signified the end of the eating and the start of conversation.

'How is trade?' Baeder asked, as one of Tusano's young nieces poured him a thimble of drink. Since the war, many thriving communities had succumbed to poverty and starvation. Those who were self-sufficient, like the Lauzon, often became the target of insurgent tax collectors, gathering a substantial portion of a village harvest.

'Very bad,' Tusano cried, throwing his hands up in exasperation. 'No one trades along the delta any more, and any food we keep in our stores is taken away by Dos Pares men.'

At the mention of the Dos Pares, a senior Kalisador who was sitting at the back of the room shot the village chief a cold, silencing glare. Tusano bit his lip and began to drift on about a lack of trade routes and inflated prices of engine oil for their river vessels. Baeder noticed the awkward exchange but said nothing about it.

'Do the Dos Pares men come often?' Baeder dared to press. Again he noticed Tusano shifting a sidelong look to the Kalisador at the other end of the hall before answering.

'Sometimes,' he shrugged. 'But it's better now that we have come to a forced agreement. We supply them with cassam plants every fortnight. What choice do we have? We are not a fighting people and they ride into town with so many guns.'

'Do they control this entire region?' Baeder asked.

Tusano poured him another drink from the urn and offered the thimble up to Baeder's lips. Baeder took the offering, knocking it back with one stinging gulp. Only then did Tusano continue speaking.

'They are more active upriver. Here, we receive the odd Imperial patrol and that keeps them quiet for a while. But there is really not much we can do. They take what they want and force us to comply. We just try to survive day to day,' Lauzon said sadly before slurping his liquor.

'I take it they don't know you are loyalist?'

Tusano shook his head. 'Oh, no. No, no, no. The Busanti people, three days' walk inland, were massacred for harbouring an Imperial preacher just two months ago. It is too dangerous.'

Baeder was not a religious man. But the idea that these people were forced to hide their allegiance for fear of death made him feel helpless.

'What choice do we have?' said Tusano as he noticed the dark look on Baeder's face. He poured Baeder a third drink and changed the topic. 'Here, drink and tell me what it is like in the Imperial Guard.'

'Master Lauzon,' Baeder said. 'I get the feeling you are trying to get me very drunk.'

Corporal Sendo Schilt had just finished scrubbing and oiling his lasrifle, uttering the last few words of the Litany of Cleansing as he did so. The rain had been hell on its working parts, clogging the delicate mechanisms with an oxidised green carbon build-up. Schilt loved his lasgun. He had even named her, and so it came as no great surprise to his squad-mates when he chose to attend to his weapon before he attended to himself. With a surgeon's precision he scrubbed and scraped his disassembled lasrifle. Only when he had performed the weapon's final function test upon reassembly, squeezing the trigger with empty clicks, did he attend to his own needs.

Like all the Riverine, Schilt had suffered under the subtropical conditions. His feet were white and swollen from waterlog and it was a great relief to peel off his wet socks and splay his toes in the cool, loamy soil. He applied a soothing balm to the sweat rash and insect stings that formed angry red continents across the surface of his skin, cursing Colonel Baeder for every bug-bite he had suffered.

His mood did not improve until he ate his boiled ration pack, a tin of ground meat and nuts in a starchy gravy. He even emptied the calorie-dense concoction into a mess tin for the purpose of dipping crackers and accompanied this with a tin cup of hot infusion. It was a far cry from eating the rations cold out of the packet on the run, and improved its otherwise questionable palatability. Overall, it was the best meal Corporal Schilt could ever remember eating.

Finally satisfied, Schilt lay back on his groundsheet, clad only in his shorts to air his aching body in the cool night air. Around him, a group of Riverine crouched around a burner, passing a hip flask back and forth. Although Colonel Baeder had expressly ordered a ban on all consumption of alcohol during the operation, the Riverine soldiers understood it differently. To them, it simply meant 'do not get so drunk that you get caught fighting and end up being court-martialled'.

'Did you hear? The colonel is a lunatic. He ran up with the assaulting platoons during the ambush today to snag a piece of the fighting,' snarled a gristly heavy stub gunner named Colder as he passed the flask over to Schilt.

'The man is a glory-hound. We wouldn't even be in this mess if he didn't drag our battalion on this suicide mission,' Schilt said as he took a long swig.

'Glory or not. As long as I die with lasgun in hand, I'll be happy,' muttered another trooper, his words already slurred by alcohol.

'Die if you want to, but I plan on living for a while longer. This colonel has no sense of self-preservation. He's going to get us all killed.'

'We already lost Neydo, Chael and Kleis today,' said Colder.

Schilt took another sip of the flask and smacked his lips. 'I wonder what would happen if I slit the colonel's throat. Mortlock too. Finish them both right quick.'

Schilt was not afraid to air his opinions in the company of these men. Although the twenty-odd Riverine sitting with him were from various platoons and companies, they formed a closely-knit fraternity within the battalion. Together, Schilt's boys shared a strong opinion on how the battalion should be run and took the ruffian pride of the Riverine Amphibious to extremes. For the most part they kept to themselves and the other Riverine steered clear of them. Each of these men had a subtle cold streak about them that was disturbing. Others within the batallion even nicknamed them the 'creepers'. In any other context, they would be called a gang and that was what made them so dangerous.

'Mortlock ain't so bad,' burped another trooper.

'Yeh, but he's with Baeder. If we smoke them both, then Pulver will take charge. It'll be smooth sailing if that happens I guaran-fragging-tee.'

'How about the company commanders? Captain Gregan, Captain Steencamp, Fuller and even that young one – Buren?'

Schilt snorted dismissively. 'They have nothing over Pulver. True command authority will fall to the sergeant major.'

The group went on like that for some time, treading a fine line between complaint and outright mutiny. As the night wore on and the drink flowed more freely, the men became louder and more daring in their protestation. Finally, a sergeant from Five Platoon stalked over and ordered them all to retire to their tents before an officer found them. Slurred and stumbling, Schilt's boys crawled into their bivouacs.

Schilt, however, could not sleep. Stirred by his fiery words and numbed with toxicity, he wandered out towards the edge of the paddy fields near the tree line to relieve himself. He tried to appear sober but he walked far too upright to remain convincing. The village chief had placed volunteer villagers as sentries on the edge of the camp, rural men armed with machetes and long, two-pronged forks used to uproot cassam tubers from their watery pits. The men greeted Schilt, who waved them away, murmuring something under his breath. The village sentries smiled knowingly and chuckled amongst themselves.

His mind fogged by drink, Schilt wandered far too long and much further away than he would have liked. Soon the sentries and the gas burners of the tents disappeared from view. Clad only in his shorts, Schilt wandered deeper into the rainforest, the undergrowth cutting open the soles of his feet. It was not until he realised that his feet were bleeding that he also realised he was lost. Abruptly, the corporal decided he was tired and he sat down beneath a large tree in the darkness.

Night was a frightening place in the jungle. Drunk and lost in its shadowy folds was not a good time to come to that revelation. Tendril vines reached out of the depths like deep-sea tentacles, and the branches suffocated his surroundings with an oceanic darkness. Schilt reached into his hip webbing and drew his bayonet. Although the corporal had forgotten his boots, his flak vest and his beloved lasgun, he had, for some reason, had the foresight to shrug on his webbing before he left. The bayonet was a wide blade, serrated along one edge with a slightly hooked tip that the Riverine dubbed a 'gretchin skinner'. Although it was no lasgun, the wirebound handle felt solid and good in his palm. He sat there with knife in hand, his desire to relieve himself overcome by the desperate need to find his way back to camp.

Suddenly, Schilt spotted a flickering light in the distance, like a mirror reflecting the moon. Schilt began to lurch towards it, groping his way through the trees. In his stupor, Schilt saw it as a light from a standard-issue gas burner. It never occurred to him that it could be something else entirely.

As he continued to stumble forwards, he saw the light again. A beam of light, white and glaring, which prescribed a slight arc before disappearing again. He wanted to call out but opening his mouth made him feel sick so he walked faster. Several hundred metres away, branches snapped and cracked, echoing loudly in the night. It sounded like a herd of beasts ambling through the undergrowth.

Then he saw it again. A beam of light. And then another. And another. Dozens of lumite beams moving in the distance.

It was not the Riverine camp.

Schilt stopped in his tracks and listened. He could hear voices now, coming closer. They were hushed voices talking in the dark, thrashing through the undergrowth towards him, but so many voices that they merged into a seething hiss. It could not be the base camp. Schilt was certain of that. Whatever it was could only be moving towards the Riverine camp. Turning, sprinting, Schilt ran in the opposite direction, hoping to reach the camp before they did. He did not even notice the weeping cuts in the bottom of his feet as he ran and ran.

Sergeant Pulver strolled along the boardwalk pier, shacks rising in tiers along his left, the muddy waters flowing by at his right. It was already late in the evening and the rickety pier was empty. Pulver was rather fond of the quiet, as it gave him a rare opportunity to gather his thoughts in between the duties of a senior NCO.

Nursing a poorly-rolled stub of tabac, Pulver walked down the pier which stretched the entire length of the river-town. The soles of his snakeskin boots thudded a wholesome, mellow beat on the warped wooden slats. It was a pleasing beat and it helped him to think about the task ahead. They were close to the siege-batteries now, close enough to warrant a large-scale ambush on their flotilla, not a minor task considering the ramshackle disposition of the enemy. In a matter of days the 88th would be at their primary objective. The fight that waited for them there would be the worst yet, Pulver was sure of it. What he was not sure about was his faith in Colonel Fyodor Baeder.

The man was a career officer, pure and simple. His mind was technically brilliant and, as a strategist, Baeder was more than sound. But in Pulver's opinion, Baeder had a fault inherited by most Imperial commanders – he tried too often to be a hero. The annals of Imperial history were richly embroidered with courageous last stands, glorious victories against the odds and dazzling displays of swordsmanship. From fleet officers to mighty Astartes, these were all grand men, Pulver did not doubt that. But he hated it. When it came down to the running of an army, Pulver wanted a stern, no-nonsense planner. The idea of following a romantic leader forging ahead towards suicidal martyrdom did not appeal to the pragmatic sergeant in the slightest.

Yet to him, Baeder was exactly that. The colonel's need to earn the respect of his men drove him to prove his worth as a true ramrod Riverine constantly. Pulver did not need that. What he needed was a commander who could get the job done, quickly and quietly with minimum loss of his soldiers. There was hope yet, however – Baeder was not all bad. Admittedly, Baeder had proven faultless so far, contrary to his chivalrous ways, and even the ambush had not been his fault, despite Pulver's heated misgivings. So far, with a mixture of luck and balls, Baeder had pulled them through intact. But it worried Pulver that sooner or later, their luck would run out and Baeder would run them all headfirst into a slaughter.

Pulver sucked his tabac and flicked the glowing end into the water. Wars were not won by officers delivering thunderous one-liners, while waving their sword against a faceless horde of enemies, Pulver mused bitterly. Wars were won by clearly written memo notes in the chain of command, efficient logistics and precisely coordinated pieces on a planning map. Men like Baeder appalled him, and it appalled him more that Imperial narratives were rife with men of his ilk.

He was lost in dark thoughts such as those for quite some time, pacing the entire length of the boardwalk over and over. Finally, Pulver resolved that if he did not occupy himself in other ways, he would likely shake out some alcohol from his men and drink himself to sleep to alleviate the tension. It was something he hoped to avoid.

After some deliberation and four tabac sticks later, he decided to explore the Lauzon township, particularly the docking sheds that he had passed on several occasions. As a soldier, he had a natural curiosity for the war-making of various cultures and to study the littoral vessels of the Bastón would allow him to analyse the insurgent spikers in their unconverted forms. It could perhaps be considered trespassing, but Pulver convinced himself that it would be an intelligence-gathering exercise. Besides, the Ouisivians had a loose concept of property.

The docking shed was a semi-cylindrical structure of corrugated metal that reached out into the eastern riverbank. Although the shed door was secured by padlock and chain, Pulver had been raised in the fen swamps by his trapper father who supplemented their meagre income by less than legitimate means. The sergeant considered it the one good thing his father had left him, and with nimble fingers he made short work of the padlock with the tip of his bayonet and the end of a webbing clip. Creaking the iron door open, Pulver slid inside and eased the door shut behind him.

Inside, a sodium lantern illuminated a clutter of mooring ropes, buckets, empty canisters and the detritus of forgotten, rusted tools. A rectangular docking space large enough to park three Chimeras side-by-side dominated the centre of the shed, and a cluster of dark vessels crouched on the water.

He moved from boat to boat inspecting each by hand, with the appraising eye of a man who had spent much of his life bobbing about on buoyant materials. They were old, these boats, perhaps close to some one or two centuries.

Pulver lowered himself into the small two-man sampans, testing their fluted hulls by rocking them with his weight. Next he moved on to the larger trawler vessels with their double outboard motors. These were the flat-nosed metal hulls that combed the Bastón estuaries, the single most important commercial workhorse for the Bastón people. But most impressive of all were the keel-hulls, capable of coastal travel and powered on a rear motor so large that it took up fully one third of the vessel's ten-metre-long frame. Pulver had come to know these as the most dangerous of all the insurgent spikers. Its heavy propeller thrust engines gave them a stability to mount support weapons that would capsize smaller sampans and canoes, but their speed was so much greater than that of the ponderous trawlers. Pulver had seen keel-hulls up-armoured with scrap metal, a scythe blade affixed to the prow and mounted by flak thrower or autocannon. In such a configuration, the keel-hulls could threaten even the mighty swift boats.

There were other boats mixed in the dock too: shuttle ferries, skiffs, scows and even a few water-bikes. Pulver climbed from one to the other, rocking them with his weight, checking their motors. Finally at the end of the docking shed, covered by a tarpaulin, Pulver came to a vessel he did not recognise as a native boat. It was low and flat in its canvas sheet, with a distinctive shape that the sergeant found strangely familiar. Pulver jumped off the end of a trawler onto a motor canoe and then onto the docking ramp to inspect the strange bundle. Gripping the tarpaulin, he hauled it off in one heavy pull.

Underneath was a rigid-hulled inflatable. The very same assault landers used by the 31st Riverine Amphibious. The regimental symbol of a long sword with the gossamer wings of a serpent-fly sprouting from the hilt was painted across the front gunwale.

'Frag and feathers. What is going on here?' Pulver muttered to himself. Even from where he stood, he could see the unmistakable smears of dried blood where someone had tried to wipe it away with a wet cloth. The inflatable was covered in it. Strings of shrapnel punctures scarred one side of the boat and the outboard motor had been stripped away. It left little doubt as to the fate of this vessel's previous occupants.

As Pulver stood, still grappling with the notion of how the bloodied remains of an Imperial vessel could end up in the storage shed of a loyalist town, he heard a rapid series of footsteps patter behind him. Pulver instantly reached for the lasrifle slung across his back. The weapon was never more than a hand's reach away. Turning, he saw that the door to the storage shed was now wide open.

A cool draft billowed from the entrance. It chilled the perspiration on Pulver's skin. Immediately, the sergeant experienced 'the churns' in his belly, a nauseous warning that coiled up in his bowels. He heard the patter of soft steps to his right.

He brought his lasgun up to his shoulder just quick enough to see a Kalisador hurtling towards him.

Pulver aimed but the Kalisador disarmed him, twisting the weapon against the hinges of his wrists. The disarm happened efficiently, with a neurological smoothness that came only with practised muscle memory. One moment Sergeant Pulver was holding the weapon up and the next it was flying into the open water, sling and all. It was then that Pulver knew better than to draw his bayonet. He knew the Kalisadors were experts at disarming their opponents, a pattern of techniques known as defanging he had already heard too much about. A refugee Kalisador had performed it as a parlour trick for the Guardsmen back on base in return for tabac.

'Defang this,' Pulver growled, grabbing the back of the Kalisador's skull and delivering a headbutt to the bridge of his nose. The Kalisador stumbled backwards, momentarily stunned. Under the sodium lights, Pulver could see his assailant was not a big man, rather he was wiry and corded like most Bastón-born. Pulver was considered a 'spark-plug' by his men but the Kalisador was even smaller than him. Pressing his advantage, Pulver clinched the back of his neck with one hand and began to hammer his face with the other.

Although he had never received any formal hand-to-hand training, no Riverine sergeant could rise through the ranks without a measure of the scrappy brawling that was well received within the regiment. The power of the bigger man surprised the Kalisador and, for a moment, the smaller fighter staggered. But muscle memory once again took over and the Kalisador squirmed out of Pulver's grip, created distance with a swift back-pedal and drew a straight-edged dagger from his waistband.

'You little bastard,' spat Pulver, backing away. His hands groped behind him for a weapon but he found none.

The Kalisador glided forwards in a low stance, tracing an elaborate pattern in the air with the glinting tip of his dagger. Then, like a coiled serpent, he struck. Pulver gritted his teeth and rushed forwards at the same instant, throwing off his attacker's timing. The stab, aimed at his liver, was jarred and Pulver took the blow on his forearm instead. Knowing that the Kalisador would not make the same mistake again, Pulver seized the knife arm in both hands and hurled himself over the edge. Both men went into the docking space and hit the water with a shuddering splash.

The water was shockingly cold. Pulver couldn't see a thing, but he maintained his grip on the knife hand. In a way, it was his lifeline and there was no way he would let it go. Twice, Pulver tried to come up for air but bumped his head against the bottom of a vessel. With one hand he clung to the assailant's knife hand, with the other, he pushed the Kalisador's head down below, keeping him beneath the water. His lungs were straining, his chest seizing up painfully.

As his vision blurred, Pulver finally emerged through the gap between two trawlers. He gasped and struggled to take in great heaving lungfuls of air. In the water below, the struggling Kalisador began to slacken. Pulver stayed there, gripping with the last of his strength until the Kalisador stopped moving. He stayed there for many minutes after. Sure that his assailant posed no further threat, he let the weight sink. With his combat fatigues heavy with water, Pulver crawled up onto the pontoon, his lungs still labouring painfully. There he sprawled out on the wooden planks, swearing and trying to catch his breath.

Even from such great heights, Duponti could see the mass of movement below. A throbbing mass of twinkling lights was converging on the 88th Battalion coordinates, sweeping in from all three sides of the inland jungle. There were so many of them converging on the position that they dispensed with stealth altogether. Down there, Duponti estimated perhaps close to five or six thousand torchlights.

'Eight eight, this is Angel One. Come in, eight eight.'

His urgent vox message was once again met by silence.

'Eight eight. This is Angel One. Multiple enemy movements converging on your position. Come in, eight eight.'

Again the dry hiss of static.

'Frag it!' Duponti swore, smashing his fist into the flight panel in frustration. The enemy were no more than three hundred metres away from the camp now. The one saving grace was that the rainforest was incredibly dense and notoriously difficult to move through, especially in the night. Duponti knew the movement would be slowed to a crawl as they chopped through the tangled undergrowth.

Retuning his frequency, Duponti began to cycle through the alternate vox-channels for the battalion. His warnings, growing in desperation, went unheard. The battalion was, after all, on temporary stand down and the only manned vox would be on the primary channel.

Duponti was almost screaming now. 'Eight eight! Enemy movements now one hundred and fifty metres from your position!'

In final exasperation, Duponti threw his voxsponder aside. He would have to go in himself. Nudging his strike fighter down, he began to level out slowly in an attempt to hide his presence from the enemy until the last possible moment.

As he closed in, Duponti fired a flare. The phosphorus flare ignited in the air, hovering in the sky like a newborn star. Amongst the showering trails of chemical illumination and the harsh artificial light, Duponti saw them clearly. Thousands of Carnibalès heretics brandishing firearms and polearms were massing together at the edge of the jungle. Thousands of them like a surging, chittering mass of soldier mites. In a creeping, pincer formation they surrounded the battalion camp. Duponti toggled his weapons to armed and primed them for an attack run.

CHAPTER EIGHT

It was already late into the night before Colonel Baeder managed to extract himself from the village chief and his hospitality. The 88th Battalion camp was silent, his men either asleep in their tents or passed out on the soil.

Baeder picked his way through the camp, careful not to wake any of his men from their much-needed rest. He could not help but notice that some of the prone figures clutched flasks or had even managed to barter urns of fermented alcohol from the local Lauzon. Baeder had ordered there to be no consumption of alcohol but he had not expected the order to be heeded. It was more an attempt to dissuade the Ouisivians from their otherwise probable excess. He himself had humoured the village chief with a sip or two of the vile local brew.

There would only be four or five hours before dawn and, although Baeder wanted nothing more than to rest his aching body before reveille, he knew it would be prudent to check on the sentry pickets. Although Tusano had volunteered nine village men and a Kalisador as sentries, battalion NCOs had also appointed a roster of five Riverine to patrol the forest edge. The unfortunate Guardsmen assigned to patrol the camp perimeter had forgone their one night of rest and visiting them would be the least an officer could do. He carried a wicker basket in each hand, laden with leftovers from the chieftain's feast, a much-needed morale booster for the on-duty Guardsmen.

Yet Baeder felt something was wrong as he neared the edge of camp.

423

He could not hear the distinct chatter of vox reports on the primary vox array that the team of five should have been manning. In fact, as he neared the gun pit where the five should have been, he saw the vox array had been tipped over in the dirt.

Baeder dropped his food baskets and went for his autopistol instead. He could see the five Riverine sentries lying face down. Each had a glistening wound on the back of their skulls, blunt trauma inflicted by blows from behind. Of the volunteer villagers, there was no sign, but Baeder could make out mud tracks leading away from the gunpit towards the camp. He considered sounding an alarm, but opted for a more subtle approach. He cocked his Kupiter .45 autopistol and slid after the footprints in the mud.

The horrors unveiled themselves to Baeder slowly. At the first two-man tent Baeder tracked the prints to, he found the occupant Riverine inside were dead, their throats slit and the ground damp with enormous blood loss. The next tent was the same. Baeder counted nine good men, lost in one night without so much as a shot being fired. Ten metres away he counted ten; Corporal Huder unceremoniously dumped into a clump of bracken with multiple stab wounds, still holding a hip flask in his hands. The corporal had likely been drinking alone at the edge of camp when he met his fate.

At the third tent in a row, Baeder stuck to the shadows. He saw four murky figures standing around the canvas tent, obviously keeping watch. Even in the darkness Baeder could see the glint of weapons. Three of the men carried machetes and a fourth leaned against his two-pronged cassam spear. They were unmistakably the village volunteers and judging by their hunched, tentative postures, they were in the act of murdering Baeder's men.

Baeder emerged from the shadows confidently, his pistol held behind his back. 'Good evening, gentlemen!' he said clearly.

The Lauzon tribesmen started. As he walked towards them, they looked at him with stunned expressions, grasping for words. Baeder knew it was the split second moment where they were deciding whether they could construct a passable excuse for what they were doing inside the battalion camp, or whether they should rush the officer and overwhelm him. Baeder did not give them that luxury. He swung his pistol out from behind his back and popped off two shots in fluid succession. Two of the murderers collapsed wordlessly. Baeder caught the third as he leapt at him with a raised machete, shooting him twice point-blank in the chest. He put down the fourth man as he turned to run. Baeder showed the murderers the same absence of mercy they had undoubtedly shown his men.

Alerted by the popping gunshots, another Lauzon murderer emerged from the tent flap, his business of killing interrupted. The machete he brandished was already wet with threads of blood. As he sprinted the several metres towards Baeder, he received a pistol shot in the abdomen. But small calibre rounds never guaranteed putting an opponent down, especially when he was running on desperation. Baeder back-pedalled and fired two more shots, both finding their mark in the murderer's torso. Yet he kept on coming. With an eight-round clip, the autopistol had one shot left. Baeder fired his last round into the attacker's neck, almost pushing the pistol barrel against him. There was a great burst of blood, but still the murderer rushed at him. A firearm's lack of stopping power was every Guardsman's worst nightmare. He remembered his power fist, locked up in the stow trunk on his swift boat, but it was too late to lament.

Baeder threw his spent autopistol aside and grappled with the man's machete. They stumbled, pushing and straining in the clinch until they toppled over into the tent. Both went down in a tangle of canvas, rope and whipping limbs. Baeder found the man rolling on top, his many gunshot wounds pouring all over him. The murderer struggled, groaning and breathing hard in Baeder's ear. It was the worst experience of combat Baeder had ever suffered. With a final heave, Baeder swept his attacker and gained top position. By then, the pistol shots were draining away the attacker's strength and the villager, with his wide crazed eyes, was beginning to go limp. His movements slowed and finally, with a shudder, he was still. Baeder released his hold on the man's machete handle and kicked him away.

The sounds of their struggle brought out the lurking silhouettes of the other Lauzon murderers from a nearby tent. But by now Riverine were emerging in various states of undress, half-asleep but gripping lasrifles.

'Insurgents,' Baeder bellowed, pointing at the Lauzon. Immediately, a las-shot snapped out and dropped one of the Lauzon silhouettes. There was pandemonium as Riverine bolted out from their tents, simultaneously tugging on boots and fatigues and loading lasrifles. A great clamour roused the battalion from their sleep.

But before the quiet was truly broken, up in the sky, a phos-flare was released.

'Angel One,' Baeder muttered to himself.

The flare hung suspended in the sky, trailing droplets of glowing white incendiary. The light it cast was a monochrome of white and stark shadow. But it was enough to reveal to Baeder what lay in wait amongst the tree line. No more than a hundred metres away, separated by just one grid of cassam paddy, Baeder saw hundreds, if not thousands, of faces staring at him. Insurgents lying in wait, their eyes white with intent, looking at him.

Then with a roar that built up into a thick wall of sound, the Carnibalès charged.

* * *

Duponti dropped his Lightning like a stone, blazing away with hellstrike missiles. He strafed the length of the enemy advance, jamming his finger hard on the trigger button. Within seconds he had made his run, gaining altitude again.

He craned his head about to inspect his damage. A wall of fire, two hundred metres in length, danced along where the farm met the forest. It consumed an entire strip of cassam paddies along with a shard of the first of the enemy wave. But from his vantage point, Duponti could see sprinting figures detach from the trees at the left and right flanks of the battalion camp. Mobs of tiny, surging people converged towards the Imperial position down below, seemingly unafraid of the Riverine las-volleys blistering them. Duponti was already out of hellstrike missiles, but he banked around anyway, determined to add his lascannons to the engagement.

'Angel One, this is Baeder,' crackled Duponti's headset. 'It's heavy down here. How many can you see from where you are?'

'They are moving in from all three sides inland, the delta is clear. I count thousands. I don't know if there are more under the canopy. Can you reach your boats?'

'My men barely have their britches on. Frag! This was a trap, the Lauzon sold us out.'

'I'm coming down to give them hell,' Duponti promised.

'Give them what you can. We need all the time we can get. Out.'

Major Mortlock threw himself down behind a low irrigation ditch and blasted a fan of las-fire to his front. Riverine Guardsmen spread out in a thin line around the camp, digging in behind the drainage canals or even the chest-deep water paddies to repel the enemy offensive. In the first few minutes of shock, the Riverine fired wildly, unleashing every firearm in their arsenal. Smoke and grit choked the air in a gagging, swelling cloud.

Yet still the insurgents came. Mortlock was uncertain whether it was the light, but some of those rushing faces were terrifyingly inhuman. There were mutants amongst them. Under his scope, Mortlock was sure that some were not even true insurgents. Some were not armed. Mobs of shrieking Bastón-born sprinted out from the rainforest, some clutching rocks, war clubs, machetes, even tools of agriculture. The insurgents amongst them, the ones who had guns and knew how to use them, blasted the Riverine lines from a distance of no more than thirty or forty metres. The short space between opposing forces soon became clogged by the dead and wounded as small-arms fire whipped back and forth.

Mortlock knew to pick his shots. Here and there, he could spot the leaders of the pack offensive. They were unmistakably tall and glowed almost white in their warpaint. These gaunt warriors directed the attacks, urging mobs of attackers towards weak points in the Imperial line.

Mortlock lined up a particularly rake-thin insurgent whose face was as white as a corpse. He breathed out and fired, dropping the insurgent as he was brandishing an autogun over his hand and yelling encouragement to his men. The pallid man rose to his knees, still screaming. Mortlock put two more shots into his chest, this time pinning him down for good.

Smoke and intense heat from the burning cassam paddies washed over them. Mortlock's eyes stung. The air became searing. Dim shapes hurtled out of the smoking haze. Mortlock tried to shoot them down before they reached the battalion lines. There were so many. Troopers Carlwin and Vere on either side of him fired on automatic. Carlwin fell, a thrown hatchet in his chest. Above the roar of gunfire, the vox-unit on Trooper Vere's back blared with competing voices. Platoon commanders were screaming orders above each other.

'Enemy are mutants,' crackled the vox.

'Enemy are not mutants. Enemy are native insurgents.'

'Enemy are mutant insurgents. Archenemy forces flanking left and right.'

Mortlock ripped the vox receiver from Vere's back. 'Shut the frag up!' Mortlock screamed into the airwaves.

No clear order could be gleaned. Communication between the various units broke down. The voices continued to step over each other. 'Clear nets! All units! Clear nets for vox silence!'

'Mortlock!' Baeder screamed as he dropped belly down next to him. 'I need Serpent Company to go and pack their belongings fast, grab ammunition and rations, ditch the rest. Then Prowler, Ghost and Seeker in that order. After we're set to go, we'll make a fighting withdrawal. Got it?' he shouted. Unable to use the vox, Baeder had taken to doing things the old-fashioned way – he was sprinting from officer to officer, heedless of the firestorm that sliced around him.

Mortlock nodded in between reloading his clip. 'Serpent, then Prowler, Ghost and Seeker, in that order. Got it!'

With that Baeder got up, without regard for the volume of enemy fire, and ran to relay his order to the other junior officers. Rounds punched the dirt around him as the colonel sprinted in a crouch. He bellowed a curse at the enemy and Mortlock soon lost sight of him.

'All right! You heard the Colonel. Serpent Company, move out!' Mortlock shouted. He pounded out sixteen shots in rapid succession to keep the enemy down as Serpent Company disengaged from the firing line to retrieve their belongings.

An insurgent with a threshing flail leapt over the irrigation ditch and into the Riverine lines. Mortlock's suspicions were confirmed – the insurgent's lower jaw and mouth merged into a tiny, spiked orifice; a certain sign of mutation. It brought its threshing flail down hard on the back of Trooper Roscher and then once across his neck, killing the man as he rolled over. Mortlock blasted up with his lasrifle, catching the insurgent underneath the chin. Without turning to look, Mortlock tore a grenade from his webbing and hurled it into the night, deterring any follow-up attack on their position. Frustrated, the enemy shredded the lip of the ditch with a flurry of las-fire as Mortlock and the men around him kept their heads down.

The fighting was the heaviest Mortlock had encountered on Bastón. It might have even been the heaviest he had ever encountered. A rocket exploded thirty metres away, showering him in mud and blood. He began to get flashbacks of the swamp ferals on Ouisivia. But those green-skins were wild, like an elemental force. The insurgents running face first into their gunfire now had a logic and belief to their sacrifice. It made Mortlock's blood run cold.

It came as a great relief to Mortlock when Serpent Company returned to the lines, now dressed and prepped. He hid his fear well as he ordered Prowler to disengage and break camp. A heavy stub gunner exposed his upper body above the ditch to give them better covering fire. He fired a long ten-second spurt before a single shot blew out his eye and sent him tumbling back into the ditch. Mortlock slung his lasrifle over his shoulder and crawled over the dead gunner. The man had been Trooper Hennel of Seeker Company, a veteran of multiple engagements; he had earned his infantryman's combat badge at the age of sixteen. He had also been one of the best snook dice-players in the battalion. Mortlock checked his pulse, making sure that Hennel was dead. He then unlatched the heavy stub gun from dead fingers and pulled out the remaining belt of rounds from the ammo-pack Hennel wore on his back. Holding the stubber one-handed while he laid the belt of ammunition across the open palm of his left, he knelt down behind the ditch and pelted out tracer in wide sweeps. In the night, muzzles flashed back at him; one shot in particular ricocheted off a rock to his front and showered him in molten pinpricks of shrapnel.

'Don't be a hero,' Mortlock said to himself as he emptied the stubber and scrambled back behind cover.

At 03.45, exactly thirteen minutes after the Lauzon Offensive had begun, the Riverine began to claw their way backwards in a fighting withdrawal.

They trampled over the remains of their tents and non-essentials as the fighting receded into the campsite. Riverine dragged their wounded with them, determined not to leave them behind as they were forced to do with their dead. It was a sad, weary retreat with none of the glory implied in a 'fighting withdrawal'. Their shots were desperate as insurgents hounded them, attacking in mobs before concentrated firepower scattered them away to regroup.

Baeder led a rearguard, two solid fighting platoons of Prowler Company with Captain Buren attempting to delay the thousands of rabid insurgents at the banks of the delta as the battalion loaded up onto their transports. Sergeant Pulver joined them from the direction of the Lauzon settlement. A crowd of emboldened villagers had followed him, hurling stones. Not at all fazed by the aggression, Pulver mustered four or five troopers, turned and directed a steady volley of fire at the Lauzon mob. The villagers broke at the sign of the first shot.

It was a messy affair and although Baeder collected eighteen frag grenades, he had used them all before they even reached the bank. By the time Baeder was rushed onto a departing swift boat, he had depleted three lasrifle mags and two clips from his autopistol.

And still the enemy followed them, surging into the water like a stampede. They hurled rocks and flaming alcohol jugs and those with crude firearms sang out parting shots. The gun-barges with their heavy flamers washed sheets of fire behind the flotilla, forcing the enemy up the banks. As they passed through the channel of the Lauzon township, some of the boat gunners began to fire on the houses in anger. Baeder voxed for them to cease fire and conserve ammunition.

They remained alert as insurgents followed them up river, hounding them for five kilometres with potshots from the trees. Each attempt was met with a thunderous volley from the heavy weapons on board the Riverine vessels until, finally, the enemy gave up.

Under the husky light of dawn, the Guardsmen finally dropped down on their decks, completely burnt out. Their faces were black with greasy ash and their throats stung from smoke. The fighting had taken a heavy toll on the battalion. Forty-five dead and a further nine wounded. The 88th Battalion lost more men in that one night of fighting than they had for the entire duration of the war.

In the following morning, aerial reconnaissance from Angel One reported an estimated six hundred insurgent casualties. Bodies littered the entire Lauzon rural fields and down into the delta itself. The grim assessment did not embolden Baeder at all. The fighting had been ferocious, the enemy had been determined, and the battalion had not even reached their objective yet.

The tribes of Solo-Bastón had lived on the mainland and surrounding islands long before the arrival of the Imperium. Indeed, they continued to occupy their traditional land in the decades after the Ecclesiarchy formally annexed the islands. Although portions of the land along the coastal regions were dedicated to administrative cities and certain land had been given agricultural leases, fundamentally the use and enjoyment of the inland by the natives continued with little disturbance from the governing authorities after annexation. As long as the natives prayed to the God-Emperor and paid their rural tithes, there would be peace.

The uprising, however, changed that. The inland and surrounding islands became red zones. It was said that the Imperium controlled the cities and the Carnibalès controlled the rainforest. It was also true that ninety-five per cent of the landmass on Bastón was rainforest. As a result, the Imperium clung to their coastal provinces while the insurgency raged like a stormy sea around them. On their small, mobile craft, the Riverine Amphibious were the first to deploy to the mainland and reinforce the remaining local militia elements. The coastal regions became the last bastion of Imperial control on Bastón. Yet slowly, even that was beginning to change.

On the one hundred and thirty-fifth day of uprising, a riot erupted in the administrative province of Union City, sixteen kilometres north-east of the Torre Gulf. Carnibalès propagandists, disguised as inland traders, whipped up a frenzy of hate in the back alleys of Union. Excited, frenzied and intoxicated, for an entire day heretics rampaged through the city, killing Imperial officials and their families. Non-natives were beaten, stripped and mutilated, their bodies tipped into the Union Quay harbour. It took three thousand Riverine Guardsmen two days to restore order to the city and by then the damage had been done. Entire blocks of Union had been consumed by fire and bodies littered the streets and hung from street poles.

CHAPTER NINE

'Look at this glorious land,' said Cardinal Avanti, sweeping his arms in a gesture that took in the expanse of broken, deforested earth before him. 'Waiting for the seed and harvest of honest Imperial folk.'

Brigadier Kaplain watched as his fellow officers Montalvo and de Ruger nodded in clockwork agreement. Inwardly, Kaplain sighed. The land before him had been freshly chain-felled by Caliguan transport tractors and the spillage of broken trees all lay in one direction like the unburied dead, the smell of sap still strong in the air. Guardsmen of the Caliguan Motor Rifles were still in the process of registering and loading native tribesmen onto waiting troop-trucks. These men and women had, until the morning of that day, been ancestral owners of this land for thousands of years. But by mid-afternoon, the Ecclesiarchy had already moved in on one of Bastón's many rimward islands and declared it annexed for the glory of the Imperium.

'Where will these people go?' Kaplain asked, pointing at the miserable line of homeless tribesmen at the edge of the clearing.

'Oh, don't worry, brigadier,' Avanti said off-handedly. 'We have settlement camps set up waiting to train them in the methods of agriculture and mining. They will soon be under the employ of the Administratum as labourers so they need not go hungry.'

Kaplain rubbed the bridge of his nose wearily. He had been a soldier for long enough to recognise a conquest when he saw one. But the people of Bastón had been loyal to the Imperium before the insurgency and now the remaining loyalists were being punished for the actions of a rebellious minority.

From their observation deck atop a Caliguan tractor, Avanti and his three senior officers watched the clearing process under the shade of servitors bearing lace parasols. Eight Adepta Sororitas bodyguards, including Morgan Fure, stood to attention with them, aiming their boltguns at the tribesmen in the far distance, although in Kaplain's opinion there was clearly no need.

'Do you think that perhaps by taking the land away from the remaining loyalists, we are aiding the insurgency with new recruits?' Kaplain asked gently.

'Are these not loyal citizens of the Imperium? What use are they to the Imperial cause if they languish in their primitive ways? Are they not better put to use on worthwhile tasks?' Avanti questioned, raising his stark white eyebrows.

Kaplain didn't answer. He could feel Palatine Morgan Fure penetrate him with her silent stare.

'Besides, this insurgency is only a by-product of our administrative efforts here in Bastón,' Avanti continued. 'It is unfortunate, but inevitable, that rebellion should arise when we are only doing it for their own good. Some people will never learn.'

At this, even Montalvo and de Ruger started in confusion. 'Your grace? The rebellion began as a consequence of your efforts?' de Ruger spluttered.

Avanti waved his hand dismissively. 'Oh, yes. I thought I might as well inform you all now, that this rebellion began as a result of the indigenous population's protest at our plans to transform their primitive island nations. The rebellion became larger than we expected, that's all.'

The revelation suddenly made Kaplain quite nauseous. The Imperial military had been led to believe for the entirety of the campaign that the insurgency had been an independent act of rebellion against Imperial authority. Now the cardinal was admitting the natives were acting in retaliation to their heavy-handed policies. Kaplain was shocked and, judging by the reaction of the Caliguan and Persepian officers, it was a revelation to them too.

'Your grace,' Kaplain began, choosing his words slowly. 'You mean to tell us, that... you started this war and made us come down to clean it up?' he said, suddenly angry. He looked at his fellow military officers but knew instantly he would garner no support from them. Both men, although surprised at the sudden turn of events, did not seem bothered. They wandered away to retrieve refreshments from waiting choral-boys, leaving Kaplain to deal with Avanti alone.

'Don't look so offended, brigadier,' Avanti chortled. 'It's not like we started cleaning them out knowing they would fight back. This war was an unexpected consequence. Who knew that a bunch of dirty indigs with clubs could cause such a fuss?'

Kaplain shook his head, trying to digest the cardinal's statement. 'You started this? This insurgency was not a revolt, but a reaction?'

'I did. I'm proud of it too. This planet was a waste of the Emperor's natural bounty. We are turning it into something productive for the Imperial settlement so that man can enjoy the fruits of his own labour.'

By the scowl on Kaplain's face, it was evident that he was not convinced.

'Brigadier, when you pick a fruit from a wild tree, does that fruit not become yours by virtue of your labours?'

'Not if my labour included genocide,' Kaplain said quietly.

There was a flutter of anger across the cardinal's face, brief and quickly repressed. 'The Emperor decreed that land unused is land wasted. What man creates by the efforts of his own labour becomes his by the laws of nature. This planet was empty when we came here, devoid of sovereign authority. Do you understand, brigadier? Or are you stupid?'

De Ruger and Montalvo, returning with drinks in hand, chuckled amongst themselves.

Then Morgan Fure began to speak. 'Regardless, brigadier, theology is beyond your right to question. You only need to know two things. One, the insurgency has escalated beyond our initial estimates and now they have betrayed us by turning into common heretics. Two, your duty is to quell these new-found cultists. Nothing else is relevant.' It was the first thing Kaplain had heard her say.

The cardinal clapped his hands in slow, mock applause. 'You can see why I like her,' he said to the three generals.

There was nothing more Kaplain could say and he knew it. One wrong word and he would end up on charges of heresy and he did not much feel like giving the cardinal and his hard-faced bitch that satisfaction.

'Besides, it seems that military intelligence has gathered enough evidence of Ruinous influence amongst the insurgency. All the better reason to deal with this heretic scum as quickly and as efficiently as possible. Would you agree, brigadier?'

Kaplain could not shake the feeling that even if the Ruinous Powers did have a hand in this conflict, it was only the result of the Ecclesiarchy's callous course of actions that invoked them somehow. The universe worked in strange ways; even as a simple soldier he knew that. But he did not voice his opinion.

'May I be excused, cardinal? If there is nothing further you wanted to show me, the weather is hot and I don't want to keep my driver waiting in this heat,' asked Kaplain.

Avanti nodded without looking at him.

Kaplain snapped the heels of his boots together with a terse thud and saluted his fellow officers. He made a conscious effort not to address the cardinal during his salute before he stamped down the ramp of the tractor towards a waiting four-wheeler.

Once Kaplain was well out of earshot, Avanti leaned in to Fure. 'Watch that man,' he whispered. 'I have a feeling he may cause some mischief before our work is done.'

The palatine, like the cardinal, had learnt to smile without her eyes. She twisted her lips and nodded obediently.

Many of the prospects were dying. They were dying through their bodies rejecting the chemical treatments or they were dying through the intensity of training. Mautista was determined not to become one of those who fell by the wayside.

The first Mautista saw die had been Abales who had, in another lifetime, been an artisan of the Ogalog peoples. They had only been three days into their Disciple induction when the artisan's blood rejected the chemicals. His joints had swelled to acute proportions as his bones had lengthened, until finally his muscles and ligaments collapsed under the strain. They found Abales dead on the fourth morning, curled up in a ball of agony. His kneecaps had split out of his legs and his shoulder blades had torn out of his upper back.

Five more had perished in the two weeks after that. The chemicals poisoned their blood, causing the veins to puff up beneath their skin in cases of angry black thrombosis. The protruding arteries were soft to the touch and minor vessels mottled their bodies. Even the prospects that survived were afflicted by the malady to some degree. It was for this reason that Mautista believed they daubed themselves in white chalk and kohl in a morning ritual. No fully ordained Disciple ever appeared before the Carnibalès soldiery without the corpse-white warpaint of their caste.

For those who survived the system shock of physical transformation, more would fall victim to the intense training methods of the Dos Pares. Early in their induction, Gabre of the Blood Gorgons led the recruits to Yawning Hill, in actuality a tiered mountain cliff in the upper hinterlands of Bastón. The sheer slabs of cliff that rose three thousand metres above the ground were all but impossible to climb. Only the hardiest foragers, searching for eggs of the rare cliff-dwelling bantam, dared to brave the ascent. The foragers worked in four- or five-man groups with the aid of securing rope and relay teams, and even then, only during the warmest seasons with well-stocked supplies for a three- or five-day climb.

The prospects were made to scale the vertical heights during the monsoon season, with no rations and only a small pickaxe. They set off alone, edging their way up the cliffsides as rain and high wind pelted them. For Mautista, the intense mental focus of the climb far outstripped the exceedingly difficult physical aspect. For minutes, even hours at a time, he would pause, splayed across the rock face as he studied his next move. The rain slicked the rocks, or loosened others, and he would reach out with trembling fingers to test the next handhold. It was like a game of rook that required unrelenting focus, a game that lasted for three whole days and in which a mistake at any point would result in death. Several times Mautista lost his grip on the slippery stones, clamping on by the tips of his fingers, clenching his cramped forearms through the sheer determination to not die. He caught snatches of sleep whenever he could find a ledge stable enough to support him, but even then never for more than one or two hours at a time.

On the third night, as he neared the peak, the wind became unbearably strong. At times it pounded him with a tangible force, pulling at his hair and wedging gaps of air between his body and the cliff. During these times Mautista would press himself against the rock and close his eyes, feeling the gale rippling across his back and howling mockery into his ears. It was only during these moments of bleakness that Mautista truly realised the purpose of this trial. He was frightened to the point of trembling. Physically and mentally he was depleted. This was what the Two Pairs wanted to know. At the final hour of the final war, would Mautista lie down and die? Or would he press on to achieve the Primal State?

Suddenly, Mautista experienced a rush of endorphins. He felt a focus that he had not felt even before the climb. He could fall backwards and let the wind carry him away, or he could climb to the top. The logic was so pure and his fate was entirely within his own grasp. He had achieved clarity of mind free of affliction. Slowly, hand over hand, Mautista clawed his way upwards. It no longer mattered to him whether there were ten metres or ten hundred metres to reach the peak. He would climb to the top, and then he would kill a platoon of Imperial Guard and climb it all over again if he had to.

When his hand finally dragged him over the edge, Mautista found Gabre and Sau had set up a base camp. Several of the other prospects had already made it up before him. They were changed men, walking with a sure, steady stride. It had taken Mautista two days and three nights to complete the ascent, surviving on rainwater and moss, but he had finally made it. Despite their newly-transformed physiques, six of the remaining sixteen had not survived the climb.

Mautista knew this was a way of culling the unsuitable. The Disciples were the backbone of the Carnibalès, the visible leaders, the field commanders and more importantly the teachers of the common insurgents. The Two Pairs made it known that ill-prepared Disciples would become a taint, polluting the insurgency itself. For the ten remaining prospects, their training as Disciples could now begin.

'Chaos is not an entity. Chaos is a state of existence. It is the Primal State.'

Jormeshu was, for the first time, in his full rig of battle armour. No longer clad in a loincloth, he appeared even larger than before, his voice made sonorous by the vox speakers housed in his enormous breastplate.

'The Ecclesiarchy has taught you that Chaos is evil. That order and the rule of law should navigate the history of mankind.'

The ten Disciples nodded in agreement. They sat in cross-legged obedience on the dirt floor of an underground bunker, watching the Legionnaire prowl back and forth like a caged behemoth. Mautista had never seen armour like Jormeshu's before. The suit had a slab-like quality to it, sheathing Jormeshu in plates thick and heavy. The colour was a deep shade of red, so deep it shone like lacquered black-brown. Yet at the same time, thorns and filigree chased the edges of the suit in leaping, energetic angles so that the armour appeared organic somehow. It was as if the suit had a life and voice of its own and had chosen Jormeshu as its host. Mautista had never seen anything so wonderful.

'But man was not made for order or law,' Jormeshu rasped. 'By nature man is flawed. It is an inevitable part of mankind. Man strives to increase his power, his influence, and he does this through his imposition of order and authority. Life is a continual struggle for one man to be better than the next man. Law and order stagnates this power struggle.'

The Disciples shouted in approval, raising their fists into the air. Jormeshu's boots, shaped like cloven hooves, thudded against the packed earth as he strode up and down, adding to the crescendo with tremendous force.

'But Chaos is change. It is a constant flux, like the delta which continues to flow, it is evolution. It is the way forward for mankind. The Imperium fears us because it fears change, it holds onto antiquated notions of sentiment. Even you, at one stage, feared change.'

He was right, Mautista knew. To become Disciples they had forgone their previous lives. At first he had held onto the memories of his life as a Kalisador and as a Taboon villager, but those sentiments had stopped him from progressing. They stopped him changing. The Dos Pares had often spoken of finding inner tranquillity through the path of Chaos and it was Mautista's ascent up Yawning Hill that allowed him to understand in part what they meant.

'Remember this. It is change through liberation; we will free you from the chains of the Imperium and allow you to exist as you want. Exist as you are in a Primal State. Morals are simply a construct of man. Yet man is but stardust, we are the same material as the earth, the sky and even bacteria. All matter does not abide by law, as nature does not abide by law. We should accept this. If you kill a man because the sight of him offends you, is it not the way of nature? Is it not as elemental as the tree that is felled by the storm? If the man you kill cannot defend himself then that is the way it is. There should be no moral attachment to it, because therein lies the stagnation of law and order.'

Mautista understood this too. Since he had become a Disciple he had already killed a man. The man had been a villager who had ridden his motored bicycle in front of an insurgent convoy. Fearing discovery by Imperial forces, as using the dirt roads was always a measured risk, Mautista and his training team had been pressed for time. They had blared their horns to force the cyclist off the road. As they passed, the man had looked at them. It was the look of disdain that had triggered the killing. In that second Mautista had decided the man should not exist any more. He was stupid; stupid enough to incur Mautista's attention and not strong enough to defend himself after a petty display of anger. Mautista ordered the trucks to a halt, alighted and calmly shot the man with his lasrifle. It had been a liberating experience.

'But if we are to lose our grasp of all else, then why do I still harbour a hatred of the Imperium for killing the Taboon?' Mautista asked.

'Hate is just a means. Emotions are the driving force of mankind. I ask you this, when you feel hatred, or when you feel love, or excitement. How do you decipher one feeling from another? Is it tangible?'

Mautista thought for a while and realised it was not. Emotions were an engine that drove physical action. The Dos Pares helped him channel his emotions into seeking the path of Chaos and liberation. It made him soar with joy and want to impart his revelations to all the people of Bastón. For those who did not understand the Primal, Mautista pitied them.

As morning came, so did the rain.

The raindrops bouncing hard on Baeder's face and neck woke him. He opened his eyes, still dreaming of combat, and momentarily forgot where he was. He rubbed his face to wake himself and realised his hands were streaked with dry blood. The Lauzon Offensive had not been a dream at all.

Having fallen asleep at the bow of his swift boat, hunched behind the mounted bolter, Baeder had sunk into the deep sleep of the chronically unrested. Around him, the flotilla was moving at an ambling speed, their crews spent from the previous night's fighting. There was a palpable weariness in the air.

He cracked his neck, stretched his limbs and walked around to the pilothouse. He stepped into the cabin and found Corporal Velder, his assigned coxswain, at the helm, eyelids hooded and half asleep.

'Morning, corporal.'

Velder started and snapped to attention. 'Sir,' he said, saluting.

'At ease, corporal. How much progress have we made?'

'We're about sixteen kilometres from the Lauzon township, sir. Northeast bearing at coordinates B15200.'

'Very good, corporal. Stand down and catch some sleep below deck. I'll take over for now,' said Baeder as he began to peel off his uniform shirt. Blood, none of it his, had congealed the shirt to his skin. He discarded the ruined article onto the deck and, for the first time, went about as most of his men did, bare-chested beneath a flak vest.

As Corporal Velder stumbled past in a daze, Baeder knew he had pushed the men beyond their limits. They had needed rest at Lauzon, they really had. They had needed the time at Lauzon to stabilise the wounded and renew the spirits of the entire battalion. But they had left with more wounded than before. Many would not make it through the day without proper treatment. Already three entire assault landers were devoted to the supine forms of those with critical injuries, the tillers manned by on-hand combat medics drawn from other squads. Aside from human casualties, several of the swift boats were so damaged they were towed along by supply barges. One of the gun-barges had sprung a leak and many other swifties, workhorses that were close to one hundred and forty years old, were beginning to show signs of wear. Baeder feared they would not hold up for the entire mission.

He agonised about their ramshackle defences and preparations at Lauzon. They were in enemy country, and the Lauzon had been coerced into betrayal. Evidence from the massacred villages along the banksides should have warned him. But Baeder had wanted so badly to believe he could rest and water his men that he had taken the gamble. He blamed himself entirely. They were deep in the lands of the Archenemy now. He could not afford any more mistakes.

Far back in the lines, Corporal Schilt was fuming. He had almost been killed in the Lauzon Offensive. He had come precariously close to dying in some backwater hamlet on some feral planet he could barely pronounce the name of.

He had only escaped death by running back into camp and hiding in a drainage culvert while the battle had raged around him. Drunk beyond all senses, Schilt had shuddered to think what would have happened had he been forced to fight. He had simply followed the main line of retreat, making sure to keep as many Riverine between himself and the insurgent waves as possible. In his hurry to flee, Schilt had climbed aboard an assault lander rather than his assigned swift boat and was now stuck aboard its cramped crowded conditions.

It was all a rather unfortunate series of events. He was sure to never let that happen again.

'I'm going to shoot him,' Schilt declared to nobody in particular.

The men huddled around, tired though they were, began to chuckle.

'Schilt. You're drunk. Settle down,' said Sergeant Emel gently.

'I'm not drunk. Just wait and see, I'll fragging shoot him.'

In reality, Schilt's temples were still viced by the after-effects of intoxication and his breath was sour with ethanol. But in his mind, the colonel would be as good as dead.

'The colonel's all right. He's got some balls considering his staff background. At least with him, we'll never spoil for a fight,' said Emel.

Schilt shook his head sluggishly. 'If you want to die then go ahead. Me, I'm not dying here, not on this planet. Baeder is nothing but trouble.'

Emel shrugged wordlessly. The others looked away in undecided silence. But although Schilt had not gathered support here he knew his boys would share his view. It was better that his comrades did not regard his threats as anything more than the aggravated rants of a drunken soldier. It would make it easier to do away with Baeder, once he and his creepers had the timing right.

CHAPTER TEN

Duponti walked out of the hangar bay with the stiff, blood-tingling limbs of extended flight. The ship was quiet. Most of the personnel were sleeping soundly except for the maintenance crew working on Duponti's strike fighter.

He crossed the long grey strip of the flight deck, small and insignificant under the shadow of towering vox-mast antennas. On board the Argo-Nautical, two thousand Persepians were at rest, oblivious to the turbulent fighting many kilometres away on the mainland. The *Iron Ishmael* carried two battalions of Nautical Infantry, a squadron of Marauder bombers reinforced by four Lightning strike fighters, as well as a crew of seven hundred sailors, crewmen and logistics units. But for now, the only man who could make a difference to the distant fighting was Lieutenant Duponti.

As Duponti made his way towards the 'iron-box' – a four-storey super-structure on the deck that housed the ship's officers – it occurred to his flight-addled mind that the operation was at a crucial point now. It was a climax. They were at war for real.

At the sentry point, two Nautical infantrymen in their neat, sky-blue waist-coats opened the enormous clam-shell entrance into the superstructure. The soldiers in their pressed uniforms, still chalky with starch, saluted Duponti as he passed. Compared to them, Duponti must have looked a dishevelled mess. He had not changed out of his flight suit for three days and thick stubble scraped his neck. For a moment, he wanted to clutch the nearest man by the shoulders and shake him, yelling as to whether he realised there was a war on. It was a momentary urge and Duponti put it down to the high spike of nerve stimms he had ingested to keep himself awake.

Duponti made his way towards the wardroom: a large officers' club that doubled as a mess hall. He had approximately twenty minutes to down some caffeine and load up on carbohydrates before his warplane would be ready for take-off again.

In the rectangular, steel container of the wardroom Duponti finally slumped down. He could not remember the last time he had straightened out his back against a real backrest. A handful of ship officers nursed cups of steaming caff at the big, otherwise empty metal tables. They shot him short, curious glances. Duponti was too weary to acknowledge them. He kept his head down between drooping shoulders and dug away at a bowl of gritty grain cereal.

He had not been eating long when he heard the loud scrape of chairs. The officers in the wardroom had all risen to their feet, sword-straight and in salute. Duponti turned around in his chair and saw Admiral de Ruger stride into the hall. The admiral levelled his gaze on Duponti and headed towards him.

Duponti groaned inwardly. He had never liked de Ruger. He found the man insufferably smug, far too smug for a soldier who had never gained his rank by earning combat pins. Like most rear-echelon Persepians, de Ruger had put far too much thought into his outward appearance as a way of distracting outsiders from the fact that he had no real front-line experience. Even now in the middle hours of the night, the admiral was upholstered in a doublet of silky cyan and a cape of translucent fur.

'Sir,' said Duponti, rising to his feet. He sat back down before de Ruger returned his salute.

'How is the fighting, lieutenant? Thrilling, I'd wager,' declared the admiral in his tone that suggested he already knew the answer.

'It's getting thicker the further out I fly. These last few days have been one continuous combat zone, so thick that it's hard to call this an insurgency any more.'

'Oh, I know. How I miss the stink of fyceline,' de Ruger said, mimicking an exaggerated shiver of delight.

He didn't, of course. Duponti knew for a fact that the admiral kept himself as far away from combat as he could and had done so ever since he had been a pampered junior officer. Being the nephew of a Persepian consul had afforded him special status amongst the peers of his day.

Duponti slopped a spoonful of grits into his mouth. 'Sir, is there anything I can do for you?'

'I've come to let you know that your services to the Riverine operation are no longer required. You may stand down and get some rest. Clean yourself up,' smiled de Ruger. He said it as if he believed it was a good thing.

'Why?' said Duponti glumly. 'It's a full-scale engagement out there. If anything, sir, I was going to request four other pilots to help fly rotations. I can't do this alone.'

De Ruger seemed slightly taken aback by Duponti's response. 'No. No, I'm not risking any more pilots for this operation. I'm letting you know that you may stand down now.'

'Sir, the battalion are going to take much heavier casualties, especially in that kind of terrain. If I'm not flying overwatch, it could get worse.'

De Ruger shook his head. 'The 88th Battalion are expecting at least sixty per cent attrition. You don't need to work yourself to death, lieutenant. Have some dignity.'

Duponti was slouched over his bowl of cold grits, his head hanging from exhaustion. But the admiral's attitude riled him. Duponti put down his metal spoon with a clink. 'Sir, they are so close to the objective now. I've seen what it's like out there in the heartland. The inland is crawling with rallying insurgents, it's like a nest of mites out there. The insurgency grows in strength everyday, sir, I've seen it with my own eyes. For the sake of my own conscience, I need to help the Riverine neutralise that siege-battery before this war becomes unwinnable.'

The admiral was unmoved. 'When they fail,' he said imperiously, 'then Cardinal Avanti will simply return to our original strategy of carpet-bombing the inland until the heavy guns are silenced. Won't that be something? The full might of the Persepian fleet taking the mainland.'

The fact that the admiral said 'when' not 'if' was not lost on Duponti. The aviator hid his face behind a cup of tea, scowling. The admiral was a true political strategist, constantly seeking to manoeuvre himself into the cardinal's favour. Maybe he truly wanted a seat by the Emperor's golden throne when he died. Whatever the case, it did not seem likely that de Ruger had the success of the Riverine objective at heart.

'Yes, sir.'

De Ruger patted his back. It was awkward, as if the admiral were not used to contact with lower ranking men. 'Good, good, lieutenant. Now you can clean up and start looking like a real man again. I hear they are serving smoked sausages and fresh local eggs for breakfast in a few hours. Make sure you're here for those. The sausages are the smoke-cured variety from the Fragment Isles, brought all the way here from home.'

Duponti stopped paying attention. The less he acknowledged the admiral, the less likely he would be to linger around. De Ruger continued to bombast, debating with himself about the merits of fine breakfast wines and whether ham in the officers' mess was better grilled or raw cured. Finally, after several agonising minutes, he left Duponti alone.

The aviator waited until he was sure de Ruger was well and truly gone. Opening a zip pocket in his jumpsuit, Duponti took out a handful of stimms. He swallowed the pills dry. Immediately, he felt his heart begin to thump hard in his chest.

He cried out involuntarily, slapping his palms hard on the table.

The other officers sitting around quietly put down their cups to stare at him. One of them shook his head.

Duponti laughed at them, tossed his chair aside, and stumbled out to find his Lightning interceptor. Admiral de Ruger be damned, the war was just beginning.

From Lauzon province, the delta widened into a basin of saline water half a kilometre broad at its widest point. But unlike the low-lying marshlands of Ouisivia, where sheets of mangroves clung to the muddy bottoms, here the rainforest continued to grow even in the water itself. According to Baeder's map, the terrain should have made for easy travel, indicating a wide expanse of water. But that was not to be.

Aquatic trees resembling stands of green coral rose out of the water and knitted a mesh of canopy thirty metres overhead. Hardy lentireeds and stringy rhizophora floated in clumps on the surface, their broad leaves speckled with salt crystals. Gas from the decomposing mud pits secreted the sinus-heavy stench of wet, rotting fruit. The foliage here had a colossal, alien quality to it, as if growth in the rough, saline waters had nurtured a strain of enormous plants that survived the conditions through sheer size alone.

The flotilla ground slowly through the aquatic forest, covering less than eight kilometres in three hours of travel. The canopy formed a greenhouse of humid air, so heavy that it could be reached out and touched like steam. Visibility was low. Sunlight that filtered through the canopy was a shade of foggy green and entire sections of boats often lost sight of each other. Fog sirens brayed constantly. After repeated slowdowns as boats sought to find each other, Baeder ordered them to maintain positional awareness through vox contact alone.

At times, Baeder felt that the entire rainforest was just an extension of the marine habitat below. Silvery shoals of fish skipped along the surface of the water, dancing on gossamer wings. Serpents slipped in and out of the water without eliciting so much as a splash. Crustaceans clung to tree bark, flies hovered in clouds and bug-eyed primates watched them from the tallest branches. The wildlife sought to claim them too; schools of tiny insects suddenly appeared on the surface of their boats, dotting the surface in hundreds, if not thousands. On closer inspection, Baeder was astounded to see that these were actually miniature frogs no bigger than his pinky nail, flitting and clustering together like condensation. Baeder brushed them away, scooping up dozens in his palm, but after a while he gave up. They simply materialised as if out of thin air.

During the height of the afternoon, at the hottest part of the day, Baeder called his men to rest. As temperatures increased, dehydration became a very real threat. Although it had not rained all day, the troopers were plastered with moisture. It was as if they had been travelling through the water itself.

Baeder himself did not rest. He ordered Corporal Velder to nurse their swift boat ahead of the battalion to meet with the scouts. The terrain was far worse than the maps had led them to believe and Baeder thought it prudent to scout ahead of the main force. Clustered and hemmed in as they were, ambush was a constant possibility.

The three scouting swifts, along with Baeder's vessel, continued sailing for a rough half hour. The going was extremely difficult and in some parts spurs of underwater roots worried their passing hulls. The boats had to navigate around miniature atolls of aquatic plants, bumping and scraping the tight confines. The water-borne jungle was like a sieve, thought Baeder, forcing the boats out of formation in order to weave around its tangled growth. The insurgents could hide thousands of men here. With this weighing on their minds, the four swifts never strayed far from each other, maintaining constant line of sight. Baeder and his coxswain stayed within the pilothouse while the boat's three other crew stayed on deck, one manning the stern stub gun and two manning the heavy bolter on the bow.

As they crept around an ox-horn bend of root systems, a village came into their view, sudden and looming. So well hidden in the jungle, the houses caught them off guard.

'Sir, was this on the map?' one of the scout boats voxed to Baeder.

'No. But this entire forest wasn't on the map either,' Baeder replied.

'Should we observe local customs and unlink ammunition from our main guns?'

'No,' Baeder decided. 'Not after last time. Keep your weapons lined up on every doorway and window.'

The village was built entirely on stilts. Support poles, some four or five metres high, kept the several dozen shack huts above the water. A system of rope bridges connected each of the various structures to each other in a web of hemp ropes and plank boards. Some of the shacks were even nestled on platforms, high in the trees, suggesting that this village was a permanent one, not just some seasonal nomadic settlement. The few villagers who squatted outside their homes fled and shut their doors as the swift boats sailed into view.

'This place looks harmless enough,' voxed the swift boat that sailed lead.

Sure enough, the town was a miserable-looking settlement in disrepair. Moss and rivers of tiny green frogs covered the walls and sloping roofs of every building. No one came out to greet them or at least regard the off-worlders with curiosity. The swifts passed in single file with Baeder at the rear, one after another until at last Baeder's boat sailed through the centre of the settlement.

That was when the enemy fired a shot.

One lonely shot that rattled from an autogun. The round danced off Baeder's starboard rear with an aggressive shriek.

Immediately, the vox-channels came alive. 'Shots heard! Location needed!'

Baeder had spotted the muzzle flash from a second storey window of a nearby shack. It had obviously been fired in anger, but it would be too premature to start igniting the entire village with heavy support fire. 'Hold your fire! My boat is going in, so cover us,' Baeder voxed to the scouts.

They drew their boat parallel with a swinging rope ladder that led up to the rope walkways. Snatching lasrifles from the stowage racks, Baeder and his crew surged up onto the platforms. The five-man team stormed up onto a lopsided house and Corporal Velder caved the flimsy plyboard door in with a fen-hammer from the boat's armoury.

The Riverine burst into a large room full of screaming occupants. 'Down! Down on the floor!' Velder yelled as he brandished the fen-hammer overhead.

Baeder took a moment to assess his surroundings. There were both men and women huddled there, along with many children. At first glance there appeared to be three or four families sharing one single room. The Riverine began to search the house while Baeder covered them with his lasgun. The women started to sob hysterically and the children followed suit.

'Sir. I found it!' shouted Trooper Keidel. The Riverine was peering into a man-sized water urn. From inside, he drew out two crude autorifles and a missile tube. 'Still warm,' Keidel said, slapping the barrel of a rifle against his open palm.

Baeder looked at the four men. The Bastón men smiled at him broadly and confidently. 'No proof,' said one of them.

Another raised his hands above his head in mock surrender. 'We are not soldiers. You cannot harm us,' he said. 'Not with our children as the Emperor's witness.'

'Emperor my arse!' Baeder spat, and was surprised by his own vehemence. 'Frag it! Cuff them all!'

Corporal Velder looked at Baeder with uncertainty. 'And then what, sir? We can't take them with us.'

'We can and we will. Let these crotch-beaters know that we won't suffer their insolence any more,' said Baeder. 'Tie them up. We're going to search this whole village. Cuff these ones and leave them here for the battalion to collect on the way through.'

In Baeder's eyes, the men in the house did not seem to appreciate the severity of the situation. They were smiling smugly and claiming to be fishermen, even as the Riverine led them outside and lashed their wrists to the house stilts with plastek cuff ties. They left the four men in chest-deep water as Baeder and his four crewmen set about searching the other homes.

They had not even crossed the rope bridge to a second house when a shot rang out from across the other side of the village. Trooper Nye yelped and fell backwards. A round had entered his neck, just above the collar of his flak vest. The others crouched or dropped flat against the rope bridge.

Suddenly, Baeder was angry. He had been a career soldier for as long as he had been an adult and fighting was his duty. He had been shot at considerably in his lifetime. But the civilians taking potshots at his men stirred something within him. The Lauzon Offensive had ignited a spark and now this remote village was stirring the embers. He had lost too many men to care. Morality was now a grey area.

Baeder got up and signalled for the three waiting swift boats providing overwatch. 'Frag this place! Kill them all!' he shouted, flashing the field signals for fire at will.

The boats opened up immediately. They fired in all directions. The force of their combined arms shook the village apart, splitting roofs and tearing down walls.

Baeder watched the men they had bound struggle loose from their cuffs. One of them began to swim away from the village. He covered no more than ten metres before bolter rounds sent a bearded cecropia crashing down on him.

A male villager from another house ran out with a machete to release the other three bound men. But Baeder felt possessed. From his position high on the rope bridge he fired down on the rescuer. He did not care what motive the man had for freeing the prisoners, he cared only that his las-rounds tore cleanly through the man's torso, sending him face first into the water.

Gun barrels peeked out from behind windows and barked out with sporadic shooting. The swift boat reply was loud and terrible. Tracer fire folded the shacks into two, three or four pieces like accordion paper. One of the remaining prisoners was hit by a round. Tied up and half submerged in water, the man began to scream. His cries of anguish drew the attention of his family. Three children emerged to see what had become of their father. Howling, arms outstretched, they ran towards him.

Baeder loosened a smoke grenade from his webbing and tossed it directly down below. He would have liked to convince himself that he did it purely to force the children away from the carnage. But in the back of his mind, he knew otherwise. He had done it to deny the father a chance to see his children one last time. The men he lost in Lauzon and all the good soldiers killed under his command had not been given the chance to say goodbye to their loved ones. Baeder would not allow this insurgent that one last mercy.

The last Baeder saw of the dying man was a frail Bastón-born fisherman, utterly despondent as he tried to find his children through the
thickening smoke. Baeder had denied him his last chance to say goodbye.
For some reason, Baeder felt a thrill of joy. It was something he had not
wanted to become. They had made him this way.

They flattened the village within minutes. Half of the houses became
sheets of corrugated metal and wood floating in the soupy water. Those
that remained standing were worried with bullet holes and las-scorch.
    The sudden and overwhelming fury of eight heavy support weapons
had silenced the village. No more gun barrels snuck out from cracks and
crevices to dare another shot. There was a strange quiet that complemented the pall of gunsmoke. But Baeder was not yet done.
    He pulled the scouts back the way they came. He would not take any
chances. Voxing back to the battalion, Baeder gave them precise map
coordinates of the village and ordered for mortar ordnance. There was
no way he would lose another Guardsman and, in his mind, there was
every chance that an insurgent could flee from the village only to follow
them later, sniping from the trees. He hated these people. He quelled any
empathy he once harboured for them. It was less difficult to do than he
thought. Baeder simply switched off.
    He could soon hear the crump of mortars and the distant whistle of
their flight. All his life, Baeder had been a non-consequentialist, caged
by an immovable moral code. He had lived as most men did, his actions
guided by decontextualised maxims. The sin of unprovoked killing. The
ethics of human empathy. The unspoken code of martial honour. Anything that may have once inhibited his actions was now nothing more
than social constructs, best kept away from the battlefield. He felt they
were distant, unreachable ideals.
    But out here, he knew all his actions had an immediate consequence
and the only consequence that mattered to him was to keep his men
alive. Several weeks ago, the thought of mortaring an enemy village
would have lurked like a ghost on his conscience. But now, the crackling
explosions of the mortars brought him a cold and curiously morbid
comfort.

CHAPTER ELEVEN

The insurgency was growing in force. Carnibalès propagandists were poisoning the provincial hamlets of Bastón through the power of print. Insurgent warbands distributed leaflets that depicted the Primal State as a patriotic religion that combined the animist culture of Bastón with new gods and ideologies. There were even rumours that the Carnibalès broadcast prayers at midnight on a certain vox frequency. Superstition held that, upon listening to the 'unholy' vox-channel, a shadowy wraith would stand in the corner of one's peripheral vision until the frequency was changed. Although the rumours were never substantiated, it was said that dark magic was at work and many who heard these prayers wandered into the rainforests, following ghosts only they could see.

The Ecclesiarchy attempted to counter the spreading rebel influence in their own clumsy, pugnacious manner. Ecclesiarchal preachers accompanied Riverine patrols into the wilderness and visited the outlying towns. Yet these preachers were overwhelmingly evangelical. They attributed the insurgency to native ignorance, and admonished the locals for their illiteracy and sins. The Ecclesiarchal methods did not fare well. The preachers were viewed as a liability by the Guardsmen. An incident in the town of Bahia became the final straw for Ecclesiarchal involvement in military patrols. A preacher's caustic oratory offended the locals to the point of riot, leading to the death of eight Guardsmen and forty-one locals. In the aftermath, Cardinal Avanti issued a decree that clerics were to remain within Imperial-controlled regions unless their journeys were approved by him personally.

'Atten-tion!' Mautista barked.

The motley ranks of guerrillas lined up before him attempted to snap into parade order. The attempt was, for the most part, sincere. Several of them were out of rhythm and one man in the rear almost dropped his rifle. Mautista, tall and white as a standing cadaver, nodded his approval as he imagined an Imperial officer would do for his men.

The band of guerrilla fighters before him was his own, the Two Pairs had given them to him. Two score men drawn from the regional villagers. The men were parading in a small grove near an inland village allied to the Dos Pares cause. They were an ill-fitting bunch, mostly new guerrilla recruits dressed in the canvas and hemp garments of rural workers. Newly-issued canvas munition rigs were strapped to proud chests and press-stamped lasguns were held upright across the left shoulder. At a distance they looked unremarkable, but from where Mautista stood, they looked fearsome enough for one reason.

Change was amongst them all.

Unlike the Disciples, each man displayed mutations of varying degrees. A few of the men carried the common gift of thorned bristles along their upper brows, while some mutations were very minor, as minor as an extra digit or three.

Yet every day, those commoners who rallied under the Dos Pares were gifted with change as long as they prayed to the shrines that the Two Pairs had erected. And what beautiful shrines they were! Tall and totemic, the pillars were of carved wood so old that they had taken on an ossified sheen. Some were the size of small busts, while others stood as high as a man. They were erected in all places, to be seen at all times, whether crouched beneath the roots of a gum-sap or nestled in a bunker shrine. Since the early days of the war, the Four had erected their shrines and, with each day, the mutations became more common.

It was not known what the origins of these totems were but Mautista knew they came from the skies. Every once in a while the totems were smuggled on board the off-world carriers that would land in the deep jungles, away from Imperial scrutiny. These off-world ships, dark and frightening, brought with them ammunition and mechanisms for the weapons the insurgency could not reproduce. Only the Four were allowed to make contact with these ships but Mautista had witnessed the nimbus of light from afar. When it came time for insurgents to carry the supplies down from the mountains to their base camps, in between the crates of weaponry would always be totems, wrapped in white shrouds and carried aloft by several men like a funeral procession.

With each shrine erected by the Four, their influence grew. Those who had joined the insurgency prayed often to these new deities, these spirits of Khaos. In turn, they experienced a change to their bodies as much as it changed their spirit. It was different from the detached and aloof religion that they had followed under the Ecclesiarchy. There the preachers had admonished them ceaselessly and in return they prayed and prayed to little effect. The power of the so-called Emperor was nothing compared to the instant gratification they received under the attentive gaze of Khaos.

'My brothers. Today we are tasked with a great undertaking,' Mautista began, drawing out each vowel in a suitably dramatic fashion. 'We are to claim taxes from a village that has not joined the cause. Although it may seem a mundane mission, I assure you it is a crucial one. The insurgency of Kaos cannot survive without the support of the people.'

An insurgent named Canao took one step forwards from the ranks. Of all those present, Canao was the most heavily mutated and therefore considered the most devout of them all. Mautista heard camp stories that, only months ago, Canao had been a very tall, very broad and very handsome village blacksmith who had courted the attention of many pretty girls, even from faraway villages. Now the muscles of his upper back and neck fused into a knotted club and his lower jaw split into two hooked mandibles. He was so very monstrous and, in his lesser days, Mautista would have envied him.

'The troop is ready, brother. We will take our payment for the cause, if not in grains then in blood.' As he spoke, the pink flesh around his mandibles peeled backwards like an eyelid and began to drool.

Mautista saluted with his long, strangler's fingers. The men fell out and began to march behind him in single file down a narrow ravine. Mautista was dressed in the cracked brown leathers of a long dead militia officer, the seams split to accommodate his height and buckled with burnished metal plates where the gaps did not meet. For the first time, Mautista felt as if he could truly punish the Imperium. He felt like a real soldier.

The target of the raid was a hamlet near the upper spur of the Serrado Basin. Known as the provincial canton of the Mato-Barea people, it was not a large town by any means, with a population of no more than two hundred. At least that was what the insurgent spies had reported. But the Four had imparted upon Mautista the importance of primary source intelligence and he was a keen Disciple.

Mautista and Canao hid their men in the forest and crept out alone to survey the area. They moved amongst waxy esculenta bushes, breaking up their silhouettes with branches and twigs as they had been taught. The hamlet was roughly three hundred metres away from their hiding place in the undergrowth. The rainforest had been felled for three hundred metres in all directions to provide space for their paddy fields, as well as to give a clear view of any desperate carnivores that might stray from the wilderness.

Mautista felt a chill of excitement deep in his stomach when he remembered that he would be the hunter today.

A stockade surrounded the circular cluster of waterfront homes. The Bastón had never been a warlike culture and the practice of fortification had only become common since the war. The barricade was an improvised effort, piled up with disused tractors, rusted engines of agriculture and hammered together with logs from the local trees. The irregular stockade was only a metre high at some points; it would not prevent any truly determined raid. It served more as deterrence than defence.

Before its walls sprawled the ubiquitous paddies and the irrigation systems that channelled feed streams from the delta. Every once in a while the workers in the paddies would look up, scanning the area around them like a herd of cautious grazers. But they didn't see the predators who waited, just beyond their view, in the greenery.

Most of the villagers appeared unarmed, or at least poorly so. The forty or fifty farmers in the fields laboured in pairs. One would loosen the cassam tuber from its watery depths with a long fork and the other would collect it with a shovel and place the harvest into a wicker basket on their back. Their tools would be no match for Mautista's twenty devoted soldiers and their rapid-fire weaponry.

'Mautista, can you see?' Canao rasped, lowering his magnoculars. 'Over there!' he pointed with excitement.

Mautista raised his own magnoculars to where Canao indicated. He saw two Kalisadors standing behind a rusted engine block in the stockade. Their dark grey armour of crab shell and coloured ribbon reminded Mautista of a life he lived not so long ago. Immediately, Mautista both pitied and hated them. The men were so ignorant in their stubborn defence of the village. They knew nothing of the enlightenment of Chaos and Mautista regretted that he would have to kill them.

'They have guns too. This will be a problem,' Canao said, clicking his mandibles with agitation. Mautista narrowed his eyes in concentration.

It would indeed be a problem. The usual method of extortion was for the insurgents to surround the village with their firearms and negotiate taxes in the form of food harvest, cloth and perhaps even recruits. Violence was to be avoided, at least in the beginning. They could not recruit for the cause if they harmed them first. Massacre would only be reserved for hard-line loyalist communities.

Yet this approach was now complicated by the two Kalisador watchmen. They were both well dug-in behind their barricade and armed with ex-militia shotguns. When the insurgency first took hold, almost a year before the war, the local forces were the first victims of killing. The poorly-trained reservist soldiers were killed and their armouries raided by Carnibalès forces. No doubt some of these weapons had drifted into the hands of loyalist communities as well during the course of conflict.

Mautista knew these weapons well, for the Dos Pares had given him rudimentary training in most small-arms. The Kalisadors each gripped a Mosgant90 tactical shotgun. These were quality weapons produced off-world and parkerised with a frosty black phosphate to prevent corrosion in the humid Bastón climate. Pump action with a six-slug capacity, the shotguns were incredibly accurate and could worry a target out at one hundred and fifty metres.

'Kalisadors carrying weapons of death? That is taboo,' said Canao.

'No. It is only taboo during times of peace. Now, it is not taboo. It means this village has recently lost members to violence and the Kalisadors are claiming the rights of retribution,' Mautista explained. He knew that all weapons in the Kalisador arsenal were designed to injure but not kill their opponent during ritual combat. Devices that caused irreversible harm were reserved only for the killing of a much-hated enemy beyond the point of conciliation.

Prior to the war, most Kalisadors would never touch a firearm for fear it would steal away their warrior spirit. It was a taboo device, and the Bastón were a superstitious people. If a villager were to touch a firearm, they must immediately bathe themselves for fear of bad luck. The act of pointing a weapon of death, be it gun or crossbow, was an insult beyond comprehension. The sight of the Kalisadors with shotguns ready meant they were claiming they were willing to inflict righteous retribution.

This presented a unique tactical challenge. The open paddy fields would become a clear killing zone for his men to approach. Of course, their autoguns and lasrifles had greater range over the shotguns, but killing the Kalisadors would simply result in a needless massacre of the village. At over three hundred metres, there was also no guarantee that their home-forged weaponry could accurately put down both Kalisadors.

'What shall we do?' Canao said.

'Hide the warband in the trees, to provide me with covering fire while I go in to negotiate an agreement. If they are hostile, I will run and the men will keep the Kalisadors down.'

Canao nodded in agreement, his humpback swaying as he scurried through the brush then hurried back to the others.

As soon as Mautista returned to his men, he began to relay what he had seen in a logical breakdown. He scrawled a rough outline of the area with a twig in the soil. The Four had taught him well, and he had an intuitive grasp for the tactics of off-world warfare. The knowledge they imparted upon their Disciples was impressive indeed and Mautista often wondered how fearsome those Legionnaires of Chaos would be in battle.

'I want five fighters covering the left arc, and five fighters covering the right arc at one hundred metres' spread. Keep hidden and have your weapons trained on those Kalisadors. You will provide covering fire at forty-five degree angles. I want another five covering our rear, facing the forest. The rest come with me, we will strike a dialogue with the Kali-sadors. If you see me raise this signal,' Mautista raised his fist sharply, 'I want the first two groups to kill them as quickly as possible. Understood?'

The men nodded.

'Good, go about it. Canao, I need you with one of the cover fire groups. Go,' Mautista said, slapping the insurgent on his knotted humpback.

The insurgents spread out and soon melted away out of sight. Mautista was left with three young recruits, boys who only several weeks ago had been simple rural types. He could tell they were scared. They had not received the vigorous enlightenment that the Disciples had experienced. They were just boys with rifles and a month of guerrilla training.

Mautista sought to say something that would dispel their anxiety. Finally, he uttered, 'The gaze of Khaos compels you.'

It seemed to work as the Carnibalès flared their nostrils while nodding with conviction. They were working themselves up, gritting their teeth and slapping their faces.

Mautista took off across the fields. His autorifle, with its chipped wooden stock, slung casually across his back. He opened his arms as a gesture of peace. Yet as the farmers spotted him run towards them they scattered like a herd of startled livestock. Mautista knew that the white Disciples had gained quite a reputation amongst the common popula-tion, a reputation that bordered on superstitious hysteria. They were regarded as ghosts amongst some, or walking corpses because of their warpaint. Others, more pragmatic, knew them as a symbol of impending death. Mautista liked to think he was both these things as the villagers scarpered over their protective walls in terror.

'Another step and we will shoot,' shouted a Kalisador as Mautista walked within one hundred metres of the township.

Mautista stopped and studied the man. The Kalisador was built like a battering ram, with a square head and no discernable neck. The decora-tive beads hanging from his torso plates confirmed that this Kalisador was a great ritual dancer who incorporated unarmed fighting into his forms very well. In all likelihood, he would be a poor shot with the shotgun. But the Kalisador who crouched behind cover next to him was younger, with a smooth intelligent face. Mautista judged, by the way the younger man held his weapon, that he knew how to fire a shotgun properly. He would need to watch him the most.

'I am a Disciple of the Dos Pares and my men are rebel fighters.'

'I know who you are,' roared no-neck. 'What are you doing here?'

The Four had often said that command of linguistics was as important as command of weapons in psychological operations. Mautista chose his words diplomatically. 'We are here to speak to your young men about joining the cause and, if you are willing to aid us, we would like to col-lect supplies.'

'We are not stupid. You are raiders,' said the younger Kalisador forcefully.

Mautista tilted his head. 'Would you shoot a fellow Bastón-born in these times of war?'

'We are Imperial citizens. We know what you lot do to loyalist settlements. Get out now or we will shoot,' yelled no-neck, thrusting his shotgun with each word.

The time for talking was over. Mautista could see it in their eyes. If he did not act quickly, the spooked Kalisadors would likely cut him down where he stood. Briefly, Mautista considered retreating and returning with more warbands in support. But the Four would not be pleased. These were just two desperate Kalisadors defending an entire village. Mautista would have to settle this himself.

He raised his fist sharply. The signal to shoot.

He found himself running in the opposite direction as gunfire cut the air around him. Rashes of volley-fire bounced out from the rainforest. For a moment, as Mautista ran towards his guerrillas, he thought they had succeeded.

But his men were not well trained. In the heat of combat, they began to fire wildly. Some of the shots kicked up the ground around Mautista as he ran. They fired without any sense of discipline, shooting in all directions. If Mautista had not spaced them out to the flanks at forty-five degree angles, it was likely he would have been caught in the teeth of their volleys.

Worst of all, the group providing rear cover forgot their orders upon hearing the gunshots and joined in the shooting. It was often a difficult task for soldiers providing cover, looking in the opposite direction of the enemy to stay on task. These men were not drilled enough and the excitement of engagement brought them running out into the open. Unfortunately, this meant Mautista was caught directly in their forward line of attack.

'Stop! Stop!' Mautista cried. 'Get back in your sectors!'

It was no use. He was too far away and the burping fire of weapons drowned out his voice. Behind him, a villager on the wall was shot down. A woman was hit in the hip and spun away. His fighters had forgotten that their objective was to put rounds on the Kalisadors to keep them suppressed. The men were firing at any target that presented itself. Mautista cursed.

He sprinted across the paddy field, hoping that he would not be killed by one of his own. His legs, little more than sinew covering lengthy bone, soon carried him far in front of his men. A shotgun blast roared. One of the guerrillas running behind was hit in the back, his entire right torso and arm smacking into the water. Mautista's plan was falling to pieces and all because his guerrillas were not putting down enough fire on the two armed Kalisadors.

It was a disaster, but it was not lost yet. Mautista sprinted into the safety of the trees and hurled himself into the undergrowth. Once there, he signalled for his men to regroup. They did so, but only after a further few minutes of ecstatic firing. When he finally gathered his guerrillas around him, their faces were flushed with excitement.

'That was a slaughter!' Canao rasped. The men raised their weapons overhead in triumph.

'That was disaster!' Mautista spat. He lost control and slapped Canao across the face. 'Why did none of you follow my orders?'

The men, suddenly chastised, fell silent.

'You five!' snarled Mautista, pointing at the rear cover group. 'Why did you not stay in your sectors? If you disobey me again, may Khaos reject your souls!' He was frothing with anger. Spittle flew from his mouth.

'We lost one of our own today,' Mautista raged, pointing at the body out in the paddies beyond, 'because you men could not follow simple orders. When I say keep those Kalisadors suppressed, you do it! Not do it when you feel like doing it!'

The sight of the ranting Disciple terrified the guerrillas. Wispy thin and white, he became a tower of rage. He scared them. He was a wraith in their eyes.

But Mautista was not done yet. He squinted at each and every insurgent, cursing, berating and screaming at each of them individually, then as a group, then individually again. He grabbed them by the scruffs of their necks and manhandled them. His wiry limbs had become surprisingly strong and he tossed them around like children.

'What do we do now?' said Suloe, a guerrilla who had developed hard, finger-like nails across his face and upper neck.

Mautista calmed himself down to breathe raggedly. He was still clouded with red rage but he was lucid enough to at least speak normally. 'We regroup and attack. What other choice do we have? At the very least, I will not return empty-handed.'

As the guerrillas refreshed their magazines, Mautista took a moment to remind them of what was at stake. 'The first fighter who fires before he is told, or breaks orders… the Dos Pares will dispose of you accordingly.'

Like shambling, grizzly primates, the Riverine emerged after two days of hard travel through the aqueous jungle. They were filthier and sicker than they had ever been before.

Their uniforms were sodden rags, hidden beneath a crust of gore, mud, salt and blood. The beard of every Guardsman had hardened into a slab of dirty, dreadlocked hair. No doubt, if Baeder could smell himself or the men around him, they would have reeked of putrid human waste. But they had become accustomed to the smell now and, for most, they were too tired to care.

A third of the men were sick with fever. The conditions had brutalised their immune systems and even the tiniest grazes were prone to rapid infection. Baeder himself had swollen glands and a head that was clogged with mucus. This was compounded by a chronic shortage of fresh water. Their supply barges were down to one-fifth capacity. They did not have enough to drink, let alone wash their infected cuts. The river water was a cesspit of bacteria and the men who had dared to drink from it had only become sicker, wracked by diarrhoea.

The steaming subtropical climate turned their discomfort into sweltering torture. The toils of the past weeks were accumulating now, wearing down their combat effectiveness. The men were not pleased and Baeder could read it on their grimaces. Even the most ordinary tasks of manning sentry guns or refuelling the motors elicited pained groans and grumbles. Many of them had doubted the legitimacy of their mission prior to deployment and now their afflictions affirmed their dissent. Once the initial anticipation of deployment had faded, Baeder could almost hear the discontented murmurs of his men as he lay awake in his bunk at night. Yet they were too deep in the enemy interior for him to be distracted by such things now. They could only go forwards.

According to his maps, which Baeder had learnt not to rely on, the siege-batteries were entrenched no more than eighty kilometres away as they exited the basin. The river system opened out into slow-moving, almost stagnant current as they left the coastal regions behind them.

Prior to the insurgency, the Planetary Defence Force of Solo-Bastón had patrolled these inland regions. The flotilla passed the remains of their outposts by the water. There were guard stations erected every several kilometres, solitary blockhouses that looked over docking piers on the water. Over the months these outposts had fallen into disrepair. Veiny creepers claimed the walls and rust had corroded the mesh compound fences. The patrol boats had long since been stolen from the now empty piers. Windows were smashed in and graffiti was scrawled spitefully on the stone walls. Looking into those dark, empty windows, Baeder wondered what lay inside. The place smelt of sadness and loss; it was like looking at a portrait of someone who was already long dead.

Baeder remembered seeing pict slides of the former militia forces during intelligence briefs, when he had been en route to planetary deployment. They were all young men clad in fresh brown leather armour. A polished metal pauldron on their left shoulder bore a cauldron crab emblem: an honorary symbol of the Kalisadors who were the custodians of the traditional tribes. They reminded Baeder of his own soldiers. It was haunting to think that most of them were now dead.

Intelligence had reported that the local forces had numbered only six thousand strong. They played no more than a peacekeeping role and were not trained for major theatres of conflict. In reality, their one true purpose had been to operate the colossal siege-battery at the centre of the mainland against phantom enemies. When the insurgency reached its greatest momentum, the PDF had been overrun and it was reported that many of them had turned and sided with the insurgency.

Baeder saluted the guard stations out of respect as they drifted by. Local militia or Guard, they were the Imperium's fighting men and they had deserved a proper burial.

'I heard some of those boys could not even bring themselves to fire their weapons. That's a sad tale,' said Sergeant Pulver, stepping up on deck.

It was highly unusual and risky for a senior sergeant to sail on the same vessel as his battalion commander. But for Baeder, it had been even more unusual that Sergeant Pulver had requested to do so. Baeder knew the veteran Guardsman would not otherwise do it, unless something was at stake, and so he had bent regulation, just this once.

'They could not bring themselves to fire on their own people?' asked Baeder.

Pulver shook his head sadly. 'No. Poor leadership. On my first patrol here, I found a squad of dead militia boys in the bush. They were all still holding fully-loaded weapons. Their squad leader was shot in the back twenty or thirty metres away. He had tried to run.'

'It's not easy doing what they do.'

Pulver chewed his tabac in silence for several long minutes. Then he squinted at Baeder, eyeballing him with steady appraisal.

'I heard about what you did back in the basin village.'

Baeder stiffened. He clasped his hands behind his back, unsure of what the sergeant major would make of it.

'It takes a lot to do that for your men,' said Pulver, pausing to spit his dip. 'Takes a lot,' he repeated.

Baeder regarded the sergeant major curiously. The sergeant major had always seemed a broad, imposing man. But now, as Baeder spoke to him, he realised Pulver was a short bundle of wire and sinew.

Baeder was by no means a big man. Back at the schola tactica he had participated as a wrestler in the sixty-five kilogram division. Yet Pulver was even shorter and leaner, despite being twenty years his senior. The sergeant major had only seemed twice as large as he was through his presence. He had the brick wall disdain of a giant.

'What scares me is that it was easier than I thought it would be,' Baeder admitted. 'Razing that entire village to the ground. I… don't feel any guilt.'

'You squashed down that part of you. That's all. You might never get that back. Those people who weren't born to be combat officers, they won't ever understand that. Some do.'

It suddenly dawned on Baeder that Sergeant Major Pulver was making peace. He was bridging the rift that had been between them ever since Baeder had been assigned to the 88th. The days ahead would be hard. The battalion was already battered and they would likely lose many more. Pulver was cementing their leadership for battle. The resolve in Pulver's sun-creased face told him everything.

Baeder wasn't sure what to say. Only now did he finally understand the hostility that Pulver had shown him. The sergeant major had seen Baeder as just another officer who regarded the 88th as tactical fodder. The battalion was a single entity and Pulver was protecting it like a herd mother against anything who would harm them, be it Archenemy or Imperial. In doing so, Pulver had made himself into a cold, logical automaton, he had given up the luxuries of compassion and choice. Baeder felt a surge of respect for the old veteran.

Pulver spat into the water. 'If we don't keep our men safe, no one will. High Command doesn't care about sending us to the meat grinder. It's us against them. That's all it is.'

'Fight and win,' Baeder said.

'Fight and win,' Pulver repeated.

The battalion moved into what was considered the red zone by late afternoon. On their tactical maps, it encompassed a sixty-kilometre radius from where the siege-batteries were expected to be hidden. This was the heart of Dos Pares territory and, incidentally, it had been the target of a relentless bombing campaign since the early stages of war.

The signs of destruction became more evident the deeper the battalion travelled. At first there was a general thinning of the dense foliage. Further on, entire patches of jungle were flattened, visible even from a distance.

Imperial bombs had been thorough. It appeared as if pieces of rainforest had been entirely uprooted, and then wood splinters had been spread where acres of trees had once been. The shockwave of explosives flattened the areas surrounding bomb craters. Gum-saps, buttress roots, flowering cynometra, were all laid down in uniform direction. There was a strange order to the systematic destruction.

Although there was a tense, fragile silence in the air, the day passed without incident. It was not until twilight, when the sun was melting to a diffuse orange, that their overwatch flier voxed Baeder with an urgent message.

'Eight eight, this is Angel One.'

Baeder had become accustomed to that voice now. Although he had never met the pilot who had helped him time and time again, Baeder had often wondered what their saviour looked like. There was an omnipotence to Lieutenant Duponti's role. A distant, gravelly voice that had, on multiple occasions, saved the lives of his men. A voice without a face who hovered in the sky.

'Come in, Angel One. I'm reading you loud and clear,' Baeder voxed from the helm.

'I thought you should know, I may have found a loyalist village just two kilometres north-west of your current position. I picked up their distress frequency through a pre-war channel. They are requesting assistance.'

'What kind of assistance?' asked Baeder, suddenly wary. He immediately thought of a trap. This close to their objective, the insurgency would be trying everything to stop them.

'They are besieged and surrounded by a warband-strength insurgent element. There has been sporadic gunfighting for the past four hours. The village has managed to keep them at bay but it seems they are running out of ammunition. That's all I know from listening in on their broadcasts.'

'Do you think it's a trap?'

'The red zone is too hot for me to go low altitude. I'd be shot out of the sky so hard it'd knock the dirt off my boots. But they sound desperate enough over the vox. Plenty of screaming and crying. I can't speak to them directly, but I've been monitoring their frequency for a good twenty minutes.'

'Could be a trap,' said Baeder, still unsure.

'Could be. Look, I'm not advising you whether or not to send assistance. But I thought I'd brief you on what I just picked up on my frequency.'

'Understood,' said Baeder.

'Whatever you decide, be careful, eight eight. This is deep hell we're in now.'

'Understood, Angel One. Stay on vox.'

Baeder heard Duponti whistle into his vox receiver. 'I can tell by your voice that you've already made up your mind to go in. I'll be on call. If things go wrong, I'll come down and hit hard. Over.'

'Right on, ramrod. Out.'

Duponti was right, of course, Baeder had already decided to gather a relief force. If these were loyalists, then he had a duty to protect them. Perhaps several months ago, that would have been Baeder's sole reason to gather a scouting party. But not any more. Now, all that mattered to Baeder was that his men needed water and, whether loyalist or not, the village would no doubt have a fresh supply. The monsoon season had faded for the past several days and they were parched. Clean water would go a long way to mitigating some of their ailments.

Try as he might, Baeder could not convince himself that he actually cared about whether the village truly needed help. It was simply a way to resupply their rations.

Baeder and Serpent Company's Third Platoon beached their rubberised landers beneath the branches of a bomb-felled cynometra. The thirty men and their colonel spread out into an open file and swept inland under the cover of darkness. They hugged the riverbank north-west, keeping low by the rushes and moving quickly.

Baeder had chosen Third Platoon not because they were the best or most experienced, but simply because they were one of the few platoons at full fighting strength. The platoon commander was a Lieutenant Hulsen, a young officer on his first off-world campaign. Although he was a combat virgin, Hulsen was keen and possessed by the wide-eyed vigour of a newly-minted platoon commander. He wore a belt of grenades across his chest, chewed tabac without pause and swore too often. He had even managed to trade a meltagun from the base quartermaster. Baeder would have to keep an eye on the lieutenant's enthusiasm lest it ran rampant during the heat of engagement.

Pulver and Mortlock had both initially protested Baeder leading the relief force. Although it was agreed that the village was a potential water source, the threat of their battalion commander going into a trap did not sit well with the others. This far into their mission, the death of Baeder would plummet morale. Yet Baeder had insisted. Neither Pulver nor Mortlock were noted for their diplomacy and the siege would likely require more than brute force.

The platoon realised they were nearing the site of the distress beacon when the crump of a shotgun shattered the night. The shot was followed by a flurry of small-arms fire. Although it was too dark to make out anything, the direction of the shooting was clear enough to practised ears.

'Hulsen. Take a knee,' hissed Baeder as he settled down behind a waxy shrub.

'They're still fighting, then,' whispered Hulsen as he crouched down next to Baeder.

'Must be. If this siege is not some elaborate set-up, then we will need to reach the village without being caught in a crossfire. It's going to be dark and I don't want to be shot at by the very same indigs that we're here to help.'

Hulsen chewed vigorously, his jaw clenching and relaxing, his eyes wide in the gloom. 'What do you want me to do, sir?'

'We need to contact the village on their distress frequency, let them know we are going in. We need them to cover us as we make a run across the open ground. Then we'll curve up along the riverbank and enter the village from the river edge to avoid the crossfire. Understood?'

Hulsen punched the side of his helmet twice in acknowledgement. He hobbled away at a low sprint to find his vox-officer. Meanwhile, Baeder turned back to survey the land with his magnoculars. He filtered the lens into night vision and took a moment to adjust his vision.

The land was a two-dimensional monochrome green. He could see the village at two or three hundred metres to his front, the lights of the town appearing as white stars. In between the sporadic bursts of fire, Baeder could make out defenders firing along the long village wall, and enemy gunmen hidden amongst the cassam paddies to the left of his platoon. It was obvious that the insurgents were amateurs. The very fact that the village had managed to keep them at bay told Baeder that the warband was too frightened to make any determined assault on the village. Instead, they skulked out in the rural fields, firing at the fortified town. They were probably hoping the villagers would run out of ammunition before they did. Any Imperial Guard platoon with good fire and movement could have taken that village in minutes.

After several tense minutes, Hulsen returned. 'Contact made, sir. We should get moving,' he hissed as he dropped down heavily beside Baeder.

Baeder immediately signalled for his men to rise. He slapped the helmets of his men as they ran past him. The platoon broke out into a sprint towards the walled town, rifles up and webbing swinging on their hips.

Kalisador Mano Mato-Barea racked his shotgun pump and fired over the barricade ledge. He crouched down quickly as the inevitable blast of counter fire kicked up sparks along the upper wall.

On the other side, he could hear the whoops and taunts of the insurgent raiders. They were creeping closer. Mano could feel them swelling with boldness as the hours dragged by, their insults getting louder and their laughter more cruel. Once he ran out of shotgun shells, the raiders would come and it would be a massacre. Mano loaded six into the breech, counting another twenty-four laid out on the ground in front of him. At the beginning of the day, the village had had five hundred shells saved up in storage, foraged and bartered over the past months. They had been a precious insurance. He never imagined they would use up everything in the span of a single day. Their situation was so desperate now it did not even seem real.

The villagers were hiding in their homes, locked and barred. If Mano strained to listen, he swore he could hear sobs, faint and muffled, coming from the houses. They knew that it was only a matter of time before the raiders came. They all knew what fate awaited loyalist villagers who refused to serve the Dos Pares.

A tracer whined overhead, followed by another ripple of laughter.

Mano breathed heavily. He was too old to be doing this. They had been fighting for four or five hours and the adrenaline had long since passed, leaving him drained. Kalisador Babaal squatted on his haunches next to him. Leaner and younger, Babaal had spent much of the day sprinting up and down the wall, firing from different positions in order to keep the raiders away. Mano had a difficult time keeping up with his younger counterpart.

'If you give up now, we will allow your women and children to live,' shouted a voice in the darkness.

'A curse on your ancestors!' Mano swore. He counted to three and shoved the barrel of his shotgun over the barricade. He fired three errant shots in rapid succession.

The exchange was followed by an awkward stillness.

Then the tiny phonetic vox placed next to Mano began to whir and beep. It was an ageing device left in the village by Ecclesiarchal preachers from when Mano was just a young man. The wooden veneer was peeling away and one of the mesh speakers was punctured. Mano was not even certain they had been able to broadcast distress pulses on old Imperial channels. Yet as the vox began fizzing with incoming signal, Mano's heart began to skip.

'Imperial channel bravo beacon. Do you read? Over.'

The voice coming through the speakers was barely a whisper, washed over by static, but Mano was sure he had heard correctly. He snatched up the metal transceiver from its stand and raised his voice without realising.

'Yes, receiving! We are the Mato-Barea people. We are in need of Imperial aid!' Mano screamed.

'We are a platoon-strength element of the 31st Riverine Amphibious. My men are on your map grid and will enter your village from the northern river-edge. Keep the enemy down with suppressing fire to your front. Out.'

Platoon-strength element. Those were the three sweetest words Mano could hope for. He decided, there and then, that the Emperor truly did watch over his people. He leaned over the barricade and fought with renewed hope, blasting shot after shot into the darkness. Babaal did the same and together they emptied out the remaining two dozen shells in an effort to aid their incoming rescuers.

The platoon arrived shortly after, vaulting over the left side of the village wall, where a disused plough reinforced multiple layers of rusted sheet. In the gloom he saw several dark figures drop over the wall. At first Mano thought they had been tricked. The men inside the barricade appeared to be no more than roughshod river bandits. They were the most ragged-looking Guardsmen Mano had ever seen. They looked nothing like the portraits of square-jawed soldiers depicted in those guidance pamphlets that their preachers used to hand out. These men wore ragged shorts and shredded boots, the remains of their uniforms faded to dirty white. Dreadlocked hair hung like manes from their shoulders, shaggy, brutal and wild.

But the way they moved showed they were unmistakably Guard. The troopers fanned out wordlessly to secure the perimeter of the wall. They moved quickly, setting up sectors of fire and creating intersecting arcs with heavy stubbers. Within seconds, the village was secured by Imperial Guardsmen who had not even spoken a word to either of the shocked Kalisadors in their midst.

Only then did a short, slim and unbearded officer approach them. Mano was not sure if it was just the waning moonlight or the angle of the shadows, but the small man seemed the most frightening out of all those hairy giants. He carried his lasrifle with bayonet fixed as if he were waiting to use it. His face was handsome, dark and slightly bat-like with an upturned nose and glinting eyes. His size was augmented by his brooding presence. In the Bastón tongue the officer had plenty of *Kamidero*, the closest translation in Low Gothic being – 'bad intentions'.

'Evening, friendo,' said the officer in a slow, drawling accent. 'Colonel Fyodor Baeder has come to save your soul.'

Baeder hazarded a peek over the barricade with his magnoculars. In the grainy night vision he could see the humps of men hiding in the irrigation ditches of paddy fields. He counted sixteen men in his field of vision, loosely scattered in an arc roughly fifty metres away. He could not see if there were others, but Baeder expected there to be more men, hidden further away to provide covering fire.

Lieutenant Hulsen and Corporal Eckert crouch-ran over to Baeder's side. Eckert was young and his eyes were wide in the moonlight. He was clearly frightened.

'What's the plan, sir?' Hulsen whispered breathily.

'Let's flak them,' Eckert said. The corporal made ready to unpin a grenade from his web harness.

'No,' Baeder said, placing a hand over the corporal's chosen grenade for restraint. 'We're too close. They'll throw the grenade back. It's too much risk.'

Eckert licked his lips and peered over the barricade. 'I can hit them from here, sir. I can. It's no problem.'

Baeder shook his head again. 'No, corporal.'

But Eckert did not seem convinced. Baeder felt like a patient father chastising his over-excited son. He understood how Eckert felt. The atmosphere was charged with a quiet, deadly tension and the corporal wanted to dispel it with firepower. It was a natural instinct.

'Sir, let's finish this with grenades,' Eckert pressed.

Hulsen did not have Baeder's patience. 'Damnit, Eckert! Shut the frag up! The colonel said no.'

Eckert fell silent with a thoroughly dejected look on his face.

Suddenly, a las-shot exploded against the barricade. The kinetic energy sent reverberations along the jig-sawed metal. Baeder sank deeper down onto his haunches and put a hand over his helmet. A flurry of shots followed the first.

'Come out! Come out!' shouted one of the insurgents in a high-pitched stringy voice. There was a crackle of laughter.

Baeder pushed his lasrifle over the edge of the barricade and fired a string of blind shots. The laughter abated.

Lieutenant Hulsen cupped his hands over his mouth and shouted. 'Put down your arms and submit to Imperial authority!'

The insurgents mocked him in heavily accented Low Gothic. *'Purt down your arms and submeet to Eemperil'*. There was more laughter from the other side.

This made Baeder angry. 'Let's give them something to laugh about,' he grumbled. He realised that both sides were deadlocked, their weapons aimed to cut down any flicker of movement. Part of him began to panic, realising that perhaps he had exposed his men and himself to danger again. Risking a platoon for a water resupply was a reckless idea. He forced himself to suppress the thought and concentrated on the task at hand.

'Eckert, Hulsen,' said Baeder. 'Sieber, Noke, Hilversum, Bosch. I'm going to call flak! Ous?'

'Ous!' affirmed the men.

Eckert's edginess was replaced by a wide, tabac-smeared grin.

'Is this a good idea, sir?' Lieutenant Hulsen asked hesitantly.

Baeder shrugged. 'What other choice do we have to break this stalemate?' He waved his hand and clenched his fist three times for the others in the platoon. 'The rest of you, fix bayonets. You move when I move! Ous!'

'Ous!'

Baeder took a deep breath. The sting of fyceline cleared his head. Gun smoke and scorched metal. The smells helped to settle him. 'Flaks out!' he shouted.

Dark orbs were tossed through the air. They landed in the dry grass beyond the ditches with dry thuds. Baeder put his hands to his ears and scrunched himself down. There was a concussive eruption of sound. The ground trembled. A drizzle of debris clattered off the back of his flak vest.

'Go, go! Move on me!' Baeder screamed above the ring of post-explosion. He rose and vaulted over the barricade. Smoke, white and solid, rose in coils. Baeder charged forwards and almost turned his ankle on the uneven ground. He slipped, but regained his balance. He couldn't see if his men were following him; he simply had to trust that they were.

The Carnibalès were surprised by his sudden appearance. Baeder found one of them crouched in a drainage ditch with his head down, fiddling with a grenade of his own. Baeder stabbed him with his bayonet between the shoulder blades and drove him into the mud. Las flashed in the smoke pall, pinks and incandescent whites. The screams were loud.

A Carnibalès rose out of the darkness. He appeared above the ditch, standing over Baeder. In the moonlight, his teeth were sharp and white, lined up neatly in a mouth that stretched from earlobe to earlobe. Baeder pulled up his lasrifle at the same time the insurgent brought his autogun to bear. But before either could react, the Carnibalès toppled sideways, his grin and half of his face crushed by a fen-hammer. A Riverine brought the hammer down again on the insurgent's prone form before rushing into the next ditch.

'They're running!' someone shouted. 'We've got them running!'

Gripping his lasgun in blood-slicked hands, Baeder gave chase across the moonlit fields.

CHAPTER TWELVE

It had been a bad day for Mautista.

The sudden barrage of fire from the Mato-Barea walls had driven his warband away from their positions. Under the swift and unexpected assault, his guerrillas lost their nerve and ran. Mautista had no choice but to run with them. As they fled back into the rainforest, Mautista could not help but lament at his ill fortune. What had been the odds that he would engage Imperial military forces on his very first raid?

Certainly, Mautista had heard rumours that a large Imperial formation had been spearing inland. But the rumours had been fragmentary, drifting from village to village. The insurgency's spy networks were disparate and news often did not travel to the leaders until it was too late to be of use.

Mautista had not expected the enemy to be in his region. The last he had heard of it, the insurgency had gathered a force of some six thousand men – both Carnibalès and commoner – and ousted the Imperial force. At Lauzon it was believed they had beaten the Imperial troops into retreat. The Dos Pares had even distributed victory leaflets showing vivid illustrations of mutilated Imperial soldiers to the surrounding villages. Mautista had seen the leaflets himself; the Dos Pares claimed to have vanquished the enemy at Lauzon and released the survivors back to the coast with dire warnings for any other expeditions that might dare to probe inland. Evidently that had not been the case.

As the enemy gave chase, Mautista's warband dispersed into

well-prepared escape holes. It was quite dark, but the enemy sent out searchers. Imperial soldiers with searchlights as well as village militia were thrashing the branches and shrubs in search of his guerrillas. Mautista lay in the hatchway of a tunnel, his upper body bare and covered by a fallen branch, watching the hunt. Not all of his guerrillas had managed to reach the tunnels that led back into the Dos Pares underground bunkers. Some, in their desperation, had crawled into prepared hiding places to wait out the search. As he lay in hiding with the torch beams of his pursuers sweeping over his hide, Mautista had a creeping doubt that perhaps Dos Pares propaganda had been inaccurate in their assessment of the enemy disposition. The armed Guardsmen that were hunting for him did not seem to fear him like the victory leaflets had claimed.

They found Balu first. Underneath some frond leaves the soldiers spotted the rim of a man-sized water pot buried in the soil. When the leaves were sifted aside, Balu was curled within. To his credit, Balu did not die without a fight. He hurled up a frag grenade from the pot. But the soldiers kicked the frag back over the rim and jumped away before it exploded. Just to be sure, the soldiers fired their lasguns several times into the pot, point-blank.

After some more digging, they found Phillero huddled within the buttress roots of a giant gum-sap. Mautista could not see what happened from where he lay, but he heard the las-shots and Phillero's dying yelp clear enough.

Then they found Caledo. Lifting a thatched lid, they discovered him wedged inside an escape tunnel that led deep into the Dos Pares bunker systems. Fortunately, Caledo knew what was at stake. He collapsed the entry by unpinning a grenade and holding it to his chest. The village militia who found him shouted in surprise and lunged away in all directions as the grenade went off.

To the relief of Mautista's rapidly accelerating heart rate, the pursuers then gave up. They milled about, laughing and talking and sharing tabac, but the hunting was done. They left soon after, their voices still echoing in the rainforest as Mautista extracted himself from the manhole. The remains of the warband reluctantly came out of hiding. There were only eleven men left.

'Everything fell apart today,' Canao said as they gathered by a camouflaged entry tunnel.

'Get in the tunnel,' Mautista snapped, his nerves fraying. The guerrillas, their faces gleaming with a day's sweat, looked at him with a mixture of fear and despair.

Canao ushered the insurgents into the bolt hole. 'Don't worry, we'll get some rest and begin tomorrow anew,' the veteran assured the others.

'No,' Mautista said flatly. 'No rest today. When we get back to camp no one will sleep until I say so. We are going to run fire and movement drills. We would not have been so shamed today if you lot had a shred of discipline,' he snarled.

There was a low murmur of complaint but no one dared to argue. They were beginning to fear their leader. Mautista was not sure whether Imperial officers ruled with fear, or whether they controlled their men through some other means. But as long as his guerrillas were terrified of him, there was hope for them yet.

As far as calculated risks went, Baeder's gambit had paid off. The 88th Battalion unloaded over a thousand empty jerry cans from their supply barges and vessels. Seeker and Serpent Company formed a work chain from the boats all the way up to the catchment silos at the edge of the village. They passed empty containers from the vessels up the line. Sloshing, laden containers were relayed back down the line. They toiled under the gaze of sentry gunners. Both infantry on land and mounted guns on the river kept a vigilant watch of their surroundings.

Baeder joined in the labour at the front of the line. His arms burned as he plunged the canisters into the water silos, bubbling and gurgling as they filled to capacity. He hauled them, one in each hand, back down the ladder and towards the waiting work teams before receiving yet more empty ones. It was tiring work and, even in the breeze of midnight, he was lathered with sweat.

It was a great relief to Baeder's cramping forearms when the villagers arrived with midnight supper. Crustaceans, simmered in brine and bay salt, were placed in fish kettles on the ground, along with boiled cassam and vinegar. Guardsmen and villagers alike settled on the packed earth to share the shellfish: rural Bastón food in its simplest form. The battalion ate on shift rotations and Baeder kept watch. An officer never ate before his men, but when it came time for him to eat, Baeder did so with vigour. The cassam tubers were floury and still steaming, filling the stomach easily when dipped in salt and vinegars. Best of all were the various crustaceans of all sizes collected along the mud banks: spiny, clawed, segmented, yet all forms yielding a sweet white meat.

So it was with great reluctance that Baeder put down his cracked tail of crustacean as Kalisador Mano appeared amongst the supping and beckoned for him. The older Kalisador, with the thick heavy shoulders and hands, was skipping with joy.

'Colonel, I have something to show you. This you must see!' he said, his words tripping with liqour.

Wiping his mouth against a frayed sleeve, Baeder followed the Kalisador through the village. It was dark in the night, except for the ebbing blush of Persepian bombers in the far horizon. Baeder groped his way to a chapel that dominated the centre of the village. He understood that Mano was likely riding on the high of surviving to see morning, but whatever was making him so joyous made Baeder more than curious.

The chapel was an upright oblong with a pointed sloping roof. It was evident from its design that the locals had attempted to emulate the sharp angles and towering scale of Copto-Gothic architecture. But the effect largely fell flat by way of poor construction. Sections of the wall peeled away stiffly, an inevitable result of the rusting metal and wood frame that was common for most indigenous buildings. The chapel sagged several degrees to the side, and its long curtained windows gave it the bearing of a frowning old face.

Stepping inside, the chapel's interior matched its outer facade. Absent were the pews that Baeder expected. Instead an assortment of chairs, some plastek, some wood and some which resembled upturned crates, lined both sides of the chapel. A patchwork of reed rugs led up the centre aisle towards an Imperial shrine at the far end. There, above the candles, was displayed a large aquila, forged from old machine parts. It spread its corrugated wings above the shrine, heavy and dignified in a rough way. The worship shrine was a mix of Imperial votive offerings and local fetishism. It was a gaudy riot of bric-a-brac, piled together in contrasting lots. Ecclesiarchal volumes shared prominence with straw dolls, dried flowers were spread over priestly robes and multi-coloured candles burned slowly above the entire display.

Mano sat down on a rocking chair and produced a flask. He rocked on his chair and took a swig, looking out of the windows as if he had forgotten what he was doing. Another rocking chair beside him was empty. Baeder sat down next to him, waiting for him to speak. There they sat, rocking on chairs in silence, staring out into the horizon as bombs flashed.

'The Dos Pares have been on this world for much longer than the Emperor's servants,' said Mano finally. His voice was lowered to a reverential whisper.

Baeder pretended to nod knowingly. In truth, it was something he had not known. As far as the Imperial war effort was concerned, the Dos Pares was a populist sentiment of the insurgency, a rebellious movement that had arisen to challenge three centuries of Imperial rule. The notion that the Dos Pares had influenced the indigenous population since before Imperial settlement was something Baeder had never considered.

Two hundred and seventy years before, Imperial settlement fleets had touched down on the tropically abundant planet of Solo-Bastón. The indigenous tribes had welcomed the settlers and their Imperial missionaries as long lost human ancestry. The settlers brought with them new methods of agriculture, new customs and the teachings of the God-Emperor. All these things the indigenous tribes had embraced, blending into the folds of their tradition.

A peace had formed over the centuries. The Imperial government secured settlement on the coastal mainland and on outpost islands, building thriving metropoles of commerce and authority. In turn, the indigenous tribes maintained semi-rural cantons along the river systems, providing the central provinces with trade and taxation. Except for the jungle raiders from the heartlands, peace had been a stable commodity on Solo-Bastón.

'The Dos Pares were here before the days of settlement?' Baeder asked.

'Far longer. Back to the time of creation,' said Mano. 'But not like they are now. They were visitors from the sun and moon. I'll show you.'

Rising to his feet, Mano waded amongst the shrine ornaments, groping in the candlelight until he found what he was looking for. Slowly, he extracted a heavy object from the mess. He blew the dust from it, polished it with a flat of his palm, then brought it under the candlelight for Baeder to see.

Baeder felt his mouth slacken with involuntary shock.

Before him was a helmet. It was old. So very old that a rocky growth of mould grew like barnacles across its black-red surface. The full helm itself was very much like the ones worn by heroes of the Astartes Chapters, but there the similarities ended. Its grilled snout and slitted eyes were sculpted into a yawning, simian visage. Horns of polished ebony curled from its brow and a coif of chainmail trailed down the nape.

'What is that?' Baeder asked. Although he already knew the answer, and already dreaded the reply, he needed to hear it voiced by another man. Just so he could know he was not dreaming.

'It is a piece left behind by the visitors from the sky. We have revered this in our village for nine hundred years,' Mano declared, patting the helmet.

'May I see it?' asked Baeder hesitantly, both repelled and yearning to touch the helmet. He reached out with trembling hands and cupped it in his palms.

It was cold and heavy. Very heavy. Baeder had to clench his upper body just to hold up the twenty kilograms of solid ceramite. Upon closer inspection, the mould growth seemed organic to the helmet itself, bubbling up from the oily black surface. Despite its great age, there was no visible corrosion and the contorted cheekbones and crooked mouth looked freshly forged.

It was common knowledge that, in Bastón superstition, all inanimate objects contained a certain spirit. Plants could be sung to, and broken machinery coerced gently into operation. Holding the helmet in his hands, Baeder understood how such a myth could have been brought about. The helmet stared at him, not as a well-painted portrait would gaze upon a viewer, but stared *at him* with expression. Baeder gave it back to Mano and brushed his hands.

'This helmet changes expression. Sometimes it laughs, sometimes it cries and sometimes it is angry,' Mano said, confirming Baeder's tingling chill.

'These visitors, what did they do here?'

'Very rarely, sometimes not at all for many years, a village may have a sighting. When they do, these ghosts from the clouds choose the sturdiest village boys and spirit them away. This helmet is said to have belonged to a guro's son from a millennium ago, who was taken away to become one of the cloud ghosts. His helmet was returned to his kin as a mark of favour.'

Baeder slumped into his seat, blinking repeatedly. It did not bother him that these loyalist indigenes did not even know they were pawns of the Archenemy. Nor that they were unwilling heretics. It did not matter to Baeder. What put the fear into his core was the prospect that the Traitor Astartes were architects of this insurgency. The implication of this revelation was too much for him. He did not know what hand the Legions of Chaos were playing in this conflict. But the thought that his battalion could be the target of a scheme laid down by Traitor Astartes invoked a bowel-churning panic that he fought to quell.

'Mano. If I were you I would burn that thing.'

At this, the Kalisador's pudgy face was drawn into a frown. He hugged the relic close to his chest and angled it away from Baeder, as if to protect it. 'Why?'

Baeder shrugged. 'I do not hold any presumptions against you. But if men of an Ecclesiarchal leaning were to catch you with it, I expect even ten platoons of my battalion would not save your village.'

Mano sighed. He put down the helmet and resumed sitting next to Baeder. Again he grew quiet. 'It doesn't matter,' he concluded. 'You will leave and the Carnibalès will return. There is nothing left for us to do.' Mano rocked on his chair, drinking, lost in his own thoughts as the faraway bombing continued.

CHAPTER THIRTEEN

The bridge of the *Emperor's Anvil* was frantic with activity. A single long-range vox from the 88th Battalion declaring that the battalion had reached the red zone had spurred the entire war effort into high alert. It was the clarion call they had been waiting for.

Above the throb of engines, the hiss of boilers and creaking of steel, boots pounded the decking. In the bridge room, movement and noise were predominant. There were too many officers wedged into a narrow space trying to do too many things at once. The relay of information between vox and staff became a slurred babble.

At high anchor on the Pan-Spheric Ocean, aboard every Argo-Nautical in the combat fleet, klaxons began to wail. It was a call to arms. All Imperial elements were to prepare for deployment.

In the officers' mess aboard the *Iron Ishmael*, onboard speakers commanded all officers to return immediately to their units. Guardsmen mobbed the corridors, all streaming towards their designated stations. As of 19.00, stand down for the Caliguan forces in reserve ended. They were to be at full readiness by midnight.

Guardsmen crowded the flight deck. A restrained sense of excitement rippled amongst the assembled soldiers. The *Emperor's Anvil* was making steam, getting ready to sail.

Major General Montalvo stood on a platform raised below the antennae masts to address the assembled men. His speech was short and direct. 'Gentlemen. After so much waiting, we announce our presence.

Make them fear us. Make their children's children remember the day they chose to fight the Imperial Guard.'

The Nautical fleet bellowed with sonorous engines, preparing to sail unmolested towards the Bastón coast. The energy was building as Guardsmen spread word that a Riverine battalion was on the verge of reclaiming the mainland's super-heavy defences. After months waiting at sea, the Guardsmen were eager to put their boots on dry land.

Within the troop holds of the Argo-Nauticals, Caliguan Motor Rifles were rousing from months of stand-down. In the cavernous docking bellies, tens of thousands of Caliguans were preparing their transports and organising their gear. Chimeras, armoured trucks, Trojan support vehicles parked in rows, were getting fuelled.

The atmosphere was one of loose, steady calm. Caliguan Guardsmen joked and talked as they went about their business. Although the call for action would likely be hours if not days away, every soldier was required to be on standby.

Guardsmen rattled through their labours, already laden with heavy webbing rigs and weapons. Over their padded brown jumpsuits were chest rigs with bulging pockets. With lasguns strapped to their chests, the Guardsmen rested their hands over their combat gear and waddled like pregnant women.

Despite their personal load, the Caliguan Guardsmen were stocking equipment up the rear ramps of their Chimeras. The cramped confines were stacked with boxes of ammunition, rations, grenade satchels, missile tubes, mortars and tanks of water. Considering the bulky personal combat load of each Guardsman, fitting into the vehicles would be an art in itself.

As the men worked, officers went from track to track, distributing stimms and dip for what would be an extended combat operation. The stimms would keep them alert and chewing dip promoted aggression. Alertness and aggression were the cornerstones of a Guard assault. Grimly, preachers followed in their wake, distributing last rites. The ship's bay sirens whooped every quarter-hour, marking down the time to deployment. There was a sense of bravado compelled by urgency that electrified the air.

Five hours after the call to deploy, General Montalvo toured the staging areas in person, travelling from ship to ship. Everywhere he went, Guardsmen scrambled to their feet. Tabac was stamped out by thick-soled boots. The men roared, a ferocious sound that was not quite a cheer nor a gesture of any civilised sort. It was just an expulsion of pent-up energy.

'It's time. It's time,' was all the general said.

For the final hours until they received word to mount up, the troops slept in their gear, rifles by their sides, on the metal decking of the staging areas. Officers tried to maintain their energy by parading them in platoon, then in company order, then platoon again. Restless, anxious and ready, the men thirsted for the call.

Sixty thousand Caliguan soldiers were at bay like hunting dogs, ready to be uncaged. Alongside the Persepian infantry, over one hundred thousand men pre-empting a single vox-signal. They would wait for the siege-batteries to fall quiet. When that time came, they would let the Carnibalès know – *'The Imperial Guard are coming for you'.*

The torrential rain doused the burnt jungle sodden. Precipitation churned the ash into a wasteland of silvery grey mud flats. The swathes of rainforest that remained were yellowed by defoliant, wilting like overcooked vegetables. Baeder found it hard to believe that the Archenemy insurgents still managed to resist from the interior despite the destruction.

But resist they did.

Strung up, crucified on X-beams of wood, were heat-swollen corpses. Initially, Baeder had spotted them along the riverbank, black and bulbous. From a distance they had looked like knapsacks and Baeder had not recognised what they were. It was only when the wind changed direction, carrying with it the saline stench of rot, that he realised they were the remains of the local troops. Evidently, they served as warning.

Ignoring the enemy theatrics, Baeder trained his magnoculars out into the distance, setting the aperture to maximum zoom. He could see the rising swell of the Kalinga Curtain, a ridge of limestone hills approximately eight kilometres to the north. Those limestone hills were layered long ago by the calcium deposits of corals and brachiopods within prehistoric reefs. Over the millions of years, monsoons had sculptured a one-kilometre chain of naturally defensible ground that the Bastón tribes had fought to control ever since the beginning.

According to intelligence, those hills would be their target. They appeared as a spine of bumpy hillocks, ravines and intrusions draped in floristic growth. Although bombing had gouged balding chunks of flora from the hillsides, the forests on the steep scree slopes were hardy. Growing in tight, irregular clumps, they clung to rock shelves and crevices, almost in defiance of the Imperial bombs.

It was little wonder that the militia had chosen the Kalinga Curtain as the housing station for the mainland's defence batteries. Somewhere among the rugged limestone blocks, the colossal super-heavy guns were bunkered down. External military compounds studded the hilltops and hollows. Kalinga would be crawling with insurgent forces. The siege-batteries were their lifeline, with which the insurgency controlled the mainland and its surrounding waters.

This close to their objective, the battalion could no longer afford to traverse the Serrado Delta. They deviated into a minor river system. According to their maps, a minor river spur to the west ended in a blunt-headed pool three kilometres upriver. The enclosed body of water would be a defensive position for the battalion to set up camp in preparation for their final push.

For once, the maps proved accurate. At the waning of the day, the 88th Battalion made camp at a river basin with the Curtain just nine kilometres to their north-west.

Baeder estimated they would reach their target in less than half a day's sail, but first they would need to prepare and survey thoroughly. The vessels were moored and the men pitched camp on land, allowing them to stretch out their sea legs.

This was a dangerous time, Baeder knew. His Guardsmen were at the limits of physical exertion. But more than physical depletion, there existed the danger of complacency. They were accustomed to the constant terror of ambush now. After so long out in the wilderness, Baeder knew men could stop paying attention to danger. At the beginning, fear and paranoia drove them to remain vigilant, guns armed and eyes keen. But after days and days, the men could begin to lose their edge. The constant grind of remaining watchful would begin to wear thin. He had seen Guardsmen forget about covering fire, disregard flank security or forget to post sentries. He worried that the extended operation made his men almost contemptuous of their situation. Baeder was determined not to allow that to happen.

As the men settled in, chemical fires were not permitted, for fear of giving away their position. Gun pits were dug and double sentries were posted. Baeder voxed Angel One and gave the aviator clearance to fire on anything suspicious. He made it clear that the overwatch flier should fire on anything that was not within the camp perimeter. The battalion was on wartime footing.

While the battalion rested, Baeder went to work.

He handpicked a ten-man squad of the battalion's most light-footed Guardsmen. Back on Ouisivia, these men had lived the lives of trackers, swamp huntsmen or thieves. But here, Baeder needed their talents to accompany him on a scouting mission, deep into the Kalinga Curtain. They would sidle up close to their enemy so they would know what they faced. Initially, Mortlock had protested Baeder's involvement in such a dangerous task. But the colonel had insisted. After all, he would be in command of the final operation and therefore would benefit most from firsthand assessment of the enemy positions.

The selected squad assembled on an assault lander at midnight. Their faces were darkened with ash mud and they had bathed in river water to scour away their heavy scent. They pushed out into the estuary and carved up a narrow channel towards the Curtain. On the map, the narrow canal was a shoestring artery that would carry them to within less than a kilometre of the Curtain, a perfect run for the scout team.

They made their way very slowly in order to minimise engine noise. Overall command of their scout operation was given to Corporal Schilt. Although there were two sergeants and a lieutenant present, Baeder made certain that no one in the squad would contradict the corporal's expertise. Schilt was by far the most experienced of them all. A ragged, skeletal man, Baeder knew Schilt had been a gun for hire in the port cities of Ouisivia. Why he chose to join the Guard, Baeder did not know and it was probably better not to ask, yet Schilt had already served in the regiment for three years. In that time, Schilt had accumulated more gretchin kills while patrolling the fens than any other Guardsman Baeder had known.

The little gretchin who infested the steaming wetlands were notoriously hard to kill; wily and elusive, catching them was likened to grappling with eels. During the hotter months, gretchin spread like an infection, swelling in numbers so great that they threatened the major trading routes between parishes. It took a special sort of man to be able to sneak behind a gretchin and strangle it dead, but Schilt was that man. He held a record of eighty-nine gretchin kills and two swamp orks, all without taking any return fire. Instead, he preferred garrotte wire.

Confident in his team's abilities, Baeder was content to let his men direct the course for once. It was a dark night, as was often the case during the wet season, with the moon choked by dark clouds. At all times, a Guardsman stood upright on the bow, scanning the canal banks. They did not want to run into an insurgent patrol so close to their objective.

Two kilometres out from the Curtain, the team powered down the outboard motor and laboured the vessel up onto the bank. Taking care to cover the inflatable with branches and sod, the team decided to cover the rest of the way on foot.

On land, the task at hand suddenly seemed far more real. The enemy would be close by. Fog clung to the ground in vaporous clouds. The team crouched amongst shrubby pinwheel flowers, bobbing from cover to cover. Schilt halted the team every so often to confer with Baeder's maps, the pace counters and team auspex. They kept up a murderous pace, shooting nervous looks at the sky for fear of dawn.

The Curtain loomed above them when Baeder's team encountered their first enemy patrol. 'Heads up!' Schilt had hissed urgently. He flashed the field signal for enemy. The team auspex began to chime and was switched off hastily in order to maintain their stealth.

Baeder went to ground along with the rest of his men. He peered intently into the night, holding his breath. He dared not open his mouth for fear that it would echo the pounding of his heart. He saw movement, like shadow puppets at first. Then, one by one, the enemy emerged from the dense fog. Baeder counted six. Six insurgents in rural garb, their silhouettes spiked with weaponry. Judging by the slump of their shoulders, the drooping of their heads and their lurching gaits, the men were tired. It was late in the night and it was probable that the insurgents had been patrolling for some time. Inexperience and weariness had dulled their alertness. Baeder aligned one of the insurgents with the ironsight of his lasgun and coiled his finger over the trigger.

Had Schilt chosen to, they could have wiped out the entire patrol. But that would have alerted the Archenemy. Instead, the team lay in wait, allowing the patrol to pass by no more than five metres in front. They waited until the last of the insurgents had disappeared back into the fog before they broke cover and continued on.

The team dared to press on until they spotted a chain-link fence intersecting the thinning jungle. They had finally reached the ex-militia compound that occupied the Kalinga Curtain. Beyond the wire netting they could see the rocky scree slopes of limestone. Around the rocky slopes sprawled a military installation. Baeder immediately began to take notes in his field-book.

The Kalinga installation occupied a fenced rectangle of roughly a kilometre in length. Its perimeter followed the jagged contours of the Kalinga Curtain, making use of the natural rocky defences. It was a large installation with rockcrete blockhouses that studded the hillsides. Many had been laid open by repeated bombing attacks and the parade grounds at the fore were scorched and cratered. Despite the damage it had endured, the compound would be difficult to assault. The only opening that Baeder could see was a docking bay which stretched out into the Serrado Delta on the west side of the compound. It would be a perfect position for them to commit the 88th's water assets, but Baeder had no doubt the pier-approach would be well defended by hidden firing positions. Further up the Kalinga Curtain, Baeder could spot large openings cut into the rock face. It suggested that the siege-batteries had resisted aerial destruction because they were deeply embedded below ground. More than that, it confirmed the intelligence reports that the compound had an underground complex as well.

The team surveyed the perimeter as well as it could, sweeping the area with the auspex. They did not linger for long, as sentry towers spread out along the perimeter probed the jungle with sweeping searchlights. They flitted like rodents, snatching in and out of the trees, never straying far from the curtain of foliage. Fear of discovery was a tense constant and, while some worked feverishly to sketch rough plans and make auspex scans, the others kept watch with their lasguns. According to the auspex, Baeder noticed that no insurgents lingered above ground in the compound's external blockhouses, save for the sentries up in the towers. They probably huddled underground, manning the siege-batteries.

In five minutes they were done. On their way back, the team avoided another patrol of insurgents. But by now they had found their rhythm.

They barely took any notice of the Archenemy patrol, going to ground and circling away from the undisciplined rebels.

The trouble did not start until they returned to their boats. By then it was almost dawn and the sky was a lighter shade of dark blue. The team piled into the inflatable and pulled on the outboard motor. Yet the motor would not catch, not even after the sixth or seventh pull.

'Chaos witchery!' Schilt spat, slapping the side of the motor.

'No, it's damn Ando Tate and his boys,' swore Baeder, thinking back to his conversation on base with his old friend the colonel. It seemed another lifetime ago. 'He never could fix a boat,' Baeder concluded.

It was a precarious situation. They paddled the boat out into the channel and Baeder began to work on the motor. Sergeant Asper, a former fen trapper with a good hand for maritime mechanics, added his expertise to the laid-open wires. They adjusted, shook and fiddled. Everyone else formed a defensive perimeter along the banks. They would have to stay alert. Dawn was creeping up on them.

As he dug around the wires, Sergeant Asper shook his head in wry amusement. 'Irony,' he said. 'I used to lay traps in the wetlands during the night. In the dawn I would begin to follow my trapping lines and collect the nets. Those rodents always looked at you with such terrified eyes. I often wondered how it felt to be snagged in the dark, knowing by morning, the huntsman would find you. Now I know.'

Finally, after a frustrating twenty minutes of the engine almost catching, sputtering and dying, Baeder gave up. The sky was a ruby pink and he was determined not to put the battalion at jeopardy so close to the end. Fear hunched the shoulders of the men around him. Not fear of death, Baeder knew, but fear that discovery would give away their only advantage of a surprise assault. Fear that they would die a pointless death out here without being able to advance with their comrades into the final fray. That thought resolved Baeder.

'We're moving out now,' he said, lowering himself into the chest-deep water. The early morning canal was shockingly cold.

The other nine slipped into the black water and with one hand on the boat, the other holding their lasguns above the waterline, they began to tread like pallbearers. The sides of the canal bank rose a metre or so above their heads and Schilt was the only one who sat in the craft. He crouched near the bow, peering above the bank onto the land so he could scout for possible enemy movement.

They had not been going long when two things seemed to happen at once. An early morning rain suddenly pummelled from the sky, so abruptly it was as if someone had turned open a tap above them. At the same time, Schilt clambered down from his perch and hissed into Baeder's ear, 'I see enemy movement along the shore, fifty metres parallel to us.'

'How many?' asked Baeder, suddenly shivering from the rain and enemy presence.

'I can't peep through the rain. I don't think they've peeped us either.'

Baeder passed the word along to the other boat pullers. Their speed increased dramatically, slogging double pace through the syrupy water, boots sinking deep into the tissue-like mud. If the Archenemy were to suddenly appear over the lip of the canal, there would be nowhere for the team to go.

Baeder closed his eyes and let the rain run over his face. Above the gushing raindrops against the canal he tried to listen for enemy movement. He strained for voices. The clatter of weapons. The sound of an autogun being cocked. He heard nothing. But although he heard nothing, Baeder trusted Schilt, and without question. He never second-guessed his men. Every man in the battalion was a combat veteran and what they said stood. It was something that many other officers overlooked.

It was a tense and tiring march. The muscles of Baeder's left arm and shoulder, pulling the boat, were soon throbbing with lactic build up. He felt as if every bone had been teased out of its socket. He could almost see waves of pain radiating out from his hands. The mud below denied them proper purchase, pulling at their boots, sinking them down and slowly draining their efforts. Schilt kept watch, ducking down every so often. It was to their misfortune that the enemy seemed to be following the canal as a patrol route. Baeder did not pray often. But he prayed to the Emperor that they would soon turn back before the rain stopped.

After an hour, the team had to rest. Their webbing was cutting their shoulders raw. Everything ached. Wallowing in the water, Baeder rolled his neck back on his shoulders and stretched out his muscles. He opened his eyes and sucked down several chest-expanding breaths. He looked at the overcast sky, still pouring with rain. What he saw made his heart skip.

There, in the clouds above he saw a winking light. Moving slowly towards them.

Baeder knew it would be Angel One, their overwatch pilot. He also remembered, instantly, that he had given Angel One clearance to fire on anything that was beyond the battalion's secure perimeter. No doubt the aviator, from his high vantage point, would see only an irregular man-made blip on his surface radar, moving down the canal in the direction of the Imperial camp. There was also no doubt that Angel One would consider them an open target.

Swearing, Baeder vaulted up onto the inflatable like a surfacing fish. 'Schilt, vox-channel to auxiliary frequencies! Right now!' he hollered, slapping the side of the boat for emphasis. All pretence of stealth was lost.

Schilt dragged the bulky vox-pack over to him and began to key frequencies. Unfortunately, it was only a small-squad level vox and Angel

One's channel had not been set into the system. They could not reach Angel One directly. Rather they could only broadcast on an open channel in the hopes that Angel One would be monitoring. Angel One was not. They received no response.

Baeder rocked back on his haunches and scratched his head. He tried to remain composed in front of his men. The team murmured in helplessness. They shook their heads. It slowly dawned on them that the Persepian aviator was going to hunt them down.

'Vox back to battalion. Have them reach Angel One,' Baeder said. He breathed out hard, trying to maintain control.

Schilt voxed but received no response. He voxed again, still no response. The winking light was closer now, dropping in altitude. Schilt adjusted the antenna, daring to unfold it above the canal edge so that it could be seen from the bank.

The vox suddenly blared to life, startling Baeder. The volume had been toggled to its highest setting on their previous desperate attempts and the response was unexpectedly loud. It cut above the rainfall and echoed across the wilderness. Cursing, Baeder dimmed the volume setting repeatedly and snatched the handset from Schilt.

'Scout element, this is eight eight. Report, over.'

'Eight eight. We are trapped in Angel One's fire zone. Danger close. Give orders for Angel One to cease fire clearance, over.'

There was a pause at the other end. The pause became agony as the winking light lurked closer. The aircraft almost appeared to glide overhead, but then it rolled a tight turn and began to head straight for them.

'Scout element, this is eight eight. We can't do it, sir. Haven't been able to reach Angel One all morning due to heavy rainfall and dense cloud cover. You should be in range to reach Angel One on your vox, but we don't have range to establish contact.'

'Fine!' said Baeder, almost shouting. 'Give me his operational frequency.'

'Sir. Uh, we'll have to find it. It's written down in a book somewhere...'

Baeder almost howled with frustration. He slammed the handset against the receiver. The strike fighter was so close now they could make out its silvery outline in the sky. The war cry of its engines was growing and it was dropping for a strafing run along the canal. Some of the team leaned back against the canal slope in resignation, still standing in the water. They began to take out tabac from soggy upper pockets and tried to light them. Sitting across from him, Corporal Schilt regarded him with a look of hatred that Baeder found difficult to reconcile.

'Sierra Echo. This is eight eight. Angel One op frequency is one zero niner, niner zero eight. Coordinate grid breaker-eight-bravo-'

Baeder cut the operator off before he finished speaking. They could hear the whine of the strike fighter's engines, becoming louder. As Baeder keyed the frequency with trembling fingers, he could imagine Angel One arming his hellstrike missiles and locking them on target.

There was a click.

'Eight eight secondary, this is Angel One. I'm a little busy right now–' said a familiar voice.

'Angel One, cease clearance! Cease clearance!' Baeder screamed. 'Don't fragging fire!'

'Affirmed,' said Angel One.

The strike fighter levelled out. It roared overhead, just two hundred metres above. Baeder could see the tips of the hellstrike missiles racked on the wings, primed for them. As an infantryman, he had never before felt so helpless in the face of complete and overwhelming firepower.

'Eight eight secondary, this is Angel One. Was that a friendly?'

Baeder lay down in the inflatable, his heart drumming in his chest. 'Yes, Angel One. Am I glad to hear your voice.'

The crackly baritone chuckled politely. 'You're always glad. When we mop up this mess, you owe me a mether.'

'Make that two or three, Angel One. Out.'

As Baeder lowered himself back into the water, amidst the backslaps and whispered cheers of his men, he could not help but wonder if the angels of prehistoric scripture were all just aviators with prophetic call signs.

CHAPTER FOURTEEN

The sight of a Chaos Space Marine thunderous with anger was not something that bore thinking about. It was akin to witnessing an earthquake, or an avalanche of multi-thousand tonnage hurtling down a mountain. There was a paralysing awe to its scale that instilled a hopeless vulnerability in those who saw it. It made Mautista feel meek and fragile.

It was worse when two were as equally displeased as each other.

Gabre and Sau seethed darkly in their command bunker, their enormous frames perched atop thrones of sandbags. They were both stripped of their armour and clad only in loincloths. Every so often they would slam their fists as they muttered to each other in a staccato language Mautista could not understand. Their white-painted bodies twitched angrily, each slab of muscle separately laid atop another muscle like overlapping sheathes of hard chitin. Sitting there as they did, they looked like furious barbarian kings, ready to cast judgement.

Ready to cast judgement on Mautista, who knelt before them.

'The Imperials have entered our region of operations, you say?' muttered Gabre, his face deeply shadowed by the sodium lanterns that burned dim.

'Yes,' said Mautista, unsure of what else to say.

'Then the Lauzon Offensive failed to dislodge them from our sides,' said Sau to nobody in particular. He gripped his big, blunt fingers into the sandbag his arm rested on. It popped like a dry blister with no effort at all.

'Tell me again. What happened?' Gabre said, placating his brother with a hand on his shoulder. The two Legionnaires had been doing so since Mautista first reported his findings. One would drive himself into a furious anger and the other would calm him down to a level of coherency. Then it would happen again in reverse. The Pair had a strange, almost symbiotic relationship that unsettled Mautista.

'I took my warband out to the Mato-Barea Canton. We encountered Imperial soldiers in the night. Judging by their firepower, I would say at least one hundred or more. We were broken and chased back into the jungles where they did not follow,' Mautista said. He was too frightened to mention that they had spent the better part of the day pinned down by two rural custodians with shotguns.

The Pair rose up from their thrones. Although Mautista's chemical treatments had nourished another two centimetres of growth from his pain-wracked body in the past week, the Pair were still head and shoulders taller than him. They were also three times as broad and Mautista was sure at any moment they would strike out with their bone-stud knuckles and break him apart. But the Pair had no intention of punishing him. They had no further intentions of even paying Mautista any attention. They crossed over to their planning maps and began murmuring to each other in low, terse tones.

'It could be a stray Imperial patrol,' Mautista offered hesitantly.

Gabre waved him away. 'Never.'

'A patrol would never come this far inland, to do so would require extended fuel and rations. That would require planning,' Sau said.

'No doubt, Imperial elements this close to our region denotes a planned mission,' said Gabre.

'They are planning an assault on the Earthwrecker,' Sau concluded.

Of course they were. Mautista had twice visited the Kalinga Curtain, once when he was issued his recruit weapon, and the second time when he was ordained a Disciple. He had seen the enormous super-heavy cannon that resided deep within the hills. The enormous machine rested on rail-tracks and could be wheeled deep into the hillside caverns to prevent its destruction by Imperial bombs. On his second visit, Mautista had even been fortunate enough to witness the weapon lob a shell hundreds of kilometres out into the ocean beyond. It had delighted Mautista when the super-heavy weapon had fired a thirty-tonne shell from a barrel so big that he had only seen the tip of it peeking out from an opening in the hillside. The muzzle flame from its discharge was a horizontal cloud, orange and black, that was actually larger than the entire Kalinga Curtain itself. The gas and smoke from the single shot drifted up into the sky and blotted out the sun for several minutes. For kilometres around, the earth trembled and the jungle fell into a hushed silence in the wake of its firing. With it, Mautista was sure they could win the war. It was little wonder that the Imperial Guardsmen were seeking to reclaim it.

'Brother Jormeshu will go and prepare the defences at Kalinga,' Mautista heard Gabre say to Sau.

'You will go too,' said Gabre, suddenly turning on Mautista. 'The Kalinga will need as many Disciples as we can spare to defend it. The insurgency will need leaders there.'

Mautista nodded obediently, glad to be given the chance to redeem his earlier failure. He rose from the dirt floor with a click of swollen knees and saluted, as he had been taught.

Gabre anchored a heavy palm on Mautista's shoulder. 'You no longer fear death, do you?'

'No, Gabre. I do not,' Mautista replied.

'Then we will have a punishment far worse than death, if you fail so thoroughly again.'

For the first time since he had followed the Primal State, Mautista became reacquainted with fear. It had become such a distant memory that he had forgotten its acidic, spiteful resonance. Not even with all the chem-treatments, mental conditioning and martial skill at his disposal, did Mautista wish to incur the judgement of the Four. He made up his mind, quite certainly, that he would rather die than fail.

By the one hundred and forty-first day of the uprising, most of the Imperial cities had barred their gates to those of indigenous blood.

Never on Bastón had the enemy been so brazen as to besiege an Imperial city. But outside the walls of Fortebelleza, thousands of heretics and Carnibalès fighters had erected a makeshift camp. Their numbers grew every day, a swollen sea of protestors engulfed the city limits. From the walls, Governor Alton relayed to High Command – 'Never before have these natives displayed such bold disregard for Imperial edict. They dare to dissent within the gates of my city in utter contempt for the authority I indisputably hold.'

They erected shrines of worship. Totemic pillars of stone. The citizens of 'belleza declared that there were mutants among those heretics, horribly metamorphic beings changed by their worship of foul idols. Military Intelligence reported that insurgency support in the rural hamlets had spiked, Carnibalès numbers were believed to have quadrupled and incidences of raid and ambush had increased to the point where it was no longer prudent to send single platoons on patrol.

At Fortebelleza, a one hundred strong company of Riverine manned the walls but could do nothing. Without supplies, especially ammunition from the Persepian fleet, the Riverine vanguard could only remain effective for so long. Yet still the insurgency grew as the Imperium watched and waited.

* * *

Jormeshu surveyed the blisters of low rock that formed Kalinga from his lookout nest. Before him the hills were strung out six hundred metres to his left and five hundred to his right. It was a long strip, rugged and broken. It would be difficult to assail the natural fortress, of this he was certain.

The plated giant was surrounded by Carnibalès veterans and painted Disciples, a retinue of forty or so who crouched or squatted around his armoured shins like scholam children. Dwarfed in his right gauntlet, Jormeshu cupped a data-slate. His left hand was bare and manipulated a tiny sliver of stylus, thick fingers sweeping angles and trajectory calculations on the display screen. The left gauntlet, segmented and bruised, was hooked to the tuille of his thigh-plate.

'The above-ground complex is poorly planned and not easily defensible,' he said, taking in the entire hill range with a sweep of his arm. 'The terrain is far too herbaceous, dense, covered. It will be no good.'

The external compound above-ground was a narrow ribbon of mesh fencing that housed multiple blockhouses the militia had once used as barracks and command posts. Due to the sloping gradient an irregular forest knotted the limestone. Small trees clung with their roots penetrating deep into the rock. The forces who had constructed the compound had a poor grasp of siege strategy, Jormeshu lamented. Even with the past Imperial bombing scarring the area into a leprous, balding carpet of greenery, there were still ample trees to provide any assaulting force with cover to advance.

'We could attempt to fell some of the jungle close to the compound,' suggested a Carnibalès propagandist, a demure man in spectacles and grey rural garb.

'No time. The Imperials could attack at any moment,' Jormeshu countered. 'Besides,' he said, pointing towards the west, 'we could not properly deny the docking bay and hangars from enemy entry. This compound was not built to withstand a siege.'

The docking pier at the further western edge of the compound posed a defensive problem. It led straight from the Serrado Delta into wide-mouthed hangars which provided entry into the underground complex. Jormeshu was a pragmatist. He would not attempt to hold what could not be held. Instead he would allow the Imperial forces to come that way and funnel them into the killzone within the compound.

'I have two hundred fighters in my warband. I can hide them well amongst the buildings and trees,' offered a shaven-headed Disciple by the name of Novera. He was one of the earliest Disciples; at least one of the surviving ones. He had received over four months of chemical treatments and it had ravaged his body, sores opening in clusters across his skin. All the Disciples who had been initiated alongside Novera were now dead, killed in fighting or dying to the mutagenic chemicals. Jormeshu valued

Novera's leadership amongst the Carnibalès: he could not spare the man to die in the initial onslaught.

'No,' Jormeshu shook his head. 'Sixty men led by two other Disciples, no more, will be hidden in the above-ground complex. The rest will be needed elsewhere. Sixty will be enough to worry the Imperial assault and delay them.'

Booby traps too, thought Jormeshu. Pit traps, grenade rigs, mines. They would seed the entire hillside and docking bay with traps. Instead of allowing the Imperial forces the open fight they no doubt craved, Jormeshu would lure them into an abandoned complex filled with traps and hidden snipers. It would sap the aggression of an enemy when they charged ashore.

It would be below ground in the hollow belly of the Kalinga Curtain that the real fighting would begin... provided the Imperial soldiers made it that far.

In the warrens below, Kalinga resembled the inner belly of a fortress. Bunkers, storage units and winding tunnels. Jormeshu knew that, since Disciple Mautista had revealed that the Imperial force was still en route to the siege-batteries, the Carnibalès had been roused into renewed activity. Within the hill fortress the troops were preparing in their own way.

Jormeshu had never seen such fervent prayer to the Ruinous shrines. Many displayed their mutations proudly, no longer hiding them beneath leather bandages. Glorious mutation was rife and over thirty of their number had received the ultimate favour of the gods, transformed into Chaos spawn. Those beasts, all maw and tentacle, were now chained in the storage basements for release at Jormeshu's tactical discretion. Within the workshops, guns and explosives were manufactured at a double pace. The rural workers did not sleep.

Of the actual defences inside the underground, gun nests were erected at regular intervals within the tunnels. Ammunition caches were hidden in strategic locations. The rebels were possessed by a belligerent certainty. They were becoming bloodthirsty.

Despite this, in his heart Jormeshu expected the insurgents to be pushed back by the Imperial Guard. In the event that the Guardsmen made it inside the hill fortress in any significant numbers, Jormeshu knew that it would degenerate into bitter hand-to-hand fighting. He had lived war for centuries and held no illusions that even with superior numbers the rural rebels would not have great difficulty in a clash with the Guardsmen. They were Imperial Guard and, in Jormeshu's experience, those fighting men proved remarkably resilient and were capable of bravery that often exceeded his expectations. Jormeshu would not underestimate them. He kept these thoughts to himself. It would be folly to dishearten his minions.

'These Imperial warriors are hard fighters. Do not mistake their false theology for poor soldiering,' Jormeshu said to his assembled retinue.

Warlords of Chaos often disparaged the fighting ability of the Imperium, considering them weak and breakable. It was, in Jormeshu's opinion, a foolish thing to do. Belittling a capable opponent brought about nothing but complacency. Complacency brought about mistakes.

'Can they compare to us? We've been winning this war, have we not?' snorted Tsivalu, an insurgent veteran whose nostrils were pugnaciously bovine, with a sloping, knurled eyebrow ridge. The retinue chorused their agreement.

Jormeshu growled, a deep sound that echoed from the cavities of his expansive chest. He commended their bravado, but no amount of faith could account for the fact that even the most hardened Chaos veteran at his command had been fighting for no more than half of a year. The Guardsmen had been fighting for most of their adult lives, ferried from warzone to warzone. He did not doubt the aggression, ferocity and fanaticism of the Carnibalès, but he held no illusions as to their discipline and training.

'You will need every edge we can muster. Do not fall lax or the blood that flows will be mostly ours,' Jormeshu declared.

Within the tunnels, vox systems had been rewired to broadcast Blood Gorgon war prayers. He intended to fill the underground with the barking, pounding rhythm of drums and Chaotic incantation during the battle. It would disorientate the Imperial soldiers and drive his own forces into a trance-like fury.

'All of you,' said Jormeshu, taking the time to look every follower who was present in the eye, 'will lead your warbands within the fortress system. We cannot lose the siege-cannon. Without it, we will lose the insurgency and all hope of liberation. Die where you stand or may the Lords and the Prince torment your undying soul.'

The assembly all bowed to him, touching their foreheads to the stone platform as a sign of affirmation. They commanded two thousand Carnibalès that Jormeshu had organised into a rough brigade-strength element. They were named the 1st Bastón Regulars. It was just a name, but it gave the rough-edged rebel fighters a sense of cohesion and purpose. They were dressed in a mix of scavenged militia leathers and peasant attire. The leather jackets were most coveted and changed hands often; in a way their shambled appearance became a source of unifying pride for the First Regulars, irregular though they were.

Jormeshu had selected the title from an enemy he had encountered in his early days with the Legion. He had been a Gorgon youngblood then, two hundred and six years ago on the agri-world of San Cheval. He and his blood company had deployed for a retributive strike on the planet's surface, aiming for a kill quota of ninety-nine thousand kills to be paid in full. They burned and massacred, offering in the name of Chaos, without resistance. That was until the company had collided with the local soldiery known as the Chevilian Regulars. They were barely men: boy-soldiers. It should have been easy. It had not been. Jormeshu still remembered, quite vividly, how he had shot a Guardsman in the leg, taking his foot off at the ankle. The young man stumbled and fell. Another Guardsman had immediately appeared in the open to drag his comrade from further fire. The wounded soldier, heedless of his missing limb, continued to chip away at Jormeshu with his lasgun. It had so surprised Jormeshu that he had hesitated before killing both of them. That was the day he had formed a healthy respect for the fighting prowess of the common man. They had all died, of course, but that was beside the point. He hoped that the title could impart their discipline to his rebel force.

For all his preparations, Jormeshu knew the only thing that mattered was the rail-mounted artillery. Without it, Chaos would lose its influence on Solo-Bastón and his warband would lose a fertile ground of recruitment which had replenished their ranks since their inception. This was as much his home world as it was the insurgency's.

In the unlikely event that the Imperial force weathered the meat-grinding gauntlet he had orchestrated and reached the battery-cavern itself, Jormeshu was personally prepared. He would defend the hangar himself. He had spent the past six days fasting and in prayer to his Lords and his Prince. He had anointed his bolter with warm blood. He had laid out his ancient arsenal of chainsword, maul, guillotine and sabre-sickle and blessed these too. The she-bitch daemon spirit of his power armour for once did not torment him. She had settled into a seething slumber, only crooning at the midnight hours.

Jormeshu could not trust the defence of the battery cavern to anything less. Of course, there would be a company-strength element under his direct command, but he was not concerned. They were a mere meat shield. Jormeshu expected that it would be his boltgun that would exact a heavy toll on any surviving Guardsmen.

'It will be a great pleasure to shoot these dogs as they come down the tunnel,' Mautista cawed. He crouched down behind the low rockcrete barrier, mimicking a rifle in his hands as he tested his line of sight.

'I've heard that Imperial Guardsmen are lobotomised. You can lure hundreds of them off the edge of a cliff with a ration pack,' said Canao as he stacked grenade crates packed with straw into their makeshift gun pit.

Another chimed in, not missing a beat. 'I've heard they are so big they can't run, the muscles on their legs won't carry them. That's why they need tanks and trucks,' he said seriously.

Mautista was not sure whether these stories were true. He surmised that many were fanciful tales sieved through the ignorance of rural farmers. Whatever the truth about the Imperial forces, he would not allow his Carnibalès to be the last to taste Imperial flesh. He had now, under his command, twenty-six Carnibalès and they held a stretch of tunnel two hundred metres long that connected the outer hill complexes to the bulk storage chambers close to the centre of the complex. It would be unfortunate indeed if he were not able to kill any Imperial soldiers, considering their advantage.

The tunnel was smooth and rounded, carved out of the porous limestone; its unobstructed length offered no cover for advancing forces while Mautista was well dug-in. Earlier in the day, Mautista had bartered for over twenty domesticated felines that Disciple Palahes had rounded up during a raid on an agri-village. It had cost him a sizeable portion of dried flesh but Mautista believed it had been worth it. They had boiled the felines alive and now strung them like bloated, white little ornaments in front of their rockcrete barriers for blessing. But not before the carcasses were squeezed to drain the cooked, curdled blood into a bowl. The congealed matter had been anointed to their various knives and bayonets, utilised as crude but spiteful poison.

Behind rockcrete barriers, his Carnibalès were going about their own rituals. Brother Jormeshu had ordered them to prepare for a protracted defence. Now many of them were praying to a small shrine they had erected to the Primal Gods. Inside a glass jar several human scalps had been placed. They were well tanned and shrunken and sitting in a solution of alcohol and oils. Each man in turn took a scoop of the liquid in his palm and slurped. They uttered incantations, kneeling down and praying. Some, the especially pious ones, had their eyes rolled back into their skulls as they swayed and chanted. Garlands of hill flowers surrounded the holy jar. As they prayed, others burned incense and bundles of human hair. The air was hot with the greasy smell of scorched protein and dry musk.

There was an excitement amongst his rebels, stirred from defeat by the prospect of killing. But it was nothing compared to Mautista's emotions. He could barely contain them. He sat cross-legged, away from the others. He uncurled a long strip of cured skin and began to wrap it slowly around his head, starting from the neck and working his way upward. Common insurgents had taken to hiding their Ruinous mutations with head garb. Mautista simply did it because it would put fear into his enemies. It dehumanised him and would not allow his enemies to recognise the familiarity of a human face. Ever since prehistoric man had gone to war, he had tried to terrify his foe with beard, or mask or sculpted helm. Warfare had changed but mankind did not.

Satisfied that his head was wrapped in an anonymous coil with only slits for vision, Mautista held the loose end over his cheekbone. With one hand he held a nail over the flap and with the other he drove the nail with a rock. The pain was white hot and momentary. He took up another nail, thin and pointed, and repeated it, this time against the soft flesh beneath his chin. Mautista did this nine times until blood wept from the cracks between the cured hide. As he drove the final nail into place, he could not help but remember a single passage from an Ecclesiarchal Primer that he had memorised as a young child. '*I am death, come for thee,*' – a passage that the local preacher had forced him to read. The words scrolled through his head, not in a preacher's sermon, but in Mautista's own voice.

In the past days, perhaps weeks, he had not only become accustomed to the idea of killing, but the very concept of life-taking gave him a surge of euphoria. Mautista was losing control. He knew it but there was nothing he could do. The chemicals that distorted his body and made him strong also sculpted his consciousness. His hands tingled with the desire to strangle, maim and pull a trigger. In fact, Mautista's hands had grown large, his fingers tingling and stretching out as if in yearning. He was not quite sure whether it was his subconscious that had rendered the mutation, or the mutations which had penetrated his subconscious. Either way, Mautista so badly wanted the Imperial men to come running down those tunnels. He would kill them with his lasgun and wrench at their limb sockets with his enormous hands.

The mutations were a poison to him. Mautista knew this too. It had occurred to him that very rarely did he meet a Disciple who had been ordained at the beginning of the war. At first he had assumed them to be casualties of conflict, but then he had realised it was something else. The chemically-induced mutations were unstable. They ravaged their once human bodies. The mutations that the common rebel often harboured were benign, a gift from the gods. But the tremendous changes that were induced in the Disciples were akin to a sacrifice.

Yet in his inevitable death, Mautista had also learnt to see purpose. It forced him to impart his knowledge upon the common Bastón-born in the few months he had. He was a better combat leader for it, because he did not think about the consequences of pain. Each day was his last and, in the primal philosophy of Chaos, there was no greater way to live. When the time came, he would kill as many Imperial meat puppets as he could. They would be terrified of him. They would remember his visage for the rest of their days and, when he died, he would ascend to an eternity alongside the Lords and their Prince. Whichever way Mautista looked at it, the killing would be glorious.

Baeder lifted the flap and walked into the officers' tent, scrunching his cloth cap from his head as he did so. All eyes fell on him expectantly. Baeder loosened his collar against the stifling heat and nodded in greeting.

Seated or crouching around a foldout table were Major Mortlock, Sergeant Pulver and the four company captains. Captain Gregan of Serpent

Company had suffered a thigh wound in the Lauzon Offensive. As a result, he was feverish, pale and sweating, yet he leaned on a fen-hammer as a crutch and insisted on being present.

Baeder laid down the scraps of notepaper on the steel fold-out. He arranged them like a card dealer as the officers leaned in eagerly to study them. Each note contained the scrawled intelligence he and the scouting party had managed to scribble in their field books and tear out. The tiny shreds of paper, containing sketches, numerical data and observations were less than ideal, but they were all Ouisivians and they could get by with much worse.

'This is the Kalinga Curtain, a range of small hills roughly three kilometres in length. A fenced, above-ground installation covers roughly a third of the Kalinga Hills,' Baeder said, tracing a graphite sketch with his fingers. 'It is our belief that the majority of enemy assets reside below ground in bunker complexes, thus avoiding aerial bombardment for the past several months.'

'Where are the fraggers hiding the big gun?' asked Mortlock.

'There are firing ports cut into the hillside. We know from the pre-mission briefing that the machine can be moved by means of an underground rail network to various firing positions. Follow the rail link and we'll find it.'

'It's a one hundred metre long cannon for frag's sake. How hard can it be to find?' shrugged Baeder.

'What entry points do we have?' Captain Gregan whispered weakly. His leg wound had robbed the young, athletic officer of his strength. Baeder feared that Gregan would not be fit to lead his company in the assault.

'Some of the structures in the above-ground installation must lead below-ground. There also seem to be certain caves carved into the hill that lead into the underground. These entry points are small, however. The most likely entry point for a large force is here,' said Baeder, tapping a badly drawn icon representing the installation's docking bays. 'These are riverside piers which lead into a large hangar that appears, from our observation, to connect directly into the underground.'

'Then that's where we'll hit them,' Captain Fuller declared. 'Hard and direct.'

'It's also where the Archenemy will expect an attack. They'll be waiting for us there,' Pulver said.

Baeder nodded in agreement. 'It's too obvious. I really would rather not fall into a well-laid trap, especially given the Archenemy penchant for deviant behaviour,' Baeder added lightly.

On Ouisivia, officers had been taught to ignore the most obvious approach to any given problem. More than likely the enemy would be prepared for it and any enemy commander would take steps to shore up their weaknesses. Illogical though the Archenemy were, Baeder refused to fall into a well-laid enemy defence due to predictability, and if the Traitor Legions truly had a hand in this, as Baeder suspected, then it would be all the more likely.

'Here, the docking pier is the most obvious approach,' said Baeder, jabbing a finger at the rough sketch laid out before them. He traced the metal docking bays that spanned a width of some two hundred metres. 'So we set the decoy assault here. The entire flotilla manned by skeleton crews will conduct an assault on the docking hangars. The enemy will expect us to land troops here. Instead, the entire flotilla will sit back and hammer them with support weapons. We deny them the assault they'll expect. Major Mortlock, I'll need you to lead this.'

Mortlock looked crestfallen. 'Sir? I lead the decoy? What about the major assault?'

Baeder took a deep breath as if the words pained him. 'The entire success of our mission will depend on the effectiveness of the decoy attack, major. We need the enemy to really feel threatened there. It will be a delicate task and, make no mistake, a dangerous one. I'm entrusting second command during the assault to Sergeant Pulver. I need you to do this Mortlock, I really do.'

Mortlock clenched his jaw and thought for a second. Finally, he nodded. 'You can count on it, sir.'

'Good,' Baeder said, continuing. 'The main assault will be dismounted infantry. We'll move inland, four hundred and thirty-five men. Once the river attack is distracting the enemy, we will secure the above-ground compound and split into company-strength elements, entering the underground through the large firing vents carved into the mountain.' Baeder indicated these on the map in turn. 'Once inside, we will follow the rail network that is used to transport the gun to its various firing positions. Remember, the battery can only traverse the rail networks so, if we follow these, we'll eventually be led to the battery. Once there, disable the battery with det-charges.'

The officers leaned back, their eyes gleaming with the thought of the final assault. They were not violent men by nature, but the past weeks of boredom and terror had made them feel like victims. Now, the thought of finally meeting the enemy barrel to barrel filled them with joy. It was a curious concept. In any other context, the thought of danger and killing was far removed from that of promise. But these were Imperial Guardsmen and war, at least to them, held a terrible allure. It gave them a chance to do the one thing they had trained so long and so hard to do. Kill.

'When do we go?' Pulver asked, ringing his dip into a spittoon.

'It's 09.00 now. We will rest and prepare. Have all companies ready to deploy by 18.00 tonight. We will break camp by 20.00 and ready positions by midnight. The attack will be 04.00 the next morning so we can make full use of the morning fog. I will give a full briefing in the afternoon, until then gentlemen, go about your business. Rest when you can. Dismissed,' Baeder said.

CHAPTER FIFTEEN

'Baeder is a stone-cold killer!' shouted a Riverine, slapping his knee.

'Yeh. Wouldn't tell by looking at him but that ramrod is a machine,' agreed another.

The word was out that the attack would begin at 04.00 and the Riverine camp was lively with cheer. The 88th Battalion had survived the long trek inland largely intact; the four companies were more or less at fighting strength and spirits were high. A leathery, grudging respect for Colonel Baeder was beginning to build amongst the Guardsmen.

Corporal Schilt, however, did not share those sentiments. He crouched in the soft leaf mould beneath the shade of a gum-sap, hugging his lasgun to his chest, and tried to keep out of sight. It was early morning and cumulus clouds gathered overhead, threatening rain again. It had been mere hours since Schilt had almost been on the receiving end of an Imperial fighter and his nerves were frayed. The clouds matched his mood.

In Schilt's opinion, it was bad enough that the battalion was led by a reckless maverick of an officer. It was worse because now Baeder had earmarked him as one of the battalion's best forward scouts and almost gotten him killed that very morning. Schilt had no intention of being selected for further special missions.

It was not that Schilt disliked soldiering. He liked it, for the most part. He loved his lasrifle and the notion of being in the Imperium's warrior caste. The uniform too seemed irresistible to women at ports of call and deployment. But Schilt had no stomach for being put in the gunsights of an enemy. What good were the benefits of being a Guardsman if he was not alive to enjoy them?

Schilt lit a tabac, content to warm his dark thoughts with lung-burning smoke, when Trooper Volk tramped through the undergrowth towards him. Volk was smiling, grinning widely to reveal the gaps in his teeth.

'What the frag are you so happy about?' Schilt murmured into his tabac.

Volk was a balding, bearded brute in his middle years, growing soft around his middle. Although he had spent almost sixteen years in the Guard, multiple infractions had demoted his rank. He was forever a rogue and, consequently, one of Schilt's most trusted in their gang of 'creepers'.

'It's a fine day today and we'll be fighting by tomorrow. It's a wonderful life in the Imperial Guard,' Volk replied, squatting down beside Schilt.

Schilt spat derisively, eyeing Volk with a hint of disgust. There were still at least eighteen hours before engagement and Volk was already prepped to go, his webbing cinched, his canteens filled and his autorifle oiled and cleaned. The old trooper had even patched the holes in his combat boots with plastek tape.

'Since when did you become one of Baeder's lapdogs?' Schilt asked snidely.

'Ain't,' Volk replied gruffly. 'I'm getting ready now so I can catch some sleep before the afternoon.'

'You better not go eunuch on me,' Schilt said, suddenly serious. 'Not now.'

The face-splitting grin dropped from Volk's face. 'Why? What are you cooking up?' he asked.

Schilt stamped out his tabac and sniffed. 'I'm going to frag Baeder.'

'Before the assault on Kalinga?' Volk asked. Judging by the furrows that creased his forehead, he did not think it a good idea.

'Of course not now, you damn pushball,' Schilt snarled venomously. 'During the Kalinga assault. I'm going to finish him there, nice and quiet like that.'

Volk didn't reply. An uncomfortable silence settled between them. Suddenly Schilt shifted forwards on the balls of his feet and gripped Volk by the collar of his flak vest. 'Damn it Volk, if you're not playing on this one I'm going to put you out. I'm going to slice you here and no one's going to shed a damn tear,' Schilt hissed under his breath. A knife was pressed up against Volk's ribs, sliding just underneath the bottom of his flak.

Despite being the older and significantly larger man, Volk stammered. Schilt terrified him. He did not doubt Schilt's threats. Besides being an excellent gretchin stalker, Volk knew that Schilt had already killed a Riverine before. Once, two years ago on their home garrison, Schilt had drowned their platoon medic for refusing to supply him with pain stimms. The regiment had put the death down to natural causes but Volk and a handful of creepers knew otherwise. You didn't turn your back on Sendo Schilt.

'All right. All right, don't get so slicey,' Volk pleaded, pushing Schilt's hand away from his neck. 'I'm in.'

'Good,' Schilt said. 'I'm going to pop him in a firefight. Make sure you and the boys finish the job. Spread the word to the others.'

Volk sighed. Up until then, he had been looking forward to engaging the Archenemy in a firefight, barrel to barrel, steel to steel. Corporal Schilt had just robbed him of all enthusiasm.

'Give me some tabac,' Schilt demanded, as Volk turned to go. 'I'm all out and look, I'm all shaken up,' he said, holding up his trembling hands for Volk to see. 'Baeder almost got me killed last night on his fouled-up scouting run.'

Volk began to rifle through his webbing pouches, trying to forage some tabac for Schilt, but he couldn't do it. His hands were shaking even harder than Schilt's.

Before the sun was high and the air grew hot, Sergeant Pulver made a roll call of each individual platoon. It took him the better part of dawn and all morning, time he could have otherwise spent resting for their attack on the morrow.

But the lack of rest didn't bother him. These Riverine were his sons. He went to each man and checked on their preparations. During his rounds, Pulver gave out the last dredges of his dip and tabac. He found out that Trooper Velder's lasrifle had a warped focus chamber. Unable to fix it, Pulver gave him his own lasrifle and checked out a spare weapon from the supply barge. It was an outdated T20 stem autogun; the trigger mech was stiff and the balance was poor. Pulver slung it over his shoulder without a second thought and went to make certain each and every man would be ready for the fight ahead.

Baeder could not remember the last time he had had more than three hours of sleep in one stretch. He was running on the last wispy fumes of energy, an energy that only lingered because they were so close to the end. Since he had returned with the scout force and briefed the battalion seniors on the assault strategy, their temporary ennui had become electrified. Guardsmen who only hours before had sprawled or crouched in sleepy, silent huddles were now up and moving with vigour. Their jungle clearing erupted with the clatter of men preparing their battle-dress, shouting orders and relaying supplies.

Following their briefing, Baeder had returned to his bivouac and tried to snatch an hour or two of rest before afternoon preparations but found that he could not. He had lain awake; his eyes open as his mind swirled with thoughts of the coming fight. Finally, unable to sleep, he rose and donned his uniform. He shed the sour rags that he had not changed for the past several days and foraged up khaki officer's shorts and a shirt of Riverine swamp camouflage. The simple change of clothes would go far in conveying his confidence towards his men. Baeder then shaved with a dry blade, scraping the coarse stubble from his skin along with a rind of dark filth. There was a ritual to preparing the regalia of war that all Guardsmen found universally comforting. As one went through the physical movements, the mind subconsciously readied itself for the trauma that would follow in the hours to come. Slowly, savouring each motion, Baeder shrugged himself into his webbing, a ubiquitous H-harness hip webbing that had served in mankind's front trenches for thousands of years. It was not the complex chest rig of the Caliguans nor the slim, side satchels of the Persepians but his webbing was slashed with the tans and cream greens of Ouisivia, and Baeder would not trade it for anything else. With a roll of plastek tape, Baeder fixed the loosened straps and buckles which had bothered him for the past few days. Satisfied with his attire, Baeder checked his wrist chron. It was not yet middle noon and he decided to make a tour of the camp before his formal pre-mission briefing.

As Baeder emerged from his tent, nearby Riverine greeted him with a loud 'Oussss!' Baeder raised his fist and hooted back. The men were in high spirits and, for Baeder, there was no better sign. The nearness of danger changed men. It was unspoken, but all the men understood it – many of them would be dead by this time tomorrow. Even the youngest, most timid Guardsmen in the battalion stamped around like ursine predators, banging helmets together while chewing dip. There was no time for fear now. The Riverine replaced it with aggression. They jokingly called each other out, snorted with crude humour and shared a gruff, intimate brotherhood. It was not an act, Baeder knew, but a way to quell the fear.

Even those Guardsmen who had never gotten along found time to sit by one another and share their remaining tabac. As Baeder walked through the camp he overheard fragments of conversation that would have been out of context anywhere else, at any other time.

'...so I left her back home, what else could I do? I didn't want to be stuck dirt farming like my old man. I hope she's found someone who treats her fine. I still think, you know...'

'...my little brother almost took my eye out with that percussion cap. It lodged there. You should have seen the look on my mother's face. I thought she was going to throw him into the water. I even cried to make it seem more serious than it was...'

'...I just wanted you to know that I always thought you were a good, solid ramrod. I just never said it before.'

'Same to you brother. I want you to have my tags if I die...'

Baeder continued on to the outer perimeters of the camp. At the edge of the water, Riverine had spread out a groundsheet held down by stones on four corners. Spread in the middle was a carpet of solid slug ammunition for autorifles. The Guardsmen sat and cleaned them by hand. Their diligence made Baeder's heart swell with pride. For soldiers who barely bathed and never shaved, they were wiping clean each individual round to reduce the chance of jamming in the middle of a firefight. Approximately one third of the men in his battalion had opted to take LH Fusil-pattern autorifles instead of their lasguns. Each of these men would carry five magazines of thirty rounds into combat. That meant over twenty thousand rounds would have to be wiped and slotted into detachable box magazines. It was a thankless job and it made Baeder glad he was a commander of the 88th Battalion.

Behind the picket line of camp sentries, a makeshift memorial had been set up around the buttress roots of a tall green giant. On sticks staked into the ground hung helmets and metal ident-tags: one for each Riverine who had fallen since their inland campaign and not been given proper burial. Guardsmen came and went, saying their last goodbyes or asking their fallen friends to watch over them.

Baeder knelt down and placed his palm on a helmet. Beside it lay the tag for Corporal Cinda Frey, Three Platoon, Prowler Company.

'Corporal Frey,' Baeder said. 'You may be eager to see your friends in the beyond, but I'm going to try and keep them away from you for a while yet. I want to keep them alive and I'm sorry I wasn't able to do the same for you. One day I know we will all salute each other again, but hopefully not tomorrow. Oussss.'

As Baeder rose and turned to leave, he started to see the skull-face of Mortlock looking at him.

'How are you feeling, major?'

Mortlock cracked him a wide grin; the sight of the smiling ork skull on his face was ironically comforting. 'I'm going to kill me fifty insurgents. Just you wait and see. I'm going to tear one limb from limb and beat his friend to death with it. It'll be a new personal record.'

Baeder did not need to feign amusement, as he often had to during the major's outbursts. This time, Baeder laughed genuinely. 'Good to hear, major. I'm going to expect a full field report when this is all over.'

Mortlock's arrogance had often bothered him. When he had first met the man, Baeder had both envied and disliked him. In the mess halls, Mortlock was loud and supremely confident. But out here, in the thick of a combat zone, the arrogance was like an anchor for morale. Baeder did not doubt that the sight of the one hundred and fifty kilo major slinging his fen-hammer could rally them from the brink of surrender.

Lastly, Baeder strolled to where the battalion's boats were waiting on the water. Riverine were making the final mechanical checks on their steeds. Others were hauling the last crates from the supply barges. For a moment Baeder considered wading into the water to check on their progress but thought better of it. He wanted the men to know that he had absolute trust in their abilities. The sergeants and soldiers were commanding the resupply with clockwork efficiency, shifting rations, water and ammunition from the vessels and over to the squad and platoon leaders for distribution.

Finally, after Baeder made several rounds of the camp, he retreated to find solitude. He sat beneath a spiny bactris and stared blankly into nothing. This was the fight he had been waiting and training for. Not only during this campaign, but ever since he had joined the Guard. Now here he was, leading a battalion into the heartland of enemy country. They were surrounded and outnumbered by Archenemy fanatics. The success of the entire war could be contingent on the operative success of his battalion within the next twenty-four hours. Despite knowing all these things, Baeder was not at all scared. The only thing that terrified him was the distrust of his own men. He did not know what they thought of him, or whether they even cared for his judgement. That one burning doubt nagged him.

He knew that this doubt, in part, had hardened him. It drove him to do terrible things. He no longer cared who he killed or how he did it. Baeder knew he would shoot women and children if they threatened the safety of his soldiers. Every shot fired against his men was a personal attempt to kill Baeder himself. When it came down to this, everything was negotiable. His world was the battalion. Fight and win.

Briefly Baeder wondered what his father on Ouisivia would think of the soldier he had become. The man had been the medical administrator of their parish, an avuncular and widely read man. Most likely, he would have been disgusted. Of course his father would not have understood the plight of command no matter how many books he read. No one would, until they stood in his boots.

The water lapped against the boat hulls. The flotilla of the 88th Battalion was on the move. From the stern of his swift, Major Mortlock could see a long column of combat vessels behind him as they manoeuvred towards the staging area. Usually, Mortlock's boat carried a crew of six men, but tonight it carried three – one to pilot the craft and two to man the support guns. Likewise, the other vessels were strangely empty to his practiced eye. Even the inflatable assault landers, usually loaded with a full squad of Guardsmen, were now guided by a single Riverine. In those landers, the squat silhouettes of backpacks were heaped to resemble the crouched forms of Guardsmen in the dark. They sailed in silence, to match the hushed, devious manner of their decoy assault.

By two in the morning, they reached their attack position. It was a sheltered cove shielded by trees like hanging gallows, just one and a half kilometres east of the Kalinga Curtain. The boats clustered tentatively there, waiting for a vox-signal from the inland assault force. The loud, steady chorus of chirping insects interspersed with the plaintive squeals of the nocturnal was the only sound to be heard.

Mortlock took stock of the men around him. In the dark, shapes coiled up behind mounted weapons. Although he could not see them, he imagined they would be chewing dip, their nostrils flared and their eyes wired open to reveal too much white. They were ready. Although they had not been granted the opportunity to join in the main assault, every man knew the importance of their objective. Their feint attack would need to be real and damaging. Damaging enough to make the Carnibalès believe them. It was not glorious but it was entirely necessary. At first, Mortlock had been offended that Baeder had ordered him to lead the decoy. He had wanted so badly to commit to the major assault. It was to have been his own *Great Crusade*. But then, slowly, it dawned on him that Baeder had separated him for a reason. Casualty rates were expected to be high. In the event that Baeder was killed in action, the colonel had wanted Mortlock to lead the battalion on their return. Mortlock could not argue with that.

A Guardsman coughed in the darkness. Mortlock savoured the sound. He wanted to remember everything he felt before the battle. If he could not participate in the final push, then he would still have his fight on the water. He wanted to remember the syrupy fog of the night, the gentle lapping of the water. This was what Mortlock had trained to do. Fight and win.

The minutes ticked on. Baeder and the battalion would be creeping towards the Kalinga now, Mortlock thought. He imagined the companies crawling into position beneath the rainforest's tall emergents. Once the battalion reached their attack point, two kilometres out from the Kalinga Curtains, they would signal Mortlock to charge. The plan was for the boats to hit the docking hangars of the installation with hard firepower. It would draw patrols and manpower in the area, allowing the main assault to stalk close enough to the installation and mount a shock raid on the Archenemy. To do this, Mortlock and the vessels would have to put up a fight for over fifteen minutes, allowing enough time for the assault teams to cover the distance.

From inside the pilothouse, the sudden crackle of vox transmission made Mortlock jump with a start. He slapped the stern-mounted heavy bolter. This was it. He could feel the heat, a spring coil in his stomach beginning to build in tension. He flexed his hands and wriggled his fingers.

But the transmission was simply a test signal. Instead, they waited. The air grew still. Riverine began to mutter, their voices drifting softly across the river surface. They waited some more. The minutes rolled by and Mortlock looked at the sky anxiously. They had maybe one or two hours before daylight. He began to wish fervently for the assault teams to hasten their task.

The vox from the pilothouse crackled again, this time so loud it echoed a metallic ring across the cove. 'Mortlock, this is eight eight. We are poised. Proceed with Operation Curtain. Over.' The voice was strangely laconic.

Their coxswain voxed something back but Mortlock could not hear the answer. The air filled with the sudden, chainsword roars of motors. It was loud and vibrated back to his molars. Mortlock settled into a semi-crouch as the swift boat lurched in gear. Churning the river white with foam, the battalion column uncoiled like a snake and crossed their line of departure.

The signal was a faraway *crump*. Gunfire strobed in the distance, flashing orange against the black horizon. The faraway chatter of guns could be heard, like a solitary blacksmith clapping hammers in the stillness of night. Men were already dying.

Missile tubes put glowing breaches in the mesh fence. Platoons hurtled through the opening. There were no visible sentries although squads trained their lasguns on empty watchtowers. The sloping hills loomed before them, dark and solid. But for the crackle of gun-fighting to their west, the hills were strangely quiet, almost serene. The sparse, bomb-shocked trees looked like lonely skeletons. Some of Prowler Company began firing up into the empty trees but a squad leader snarled for them to be quiet.

'Lieutenant Hennever! Take that building!' Baeder commanded, indicating towards the closest structure, a boxy rockcrete block with high slitted windows.

Baeder pushed up the hill as the companies spread out into an open file advance. Despite the feint assault, Baeder had expected at least perfunctory initial resistance. But there was not a single gun platform, nor even a Carnibalès fighter in sight.

As the battalion advanced, Lieutenant Kifer's platoon consolidated their position behind an empty blockhouse. Baeder pushed the battalion line another fifty metres up the slope, their left flank anchored by Kifer's platoon. Baeder sprinted over to a heap of brick rubble, no doubt the result of an Imperial sortie in the preceding months. He crouched down behind a splinter of rockcrete and scanned uphill with his magnoculars.

'Where are they?' Baeder whispered to himself. Further up the installation, a string of five blockhouses surrounded the bowl shape of a vox dish. A berm of sandbags oozed down the hill like sand dunes, providing defensive positions, but there were no gunmen behind them. According to his tactical maps, the cluster of buildings provided an entrance point into the underground facility. Although the maps were blueprints of the facility during its tenure as an Imperial outpost, it was unlikely the Archenemy could so easily reroute the complex tunnel systems. Turning to his companies, Baeder gave them the signal to advance. As they had planned, the four companies dispersed. Prowler and Serpent split away, clattering off into the trees towards the eastern slopes.

They continued up, almost at a stroll. Baeder aimed his Kupiter autopistol at the undisturbed trees. For a few seconds, Baeder wondered if Mortlock's decoy attack along the river had really been so effective as to have drawn the entire enemy defences away. It was only momentary, as a slicing round stole his thought away. He dropped as a trooper advancing several paces behind him pitched over and rolled down the slope.

'Did anyone see the shot?' Baeder shouted.

'Contact at left flank! In those trees!' shouted Captain Fuller, indicating towards a stand of white barks which appeared unnaturally bright in the moonlight. Immediately, the advancing line erupted into a mad splintering of las-fire. Branches were whipped away and leaves burst into flame as the fusillade tore into them. Baeder was not sure, but he thought he made out the shape of a gunman drop from the tallest branches under the searing flashes of las-fire.

'Cease fire! Conserve your ammunition,' Baeder commanded with a chopping motion of his hand. He was thinking that the Archenemy were playing smart. They were digging in with hidden snipers, presumably because they knew that a head-to-head clash with Imperial forces would be too much to risk. Most likely the Carnibalès were concentrating their forces at critical strong points and leaving hidden gunmen to harass them. In such conditions, even a single gunman could be a force multiplier against an entire battalion advancing in open terrain. It was a shrewd decision and Baeder would have done the same.

Mortlock's littoral assault powered up the wide delta channel and banked hard towards the Kalinga Curtain. Beneath the harsh roof lights of the docking hangar, the Archenemy were lying in wait. A bombardment was launched from the pier by sentry mortars but most of them fell short of the rapid Riverine vessels, punching high geysers into the river. The hangar appeared as a wide maw at the base of the hills, almost one hundred metres wide. From within that maw, twenty ex-militia cutters and a shoal of insurgent spikers spread out into the river basin, crackling with weapon fire.

The Riverine met them head on and engaged three hundred metres out from the piers. Mortlock ordered his forces to scissor into and through the Archenemy squadrons, diluting their forces into a mingled dogfight. In doing so, Mortlock denied the Archenemy a clear line of fire from the manned guns and troops lurking within the cavernous hangar. Mortars and autocannons barked loudly regardless.

Vessel fought vessel, swirling and circling like fighting fish. The improvised spikers were no match for the rugged swift boats but their numbers were telling. Las-fire slashed in every direction and lit the night into a coloured display of pink and white. The firepower of support weapons pounding each other from point-blank range shook the river. Muzzle flash touched and turned into columns of clashing flame. A cutter flanked Mortlock's swift boat, wedging it between two frilled trawlers. The trawlers poured las-fire up into the stern, ricocheting off the railings as Mortlock ducked behind the mantlet of his bolter. Behind them, the cutter aligned the swift boat under the sights of its turreted autocannon. Out of the night, another swift boat rammed the cutter's portside, throwing its aim. A Riverine gunner tossed three grenades onto the cutter's deck. The explosion was swallowed by the chatter of guns. Beneath the light of predawn the boats continued to fight, jinking, ramming and burning.

It took Sergeant Major Pulver seventeen minutes to breach an entrance point and lead both Prowler and Serpent Company into the underground complex. During those minutes, he lost thirty of the one hundred and eighty-five men under his command and they had not even engaged the bulk of the Archenemy yet. Rather, the ground had been seeded with spike pits and shell mines. Hurried boots in the dark could not discern the freshly-laid traps from solid earth and the traps had claimed many of his boys.

Pulver grabbed the vox handset from his vox-officer's backpack. 'Breached! Serpent and Prowler are in,' he said, as he eyed his surroundings warily.

They were in a sub-ground hangar of the Kalinga Complex, a domed belly hewn into the limestone. The space was large and white grid markings on the expanse of concrete ground suggested that the sub-hangar had once been a motor pool for the militia garrison. Overhead, extractor fans thumped and ventilated air into the multiple exit tunnels that led out deeper into the underground installation. According to his memorisation of the blueprints, it would be a two thousand three hundred metre distance to reach the facility's central core.

With Lieutenant Fissen's platoon spread out for covering fire, Prowler Company moved towards a large ovoid tunnel. A railed conveyance track was laid into the floor of the tunnel, stretching away to disappear out of sight. Captain Buren led Prowler Company away, stalking the railed track like a huntsman tailing spoor.

Pulver checked the schematics on his data-slate before forming up Serpent Company into three full platoons with at least twenty Riverine each.

Emergency sirens were braying, while flickering hazard lights alternated brief moments of darkness and neon yellow.

'Leap frog on alternating sides of the wall,' Pulver commanded.

The three platoons crossed the sub-hangar and entered a carriage tunnel that sloped at a downward angle. The railed track-line down its centre had obviously been used to cart supplies and a pulley wagon had been abandoned halfway down the tunnel. The platoons bounded each other, one moving forwards, while the other two provided covering fire from opposite sides of the limestone walls. Of the Archenemy, there was still no sign. Pulver was sweating in sheets. Partly, it was due to the dry, artificial air, but also because the lack of resistance gave him the churns. He felt his heart fibrillating rapidly yet weakly in his chest. He had never before felt so acutely vulnerable in a combat zone.

His fears were not unfounded. The company had bounded down half the hallway before Lieutenant Hulsen signalled for them to halt. At first, Pulver felt a spark of irritation. Why the frag was Hulsen calling for a halt when they were stranded in an open tunnel without cover? But then he remembered that these men had been blooded before. They were not rawhides that needed minute management and he needed to trust their judgement. Pulver called a halt and sprinted at a low crouch towards Hulsen and his forward platoon.

'Report!' he snapped, wasting no time.

Hulsen pointed at the pulley wagon abandoned on the rails with a hunched, mischievous demeanour, almost like a boy who had found a guilty secret. It was a boxy, slate-grey six wheeler with a carrying capacity of half a tonne. Around it, a web of wire had been arranged to form a complex lattice that stretched from wall to wall. Under the flashing siren lights the wire glinted as fine filament. There was no doubt the half-tonner would be rigged with explosives.

Pulver's eyes widened. 'Get back!' he shouted, rising suddenly. 'Back! Back!' he waved. Serpent Company rose unsteadily from their positions and began to back pedal. In withdrawal, the men were confused but nonetheless obedient.

That discipline saved many lives. A squad of Carnibalès fighters clattered into the far end of the tunnel, shooting up at them. Their faces, distorted by the heavy brow and slit grin of mutation, glowed in the wash of their muzzle flashes.

'Find cover!' Pulver shouted, shooting as he retreated. 'Keep moving!'

The Carnibalès were firing at the rail wagon in an attempt to trigger the explosives. Each shot rocked the carriage on its suspension, lurching it and denting its thin metal hide. With each shot, Pulver flinched inwardly, expecting the carriage to detonate. The cluster of insurgents now solely concentrated their fire on igniting the det-trap, pouring las and solid slug into it. From his experience, Pulver knew that even two

hundred kilograms of poorly mixed det-powder would likely collapse
the entire carriage tunnel.

Serpent Company had only moved sixty metres back up the tunnel
when a las-round finally caught the det-trap. It erupted. A tidal wave of
concussive force, heat and sound tore through the tunnel. Pulver was
bowled onto his back, his eardrums popping with agony. Fragments of
limestone peppered his face and for a moment Pulver thought he was
dead. He rolled onto his side but quickly found that he was intact.

Smoke filled the tunnel. It burned his eyes and seared his throat. He
tried to clear his vision by rubbing his eyes but only succeeded in smearing ash into them. He began to wonder if perhaps everyone else had been
killed and he was the only survivor. Slowly the smoke began to settle.
Pulver blinked and his company came into view. The familiar shapes of
Riverine, swaying and groggy but otherwise unscathed, rose into sight.

'Serpent Company. Report injuries!' Pulver cried hoarsely. His throat
was seared and his voice raspy and weak.

It was a small miracle, but the men only grunted. There were no
screams of pain or wailing reports of casualties. Pulver had been furthest
at the front and therefore the closest to the blast. Serpent Company had
survived the first attack of Operation Curtain. The thought had barely
registered when las-fire stitched into the limestone overhead, eliciting a
downpour of rock drizzle and dust.

Suddenly, Serpent Company opened up, the bounding platoons pouring their fire at the Carnibalès at the far end of the tunnel. The tunnel was
still smoking and beams of las seemed to flash out from the clouds. Pulver hammered a series of blind shots in the opposite direction. Trooper
Kleiger took aim next to Pulver and racked off a trio of grenades from his
launcher, the drum magazine cycling with a hollow *foomp foomp foomp*.

Baeder and Seeker Company progressed steadily down Kalinga's main
service shaft, following the wide rail tracks that transported the siege-
battery. The service shaft was thirty metres wide, its cavernous roof
buttressed by girders. From these girders, the Carnibalès had hung row
upon row of poorly cured human scalps, which hung like a colony of
rats. From all directions, speakers grated out the electric beat of drums,
fast and pounding. The sound was distorted so it sounded like the rhythmic barking of hounds. The unwholesome sounds unsettled their focus.
Their temples pounded with a distracted urgency.

The company moved in squads, bounding from girder to girder behind
cover. Baeder moved with a platoon of twenty-six, leading them on with
his fen-hammer. For twelve straight minutes, they encountered nothing
in the service shafts, nor movement in the winding sub-tracks. They
checked and rechecked their auspexes, cross-referencing them with their
tactical maps every fifty metres. Following the service shaft for a full

kilometre would take them halfway to the inner core and the way was eerily clear. Baeder was beginning to believe they were being lured into a trap. The waiting was intolerable.

Then, without warning, the Archenemy opened up on them. From behind sandbagged cubbies embedded into the alcoves, tracer snapped at Seeker Company. Caught in the open, six Riverine buckled and collapsed. Under the splinter of fire, others ran out to drag them behind the rockcrete girders.

Suddenly the Archenemy seemed to be all around them. The Riverine, squatting beneath the wide support beams, traded shots in multiple directions. The Archenemy were thoroughly dug-in and had been waiting. Huddled down next to Baeder, Corporal Velson dared to lean his upper body out from behind the girder and fire a shot from his autogun. He swung back behind cover as the enemy answered with a salvo of shots, crazing the rockcrete near his shoulder with puffs of dust. Then a las-shot coming from his exposed right side tore out his throat.

Velson's legs swung out and he slid down into a sitting position; his chin dropped into his chest and his helmet rolled off his head. Baeder swore and fired his pistol in the direction of Velson's killers. The Archenemy had outmanoeuvred them through a sub-track along the main shaft. They had drawn them into a killing zone. Above his men the drums continued to pound.

They were saved only by discipline. The company held their positions, laying down defiant counter fire. Lieutenant Hulsen's platoon fixed bayonets and charged an enemy emplacement with a barrage of grenades. They ousted the Carnibalès like rodents from a burrow, stabbing and kicking into the emplacement. Under the determined cover fire of their company, Hulsen's platoon moved on to the next nest of insurgents. Hulsen himself was shot in the arm and chest but he kept standing, ordering his men onwards with his remaining arm. It took more than twenty minutes to clear the service shaft of Archenemy defences and, even then, lone Carnibalès continued to harass them. Lieutenant Hulsen collapsed at the end of the skirmish, finally succumbing to multiple shot wounds. Although Hulsen was not the only casualty in that engagement, his platoon tried to drag his body with them, refusing to leave him behind. An officer from One Platoon finally had to order them to leave Hulsen's body, citing that it would not be fair to all the others that had fallen.

Sergeant Petero Slater was the oldest man in the battalion, if not the regiment, at the age of sixty-eight. His beard was silver and the knuckles and joints of his trigger finger were rigidly fixed in the coiled position, a result, he often said, of a lifetime behind the lasgun. Slater had joined the 26th Founding of the Riverine when he had been a slum youth. He fought and bled with his comrades on the beaches of Bilsbane to the outer reaches of the Canis Cleft Sub. For forty-one long years, he fought with the 26th Riverine, watching his friends die one after another until there were less than a company's worth of men surviving. The old veterans were retired from service in the Austral Subsector and Slater had scrimped his savings to purchase a voyage back to his home of Ouisivia. It was every Guardsman's dream to survive his service and one day return home. But upon his return, Ouisivia was a strange and foreign place. The only home he knew was with the Guard. Old, tired but seeking purpose, Petero Slater reenlisted with the Riverine and joined the 31st Founding.

The solid slugs gouging craters in the rock around Slater brought serious doubt to the wisdom of that decision. Ghost Company led by Captain Steencamp followed a railhead that merged into a sub-track, parallel to Seeker Company's advance. Unlike the other companies, Ghost had suffered heavy fighting upon first entry. The Archenemy waited for them at every corner.

At one particular intersection, the Archenemy had erected a catapult that launched the rotting corpses of militia soldiers at them. For Slater, being crushed by a blackened hunk of flesh was worse than a shot from a lasgun. But Ghost Company pressed on, desperate to keep pace with Seeker Company only fifty metres ahead, yet separated by impenetrable walls of rock.

Likewise, Slater fought to keep pace with the younger men. His joints were not as young as they used to be and a blade wound from an eldar pirate in his thigh had never healed properly. As a result, Slater moved with a galloping limp.

The Archenemy appeared in small, fragmented groups, barrels firing at them from corners and then disappearing. It was almost as if the Carnibalès were baiting them to give chase. Sergeant Slater was wary of this and warned Captain Steencamp. Slater had wanted to adopt a more wary approach. The eldar pirates on Sumudra had employed similar hit and run tactics against the superior grinding advance of the Imperial Guard. Entire companies of Guardsmen chased those stick-like creatures, snatching at shadow puppets, only to be lured en masse into clever, wicked ambushes. But Steencamp had not relented. Seeker Company might need mutual support in adjacent tunnels and Ghost Company had to keep pace.

In their haste, the company never saw the insurgents lurking on gangways built into ledges of the limestone above them. Slater noticed movement above, even felt the prickle of heat on the nape of his neck, but it was too late. As the Riverine swept down the track, the enemy upended vats of boiling tar into the narrow sub-track below. A torrent of bubbling pitch cascaded down onto the heads of the forward platoon and flooded down the sub-track. Steencamp withdrew his remaining three platoons as the resinous sludge chased them back down the corridor. He had no choice but to leave his first platoon, their cries merging into one keening scream as their skin and fat cooked off them. Above the clash of drums and screams for mercy, the insurgents laughed mockingly at their suffering.

Sergeant Slater died slowly. He clawed at the scalding pitch but only tore away strips of skin and resinous uniform. His only comfort was knowing that, this time, he did not outlive his young comrades of the 31st Founding. It would have been a terrible shame if he did.

CHAPTER SIXTEEN

Eighteen minutes after the Riverine entered the porous stronghold that was Kalinga, the Archenemy began to suspect the water-borne assault against the docking hangar contained no landing elements. Pale-faced Disciples decided it was a decoy and abandoned their meticulously rigged traps and carefully measured firing lanes. They immediately withdrew their troop strength from the docking piers to join the heavy fighting within the complex itself.

The short delay was all the Riverine had needed. The 88th Battalion had lanced deep into their heart. Seeker and Ghost were stalemated at the inner core of the stronghold, fighting barrel to barrel amidst the former barracks and mess halls that were now desecrated by the enemy. According to their auspexes they were less than fifteen hundred metres from the central belly that contained the siege-batteries. Yet the gridwork of the tunnels had been constructed as a maze by defensive design. Even with the aid of navigation tools and maps it was utterly disorientating. It would be the longest fifteen hundred metres of tunnel that any man would travel. Meanwhile, Prowler and Serpent in the western rail network found themselves pincered by dug-in Carnibalès to their front, and more insurgent reinforcements withdrawn from the docking hangars from behind their advance. The enemy pushed before them wheeled heavy bolters and replicate guns on treaded tires. Despite their dubious workmanship, the guns tore chunks out of the limestone with their spread of fire, pinning the Riverine elements into cover.

In that sudden, violent spike of fighting, Seeker Company lost both commanding officers to a single, tragic missile attack. Captain Fuller and Lieutenant Kifer had been working the company vox when the warhead blew out the pillar they had been crouched behind. Had it not been for Colonel Baeder, who strolled upright amidst the snapping rounds, rallying his men to hold, Seeker Company would have lost all sense of order.

Corporal Schilt crept low amidst the long, empty barrack halls. Rank upon rank of bunks, four stacks high, lined the long hall. Yellowing papers full of text caked the walls like papier-mâché. Their seniors ordered them not to study the text on the walls, but Schilt had a good look anyway. They were prayers to the Ruinous Powers, written in a basic Low Gothic. The words were soothing and easy to memorise. Once Schilt read a sentence, he found it hard to shake it off. It was as if the words were like a melody he could not stop chanting in his head. The rhythm was intoxicating.

It took no small measure of willpower to focus himself on the task at hand. Schilt wiped his forehead with the back of his hand and pushed the wad of dip beneath his upper lip. The enemy were in front, and the enemy were behind. Stripes of las-fire left searing afterburn in his vision and he blinked them away. Carnibalès bolter teams pounded them with support fire, forcing the Riverine into huddled clusters, seeking shelter behind whatever they could put between themselves and the enemy. To Schilt's direct front, squatting behind wadded stacks of propaganda crates, a squad of Riverine returned fire with a heavy stubber. With a flash, an enemy missile streaked in from the darkened corridor beyond. It exploded above the squad, hitting them with shrapnel and a wave of concussive force.

The men were dazed. Seizing the advantage, a warband of shrieking Carnibalès swarmed over the squad. Schilt saw the flash of machetes and sprays of blood. A Carnibalès leader whipped his skeletal limbs back and forth, laying about him with a scythe-bladed sabre. Schilt was paralysed with fear as he watched the entire squad being systematically dismembered. The wet thud of metal on flesh could be heard above the clatter of small-arms fire. Then, out of the pandemonium, the Carnibalès leader locked eyes with Schilt from across the hall. His face was white and equine in length, his eyes and mouth blackened like empty pits. The Carnibalès opened his mouth, displaying pearly white teeth. Schilt turned and ran.

With his back against a bulbous copper heating furnace at the centre of the hall, Baeder continued to direct his retreating squads into some semblance of a counter-attack. 'Sergeant Galhorn, lead your men up to that alcove. Hold position and pin the bastards in place!' Baeder shouted, pointing towards the Carnibalès.

Fifteen metres to Baeder's right, Galhorn and two squads of Guardsmen were lying down miserably behind a row of metal bed stacks. They clutched their helmets as if trying to force their heads deeper down into their necks as gunfire whistled above them. Galhorn looked at Baeder in disbelief. It was not that he was disobeying the colonel's order, but his face was locked in such blank shock that the sergeant did not respond.

'Frag it!' Baeder shouted. As calmly as he could force himself to, he walked out into the open towards Galhorn. A las-shot fizzled on the ground before him. A bolter shell kicked out a chunk of limestone on the ceiling above. Baeder's instincts screamed at him to scamper back into cover but he focused on placing one boot before the other. 'See, sergeant,' Baeder said, as he finally reached Galhorn's position. 'These fizzheads couldn't hit the wall of a hangar if they were inside it.'

Spurred on by Baeder's contempt for the Archenemy, Galhorn and his men picked up their weapons and surged towards the direction of flashing muzzles. They dropped into position after a short thirty-metre sprint and began to return enfilade fire along the advancing enemy flanks. Carnibalès fighters were caught in a crossfire and fled from the long hall back up the corridor, leaving behind the mangled husks of over twenty insurgents.

'On! On!' Baeder urged. 'Don't give them breathing space!' At his command, a platoon clattered down the hall under Riverine covering fire and entered the enemy-held corridor with bayonets fixed. There was a grenade flash followed by the grunts, exertions and clash of body on body.

'He's going to get us killed,' Schilt muttered under his breath. From his position at the rear of the Riverine advance, all he could see were the lurking shapes of Carnibalès, and Riverine pushing forwards against the hail of enemy munitions. As a Riverine fire-team sprinted forwards, an autocannon round erupted in their midst, punching a jagged spear of limestone into the air. Bruhl and Drexler literally fell apart at the joints. Fragments of stone and metal shredded Daimler's flak vest from his torso along with much of his skin. Daimler skidded onto his rear, clutched his bleeding upper body with his arms and began to scream. Half of the squad halted and returned to drag Daimler by his boots. The Archenemy had expected this. They landed another autocannon shell in the exact same position. Haber, Landau and Riese disappeared in a mist of red.

Carnibalès rushed back into the barracks room, spraying wild gunfire. The fire-team closest to the corridor entrance faltered. Sergeant Ohm and Trooper Vasmer crumpled, spurting blood across the floor. Schilt never ceased to be amazed by how much blood the human body could leak. He saw Zermelo manage to fire back with two shots before a wraith-like commander of the Carnibalès chopped him from shoulder to sternum with a machete. The Riverine advance was blunted. It looked like the slight gain they had pushed for would be lost.

Then Schilt saw Baeder bring up the remains of Lieutenant Kifer's platoon. 'Don't fall back one step!' he bellowed. 'Bruhl and Drexler didn't die so you could fall back!' Baeder palmed a rushing Carnibalès in its face so violently that the insurgent's upper body folded backwards at ninety degrees. Combatants fired their rifles directly into the faces of their enemies. Bayonets clashed with machetes. A grenade went off, blowing apart Riverine and insurgent alike.

Schilt had had enough. In his opinion, Baeder was pushing them into a meat-grinder, churning able-bodied Guardsmen into loose shreds of uniform and gore. He lurked behind a stack of paper crates well behind the main thrust of advance. Inside the crates, there were pamphlets depicting a rosy-cheeked rural boy with the stencilled words – '*Question Imperial authority*'. If Schilt stared too long at the boy, the picture seemed to melt softly and blur, the boy's soft cheeks whitened and his eyes became dark holes. It was either a trick of the light or foul magic.

Spooked by the prophetic symbolism, Schilt crawled away from the crates and lined up his lasgun on Baeder. The melee was now a heaving scrum of heated gun barrels and flashing blades. Schilt saw Baeder plough his power fist into the Archenemy pushing down from the corridor. The colonel had established a solid brawling stance with his legs staggered, throwing looping punches from the hip. A Carnibalès rushed at him with a raised machete and the colonel put him down with a wound-up punch. Two more insurgents charged forwards and Baeder crushed their sternums in rhythmic succession, one – two. Schilt lined up Baeder's back with his cross hairs. He breathed out, releasing all the tension through his nostrils.

'Snap. I got you, you fizz-headed fragger.'

And with that, Corporal Schilt clenched the trigger.

Murals on the mess hall walls had once depicted soldiers standing side by side with Bastón natives as a symbol of solidarity. Now they were smeared with the blasphemous runes of Chaos. Dark daemonic shapes had been painted into the original artwork, wraith-like apparitions that seemed to shift and move if one looked upon them for too long. Steencamp ordered flamers to be put to the walls, peeling and blistering the murals from the rockcrete. Some Riverine swore that the walls screamed as they were torched.

The fighting had ebbed and floundered in their advance. Steencamp consolidated his remaining men, just over sixty Riverine, in the empty mess hall. The Carnibalès had been filthy, carpeting the entire floor space in refuse. Gnawed bones, rations wrappers, crockery and plastek had been mashed into a splintered carpet of detritus. Steencamp thought he saw a human fingerbone amidst the mess and hurriedly kicked it away. He set up fire-teams on the three double door entrances and reorganised his battered company.

From vox reports, Baeder and Seeker Company were mired in heavy fighting in a barracks facility just two hundred metres west of their position. Supposedly, they were close to the core and the Carnibalès were throwing up a stiff resistance. Prowler and Serpent Company were bringing up movement to their east, lagging several hundred paces behind in the bowels of sub-tunnels. Those companies were drawn into a savage firefight with Carnibalès elements flooding up the tunnels behind them. According to reports, the enemy reinforcements were troops withdrawn from the docking hangars away from the decoy Riverine assault. Steencamp noticed that, for the first time, the vox-officers referred to the Archenemy insurgents as 'troops'. If anything, this hellish fight in the rail tunnels had earned the rebels a measure of bitter respect.

Steencamp recharged his lasrifle with a fresh clip and tucked the spent one under his flak vest. 'All right, ramrods,' Steencamp drawled in his vowel-heavy Ouisivian accent. 'Colonel Baeder and Seeker are close to the Earthwrecker. The Carnibalès are soiling their rags now and throwing up everything they have left. We're going to move in and support them. Prowler and Serpent are going to defend our rear.'

Steencamp led the sixty men off into the darkened tracts which fed into the core of the subterranean fortress. Murals were there too. The Archenemy had painted depictions of their idols into the brickwork – wispy, daemonic faces that danced and leapt and whirled. The overhead luminite strips gave the paintwork a surreal backlit quality. Their world seemed to consist of only three colours: black, crimson and ruddy ochre.

As the company pressed on in squad order, Steencamp could not help but stare at the paintwork. As a child, he had always been frightened of particularly realistic portraits of stern ancestors that dominated the hallways of his family home. He had been convinced that those stern oil painted features would move, and those hands, clasped so demurely in their laps, would lunge out to seize him. Now, in the intestinal depths of the Archenemy lair, those fears suddenly seemed very real. So real, that when the paintings began to shift and move, Steencamp refused to believe it.

The paintings peeled away. The shadowy forms came unstuck from their two-dimensional moorings and moved towards him. Steencamp was paralysed by fear.

'Sorcery!' screamed a Riverine. A las-shot cracked out.

The snap of gunfire broke Steencamp's stupor. It was Archenemy magic indeed. He had never seen it, but he had heard the Ruinous Powers were certainly capable of such things. Carnibalès fighters seemed to melt from the walls, camouflaged amongst the paintings. They were daubed in blacks and reds and ochre chalk to blend in with their surroundings. Heretic sorcery had done the rest. It was an ambush that no passage in the Ecclesiastical Primer could have prepared him for.

Carnibalès troops crashed in on both flanks with the tools of close combat. Blades rose and fell. The company fell into disarray. Dozens of Guardsmen were run through before they could react coherently. Steencamp's nightmare was now reality. Where there had been a particularly obscene painting of a red tribal dancing with a black daemonette, a Carnibalès wielding a machete materialised in its place. The heretic was naked, his skin reddened with inks. When he smiled, he showed the whites of his teeth and eyes.

The captain brought up his lasrifle, but the heretic jammed the rifle at chest level with his machete. Something surged into him from behind and Steencamp lurched towards the red fiend. They fell against the wall, clinched up, lasrifle locked against rusty blade. Another Carnibalès appeared at his side, this one entirely black and wielding a scythed sabre that resembled the crooked claw of the painted daemonette. Steencamp screamed as the sabre carved into his lower back. His vision dimmed from the pain. The metal plunged into his side was shockingly icy. Another blade hacked into his upper legs. Steencamp crumpled into the swarming press of bodies. Painted fiends looked down on him as his vision tunnelled. More blades stabbed downwards. Just like that, the paintings swallowed up Ghost Company.

'Schilt! Don't do it!'

A boot kicked Schilt's perfectly angled elbow from its shot. The bolt of las-fire went wide. Colonel Baeder continued to fight, unaware of how close to death he had come. Schilt snarled and rolled onto his back and, for once, it was he who was surprised.

Standing behind him, eyes still wide with surprise, was Volk. The big man seemed to be awed into disbelief by his own actions.

'Damnit, Volk. Why'd you have to go and spoil it?' Schilt growled.

The dissident Riverine, usually foul-mouthed and pugnacious, stammered for the right words. 'You can't kill our colonel,' Volk finally replied.

Schilt narrowed his eyes. It was a familiar experience. It slitted his face into a serpentine glare. '*Your* colonel?'

'He... he's not that bad, Schilt. I didn't join the Guard to duck fighting. A bad officer can get us killed, I'll throw my hat in with that. But Baeder, he ain't so bad. He's a gambler, but he does the job.' Volk took a deep breath, as if summoning words that had been bottled up inside him for a long time. 'Schilt,' he said, exhaling, 'you've got your priorities all messed up.'

Schilt's expression softened. It was a strange contrast to the roaring gunfight around him and the pounding drums of the Archenemy. He stood up and pulled Volk behind a support column as stray shots whined past them. 'You're right. I'm a Guardsman. Damnit, what was I thinking?'

'You weren't!' laughed Volk in relief. He slapped Schilt on the back. 'If either of us get out us this alive, you'll thank me.'

Schilt leaned in and smiled. 'I know *I'm* getting out of this alive.'

Volk's eyes widened. Schilt had already stabbed him in the chest. Volk gurgled. His eyes bulged. The stub gunner tried to push away, but his left leg began to spasm. Schilt leaned in with his blade and twisted. After more seconds of trembling, Volk stopped struggling and sagged towards the ground. Schilt laid him down in a seated position, well hidden behind the column. He wiped his knife clean on Volk's uniform and resheathed it.

Warily, Schilt peered around the column to see if anyone had witnessed the killing. No one had. Fire-teams were clattering towards the corridor. A squad sergeant spotted Schilt and waved him on. 'Leave him, he's done for,' commanded the sergeant, pointing at Volk's body.

In the smoking aftermath of their skirmish, Baeder had broken the stalemate at the corridor and the company was moving up to support him. The shooting had finally subsided. Still cursing the misfortune of his spoiled shot, Corporal Schilt picked up his lasgun and ran to join his company.

Pulver didn't feel like the aggressor. It certainly did not seem like the Carnibalès were fazed by the suddenness of their assault. The Archenemy had reeled like a wounded ogre stung by a needle, but they had rallied swiftly and were now mauling them, lunging and trapping them from all directions.

The sirens were whooping. Emergency lighting flickered. The tunnels were hot with the shimmering haze of flame. Pulver's Serpent Company became lodged at a main carriage tunnel, pinned ahead by emplacements dug into the railhead and assaulted from the rear by reinforcing units. They simply did not have enough guns to cover all areas. The Riverine clustered in the open. Las-fire scythed down dozens of men, each of whom Pulver knew by name and had served with for many years. A bolt shell glanced off Trooper Freige's leg at the shin. Freige fell on his backside, swearing at the enemy who had just changed his fortunes forever. Corporal Klader ran to put himself between Freige and the enemy line of sight as Medic Lowith tried to stem his blood loss. Freige swore at Lowith and he swore at Klader. 'Roll me onto my stomach and give me my gun you fraggers,' bellowed Freige. Klader did as he was told and Freige began to bang shots down the tunnel at the enemy. A grenade exploded overhead and Pulver lost sight of them all in a dense shower of smoke.

Baeder had voxed them and ordered them to hold their position. Seeker Company was close to their objective, Baeder promised. He just needed Pulver to halt the Archenemy for another fifteen minutes. Pulver had spat. 'I'll give you thirty,' he had said.

Pulver simultaneously led the fighting on both fronts. He directed fire-teams heavy with flamers to hold the Archenemy at bay to their rear, while he assaulted the railhead to the fore with bayonet.

At two metres tall, Lieutenant Vayber led the charge, crashing his fen-hammer into the Archenemy barricade. The Carnibalès shot at him as he ran, but big Vayber did not stumble. The enemy lost heart and fell back. Once they claimed the railhead, Vayber folded to his knees and allowed himself to die.

Pulver surveyed the carnage. A landslide of bodies littered the sloping carriage tunnel they had come down. Riverine and Carnibalès alike were twisted in the stiff-armed poses of the dead, their legs straight and stiff while their arms were locked up, some pointing upwards, others reaching out for something. The air stank of blood and faeces. The Riverine were taking up defensive positions at the railhead, kicking and rolling bodies off the barricades and firing points. Pulver jammed a wad of dip into his mouth in preparation for the inevitable counter-attack. Just thirty more minutes, he thought. Thirty.

Thirty-one, thirty-two, thirty-three...

Trooper Kesting counted the dead felines the Archenemy had such a fondness for stringing up. It kept his mind off the grinding fear of death. The deeper Baeder led them, the heavier the fighting had become. A crackle of shots lit up their front.

The column stopped and Guardsmen scrambled for cover. Kesting followed his squad behind a stack of locomotive machinery. Support weapons spilled out to cover the various angles of approach. The entire company fanned out before a blast door, wide enough to accommodate the girth of a super-heavy artillery piece. The grid-toothed shutter that towered above them was half open like an iron jaw, inviting them in. From side tunnels, Archenemy troops fired sporadically. Kesting watched rounds shatter off the limestone with an almost bored detachment.

This was it. The final push. The Earthwrecker, by all accounts, lay dormant beyond those blast shutters.

I wonder if they've sacrificed more felines in there, Kesting mused. A lasshot skimmed his helmet, the kinetic force slapping the top of his head as if reminding him to keep behind cover. It was absurd but Kesting was not at all frightened. They had come too far to be panicked. Even the lurking enemy gunmen, sniping from their posts, no longer really fazed him. He looked around. The enemy fired at him again, this time missing by a wide margin. Kesting spotted the muzzle flash and calmly pointed it out to Ruslet who carried the squad's grenade launcher. Ruslet plopped a round into the distance and settled back, quite pleased with himself.

This war is absurd, Kesting decided. A missile shook the chamber. The Riverine answered back with heavy bolter and stubber. As they did, Kesting rocked on his haunches and thought about felines.

* * *

'All companies, this is Seeker. We are in. Push towards us and hold the Archenemy reinforcements off our backs,' came Baeder's command over the vox.

Pulver fired a shot with his autogun in one hand and gripped the vox speaker with the other. His lasgun, spent of all clips, lay discarded by his feet. 'Seeker, this is Serpent. Prowler and Serpent are holding the tunnels to your direct rear but we are low on ammunition. Enemy presence is thick.'

'What about Ghost Company?'

Pulver hesitated, surprised that Baeder did not know. 'Ghost Company are gone, sir. They were ambushed in the main carriage tunnel parallel to your position about a quarter hour ago. We've since lost contact.'

'Hold position, sergeant. We're in,' Baeder repeated before static swarmed the channel.

Pulver dropped the handset and edged his head above the ridge of sandbanks. Carnibalès elements ghosted in the carriage works, less than forty metres away, flitting from shadow to shadow. The fighting had waned to a drizzle of half-hearted las-fire. The Carnibalès were sending four- and six-man teams down the tunnel, probing their strength, testing their resolve. The Riverine dug in behind their captured fighting positions to conserve ammunition. They could see the Carnibalès out there were gathering, swelling for another surge.

Sliding a new clip into his laspistol, Pulver made a mental checklist of what he would do in the final delaying action. He had one spare clip in his webbing and a half clip he wedged into his harness strap. A missile launcher was propped against the sandbag within reach, two warheads laid out beneath it. His tools were rudimentary, but the hand administered to him dictated the result. He would try to kill as many of them as he could before they killed him.

It was an ammunition bunker adjacent to the core where the Carnibalès walled up the fiercest resistance. Amidst the stacks of Earthwrecker shells, Archenemy fighters laid down a furious web of las. Resembling coned silos, they stood ten metres tall, enamelled in the pitted black of a ship's anchor. Ordnance stood in rows like sentinels, dozens and dozens of them.

Within the maze, Baeder directed the remaining squads of Seeker Company. Las hissed into the munitions, rounds ricocheted off the thick black skin. Baeder flinched inwardly every time one of the shells was struck. These were not simple ordnance but self-propelled rockets capable of long-range ballistic trajectory, each carrying a fission charge. It would only take one ruptured shell to devastate the entire bunker. Perhaps that was what the Archenemy were trying to achieve, he thought.

To his left, Sergeant Bering's squad was getting hit hard. A Riverine was bleeding out on the floor as Bering and the medic fought to clip the artery. The squad huddled around them were sprayed with blood. Distressed, Trooper Tuton crept around the cover and squeezed off a long burst. A bolter round exploded from his lasgun. The broken weapon flew off in one direction and pieces of his hand sprayed out in the other. Tuton fell back to his squad, clutching the stump of his wrist.

To his right, Baeder saw Corporal Helvec's squad pinned out in the open. Carnibalès trapped them in three directions. Rounds popped at them, slicing between the Riverine, over their heads, around their shoulders, glancing off the ordnance with metallic rings, punching smoking holes into the enamel. It looked as if rain was kicking up chalky clouds of limestone around their feet. Helvec held the platoon together by example alone. He stood up in the firestorm and coordinated his men to fire in disciplined volleys.

Baeder was aware that if they did not advance their position, the Archenemy would pick them apart and overwhelm them. He spotted an enormous locomotive carriage on the rail grid that ran the length of the bunker into the tunnel beyond. It was a payload tractor, a flat-nosed hulk of yellow metal and railing that carried six Earthwrecker shells on its flatbed. If he could get at least one platoon behind that thing, they could drive it before them as cover. To reach it, however, they would have to expose themselves in the open. As Baeder considered his decision, he saw Corporal Helvec picked off his feet by a bolter round. The shot slammed him backwards and left a smear of blood on the shell behind him. Baeder's mind was made up.

Baeder lifted his power fist. 'Three Platoon, on me! Go!'

Baeder broke cover and ran. He could feel his legs shaking from fear. He squinted into the line of Archenemy muzzle flashes. Some of them definitely were not human any more. Their faces were mummified in strips of leather and some bore inhuman appendages. These were not peasant rebels. At least not to Baeder. He expected to be pole-axed by a well-aimed round, but the killshot did not come.

Instead, Baeder ran into the rail tractor so hard he clashed his elbows into the rear of the machine. Three Platoon piled in behind him, shooting in all directions.

'Release the braking system!' Sergeant Melthum yelled hoarsely. Several troopers put their weight against a rusting track lever that locked the tractor in place. Shots whipped into the platoon, dropping three men. The lever would not give. Archenemy troops scurried into the open, dozens at a time, firing volleys and then ducking back into cover. Still the lever would not give. The Archenemy reappeared, ready to catch them again. This time the platoon's heavy stubber was waiting for them. He emptied what must have been an entire drum of rounds in their direction, firing long after they had rushed back into hiding.

In those brief few seconds of respite, Baeder tore away the track's braking pads with his power fist. He gouged them away with his armoured fingers, tearing off strips of metal like strings of melting rubber.

'Get up, ramrods!' Baeder ordered. Sergeant Melthum was already in the cab by the time Baeder clambered aboard. The rest of the platoon piled onto the flatbed or stood on the running boards with one hand on the side railing and the other firing their lasguns. Melthum roused the gas engine. The tractor jolted and began to pick up a grinding, steady speed. A shot crazed the cab windshield. A Carnibalès insurgent with a flamer ran out into the open and aimed his flickering ignition flame at them. Baeder leaned out of the open cab door and flattened him with a burst from his autopistol. As the tractor advanced, the rest of Seeker Company fell in behind the locomotive.

The tunnel loomed ahead. That was when the killing started.

It began with a roar. A bestial yell that temporarily silenced even the stutter of weapons. The sound rebounded off the walls in waves.

Heavily mutated Carnibalès fighters surged down the tunnel. Warped, their features melting, skin sloughing, bodies scaled, horned or fanged. They appeared barbaric in their looted leathers, many draped with chain-mail surcoats or bolted with oblongs of beaten iron. Baeder gathered that these would be veterans – such a level of warp-touch required lengthy devotion to the Ruinous Powers.

A shadow darkened the corner of his vision. There lurked a phantom, solid in his plate like a citadel given human form, a heretic of the Traitor Legions.

It issued its challenge, that same resonant roar. A comb of membranous spines flared from its helmet. The crest raised up, trembling and fearsome.

Riverine redirected their fire onto it. Burning flashes radiated from the Traitor Marine's armour where nearby Guardsmen shot at it. The monster appeared unfazed. It raised a boltgun and fired six shots. The first gauged its aim. The subsequent rounds chopped down five Guardsmen off the tractor running board.

Then it was on them, ploughing into the side of the tractor cab. The chassis crumpled. Glass exploded. The metal punched inward. Riverine shouted. The monster snorted like a raging grox. Baeder backed away from the buckled left-side of the tractor cab. A Riverine leapt off the running board and fired up at the Traitor Marine's armoured back. The Traitor torqued its immense torso and chopped out with a crescent blade the size of a harvesting combine's industrial cutter. The Riverine was cleanly separated with a curious puffing sound.

Baeder drew his bayonet, unsure of what he hoped to achieve with it. He clenched his power fist with the other hand. This would be it, he realised. If he hesitated now, then he could never look his men in the eyes again. He could never give an order or be saluted. All the privileges of command would now be repaid. Biting down on his tongue, Baeder leapt out of the cabin and drove his fist at the Legionnaire's chest.

Jormeshu slammed his weight into the tractor cab, rocking the multi-tonne locomotive. Through the splintered glass, Jormeshu's ancient helmet focused its visual scanners on the rank slides of their occupants. If his knowledge of Imperial soldiery did not fail him, one was a squad-level leader and the other was the force commander. Punching his fist through the windshield, Jormeshu screamed into the cab with the sonic blast of his chest speakers. The door of the cab was too small to facilitate the width of his shoulders and the Legionnaire peeled off chunks of twisted metal in his fury to get at the Imperial commander. The man was terrified. Jormeshu's olfactory glands could already smell the sour spike of fright musk.

Jormeshu reached out with a gauntlet, the clawed tips of his glove plucking at the soldier. The man recoiled. A peal of laughter escaped from Jormeshu's vox-gills. Imperial soldiers had never been much sport for a Traitor Marine. The only time they had threatened his existence had been nine decades ago when Jormeshu and his gene brothers had fought a regiment known as the 'Valhallans' on some wastrel ice-world. Those tenacious long-coats had actually forced the Blood Gorgons to retreat down frozen slopes. Still, the Blood Gorgons had wiped them out within the hour and their bones were now entombed in some forgotten glacier. As empires went, the Imperium's standard of soldiery was woefully incapable when compared to a Traitor Marine.

So it came as a great surprise when the commander launched himself at Jormeshu. Caught off-guard, the commander's power fist rammed into his chest. Sparks lashed out from his ruptured plating. The armour's daemon spirit shrieked in shock. Bones in his chest cavity snapped. A rib punctured his secondary heart. The visual read-out on Jormeshu's helmet flickered and hazed as its spirit voice cursed him for his carelessness. The Legionnaire staggered, the columns of his legs churning for purchase as he lurched off the tractor.

A Guardsman shot him in the side. Without looking, Jormeshu fanned out his sabre to the left and silenced him. The Imperial commander actually had the gall to follow him off the tractor and strike him again while Jormeshu's genhanced system was stabilising the shock trauma in his secondary heart. Jormeshu turned with the punch and the power fist pounded a crater into his shoulder pad. Furious, yet stunned, Jormeshu simply threw his weight into the commander. With five hundred kilograms of post-human sinew and augmetic plate, Jormeshu collided with his opponent and ran him into the ground. A volley of las and solid slugs drummed against his chest and bit shrapnel off his helmet, forcing him backwards before he could deliver the deathblow.

Then the Carnibalès veterans rushed onto the tractor, attacking the ponderous yellow beast like a swarm of tiny predators. The Imperial soldiers fanned out to meet their charge. To their credit, the soldiers held a thin line bristling with bayonets. Veteran Carnibalès fighters pushed forwards in a solid block, thrusting behind tower shields of cold forged iron. The clashing forces resembled warrior formations of prehistoric Terra, metal rasping against metal, shouting to be heard above the crack of splitting bones.

With only sixty-odd men in the company, the surging Archenemy spilled around them and viced their flanks. Face to face with the Guardsmen, the Carnibalès howled and spat from fish-toothed maws. They threatened to eat the livers of the Imperial fallen and put their spines in soup. The Guard struggled to hold their line, thrusting bayonets or hammering out with the butts of their rifles. A heavy bolter opened up at point-blank range, flattening a semi-circle of Carnibalès fighters before the crew were wrestled to the ground, hacked, stabbed and swallowed by the crushing advance.

Bruised and shaken, Jormeshu cursed. In the press of combat he had lost sight of the enemy commander. Never in his centuries of service to the Legion had he ever not been able to kill what he set his focus on. Furious, Jormeshu discarded his bolter and whirled his sickle-sabre two-handed. He waded through the press, shearing limbs and bisecting torsos with a horrible, fluid ease. The sickle winnowed as he looped it back and forth. Guardsmen fled before his warpath, the line folding in panic.

Fear, warm and tangible, ran down his legs. Corporal Schilt sagged to the ground as his throat constricted from panic.

Schilt considered running, but there was nowhere to hide. Instead he curled himself down and began to drag a corpse over himself. The body was that of Trooper Eschen, a rifleman of Eight Platoon. Eschen was still largely intact except for a bite wound that had separated most of his right cheek and forehead from his face. The blood rolled onto Schilt, still hot with vitality. Closing his eyes, Schilt tried to imagine he was somewhere else. Anywhere else but here.

'Fight and win, ramrods! Fight and win!'

Even as the words left Baeder's mouth, they felt hollow and devoid of conviction. In the tide of combat, Baeder had been knocked into the rear lines, lurching as he tried to regain his bearings. The colours of the fen were on all sides of him, Riverine with their bayonets braced like spears. Rising like a leviathan above the sea, the Traitor Marine raised his reaping sabre. Blood drizzled off the slick surface.

Baeder raised his autopistol and emptied the entire clip at the Traitor Marine from a distance of twenty paces. Although a dozen skirmishing bodies separated him from his target, every shot found its mark on the Traitor Marine's chestplate. Yet the shots did nothing. Most ricocheted away from the ceramite slab and the sparse few which penetrated opened up pinprick wounds on the expansive pectorals. The Traitor Marine did not even spare Baeder an irate glance as he continued to chop his way through the Riverine.

Captain Buren and the last twenty-eight of his one hundred and twenty man company limped into the ordnance bunker to the sounds of throbbing combat. The bunker was high and wide, Earthwrecker shells lining the walls like monument stones. The sounds of fighting climaxed to such intensity that even those stoic black sentinels began to shiver, warheads shuddering rapidly against one another. The very ground seemed to shake.

'Forward, men. Not long to go now,' said Buren with renewed vigour. The Riverine, beards soaked in blood, uniforms hanging off their slumped shoulders in loose shreds, jogged forwards, suddenly alert.

At the opposite end of the bunker's cavernous womb they could see Seeker Company fighting to the last, a ragged fighting circle anchored in the centre by a rail tractor. Heavily armoured Carnibalès fighters assaulted them from the front, while Carnibalès regulars engaged them from the rear. They could not see much of the Riverine, except for brief flashes of swamp camouflage. The Carnibalès were all over them, a heaving, swarming, disjointed mess.

Buren, the youngest of the company's captains, was a stranger to warfare so ugly. He had been an academic in his youth and had served his early years as an artillery officer with the regiment's floating gun-barges. His expertise lay in trajectory, range-finding and the variable gravity of planets. The violence of close combat frightened him.

It was precisely his fear of a hand-to-hand engagement that had forced Buren to salvage the support weapons of their decimated company. The men clattered, not only with their own small-arms but with spare barrels and disassembled heavy guns. Those who did not strap a spare weapon to their backs were draped with coils of ammunition or hung hands of warheads like fruit from their webbing for those who did. Buren's prudence now proved its worth.

With great haste, Prowler Company uncased their missile tubes and unwrapped stubbers from canvas cloth. Bolt belts were connected to bolter feeds and arcs of fire established. Buren put his expertise to use, directing missiles into the rear of the Carnibalès formation, dropping the warheads just short of the melee so they lacerated the Archenemy with shrapnel and flattened them with the force of explosion. Meanwhile, three grenade launchers pumped forty millimetre rounds in curving arcs, dumping their payloads into the Archenemy shield formation at the fore. Concussive bursts split the tightly-packed heretics so hard that shields flipped high into the air. Four heavy stubbers drilled cyclical fire, chopping Carnibalès' legs out from underneath them. Prowler began to carve a path towards the beleaguered Seeker Company.

The Carnibalès assault began to disperse under the sudden salvo of heavy munitions. Carnibalès broke away, scurrying to avoid the relentless bombardment. A missile misfired and exploded against an Earthwrecker shell; its thick skin unperturbed, the shell toppled onto a rank of shield-bearing Archenemy fighters. Shrapnel whistled through the air like buzzing silver hornets. In the mayhem, Buren began to appreciate the brutal artistry of his craft.

The first barrage hit the outer lines of the Archenemy and rippled panic through their ranks. With the certainty of slaughter suddenly denied to them, their barbarous ferocity weakened. Baeder climbed aboard the wrecked tractor and raised his power fist like a standard, its energy field shining outward in a perfect circular halo. 'The fury of Ouisivia renewed! Let's quash these heretics under a soldier's boots!' bellowed the colonel, reciting a line from a folk poem of the fen.

Less than forty men were able to drag themselves, bleeding and bruised, around the colonel. They discharged the remaining rounds from their rifles at the retreating foe. Rocket and fragmentation erupted around them, dangerously close, but they held firm.

As the Archenemy receded, Schilt rolled out from beneath the corpse of Trooper Eschen. The Archenemy left their dead in trampled piles. The Traitor Marine, wounded and bellowing in rage, lay amidst a tumble of dead Carnibalès heretics.

Schilt edged towards the Traitor Marine slowly. Both its legs had been shorn away at the kneepads, the jagged ends of ceramite scorched by rocket flame. Numerous gunshot wounds punctured its upper chest and arms, a mixture of syrupy blood and black fluid leaking from the gaping holes. In between its brays of outrage, the Traitor Marine's breath was ragged and irregular. Electrical sparks spat from the gargoyle vanes of its powerpack.

Despite its weakened state, the Traitor Marine was still dangerous. Schilt circled warily until he was behind the armoured beast. Despite Schilt's notable stealth, the Marine snapped its head around. The helmet had been worked into the shape of a long-faced female with a harlequin's grin. The mask regarded Schilt with a frozen, long-toothed smile. It snorted a metallic chortle through its vox-gills.

'Well done, Emperor's soldier. Your commander has outplayed me. But I am just one Legionnaire. How many of your friends have I killed today?' it rasped.

'They weren't no friends of mine,' replied Schilt through gritted teeth. He raised his lasrifle to his shoulder and aligned the ironsight on the Traitor's helmet.

The Traitor Marine grunted in resignation. Schilt savoured that. The monster that had robbed him of his dignity had now been reduced to Schilt's mercy. He squeezed the trigger. Automatic las-fire whined from his muzzle in whickering, white flashes. Molten droplets fanned out like a welder flame to iron. Slowly, the faceplate deformed and split, flesh parted to fortified bone. The bone gave way and finally the Traitor Marine slumped.

'Corporal! It's done! It's dead. Let's move!'

Schilt spun and saw Baeder waving him on. Seeker and Prowler Company had formed up and were following the track bend out of the bunker before the Carnibalès could regroup. Stray rounds were already hissing towards them from behind the cover of Earthwrecker shells. They did not have the luxury of time.

'Yes, sir,' Schilt replied, breaking into a jog. 'You're next,' he added under his breath.

The Earthwrecker was an ugly behemoth. It was sixty metres of barrel supported on an arachnid grid of gas valves, shock dispersal coils and pistons the size of cathedral columns. The entire weapon was self-propelled on a locomotive engine of heavy steel and grease. Structurally the interlocking support beams had to withstand the pressure of seven hundred tonnes. The Earthwrecker, Baeder decided, was a monument of destruction.

It was dormant now in its firing station, the muzzle locked into a crane system that delivered shells down into its iron gullet. Eight vertical apertures carved into the circular chamber allowed the Earthwrecker to steam forwards on a U-shaped rail track, once loaded, and slide its cannon barrel into a balistraria. The view from the apertures was shockingly beautiful: a broad vista of the jungle canopy below, a flat pane of green that reflected the rosy hue of dawn.

The survivors of Seeker and Prowler Company were laying a web of detonation cord and clamp charges on the war machine under the direction of Trooper Leniger. At thirty-eight, Leniger had been a bridge builder back on Ouisivia before he mustered for the Guard. The man often referred to himself as a mechanic of the landscape, laying down bridges, roads and swamp crossings. In Baeder's experience, Leniger was as good as, if not better than, combat engineers from more specialised regiments. Under his supervision, the Earthwrecker would not fire another shell.

Baeder climbed the ladder to the loading gantries as the few remaining officers of the 88th climbed after him. From the upper gallery of the circular chamber they trained their weapons on the blast doors, expecting one last Archenemy push. But none came.

'Sir, it's done!' Leniger shouted from below.

As the charges were placed and timers set, the Riverine evacuated the chamber. Baeder was the last to leave. He took one last look at the Earth-wrecker. He tried to envisage the immensity of its recoil, threatening to split its structural girders. He imagined the cranial-pounding roar of its gun as it was fired in the confines of that chamber.

'Sir!' Leniger repeated. 'We have two minutes, sir. This chamber is rigged to collapse.'

Baeder lingered, casting the Earthwrecker a final look. A look of equal parts awe and hatred. The machine was silent in its execution, indomi-table and unmovable.

'Can't hate the gun, sir,' Leniger said, tapping Baeder by the elbow. 'It didn't kill the men. The gun didn't send us alone into a meat grinder. The Ecclesiarchal fizzheads did.'

Leniger's accusations shocked Baeder. It was borderline heresy and, by all rights, Baeder should have given him *the heretic's court martial*, four rounds to the body forming the points of the aquila. Yet, startled though he was, Baeder could not find a reason to disagree.

All sound was drummed out by the tectonic quaking of earth and tunnel. The Earthwrecker was dying, consuming in its pyre the exposed shells. A chain of explosions trembled the stronghold. Carnibalès tried to gather their shrines and flee above-ground like drowning rodents.

Seeker and Prowler retreated to the docking hangars, passing the aban-doned war machines of the rebels. Aimed at the landing piers were quad-linked support guns and a dozen missile batteries. Facing the mouth of the hangar, an Earthshaker cannon was aimed squarely out towards the water. It was only then that Baeder recognised the wisdom of his judgement. Had the 88th Battalion elected to storm the exposed pier as expected, the waiting enemy would have decimated them.

Major Mortlock and the flotilla waited for them thirty metres from the shore. Of the 88th Battalion's five hundred and fifty men, ninety-six remained. Ghost Company had been entirely lost. Casualty rates had exceeded even initial estimates and stood at eighty per cent. So deci-mated were they, that fully two-thirds of their vessels were abandoned for lack of crew. The survivors were feverish with infection and malnutri-tion. As adrenaline drained away, the last fumes that had propelled their weary frames deflated.

Baeder was the last one onto the boats. He waded through the water and had to be pulled up onto the vessel by others. He simply lacked the strength. They were paper soldiers now, thought Baeder as he passed out on the deck of his swift.

The 88th who sailed down the Serrado, victorious though they were, sailed with the dreadful silence of the defeated.

CHAPTER SEVENTEEN

The Persepian Nautical Fleet sailed into Union Quay like silver blades against the flat grey pane of ocean. They were greeted by the great fanfare of the local administrates, docking for the first time in months amidst multi-coloured blizzard streamers and the pomp of brass bands playing Vinevii's *Hail to the Cavalry*. Imperial citizens who just days ago had been hiding in their habs now flooded the dockside in force. Mothers carried toddlers who waved paper banners. Acrobats vied for attention alongside preachers who praised the grace of the Emperor in righteous bellowing voices. The clap of fireworks painted streaks of pink, green and yellow into the sky.

The festivities were cut abruptly short. Military command was in no mood to rejoice. Admiral de Ruger ordered the port cleared of all civilians for the disembarkation of the landing forces. Thousands of stern-faced Guardsmen, hungry for combat, were released onto dry land. Columns of Chimeras churned down the eastern viaduct of the city, the graffiti of the previous week's rioting covering the damaged structures that towered above them. Loyalists stood on the streets and leaned out of windows to watch the Guardsmen pass by. Tall shaven-headed soldiers rode on the roofs of their armoured transports, their faces expressionless. The population of Union City was convinced that the insurgency would soon be over.

Within two hours, twenty thousand Motor Rifles had rolled into the rainforests of Bastón. Hamlets were crushed under the treads of APCs while truckloads of dismounted infantry chased down the villagers. It was like a hunt, the Guardsmen crushing their way into the forest and shooting down anything that fled from the disturbance. No distinction was made between loyalist and heretic. In the eyes of the Ecclesiarchy, they were all tainted. According to Montalvo, it simply made for an effective military strategy.

Persepian Poseidon-class patrol boats, off-shore combat vessels forty metres long from bow to stern, were released into the river systems under orders to 'reclaim the waterways'. Beyond that, orders were flexible and the Persepians rampaged in the coastal estuaries, volleying broadsides into river villages. Their destruction was only restricted by shallower waters further inland.

Despite this, insurgents continued to fight. Mortars, preceded by hit and run strikes, were the preferred method of engagement. Small groups, sometimes as little as two or three Carnibalès, harassed the grinding Imperial advance. By afternoon, the Guard reported an estimate of two hundred dead enemy combatants. Yet they also reported forty-five Caliguans and three Persepians killed in action. An Orca was further immobilised by a mortar round and grounded its keel in the muddy Serrado. As the advance continued inland, casualties were expected to escalate.

Thunder rolled across the ocean, its approached heralded by tides crashing against the quayside. A strong gale dragged a sheet of darkening clouds overhead, pulling black and grey over the blue sky. On the harbour, the deployment continued. Wind lashed and pulled at the Guardsmen as they guided trucks and Chimeras off the carrier ramps. They thought this a bad omen and pointed their thumb and smallest finger towards the encroaching storm, shouting *'Misfortune and mischief, away away'* as the keening wind stole their voices. It was only an infants' story but it seemed to give the Guardsmen some comfort.

Lieutenant Duponti clambered down the side of his Lightning and sucked the cold, un-recycled sea air into his lungs. It was a welcome change, after having spent the majority of the previous weeks in the pressurised cockpit of his strike fighter. But finally the 88th had broken the stalemate. Duponti's duty, for now, was fulfilled.

The flight deck was empty except for a small huddle of officials waiting to greet him. Duponti was in no mood for ceremony. His limbs were stiff from poor circulation and the stimulants were intoxicating his system. He felt giddy and light-headed. As he approached the group, Duponti's heart sank. It was an Ecclesiarchal gathering, no doubt ready to save his soul when what he really needed was for them to have saved him a shot of dramasq and some eggs and ham.

Cardinal Avanti stood in the centre, flanked by two altar bearers, regarding him with cold, flat, watery eyes. A cope of gold thread bound him together and kept the wires and machines that sustained him hidden from view. A mantle of sea-bird feathers was draped across one shoulder and embossed rings of blocky gold lined his well-manicured hands. The altar bearers wore only tabards of parchment despite the storm winds, their chem-nourished arms oiled and scraped. As much for intimidation as they were for clerical service, one bore the cardinal's sceptre of authority and another a gilded trident.

'Let me be the first to commend you on exemplary conduct in the course of your duties,' Avanti said, spreading his bell-sleeved arms.

It sounded like rehearsed babble to Duponti. The aviator eyed the cardinal warily. He had defied the admiral's orders and he doubted the cardinal was unaware of this. It was common knowledge amongst the Persepian soldiery that the cardinal's attention was best averted.

'The Emperor and His saints have smiled upon you. Surely were it not for them, you would not have succeeded in this arduous task,' Avanti continued, clearly enjoying his own impromptu sermon.

No, Duponti thought, it was a dangerously high amount of stimms and my own brass balls that got the job done. Yet he bit his tongue and nodded, forcing up a thin smile.

'The 88th's sacrifice in allowing my campaign to proceed will surely earn them the Emperor's forgiveness. In fact, I myself may give personal admiration for their deeds,' Avanti continued, seemingly addressing an audience of thousands rather than a lone weary aviator.

'Of course. Your respect is invaluable to front-line Guardsmen,' Duponti said.

Avanti dropped his glacial stare level with Duponti. 'How tainted were the 88th by the end of the mission? I expect them to be turned stark raving mad by the Ruinous Powers after having been in such close proximity.'

Something was not right. A sudden menace crept into the cardinal's cold, detached manner. Duponti decided to pick his words carefully. 'No, sir. They were coherent and unaffected. I can attest to that as we maintained vox contact up until twelve hours ago.'

'No. The Ruinous Powers would have changed them, just as they have changed the people of Bastón.' The cardinal spoke with a knowing tone that foreclosed any further argument.

Duponti gritted his jaw. Who was this Ecclesiarchal bureaucrat telling him what he knew? He had been out there in the field flying through flak while the cardinal had been pampering and manicuring himself in a stateroom.

The cardinal laid a palm on Duponti's heart. 'My poor child. It seems your judgement has been clouded by your close proximity with the Ruinous Powers as well.'

There was something in his voice. Something that suggested Avanti was playing a game with him. That the outcome of their conversation was predetermined and the cardinal was only going through the motions.

'I'm fine,' Duponti said, suddenly trying to walk around the trio. He was too tired for this.

'You are not. Do you hear voices and daemons?' Avanti asked, his voice raising several octaves and his eyes widening.

Duponti stepped backwards, knocking the cardinal's hand from his chest. He was being played with, he was sure of it. Something was conspiring against the 88th, and his insubordination had drawn him into it. Duponti darted his eyes about, hoping to see a fellow Persepian, but the wind howled across an empty flight deck.

'What do you hear?' Avanti repeated, eyes wide as he glided forwards.

Before Duponti could speak, the altar servant with the sceptre swung at his neck. Four kilograms of solid bronze landed with a jarring crunch on the top of Duponti's spine, whiplashing his head and sending him down.

'He is possessed, the poor child,' Avanti said with genuine concern. The altar servant with the sceptre continued to pound down with the holy relic as the aviator tried to shield the blows with his arms. The sceptre continued to rise and fall, breaking his forearm and forcing a scream from Duponti that was muffled by the buffeting northerly. Droplets of blood danced in the air, the wind carrying them into Avanti's face. The altar servant laid about, heaving and spitting with exertion until Avanti commanded him to stop. By then, Lieutenant Duponti was no longer moving.

'Give his daemonic soul to the sea. Let him drown for eternity,' Avanti said. He watched his servants tip Duponti's unconscious body into the waves. Satisfied, Avanti gave praise to the Emperor and wiped the blood from his face and his vestments.

It had been less than one week since the Guard had landed on the inland and already the Dos Pares cause was on the verge of collapse. Somewhere in the forest, Mautista heard the rustling snap of a felled tree, and the steady grumble of engines.

Mautista peered through a thicket, keeping amongst the leaves. He could see nothing in the distance. His eyesight had deteriorated in the past days, blood spots blanketing his vision. He knew his veins were haemorrhaging. His body had continued to warp, tearing and re-knitting his muscles. Most painfully, his bones had grown barbs, the tiny growths puncturing his skin like translucent quills. The internal bleeding was hazing his eyesight and swelling his flesh. It was agony to simply walk upright, let alone navigate the jungle.

His warband squatted miserably at his feet, wrapped in blankets of beaded fabric and dirty sheets of plastek. They had spent the last several days wandering from village to village in search of food. What they found were abandoned settlements as the Bastón fled before the march of the Imperial army, spurred on by tales of massacre along the coast and river regions.

The insurgency had relied on the support of the native population. It drew its strength, its resources and its powerbase from those native provinces. Indeed, its survival depended on the anonymity afforded by a network of Dos Pares agents seeded within the civilian population. But the Guard were razing and burning them, uprooting the insurgency from the ground. Just two days ago, Mautista tried to negotiate for ammunition from a local Disciple based in Manecal province. But word had arrived that their Disciple had perished and already been buried. The mutations had finally killed him. He had only been in service of the Dos Pares for forty-six days.

Worse still, when Mautista led his warband to seek medical supplies from the village of De Pano, they found an empty ghost town. Bodies of Bastón-born littered the streets, stiffened with their arms up to ward off their murderers. Province by province, the insurgency lost their network of influence. Where once there had been well-established lines of supply there were now scorched blisters of wasteland.

Communication lines had broken down throughout the network. Rumours were abounding that Carnibalès fighters were withdrawing from the coastal provinces to consolidate inland. Conflicting rumours suggested that other Dos Pares warriors were going to face the enemy head on.

Thus far the only tactical advantage possessed by the Carnibalès was their mobility and knowledge of terrain. The Four directed the warbands to avoid the Imperial combat elements and harass their supply lines. The inevitable tail of fuel trucks and logistics trains that followed the wake of the motorised divisions was firebombed and ambushed. Yet the war could not be won that way and, in six days, the Imperial Guard had reclaimed provinces almost two hundred kilometres inland.

'Mautista, do we flee or do we fight?' asked Canao, tilting his sloping cranium and clicking his mandibles nervously.

His question was punctuated by a sudden burst of cannon-fire. It sounded close, the rolling blast sending a burst of birds into flight. It was followed by flutters of small-arms. If Mautista strained, he could almost hear the agonised shouts of men.

'There,' Mautista said, pointed into the tangle of jungle where the river met the trees. 'There is fighting there.'

The rebels threw off their blankets and rose to their feet wearily. They cocked their weapons. Mautista did the same. 'We should join the fighting,' he said, but there was no need. The rebels were already slinking into the undergrowth.

* * *

The river stretched out like a soupy brown thread towards the coast. Behind them, the dog-toothed silhouette of the Kalinga Hills faded into the distance. Monsoon season was fading too, yet the morning showers lingered reluctantly, desperate to exert the last of its sodden influence over the canopy.

The 88th travelled west, branching away from the Serrado river. By all accounts a Persepian naval picket had deployed Guard forces into the western seaboard. It was only a three day pass from their original route and an Argo-Nautical would pick them up. The thought of extraction was the only thing that kept Baeder's ailing body going forwards.

He dreamed of a scalding shower to dislodge the dirty crust from his body on board the Nautical's hygiene facility. Perhaps a full breakfast with extra servings of ham and eggs in the officers' mess. He reasoned that he could fall asleep in the infirmary while medics attended to his accumulated cuts, bruises and tropical agues. He would sleep for a long time.

Until then, Baeder instructed the 88th to remain alert. The Carnibalès were desperate now, cornered and wild. Although the region was dominated by the presence of an Argo-Nautical just off its shores, the threat of ambush was ever persistent.

By afternoon, when the heat extracted steam from the rain-slick surfaces, a forward scouting swift boat reported sighting a Persepian Nautical picket at a fork in the river where the ocean currents branched out into twigs of minor rivers.

'We've broken the stalemate, men. The 88th ended this,' Baeder proclaimed on the battalion vox. There would be a time for speeches later, for now it was a simple congratulatory remark that lifted a burden of tension from their shoulders. Riverine appeared on deck, embers of tabac hanging from mouths. They sagged against the gunwales, craning to catch a glimpse of the Persepians like lost sailors sighting land.

The last boats of the 88th linked up with the waiting scouts and rolled in to announce their arrival together. Baeder watched the men of the 88th gather on their bows. They looked less than human, like badly-drawn outlines of men. Wild dreadlocked manes and beards that appeared ridiculously leonine upon their slouching bodies. He could see Mortlock too, his head wrapped in gauze from where a bolt-round had bent his ship's rear railing in half and sent tiny particles of it into his scalp.

There was no cause for celebration. Instead, as they neared the extraction point, the 88th mourned. They remembered those who had set sail but not returned. Pulver, Steencamp, Vayber and hundreds of men they had known for years. It was doubtful that the 88th were even a functioning battalion any more. They were done. The war, at least for a while, would not include the 88th.

Closing the distance, a Persepian Orca-class patrol boat broke away from the picket. Long and lean with a towering cluster of vox-masts and auspex sweepers, it was larger than five swift boats in length. A trio of twin-linked autocannon turrets was tiered on the vessel's short stream-lined superstructure.

It hailed them on a direct vox broadcast. 'Halt your position. On orders of the Imperial Guard.'

'This is eight eight battalion. We're coming in for extraction,' Baeder replied into his handset.

The Orca continued its path towards them, not appearing to slow. In the distance, another Orca peeled away from the picket and sailed towards their flotilla.

Baeder tried again. 'This is eight eight. Do you receive? Over.'

The first Orca was less than one hundred metres away and still closing fast. It split a frothing bow wave, breaking the smooth pane of brown water with its momentum. The men grew uneasy. Hesitantly, with no small amount of confusion, some of the Riverine settled behind their bow guns, unsure of why they were doing so.

Finally, the vox clicked and the Orca transmitted. 'Colonel Baeder, this is Lieutenant Commander Nemours of the Persepia 17th Patrol Group. I'm sorry. Soldier to soldier I'm sorry. But the cardinal's orders…'

The Orca smashed into the front rank of the flotilla, the sharp prow tilting airborne as it sliced into a swift boat, spilling Riverine into the churning water. The larger vessel's bulk landed like an ursine amongst pack dogs. Once it had entered the formation the Orca's turrets thudded, slashing 25mm rounds in a wide fan. Plumes of water misted the air, Riverine vessels broke apart, blood and debris fluttered down like an autumnal gale. Baeder stood still, for how long he did not know. After his ordeal, his mind did not comprehend the reality of what he saw.

The Riverine responded aggressively to the carnivore in their midst. Several missile tubes clapped, and warheads blossomed against the Orca's blue hide. A gun-barge drew parallel with the larger vessel and began to wash the length of it with a heavy flamer, fanning its weapon up and down. An Orca turret swivelled and unleashed a loud burst at the gun-barge, igniting its fuel tanks. The resultant explosion crumpled the Orca's starboard and it listed, the jagged wound taking water rapidly.

Regaining his senses in the white-hot fury of the explosion, Baeder pressed the handset to his mouth. 'Turn and move! Disengage upriver!'

Speed and manoeuvrability were the only things that would keep them alive as the second Orca surged in, with a third and fourth chasing its tail. The flotilla reversed direction rapidly, stern guns chattering defiantly. Three tubby gun-barges, all flamer vessels, intercepted the lead Orca to buy the other vessels time to escape. Smaller and faster, the barges circled the Persepian craft like piranhas worrying a sword-snout. They spat spurts of flame as the turrets swung in to track them. It was a brave but sacrificial gesture as more Persepian vessels flanked them and locked on with their targeting systems.

As the 88th fled from the Persepian picket, the flashes of the burning gun-barges shone orange on their backs. Their triumph burning away to tragedy, Colonel Baeder led his survivors inland. There was nowhere else for them to go.

Brigadier Kaplain was lying awake in his tent when he heard the first shots. Wary, yet curious, he tugged on his boots and slung his chest holster over one arm. The single shot crackled into a sustained splinter of gunfire that echoed in the still night. Shouts, sirens and then an explosion. Sweeping up two loaded pistol clips from his writing desk, Kaplain lifted the flap of his command tent.

Riverine Base Camp Echo was in a state of panic. Guardsmen sprinted in their undershirts to man battle stations. A storage hangar was up in flames. The klaxons were whooping on double-time, signifying red alert. The base camp was under attack.

The enemy were already among them. He could see shapes, backlit by vaporous curls of flame and smoke. In the distance, he saw the outline of a Rhino-pattern APC shooting bolter-rounds like star clusters into the barrack lines. Kaplain strode into the path of a sergeant running towards the flames with a canister of compressed extinguisher. 'Report, sergeant,' Kaplain commanded in a soft even tone.

'They're in the perimeter, in amongst us,' gasped the sergeant, coughing between words on smoke-clogged lungs.

Kaplain remained calm. 'Who? Who is amongst us?'

'Adepta Sororitas entered the camp. Sentries had no reason to deny them entry,' the sergeant replied. As he spoke, his eyes flickered about in fear. A crackle of las-fire lit up the western perimeter of the base camp, just beyond the boat sheds.

'The Adepta Sororitas?' Kaplain echoed in confusion, his composure fracturing for a second.

Before the sergeant could reply his head disintegrated in a puff of blood, following the distinct report of a bolter. Kaplain blinked the red back from his eyelids. Tiny, clustered dots of blood fanned out in a circle ten metres wide.

'Brigadier,' said Palatine Morgan Fure, rising like a phantom out of the dense smoke pall. Five, ten, twelve battle-sisters followed her from the smog, marching in unison like automatons. Kaplain felt hopelessness when he saw them, a sheer weakness that he had never felt before. The Ecclesiarch had ordered the death of him and all his men. He was sure of it.

'Brigadier, we've come to take you. Do not resist us,' said Palatine Fure. Her sisters clacked their bolters into place against their shoulders like a firing squad. Each was clad from helmet to sabaton in plates of iridescent pearl that caught and reflected the flames like burning oil. The armour of their torso had been shaped into rigid corsets, studded lamellar plates that gave them feminine form, yet there the humanity ended. Their full helmets had visors worked into the hook-nosed grimace of Ecclesiarchal gargoyles. Crease-heavy cloaks of lavender velvet trailed from bulky power-units on their backs, fluttering like banshees. Their bolters, lacquered in black panelling, were tangled with coils of piety beads.

'You cold bitches. These men you're killing would have given their life for your damned cardinal,' Kaplain said evenly.

'No they wouldn't, brigadier,' said Fure with a smile. 'Your men and yourself are tainted by the dark influence of the interior. We can't afford the risk.'

'That's grox dung and you know it,' Kaplain said, reaching into his pocket for a tabac. The sudden movement caused the sisters to thrust their bolters meaningfully. Kaplain slid the tabac stick out without missing a step and lit it with a clink of his igniter. 'I suppose I'm not surprised the cardinal would do something. I just didn't think he'd be so brazen.'

'He is the Emperor's authority,' Fure said in a tone that suggested rote learning.

'What's the real reason. The 31st were a liability? We landed on the mainland as a self-sustaining vanguard and as soon as the cardinal's men arrive we become a liability. Shoot us all while we sleep and be done with it. Is that it?' Kaplain said, blowing smoke in Fure's face.

'We are cleansing the mainland. You would have refused,' Fure added, suddenly hesitant. 'Wouldn't you?'

'Yes. I would have refused,' Kaplain said, with a hint of pride. In the distance the ammunition stores cooked off in a great mushrooming cloud of white flame. Kaplain swore and slowly, steadily, put a hand to his pistol.

'Don't do it,' Fure warned, raising her bolter.

He drew it out a centimetre, as if daring the sisters to shoot.

'Last warning, Kaplain. The cardinal prefers you alive. It doesn't matter to me.'

Kaplain, in agonisingly slow fashion, unsheathed the autopistol from his holster. Fure and her line of white-clad executioners fired. Kaplain died instantly, pulled apart under a volley of bolt shells.

For a full day following the failed extraction, the 88th Battalion fled inland on foot. They abandoned their vessels sixteen kilometres east of their extraction point as arrowheads of Persepian aircraft shot overhead like migrating flocks.

The rainforest near the coast was a humid wilderness of sagging trees and mossy emergents. Without the use of machetes, the Riverine sawed

their way through the vines, branches and entanglement with their bayonets. Sprightly, simian forms watched their piteous advance from the
treetops. Palm-sized beetles vibrated their wings in a dry, clicking chorus
and the air smelt of mildew and soil.

The last sixty-five men of the 88th Battalion slumped in a single file.
Some of the troopers were so sick they could no longer walk without the
support of a comrade. Finally, as exhaustion became total, some Riverine
began to shed their support weapons, leaving them to rust in the jungle
as they clawed their way forwards.

With his head down, speaking to no one, Colonel Baeder began to
think. He thought first of the Imperium, of the empire that his men had
died for. He was a soldier of the Emperor and he had given his entire
being to serving His Grace. Yet in his finest hour of service, the Imperium
had abandoned him. No, they had betrayed him. Even then, betrayal
could not encompass what had occurred. The Imperium had tried to end
him as if he had never existed.

It dawned on Baeder that, for his entire life, he had been fooled by the
Ecclesiarchs, the historians, even his fellow officers, into believing the
Imperium existed as a bastion of 'good' against the evils of the universe.
There was no such thing as good or evil. There was just perception. Various, multitudinous, infinite modes of perception. That was all. Moreover,
the death of his men had shown Baeder that the Imperium's perception
of reality was not infallible.

Under the vastness of the rainforest, he saw himself as a lone individual whose perception had been pressured and sculpted by the Imperial
system.

The rainforest thrummed with life, breathing as one vast organic mass.
Each part was the constituent of a whole: the mammals could not survive
without the nourishment of the wild, the greenery would not flourish
without the seeded droppings of birds and herbivores. Even the mighty
carnivore could not live without the insects, moss and microorganisms
that sustained the lowliest of prey. Just as Baeder could not survive without his men, the battalion existed as a single, living beast. Where the
Imperium fit into that equation, Baeder did not know.

He began to understand why the Bastón-born fought against them.
The ferocity of their resistance seemed apt now. The way rebel provinces
formed a network to shelter, provide and recruit for the insurgency. The
way they willingly sacrificed their rural sons to fight trained Imperial
soldiers. They fought for their right to existence. Their right to live or
perceive the world as they chose to, not the perception that the Imperium
imposed upon them. They had nothing to lose beyond that.

There was no good nor was there evil. The Ruinous Powers were the
Archenemy, but they were not *his* Archenemy. As far as Baeder could
discern, the only true enemy were the ones who fought to deny Baeder's

right to existence. As that Orca had ploughed into his men, rewarding their triumph with an ignoble, shameful execution, Baeder had come to hate the Imperium.

The colonel tore the silver Imperial eagle from his lapel and cast it into the deepest hollows of the undergrowth. He stripped the rank slides from his epaulette and discarded those too, crushing them into the mud with his boots. Cursing, he stumbled forwards, lurching only through the forward momentum of his slumping head.

Something was crushing his chest from above.

Baeder could not move, could not even snatch open his eyelids. The weight on his chest was nauseatingly large in measurement. Hundreds upon hundreds of kilograms. The thought of trying to imagine the scale gave him a curiously sickening feeling in his stomach and made his temple throb.

Someone had taken the Earthwrecker, barrel and all, and then balanced the entire machine on his sternum. It compressed the blood from his torso out into his limbs, pulsating pressure into his fingertips. Baeder tried to force his eyes to open. He tensed his muscles, coiling them for one almighty push.

Baeder spasmed. He awoke from his fever and rolled onto his stomach. Phlegm clogged his chest and he gagged, dry-retching to clear his airways. Even the task of coughing fatigued him. He was slick, almost slimy with sweat and blackened grease. It dampened his clothes and made him shiver with cold, yet his head was searing with heat. Every breath he took, he felt as if were breathing pure steam. He dry-retched again.

Night was falling. He was in a clearing of sorts: a dell created by a depression between the tendril roots of tall blackspurs. A festering pool of water had collected in the hollow, its unmoving surface waxed with a dirty film. The waning indigo sky was fading between the blackspur canopy above.

Baeder could not remember, but it was likely they had chosen to rest here in search of water. The remnants of his battalion lay slumped, supine or curled up. They looked like battlefield dead, collapsing in a jumble of fatigued heaps. Major Mortlock lay next to him, his chin slumped into his chest, the bandages on his head dark red. Baeder thought he was dead until his eyes popped open.

'Sir,' Mortlock croaked. His lips were cracked from fever, peeling his tattooed ork's teeth into bleeding scabs. 'What now?'

It was a loaded question. *What now?* It asserted how directionless and devoid of purpose they had become. Baeder shook his head. 'I'd like to say we die fighting against the bastards who did this… but I just don't have the strength any more.'

'Who do you think will get us first? The Carnibalès or the Guard?'

Baeder knitted his brow in concentration. 'I'd rather die to the heretics than be killed by our own,' he decided.

'Can you imagine the memorial at Centennial Park back home? *In the memory of the 88th Battalion/31st Riverine Amphibious lost in action to fellow Guardsmen. May we forget them.*' Mortlock sighed. 'What a way to die.'

'They think we're tainted now, don't they? I don't think they erect memorials for renegade mutants,' said Baeder.

Mortlock suddenly held up a hand. 'Do you hear that?'

'No,' Baeder said.

Mortlock held a finger to his lips and motioned for silence.

Baeder sat very still, trying to make sense of the croaking, chirping choir of insects and amphibians with his feverish brain. Then he heard it. The heavy rustle of undergrowth, boots trampling the crisp stalks of tropical succulents. There were voices in the twilight. Then the distinct, echoing clack of an autogun being chambered.

A figure emerged over the crest of the dell, peering down at them. A face mummified in shreds of coarse leather. Loose canvas clothing. A lasrifle of raw metal.

Baeder closed his eyes. The Carnibalès had come for them. Some of the Riverine stirred, groping for their weapons. Strangely, Baeder felt neither fear nor panic. His temples were throbbing and that bothered him more than death.

They crashed down the slope, sliding and slashing through the foliage. Baeder clenched his power fist but realised the fusion generator was depleted, its display screen chipped and clouded with water. It was dark but Baeder could see the Carnibalès surrounding them, weapons drawn. The babble of foreign dialects hurt his head.

'Put down your arms,' commanded their leader. It hardly needed to be said. Caught off-guard, the Riverine had no fight left in them. Some looked up despondently and surrendered with their hands in the air.

The Carnibalès picked his way over to Baeder. 'I smell the aura of a leader in you,' he announced, pointing a finger at him.

Their commander had the characteristic corpse face and long-shinned bones of a Carnibalès warlord. He was tall, so very tall and thin that he seemed like a shadow thrown out by a setting sun. He wore the husk of ex-militia leather with small discs of metal riveted over the torso and upper thigh. Black, swollen veins pulsated across white forearms in stark contrast. The moonlight reflected off the flat, angular planes of his face. Mutations had distended his jaw so that it jutted downwards and into a point, revealing long equine teeth. He couched a long-barrelled autorifle upright against his shoulder.

'I am,' said Baeder calmly.

'You are Fyodor Baeder. We have been looking for you. I am Mautista.' Those words cut through Baeder's sickened state with startling clarity.

He suddenly rose to his knees. 'How do you know my name?'

'It doesn't matter,' hissed Mautista, suddenly springing forwards into Baeder's face. 'You and your men will come with me now.'

'Just kill us here and be done with it,' Mortlock interjected with his head still sagging.

'Believe me, I want to eat your livers here while you squirm,' said Mautista. 'But the Dos Pares command otherwise. Come with me.'

'Why?' Baeder asked.

'I can't answer that. The Dos Pares see things that others cannot see. Gather your men and come with me.'

Several dozen figures loomed over them, guns drawn like spears in the fading light. Baeder thought about the Carnibalès's words. Surely, if they had wanted him dead, they would have killed him already. But they knew his name and evidently needed him for a purpose. He had no choice. He could not think of anything worse than being still alive while heretics chewed at his organs. At least playing along with them would give them all a chance to avoid that fate.

'All right.' Baeder rose unsteadily to his feet, feeling faint.

Mautista nodded. 'I will say this now. The Four have called for you. I have not. I will not hesitate to kill all of you if you try to harm me.'

The Gouge had many names – *Machanega* in the indigenous tongue, the earth's scar, split valley, although Imperial cartography referred to it simply as a gorge. Like most fluvial landforms, it was the product of prehistoric erosion, a deep canyon in the heart of Bastón mainland. A narrow tear, eighty metres deep and almost one kilometre in length, it resembled a mouth in the landscape. A ridge of forest emergents formed its outer maw and stunted, hardy tendril growth lined the rocky interior. Dark and sheltered, the gorge festered with spore-bearing growth, polyphore and stalked fungi fighting for nutrients with horse root and flowering creepers.

There was history here. The earliest footsteps of mankind on Bastón were fossilised upon the mud. The early tribes believed the gorge had been caused by the crash of Dark Age exploration craft, the ancestors who had raised a human colony on that wild planet.

Petroglyphs depicting the creationist myths were carved in varying sizes into the sandstone. Anything from pictorials chipped into pebbles and discarded in the quarry, to carvings cut into the gorge face soaring sixty metres up.

Millennia later, the Bastón warrior-king Machad had united the kin groups in the fabled forty-year war against a band of alien pirates from the sky. Although the fey-like aliens had been few in number, they inflicted thousands of deaths upon the Bastón, until finally, with club and machete, the indigenous tribes trapped the aliens in the Gouge and starved them. Chalk paintings of stick-like creatures with leering pointed faces cavorting with spiked rifles, fighting ranks of ancient Bastón huntsmen, spanned five hundred metres of rock shelf. The paintings imparted legend into the history of the Gouge and, indeed, into the history of all the Bastón archipelagos.

It was here that the Dos Pares rallied their fragmented cells and prepared for their major counter-offensive. From across the mainland and its satellite islands, insurgent warbands gathered in the Gouge. But it was not only Carnibalès fighters that collected there. Refugees, many Dos Pares sympathisers, were there too and they aided the fighters in the industry of war. Crude munitions workshops set up in rock niches produced pipe bombs and fyceline. Production lines rushed to press-stamp lasgun components throughout the day and night.

All told, the Carnibalès fighters mustered a force of four thousand, many of them veterans from the previous months of conflict. At least one hundred were Disciples of the Four, their unstable mutations afflicting them with such physical pain that they raged and slavered, eager to die for the Primal Cause. The Four were also present, although now there were only three: Sau, Gabre and Atachron. Their very presence emboldened the Carnibalès. Every night, both fighter and tribal sacrificed livestock and rodents in their honour, spraying the blood against totem shrines. Even the children vied for favour by catching beetles and winged flies, dissecting them and pinning their wings onto the totems.

Despite the inevitability of the Imperial conquest, the Pair and Atachron promised them victory. They swore solemnly upon the great Ruinous Powers that Bastón would not fall again to the Imperial colony. Not even the pounding artillery of Persepian fleets, nor the avalanche of infantry crushing through the rainforest, could convince the Carnibalès otherwise. The Blood Gorgons had spoken and their word was as good as the word of Khornull, of Slaan'esh, Ni'urg and of the great Changer in the Sky.

They marched for three nights, hiding during the day. Baeder, the survivors and their captors followed an unmarked trail through thick walls of thorny bromeliaceae and barely navigable trees so densely packed they formed curtains of mossy wood.

Baeder counted three dozen captors, all men who hid their facial mutations beneath swathes of leather binding. Although they did not attempt to tie or restrain the Riverine, they had confiscated their weapons and marched both in their rear and front. They did not speak, but gestured their directions and intent with the thrusting of lasguns.

During the day, they smeared their bodies in mud and wedged themselves in the thickets to sleep. In the distance could be heard the pounding of Imperial artillery, the low moan of engines and thudding flight of

Vulture gunships. Many times Baeder awoke to hear Caliguan Guardsmen on foot with tracking hounds, hunting ahead of the motor columns. Those were moments of tense, terrifying silence as boots *crumped* closer and each bark of a hound elevated his heart rate. But the wet mud hid his scent and the barking would fade, leaving Baeder to drift back into fevered dreams.

At night, the going was difficult and taxed the frail constitutions of the 88th survivors. Three men died on the first day, falling down and no longer rising. To Baeder's surprise, their Carnibalès captors began to treat their tropical agues and infections. The insurgents pounded foraged roots and berries into salves, oils and powders, tending to his men in a rough but thorough manner. Some of the Riverine refused treatment from the heretics, believing it to be Chaos sorcery. Baeder did not blame them, but he reluctantly accepted a slimy paste of gum-sap and bitter roots to smear into the festering wounds on his skin. As he awoke on the third night, he expected horns to sprout from his brow but, to his astonishment, found his forehead cool for the first time in weeks. Even the wracking pain in his joints had receded.

Although the indigenous medicine had alleviated his fever, his fatigue was total and the lack of full nourishment did not abet his condition. Baeder's left arm had developed an uncontrollable twitch and the sweat rash on his chest had become so severe the upper dermal layers were peeling off in filthy, brown strips. His stomach was empty but for phlegm. The Carnibalès had pilfered the rations from their webbing and distributed meagre quantities before dawn as they prepared their hiding places. Those who were sick, much sicker than Baeder, were given larger quantities and even supplemented by broth from a kettle. It occurred to him that the heretics were keeping them alive.

On the fourth dawn, as Baeder was slathering cool mud over his limbs, Mautista came and stood before him. In his segmented fingers he held a cold gruel of cereal, tinned meat and jellied broth. His face, constantly split by a mad daemonic grin, was unreadable, yet something in the way he stood told Baeder that the heretic wanted to speak to him.

'I should hate you for what you've done to my home,' Mautista began, 'but I don't. Every thread of your fate has already been designed by the Great Changer. I cannot hate you for what you've done, for those are the plans.'

Baeder didn't touch the food. He simply stared at Mautista, unsure of the heretic's purpose.

'But I do hate you when I see you. You *Guardsmen*. You have tried to kill all my people and take our land.'

'We did not participate in genocide,' Baeder said, rising. 'That was the Caliguans. We were raised with more manners than that.'

'Yet you stood by and did nothing. That makes you just as accountable as those who carried out the executions,' Mautista declared. By the tone of his voice, Baeder knew it was something that the heretic had carried on his chest for a long time. He had wanted to say it ever since he had laid eyes on Baeder.

'I thought you said our actions are devised by the Great Changer. Everything is simply a thread of his plans.'

Mautista smiled, unnaturally splitting his face from ear to ear. 'Your perception is very good, colonel.'

Baeder sat back down, suddenly very tired. The blasphemy of his words shocked him. Before the insurgency on Bastón, such an insight would have been sacrilege. But his world had changed now. Everything was different, somehow. He no longer felt confined by dogma or Imperial law. Despite his pitiful state, lying in rags on the forest floor and held captive by the Archenemy, Baeder had never felt more liberated.

CHAPTER EIGHTEEN

The skies belonged to Nautical flyers. Lightnings and Marauders dominated the troposphere while Vulture gunships hunted above the canopy.
The drone of engines became a constant, interrupted only by the pounding of bombs. With the Argo-Nauticals now anchored off the coastal
mainland, sorties increased twenty-fold. No longer were they restrained
to long-distance probes. With fuel stations and rearmament well within
flight range, de Ruger was able to conduct the sustained aerial campaign
he had craved.

By the one hundred and sixtieth day of the insurgency, the Imperial
ground advance had secured one-fifth of the Bastón mainland, no easy
task considering the choking terrain. The coastal Imperial provinces previously threatened by rebel attack were declared green zones of safety.
Along the northern coastal tip, the provinces of Fontabraga, Fuegos,
Uventin and Mentulo were secured by elements of the Caliguan Second
and Tenth Brigades. Likewise, the littoral channels and port city of Del-
lavio were held by Persepian Orcas, while the roads were blockaded by
Caliguan sentries drunk on pilfered liquor.

Every indigenous village encountered was put to flame. Charred rubble was reconsecrated by preachers who followed the Imperial advance,
rendering the bone-rich soil ready for replanting and immediate
resettlement.

Insurgent junk fleets retreated to the inland estuaries where the
larger Orcas and Persepian naval hunters could not follow. Many other

545

Carnibalès were driven underground into their system of fighting tunnels. Initially, Caliguan foot troops sent forays underground but traps hidden within the labyrinthine tunnels soon convinced them otherwise. Rather, the Imperial Guard were content to collapse the hidden entrances when they stumbled across them. Imperial intelligence estimated the war would be won in five weeks.

On the sixth day of their march the 88th Battalion reached the Gouge. From afar, the knitted tree line dropped away suddenly into an almost vertical decline. Yet deciduous growth defied gravity and continued to grip the rock with horizontal roots, their branches bent and twisted as they struggled to reach the sunlight. It was only the purchase afforded by the stunted, multi-stemmed trees that allowed the 88th and their captors to descend into the gorge.

On the valley floor, the gathering war camp resembled a barbarians' mustering army mixed with equal parts refugee exodus. White canvas tents were mixed with lean-tos of flapping plastek sheets. Carnibalès fighters and leashed canines picked their way between the huddled rags of non-combatants. Forges embedded in rock shelves smelted and hammered. Villagers stirred cauldrons. The tents formed circles, cowering at the base of totems that towered like monoliths. The stony obelisks were festooned with offerings of dried human remains, bones and plundered Guard equipment. Judging by the campfires, Baeder guessed five or six thousand were settled here.

At the centre of the camp, rising thirty metres into the sky, was by far the largest totem. The stone was roughly hewn at the base, blending into a colossal human face at its upper portion. Androgynous and smooth-skinned, the face had no features but square-cut cheekbones and a sharply-pointed chin. The broad, sweeping panes of granite gave the totem crude, powerful dimensions. Bloodied Imperial Guard helmets were stacked a dozen high around its base: Persepian pickelhaubes, padded Caliguan R-61 anti-ballistics, cloth-covered FEN-Cam helmets of the Riverine. Along with the helmets were shreds of torn fuselage, the turret of a burnt Chimera and even a string of severed hands.

It was under the central totem that the 88th finally met the Dos Pares.

Three armoured superhumans, the tallest almost three metres in height, waited for them. Like the totem, there was a broad, uncompromising presence to their frames. Their power armour was blackened umber with a glossy carmine sheen that caught the morning light. Each panel was etched and worked into the organic, stylised texture of flesh. Bronze charms, monstrous talons, opalised jewels, braided scalps and trophies from untold warzones hung from the armour plates. Their helmets, like their armour, were individually unique in design. They resembled theatrical masks with furrowed foreheads, wickedly-beaked noses and warped venting grilles that symbolised howling mouths. Baeder knew they were Archenemy, yet the soldier in him was humbled by the might of these superhuman warriors.

Mautista halted them at a respectful distance from the totem. The Riverine were silent. They settled around the totem with wide-eyed expressions. Carnibalès began to light incense from iron braziers, fanning the smoke with dried palm fronds. Mautista approached the Archenemy warriors alone. He opened his arms wide with his palms facing the sky and knelt down. The shortest of the warriors plodded forwards. He was slightly taller but many times wider than the rake-thin Mautista, with antlers that branched wide from the brow of his helmet. Reaching down he gripped Mautista's throat in his gauntlet and said something to him that Baeder could not hear. Mautista smiled in glee, despite the fist encircling his crookedly narrow neck. Baeder guessed it was some sort of a greeting ritual.

The antlered warrior withdrew his hand from Mautista's neck and pointed at Baeder. 'Come forward.'

The voice was soft and sonorously rich. It was startling. Baeder stopped several paces away from the antlered one and swore he would not kneel. The antlered one stared at Baeder with black visors like deeply sunken eyes. Suddenly, without realising, Baeder found himself sinking down onto his knees. It was not even a conscious effort.

'Fyodor. I know your name and it is Fyodor Baeder. May I call you Fyodor? Good. You may call me Gabre.'

'Yes,' Baeder said, not finding the words to say anything else.

Gabre gestured at his fellow warrior who had a helmet visage that resembled a lamenting crone. 'This is Atachron the Old.' He turned and pointed at his other side, at the last warrior with torso armour that was worked to resemble a black-faced daemon with a flat nose and a thin, darkly secretive smile. 'This is Sau, of Poisoned Mischief.'

'How do you know my name?' Baeder asked, immediately feeling weak for doing so.

'We have had visions of you, Fyodor,' replied Atachron. 'You are a great man. An admirable man. The gods show you unprecedented favour.'

Baeder rocked back on his heels, unable to comprehend what they were saying. The fever was throbbing in his sinus cavities.

'You must be tired,' Gabre said.

'Yes,' croaked Baeder, nodding weakly.

'Do you wish to feed and water your men? Perhaps have us tend to their wounds and ailments?'

Baeder nodded.

Upon his assent, Baeder's men were led into a shallow cave at the edge of the camp. The Guardsmen went mutely, whether silenced by exhaustion or fear of the Chaos Marines, Baeder did not know. The cave was wider than it was deep, a gap of shade at the bottom of the canyon. Beards of climbing creepers drooped across the sandstone entrance.

Inside it was cool and sheltered from the tropical heat. The temperate clime instantly felt soothing on Baeder's blistered skin. Rush mats were spread out on the rocky ground. Someone had prepared for their arrival and incense smoke wafted from wood lanterns.

Without being told, the Riverine lowered themselves onto the rush mats, hushed and expectant. The Carnibalès brought them pails of sloshing water and set them around the rush mats alongside strips of washing cloth. The sight of the clear water almost made Baeder give thanks to whatever Dark Gods the Carnibalès worshipped. Despite their fatigue, the festering state of their bodies warranted immediate attention. The Riverine clambered for the pots, dredging up slopping handfuls onto their faces. Baeder clawed at his skin, scraping away pieces of dried dirt with his nails. The cold water on his heat-rashed skin took the edge off the stings, the itches and the prickling burns. Scabs, gore, mud and sweat all fell away from them like a layer of hardened clay. Some scrubbed so hard their skin began to bleed. The pails of water soon turned black and were replaced with fresh ones.

When the Carnibalès finally took away their pails, they distributed jerry cans full of distilled spirits that smelt strongly of kerosene. The men tipped them into their mouths, alcohol spilling out and down their fronts. After having taken their drink, some sat around in a stupor with their eyes closed in a state of half sleep. Baeder dabbed some of the spirits onto the infected cuts that criss-crossed his body. He did not remember sleeping, drifting off with the wash rag in his hand. He simply woke up fitfully to the smell of incense several times. The Riverine were sprawled on the mats around him, in various states of intoxication. Some were laughing incoherently. Trooper Roschig was squatting over an incense lantern dragging deep, chest-heaving inhalations. His eyes were rolled up to the whites and he was babbling. As an officer, Baeder wanted to get up and wrench Roschig away from the incense. But his limbs wouldn't respond. He closed his eyes and didn't remember falling back asleep.

The smoke rose and fell in coils of purple. Outside the air was filled with the chirp of valley beetles and birds shaking off the morning rain. Sun spilled through the cave mouth onto mats and smoke and bodies.

In the furthest corner, away from the others, was crouched Corporal Sendo Schilt. He breathed short gasps through his mouth, trying to inhale as little of the incense as possible. The fumes were dark magic, perhaps even spirits trying to invade his body. Some of the Riverine were going mad. Schilt was sure of it. They lay on the mats, giggling in childish glee.

Schilt would not damn his soul like those fools. Perhaps the Ecclesiarchy had been right about Baeder. Maybe the mainland had tainted him. Perhaps the entire battalion had been tainted. But he was not, and he would not be damned with them.

Schilt gnawed at his nails as his mind tried to find a way to keep him alive. Perhaps if he brought back proof he had killed Baeder, the Ecclesiarchy would pardon him. Surely Cardinal Avanti would reward him for his piety? Perhaps a dog tag and an ear would suffice? Yes, thought Schilt, that would buy him his pardon.

He would wait until nightfall. Then he would strangle the bastard colonel in his sleep. Schilt had strangled many living creatures to death and it never bothered him. He would have to bite off Baeder's ear too, for the Carnibalès had taken his blade, but that didn't bother him either. The hardest task would be escaping the Archenemy camp. But he would come to that when the moment arose. The incense was making it hard to think. Schilt just wanted to lie down and close his eyes for a while. When he did, the backs of his eyelids were illuminated in complex spirals with a mathematical significance that Schilt didn't understand. Outside the cave, he began to hear chanting. The shapes in his eyes pulsated and oscillated in sync with the chants.

He would kill Baeder after he rested, Schilt decided. Then he would be given the Emperor's Forgiveness.

At night the war camp was still. The campfires were put out to prevent aerial observation and not a sound was heard. Noise discipline was absolute. The shadowy outlines of Carnibalès sentries and their canines patrolled the upper edge of the Gouge.

It was during this period of darkness and quiet that Mautista came for Baeder. They woke him from his slumber and marched him foggily back to the central totem. A large Munitorum-issue tarpaulin had been stretched around the monolith, with the totem providing central support to form a circular tent.

Inside, the air was dry and stale. Nothing moved. Even the motes of dust that flitted before the sodium lamps seemed suspended. The ground was layered with rugs of woven wool, exotically off-world and, judging by the faded tones, very old. The offerings of dead Guardsmen were still stacked around the central pillar, although now other items adorned the room, items that Baeder had never seen before. A yellow Astartes helmet hung from the roof, a round shield of layered bone and iron was hooked on the wall, even the fanged skull of a xenos creature two metres in length was anchored against a support beam. There were other trophies too, but these were just unfamiliar outlines lost in the shadows of the great tent.

Beneath the sodium lamps stood two Chaos Marines. Baeder recognised Gabre and Atachron. The two stood in the thick shell of their armour with their helmets curled beneath their arms. Their faces were bare and chalked in white. Lips and eyes smeared in kohl gave their features an unnatural depth. In the pale light their faces were all cheekbones and stern jawlines.

Baeder knelt this time, if only out of neutral respect to their martial prowess.

'You don't have to do that,' Atachron intoned.

'Rise please. We only want to talk between soldiers, as equals,' said Gabre.

Baeder knew as soldiers they were anything but equal. The presence of leadership radiated off them, instilling calm and confidence with every slightest gesture or tonal inflection. He remembered the Chaos Marine who had ambushed Seeker Company at the Kalinga Curtain and the raw measure of its combat power. Baeder had hated the Chaos Marine for killing his men. But in retrospect, he had been acting only as he would have done, protecting the men under his command. Perhaps in a strange, indirect way, they were indeed just soldiers.

Baeder rose. Gabre picked up an autopistol from the trophy stack behind him. It was a Brickfielder-pattern, a local replica used by Bastón officers. The body was finished in contrasting wood grains of gum-sap and blackspur panels with a frosty black parkerising on the exposed metal components. Gabre released the magazine, checked that it was fully loaded and slammed it back in. He racked the slide. Holding it barrel first, he handed the weapon to Baeder. No soldier could be whole without his weapon. It was a gesture of absolute trust. Either that, thought Baeder, or the Chaos Marines were so confident in their abilities that even armed he would pose no threat. Whatever the gesture signified, it humbled the colonel.

'The Imperium has betrayed your men. How does that make you feel?' Atachron asked.

Hopeless, utterly hopeless. But Baeder kept these thoughts to himself. Instead he remained silent.

'The Ecclesiarchy has condemned your regiment to death. We offer you a chance to keep your soldiers alive. But let me make this clear, we do not need your alliance. It is a privilege we grant you.'

Baeder stiffened. He was speaking to the devil, he realised. They were asking him to damn his soul. Baeder had always imagined the lure of Chaos to be seductive, but he never before thought how.

As if reading his thoughts, Gabre chortled. 'We are not inviting you into our way. We are allowing you to fight your enemies. An enemy of my enemy is another sword at my side.'

'It is simple, Fyodor,' said Atachron. 'We are going to end this war now. Solo-Bastón will be reclaimed in our name, no matter what role you play. But we are letting your men, betrayed and sacrificed, exact revenge.'

'The end justifies the means?' Baeder asked, mostly to himself.

'Ask yourself this. On what basis, by what authority do you decide your moral prohibition or ethical imperatives?' said Gabre.

Had he been asked that question before the insurgency, Baeder would have answered '*the Emperor*'. 'None,' Baeder began, but halted his words and corrected himself. 'Or rather, my own. As an officer to my battalion.'

'The authority of human reasoning thus replaces high authority. A philosopher of old said that, Iman Kant, I believe. I ask you again, what prohibits you from keeping your men alive?'

'Nothing,' Baeder found himself saying. 'I...'

'Fight with us, Fyodor. We have seen things you have not.'

Baeder took a step away, shaking his head. 'Why did you invade this world? It was Imperial territory. Your actions brought about the death of thousands,' he said.

Gabre seemed slightly amused. 'We did no such thing.'

'It was the Imperium that instigated this,' Atachron said. 'The Ecclesiarchy began removing kin tribes from their native land, herding them into work camps so their soil could be tilled by Imperial agriculturalists.'

In truth, Baeder had suspected this. But it seemed like everything he had known had fallen apart over the past few months. His loyalty to the Imperium; his faith in the God-Emperor. Now he clung to the last vestiges of his reality. The new truth that these Chaos followers showed him was overwhelming.

'The Bastón fought back, but against local militia guns and machines, they only escalated the violence,' said Atachron.

'What they did not know is that Solo-Bastón has long been one of the recruitment worlds of our Legion, ever since the days of the Fragmentation. We came to the aid of our benefactors.'

'Just four of you?' asked Bader, suddenly drawn to the narrative.

'We did enough, didn't we,' snorted Gabre.

'Avanti is a sick, cruel little man. He embodies the corruption of the Imperium. Exploitation, hierarchy, materialism, all hidden under a veneer of Imperial benevolence.'

It was enthralling to hear such physically powerful beings belittle the cardinal. These were thousand-year-old warriors, mocking the desiccated puppet master of Imperial Bastón. There was a righteous, natural law to their judgement. Baeder could not help but agree.

'You are at a crossroads, Fyodor Baeder,' said Gabre, using his birth name.

'One road, you can fight for your men again. Avenge those who have fallen and impel those who still yet live with purpose. We can give you this.'

'The other road,' Atachron intoned, 'the other road leads you to an anonymous death, dying for a cause that has betrayed you, and holds no meaning.'

'Will I need to worship your gods?'

'You do as you wish. Piety is witnessed through action, not in scripture and cathedral stone.'

Baeder held out his hand. The great, segmented gauntlet folded his within its palm. 'I will fight side-by-side as long as only I command my men and no one else,' said Baeder.

He was not the only one. Riverine survivors were getting rounded up. The Carnibalès had learned to ghost on the trail of fleeing, desperate Guardsmen.

Along the banks of Serrado Minor, the remains of Sierra and Bravo Company 31st Riverine were overrun by forward elements of the Caliguan Sixth Motored Regiment. The Riverine fought a desperate last-ditch engagement from between the trunks of a rubber plantation. Despite forcing the Caliguans to dismount, the Riverine were vastly outnumbered by some two thousand Calig Heavy Infantry. It was only the timely flanking interference of a Carnibalès warhost that drove the Caliguans out of the plantation. Missiles wove between bowers, mortar fragments whistled through leaves, breaking the Caliguan formation and forcing them into the river.

In the aftermath, the Riverine Sierra and Bravo were extended a temporary alliance by Disciple Thaleis. Captain Thorn, the stiff-backed commanding officer, refused, declaring stoically that he would rather die at the hands of fellow Guardsmen than dance with the devils of Chaos. Following his wishes, the Riverine shot him and offered Thaleis their allegiance. Pragmatically, if the Ecclesiarchy had accused them of taint, the Riverine would not die trying to prove them wrong. Tainted they would be.

Three hundred kilometres away, a swift boat squadron led by Sergeant Gamden was trapped by a blockade of Persepian littoral vessels in the channel and ambushed by Caliguans from the bank. They lost three boats to the Chimera-mounted autocannons before the enemy fire slackened and seemed thrown into disarray. To Gamden's astonishment, Carnibalès fighters exploded from the tree line. Firebombs splashed in fiery liquid rivers across the Chimera hulls and Caliguan infantry were cut down from behind by sustained las. Trapped in a crossfire, some Caliguans threw themselves into the water and attempted to swim upstream. Gamden ordered the flamers onto the water, bringing the temperature to a rapid boil.

The Carnibalès insurgents signalled for ceasefire from the land. The Persepian blockade closed in, turrets traversing for range. By then, Gamden had little choice. He had no food, no water and sparse ammunition. To keep his men alive, he went inland with the Carnibalès.

Up and down the coast, the hunted remnants of massacred Riverine base camps were offered a second chance by the Disciples of the Two Pairs. Some resisted, others regressed to outright hostility, answering the offers with bullet and bolt. Many entered an alliance with the Archenemy, a heretic pact made by desperate, hopeless men.

In the morning, Baeder returned to the cave and brought with him kettles of food. Clay pots of rice, stirred with lard and salt. Whole birds stewed in a clear broth. Then came trays of raw, diced onions and leafy, bitter herbs floating in dipping vinegar. The Guardsmen stared at the food as it was arranged on the rush mats as if their extended period of famine had made them forget how to eat. Baeder had to command them to eat before they began to dig at the food with their bare hands.

Hot and greasy, the food plugged the cold, painful void of their stomachs. The Riverine ate in silence, intensely focusing on the bowls of food in front of them, careful not to drop a single grain.

Schilt could smell the food, the savoury aroma cutting through even the constant smog of incense. Yet he refused to eat. He did not trust the fruits of the Archenemy, or Baeder for that matter. He had, however, risen to retrieve something from the food kettles. A serving fork.

Now in his corner of the cave, Schilt nursed the eating fork to his belly. It was a fork of long and narrow design to spear food from scalding cauldrons. The two tines were five centimetres in length, protruding like clawed fingers from a wooden handle the length of his forearm. He hid the utensil from the others. It was to be his pardon.

Schilt had always been a survivalist. As a young ganger in the wayside drinking dens of the bayou he had purposely sought trouble to hone his gutter-fighting skills. Those watering holes, filled with fen labourers, juve gangers and the surly, wasteful outcasts of the swamp had been tinderboxes of aggression. Fights erupted over bumped shoulders and men were stabbed over spilt briner. As a lanky pubescent youth amongst burly men, Schilt had not only survived but became feared in many establishments for his murderous intent. They quickly learnt not to pick a fight with Sendo Schilt. He was the sort who could receive a thorough gang beating, but unless his attackers managed to kill him, Sendo would eventually be waiting around the corner with a hammer for the knees or a shiv for the neck. No one ever got the better of an engagement with Sendo Schilt.

Slumping against the cave wall, Schilt fell into a fevered, delirious dream. The memories of his youth on Ouisivia filled him with determination. He would kill Baeder and escape from the Carnibalès. They would not find him for he was Sendo Schilt. The cardinal would personally commend him for his actions, perhaps even award him with the Cross of Saint Tarius. Perhaps he could even buy his freedom from the Guard and return to Ouisivia.

* * *

'Listen up, ramrods,' bellowed Baeder.

He crouched amongst the feeding Guardsmen and scrutinised each and every one of them. The survivors now looked at him expectantly. Despite their grease-slick beards and dishevelled uniforms, they had the air of soldiers waiting on the parade ground. The resentment and distrust that Baeder had feared was gone. At some point during their ordeals, they had put their lives into his charge.

Just months ago, Baeder would have been hesitant to issue the slightest commands. He had not even dared to press for uniform infractions for fear of aggravating the notoriously roguish Riverine Guardsmen. But now, he wielded absolute command. The Guardsmen obeyed simply because they respected his orders. Baeder treated his battalion as an extension of his body, as one would preserve one's own fingers or limbs, not as anonymous units to hurl into the meat-grinder.

Colonel Baeder nodded to himself. 'Men. Gather your arms. The cardinal has written us off, so let's remind him what we can do.'

Mortlock grinned his skull-faced grin. Most of the Riverine nodded. Others simply gazed at him with blank expressions. They were prepared to follow.

'The Carnibalès insurgency are consolidating for a counter-attack against the Persepian flagship *Emperor's Anvil*. We will fight, not for them, but alongside them. I will maintain full command of Riverine elements. Any objections?'

There was a moment of silence. Some smiled amongst each other, suddenly motivated by the purpose it gave them. Many others seemed too spent to care. 'The Ecclesiarchy have excommunicated us as damned souls. What more have we to lose? It's better than dying from starvation,' said Mortlock, breaking the silence.

'Heresy!' came a weak lonely voice from the rear of the cave. Shaking his head and muttering, Schilt stood up. He had never been a brave man but he acted now, without thought. 'Heretic! I am a soldier of the God-Emperor. You will not sin!' he shouted. Froth gathered at the corners of his mouth. The whites of his eyes surrounded his contracted pupils.

As a boy, Baeder had often accompanied his father in the medicae clinic. He remembered that once a mad man had been brought in to see his father. He was bound at the hands and had to be held down by three strong fishermen. The patient had been stabbed by a gretchin spear when their fishing boat had wandered too far out into the uncharted fens. The wound had become infected and the man had fallen into a howling, delirious madness. There was nothing his father could do for the man and the fishermen took him away. When Baeder was much older, he learnt that the fishermen had taken their friend out to the bayous and drowned him to end his misery.

'The cardinal will pardon those who prove their worth. We can survive this,' Schilt ranted, wiping his mouth on his sleeve. He approached Baeder, murmuring under his breath in rapid yet incoherent syllables.

'Corporal Schilt. The Imperium, the Ecclesiarchy, they treat us as meat puppets. We survive as a battalion or not at all,' said Baeder.

Schilt came closer. He pushed the other Riverine aside with his hands but his eyes were transfixed on Baeder. 'The Archenemy killed my friends. They tried to kill me.'

'No,' Baeder shook his head. 'The Carnibalès fought for the same reasons we did, to protect their comrades and their homes. We are not so different. It was the Imperium who condemned us all.'

Schilt moved to within an arm's length of Baeder. His skin smelled of rot. Raw, bleeding blisters covered the corporal's face. He was a very sick man, Baeder realised.

'The cardinal can forgive us,' Schilt rasped. 'But not you. Never you,' he spat at Baeder.

Suddenly, Schilt uncoiled his right arm. A flash of metal glinted. He stabbed hard at Baeder's heart. Acting on instinct, Baeder burst forwards, jamming the stab with his left forearm. Pain exploded all the way up into his left shoulder. Although unarmed, several nearby Riverine made ready to lunge at Schilt.

'Stand back!' Baeder ordered as Schilt stabbed at him again. The Guardsmen paused, hovering in a circle around them but staying at bay.

Schilt was practised in knifework. The corporal adopted a low gutter stance and darted forwards with a double stab. Baeder circled away, maintaining distance by footwork alone. The long fork in Schilt's hand was already glistening with red. Baeder's left forearm was feathered in rivulets of blood. Despite Schilt's decrepit state, he fought like a cornered rodent.

'You condemned us, Baeder. I just wanted to live but you won't let me!' Schilt accused, almost plaintively. He lunged forwards like a fencer.

'Trying to keep you alive was all I did,' growled Baeder as he stepped into Schilt's thrust. He jammed the fork into his arm again. This time the tines sank deep. Gritting his teeth against the electrical pain, Baeder wrenched the blood-slick fork away from Schilt's grasp. The tide of the fight changed abruptly. Terror replaced Schilt's maddened grimace.

The corporal back-pedalled, almost stumbling. In the shadows of the cave, it seemed Baeder's presence grew. He was not tall, nor broad, but there was a change in the way he moved, a slight stiffening of his shoulders and a rolling menace in his gait. Advancing, he cut off Schilt's retreat and flattened him with a left hook.

Schilt scrambled away, clutching his jaw. Baeder stalked forward, slowly. His shoulders were rounded and his fists raised like a pugilist, circling his downed opponent. Schilt reached out and seized a wooden lantern, hurling it at Baeder's head. Side-stepping contemptuously, Baeder followed up with a knee to the side of Schilt's head. The corporal folded over. Baeder did not relent. He followed Schilt down to the mats and dropped hammerfists to the side of his head. Schilt tried to turtle up, curling his arms over his head. Baeder began to stamp on his ribs. Schilt squealed. To the watching Riverine, Baeder was possessed. His methodical assault on the corporal was animalistic.

As Schilt struggled to rise, Baeder caught him in a reverse headlock. He arched his back up high, cranking Schilt's neck, guillotining his throat with his arm. There was a snap that echoed in the cave. Schilt's neck broke. Baeder had killed one of his own, in order to protect the rest. In keeping his battalion alive, everything was negotiable.

As Schilt died, the Riverine were up and shouting. They were shouting for him. The men chanted his name. There was respect, but now Baeder saw something else. The same thing that the Carnibalès showed in the presence of the Chaos Marines. There existed an unmistakable widening of the eyes and tense shoulders of uncertainty. Fear. His men feared him.

CHAPTER NINETEEN

The Union City governor's palace was like many colonial estates on Bastón, or any other remote Imperial outpost. It stood in stark contrast to the environment, floating pale and sharp against the sea of green.

Rising above the warren of shanties and concrete hab-blocks that spilled down the harbour side, the palace was a sixteen-storey artifice of Latter-Orient Gothic architecture. Wide, open-aired mezzanines and over a hundred interlocking balconies afforded a panoramic view of Union Quay harbour. In order to dispel the tropical heat, cold cream tiles covered every surface, each piece individually painted with flower and beast by off-world artisans. Gated awnings were unhinged over windows and fanned by native servants to induce airflow.

The central reception hall was small but neatly ordered for the purposes of business. Pink gauze curtains filtered the sun through open windows, muffling the sound of Guardsmen assembling on the parade grounds below. A small gilt table laden with imported teas and chilled cream was carefully arranged, surrounded by caquetoire chairs at neat angles. The sacred armour of a Kalisador casually adorned the wall alongside a chalkboard of teatime menus. In the soft, rosy haze, Cardinal Avanti lounged with a collection of rogue traders, subsector trade barons and starch-collared representatives from investment holdings.

Despite the hushed civil tones, the meeting was a subtle war of words. Solo-Bastón was being carved up, each fertile piece of land being wrangled, negotiated and traded, with Avanti at the head of the feast. Opposite him sat Octavus Sgabello, most esteemed of all the rogue traders present. Sgabello held trade charters from the Bastion Stars to Medina and back to the Lacuna Stars, earning him the title of Tri-Prince. He sat cross-legged in velvet hose with one pointed slipper bobbing jauntily.

Next to him were the trade barons. Stiff, humourless men ruffled in finery – slashed and puffed sleeves, periwigs and hundreds of yards of ribbon. For these men, the domain of anything exportable – fabric, spice and even wood pulp – was theirs and theirs alone. Such was their influence on the subsector that the wealth of planets relied on the accuracy of their calculation servitors and the shrewdness of their minds. Accompanying these oligarchs were the mercenary-explorers of the Weston-East Phalia Holding Company. Jack-booted and moustachioed, the explorers were represented by Commandant Amadeus Savaat. Resplendent in their frock coats of reds, blues and yellows, bastion loops lacing their chests and pewter buttons on their cuffs, the mercenary-explorers each bore a lance with their company heraldry.

Amadeus Savaat, loud and militant, had been by far the most vocal of the group and it was he who protested the most. If anything, Avanti would have preferred to have had the man shot for his insolence, but such an undiplomatic act would not go down well in negotiations.

'We have heard rumours that the inland is tainted by Chaos,' Savaat rasped. He touched the laspistol at his hip to ward against bad luck before continuing. 'If this is true, then not even with all the Chapters of the Astartes will I send my expeditions into the jungle.'

'Simply not true. Local superstition,' Avanti dismissed flippantly. 'If your company maps and charts the inland, then the Ecclesiarchy is prepared to offer you a sum of sixty-four million, half to be paid in advance.'

'There could be an appreciable risk,' Savaat countered. 'Sixty-four million including a right to levy slaves from the indigenous population. A quota of forty thousand males and twenty thousand children, cardinal. That is my final offer, my company knows where we stand.'

'It's only fair,' chimed Rogue Trader Sgabello. 'There is after all, an appreciable risk,' he said, smiling with his laminated teeth.

Avanti transfixed Sgabello with a stare he reserved for the most unrepentant of sinners. He knew the only reason Sgabello supported Weston-East Phalia was due to the fact that any slaves gained would require transport on Sgabello's fleet. Such transport would likely net the rogue trader a ten to twenty per cent cut of slaves on top of transit fees. In response to Avanti's withering attention, Sgabello looked away, still smiling although with much less mirth than before.

'That's out of the question,' murmured Baron Cuspinan in between sips of his tea. 'I have already invested a sizeable amount into agrarian land once the jungles are cleared. We will need slaves to till the soil and I can't have you shipping them all off-world, Master Savaat. The pinseed is not going to pick itself.'

'And your trade blocks will need our logistic expertise in order to establish and build your farms and mills,' Savaat snarled aggressively. 'Unless you are willing to compromise.'

Cuspinan sighed and put down his teacup with a rattle. 'You can enslave all the children you want. Their little hands are terribly labour inefficient. I am also prepared to sign a ten-year treaty guaranteeing you five per cent of all agricultural stock on the southern mainland payable in bond.'

Savaat grunted, apparently satisfied.

Avanti clapped his hands. Although a five per cent cut to Weston-East Phalia meant a five per cent reduction to the Ecclesiarchy, the Imperial church would still hold forty-five per cent of all rural profits on Bastón. Indeed, it would be a new age of enlightenment and civilisation on the world. Avanti was still bathing in the glow of his triumph and the afternoon sun when a Persepian aide appeared at the accordion door and bowed.

'Your grace. We have intercepted a vox transmission from the renegade Riverine forces.'

Before Avanti could respond, Savaat swore aloud. 'Renegade? You promised us no threat of Chaos taint.'

Suddenly, the trade barons and investors all looked to him expectantly. Avanti cursed the stupid aide for being so candid. Undermining investor confidence now would be disastrous. He would have to choose his words very carefully.

'Explain the situation,' Avanti ordered the aide calmly.

'At 14.00 today, Persepian vox-officers intercepted a broadcast from one Colonel Fyodor Baeder of the 88th Battalion, 31st Riverine. He claimed to be the highest ranked surviving officer of the Riverine and issued an order for them to rally to an unknown location. They used Ouisivian slang or local dialect and we were unable to discern the location.'

'You never mentioned that the Guardsmen turned renegade,' Savaat cut in. Sgabello mewed in agreement.

Avanti sighed. 'It was not worth mentioning. The Riverine only comprised a smaller section of the overall campaign force, roughly eight thousand in number. They were disobedient and a raucous lot, complete savages. Their superiors had disagreed with the conduct of the campaign and we dealt with them accordingly.'

Turning back to the aide, Avanti waved him away. 'This is such a minor, inconsequential threat that it requires no pre-emptive action.'

The Persepian junior officer shifted from foot to foot, wringing his hands. 'But your grace, the Riverine are gathering and reassembling. Intelligence estimates that anywhere between one to three thousand are unaccounted for amongst the Riverine war dead. It is a matter my superiors would like clearance to investigate further.'

Outwardly, Avanti smiled at his guests. 'One thousand? That's nothing. We broke them. The Riverine are scattered and directionless. What could they possibly do?'

By now the assembly no longer cared. Indeed, they seemed to share Avanti's opinion that the matter was trivial. The trade barons had lost interest in military matters and now talked of output data and statistics amongst themselves. Sgabello nibbled on a biscuit and laughed quietly amongst his rogue trading fops. Only Savaat and his damned explorers seemed to be paying any attention.

'My expedition will not fight rogue Guardsmen. That would incur a greater risk, cardinal.'

'So few remain and they will all be swept from the mainland well in advance of your endeavours. Take my word for it, commandant.'

Rising from his seat, Avanti clapped his hands for attention. 'To assure your interests are secure, I would like to invite you aboard the Argo-Nautical *Emperor's Anvil*. The Persepian fleet spearheads the campaign on Bastón and will remain long after the war is done in order to protect your investments.'

With that, Avanti left the chamber and the assembly rose to follow. Indigenous house servants wearing liveried tabards swept in from adjoining chambers like clockwork birds in waiting. The dishes were cleared and the furniture polished as the self-appointed rulers of Bastón left, leaving crumbs in their wake.

A coastal inlet, thirteen kilometres south-east of the docked Persepian fleet, was the weakest and most viable approach. The system of saltwater estuaries fed into the ocean where the Persepian flagship *Emperor's Anvil* was anchored ten kilometres off Union Quay. That was where Baeder planned to strike.

In the days subsequent to his vox broadcast, Riverine emerged from the rainforest as skeletal wrecks bearing with them stories of massacre and Ecclesiarchal betrayal. They joined the gathering Carnibalès war camp, their spirits resurrected by the prospect of revenge. In all, they formed a force of eight hundred able-bodied Riverine and four thousand Carnibalès veterans.

On the one hundred and seventy-sixth day, Colonel Baeder stepped onto his swift boat and cast away from the riverbank. The last survivors of the Riverine deployment, Guardsmen whittled thin and sharp by experience, followed him in a convoy. They were feral soldiers in the milk green and tan fatigues of the swamp, their weapons freshly oiled and clean in stark contrast to their barbaric appearance. Behind the fleet of Riverine combat vessels came a mixed flotilla of Carnibalès spikers, commanded by the architects of the insurgency, a trio of Traitor Marines. Those insurgents were also the veteran survivors of war. They hid their mutations under coiled face-wraps, yellow eyes peering from within the folds of their bindings. These were not rural rebels any more, but Archenemy warriors in leather armour and chainmail, holding lasrifles at the ready.

In the centre of the column were over two dozen spikers, stripped of their armour and any excess weight. The vulnerable vessels were hemmed in and escorted. Each carried a payload of raw, crudely manufactured explosives. Their pilots were martyrs, a single Carnibalès who would ram the spiker to a glorious death. Some were insurgents, their faces wound in strips of scriptured cloth and prayer seals. Most were Disciples already dying; their physical bodies deteriorating as their mutations spiralled, shedding their skin, hardening muscles, melting their organs.

The combined fleet embarked under a supernatural storm, its ferocity blackening the skies with cloud and thunder. The tongues of lightning and sleeting rain were not a coincidence. There was Ruinous influence at work, and even the Riverine knew this. They could feel its ominous presence in the air, like spirits watching them from afar. The clouds had boiled so black that they resembled ashen smoke. Rain curtains smeared visibility to a grey blur.

The fleet dispersed into the smallest littoral channels, its advance masked by the clashing storm which did not abate. Once they reformed out from the inlet, the flotilla emerged warily onto open waters, circling wide to avoid coastal patrols, and began a hard two days' sail towards Union Guay.

In their maritime tradition, the storm was a bad omen to Persepians. The clouds were so dark and so heavy, they dragged with them a sinister presence. The rain was a constant torrent of water from above, clattering the ships' decks like a tin drum. It confined the coastal patrol Orcas to sheltered ports and threatened aerial patrols with such ferocious gales that bombing sorties were temporarily suspended. Whenever that thunder rolled, Nautical armsmen touched the iron tip of their helmets and made the sign of the aquila.

On the one hundred and eighty-second day of the Bastón Insurgency a bridge operator on board the *Emperor's Anvil* noticed a suspicious blip on his auspex. The blip soon turned into two, then a dozen, then several dozen. Within a minute, the screen showed a mass of several hundred green pixels sweeping in on Union Quay. An alert was sent out two minutes later on board the *Emperor's Anvil*, and relayed to the only other Argo-Nautical docked at Union Quay, the *Barbute*.

Six minutes after initial contact, Admiral de Ruger, aboard the *Emperor's Anvil*, ordered all personnel of both ships to their respective stations. In anticipation of impending attack, gunners peered from behind autocannon turrets, while torpedo crews and deck gunners gathered at their battle stations. Range-finders leaned forwards into rubberised eyepieces, trying to make something out of the rain.

Lightning strike fighters were scrambled despite the high-pressure wind, yet there was no time for them to respond with any measure of effectiveness. By the time they took to the air, the Carnibalès were within bolter range of the Argo-Nauticals.

It all happened so quickly. Out of the crashing storm, a swarming fleet of river vessels bobbed on the swollen waves. The coastal patrols, pressured by the storm, offered no warning.

The range closed on the auspex. The *Barbute* sighted a spearhead of Riverine gun-barges to starboard, materialising from the rain well within range. The deck-mounted storm bolter batteries drummed out a salvo of ranging shots, throwing glowing tracers over their heads. Both Argo-Nauticals opened up with broadsides, large naval guns sending a curtain of shell-splashes into the sea. The gun-barges sailed on in a widely dispersed formation, the heavy shells crashing between the skirmishing Riverine vessels. Yet the ordnance which found their mark tossed gun-barges upwards on towering geysers of steam. In a futile effort, gun-barges bounced heavy bolter, autocannon and bursts of flak off the Argo-Nautical's thick hide.

Although it was afternoon, Persepian searchlights groped out into the cauldron sea in order to illuminate the storm. From behind the gun-barges came a flotilla of brown water vessels. Some were Riverine combat boats but many were the improvised Archenemy spikers. They spread out and around the Argo-Nauticals like shoals of carnivorous fish. The Persepian main cannons were not meant for tracking such small and fast-moving targets. Instead, deck gunners sprayed the ocean with waves of smaller calibre weaponry. Hundreds of men died within seconds, their corpses swallowed by undulating crests of water. It seemed the enemy attack was suicidal. Their small-arms could not penetrate the armoured skin of the Nauticals. Commander Stravach gave the order to conserve ammunition and 'pick the bastards off in our own time.'

At that moment, over a dozen spikers broke away from the main formation, surging ahead. Unbeknownst to the Persepians, each carried a volatile cargo of compound explosives towards the *Emperor's Anvil*. As they neared, deck gunners tracked their approach with tracer, lashing out at the approaching spikers. Two were hit, igniting and exploding in blossoms of super-heated gas and flame that far exceeded the size of the vessels. The Persepian officers on deck immediately realised the error of Stravach's judgement. The incoming vessels were burdened with explosives, although by then the revelation was entirely too late.

Five collided simultaneously into the hull of the *Emperor's Anvil*. Explosions bloomed with such force that tonnes of seawater crashed onto the decking. The silver corpses of fish floated up for a hundred metre radius. After the clouds melted away from the ocean surface, two gaping wounds were exposed in the Nautical's midship and several minor scars opened her blunt-nosed bow. Water filled the wounds, listing the great ship to port. Into the breach, assault landers and spikers surged along with the flooding tide.

The bulkhead was flooding with seawater and oil as the Argo-Nautical continued to list. Baeder leapt off his swift boat into the chest-deep water. Pieces of flesh and charred Persepian uniforms floated with twisted steel debris. He found himself in the hull's bulkhead, support girders ribbing the steel compartment. The bulkhead door with its wheeled lock was blasted off its hinges and inside could be seen service elevators and the tubes, piping and gas valves of the ship's corridors.

Baeder splashed his way to the door and took a knee. Shaking his lasgun free of water, he aimed the weapon out into the corridor. Major Mortlock crouched down next to him, slinging a fen-hammer across his shoulders. Behind them, assault landers poured into the breach, disgorging mobs of Riverine, creating a jam of empty vessels which the flooding tides pushed away. There were no platoons, nor were there companies. Their only objective was to rend their way into the ship's superstructure, inflicting as much destruction as they could.

Baeder crossed the corridor into the next partitioned chamber and met Persepian Nautical infantry running towards the breach. Spike bayonets polished to a gleam, they lowered their lasguns and fired a volley. Baeder swung behind a bulkhead frame as las-shots punched the ventilation pipes, spurting cones of steam.

'Isn't this what we came here for?' Mortlock shouted to Baeder as he ran past into the open. Flexing his arms, he wound up and hurled a fragmentation grenade into the Persepian position, scattering the firing line. The resulting explosion sounded like a pressurised clap and a burping gurgle of water. Seizing the brief seconds of respite, the rebels charged down the corridor, heavy stub gunners running point with cones of suppressing fire.

With the way cleared, the Riverine advanced into the next compartment. The retreating Nautical infantry, a platoon-sized element, waited for them in the valve chamber beyond, now reinforced by more of their number. The hatchway created a bottleneck and four Riverine were shredded by las-fire as they attempted to enter.

'Shoulder charges!' Baeder bellowed as he strode towards the hatch where the Nautical infantry sought shelter. Troopers Fendem and Olech clattered forward with missile tubes pressed against their shoulders. Fendem took a knee and put a hand to the trigger spoon. A Persepian round zipped out from the doorway and blew out the back of his head before he could aim. In turn, Olech managed to fire before Fendem had hit the decking. There was a deafening back blast as the missile hurtled less than twenty metres into the compartment beyond. It was such a close range shot that Olech was caught at the hatch and torn apart by an explosion of super-heated gas. From where Baeder leaned against the partition, the metal warped outwards from the force.

Mortlock tossed two grenades inside for good measure before Baeder led the charge into the compartment. Slumped against walls or thrown across the room were the charred corpses of Persepians, fused to the melted, waxy fibre of their blue uniforms. A Nautical officer had been tossed face first into a corner, his back twisted at an obtuse angle. He moaned as Baeder stepped past. Halting, Baeder turned back and fired a clean shot through his head. The man was dead before Baeder realised what he was doing or why he did it. He had always been a calculated thinker, but now he was falling more and more often into wild, frantic lapses of control. The reason and restraint which had made him human now seemed replaced by an animalistic urge. He did as he wished, and it filled him with a euphoria that started in his chest and spread to his limbs. Spraying a side compartment with las-fire, Baeder moved on, leading the column deeper into the *Emperor's Anvil*.

Mautista entered a rent in the bow and fought his way abaft of the collision bulkhead. He led fifteen Carnibalès fighters into the dry provision stores and began to burn the rations with flamers. In the pandemonium, Mautista had linked up with eight Riverine and pressed on.

A large number of transverse, watertight bulkheads extended from the outer shell of the vessel to the deck compartments. There, groups of crew ratings fought to keep the pump valves working in order to counter the seepage of water. Unarmed, almost forty of them surrendered to Mautista. The Carnibalès executed every one and Mautista had to physically restrain some of his men from carving strips of flesh from their enemies. There would be time for trophy taking later.

In the ship's berthing spaces, damage-control parties were hosing down oil fires with compressed air pipes. Ratings with buckets tossed up water from the rising pools into the flames. Mautista shot down three of them before they realised where the shots were coming from. The rebels massacred their way onto the third deck before meeting concerted Nautical resistance at the junior officers' quarters. From within the cabins, pockets of Nautical infantry and provosts savaged them with heavy support weapons.

Mautista dove into a cabin as a bolter round chopped down Mader, a former Kalisador. The cabin was cramped, with a single foldout cot on the far wall and a footlocker. A pair of socks lay on the pillow and a framed photolith of a girl with a high forehead and a single braid wound in her hair sat on the footlocker. Mautista peered around the cabin door and dared expose his upper body. He fired a sustained burst at the Imperial positions. It was a reckless move, but Mautista no longer cared; his heart pumped poison into his bloodstream and the agony had become constant. He knew he was not long for this world.

A shot sheared away his forearm. The limb, including his gun, skidded away down the corridor. There was no pain. Falling back into the cabin Mautista looked at it curiously, even probing at the exposed bone. Blackened, curdling blood leaked weakly from what should have been a shocking wound.

A Riverine sergeant sprinted into the cabin with Mautista, tearing at a gauze pack from his webbing. 'Critical grade four injury here!' bellowed the Riverine as he fumbled out a coagulant powder from his med pouch.

'I'm fine, I don't feel it,' said Mautista, staring at the stump of his arm. The mutations that tortured his body from the inside out numbed him to external pain. He looked up from examining his wound to see the Riverine's mouth agape in horror.

'What is that?' the Riverine asked in hushed, drawn out tones.

'It is the lifeblood of a Chosen Prince,' replied Mautista.

Blood continued to dribble from the stump, pouring like wine from a gourd when Mautista lowered his arm. Daemon's blood. The very same which had been injected into his veins for the past months of his induction.

'You are a daemon?' shouted the Riverine, suddenly startled. He backed away, almost falling out of the cabin door into the splinter of enemy fire. The sergeant dropped the bandages and touched the metal of his belt buckle.

Mautista shook his head sadly. 'I am a human. But we humans cannot contain such noble blood. It eats away at us, finding a way to claw out of its flesh vessel. But it is a worthwhile sacrifice for the fleeting clarity of vision and strength it gives us.'

The Riverine seemed puzzled. His knitted eyebrows showed he did not understand. But Mautista no longer had any time for him. He unsheathed a machete from a scabbard on his back and shouldered past the sergeant, back into the fight.

Baeder and Mortlock cut their way through the bulkheads and structured compartments, driving the Nautical defences back through the navigators' stores and into the torpedo bays.

'What's beyond, sir?' Mortlock asked.

Baeder craned to look over a fire control panel as stray las snapped the air. Beyond could be seen a hatch and a corkscrew staircase that spiralled into the upper decks. But before that came a block of Nautical provosts. They wore grey, fire retardant overalls and Persepian pickelhaubes. The provosts fought in two-man teams, one bearing a full-length oblong shield while another fired around it with a shotgun.

'Ship marshals and shotguns,' Baeder replied. 'We need some heavy support fire down that way.'

'Save the big guns for later, sir, we'll need them,' Mortlock said. He patted his fen-hammer. 'Give the order to fix bayonets.'

At first Baeder hesitated. A frontal assault without cover into well-defended Imperial positions would be suicide. But he had also come to know the importance of trusting his subordinates when they were sure. He owed them that much. In any event, Mortlock did not attain the rank of major by making mistakes.

'Are you sure?' Baeder asked.

'Ship marshals aren't Guardsmen. This will be too easy,' said Mortlock.

'All right. I'm coming with you,' Baeder said. 'Fix bayonets!'

Mortlock swung out from behind cover and swung his fen-hammer in a wide arc. Baeder signalled the advance with his power fist. The Riverine roared, pouring towards the partition. The ship's emergency lights caught the flash and glint of naked steel.

The Nautical provosts gave out and broke. Not a single shot was fired. The sight of the wild men clattering towards them with drawn steel had overwhelmed them psychologically. As Baeder chased down a fleeing provost and clubbed him down with his power fist, he smiled. A drill sergeant had once told him that an officer was only as great as the men around him. Only now did Baeder realise the truth of his words.

CHAPTER TWENTY

The Penitent Engine activated with a squeal of hydraulics and hosed the boiler room with cones of flame. Riverine scattered at the machine that had arisen in their midst, falling away in all directions. Fire blistered paint from the walls and churned the ankle-deep floodwaters, boiling up a solid curtain of steam.

'Heavy weapons! Heavy weapons on target!' shouted Baeder as he bounced shots off the Engine's frame with his autopistol.

Three and a half metres tall, the Penitent Engine had collapsed its hydraulic legs and crouched amongst the generators, purifiers and compressors of the boiler deck. It had hidden there, camouflaged amongst the raw metal machinery.

When it rose, the Penitent Engine rose as a solid walker frame, its hardwired pilot crucified across its central chassis. From afar, it resembled a hybrid between an industrial servitor and a chapel organ. Banks of pistons powered its theropod legs and smoke stacks were arrayed along its upper back. Tilt cylinders engaged the use of its upper appendages, both ending in flamers.

Trooper Gresham managed to circle off behind the Engine and squeeze off a long burst from his heavy stubber. The solid slugs had no visible effect. Shuddering on stiff, rotary joints, the Penitent Engine about faced and fired. Gresham disintegrated under a sheet of white heat, his black outline visible for a split second beneath the fire.

Baeder knew they were in trouble now. The boiler room was packed tight with the ship's vitals. Silo furnaces dominated the chamber and what little space remained had been devoted to nests of piping systems and bulky, thrumming generators. The main Riverine assault was now bottlenecked with no space to utilise explosives or armour-piercing rockets. The flamers of the Penitent Engine were devastating them in those confines. Tactically, it was the worst possible position for them to be in.

'Sir!' cried Mortlock.

Baeder flinched. He recognised the panic in Mortlock's voice. He had also come to know that anything which could panic the indomitable Major Mortlock was probably very bad indeed. Baeder turned around and froze. From the space between two welded air compressors, a second Penitent Engine clawed up from its dormant state. A third was cutting off the boiler room entrance, suppressing the hatch with its twin flamers.

It was as if Baeder's rational mind chose that very moment to shut off. His mouth roared a war cry that he didn't hear or understand. He vaulted over a turbine generator and rolled directly into the path of the first Penitent Engine. Baeder tried to get inside the Engine's flamers, looking to trade blows at close range. Industrial chainblades, painted with yellow and black hazard stripes, underslung each flamer. They revved up into a high-pitched whine and swung in a rhythmic, clockwork pace.

Baeder bobbed underneath, as he had drilled often in the regimental boxing yard. He lunged with his power fist but the Engine back-pedalled with a speed that was at odds with its size. Piston banks pumped its bird-legs backwards as Baeder doubled up on his punch. The chain fists snapped together like scissors. Baeder ducked low, almost bending his knees into a full crouch. A coxcomb of sparks splattered down over his shoulders as the chainblades collided.

In the corner of Baeder's vision he saw a second Engine thud towards him. The remaining Riverine in the boiler room were now trapped by the marauding machines. The men aimed at the Engine's exposed pilot, a female in a white shroud racked into the machine's frontal chassis. Yet even with their lasguns set to the highest output, punching cauterised holes in the pilot, she continued to shriek and babble in pseudo-prayer.

Baeder knew the Ecclesiarchy was not above the use of chemical drugs. He was reminded of the time his tutor had taken him to witness a public execution that the Ecclesiarchy had staged in a local theatre near his scholam-house. The brutality of the punishment meted out by the preacher had stunned his young mind. By the time the man was limbless and screaming for penitence, Baeder had been retching bile. The preacher then shot him three times in the chest with a pneumatic stake and declared the exhibition over. However, Baeder never forgot the look in the heretic's eyes as they snapped open and he shrieked even louder. Through bubbles of blood he asked why the preacher had not allowed him to die after his penitence. The preacher fled the stage in a fright.

Chemicals had kept the victim's heart pumping despite the horrendous trauma. He saw that same glazed look in the eyes of the hard-wired pilots.

The Riverine had nothing to match them.

Baeder was pincered between two Penitent Engines, their chainblades buzzing from every direction. He was alone. There was no room to escape. Pipes and ventilation tubes caged him. He dived low as a chainblade soared over his head. When he came up his heart was pounding hard. Somewhere in the thin pool of water he had dropped his autopistol. Yet still he raged. It was a volcanic build-up from months of carnage and mental anguish. He physically felt his veins swell in hot, angry flushes. His power fist suddenly felt light. He was no longer in control of his own body. Baeder hurled himself at the Engine to his left and reached for the chainblade with his power fist. The fist's disruption field collided with the whirring chain teeth. The external generator on his wrist spiked in voltage and snorted a plume of sparks. Violent tremors shook Baeder all the way up to his shoulder socket. He wrenched the Engine's left appendage away with a squeal of twisted metal and wire. As he did so, the corona of energy around his fist flickered and died. The power fist was spent.

Baeder stood very still. The battle rage ended, whisked away like a shroud from his head. Rationality set in. As the Penitent Engines raised their arms in execution, Baeder could only think that struggling as he died would be an undignified death. He wondered if he would truly be damned to the warp for all eternity.

The Penitent Engine to his rear was suddenly smashed aside. Chips of metal pelted his back. He felt the force and sound of a locomotive collision. Turning, Baeder saw the Penitent Engine lying on its side, embedded into the dented heap of a purifier tank. Atachron straddled it like a triumphant wrestler, hammering away at its chassis with strokes from a double-headed axe.

'Down, Fyodor!' shouted Gabre as he wedged his enormous shoulders through the boiler hatch entrance. Acting on instinct, Baeder threw himself flat onto the decking. Gabre released a tentacle of thermal rays from his meltagun into the one-armed Engine at Baeder's front. The Engine's pilot began to steam as the molecules of her body cooked off. It collapsed to one leg as the metal bubbled and warped, crashing the machine out to the left. Gabre continued to play his meltagun over the wreck until it had fused with the metal of the decking, spilling out in wide, molten slags.

'I owe you a blood debt,' Baeder said as the Chaos Marines approached him.

'Everything will be repaid in full,' replied Atachron, his voice meaningfully passive.

Baeder wanted to ask what he meant, but Atachron waved his great axe onwards. 'The gods tell me our prey lies beyond these hatches. Your men will need you to lead them. The cardinal has much to answer for.'

Stripping off the inert power fist, Baeder pried a fen-hammer from the fingers of a fallen Riverine. It was a weapon that he was not familiar with. Yet the striking head gave the hammer a sturdy weight and the padded grip felt good in his palms. It felt right. 'Let the cardinal answer to this then,' said Baeder. He looped the hammer over his head like a drill sabre and advanced at the head of his Riverine.

Admiral de Ruger was indignant. His grand ship was being sunk by filthy indigs and estuarine corsairs. The greatest pride of his entire fleet was being invaded by barbarous heretics who had no right to tread on its hallowed deck plating.

'Sir, we have to abandon ship,' shouted one of de Ruger's aides. The bridge room was tilting at a twenty-degree slant. Console displays were flashing urgent red warnings. The smell of burning petroleum was on the air, cut with the dry aftertaste of sea salt.

De Ruger tried to protest but he had no more ideas. For all his political wit and cleverness, the admiral became stricken with fear. 'These filthy, landless thieves are sinking my ship,' he repeated in disbelief.

'Sir, they're boarding us. We have to head for the preservation rafts now,' the aides insisted.

'Come then,' de Ruger said, waving them on. 'Before they fall upon us.'

His three aides led the way through the compartments which were rapidly filling with smoke. The three junior officers had discarded their frock coats and boots, rolling their jodhpurs up to their thighs as they waded through the rising flood. De Ruger followed behind, weighed down by his silver chestplate and lobster tail tasset. His black riding boots filled with water and the blue and white ostrich plumes on his burgonet wilted with moisture.

By the time they reached the deckhead, the battle had caught up with them. Nautical infantry jammed the wide corridors in their bayonet formations, bristling outwards in a phalanx of lasgun and boarding pike. The insurgents seemed to be attacking from all directions without any sense of order, appearing only to inflict random damage. The way onto the deck was blocked by heavy fighting.

De Ruger drew his sabre, a basket-hilted briquette, and waved his aides into the fray. 'Go on! Make a path!' His only means of escape was a cage elevator at the end of the service corridor, but a melee between ten Persepians and a handful of rebels degenerated into a mauling close quarter fight before him.

'Sir! Beware to your left!' shouted an aide as he tried to pushed the admiral away. De Ruger shrugged him off and smoothed his great coat.

Five Riverine emerged from a bulkhead hatch no more than a dozen paces from de Ruger. Although they did not know him to be the fleet commander, they recognised the rich gold braiding across the admiral's chest and the inlay on his burgonet helm. A square of silk embroidered with a cartographer's depiction of the Persepian seas, was plastered wetly across his back. 'That's the bastard,' growled a shirtless Riverine, pointing at de Ruger with the thick chopping end of a machete. 'That must be him.' Rebel Guardsmen clattered out from the same hatchway, eager to claim the liver of an Imperial high-ranker.

De Ruger puffed his chest as he heard the rebels sloshing through the water towards him. An officer's pride prevented him from retreating in the face of heretics. He stood his ground and flourished a glittering arc in the air with his sabre, a formal salute of the Persepian sword duel.

'Let's have you then,' challenged de Ruger. He stood straight-backed, sword parallel to the ground in a classic swordsman's stance.

But the Riverine running point simply dropped to his knee and fired his autogun into the admiral's chest. De Ruger fell sideways, smoke wafting from the punctures in his ceremonial plate. The burgonet tipped over his face and the sword clattered from his hand. His mouth was open, frozen in an expression of dignified shock. As if he could not believe that he, Admiral de Ruger, supreme commander of the Persepian Nautical Fleet, had just been slain by a Riverine wearing a corporal's chevrons. Blood soaked his powder-blue dress coat and clouded the water around him. Looking up, de Ruger clawed weakly at the Riverine as they fell upon him, tearing at his dress medals and hacking him with machetes.

Explosions trembled the decking. Steel groaned with pressurised creaking. More of the rebels were breaching the hull. Avanti almost lost his footing as the Nautical listed again, sliding candles and papers off his stateroom desk.

'Cardinal, what is happening?' demanded Amadeus Savaat. For once, the cardinal's esteemed guests shared Savaat's outrage.

'The Persepian armsmen have everything under control. They are exemplary soldiers, I assure you. I would not have your investments protected by anything less,' Avanti said, holding onto the edge of his desk.

A trade baron – Groseph Uhring – began to cry. Uhring was the first-born son of a grain and textiles magnate from the inner Mesalon sub, heir to an illustrious line of merchant aristocrats who owned five per cent of all shipping along from the Bastion Stars to Medina. He sobbed into his tricorn and began to shake. 'Forget the investments!' he wailed. 'Just let us live. Take us to safety and my father will donate untold amounts into the Imperial coffers.' As if to punctuate his plea, there came another distant rumble in the ship. Faint, muffled screams of men echoed in its wake.

Avanti silenced him with a turn of the wrist. 'There is no need to panic. We will proceed to the saviour deck. Valkyries will take us to the mainland, although I doubt the necessity of such precautions.'

'Necessity, cardinal? You promised us this war was as good as over. From what I can see, it is anything but over!' Savaat raged, stamping the plush carpet with his badge-lance.

'We are going to die! I smell leaking gas!' wailed Uhring, throwing his hands up into the air. He was right. Even Avanti could scent the heavy odour of propane. Somewhere, the pipes which provided heating of the staterooms had burst. There was a murmur of worry amongst Uhring's fellow trade barons. Some began to take pinches of snuff from locket pendants in an attempt to mask the stink.

'Gentlemen, please,' shouted Palatine Fure. She was like a siren of calm amongst the babble of panic. 'Follow me. My sisters and I will accompany you all off this Nautical until the situation can be placated.' She signalled to her retinue of Sororitas who began to move out of Avanti's stateroom in a herring-bone formation.

'We are going to die. I can smell it! Can anyone else smell it?' Uhring cried. No one answered but even the hardy mercenary-explorers of the Phalia Trade Company made signs of the aquila.

The cardinal could feel his subsectoral investment slipping through his fingers. Who would be willing to bring trade to a war-torn planet? He could not let such a thing happen. It had taken him the better part of six years to provoke the natives into rebellion alone. The Ecclesiarchy would not look on him fondly if he failed to bring this world to heel.

'Kill that man,' Avanti ordered, pointing to the hysterical baron. Before the oligarchs could fully process what had happened, Palatine Fure crushed Uhring's face with a blow from her flanged mace, collapsing him instantly.

'He needed to be quiet,' Avanti muttered. 'I'm under quite significant stress right now and I need to think. My apologies if you thought that was crude, but Palatine Fure cannot risk combusting the leaked gas with firearms. Now please be quiet so I can think.'

The assembly fell very quiet. Even Amadeus Savaat stared uneasily at Groseph Uhring's body, leaking fluid from a split down his face.

'We must proceed to the saviour decks. May I remind you gentlemen, if you have any firearms on your person do not use them while the threat of leaking gas lingers. My devoted bodyguard here will keep us quite safe.'

To prove his point, the Adepta Sororitas lining the stateroom corridor slung their bolters in front of their chests and drew personal arms. Maces, morning stars and chain flails were unhooked from plate girdles. They snapped the gargoyle visors down over their helmets as Palatine Fure took her position at the head of the fighting column. 'My Celestian bodyguard,' announced the cardinal proudly. 'Gentlemen, despite this interlude of excitement, we will be dining on shellfish in my palace tonight. The Emperor protects.'

* * *

Baeder flipped open the deckhead hatch and emerged in the ship's upper structure. Here the Argo-Nautical more resembled the interior of a ducal manor than the structure of a warship. The staterooms were divided into three separate decks with swirling ceramic staircases connecting the mid-tier mezzanine.

Baeder, Mortlock, some forty Riverine and the Carnibalès found themselves in the ground lobby of the state ward. Thickly-padded carpet of Berberian tapestry covered the expansive floor upon which bobbed a family of divans. The regimental flags of various boat squadrons, battle fleets and armadas were draped like heavy curtains on the wall in proud colours of sky blue, white and golden thread. High overhead, a crystal chandelier flickered as the ship's main power stations shorted. The air was hot and appeared to haze. Several gas pipes that provided the state ward with warmed water and heated flooring had burst. The air was pungent with a sulphurous stink.

'I'm getting a high read-out of combustible gas in the atmosphere,' Gabre announced.

'Yes, brother,' confirmed Atachron. 'As high as thirty-five per cent in some parts. Set firearms to safe,' he commanded.

As the rebel Guardsmen toggled their weapons from ready, the double doors at the far end of the lobby crashed aside. A female in pearl-white power armour entered the chamber. Her visor was open. Palatine Morgan Fure. Baeder recognised the cold witch from their deployment parade. She led a column of some thirty Adepta Sororitas flanking a procession of extravagantly dressed off-world dignitaries.

There was a shocked, split second of stillness as Fure saw the rebel raiders. The sisters encircled the flock of dignitaries like low, growling hounds. The Riverine began to bay for blood, clashing machetes against their bladed rifles. Baeder snorted through his nostrils, barely able to contain the angry shudder in his hands. Avanti was amongst them. The man who had decimated the 31st Riverine Founding. He could see the cardinal's purple robes. He wanted to remember every line and every crease on the ancient planes of his face. They locked stares and Baeder saw no fear in the old man's eyes. Just a righteous glare of hatred. That compelled him more than any fear. He hated Avanti more than anything. More than the orkoids of the swamp. More, even, than the Carnibalès. Cardinal Avanti personified the Imperium and the entire, rotting hierarchy that had spurned his soldiers.

In the haze of gas, the battle-sisters formed a solid wedge of warriors in front of the Imperial dignitaries. Without the threat of projectile weapons, fighters squared, shoulder to shoulder. Like jousting knights, both sides lowered their weapons and charged. Baeder could see his enemies in intimate detail. He could count the brass buttons on their mantles and smell the frankincense of their bodies. Most Guard regiments were not accustomed to combat at such a range but the Riverine howled for it. The forces met in the centre with a grinding crunch of bodies.

Palatine Fure stood at the front of her formation, face to face with Atachron, who towered over her like a rising black tide. Brandishing a holy war sceptre in her left and a plasteel combat shield in her right, she darted at Atachron. The Chaos Marine swept from left to right with his axe, cleaving through the gas curtain in a trail of liquid ripples.

Gabre threw himself into the power-armoured wall of battle-sisters. He slashed with a double-edged chainsword, the brute strength of his swing cracking Sororitas armour.

Baeder fought his way to Gabre's side. He brought his fen-hammer down in a downward arc directly onto a battle-sister's helmet. She raised her mace in a horizontal block but the weight of the fen-hammer simply crashed through. Neck buckling at an awkward angle, her head tilted almost ninety degrees and she fell backwards, throwing her hands into the air. He swung the hammer up again like a woodsman and sent it crashing back down. His swings were long and almost comical in their method, despite throwing up plumes of blood and armour fragments with every downward arc.

Despite Baeder and Gabre holding the centre of the line, the rebels were retreating under the crush of mace and flail. The Sororitas's pearl ceramite deflected all but the most fortunate of blows from their opponent's rusting machetes and bayonets. At such range, the sisters' advantage of armour was undeniably telling. Moving as one solid block, the sisters pushed through the rebel mass. Baeder saw Mortlock bouncing the end of his fen-hammer from foe to foe, bellowing in his attempt to rally the men.

There came a sudden, sharp bellow, like the spearing of a bull oxen. Atachron stumbled backwards. Palatine Fure's power sceptre was sizzling beads of blood off its crackling disruptor field. Atachron's battle axe and his arm lay some metres away, a black, segmented limb lying in a pool of darkening fluid. Fure took two steps forwards and brought her mace in a backhand across Atachron's antlered helmet. With a final, sonorous cry, the ancient warrior spilled onto the ground like an avalanche.

'For the Emperor! And the glory of the cardinal!' shouted Palatine Fure. Her battle-sisters warbled curious whistles that bridged into the first high-pitched notes of a hymn. As they sang, their fury was renewed and they pincered the beleaguered Riverine.

'For the fallen!' Baeder bellowed, throwing himself deep into the enemy lines.

Mautista's heartbeat was more a convulsion than a pulse. It soared up to three hundred beats a minute, drumming agony and the hard buzz of adrenaline into his system before slacking down to a weak tremor or two every few seconds. The daemon in his curdled blood was whispering sweet promises in his mind.

Mautista would find death soon.

Four score rebels rampaged through the deckhead with him. They slaughtered any unarmed crew ratings they encountered. Some tried to flee past them onto the deck, while others just curled up and surrendered. None were spared. The Persepian resistance they met was sporadic and cursory. It seemed most Nauticals were more concerned with evacuating the sinking warship than defending it against attack. The few Nautical armsmen they encountered put up a few stray shots before scurrying away.

'Mautista! There!' Canao pointed eagerly. There was a corkscrew stair-case leading out of the deckhead into the upper structures. The aperture was open and they could hear the intense clash of metal and cries of pain and anger, even above the creaks and booms of oceanic warfare.

'I can find rest up there,' Mautista said, smiling crookedly. He clawed up the corkscrew and into the hatchway, limping into the plush ground floor of the state ward. Structural damage to the ship had loosened valves and cables. The air was swimmy with a haze of combustibles, but through it Mautista could see a pitched and desperate struggle. Instruments of cut-ting and clubbing rose and fell. An armoured female lay on the carpet, bleeding from a stab wound to the rubberised underarm of her shoulder plates. An off-world Riverine was slumped on a divan as though asleep, his lower body twisted around unnaturally. Dozens of Riverine bodies lay on the carpet, their arms locked stiff as if trying to ward away the final blow. Several white-armoured bodies were interspersed with the Guardsmen. Mautista followed the carnage with his eyes until he saw the behemoth of dark armour in the centre of the room. It was Atachron.

Mautista's ruptured vision immediately tunnelled. His heart rate esca-lated to five pulsations a second. He felt a hot, swelling bulge in his stomach. He nursed that hot rage into a fury. For a moment all he could see was the broken shell of Atachron. He had been one of the Two Pairs of visionaries who had given Solo-Bastón the means to fight. Were it not for them, Mautista would have never reached enlightenment. He owed them everything.

The remaining rebels emerged out of the floor hatch. Less than eight-een mixed Carnibalès and renegade Guardsmen. They would suffice. With a sharp yell, Mautista the Disciple charged into the melee.

The battle-sisters laid about themselves with maces and chain flails. They were like ancient knights driving back the feral hill hordes. The colonel's men were the faceless animals to be felled for their legend.

Baeder fell back into a ring with the eight remaining men in his unit as Fure's Celestians hemmed them in. Baeder ducked a lashing chain flail and swung his fen-hammer low. It caught the battle-sister in her shins and swept her legs out from underneath her. She came crashing down, her legs shattered. Prayer – fervent and pained – escaped from her helmet vents.

Another mace cut the air and this time Baeder had no room to evade. It hit him square in the ribs, the flanged mace-head bouncing off his flak vest. Baeder heard bones break and scrape against splintered ends. He fell. He heard harsh incantations. Baeder expected death. The sisters were intoning his death prayer. But the killing blow did not come.

Instead, the sister turned away, her attention drawn as more rebels had fought their way into the state ward. He saw Mautista, the skeletal Disciple, decapitate a battle-sister with a scything machete. A second wave hit the scrum – Soder, Barlach, Boetcher and a mob of Carnibalès. They hit the Celestian flank and threatened to spill over to where Avanti and his assembly hid in the rear. Once again, Baeder realised, the powers above had chosen to keep him alive.

He rose to his feet. Broken ribs grated. Every breath brought a stab of pain in his right side. Clawing his way up, he led off the remnants of his group. Mortlock moved to his side, slamming a battle-sister into the ground with a downward blow. 'Where to, boss?'

'Find Avanti. I need to see him die.'

The cardinal hid behind a fighting square of his bodyguard as they fought their way beneath the mezzanine towards the foredeck. They had almost broken free until Mautista's party engaged them. Now the cardinal was hollering about the ship sinking. He was probably right, the Argo-Nautical rocked dangerously. But Baeder's focus became one of such singular aggression he did not hear any words.

Gabre bowled into the Celestian flank. He tore at them, picking up the armoured form of a battle-sister and shaking her like a deranged simian. The Celestians rushed to meet him, creating a gap in the formation.

Baeder staggered towards the breach, fen-hammer loose in his hand. Mercenaries rushed to plug the gap with a forest of flagged lances. Each bore a handlebar moustache and neatly-waxed hair. These were no fighters. To Baeder they were typical of the Imperium's ruling elite. Baeder smashed the ceremonial weapons aside with contempt, splitting the polished wood staves and trampling their pennants. Avanti was close now. Baeder looked into his eyes. There he saw not fear, but a flicker of uncertainty. It elicited a thrill of delight in Baeder. He was slavering now, but he didn't care.

'He's mine!' howled Baeder. 'Mine!' He hurled himself against the aristocratic lancers, breaking apart two of them. The burning in his ribs was forgotten. He snorted, blowing strings of blood from his nose. A lance plunged into his thigh. Something collided with the side of his head. Baeder felt none of it, he could see only Avanti and his cold blue eyes, clear and vivid amongst a periphery of grey shapes. He was reckless. He would die here.

'No!' screamed Mautista.

A hand seized Baeder by the back of his jacket and pulled him away from the front-line. Baeder lashed out instinctively, punching Mautista in the face and exploding his nose in a spray of blood. 'What? What?' growled Baeder through his teeth.

'There!' said Mautista, pointing to the mezzanine stairs. Platoons of Persepian Nautical infantry were clattering down the steps, bayonets couched at the hip. Nautical officers blasted their bugles in the cardinal's rescue. A company-sized element at the very least. Several of the vanguard threw themselves into the churning fight, spearing Riverine from behind with their bayonets. He saw Sergeant Colborn sink as a Persepian blade transfixed his spine. A Nautical officer's sabre parted the head of Trooper Bantem from his neck. A Carnibalès screamed as he clutched a stomach wound.

The realisation of sudden defeat sobered him. Mautista pulled Baeder back from the melee as the man continued to protest. 'I have to kill him. To rest the souls of my men, I have to kill him.'

'Let me do it. Gabre needs you to go with him. The ship is sinking.'

Baeder shook his head. 'Damnit Mautista, no. I will not. This is what I came to finish. This is everything I have left.'

'No, this is not why. The Four know there are greater designs for you yet. The gods have promised.'

'This is my fight,' Baeder shouted into the Disciple's face, lashing him with spittle.

'Fyodor, leave! The gods have marked you as their own now. As for me, the gods have chosen to end my mortal life. I am dying already.'

As if to prove his point, Mautista wrenched open the buttons of his leather jacket with his remaining arm and bared his chest. Beneath a cage of distended ribs, his heart was a visible black stain beneath paper skin. With each slow, irregular beat, the black stain pulsated like a convulsing ink blot. 'I have been infused with the blood of daemons. My life purpose is to serve the Dos Pares. Yours is a greater purpose. Go Fyodor, do not anger the gods.'

Baeder could not look away from Mautista's heart. Arterial spider webs of black were spreading out across his skeletal chest. Whatever daemonic entity had been imparted into Mautista's body was claiming the flesh vessel as its own. Baeder was not sure how he knew this, but he was sure he was correct.

A mace slashed towards his head. A black armoured shape took the hit against its ceramite hide and eviscerated the mace-wielder with his chainsword.

Gabre.

'Fyodor. Come with me,' he said, holding out his great gauntlet.

Bader looked around at the crashing battle. More of his men were dying. The last of the 31st bleeding out, dashing themselves against the wall of pearl amour. The entire Persepian company had reached the floor level now. They were surrounded and overwhelmed.

'Riverine!' Baeder ordered. 'Fall back on my mark.'

Mautista saw the last of his warband fall. He knew he would fall too, soon, but not quite yet. He knew his purpose and he would play it out to the end.

The ship boomed again. Perhaps an ammunition store had cooked off, or perhaps the boiler room had erupted. The she-warriors in pearl, their polished ceramite dented and stained, maintained a tight circle around Cardinal Avanti, leaving the flock of beribboned oligarchs scurrying in their wake.

Mautista cut diagonally with his machete and sheared a Persepian apart from shoulder to waist. He leapt clear of a toppled divan and sprinted towards Avanti. The last three survivors – Canao, Estima and Azuilgur – followed him, hacking left and right as they ran.

Estima was transfixed by a Persepian bayonet. Stopping to parry a Nautical officer's sabre, Canao was dragged down and lost. Only Azuilgur and Mautista reached Palatine Fure.

The palatine's power sceptre knocked Azuilgur sideways, five metres across the room. His torso ruptured, beads of blood seemingly hanging in the air before pattering to the carpet. Mautista knew, despite the unnatural augmentation in his bloodstream, he could not match the martial skill of the Palatine. He reached for a stub pistol at his hip, a small six-shot revolver. Fure swung her sceptre, gouging away a portion of Mautista's lower torso. As the holy weapon met daemon blood, there was an audible hiss as if the wound itself was crying out in pain. Steam ejected forcefully from the open wound, boiling and bubbling with effervescence. The shock alone would have been enough to kill a normal man, yet Mautista was numb. His legs buckled and he toppled backwards, his stub pistol still clutched loosely in his fingers.

He saw Avanti, now at the front of the procession. The cardinal's eyes were closed, his hands clasped in prayer. He seemed impervious to the carnage around him.

Fure loomed over him to deliver the killing blow, but Mautista was faster. He jerked his finger on the trigger, willing his muscles to contract one last time. The percussion cap struck the round and the stub gun barked. Mautista saw the muzzle glow before the bullet had left the barrel. A discharge of hot, high-pressure gas flickered. It sparked the volatile gas and ignited. The flame expanded outward, a horizontal sheet of flame that erupted instantaneously from wall to wall.

There was no sound. Mautista felt nothing. He saw, before his death, the room grow white and Avanti open his eyes. Mautista saw fear there. In the fraction of a second before his death, Avanti's eyes quavered. His soul was damned, and he knew it. The cardinal opened his mouth to scream but blooming fire sucked the oxygen from his lungs.

EPILOGUE

The Imperium's inland campaign pressed on for a further ten months, well into the dry season. Robbed of its initial momentum, the land forces were drawn into a lengthy guerrilla war with the natives of Solo-Bastón. Outmatched by Caliguan heavy armour, the indigenous fighters expanded their tunnel systems and continued to fight, drawing numbers from the sudden influx of refugees dislodged by fighting.

Although the death of Cardinal Avanti did not have any strategic impact on military planning, its impact on the overall campaign was considerable. He had been the embodiment of the holy campaign on Solo-Bastón and the architect for the creation of a post-war industry. Without him, the campaign lost political influence and financial investment fell away. Prospective shipping and holding firms declined to enter into any chartered agreements on the unstable planet. The Weston-East Phalia Company reneged on their contracts and ceased negotiations to explore the mainland interior. House Uhring, furious at the loss of their heir, lobbied for a protracted trade sanction against Solo-Bastón. The Ecclesiarchy severed their ties with Solo-Bastón and were quick to wash their hands of Avanti's mess.

Without the support of powerful vested interests, the Imperial Guard were left to conduct a war with limited resources. Major General Montalvo succeeded as operations commander upon the deaths of Avanti and Admiral de Ruger. Despite the initial successes of an inland assault, he inherited a stagnant campaign. His men were unused to fighting an insurgent war in such inhospitable terrain. Demoralised and without cohesive leadership, Caliguan crews hid in their tanks and Chimeras away from the heat and disease. Dysentery afflicted one in two men while tropical agues became a conditional norm. Significant quantities of medical supplies were requested, but none were forthcoming and their pleas were ignored. No Imperial officials in the region wanted to involve themselves in the cardinal's disaster.

Despite Imperial superiority in firepower and numbers, the Carnibalès fought an obstinate war on their home soil. With no end in sight, the Imperial Guard lost the will to fight. They languished in camps, unwilling to advance and unable to retreat. However, the poorly equipped Carnibalès were unable to press the advantage and the fighting stalemated into intermittent skirmishes and constant ambush.

The war on Solo-Bastón ended exactly eighteen months after initial deployment. In its aftermath almost a third of the planet's population had perished from conflict, disease or malnutrition. The Imperium declared it a victory. Streamers and processions lined the streets as far as the Bastion Stars. A soapstone statue of Major General Montalvo was erected in Union City. With its arms raised towards the sky in victory, the forty-metre sculpture was clearly visible from the Solo-Bastón coast.

However, only the inner administrative officials knew the truth of their triumph. They had lost Solo-Bastón. The war was an Imperial catastrophe that could ruin Ecclesiarchal legitimacy within the subsector. Restriction of information was imperative.

Many years later, military theorists wrote of a guerrilla network concealed within the rural populace led by daemon-blooded heretics known as Disciples. These Disciples disseminated knowledge of guerrilla warfare far in advance of anything the rebels would otherwise have known. Yet more importantly, the success of the insurgency relied on the support of dissident villages who supplied raw produce, food, labour and concealment for the Archenemy host.

Imperial historians legitimised the massacre of thousands by citing the local support for heresy. No mention was made of the wholesale genocide of loyalist groups. A complete history of the Solo-Bastón Uprising was commissioned by Cardinal Heitor de Silva which omitted the violations committed against the indigenous groups of Bastón. Instead the campaign was repainted as a struggle between Caliguan Guardsmen and Persepian vessels against the barbaric hordes of Chaos cultists. No mention was made of involvement from the 31st Riverine Amphibious.

In actuality, it would be the arrival of Traitor Marines that broke the stalemate on the eighteenth month. Blood Gorgons, in company strength, deployed via a fortress fleet that broke the Imperial picket at Midway Reach. They deployed by Thunderhawk and Raptor into Bastón's interior, pin-pointing strikes against command and communication centres.

Quick and brutal, the Blood Gorgons routed the Guardsmen back out into the sea, drowning them in their thousands. The colossal monument of Major General Montalvo was demolished by the Archenemy, less than three weeks after its completion.

Khorsabad was both title and forename. It was derived from the Bastónese word *'Khorsa'* meaning corsair or renegade and the honorific *'Habad'* meaning 'the King'.

Maw or *'Mau'* was his true name. It was a name that Gabre of the Blood Gorgons gave him. A derivative of another name, Mautista, whose very fate was intertwined with that of Khorsabad Maw as much as Maw's own organic birth mother's. The threads of fate criss-cross and interlock. Although Mautista's thread had ended, it converged and continued along the thread of Khorsabad Maw. His actions in life had bound them. Without following the destiny of Mautista, there could be no Maw.

Fyodor Baeder was a past name. With the passage of time, it was a name that would be forgotten. There existed a young Fyodor, much younger, who had sailed paper yachts in the marsh parks of Ouisivia with his father. Another Fyodor not quite yet a man who had greased his hair, worn leather crêpe-soles and taken a dark-haired girl to the slump dances. The last Fyodor has been the colonel who led his men into interiors of a distant, war-torn jungle. All of those Fyodors would in time be forgotten too.

His title Khorsabad and his true name Maw were chiselled into the newly-forged plates of his armour: miniature, heretic script that adorned every pane of his shoulder, torso and thighs like the cauldron crab shell of Kalisador fame. The ragged remains of his military uniform fluttered like ghostly vestiges, the death shroud of man entombed in a crypt of new armour.

The Blood Gorgons gave him his armour and much more. They gifted him with a mask of iron, so he would not suffer memories of the past each time he faced a mirror. This they welded to his face, forever, as a pledge to his new life. Bands of steel looping like serpents, their tails began sharply at his chin and their heads met atop his crown. They gifted him with a falchion, sculpted from the rending claw of a tyranid specimen, and many accoutrements of war from the Eye of Terror. But most of all, they promised him immortality so he could pursue his vendetta against the Imperium.

Khorsabad Maw lowered himself unsteadily, touching his forehead to the soil. 'My benevolent creator.'

'There is no need for that,' replied Gammadin, Ascendant Champion of the Blood Gorgons. When he spoke, the rich voice that oozed out of his amplifiers reverberated among the ancient gum-saps. Flocks of tiny, dark birds were startled from epiphytic perches. Unseen amongst the broadleafs and tangled roots a panthera roared, as if recognising the power behind that voice.

The Traitor Marine stood before Khorsabad, as large in physical presence as the totemic pillars that surrounded them. Gammadin stepped forward, caped in the severed wings of a giant bat. Stooping slightly, the Ascendant Champion guided Khorsabad up by the elbow. 'We are allies, equals. An enemy of my enemy is to be treasured,' Gammadin said gently.

Khorsabad nodded. 'Fighting is all I know. It's all I've ever done. If you will give me the arms and the purpose, we will fight for you.'

'There will be plenty of opportunity to fight,' Gammadin said. 'The Imperium is vast and the Eastern Fringes uncharted. Harass them. Plunder and worry their shipping lanes, cut them where they are weakest. Fight and flee and fight some more. Can you do that?'

Although Khorsabad's iron mask could express no emotion, his shoulders lifted visibly. 'It will be the only thing we do.'

'You have my patronage in this pursuit. Arms and ships I can give you, but your men will need you to lead them.'

'I can do that.'

Gammadin drew his scimitar, an immensely old weapon. The length of its two-metre blade was pitted and notched, beaten and scarred. He brandished the weapon horizontally towards Khorsabad Maw. In reply, Maw struck the back-edge of the blade with his own lacquered falchion. He did this thrice, gouging teeth marks into Gammadin's thickly rimmed blade.

'That is all?' Khorsabad asked. 'No blood oath? No pledge?'

Gammadin shook his head, the recurved horns on his crown rattling against his armour. 'We are not the barbarians the Imperium thinks we are. I don't need your blood when I already have your word as a commander of men.'

BLOOD GORGONS

CHAPTER ONE

Come dawn, the small craft settled on a disused runway sixteen kilometres east of the Belasian capital. The landing struts sought purchase on the broken rockcrete and Gammadin of the Blood Gorgons emerged purposefully. His men followed him, stepping down the landing ramp into the quiet morning. He led the way, parting the tall weeds that choked the landing strip as they threaded west towards the distant city lights.

The sun was rising, spilling a weak light over the disrepair of Belasia. Along the way, rockcrete blockhouses struggled out from the bushes. Their windows were broken, their roofs collapsed, and they had been abandoned long ago. The wind moved amongst the yellowing plant life, rustling the dead grass and shuddering the knotted, leafless brambles. In the distance, the rusting frame of an air mill lay on its side, its skeleton scorched white by bomb blasts.

Gammadin and his Blood Gorgons scanned the broken panes of glass, their helmet arrays searching for thermal heat. There was none to be found except the tiny, skittering signatures of rodent life.

'All clear,' reported one of Gammadin's companions.

'Remain alert and adjust your auspexes,' replied Gammadin. 'They may mean to deceive us yet.'

Heeding his words, Gammadin's men spaced themselves out into a wide echelon. They bent low, the butts of their guns locked tight against their shoulders. At the fore, Gammadin walked upright, almost nonchalantly, as he led them to the Belasian capital. He held out his palm, skimming the tall grass with one hand as he walked. In the other hand, held tight behind his back, he gripped the handle of a heavy tulwar blade.

They were large, these men, and some would say they were not men at all. They were post-humans – living constructs that evolved the human form into a singular purpose of warfare. They were mortal things, but most whispered their names with a superstitious fear reserved for phantoms and daemons.

There were nine such warriors following Gammadin. Encased in plate and horn, they moved slowly and deliberately, as if they lived by their own rhythm and the world simply orbited their presence. Like their lord, each Traitor Marine wore power armour the colour of burnt umber. Barnacles and fossilised organisms spread across the sweeping surface of each plate. There was an organic element to their regalia, accentuated by the mutant growth of dorsal fins, quills and hard, segmented shells. Shambling ancients, slow and terrible, the eight Impassives appeared not to move at all as the landscape glided beneath their feet.

Behind them, almost as an afterthought, ghosted the witch, Anko Muhr, following behind in a tower of rigid armour with curtains of black silk trailing from his shoulders. Unlike his brethren, Muhr was pensive, his fists clenching and unclenching. Unhelmed, his equine face was painted white but the war markings could not mask the agitation in his eyes. He watched the still grass and blinked against the rising sun. Nearby, leafhoppers chirped, promising a hot, quiet day. There was a still tension in the dawn, a fragile peace that could not last. Muhr could feel the taut energy on the wind.

Picking up speed, Gammadin and his warriors cut through the yellowing hills that bordered the capital. They stopped every now and again, trying to catch the scent of a human; a pack of blackened hunters, crashing through dry branches, lifting their heads to taste the air. Belasia lay ahead, a shoulder of rockcrete that surfaced above the flatlands and pastures. In the distance, yet clearly audible, the early morning was accompanied by the waking screams of thousands.

The weather was unusually fine in the Capital State of Belasia. The sun shone lime-bright on the highways and gridded, austere buildings. Such temperate weather only contrasted with the depressive state of each precinct. The air was hazed with heat and summer dust. There was not a single window within the rectangular ministry blocks and tenements that remained intact. Life still dwelled there, but it was sporadic and rare. The long silence of the day was interrupted only by sudden and intense swells of gunfire.

Belasia had once been a stable world of the Imperium. High density city blocks dotted efficient highways that traversed the wide plains of chemically wilted flora. It was neither a metropolis nor a thriving port of trade, but its governance had been effective. A modest export of carbon fuel and non-ferrous metals to the domestic subsector maintained a reasonable standard of living for its large labouring populace. Like their plain proto-Imperial architecture, Belasians were an uninspired group. Austerity, order and economic prudence were the prevailing ideology, alongside honest work for the Emperor's glory.

But this stability had been undone by the discovery of rich mineral seams along the Belasian Shelf and the civil war that followed. As with all civil wars, it became a battle of interests. The wealthy collared the poor and the poor fought amongst themselves.

The military chieftains of the Belasian were quick to declare their interests in the mineral wealth, mobilising Belasia's 'Red Collar' regiments to forcefully secure mining sites. In reaction, the Imperial administration levied a conscript force and transformed their modest primary production sectors into industries of war. The ensuing conflict wiped out thirty per cent of adult males in Belasia within a decade. When the number of able-bodied young men dwindled, both factions turned to recruiting boy soldiers to continue their campaigns.

Rebels, looters and activists added to the degeneration of society. The entire infrastructure of Belasia deteriorated as her people descended into violent madness. It was not long before boy soldiers roamed the streets, proclaiming themselves rulers, brandishing lasguns. With the sudden proliferation of arms, no one argued with them.

By virtue of their obscurity within the star system, the Belasians fought a vicious war amongst themselves for seventeen years. Neither militants nor the local government requested aid from Holy Terra, for neither wanted to share the spoils of victory. By 855.M41, entire cities were held by local warlords and their gangs. The Red Collar regiments became mere mobs of heavily armed children fighting for food and ammunition.

That was when the dark eldar chose to strike.

Not much can be remembered of the invasion, for nothing was recorded. Although the xenos were few in number, the population of Belasia possessed no means to repel them. The Red Collars and child rebels, soft from plundering unarmed civilians, fled at the advance of the dark eldar. In the days following the xenos landings, the remaining military vox-channels spread tales of alien raiders and mass murders. People hid in their public shelters or fled from the cities.

In the years that followed, the dark eldar cultivated Belasia as a farmer tends an orchard. They harvested slaves from the pockets of life, never taking more than the population could replenish. They indulged in orgies of bloodletting to keep the humans fragmented and fearful, but never pushed a region into extinction. These slaves were sold on to other dark eldar kabals, to Chaos cults in neighbouring subsectors and even to Chaos Space Marine warbands such as the Blood Gorgons.

* * *

It was the first meal Jonah had eaten in three days. That in itself was not uncommon on Belasia. Not many dared to forage wild cabbage in the city outskirts when pressured constantly by the fear of being hunted.

But finally Jonah had succumbed to hunger, and under the cover of darkness he left the shelter of his basement. From the local chemical mills, he would gather fungi that spored in the rubble and rust of demolition. Over where the highways led out to the district outskirts, he knew of a spot where string vines grew in patches, between the cracked pavement slits. They were palatable enough if boiled with salt.

Travelling light, Jonah tucked the scavenged vegetables into a plastek bag and stole his way through the darkest lanes and drainage pipes. At all times, he watched his back carefully, looking for a glimpse of the stick-men. Jonah remembered a time when it had only been a brisk stroll from his hab to the outer townships. Now the creeping, hiding and constant panic took him hours.

Back home in his basement, his family waited for him – his daughter, Meisha, and his wife in the corner, looking mousy and long suffering.

They ate in silence, concentrating on the task of spooning, chewing and savouring. It made the food last longer that way. Quietly they ate, hidden from the outside world.

It was not until they finished that Jonah heard a cracking on the floorboards above. A low groaning of the wood, soft at first but growing persistent as it crept close. It sounded, quite dreadfully, as if someone was treading across the abandoned rail station above them.

Had he been followed? He had never been careless when foraging for food or water in the city.

They held their breaths. A shadow glided across the boarded up windows, rippling through the tiny slits between the planks.

The fear in him was so great. Jonah knew very well what those stick-men did to people. Pushing the sinking fear from his mind, Jonah closed his eyes and began to count. Slowly, with his breath still and taut in his chest.

The footsteps faded.

Meisha hissed a low wheezing breath. It was too soon.

Suddenly and without reason, the lone candle flickered out.

The door buckled with a sudden crack. Jonah screamed in shock without meaning to. The door warped under the pressure before popping uselessly off its hinges. Meisha began screaming because he was screaming. Soon his wife followed suit and they were all shrieking in terror as the stick-men skittered into their shelter.

Their limbs shot through the door first, long and fluted like finely carved lengths of ebony. This was followed by the uncurling spindle of their torsos as they swooped beneath the door frame. They moved so fast that they seemed to flicker.

Jonah fumbled for the shotgun beneath the blanket trunk. He had once been an enforcement officer, when Imperial law had still been relevant on Belasia, and that weapon was the last remaining vestige of his pride. It had pained him when his wife had insisted he keep it locked away from the children. Now it was too late. Jonah never got to the shotgun.

They came to him with such speed, kicking him in the jaw with a finely pointed boot and sprawling him onto the floor. In a daze, Jonah could not see how many there were, he only saw the whirl of tall thin bodies. In the dark, their armour matched the hue of a midnight sky and their faces were enclosed in tusk-shaped helmets.

'Pa!' shrieked Meisha. 'The ghosts are here! The ghosts are here!'

A stick-man aimed his rifle at her, the razorblades that edged the weapon flashing with his movement. It was said by some that their guns spat poison. Jonah leapt to his feet, his fear suddenly forgotten, and lunged for his daughter. But the stick-men were too quick. An armoured fist punched him on the chin and blackened his vision entirely. The last thing he remembered was the shrieking.

Jonah awakened slowly to pounding pain in the back of his head. He was groggy and it took him a moment to realise he was not in his own home any more. He panicked with a start and began to fight against the paralysis of sleep. With a thrust of conscious effort he forced his eyes to open.

He lay in an old armoury of some kind, likely the local militia staging station in St Orlus Precinct. The tin shed was unlit except for the bay of small windows that let in hazy shafts of sunlight. A thick patina of blackened soot covered the inside of the corrugated tin shed while old tools still hung from the roof racks in cocoons of dust and spider webs.

The place had been stripped of its equipment during the civil war, likely many years before the coming of the stick-men. Civilian vehicles, uparmoured and customised, replaced the old tanks and carriers of the Red Collar regiments. Jonah could make out a road hauler with a heavy bolter mounted on its bonnet and a Chimera, its hull sprayed with skull motifs in the manner of the child soldiers.

As his vision began to focus, Jonah realised there were others with him. There were bodies shifting under the scant light, packed into the armoury. Jonah recoiled in fright, but hands pushed back at him, intruding on his space. In such tight confines, he smelt sweat and the oiliness of human hair.

There was a man of middle years next to him, his shoulders pressed together. Squinting, Jonah saw the silhouette of a beard and matted hair. The man said nothing, but Jonah could feel his shoulders tremble softly as he cried. Jonah looked away, suddenly ashamed. There were many others around, moaning and babbling.

The noise rose as more captives regained consciousness. The nonsense sounds of human misery grew louder until suddenly Jonah heard a sting-ing crack. The moans turned into howls.

Something was amongst the writhing captives. A tall figure, standing above them, lashing a whip into the mound of bodies. Following each snap of the whip came a protest of humiliated pain. Jonah tried to move away as the stick-man picked his way through the captives, thrashing his whip. There was a final, sinking pain in Jonah's chest as his fears became real. He had been captured by the stick-men; there was no denying that reality any more.

The stick-man's face had the pallor of the dead and his eyes were large and almost entirely black, their pupils seeming to swallow up the whites. Narrow and vulpine, his features had a wicked upward slant that were locked in a darkly comedic grin.

Jonah started to yell. He did not mean to, but he became caught up in the panic around him. It was the deep, bawling cry of a terrified human adult, equal parts a sound of distress and the loud roar of an animal try-ing to frighten away its tormentors.

The armoury erupted with shrill, maddening laughter. Jonah realised there were more stick-men watching him than he had realised. The laughter came from behind him, and even seemed to drift down from the darkened rafters and furthest corners. Bladder muscles loosening, Jonah sank back into the floor as the whip crashed against his back.

The water was an unctuous yellow. It was so heavy with pollutant that the liquid sat with an unmoving viscosity. Stringy, grassy vegetation scummed its surface, collecting in progressively larger bales towards the centre of the lake, gathering into a morass of dark, hairy fibres.

Standing on the banks, Lord Gammadin watched as Captain Ham-murabi descended shin-deep into the water. The still surface rippled awkwardly, bubbling and frothing in fits. With one mighty stroke of his broadsword, Hammurabi collapsed an entire copse of small bushes.

Gammadin had a great admiration for the captain of his personal guard, the eight Impassives. Hammurabi had a good sword arm, and was loyal as far as a worshipper of Chaos could be termed so. He followed his duties as Gammadin's first blade strictly. He executed those duties well now as he sloshed deeper into the water, parting reeds with heavy blows of his sword.

Gammadin waded into the water. The disturbance rocked the water grasses and they rustled a collective sigh, swaying gently back and forth. The sun caught the water and flickered. For a moment, Gammadin thought he saw a face, but then it was gone.

Blinking his hooded eyelids, Gammadin studied the grasses but found nothing. His hand slithered over the hilt of his tulwar and there it stayed. The air was hot and still, the sun steaming off the lake's surface. The water seemed to murmur, furtive with secrets. Suddenly, Gammadin sensed a presence. He felt a chill in the base of his neck.

He advanced waist-deep into the water, the ancient servos of his power armour whirring as they churned his legs through the muddy bottom. Yet still that feeling would not leave him.

'My Khorsaad,' Hammurabi said, gesturing respectfully for Gammadin to follow. The captain had already advanced several dozen paces ahead, cutting a swathe through the bog.

Gammadin raised his ceramite palm. 'Wait.'

Despite the stillness, there was a restless quality to the atmosphere, beneath the surface. Long ago, the gods had gifted Gammadin with enlightenment, and his psychic abilities had since matured into a fearsome prospect. Gammadin could see the arcs and mathematic patterns in the air that modelled the space and materium of this world. He could channel his will into displays of physical force. But above all, he could sense the consciousness of the world around him – the rocks, the soil, the trees. He sensed, now, there was a hidden danger. The lake seemed to tremble with anticipation and the air was coarse with a lively, barely contained static. Hidden energy surrounded him everywhere.

The water stirred behind Gammadin. The lord turned slowly to see Anko Muhr enter the lake with Gammadin's retinue, an elite core of venerated seniors bonded in the ritual way of the Blood Gorgons. There were four pairs in all, each pair having shared organs and tissue to produce a symbiosis of shared battlefield experience.

What manner of beast or man could ever overwhelm the eight Impassives?

Gammadin quelled the troubling instinct and began to walk across the lake. Together they fanned out into a staggered formation, waist-deep. The lake was wide, but drought had evaporated its depth. Heavy minerals crunched underfoot, feeding the floating water grasses that obscured the distant shoreline from view. They did not travel far before Gammadin felt it again. Stronger this time, a palpable warning that drummed with percussive urgency in his temple.

'Halt!' Gammadin called. He spied movement in the water to his immediate left. The grass parted softly, tentacle roots bobbing listlessly away in the water. Their steps had disturbed the soil. Something dark and round bubbled to the surface.

Gammadin gnashed the spined pincer of his right arm with a loud click. The Impassives dropped low, their bolter barrels chasing the grass for a target. Sliding his tulwar from his waist, Gammadin slapped the flat of its blade against the mottled shell of his right arm.

The object burped to the surface with one final pop of oily water. A black hat. It sat still on the surface. A black felt hat with a round crown and wide brim.

Hammurabi slid through the water and flipped it over. It turned, floating like a high-sided boat, revealing blood and hair on the underside. The blood was still fresh and soaked into the felt like an ink stain.

'How curious,' Muhr observed. He seemed to drift. His dark brown cloak, sagging with charms and fetishes, clung to his power armour wetly as he waded closer.

Gammadin eyed the witch warily. He did not trust Muhr. Not only because he was a sorcerer, but also because Gammadin could sense a jealous ambition in Muhr's black heart. Muhr was the Chapter's senior Chirurgeon and high priest of the witch coven, and Gammadin was aware of his power lust.

'Leave that,' Gammadin commanded.

"Tis truly a gods-damned omen,' Muhr said theatrically, rubbing the wreaths of knuckle bone necklaces that coiled down his breast. 'A dead man's hat, drifting in the current.'

The troubling fear still weighed heavily on Gammadin's brow. He was not one to listen to the witch's superstitious meanderings, but there was something in the air.

'Let us beseech the protection of the gods,' Muhr said. 'Only they can convert ill-luck to fortune.'

Gammadin scanned the lake, motionless now. He agreed reluctantly and signalled for the witch to go ahead.

As the chanting began, Muhr's black craft unsettled even the eight Impassives. He swayed, rocking gently at the waist. A monotonous prayer rasped from his vox-grille. It had a steady, hypnotic cadence. With the raising of his voice, a light wind picked up which brought grit and dry leaves on its draught.

The Impassives grew ever more restless. They breathed heavily. The Blood Gorgons were renegades but they had not been lured into depths of arcane lore like the warbands of their more superstitious brethren. They considered themselves a warrior band first and foremost. Despite their worship of the Sects Undivided, sorcery was a fickle and dangerous thing to be feared and respected from a distance.

Muhr finished his chant and began to splash oil from a ceramic gourd. He splashed some against Gammadin. The droplets felt like intrusive hammer blows, and Gammadin immediately felt drowsy, as if his eyes were blinking through the haze of half-sleep.

'What have you done, witch?' Gammadin asked brusquely. He felt his muscles unknot involuntarily as the ominous urgings dissipated. Yet it did not quell his instincts. He simply felt blinded now. The trouble did not seem to go away, it felt to Gammadin that he simply could not feel it any more. As if it were hidden from him now, just out of reach, as if someone had hooded his psychic abilities.

'The gods have dampened our souls against the daemons that watch us.'

'I feel–' Gammadin took a deep, clattering breath. 'I feel like a dull razor.'

'A mere blessing of the gods' gaze. They watch over you now, so you do not need to watch for yourself,' Muhr replied.

'Khorsaad, there is movement,' Blood-Sergeant Makai announced, pointing his boltgun warily.

As Makai spoke, the reeds to their immediate left parted and a man hurtled through the water. He was dazed and bleeding, running wild. He did not even seem to register the presence of the Traitor Marines. He simply tried to churn his legs wildly through the sluggish water.

Makai cut down the man with a burst of his bolter.

'No!' Gammadin said, his voice rising slightly in anger. The man was already dead, bobbing softly over a dark patch of aquatic weed. It was not like Makai to be spooked so easily. Something was irritating all of them.

'I acted hastily, Khorsaad,' Makai replied.

Hammurabi interjected, shaking his head as if to clear it. 'Be still, Makai. We came here to test this world for genestock. This is not a kill-raid.' As Hammurabi spoke, he flipped the dead man onto his back.

For a brief moment, Gammadin's flesh tensed. He thought he saw fear in the man's rigid features. The man had been running and frightened before he had even seen them. As Gammadin studied the corpse, he began to wonder if the Impassives stood on the same soil as something even more terrifying to these humans than an Astartes. Perhaps there was more on Belasia than the topographic scans had revealed. From orbit, the planet had appeared to be a prime slave colony, but now they were on-world, he was not so sure. There was just something in the air…

'This is a lawless world and this human's suffering is no uncommon thing,' Muhr said, pointing at the dead man. 'We should make haste and think nothing of it.'

Gammadin slapped his thigh decisively. 'Come then. We go,' he said, resuming his steady wade.

Standing amongst the chemical-churned mud and dead reeds of the shoal, Jonah was stripped of his clothing. There was no dignity, no modesty. The captives stood close together, each trying to hide behind the person in front. A cold draught blew across the lake's surface, drawing goose bumps across Jonah's forearms.

The stick-men surrounded them. Perhaps two hundred slaves, shepherded by tall, thin shapes. Jonah dared not look at them directly but he felt them in the corners of his vision. Stick-men enslavers hauled against the straining leashes of their hounds. Further behind them, Jonah could hear the high-pitched machine hum of their war engines. A fleet of four or five craft hovered metres above the ground, their long ship-like chassis sharp and narrow. Poised for speed, they rocked gently under the gravitational pull as the stick-men clung to the running boards, shouting and keening in anticipation.

When it finally happened, the stick-men gave them no instructions. They simply pointed across the lake with long, clawed fingers. The meaning was clear enough. Slaves were to run, make a break for freedom across the lake.

And then the stick-men unleashed their animals.

Jonah could not avert his gaze any more. He looked up and saw a hound pounce on a man at the edge of the mob. They were not like any canines that Jonah had handled in his enforcement days. These were hairless things, all naked flesh and gristle. Teeth with jagged regularity snapped closed as the creature began to savage the man into the mud, grinding the man down with its weight and mauling him.

Jonah ran. They all ran, a stampede that crashed into the water and moved as one. Blinding fear forced them to stay together.

Flanking them, running parallel, the hounds chased the slaves, forcing them to run in the same direction. The animals did not bark, but they laughed with a shrill yapping as the pack communicated to each other, herding the running humans along the lake bank.

A slave went over, tackled from behind by a hound and nailed into the mud face first. On impact, the hound flipped over its victim, hurtling through the air with its legs upturned and twisting. Before the captive could rise, the other hounds were snapping all over him.

Gammadin stopped mid-stride, his boot sinking into a mud crater. He raised his hand.

The shore grass swayed beneath a sudden bar of wind. He could smell the scent of humans on the gust, but there was something else too. More than the gamey, mammalian oil of human skin, there was something organic that stung Gammadin's olfactory glands.

He realised that they were not here simply hunting for slave samples any more. Without a doubt, there was something purposeful manifesting itself. Something knew of the Blood Gorgon presence and was prepared for it, this Gammadin could feel. He knew.

Gammadin's helmet optics were already scanning the surrounding area for danger. The banks of the lake were wide and flat, covered in clumps of dry grass and semi-aquatic rushes. There could be danger there. A fluid stream of information was filtered from his helmet's sensors into his neural relays – wind current, visibility and metallic resonance.

Hammurabi sank into a squat beside Gammadin, leaning on his sword. 'I feel it too, Khorsaad. There is a background roar in my ears.'

Probing psychically, Gammadin attempted to expand his consciousness into the surrounding environs, but he found himself mentally disorientated. The air and slight buzzing of insects made him listless, almost distracted. He had felt the same way ever since Muhr had invoked his black arts.

Muhr. Gammadin growled deep within his blackened hearts. What did he know of the events here?

'Khorsaad!' Hammurabi began, rising suddenly.

They came over the crest, hugging the line where the water met the earth. Slashing, frothing and flailing as they went, a stampede of people.

It was unclear who fired the first shot. A bolt-round exploded in the midst of the rapidly advancing human tide, but they ran undeterred. Closer now, Gammadin could see their faces, contorted in fright and utterly unaware of the Blood Gorgons in their path of flight.

'Formation!' Gammadin shouted at his Impassives.

The Impassives tightened into a defensive shell around Gammadin. In a circle, they fired into the oncoming avalanche of thrashing limbs, flashing bursts of ammunition into the mob. The horde rushed into and directly over the Blood Gorgons. Naked bodies collided against the anchored warriors, bouncing off their solid weight and swarming around them like an estuary.

'We are being fired upon,' voxed Bond-Brother Carcosa as he placed a hand to his suddenly bleeding neck.

'We are receiving fire,' Khadath affirmed as panicked bodies drummed and bumped against him.

From the distant slopes, a high-pitched whistling could be heard as high-velocity missiles whipped through the grass. They came from every direction at once, slicing into the enamel of his armour. It was an indiscriminate volley, slicing down the fleeing humans as it ricocheted against their plate.

Gammadin magnified his vision threefold towards the slopes. He saw thin humanoids in dark blue carapace standing up from the grass, darting from position to position. They raised long rifles and moved with the fluid coordination of trained marksmen. Gammadin recognised their attackers as dark eldar and knew there was treachery on this world.

He threw the tulwar blade in his palm underhand; the heavy dagger shot out in a wide arc before meeting a dark eldar almost forty metres away, sending it sprawling into the grass. Before his blade had found its target, Gammadin had already picked out several shots with his combi-bolter. The mag scope of his vision lens spun and whirled as it tracked multiple targets before seeking a new one as Gammadin put them down. His rage was building. A xenos round, a crystallised shard of poison, sliced through the back of his knee joint. The toxin tingled in the wound, potent enough to have immediately paralysed any normal human being. The wound only enraged Gammadin further, his killing becoming methodical as he picked target after target.

The eight Impassives fanned out to lay down a curtain of fire. Like

Gammadin, they were not pressured to shoot wild. Even as a constant shred of dark eldar weaponry hummed through the air, they picked their shots. The Blood Gorgons refused to give ground, despite the fleeing humans who were adding to the confusion. Growing bold, the dark eldar emerged from the grass to charge down the sandy gradient in a ragged line. A grenade went off at close range, shaking the world and jetting up sheets of mud.

Gammadin's withdrawal was being cut off. The dark eldar hooked around their flanks as the stampede of captives blocked and hemmed in the Impassives. Gammadin nearly lost his footing in the treacherous mud as the storm of xenos weaponry thickened considerably. Splinter rifles rippled shots across the mud flat, steaming up a fog of dirt particles. The airborne mud hung in swirls and lazy drifts, choking the Blood Gorgons' targeting systems.

'We must withdraw,' Gammadin voxed over the squad link.

As they fell back, the dark eldar pressured them, staying in their pocket and exchanging a blizzard of shots. Blood-Sergeant Abasilis and his Bond-Brother, Gharne, moved to intercept the dark eldar flanking pincer on their left, banging off crisp, precise shots. Gharne had been blinded in the firefight, his helmet discarded and his eyes shorn by shrapnel. Abasilis called out coordinates to the sightless Gharne, directing his bolter wherever the enemy gathered to return fire.

Movement was the only thing that prevented the Blood Gorgons from being pinned in the open. Gammadin, still facing the enemy, moved backwards into the lake. His combi-bolter was spent of bolt shells. The dark eldar chased him, daring to rush so close that Gammadin could see into the vision slits of their helmets. Easily excited, the dark eldar were growing careless in their pursuit. Gammadin raised his right arm, the monstrous chitin of his pincer, and caught them as they lunged in. With his left he expelled the last of his flamer.

The dark eldar caught in the high pressure stream shrieked and died loudly, their inferior carapaces charring under the chemical flame. Capable of stripping paint off a tank-hide in its raw form, when ignited the palmitic acid burned to a glowing white two thousand degrees. Within seconds the dark eldar were melted into stumps of fused plating and flesh. Corrosive fumes billowed out in a thick, cloying raft, driving back those dark eldar who were hounding Gammadin too closely.

Behind Gammadin, Blood-Sergeant Khadath, Carcosa and Blood-Captain Hammurabi escorted Muhr, who was extracting Nagael's gene-seed with his scissor-like hands. The trio surrounded the witch-chirurgeon, firing outwards as they fought their way towards Gammadin. A dark eldar raider, too confident in his abilities, darted low at Hammurabi, twin blades trailing. The ancient captain dismissed him with a back-handed slap, breaking the dark eldar's neck while he continued to cycle through his bolter. Khadath suddenly fell, his neck ruptured. Carcosa caught him by his bolter sling and dragged him backwards.

Gammadin milked the last of his flame chambers as he watched the dark eldar close in. How many of them were there? Hundreds? Certainly, judging by the bodies that were beached on the shores.

The remaining Impassives, their bolters now slung, slaughtered their way deep into the lake with mace, axe and hammer. They drove a path through the dark eldar who tried to engage them hand to hand. For all the speed and deft blade-skill of the xenos raiders, the Impassives crushed them with brute strength. Bond-Brother Gemistos led the way, sprinting at full speed, all three hundred kilos of him. An ironclad juggernaut crashed through the dark eldar, swinging his antlered helmet from side to side.

Together the Impassives clustered around Gammadin like a shield wall. They became a solid phalanx of ceramite. The dark eldar could not manoeuvre close enough to surround them. Bolt shells whistled and spat through the water grass.

And that was when Muhr revealed his hand.

Trailing behind, the witch moved away from his lord. The dark eldar around him did not strike nor fire upon him, even as he raised his arms to summon his powers. A sudden wind gusted across the river, flattening the grass on the banks as it reached a high-pitched crescendo.

'Witch!' shouted Gammadin. 'What manner of–'

Gammadin was cut short as Muhr clapped his hands. The air pressure dropped as if in a vacuum. Shadows began to rise out of the boiling current, humanoid in shape, with multiple reaching hands.

The water frothed violently around the Impassives. Shadowy apparitions bubbled forth from the river and began to swarm over them. The mud beneath the Chaos Space Marines' feet gurgled wetly, slipping and sliding as if falling away.

'Muhr. You are not worthy of the Blood Gorgon title,' Gammadin whispered on the squad link.

The lake bottom suddenly imploded with a thunderous gurgle. It yawned like a sinkhole, thirstily draining water into its aqueous abyss. Four Impassives were carried down by the crashing flood of water. Gammadin sank down on one knee, fighting for purchase in the mud. Warning lights flashed across his vision as the spirit of his armour began to babble nonsense in his ears. The ground beneath him continued to give way. Sensing his weakness, warp hounds began to paddle across the lake towards him.

'I have plenty left for you!' he roared, drawing a scimitar from his back scabbard. The pitted blade was almost two metres in length, scarred and nicked from centuries of service. It resembled a tool rather than a blade, a piece of metal stripped of any elegance in favour of the utility of killing.

Dragging it to his left he met the charging hounds with three horizontal strikes, rushing past them as they leapt into the air and leaving severed corpses in his wake.

He turned to meet Muhr the betrayer. The sorcerer was wise to keep his distance, stepping away even as his hands throbbed with black, sorcerous fire.

'Witch. What have you done here?' Gammadin demanded.

'You're a tiresome one,' Muhr replied. 'The Blood Gorgons need leadership. I tire of roving like vagabonds, adrift in space with no purpose.'

'We are raiders, Muhr. That's our way of doing things,' growled Gammadin. He tried to rise to his feet, but the lake bottom sucked and slurped. The waterline lowered visibly as the Champion Ascendant planted his foot into solid mud, but it yielded completely. The gushing water pushed against him and suddenly Gammadin was going over.

'You're going to die now,' Muhr said.

It was the last thing Lord Gammadin heard as the lake opened up to swallow him whole.

CHAPTER TWO

Gammadin was dead.

Those were the words that echoed aboard the *Cauldron Born*. From the fortress-ship's hammerhead prow, word spread quickly of their champion's death. Cries of alarm could be heard in the ship's temple bowels, and sorrow radiated out into thousands of chambers and connective corridors of the floating fortress. The daemon bells were tolled and the ship fired broadsides in salute. Many did not believe the news. It should not, nay, it *could* not have happened and some refused to accept it.

Lord Gammadin had been their master when the Gorgons were first created in the 21st founding. He had been their shepherd when the Imperium declared them renegade – *Excommunicate Traitoris* – mere centuries later, and it was he who parted the warp-sea to lead them into the Eye of Terror. The Blood Gorgons knew no other commander.

Even the ship itself strained in mourning. As an artefact of Blood Gorgons biological experimentation – pseudo-surgery and daemonology – all eight kilometres of the vessel seemed to tremble. It was said that the floating fortress had been grafted with the flesh of a daemon prince and that organic matter had been cultivated to merge with the ship's engines, spawning a spirit that inhabited the circuitry. Gammadin was its master and the ship was his steed.

Panic and disturbance accompanied the news of his passing. The captains of the companies, nine in all, retreated to their lairs within the labyrinthine depths, drawing around them their most trusted warriors.

None knew what the following days would bring, but they knew well enough not to act in haste.

Sabtah the Older, Chapter Veteran, slipped into a berserk rage. He had been Gammadin's Bond-Brother, having exchanged excised organs and blood with him in the Rituals of Binding. The death of his bond drove Sabtah insensate with grief and fury.

It was recorded in history that when Gammadin had first begun to experiment in daemonology and the rituals that would form the Blood Gorgons custom, he had been bound to his most trusted lieutenant, Monomachus. Utilising the superhuman constitution of an Astartes, Chirurgeons had transfused blood and nurtured organs from excised tissue into prospective bonds. Using Gammadin's knowledge of arcane lore, rituals of the forgotten text were followed, creating an almost supernatural connection between those who survived the procedure.

Together, Gammadin and Monomachus led the Blood Gorgons to raid and terrorise the shipping lines of the Segmentum Obscurus. So attuned were they, that in battle the pair could orchestrate intuitive tactical decisions without communication. During the War of the Wire, Gammadin had sensed Monomachus's beleaguered disposition and sent reinforcements from two star systems away, despite the oceanic gulf of distance.

For four centuries they fought as parallel twins until Monomachus angered the gods and his form was corrupted into that of a spawn. It was said that Gammadin was greatly shamed by this and slew Monomachus himself, an act that would have caused him considerable physical pain. By now, Gammadin was a warrior so great, with blood so rich and vibrant with the power of Chaos, that no mere aspirant could hope to be blooded to him.

Following Monomachus, numerous unsuitable aspirants were killed by the rich blood of Gammadin. Rituals of Binding were dangerous, both through the traumatic shock of surgery and the whims of daemonic spirits. Although Gammadin's experience was vast, he could not share it, for dozens of aspirants died or went mad in the rituals of transfusion and excise.

It was not until Sabtah – an inductee from the legion plains of Symeon – that a bond showed promise. The aspirant endured months of torture on the operating slabs, his body sent into shock by the process of plasma binding, until he emerged as a young charge of the great Gammadin. For the next three thousand, six hundred and fifty-one years, Sabtah the Older had become Gammadin's brother, growing stronger and wiser through their synergy.

And now Gammadin was dead.

The Maze of Acts Martial, a sixty-hectare section of interior combat facilities set beneath the engine decks of the *Cauldron Born*, was littered with corpses. Narrow ossuaries meandered into charnel houses where the bones of slain 'training prey' filled the walls. These macabre displays formed neat lattices, while bare skulls of all species formed low pyramids. Even the floors were snowy with a build-up of bone powder. Each time prey was released into the maze, the Blood Gorgons interred them where they fell, and in the preceding centuries, the Blood Gorgons trained often.

'Push to the left. The prey is on your left, at thirty degrees,' Sargaul whispered into his vox-link.

But Barsabbas didn't need to hear the command. He could already judge by the way Sargaul stood, the angle of his helmet and the urgency in his voice, that their prey was on his left. Such was the shared experience of a blood bond that Barsabbas fired before he took aim through his bolter scope, so sure was he of Sargaul's warning.

The termagant was shredded by the salvo of shots. The plates on its forehead crumbled away as its frontal lobe exploded. Its bulbous hind legs loosened out from underneath it and the creature collapsed, its thick tail straightening. As it died, its thigh muscles continued to work, twitching and kicking the last of its life away.

A kill counter chimed in the corridor, signalling a successful training shot. 'Perfect,' Sargaul said, slapping the back of Barsabbas's bulky power pack. 'But next time, do not wait. Aim your shot if you can spot it. Our blood bond allows us to kill efficiently together, not through some rigid singularity.'

Barsabbas nodded intently as his blood bond spoke. Bond-Brother Sargaul was an experienced warrior with many years of service to his trophy racks and although Barsabbas had been bonded to him since his early days as a neophyte, they were markedly different. Barsabbas was young, at least for a Traitor Marine. He had been plucked from his family as a child and survived the test and ordeals required to become a neophyte. At the cusp of adulthood he had been selected to bond with Sargaul and survived the ritual of excise that transplanted their major organs and homogenised their blood. Since then, he had only served as a fully fledged bond-brother on two major tours and a dozen minor raids.

Physically too, Barsabbas differed from his bond. Where Sargaul reached almost two hundred and fifty centimetres tall in bare feet, Barsabbas was short for a Traitor Marine, topping out at two metres thirty in plated height. While Sargaul was long in the hamstrings and forearms, Barsabbas was wide and thick in the legs. Although their differences would go unnoticed among humans, who viewed all Astartes as uniform giants, a Space Marine perceived such subtle differences in stature and interpreted accordingly. Theirs was a martial culture and Barsabbas had often felt the lesser of the bond. The pair were anything but the same.

'That was sharp, brothers,' said Sergeant Sica. 'Gather on me for post-training evaluation.'

The six Traitor Marines of Squad Besheba took a knee and began to break down the entire training session, from movement formations and firing patterns down to the finite details of xenos psychology and communications theory.

As the youngest of the squad, Barsabbas scribbled notes on a data-slate while the others listened with the casual confidence of experience. There was the pair Hadius and Cython, impetuous and helmet-less, both displaying knife scars on their cheeks and nose bridges, mirror images that perfectly aligned. There was stern Sergeant Sica with his chainaxe slung across his shoulders. Crouched next to him was Sica's bond, Bael-Shura, clacking his metal jaw, an augmetic replacement that had been purposely left jagged and rough-cut. The downward point of his stalactite chin cemented Bael-Shura's face into a morose, forlorn grimace.

The sirens in the ossuary blared again, signalling the end of the session. Having dispatched the last of their prey, the six members of Squad Besheba picked their way down the corridor towards the caged exits.

They followed the trail of dead, the remains of those they had felled that day. Most had been lower organisms of the tyranid genus, smaller wiry animals that had been herded from the slave pens into the maze. The Chapter had recently procured a large quantity of such creatures from xenos slave drivers on the Edge Rift Worlds, and it seemed as if every training drill since then had involved using the captured tyranids. In truth, Barsabbas had grown bored of killing them. At first, the flocks of skittering, agitated little creatures had been a challenge. They leapt and bounced in defiance of the ship's artificial gravity, running vertically up walls and racing across the ceilings like paper debris ejected from a venting pipe. But it had not taken Barsabbas long to recognise their patterns of movement and adapt his bolter drills accordingly. Soon, the challenge of shooting them became a chore, a mere series of 'trajectory calculations' to be hard-wired into Barsabbas's muscle memory through repetition.

The trail of dead was kilometres-long. The Maze of Acts Martial needed to be large in order to accommodate the training requirements of the Blood Gorgons Chapter. Only in these rambling tunnels could the Blood Gorgons simulate the violent claustrophobia of a ship boarding action. A system of concentric corridors, murder holes and dead ends, it was perfectly adapted for the boarding actions of the piratical renegades.

The maze was so vast that slaves released into the labyrinth could hide for days, if not months, before Blood Gorgons squads found them again. At times, the slaves would be supplied with weapons and rations, so they could better mimic enemy action. It was not uncommon for slaves of higher intelligence to survive for periods of time, subsisting on fungus and condensation. They often converged into groups for survival, leaving behind the unmistakable remains of food scraps and refuse. Some lost their sanity and were driven to cannibalism. Humans and orks were especially susceptible to such madness, prowling the maze in ghoulish packs.

Barsabbas led the way as the maze sirens barked again, more urgently this time. The corridors were unlit and lined with porous granite that seemed to soak up light as well as it did blood. Relying only on the dimmest vision setting, Barsabbas probed the way with his chainsword. The persistent tolling of the bell swelled into an imperious clanging. This was no longer a signal that the training drills were over, Barsabbas realised. Somewhere, deep within the Temple Heart of their ship, a call had been issued for Chapter formation. Barsabbas did not know why, but he knew Sargaul echoed his confusion. The temple bells were never rung, except in the event of Chapter-scale war or calamity.

Quickening his pace, Barsabbas slashed away at a solid, gossamer curtain of spider webs through a passage that had been disused for centuries. Barsabbas was not sure what was happening. Stomping through the carcass of a termagant, he threaded his way towards the ship's Temple Heart.

Deep within the ship's core, the bells were sounding again and again. The twin bells swayed ponderously in their chancel arches, pounding out Gammadin's swansong. Carved from ore stone, each bell was fifty metres from crown to lip and their echo could be heard clearly in the furthest points of the fortress-ship. The Blood Gorgons knew the sound as the *Apocalypse Toll* – a herald of calamity.

For the past several days, the bells had been sounded at the passing of each ship cycle. Now they were hauled with a climactic urgency to mark the Summoning. Gammadin's death song would end only with the invocation of the Chapter's patron daemon – Yetsugei.

Their peal woke the Dreadnoughts from their rusting slumber. The sixteen Dreadnoughts of the Blood Gorgons shifted sleepily as servitors anointed their machine joints. They were old bondsmen – some four thousand years old – locked in their coffins of war. They had earned their rest and did not wake for petty foibles, but even they recognised the Apocalypse Tolls.

The knells radiated outwards and down to the ship's bowels, where the Blood Gorgons berthed the few rare armoured machines they still maintained. These Rhinos and Land Raiders from the ancient past were now hollow shells inhabited by dormant spirits. At the crack of the bells, the engine daemons started, their motors throaty with promethium-phlegm. Some of the armoured carriers jolted forwards, pulling against the shipping chains that lashed them to the decking. They growled and revved, suddenly excited, like leashed dogs straining towards bait. The *Cog's Teeth*, a Rhino-pattern armoured carrier, broke free of its moorings and crashed into a far wall, crumpling the bulkhead. Servitors rushed forwards to calm the daemon spirit within, splashing its tracks with blood to satiate its rage.

All throughout the *Cauldron Born*, from the central barracks to the most crooked of forgotten passages, all were summoned to the temple at the core of the cruising leviathan. The temple matched the bells in their size and grandeur. The ribcage of a dead beast ridged the domed ceiling; intercostal spaces were filled with personal shrines, each maintained daily by one of the nine hundred Blood Gorgons. Some were tall and narrow, like grandfather clocks, while others were squat cubbies brimming with offerings of spent bolter casings, ears, teeth and baubles.

The Temple. The Pit. The daemon's cage.

Muhr and his coven were painting the geometrics onto the marble floor with careful strokes of their ash brushes. The Chirurgeon-witches, nine in number, were barefoot and clad in loose black robes. They appeared as ants against the wide, featureless expanse of the marble dais, yet they painted with tiny brushes, tracing precise triangles and interconnected pentagrams. These wards had been inscribed on the domed walls too, painted via scaffolding that swayed gently in the gravitational lurch.

The pit smelled of sorcery – incense, braziers, oil and acidic paint. Of slow, focused intensity. Muhr and his witches could make no mistake. The slightest error in the wards would be unthinkable.

Elusive and ever clandestine, the Chapter knew to leave the witches to their own rituals. The coven were not blood bonded like their brethren, and from this there grew a rift between the witches and the companies. It was a respectful rift but a rift nonetheless.

Unseen by others, the witches had cleaned themselves first, a ritual cleansing that washed away all their scent. The skin files and dermabrasion had left them pink and newborn, which would not give away their musk to the warp ghosts, or so the ritual claimed.

Once the last wards were laid, and the bells finished tolling, the Chapter would gather for summoning.

Yetsugei was an old daemon. Older than the Imperium, than Terra, old even when men still fought with sword and shield. He was known by many names, and had appeared under many guises throughout the history of man.

But he was not strong. Not strong in the way a greater daemon, or even a warlike daemon prince, was strong. He was a mischievous daemon, a trickster.

He was also a patron. He had chosen the Blood Gorgons, for they, much like him, were rogues. They came to him for his prophecies and his knowledge, and he chose to humour them for he yearned for human company. Yetsugei enjoyed the petty foibles and insignificant dramas of their short lives.

When they summoned him, as they had done so for the past three thousand, six hundred and fifty-one years, Yetsugei roared. As his avatar materialised on the prime worlds, Yetsugei spread his arms and shrieked. In truth he would have preferred a quiet summoning, but the humans responded well to theatrics.

There was a maelstrom of warp fire, coalescing into a spiralling column. With a clap of crashing air it disappeared and Yetsugei found himself in the familiar Temple Heart. Pentagrammic wards criss-crossed his vision like the interlaced bars of a cage. They sprouted from the wide marble floors and lanced down from the domed ceiling. Beyond the dais he could see the souls of the assembled Blood Gorgons. Patron or not, Yetsugei could not deny his daemon hunger. Given the chance, he would devour them all.

'You intrude upon my slumber again?' Yetsugei cawed, feigning shrill indignity. In truth, he had grown tired of the warp and a glimpse of the prime worlds was a welcome respite.

The Blood Gorgons psyker he knew as 'Muhr' stepped forwards and onto the dais, stopping shy of the external pentagram. 'Yetsugei – the most grave and reverend. Baron of the Reef of Terror, what deeds you soon must hear! What sorrow you must behold, for we mourn the passing of our Great Champion.'

Yetsugei rolled his ropey shoulders. 'Most dreadful to hear and even more so to see. But first, loosen my bonds, they are too tight.' Yetsugei pretended to contort his daemonic form in discomfort.

Muhr crouched down and brushed a line with his hand. Pigment came away from the marble onto his palm. On his hands was a tiny smear, almost imperceptible considering the immense size of the marking, but it broke an external seal. It was a calculated risk, and a dangerous one at that, but Yetsugei knew the humans needed something from him and Muhr did not dare to antagonise him. He had other plans.

Yetsugei felt his confines loosen ever so slightly. Their souls grew brighter to him.

The daemon stretched languidly. 'Ah. How these bonds make me weary.' He yawned and opened one eyelid coyly. 'Perhaps you can loosen another?'

'So you say,' Muhr replied coldly. He stepped back from the dais.

The witch was no fool, and he knew better than to trust a daemon. Although Yetsugei was their chosen patron, he was a deity and they his mere humans. He appeared to Muhr as a leaping shade, narrow-waisted and smoky, with horns that formed an intricate crown atop his head – a towering pillar of unreality – a thing from another existence. They trusted him for his prophetic knowledge but not with their lives.

'Amuse me, then. What favour would you crave of me?'

Muhr cleared his throat. 'Lord Gammadin is dead.'

Yetsugei yawned. 'How did Gammadin die?'

Muhr lowered his head solemnly. 'Lord Gammadin and his warrior few embarked across the warp-sea to claim a new slave world for harvest. But the pirates of the eldarkind had long ago colonised this world in secret. They were prepared and the battle was their theatre, their stage. We were ambushed and fought on their ground. I was the only survivor.'

Yetsugei steepled his fingers and fixed his eyes on the witch. Muhr was a good liar, and it was clearly a story he had rehearsed and no doubt recounted many times. But a daemon could see deception against the fabric of reality. Although this was the story Muhr had told the Chapter, Yetsugei knew the witch was hiding his own involvement.

'Yes, so you spake of his demise, that is not your present plight,' the daemon purred. 'It matters not the death of an old champion. Merely that you present a new one to the gods.'

'Gammadin has appointed me sole guardian in his stead,' Muhr recited.

The daemon knew this to be a lie too. There were other factions at play here and Muhr was simply one such cog in the machine. But Yetsugei did not reveal Muhr's lie. He would enjoy whatever plot was to unfold.

'Tell me, witch. How did he die?' the daemon asked, baiting the witch to reveal more.

'Slain by treachery,' Muhr responded.

That was the truth this time. Yetsugei smiled.

'I challenge that claim!' said a low voice. 'The witch has no proof.'

Yetsugei knew that voice. Sabtah! The daemon clapped with glee. 'The bond of Gammadin! Come forth! Come forth!'

Sabtah stepped onto the dais from the audience. Yetsugei could see raw aggression rippling from the old warrior. 'The wardship is mine to hold,' he stated boldly.

'So it should be!' Yetsugei agreed eagerly, straining against the circle of ash and paint. As he writhed, paint faded from the walls and several of the wards disappeared from the marble. His constraints were breaking. Souls grew closer, brighter.

'Then denounce this man as a liar,' Sabtah said, stabbing his forefinger at Muhr.

Yetsugei cocked his head. 'I sense this witch has some power. A foreign power. Perhaps Gammadin has given you this power... or perhaps another...?'

Yetsugei could tell Muhr was beginning to wither under his attention. The witch was being influenced by greater powers, a rival patron perhaps? There was something more to this tale. Gammadin had not simply been slain by the dark eldar in an accident, leaving the witch a sole survivor.

Muhr's eyes narrowed defiantly, as if sensing Yetsugei's intent. 'Gammadin chose me.'

Biding his time, the daemon leaned forwards and smiled at the witch and the old wolf. 'You must enthrone an Ascendant Champion. Hear me this – do not displease the gods or there will come bad spirits. They will snatch good fortune from your grasp.'

Yetsugei was cracking the seals now. He strained against his weakening confines. He hungered for their souls. Reaching out with his hand, Yetsugei beckoned Muhr closer.

'Daemon, begone!' Muhr shouted suddenly, as if angered. He dispelled the coven's bindings and unravelled the daemon back into the warp. There was a swirl of cold and the wards blackened to ash.

CHAPTER THREE

On the first day of Swelter, in the Central Territory of Hauts Bassiq, herdsmen of the plains were mustering their caprid for the early morning drove. When they looked up, they saw a dark ochre cloud hidden amongst the swells of the light dawn cumulus. It was the colour of powdered groundnut and seemed to have the same grainy texture. Heavy and brooding, the strange cloud spread out and descended to cap the distant ridges.

The herdsmen thought little of it, rushed as they were to return to their kinships with caprid milk for breakfast. Yet there was something about the cloud that troubled them. The season of Swelter brought with it brutally clear skies, bathed almost white by the harsh suns. By morning, the red rocks of the plains would be hot enough to curdle lizard eggs. Seldom did the storms come until evening, and even then only briefly.

When the cloud landed, far away from their eyes, it began to kill. More clouds like it soon followed and the microfauna began to die first. Across the plains and dunes of Bassiq, beneath the layer of red iron oxide dust, ore beetles shrivelled up into husks and died. The microscopic filing worms that inhabited the top layer of ferric sand writhed in toxic pain, burrowing deeper to no avail.

The cloud savaged the earth. Distant Ur, the sealed city, cocooned its gates and weather-shields against the encroaching clouds. For as long as Ur had stood, it had been sealed and silent against the outside, opening only intermittently to trade with the plains nomads. Now it sealed itself permanently.

A light southerly carried the fumes across the dry clay seas and dispersed the poison across the lower part of the continent. Ancient boab trees whose swollen trunks and leafless branches had survived centuries of remorseless sun and drought sickened visibly, their silver bark peeling like wet skin. Amongst sheltered gorges that had resisted the climate, patches of coral brush and cacti wilted upon contact.

Only when the clouds began to affect the caprid herds did the plainsmen become concerned. The leaping caprid was the lifeblood of the Bassiq kinships. In ages past, when the mining colonies of distant Terra had harvested the ferrous-rich planet of Hauts Bassiq, these goat-antelopes had been brought with them as a hardy food source. It had been a wise choice, for the horned bovids proved remarkably resilient in the scorching desert, surviving off runt flora while providing the settlers with milk and meat.

Even when the colonists began to leave Bassiq, abandoning its ultraviolet heat and its isolation from the Imperium, the caprid flourished. With their musterers gone, they escaped their pens and became wild, their numbers multiplying. The industrial mines fell silent and the colonists who remained were too few to operate the earthmovers or tectonic drills. Some retreated to the walled city of Ur and sealed themselves within against the heat, drought and radiation. Their fates became unknown, their envoys only emerging from their sealed city to trade. An isolationist Imperial cult, Ur became a forgotten bastion of the early colonists.

Many others wandered the plains in loose familial bands known as kinships, gathering petrochemicals in a vain attempt to keep their machines running and resist their decline into savagery. Soon the Imperium had forgotten that scorched, thermal planet of Hauts Bassiq and Bassiq, in turn, forgot the Imperium.

Even then, the caprid remained a key factor of their survival. From their shaggy long hair sheared in the Swelter Seasons the colonists-turned-plainsmen wove their fabrics, and from their curved horns they crafted tools. Although official history had largely been forgotten, it was said, by word of mouth from kinship to kinship, that the caprid were the true settlers of Hauts Bassiq.

The animals' death was of great concern to the plainsmen. Affected caprid refused to eat, wasting away within a matter of days. The herdsmen could not bear to watch the caprids shrink away until they could barely lift the thick horns on their heads, stooped and bent as they stumbled about. Before succumbing to the disease, the caprid would become aggressive, their eyes rolling white as they bit and kicked in a frenzy. The herdsmen soon realised it was better, and safer, to kill any caprid they suspected of being ill before they could become 'possessed by the ghost' as the plainsmen coined it.

In due time, the sickness spread from the caprid to the plainsmen. At first there was panic amongst the nomadic kinships. They sent emissaries to the north, to the only permanent settlement on the continent, to the Mounds of Ur. But the city hid behind its walls, blind to the fate of wandering nomads. The denizens of Ur had never considered the plainsmen worthy of anything more than infrequent trade.

Although the nomads had no central king, an elder named Suluwei gathered all the wisest elders of the North Territory to discuss this great catastrophe that had befallen them. Suluwei was not a king, but he was the elder of the Ganda Kinship and he owned a great many head of caprid. His possession of so many herds earned him a respected place among the leaders of other kinships and they acknowledged his word.

At his request, the wisest men of the Northern Kinships gathered to discuss the disease that was spreading so rapidly. As was custom for the plainsmen, stories were abundant. Some spoke of black skies in the extremities of the north, dark clouds that besmeared the sky even during the hottest midday. Others spoke of famine and entire kinships disappearing. Others still muttered of ghosts and the restless dead. It was difficult to separate fact from fiction amongst a nomad's word of mouth, but it was clear that strange and frightful things were occurring.

Suluwei spoke briefly of summoning the Godspawn, but the elders, grave though the situation, dared not resort to such measures. In the end, nothing came to fruition from the meeting and the elders returned to their kinships. Within two days, Suluwei was sick, his brain wracked by fever and his eyes rolling white as he succumbed to a sickness he had likely contracted during the meeting of elders. He died soon after, not remembering his own name or where he was. Within ten days, fully half of his kinship fell ill. Even Suluwei's slight exchange with the other kinships had been enough to infect them all.

Yet most frightening of all was the story of Suluwei after his death. It was passed, from word of mouth, by kinless herdsmen to the Southern Territories, and there were many variations of the tale, but the core of it always remained the same. It was said that Suluwei's kin buried him in the hollowed bole of a boab tree, as custom required, and sealed the hole with many heavy rocks. They performed the ceremonial dances to calm his spirit into the plains and buried him with his warbow, hatchet and saddle so he would not need to seek his possessions in the afterlife.

Yet despite their precautions, Suluwei returned many days later. Here the tale differed, for some said Suluwei returned to his kin with his eyes white and a smile on his face, asking them for one last meal. Others spoke of Suluwei returning at dusk, a flesh-hungry ghoul who tapped on the carriages of his kin, pleading to be let in with a beguilingly sweet voice. Whatever the truth, the story spread as rapidly as the sickness.

When this story reached the ears of Suluwei's brother-in-law, Chetsu, an elder of the Zhosa Kinship, it was decided that they could wait idle no more. Although Chetsu did not own many caprid, nor did his kinship boast many young men, the Zhosa were a brave family. There was evil in the northern tip and Chetsu was resolved to ride out and find those kinships that had fallen silent there.

Chetsu chose five of his kinship's most robust men, all of them his own blood cousins. He made sure they groomed and saddled their talon squalls properly, preening the black feathers of the flightless sprint-birds with oil until they were glossed against the sun and hooding their beaks in sheaths of leather. As usual, young Hantu neglected to oil the bare legs and long neck of his bird, featherless parts which were especially susceptible to sunburn, and Chetsu had berated him furiously, dashing a clay bowl onto the ground in anger. Chetsu was in no mood for slothfulness at a time such as this.

The riders were dispatched in the dawn before the suns could grow thermal. Each man wore a *shuka* of brilliant red wool, a loose sarong worn by all the plainsmen across the territories. Red was a favoured dye and it would give Chetsu and his riders much bravery and aggression. They rode with bows across their saddles and weighted hatchets at their hips. The kinship saw them off with dancing and singing, jumping up and down on the spot to clatter their wrist bangles and necklace wreaths. The plainsmen were not a warlike people and the departure of five warrior braves was a momentous occasion for the Zhosa.

Chetsu rode to the north and that was the last time his kinship saw him. The days passed and the riders did not come back. Chetsu's wife waited for his return, watching the horizon. For as long as she watched, the sky in the distance was ominously dark, contrasting with the harsh white everywhere else. Some of the clouds were pileus, rolling like caps of toxic amber; others were low stratus clouds, coating the horizon in a flat, featureless black rind. They uncurled ponderously, boiling themselves into monstrous shapes that resembled faces, always creeping closer. It would not be long, she thought, until they blocked out the many suns.

The temple had no name. It had no name because it was the only temple they knew. From outside, it resembled a pylon of uncarved red rock, like a ridged tooth that rose from the flat ground around it. If one were to carve away the exterior, to tear away the rust storms and ferric build-up that cocooned its outside surface, one would find a cathedral of grand design, an edifice built to worship the double-headed eagle from another era. Within its cool interior was a vaulted ceiling of coloured glass, arches and columns – designs that the plainsmen of Bassiq had forgotten how to construct.

By the time the elders of the various northern kinships met in this temple, only three weeks after Suluwei's first summons, there were very few of them left.

Many of the kinships had never responded to the ageing hand-wound vox-casters, nor had they responded to the secondary smoke signals. Although it had not been spoken, they were already counted among the dead.

All the elders waited in reverential quiet, sometimes expressing their concern in hushed tones. The temple was dark and only pinpricks of sunlight managed to pierce gaps in the rocky crust that covered the windows. The darkness did not matter, for the attention of the assembled elders was centred solely on the single shaft of light at the centre of the temple.

Captured beneath the beam of an open skylight above was a curious machine piece. All the elders had seen it before; some had even prayed to it, but never had they seen it used. There had never, in all their collective memories, been a time that required it.

It just lay there, on the ground, an oblong of tin no larger than a block of compacted nut flour. It was inert, like a sleeping beast, with a thick skin of dust that covered its dials and press pads. In all the time it had been there, no one had dared to touch it. A cranking shaft, delicate and small, protruded from one end of the machine, as if waiting to be turned.

Around the machine, a wide circle had been marked in the stone and simple illustrations of armoured warriors in bulbous helmets had been scratched into the floor. They depicted the helmeted warriors slaying a double-headed eagle, smiting it out of the sky with stylised tongues of fire. Like the machine itself, this circle bore no footprints in its dust rind, although the stone outside its circumference had been worn smooth by pedestrian traffic.

'Someone has to do it,' croaked a toothless elder of the Muru kinship.

'Nay, you are older than I, so the honour is yours!' rebuked another elder.

'Do not be frightened, you are young and vital. You should do it!' another countered.

Soon the congregation were openly shouting and it became clear that no one wanted to touch the machine. No one knew what it would do.

'I'll do it!' shouted a young man as he stepped forwards. 'I'll summon the Godspawn.' The brave's distinctive plaited hair marked him as a brave of the Kosi kinship, reckless riders from the Western Plains. No one argued with him as he pushed his way through the assembly and made his way towards the centre of the temple.

The plainsmen had once worshipped a God-Emperor in the darkest reaches of their dimmest histories. But that had been during the time of the Colonies, a time of dreaming for them. Isolated as it was, Hauts Bassiq suffered many raids from alien invaders and human pirates. For a time, the plainsmen had lived fearful lives, constantly nomadic to avoid conflict. But then the Godspawn came to drive away the xenos. The Godspawn had been their protectors and so it had always been, as far as the plainsmen were concerned.

The Kosi brave took a deep breath and planted a foot inside the carved boundary. The crowd inched back, fearfully expectant, but nothing occurred. Exhaling slowly, the Kosi entered the circle fully and knelt down to inspect the machine.

The machine seemed intuitive enough and there was nothing for the brave to do but turn the cranking handle. Gingerly gripping it with thumb and forefinger, he started to wind it. To his surprise, it began to turn smoothly despite its considerable age. He began to turn it faster, feeling the gears within the machine tick over, building up momentum as a soft purr began to emit from the tin box.

With a sudden flash, lights within the temple came alive. Some of the elders exclaimed in wonder while others screamed and covered their heads. High up in the vaulted ceiling, light they had never known existed flared after five thousand and seven hundred years of dormancy, lighting the temple with a bright orange radiance.

The brave continued to turn, as if he had known all along what to do. The purr become a loud, steady hum. Acoustic resonance thrummed the air, shivering the skin with its building pressure. In the back of the assembly, someone begged the brave to stop turning the handle but the Kosi could not stop turning even if he had wanted to; the cranking wheel was now spinning on its own, moving so fast the man could not lift his fingers away.

Then it stopped turning with a click. The temperature in the temple plunged. The breath of the elders plumed white as they waited in expectation. Even the alarmed ones who had screamed were now still. Frost did not exist on Hauts Bassiq, except for when mind-witches used their mind powers. But frost now coated the temple, a thin furry sheet that covered the walls and even the wool of the elders' shukas.

But nothing happened. Except for the winking sequence of lights that played across the machine's press pad, nothing happened. The Kosi brave backed out of the circle and the elders leaned forwards, eager to get a closer look now that the work was done.

That was when a seismic rumble flattened the entire congregation. A wall of energy pushed them down and the machine rose up into the air, suspended for a blink before it clattered back down. This time, everyone shouted in fright. The lights winked out and the temple dimmed, as if a shadow had passed overhead. The elders felt exhausted as they tried to claw their way upright, groping lamely in the darkness.

All of them, even the most dim and psychically inert, could instinctively feel what had happened. Although they could not truly understand it, they knew that the power from the little tin machine had been real.

'I think I have summoned them,' the Kosi brave said, staring at his own hands as if they were sacred objects.

* * *

The slave scratched at the scar on his cheek without thinking. It was a habit he had developed without ever realising. The small incision, shaped like a ringworm, had been cut below his cheekbone. Every slave bore the same mark as a sign of servitude.

Although he had been a slave for many years he had never become accustomed to that scar. It worried him. He could feel a lump in his face, if he dug his fingers in and felt past the skin, fat and flesh. Inside, the Blood Gorgons had buried a small larva, a thread of white worm no bigger than a fingernail.

For now the larva was inert, hibernating within his flesh. The slave was not sure how it worked, for it was not his place to know such things, but he knew that each larva was genetically coded to a particular Blood Gorgon, so that if a slave ever strayed too far from his master, the larva would hatch.

What occurred thereafter was the stuff of speculation. Slaves did not wish to talk of such unfortunate things.

Their masters told them often that it would take many hours for the larva to reach the pupal stage, but from there, growth to the final stage was instantaneous. Self-destructive death and engorging of human flesh was its final stage of development but by then, as far as any slave was concerned, escape would be impossible.

It meant he was bound to Master Muhr. Even when he was more than a sub-deck away from his master, the beetle often itched, a sign that the creature was waking and growing hungry.

He scratched again and quickened his pace.

The slave climbed the stairs from the *Cauldron Born*'s cavernous lower decks and began the long trek towards the upper galleries. The ship's size was immense and even after nineteen years of servitude, the slave still found himself lost if he did not leave glowing guide markers to retrace his passage. Some of the passages had been disused for so long that they had developed their own ecology. Softly glowing patches of bacterial flora crept up the walls, while shelled molluscs sucked on reefs of neon dendrites. There, the plant life wept a weak organic acid which corroded the metal bulkheads, forming small grottos and burrows for the darting lantern-eels and other flesh-hungry organisms.

It was a dangerous walk for a slave and he thrashed the darkness in front of him with an ore stave in one hand and a phos-light in the other. He found one of his guide markers at every bend in the tunnels: little glow stones that he had put down when he had walked this path the first time. The walk had taken much longer than expected, and he was afraid his master would punish him for his tardiness. He picked up the glow stones and returned them to his satchel as he found them, until finally he reached a clamp shutter at the end of a tunnel, wreathed in gently nodding anemones of pink, purple and electric blue tentacles.

'Catacomb serf Moselle Grae,' the slave said to the brass vox arrays overhead. 'I have the nutrient sacs that Master Muhr requisitioned. Hurry please.'

The clamp shutters shot upwards with a clatter of machine rollers. On the other side were two guards in brass hauberks and black, tightly wound turbans. They too were slaves and their cheeks were scarred by scarabs, but to Grae they were imposing nonetheless. Grae nodded at them briefly and scurried beneath their crossed halberds.

The guards stood at the threshold of Master Muhr's personal chambers, a towering spire that jutted from the upper tiers of the *Cauldron Born*.

The neotropical flora grew less abundantly here, as if the organisms dared not anger the sorcerer. They were tamed to a fluorescent garden that flanked the winding path towards the spire's lower entrance. Thousands of luminous ferns, swaying like synapses, were surrounded by ponds of condensation from the ship's circulation systems. Only the lower portion of the spire was visible, for its height protruded from the ship's hull, rising through the inner mantle, vacuum seals and the hemispheric armour. The strip path led to double doors of old wood, a rarity aboard the ship, and likely plundered as a trophy on some past raid.

'Emperor bless me,' Grae muttered to himself while touching the iron of his slave collar three times.

The spire of Master Muhr had always made him feel a nauseous fear, no matter how many times he had been there before. It was different from the other parts of the ship. The air here seemed sorcerous, alive with a hateful presence. Grae likened it to a feeling of walking through the site of some terrible past massacre or touching the clothes of a murder victim. Things had happened within these walls, horrible blasphemous things that had left a psychic imprint.

As Grae crept down the path, he found the doors to be ajar. He hesitated, unsure of whether to enter, but decided that it would be an evil day if he did not bring his master the nutrient sacs on time. Easing the door open, he crept inside.

'Master Muhr?' he called out.

There was no answer. As his bare feet padded into the antechamber, glow strips reacted to his movement and permeated the area in low green light. The walls were honeycombed with preserved specimens immortalised in amniotic suspension. Grae went about his business quickly, trying to avoid eye contact with the jars and tanks containing Muhr's creations.

It was like a horror house Grae had visited in the travelling rural fairs, when he had been a child growing up in the tableland counties of Orlen. He made sure to scurry past an open display at the entrance to the west corridor. From afar the display looked like thespians frozen mid-scene. Up close, they were taxidermed slaves, posed in a sickening recreation of a scene from the stage theatre *Ransom of Lady Almas*. Thankfully their glass-eyed faces ignored him, their waxy skin frozen permanently in their rigid poses.

Grae began to check all the chambers in the lower levels, working his way from the lower laboratories into the trophy galleries. There, glass display cases housed the relics Master Muhr had collected on his campaigns. Orkoid teeth, rusting blades, eldar jewellery, polearms, xenos attire and ceramics, all neatly labelled and well dusted. Yet Master Muhr was nowhere to be found.

From these galleries a spiralling staircase of black iron led to the upper levels, but Grae had never been that far up before. Briefly he considered leaving the nutrition sacs at the base of the staircase for Master Muhr to find, but he feared such a gesture would be seen as a sign of disrespect. In fact, many of the jarred experiments had been slaves who had shown Master Muhr disrespect. He thought better of the idea and climbed the staircase.

It was the first time he had been up this far, and frightened though he was, it was difficult not to be awed by the view. He stood in a circular observation deck. The heavy drapes had been pulled back and beyond the void glass was a three hundred and sixty degree view of deep space. It was a never-ending darkness, an infinite deepness interrupted by the fizz and pop of billions of stars. Thousands of kilometres away, a pillar of gas was ponderously exhaling, its plume resembling the head of a horse. Grae knew its unfathomable distance, yet it seemed to rise so close, almost eclipsing his vision. It felt as if a horse-headed god was peering into the tiny viewing glass of his interior.

'The void glass will need resurfacing and cleaning,' Grae muttered to himself as he climbed higher up the staircase. He was talking to himself out of fear. Shaking his head, the slave began to climb to the top level.

But that was when all the glow strips faded out.

Grae almost dropped his satchel there and then. Startled, he fumbled to turn on his phos-light but the bulb had fizzed out. It was strange, as he had made certain to place a fresh bulb into the hand light when he set out. Shaking his head, Grae began to grope his way upwards, cautiously tapping the ground before him with the ore stave.

The air was coarse with chill and Grae became acutely aware that he was shivering. The loincloth and studded iron belt he wore afforded no warmth and he wore nothing else, for his masters were wary of concealed weapons. As he ran his hand along a wall panel, it left a furrow in the hoar frost there.

'Witchcraft,' Grae moaned. He felt as if he were going to be sick.

Grae had been a governor's aide before the Blood Gorgons ransacked his world. His daily job had been receipt of aerial parcels and message wafers for the governor's Chamber of Commerce. It was dreary work for the most part, but once Grae had seen an adept of the Astra Telepathica transmitting urgent interstellar messages from the governor's office. The eyeless man had spooked him, and Grae had become withdrawn in his presence, showing more timidity than he would have liked. By the time the adept had finished his work Grae remembered vividly that the room had become freezing and he'd spent considerable time mopping up the after-frost. The adept had wet the parcel shelves and frozen the ink in his typographer.

He was shocked out of his thoughts as something brushed past him. Grae turned around but saw nothing, or rather, could see nothing. It had been astonishingly quick, like a brisk tug of his clothes.

'Master Muhr?'

He climbed the next few levels slowly, calling for his master the entire way. The air grew colder. He almost lost the skin of his left palm when he placed it on the hand rails.

'Master?'

At the upper atrium, Grae froze. He heard voices. Master Muhr was talking to someone. Not daring to interrupt, Grae crept to a standstill at the top of the stairs, glad that he was hidden within the shadow. He stood within the folds of the curtain with his eyes fixed firmly on the floor. In the periphery of his vision, Grae could see the atrium was bathed in a green light. A forest of black curtains as tall as trees hung from the ceiling; beyond that, he could see nothing else.

'Then it is done. The ambush was clean and the dark eldar performed excellently. Gammadin is dead.'

'That's a good start, Muhr, but we need better assurance,' said a voice that Grae could not recognise.

'Only a start,' Muhr rasped. 'The Crow has begun the sowing of Hauts Bassiq.'

'Plague and famine, Muhr – you've promised plague and famine for so long.'

Grae tried not to listen, he even blocked his ears. These were things a slave had no right to know, he was sure of it.

'The Crow will maintain his side of the bargain,' Muhr retorted. 'He needs our hand in this as much as we need his.'

'And what of Sabtah?' the voice inquired.

'I will kill Sabtah myself,' Muhr answered.

Grae squeezed his eyes together and held his breath. Most of what he heard he did not understand, but there were glimmers of things that he knew he should not be hearing.

'Who else knows about this?' asked the voice in the curtains.

Muhr cleared his throat. 'Only you, a handful of unnamed squads in Fourth and Sixth Companies... and a slave named Moselle Grae.'

The reply jolted Grae. Frightened, he looked up and realised Muhr was already looking at him. The witch's eyes sought him out in his hiding place, boring into him.

'Did you think you could hide there, little mouse?' Muhr asked, addressing him directly.

Grae's nerves could not hold out any longer. He was done. He turned and ran, taking the nutrient sacs with him. There was no logic to what he did, but the fear he felt was deeply primal. It was the same flight instinct that early man had relied upon, a thoughtless, baseless need to just run. That voice was too much for him.

He clattered down the spiral stairs but only made it to the third step.

+*Stop,*+ commanded Muhr.

Grae's legs instantly seized up, his mind overwhelmed by Muhr's psionic will.

+*Turn around.*+

Jerked like a marionette, Grae spun around without consciously doing so. He saw Muhr rise from the ground, utterly naked except for his mask. A grotesque mass of scars ridged the muscles of Muhr's abdomen, long and thin like the deft cuts of a razor. Grae wanted to scream but he no longer had control of his own body.

Muhr hovered over Grae with his towering stature and studied the slave. He inspected his shaven scalp and tested the muscles of his arms like a rancher inspecting stock. Apparently satisfied, Muhr nodded.

'You are a strong slave. We Blood Gorgons do not waste the lives of our slaves needlessly,' Muhr remarked. 'So you will live.'

Grae was so relieved his left eye began to twitch. It was the only part of him that Muhr's psychic paralysis had not affected.

'But we should lobotomise you. I do not want my aspirations undone by gossiping slaves,' Muhr said sagely.

Grae's left eye widened. There was pure terror in his pupils. The veins on his neck bulged visibly as the slave struggled to move. But Muhr would not let him go.

'We have need for workers such as you on Bassiq. Not living like you are, of course, but dead, yet obedient all the same,' Muhr muttered as he parted the curtains and moved out of Grae's paralysed view. He rustled through the atrium, clicking his eyelids rapidly to adjust to the darkness. With a satisfied whistle, Muhr picked up a sliver of long surgical steel from a trestle table – an orbitoclast.

'This is harmless really. I'm going to insert it through your eye socket and puncture the thin wall of bone to reach your frontal lobe. A few medial and lateral swings should separate your thalamus,' Muhr stated. 'You will not feel much after that.'

CHAPTER FOUR

Nine hundred Traitor Marines in congress was unsettling. The Temple Heart barely seemed to contain their wild, exuberant ranks. They stamped their feet like bulls and boasted on vox-amp of their scars and trophies. Silence only fell across them when Sabtah ascended the central dais.

'Chapter-strength deployment,' announced Sabtah the Older. The declaration was momentous and all of the Blood Gorgons, all nine hundred of them, roared their approval.

'Hauts Bassiq is an ancestral world. Many of your brothers can trace their blood line to the lineage of the plains people. I'd wager many more of you have infused Bassiq lineage in your veins through the blood bond.'

The gathered Traitor Marines howled in approval. They sat, lounged or crouched about the temple without any particular display of company order. Congregating in six-man squads, each formed by three blood-bound pairs, each of the pairs were attended to by a train of retainers – black turbans, armour serfs, helm bearers and dancers.

'With Gammadin's death there is a void in rulership,' said Captain Hazareth in his deep metallic bass. 'Until such time as a warrior will be chosen to reign, I pledge wardship of my company in your hands. Whoever else may do so is not of my concern. For now, my swordarm is yours.'

Hazareth the Cruel, Captain of 1st Company, was an embodiment of the Blood Gorgons Chapter. Wild and boisterous, he was a violent thing. When he laughed, and he did so often, the humour behind it was black and bitter yet genuinely mirthful. His face had been melted by fire and his cheek pockmarked with bullet scars. Hazareth wore them like laurels of honour, for his men feared him and the gods favoured him well. A tortoise-like shell had solidified around his shoulders and power pack like a hunch-backed mound of bone, a powerful sign of daemonic favour. The shell ended in a short, muscular tail that sprouted from the base of Hazareth's spine and ended in a knot of fibrous growth. So monstrously thick-framed that he resembled a Dreadnought, Hazareth had his club tail swept low to balance his ponderous steps.

'Hazareth, your words stir this old heart,' said Sabtah. The verbal dance was almost theatrical, more of a symbolic gesture than any meaningful exchange. Despite their piratical nature, the Blood Gorgons were traditionalists at heart and Sabtah was a piece of their long history. To the assembly, Sabtah was the old grey ring-wolf they had always known. He was carefully presented in his Mark II Crusade armour, the articulated hoops of the relic lending an impressive bulk to his already broad girth. Most impressive was his beard, a tiered cascade of uniform ringlets that reached the bottom of his chest guard, black and well oiled. There was no doubt that Sabtah was venerable, but more than that, he would ensure the proper functioning of the Chapter beyond the death of Gammadin.

'Full Chapter strength deployment,' Sabtah repeated. 'But understand this – I know that there are those of you who do not support my custodial rule of my fellow brothers.' Sabtah paused to let this statement sink in.

There was an uncomfortable silence from the assembled Blood Gorgons. Amongst them were younger squads who showed fealty to the witch-psyker Muhr. Others still gave tacit support to the few rogue captains who were rumoured to harbour aspirations of Championship. It would be a volatile time for the whole Chapter.

'This is not the time for petty conflict and spiteful loyalties,' Sabtah continued. 'An unknown threat has chosen Hauts Bassiq as a target. Whatever is making our world their playground will soon have nine hundred Blood Gorgons crashing down around their ears. This, this will be a good fight. One that will be remembered, as the ancients remember the massacre at Dunefall!'

Hazareth barked hungrily at the thought, a loud war-mongering belch issued from valve amplifiers. They all cheered, stamping their traction boots in a deep raft of applause.

'That will not be happening,' declared a psych-amped voice. They turned to see Muhr descending the stairs into the pit of the Temple Heart. His long black hair was slightly wild and his eyes were still milky with the aftergleam of recent psychic strain. 'This will not be happening,' Muhr repeated. 'Gammadin has entrusted the Chapter to me. I will not deploy my Chapter blindly into an unknown threat. Certainly you do not mean to commit and risk all of us to save some *nullius* world of primitives?' Muhr asked as he reached the assembly.

'As great as Lord Gammadin was, he did not have the authority to make you our lord,' Sabtah responded. 'That is the way it has always been. If you seek to rule, then declare it openly. I will challenge your title.'

'I declare it!' hissed Muhr.

As he spoke, Sabtah levelled his power trident at Muhr. The three-pronged *trisula* hummed like a tuning fork as the disruption field vibrated up and down its length.

'I accept your challenge,' Muhr shrieked. The witch-psyker was already amping, his eyes and mouth streaming a harshly unnatural light. He screamed to emphasise his potency and vomited a beam of energy into the ceiling. His own battle-brothers backed away and slaves scattered in mobs. Nearby, a dancer collapsed, her brain haemorrhaged by the psychic build up.

In response, Sabtah fired a quick burst from his bolt pistol over their heads. The gatling burp punctured the far wall, pushing deep holes into the basalt veneers. This was ritual posturing amongst the Blood Gorgons, a slow escalation of violence that could either end in death or the submission of one of the challengers.

The Blood Gorgons were cheering hard now. Amongst the chaos of gunfire and confusion, above the screams of slaves and performers, the bond-brothers were shouting the name of Sabtah. There were others amongst them, a minority of Muhr's allies, who drew concealed blades and punch daggers. The atmosphere became volatile. Muhr pressed forwards until he was within arm's reach of Sabtah, putting his skull directly in front of Sabtah's pistol. In the background, an eager bond-brother emptied his bolter clip into the ceiling.

Sabtah aimed his bolt pistol at Muhr, his trident arm poised like a javelin thrower.

Muhr feinted forwards, provoking Sabtah. The old veteran's nerve held steady; he did not fire. The trident darted forwards, calculated to miss Muhr's neck by a razor's breadth.

Muhr flinched.

'Not now!' Hazareth boomed into the squad links. 'We can't afford this now.' The deep bass tones were so loud that they glitched the broadcast with shrill feedback.

'This is not how Gammadin would have led us,' said Hazareth. 'Is this leadership? To divide the Chapter when our ancestral grounds are threatened?'

'Ancestors? Bassiq is nothing more than a harvesting site for genestock. We can find others,' Muhr said dismissively.

'You are a petulant child,' said Sabtah, his trident still rearing. 'Where is your pride?'

'I am a realist. We don't need to risk ourselves at the summons of some distant, half-remembered populace,' Muhr responded.

Sabtah looked clearly disgusted, as if Muhr was speaking about something else entirely. 'This is not about that. Someone has touched our chattel and property. We don't turn a blind eye. We hit them with the weight of our entire arsenal and inject the fear of angry gods into them.'

Hazareth drummed his heavy tail-end against the ground in agreement. 'Without history we are nothing. We are nomads, and history should mean everything to us. Without pride or connection to our roots we are nothing.'

Muhr was not convinced. The psy-fire did not leave his eyes. If he chose to, the rites of challenge allowed him to slay anyone who opposed him. Even Hazareth, but that would not be wise now.

'I propose a scouting deployment. Five squads,' said Sabtah, bristling. 'You cannot deny us that.'

'I will personally answer to that,' Hazareth agreed. 'I will select the squads from my own company.'

There was no more Muhr could say. Hazareth's company was his to command and only Sabtah could countermand such an action. Several dissident Blood Gorgons leapt up and began to voice their protests. Others howled them down. Muhr hissed and recoiled, displaying displeasure by baring his teeth.

Unseen amidst the pandemonium, Sabtah squared up to face the sorcerer. The old warrior was in his face, his jaw set grimly. 'What do you know of brotherhood?' Sabtah growled. 'The witch-psyker takes no bond. You know nothing of brotherhood. Remain with your coven and leave the business of war to us.'

The *Cauldron Born* prepared for warp jump at first cycle. The reclamation of Hauts Bassiq was under way.

The coven summoned Yetsugei for his blessing. The witch-surgeons sang and chanted to the gods. Gun-servitors were anointed and their nerve receptors plugged to the vessel's lance batteries, ordnance turrets and the hull-bound gun citadels that studded the vessel's orange hull.

The floating fortress shifted on its gravitational axis as its warp drives gathered power. Even in the expanse of space, the space hulk was a leviathan. From a terrestrial telescope, the *Cauldron Born* resembled a blend of paleo-gothic shipcraft and oceanic fish. High exposure to the warp and the Eye of Terror had mutated the vessel's structure. The neo-tropical flora that infested the ship's interior had expressed itself on the ship's exterior, but on a mammoth scale. Barnacles of lamprey lights clustered like eyes on its hammerhead prow. Large sail-like fins edged with delicate, translucent fronds rippled along its flank. Muscular ridges and weeping fungal colonies contrasted with the architecture of its hull.

It entered the warp-sea slowly, laterally decompressing a void into the fabric of the materium. It sent ripples of gas flowing outwards and disturbed the orbit of minor asteroids and moons. Then, with a final, trembling burst of its engines, the warp-sea swallowed the fish whole.

The middle-day suns of Bassiq seemed to burn the air, boiling it so hot that every breath stung the nostrils. It grew so hot that sleep during these rest hours was impossible.

Roused from a fevered dream, Ashwana woke up feeling ill again. Her armpits and neck were burning with a throbbing, almost rhythmic pain. Rolling over she tried to bury her face in the straw mat but the clattering became persistent. For a while she blinked, angry at her grandmumu for having woken her. A final, loud clatter brought her up and Ashwana snapped back the curtain that separated her sleep nest from their carriage.

'What are you doing?' Ashwana groaned.

'Going hunting,' muttered her grandmumu, rummaging through a barkskin case of tools.

'*Eish*! We've talked about this. It's too dangerous,' Ashwana whispered.

Her grandmumu Abena wasn't listening to her any more. Her old, creased face was stern with determination. She discarded a flint stone from the case, tossing it to the pile of unwanted tools at her feet.

Ashwana tried to stand up but she was too weak and the head rush brought her back down onto her haunches. 'Don't go,' she pleaded.

'You've not eaten in two days,' scolded Mumu Abena. Braced between her stout legs, a recurved bow was being strung. The bow had once belonged to Ashwana's father and it was a beautiful piece. It had an accentuated curvature and was detailed in the ridged horn of a caprid. For years it had resided, unstrung, in the barkskin tool case.

'Mumu, I'm not even hungry,' said Ashwana. She was telling the truth. She could barely sip on water without nausea. The sickness had caught her swiftly, as it had the rest of her kinship. Three weeks past, the hunter Bulguno had been the first to catch the illness upon his return from a hunting trip in the Central Craters. In that time it had spread and almost all of the kin complained of fevers, pains and insomnia. Within days, the kinship had its first death – it had spread from there.

Lying back down, too tired to argue, Ashwana looked about their carriage – the rusting iron walls, the mesh ceiling, the familiar plastek curtains. It was a small space, a mere cubicle within the road train of their kinship. She could not remember how long they had been camped. They moved with their nomadic road trains, the relics of early prospectors. Many of them still had working gas engines that were thousands of years old, retained and cared for by the shamans. The engines failed often, and they camped until the shamans could coax life back into the valves and pistons that were beyond her understanding. She could not remember how long they had been camped there.

Ashwana's aimless gaze fell upon the shrine that hung above the boiler stove at the centre of their cabin. Hanging from a length of rope was a square clay face, framed by charms of squall feathers and the dismembered hoof of a male caprid. The face was of the Godspawn. A tiny wooden dish of acid berries and gourds was placed beneath it as an offering. Despite the fact that their oven had been cold for days, and there was no other food in the carriage, Mumu Abena had spared enough for the Godspawn. It seemed all they did these days was appease the Godspawn, but in return they received nothing but suffering.

Ashwana had lived with her grandmumu for all the twelve years of her life that she could remember. Without her parents, life had been hard within her nomadic kinship. The community moved often, following the migration patterns of the horned caprid, and it was difficult for her mumu to keep up without the help of anyone else. By all rights, Mumu Abena was an elder, and an elder's immediate family had a filial duty to ensure she was well cared for. But Abena had no other family except little Ashwana and she was too young to do much.

Of course, that had not stopped her from trying. Every day, she tried to tend and milk the caprid, but her hands were too small to placate the wild, shaggy-haired animals. She tried to gather sticks for the communal fires, but she had not been strong enough to carry the enormous bales on her head like the other women. Mumu Abena often laughed and told her that she was not yet old enough and she should play clap sticks with the other youths.

'Your skin is not old and dark like mine,' her mumu would say to her, while pointing to the deep, leathery bronze of her own skin. The sun of their land was exceedingly harsh and while bronzed skin was a sign of seniority among elders, tanned children were a sign of impoverishment. It meant the child had to work, and was a source of great shame. Her mumu was too proud a woman to live with that.

So it was that Mumu Abena, old yet spry, tended to their few domestic caprid, cooked, wove and contributed to the kinship in every way she could. It was a burden she should not have had to bear given her age.

But in the past season, things had become progressively worse. Since the strange lights in the sky, there had been little to eat for weeks. Travelling herdsmen from distant kinships had brought word of a plague spreading from the Northern Badlands. Ashwana's kinship had dismissed it as the panic of isolated northern plainsmen, but they had been wrong to do so. It was not one plague, but many. A blackening wilt had destroyed what meagre vegetation the red plains had offered. Rinderpest killed the caprid herds, causing the animals to be so fatigued they could no longer dig up the roots beneath the clay. Animals died in masses, flocks of birds fluttering down from the sky to die amongst the droves of upturned, sun-swollen caprid bodies.

Travellers told tales that the city of Ur, the only city on the planet of Bassiq, had sealed its great walls for fear of the black wilt. But that did not matter to Ashwana. She had only ever seen Ur once, and even then, only from a distance. The denizens of Ur did not often make contact with the kinships of the plains. Most plainsmen were not welcome there.

Now, finally, the plague had come south. It started with an innocuous cough and an inflammation of the throat. From there, like the others, Ashwana developed a persistent fever and painful swelling in her neck and underarms. Some languished for weeks while others began to die in a matter of days. But it was no merciful death. The sick slowly lost their memory, their eyes becoming dull and their minds deteriorating. There seemed to be no cure and even the medicine men were helpless. White stunt grass did nothing to alleviate the pains and even brewing gecko skin and sunberries only brought temporary relief from the joint pain.

Ashwana still hoped that her sickness was not the plague but a simple condition brought about by weeks of malnutrition. It was a forlorn hope, as the buboes in her neck suggested otherwise. Already, she had experienced brief moments where fragments of her mind seemed to slip, a tell-tale sign of the plague. She forgot simple things like whether her mumu had put oil on her mosquito bumps or what time of day it was.

'I don't need food,' Ashwana murmured again.

Her grandmumu shook her head, the tightly beaded coils of her white hair rattling. 'Some roast talon squall,' she suggested, 'or maybe a bush tail soup.'

'It wouldn't matter. I could die soon.' Ashwana said. The words hung in the air. The bar of honeyed sun shone through the roof hatch, holding tiny motes of dust in suspension. Neither said anything else and Ashwana immediately wished she'd never let the words out. She closed her eyes and silently wished her grandmumu had not heard it.

'You'll be better, my little *duumi*,' said her grandmumu finally. She swung the bow over her shoulder and secured a quiver of long arrows across her hip. Mumu Abena put on a brave face, the same stern face she used when Ashwana refused to drink her bitter bark soup. 'This will pass soon,' she said soothingly.

Overwhelmed by fatigue, Ashwana rolled over. She couldn't remember what they had been talking about. It seemed there was a dark patch in her memory for the past several hours, perhaps even days. Watching with hooded eyes, Ashwana saw her grandmumu step outside their carriage into the white sunlight outside, a bow across her back and a pail in her hands. Try as she might, Ashwana did not know where her grandmumu was going or why.

Grandmumu Abena left the camp at the base of the crater-like cirque and climbed the highlands with the suns at her back. Before her lay endless longitudinal sand dunes interspersed with shining white salt lakes. Chenopods and the salt-tolerant eragrostis grasses dominated the fringes of the basins.

Despite her age, she was surprisingly nimble and her old legs carried her well. She crossed the dry remains of a creek, remembering that just two seasons past, broods of barraguana, with their long fleshy tails and webbed feet, had basked in the shallow waters. It seemed that even before the plague, the climate was becoming harsher and more untenable, or had it always been so?

She was old now, and she could only remember better times and more glorious days. The plainsmen of Bassiq had always been a hardy people and there had been times in her youth, during the harshest season of Fume, when her kinship would scrape the bark from fissure trees. The bitter bark would be boiled into soup so that its numbing qualities could dull the hunger pains, nothing more. Even then, life had been good. She had been allowed to ride talon squalls and help muster the caprid droves, drink from the communal water jug and sleep on the ground when it rained.

Abena could not remember anything as bad as this before. The plague had taken so many of the kinship and already some were whispering that the world would end. It was not a life she had wanted for her children's children.

She left the creek bed and began to cross the Great Northern Plains. Although there were no roads, she navigated a thin track ridge through the clay desert. Such ancient tracks had been made during seismic surveys for gas and fuel deposits by early colonists, or so the tales went.

After several hours of walking and a short water rest in-between, she approached a familiar place. She was in the territory of the Nullabor, a neighbouring kinship. During the cooler seasons, the Zhosa and the Nullabor had feasted together and performed their traditional dances to celebrate the defeat of the double-headed eagle by the Godspawn, as the suns of Swelter were eclipsed by a red gas giant, marking a twilight and celebration that lasted for an entire lunar cycle.

Perhaps they would know of fertile gorges in the region, or even of karst caves with edible rodentia. Better yet, Abena hoped that despite the famine, the kinship would honour their ties and perhaps spare her a cup of fermented milk for Ashwana.

Through the haze of noon dust, she could recognise the distinctive silver of their long carriages. The road trains, mechanical beasts from a lost age of mining, were drawn like protective wagons in a circle around the settlement, the rusting bulk of their segmented carriages protecting the tents and lean-tos that clung to their bellies from wind and sandstorm. In all, Abena remembered the Nullabor as a generous but poor kinship. They did not own many heads of caprid, and their road trains were in

disrepair, the engines temperamental after sixty centuries of maintenance. They owned only early prospector models with loud engines and
noisy wide gauge tracks. Some of the corroded carriages had been shored
up with hand-painted wood panelling, giving them a roguish, antiquated
air. Yet Abena knew the kinship would still share whatever meagre supplies they could.

Drawing a zinc whistle from her belt, Abena blew a long, warbling
note. It was to herald the arrival of a peaceful visitor and its sound travelled far across the sandscape. Yet there was no response whistle from
the Nullabor.

Unsettled by the silence, Abena shielded her eyes with her hand and
tried to search for the tell-tale signs of carrion birds in the sky. If the
Nullabor had fallen ill to plague then surely she'd be able to see carrion
birds. Yet there were no birds, just a pervasive sense of lifelessness from
the clutch of carriages.

She stood for a while, unsure of whether to enter the settlement or turn
back. But Ashwana needed the food, and her old painful knees would
not allow her to hunt game so late in the day. Easing an arrow out of
her quiver, she rested it across the strike plate, ready to loosen. It was the
custom for women of the plains to participate in hunting and herding as
much as the men engaged in domestic chores, and although she could no
longer run or jump like she used to, her arms were strong from carrying
pails of water and stone-milling, more than enough to draw the recurve.

The carriages were occupied. Huddled around their protective bulk,
light wooden frames had been erected and then draped with heavy
cloth to form lean-tos. Plainsmen would take off their red shukas and
spread them over the frame of their tents before they entered a home.
The purpose was twofold: one was that the red cloth would ward away
evil spirits who would see that a house was already occupied, and the
second, perhaps more pragmatically, was to prevent dust and dirt from
being carried into the home.

The carriages were hoary with a film of red dust. Dust storms were
worst during the night and any respectable plainsmen would have beaten
the walls with a stick by morning. The fact that the carriages had accumulated so many days of red dirt meant the kinship had not moved for
many days, perhaps weeks. As that notion slowly crept into her mind,
Abena suddenly became aware that all the Nullabor could have perished.

'I do not wish to harm you. Restless spirits, do not harm me,' she
chanted under her breath as she stepped towards the nearest carriage. At
that moment, as if roused by her superstition, a brisk south wind picked
up, gusting oxide dust in her direction and flapping the cloth draped
across the carriage frames. With it came the sudden stink of rot.

Abena held her breath in fright as she recognised the smell. In her
younger days as a shepherdess she had come across a caprid that had

strayed from the herd and been mauled by some plains predator. The stench of that carcass under the thermal suns had been horrendous, bloated as it was with gas. The smell coming from the carriages was almost the same.

'Ashwana's grandmumu? We must eat soon before the food is cold,' said a voice from behind her. It was a quiet voice, a young voice.

Startled, Abena turned quickly, drawing her bow smoothly. But when she turned there was nobody there. Perhaps the voice had been carried by the wind? She strained her eyes against the gust of wind to look at the other carriages, set in a concentric ring around a communal firepit.

Whip-fast, in the furthest corner of her vision, she sensed movement. She did not quite see it, but felt that sudden absence of stillness.

'*How de body?*' Abena called out in customary greeting. 'I cannot see you.'

The wind gust picked up, drawing a veil of rusty particles across her vision. No more than twenty paces away, she saw a figure stand up from between two carriages. Judging by the raw-boned shoulders and narrow torso it was a young plainsmen of the Nullabor, but she could not see him well.

'What is your name, little son?' Abena asked the man, making known that she was a person of elder seniority.

'I can't remember my name. I remember yours. You are Abena. We should put out the fire pit so the others can sleep,' said the silhouette.

The man must be so feverish he was talking nonsense, Abena realised. Her grandmotherly instincts wanted her to tell the boy to sit back down until the rust storm had passed, but something cautioned her to keep quiet. The silhouette began to stumble towards her, speaking fragmentary phrases that made no sense.

'Remember to lock the talon squall pens,' he ordered angrily, before lowering his voice and chuckling. 'This is my best and most favourite shuka.'

Abena was wary. She remembered folktales of the dead who returned to their homes with only fragmentary memories of a past life. *Vodou* they had called them, and although they had no minds, they retained enough fragments of their past – things they had said often in life, or certain things people had said to them, and they mimicked the living with their vocal cords, luring out distraught relatives with pleas and familiar phrases. She had never believed in such things – raising Ashwana on her own had required a sturdy head – but now she was not so sure.

'I do not know you,' Abena shouted.

The rust storm died away, leaving the particles to twirl and settle. Like a curtain falling away, Abena saw the corpse that was walking towards her. That was what shocked Abena more than anything, the corpse walked with a loping gait as it had in life. Despite the fur of mould that grew across its pale, bloodless skin, it was walking. It appeared unhurried as it approached her, although its face, bloated by fluid beyond all recognition, was angled away towards the sky. It was as if the man was stuck between life and death, the skin and flesh rotting away while it talked of a past life and moved like the living.

Abena aimed and fired a hunting arrow into its chest. The dead man wheezed painfully as one of its lungs collapsed, but it kept walking. It was close now and Abena found herself paralysed by a mixture of fear and fascination.

It was so near, she could see the man was dressed in a sarong of undyed funeral wool. It meant the man had been buried and sealed in the bole of a boab tree. Somehow, it had clawed its way out and had returned to its home. Perhaps the tales were true.

It reached out a hand towards her and touched her upper arm. The coldness of the palm on her warm skin shocked her into movement. She ran several steps, her bow already drawn before she swung around and released another arrow. The copper head cut deep below the dead man's ribcage and punched out through his back with a dry, meaty thud. Entirely unfazed by the wounds, the man snatched for Abena with stiffened fingers. She wrenched away, frantic with adrenaline. She began to run, racing down the dune slopes.

Wordlessly, the corpse pursued her. She could feel its presence on the nape of her neck. It no longer tried to talk to her, its intent had become singular. It hit her hard from behind, knocking her down the hill, sending her rolling down the rocky slope. She came to a jarring stop as the creature loomed over her. As it reached down to seize her, Abena thought about Ashwana, lying in her hut alone. How long would it be before these ghosts came for her?

CHAPTER FIVE

Barsabbas woke from his sleep to an aching in his left primary lung. Abruptly uncomfortable, he sat up and swung his legs over the edge of his cot. Grimacing, he rubbed his lower ribs slowly. It was not real pain, not real damage, but it seemed real to him nonetheless.

'Your lung is troubling you again?' Barsabbas called out.

Sargaul appeared in the door frame, dressed in a bodyglove for early sparring. 'The same. I feel it most in the mornings. The Chirurgeons were not thorough in purging the residual shrapnel.'

Barsabbas nodded thoughtfully. He was feeling the old wounds of his blood bond, a common experience between pairs. After all, it had been Barsabbas's left primary lung they had excised and transplanted into Sargaul in their rituals of pairing.

Years ago, as a young neophyte, Barsabbas had not fully understood the rituals performed upon him. He remembered vaguely the surgical pain. The multiple waking horrors as the Chirurgeons sheared his bones for marrow and opened his muscles like the flaps of a book. There were not many memories from that time, but those were the ones he recalled.

Now, as an older, wiser battle-brother, Barsabbas still knew little of the secret bond. The process itself had become blurred with folklore and mysticism, to the point where effect and placebo became one. Paired with the veteran Sargaul, Barsabbas would become strengthened by their shared experience. He would inherit not only Sargaul's genetic memory, but also his bravery and ferocity. There was an element of witchcraft in this, but whenever Barsabbas felt that twinge in his lung, he was convinced there was substance to their ritual.

'How is your knee?' Sargaul asked, flexing his own.

Barsabbas stretched out his right leg, the thick cords of his thigh rippling. 'Better today,' he shrugged.

'I thought so,' nodded Sargaul, flexing his own right leg. 'They were ferocious, those tau. Much better at war-making than I expected.'

Barsabbas had almost repressed the memory of defeat but Sargaul's words invoked the images back to wakefulness. Just ten lunar cycles ago they had deployed on the tau world designated 'Govina' – a planet targeted for its lush natural resources and relatively weak military presence. It should have been a simple plunder raid for Squad Besheba: hit hard and retreat with a mid-grade quota of slaves. But they had underestimated the aliens, and the tau military presence proved entirely capable.

They engaged on the tundra, trading shots between dwarf shrubs and sedges, low grasses and lichens. By the hundreds, the tau had come, their firing lines disciplined and their shots overwhelming in sheer volume. Pulsating blue plasma hammered them so hard their armour systems had been pushed to failure, and Barsabbas's suit had reached seventy per cent damage threshold within the first few volleys.

The squad had fought with customary aggression and speed. They had burst amongst the tau infantry squares, ploughing through their chest-high adversaries, splintering their helmets and bones. They had killed so many.

But it was the tau's home and they did not flee. Squad Besheba had been driven back, overwhelmed by sheer numbers. In the end, they had fled, chased by ground-hugging tau hoverers. They escaped, but without dignity and their wounds were many. Like Barsabbas's disintegrated patella and Sargaul's collapsed lung, the shame had stayed with them, agonising them for the past ten months.

Thousands of slaves woke to the pulsating itch in their left cheekbones, scratching their scarred faces. It was an urgent, pressing discomfort that could not be ignored.

Beneath each scar could be seen the outline of a flesh burrowing thrall-worm. Agitated during sleep cycle, when the slaves were at a distance from their masters, the thrall-worms bulged against their cheeks like distended tumours. With clockwork precision, at the six-hour mark, the parasites would rouse their hosts by feeding on the rich fat beneath their skins. Sleepy-eyed, fatigued and forlorn, the slaves would wake to their daily work.

The workforce were of all kinds and pasts, both strong and feeble, soldiers and clerics, shift workers or merchants; here an artisan, over there a human Guard colonel, all of them slaves to the bonded brotherhood.

Those strong and young set about the tasks of burden, carrying equipment lockers and hefty pallets. The old and feeble, those who had been branded many years ago, fanned out into the corridors to light the upper halls with sconce lanterns. Others fetched haunches of roast for their twin masters, for although the post-humans did not need such food for sustenance, they enjoyed the taste of rare meat.

The most unfortunate of all were those who formed the work teams – the *delvers*. They were given the impossible duty of clearing the encroaching bio-flora that threatened to overwhelm the ship. Such teams often disappeared into the forgotten sectors of the ship, which had become a cavernous ecosystem. Those regions became wildernesses and the delvers with their hatchets and chain cutters could do little to stop their spread. Many were lost to the apex predators that flourished in the abyssal depths of the space hulk.

Slaves who had become favourites were allowed to rise one ship's cycle later than the rest. The black-turbaned sentries in their hauberks of brass, the gun ratings, the deckhands and pleasure pets were all among the number who enjoyed relative luxury.

But on this day, all the slaves, regardless of hierarchy, would forgo sleep or food for the Blood Gorgons mobilisation. It was not full Chapter strength deployment, but it would still be a time of solemn ritual and ceremony. The drop chambers would need to be cleaned and the vacuum locks cleared; weapons would be oiled and armour polished. Sacrifices would be made. There was much work to be done.

It was not yet dawn cycle, but Barsabbas and Sargaul were already in the Maze of Acts Martial. Squad Besheba had set up a three-point fire pattern in a little-used section of the maze.

The ceiling of the tunnel had collapsed under the bacterial acid, forming a natural cave shelf. The collapse had also breached several water filtration pipes and the resultant fluid had allowed a host of microorganisms to thrive and grow. Through the thermal imaging of his helmet, the interior wilderness appeared to Barsabbas as a low-lying pattern of fronds, reefs and fungal caps. He opened the vents of his armour and allowed the moist, external air to creep into his suit. Tasting with his tongue, he judged seventy-two per cent humidity in the air combined with a high blend of toxic carbon, likely released by the nearby floral growth. There was something else in the air too, the animal scent of sweat or something similar.

There was a flash of thermal colour to his left and Barsabbas turned to meet it, his ocular targeting systems already synchronising with his bolter sights. A human shape rose from behind a mound of viral lichen and opened fire. The first shot went wide, a ranging shot that left the searing after-image of its trajectory across Barsabbas's vision. The next one clipped him on the hip, ricocheting with a whine off the ceramite plate. His armour's daemon spirit groaned sleepily in protest.

Before Barsabbas could return fire, the human was already dead. Sargaul had finished him with a clean chest shot. Bond-Brothers Hadius and Cython shot him repeatedly, tearing him down to constituent fragments.

'Cease fire!' called Sergeant Sica, waving down their violent excess. Hadius and Cython whooped with glee.

'That's it, we're done here,' added the sergeant's blood bond, Bael-Shura. 'Thirty kills. That's the last of them.'

'No,' said Sargaul, holding up the auspex. 'Squad, hold. I'm getting ghost readouts on the auspex.'

A caged pen of thirty Guardsman captives had been released into the maze less than two hours ago. They had been a platoon of Mordians guarding a merchant vessel en route to Cadia. The men had put up a stoic fight, but by Barsabbas's count, they had killed all thirty. There shouldn't be any more targets within this section of the maze. Yet their auspex was pinging.

Barsabbas took the auspex from Sargaul and studied the tracking device. Whatever it was, the target was large and moved with expert stealth. Several times it moved so quietly that the auspex sonar reflection lost track of its movement. It closed in, only to disappear, then reappear, slightly closer than before.

'A maul mouth?' Sargaul suggested. He was referring to the apex predator that had evolved in the confines of the *Cauldron Born*.

Barsabbas shook his head. Maul mouths were light-framed creatures, their slender, hairless bodies suited to hiding within circulation vents and underneath walkways. This was too big.

Abruptly, the auspex began to ping again. 'Fifty metres!' Sergeant Sica hissed urgently. As quickly as the warning came, the auspex settled again.

The squad fell into interlocking arcs of fire. They couldn't see any targets. Except for the bubble of a dimorphic yeast fungus as it corroded the tunnel walls, there was no sound.

'Thirty-six metres,' Sargaul voxed through the squad link as his auspex caught a fleeting glimpse. The target was moving fast, darting between the auspex's blind spots.

'Eighteen metres.'

Barsabbas toggled between thermal imaging and negative illumination. Neither showed a target. He loosened the muscles of his shoulders and placed one hand on the boarding axe sheathed against the small of his back.

'I've lost target,' Sica voxed, his voice laced with frustration.

Without clearance, Hadius and Cython loosed a quick burst of their bolters. The distinct echo of the jackhammer shots signalled they had hit nothing.

'Cease fire, you soft-backs!' Sica barked.

Suddenly, Cython was flying backwards, as if struck heavily. Hadius lumbered to the aid of his blood bond, but he too was sent sprawling. It was happening so fast that Barsabbas cursed as he tore the hand axe from its casing and looped small circles to warm up his wrist.

Sergeant Sica aimed his bolter at a large dark shape that was suddenly in the middle of their position. Sargaul did the same while Bael-Shura brought the squad flamer to bear. The shape was black, its negative luminescence making it appear colder than its thermal surroundings.

'Hold your weapons, Squad Besheba,' came a familiar voice through their squad's direct link.

Sica lowered his weapon hesitantly. 'Captain?'

'Aye, sergeant.'

Spitting in relief, Barsabbas switched off his thermal imaging. It was dark and he blinked several times, rapidly dilating his pupils to increase visual acuity. The formless black shape immediately became that of Captain Argol. Even in the low light, he was unmistakable. Horn plates cauliflowered up his neck and the left side of his face, sprouting, branching and multiplying like saltwater coral. Argol was immensely proud of his gifts and seldom wore a helmet to hide them.

'You caught us,' Sica admitted. As if on cue, Hadius and Cython staggered back to their feet, their earlier bravado neutered by the ease of their dispatching.

'Learn to adapt quickly. Never become comfortable with one kind of enemy,' said Argol.

Barsabbas knew their captain was right. Space Marine armour was an insulated exterior of ceramite and adamantium, almost invisible to thermal or heat detection. Had they relied on their own hyper-sensitive vision, perhaps they would have spotted their attacker.

'That's what makes us dangerous. We are the symbiosis of war machine and human ability,' Argol continued. 'Do not rely on gears and motors, remember that you have two hands and a brain.'

Sica unlocked his helmet to reveal a face of heavy cheekbones and long matted coils of hair. His heavy brow ridge was pinched in a grimace. The sergeant did not like being made a fool of, even by the venerable captain. 'You didn't come all this way to lecture us on battle theory, my captain. What do you need from us?'

'Sergeant Sica. Your squad's performance was less than notable on Govina.'

The mere mention of it made Barsabbas wince inwardly. He knew Sargaul would feel the same.

'What of it?' Sica snarled.

'I know you fought hard. Post-operation data showed pict evidence of heavy tau casualties. Have you had the pleasure of viewing the aerial surveillance? There is a pict-capture of a rock ridge lined with tau bodies in a neat little line. All of them, gunned down in a straight line just like that. Pop. Pop. Pop.'

Sica was not amused. 'We faced almost five hundred tau foot-soldiers. They are pliable and break open easily, but their guns are difficult to trade shots with. Even their basic infantry rifle cuts through a clear thirty centimetres of brick.'

'The fact remains – you were defeated, beaten, driven back. It's brought shame to your squad and, by extension, my company.'

Barsabbas heard Bael-Shura hiss, as if warming up the Betcher's gland beneath his tongue. For the past ten months, Squad Besheba had become pariahs within the Chapter.

'What do you need from us?' Sica repeated warily.

'I'm giving you a chance to redeem your performance. Five squads from Captain Hazareth's First Company will be deploying to Hauts Bassiq. Sabtah and Muhr have, for once, agreed to this course of action.'

Barsabbas kept quiet, but his breathing quickened with quiet anticipation. Although it was left unsaid, there was no doubt Captain Argol had requested their presence on this mission. It meant the company, despite their misgivings, still believed Squad Besheba was an effective and dependable squad, but they would need an act to redeem their reputation.

'This is your chance. I have petitioned Captain Hazareth to augment his forces with Squad Besheba. Hazareth has accepted,' Argol finished.

Beside Barsabbas, Sargaul slapped his palms in anticipation. A hush fell over the squad.

'Second Company's honour is at stake here, Sergeant Sica. There existed a long and violent history when I inherited this company, a reputation for being monsters in fables. Bastion, Cadia, Armageddon, the Medina Corridor, the actions at Dunefall. I hope these wars mean as much to you as they do to me, but Second Company have never been found wanting. Good, noble men fear us. Soldiers of alien cultures know us by name and know of our brutality. We make their warrior castes feel inferior.'

They all nodded.

'I won't pressure you, Sergeant Sica. But you must know Squad Besheba carries our history on their shoulders.'

The Blood Gorgons were deploying. Despite the nature of a scouting deployment, the entire *Cauldron Born* was thrumming with activity.

Muhr's coven was coaxing the warp drives and daemon spirits. Alarm sirens were blaring, engine slaves were sweating. There was no rest, no pause in labour. Freight docks were ramped, shrines were tended to and everywhere was the synchronised stomp of boots as black turban patrols doubled.

Weaponsmith Linus knew he would not be sleeping for several rotations. The deploying squads had equipment that needed to be repaired and readied for war and already his apprentices were bowed in focused work. Alcestis was stooped at her work bench, a portly woman in her fifties who had once been a respected dollmaker in her home hive of Delaphina. Her hands worked quickly, darting between whetstone, file and a Traitor Marine's cutlass. At their benches, others were hammering the dents out of water canisters, re-meshing buckle straps or cleaning trophy racks. These were not the sacred power armours or bolters of the Blood Gorgons, for no slaves were allowed to touch, much less be entrusted with, such artefacts. Rather, these were the various tools of the Traitor Marines.

The slaves worked by the light of small gas lamps and candle flame. It was slow, agonising work, but it was better than being a menial. Although their work chamber was a dark box in the ship's dilapidated lower halls, they were allowed to sleep under their work benches after rotation and were rationed one and half standard meals per day. The walls were covered with old sheets and shredded waste to insulate against the sub-zero space climate. Through an ever-present haze, tabac smoke was chain-lit to help them through their work shifts. Despite these conditions, the mending slaves had come to accept the cubic little chamber as their home. They had learned to make the best of what they had become and even named their portion of the ship *the smokehouse*.

An entire half of the smokehouse was cramped with racks of axes, boarding pikes and gaudy blades that had been delivered there since morning cycle. Varied were the weapons in the collection, as no two Traitor Marines possessed the same arsenal. These were personal caches collected by each individual over their decades or centuries of service, a veritable history of their achievements. Each Blood Gorgon took great pride in their exotic collections, and any fleck of dust or slight damage would cost a weaponsmith one finger. Already, Linus, meticulous with his work though he was, had lost a little finger and a ring finger, once for sharpening an axe blade against the grain and another for leaving carbon build-up in the pommel of a sword that he could not reach with his tools.

'There is a boarding axe which needs sharpening and rebinding,' a young apprentice told Linus. 'Would you like me to finish it, boss?'

Linus shook his head. The apprentice was a mere boy. In time he would learn the finer points of regraining and weave binding, but for now he was too clumsy to be entrusted with so dangerous a task. 'Not now, lad,' replied Linus. 'Squad Brigand needs a half-hundred leather pouches to be oiled, you get along with that.'

Picking up the short-handled axe, he ran a palm along its edge. Although the slaves were told nothing about the nature of deployment,

Linus had been enslaved for long enough that he could judge, by the tools the Traitor Marines chose, what the nature of their mission would be.

This time, there was a predominance of light and concealable weapons. The absence of heavier weaponry such as halberds or polearms suggested that it would be no quick, frontal assault. There was no preponderance of boarding pikes to be re-toothed as there often would be before a boarding raid. Lighter weapons meant utility.

Perhaps a long-distance campaign? A planet of smouldering fields and ash plains? Linus remembered distant planets, exotic in plant life and fauna. He remembered when he was younger, the fields outside his hab had been covered in green grass and the swaying growth of trees. But try as he might, he could not remember what they smelled like or how they felt to the touch. He knew only the *Cauldron Born* now and nothing else.

Linus sighed. He often wondered where these Traitor Marines went – even if they were horrifying warzones. Surely anything would be better than a lifetime of enslavement, subsisting on gruel and watery yoghurt?

Barsabbas and Sargaul summoned their retinue sometime around mid-cycle.

Situated in the *Cauldron Born's* middle decks the Blood Gorgons' interior citadels rose along the cliffs and numberless ramparts of the ship's interior structure. Turreted proto-fortresses loomed along the dark rises and shelves of the superstructure, each housing one pair of bonded brethren. Lighting their way with lamps, the personal slaves went quickly and urgently, together in a hurried flock.

There were the two black turbans in their brass armour, Ashar and Dao, striding imperiously in their upturned and pointed boots. The helm bearers came next, little more than young boys in stiffly embroidered tabards. A train of munitions and armament servitors clattered behind, guarded by a trio of scale hounds. Behind them, appearing unrushed, came the litter of pleasure pets, collected from a double dozen planets, each of the women chosen on the nine Slaaneshi principles of exotic beauty.

The fortresses remained unconnected; the chain-link walkways that had connected them had been destroyed centuries ago and never rebuilt. The Blood Gorgons had not always been a unified Chapter before the reign of Gammadin. During the early stages of their excommunication, intra-Chapter conflict had reduced them to little more than a band of thieves escaping together for survival. It had been a time of turmoil, during which the Blood Gorgons had turned upon one another and walled themselves up within their drifting fortress. Even after Gammadin united the Chapter after the Reforging, the citadels remained as a memorial of past failings.

The retinue of Barsabbas and Sargaul arrived at a grated walkway.

Beyond them, spanning an abyssal drop, the walkway led towards blast shutters set in a wall that dropped away like a cliff edge. Swathes of rust honeycombed the citadel across the pit. Flat and imposing, it swept four hundred metres down into shadows and dim pinpricks of strobe lighting.

By the time the retinue had cleared the muzzled gun servitors at the entry shutters, they were already late. Barsabbas and Sargaul had begun their anointments and the seven rituals of predomination were about to begin.

Barsabbas met them at the draw gates, unarmoured and imposing. 'Do not be late. Tardiness erodes my efficiency. Entirely erodes it. Understand?'

'Yes,' the slaves said, bowing and hurrying to their positions.

Each slave within the retinue had a personal task in the pre-deployment rituals. Gammadin had coined them 'the Sacrifices of War', but Barsabbas had quietly referred to them as 'the Tedium before Battle'.

With a dismissive wave from Sargaul, the sacrifices began without much fanfare. To Barsabbas, it was slightly deflating. The rituals grew tiresome to him. He attributed the tedium to the reverence in which the senior Blood Gorgons held the rituals. The veterans built up such a sense of solemnity and ceremony that when the younger ranks performed it, half-hearted in youth, the sacrifices seemed to lose all meaning.

Barsabbas sighed wearily. First, he and Sargaul reswore their oaths of brotherhood. The Astartes implant known as the omophagea allowed for learning by eating. Through the implant they were able to 'read' or absorb genetic material that they consumed, the omophagea transmitting the gained information to the brain as a set of memories or experiences. The Blood Gorgons remembered a time when they had fought against one another. Although they had always been one Chapter, the Reforging was part of their Chapter history. The oaths reminded them of this, or so the veterans said.

Barsabbas could not remember the Reforging. That was before his time and no more than a curious relic of history.

Barsabbas cut a small piece of flesh from inside his cheek while Sargaul sliced open the meat of his right thumb. A tiny sample of blood and flesh was collected into a brass bowl and the bloody tissue was diluted with an alcohol solution. Apparently, the blood was traditionally mixed with fermented mead. These days, honey was a rarity for the Chapter and it was simply more efficient to manufacture an alcoholic solvent. Perhaps Barsabbas would appreciate these rituals if they were not some mere nuisance to be observed for the sake of tradition. He shrugged and slugged down the caustic mixture.

The Sacrifice of Armament followed. Barsabbas and Sargaul were stripped naked and lowered their bodies into a simmering cauldron. The water was hot enough to par-boil the outermost layers of skin. Once bathed, the inflamed skin was then vigorously rubbed with coarse-grained salts. Lastly a thick white salve of *woad* – a mixture of animal fat, minerals and bio-chemicals – was applied to toughen the skin, numbing it.

Again, Barsabbas found the process unnecessary. The skin was more prone to infection in humid combat zones. Yet they did not argue the procedure. It was something that had always been.

After the skin treatment, the Traitor Marine's suit of power armour was fitted into place, segment by segment. The plugs, stem cords and synapse wires were connected from the armour to the black carapace. All present began to chant a simple, almost child-like rhyme, in order to placate the armour's spirit as it was coaxed from its sleep.

Fully suited and armoured, Barsabbas could not help but notice the subtle reaction from his servants. They shied away from him, afraid to be close. It happened often. It was as if normal humans had an instinctive fear of Space Marines, a deeply seeded biological aversion to being close to something so dangerous, so powerful.

Finally came the Sacrifice of Smoke. This was the ritual that Barsabbas found most pragmatic, despite its superstitious nature. While in warp transit, objects were likely to go missing. To a warrior-mind, the phenomenon was unexplainable and oddly disturbing – small items left unlocked or unbolted would disappear. Sometimes these could be vital pieces of wargear, or even the firing pin of a bolter. In order to prevent such warp poltergeist activity, most loyalist Chapters prayed and erected gargoyles.

The Blood Gorgons observed this superstition in their own way by discharging firecrackers and parading in their war helms. It was the Blood Gorgons' belief that war helms needed to be terrifying enough to scare even the daemons of Chaos, or ill fortune would be invited. Barsabbas's helmet was terrifying indeed, a screaming bovine sculpt with a narrow slitted vision lens and wide antlers like arms rearing up to frighten away mischievous spirits. He danced a strange, spasmodic dance, executing clumsy movements in his power armour. Their retinue beat drums and cymbals while singing.

With the final sacrifices complete, Barsabbas and Sargaul stood in their full finery of war. He stole a look in the gilded mirror in their chambers. The creature that looked back at him appeared monstrous – a broad framework of engineered bone and muscle. Theatrical yet pugnacious, his mask was strangely emotionless, its exaggerated scream frozen into the rigor mortis of sculpted brass.

He realised he was the most feared fighting unit in the universe. He allowed that thought to settle upon him for a moment. It was intoxicating. They were mobile fortresses, able to bull-charge head first into a storm of enemy munitions unscathed. They were destructive, the firepower at their immediate disposal able to flatten urban blocks. With his hands, gloved in ceramite, he could crush and pry open sheets of metal, maybe even the support girders of a building.

'Master,' cried the slaves as the ritual preparations drew to a close. They mewled collectively, scratching pleadingly at their faces as if Barsabbas and Sargaul had forgotten.

Barsabbas watched Sargaul slide a black metal piston from a leather carrier at his thigh plate. The slaves lined up eagerly. One after another, Sargaul viced their jaws in his hand, turning their faces ever so slightly upwards. The piston punched into their cheek scars with a meaty thud. The slaves would wince, flinching away from Sargaul's grasp with a weeping wound in their cheek.

They liberated the slaves in turn, extracting the larvae from their flesh. Sargaul hurried through the process without veneration, his movements deftly practiced, yet rough and bored. A young girl with a graceful neck was next in line. Barsabbas had never learned her name. She was just a menial.

Sargaul trapped her timid face between the vice of his fingers. The black tube slid into her cheek like a monstrous syringe. She remained stoic as it retracted, leaving a neat incision below her cheekbone. A hard tap of the piston dislodged a tiny white larva onto the floor, oozing with fluid and pus. It trembled fitfully upon contact with the air, expanding rapidly, its membranous cocoon stretching and straining. As the egg skin peeled away, a fleshy nub of fingers and teeth emerged. The newly birthed creature resembled an arachnid, with a swell of bone-shearing mandibles above its abdominal sac. Black hair, coarse and wet, sprouted wirily from its throbbing skin.

Sargaul set his heel down and crushed the skittering mess.

'You are all free until our return,' Sargaul said.

The slaves, some amongst them wadding their palms against bleeding faces, stared at them like a lost herd of particularly dull sheep. Most of them knew no other life than servitude. Some had been born into slavery, their ancestors having dwelt in the slave warrens for many generations.

'But if we do not return, then you will all die with us, for this is the way the gods will it. You serve only us, and live by virtue of our existence. Without us, you cannot be allowed to live,' Sargaul announced. 'It may not make sense to you, but it is our only way.'

In steaming cauldrons and platters on carts, the food was served in the Hall of Solemn Supper. Teeming like colony ants, scullery slaves toiled, the patter of their steps strident across the ancient floorboards.

The Hall of Solemn Supper was a narrow, antiquated chamber deep within the ship's furnished core, with great wooden beamed ceilings dating from a time when the ship was an abandoned drifter. Arched windows framed with sculpted mer-maidens and harpies were spaced evenly, allowing the hall full view of distant stars and galaxies.

Here the Blood Gorgons came to feast before deployment and, as was customary, receive their pre-mission assembly with the company commander. Although it marked the last stage of squad-level planning and tactics, it was also a sombre time to gather and feast among brothers.

It was only a small deployment, with five squads. Many of the long tables, arrayed in one-hundred-man company lines, were empty, yet the food and wine were nonetheless bountiful. The kitchen crews had been diligent in their preparation of the Traitor Marines' pre-war nutrition. Loaves of fibre-dense wholegrain breads steamed in baskets. Creamed soups from the vessel's fungal colonies were wheeled out in cauldrons. Roast and furnaced meats of all kinds were hauled out in hand wagons.

The five squads sat together at the long table, with Captain Hazareth at their head. Gathered were Squad Besheba, Squad Hastur, Squad Yuggoth, Squad Brigand and veteran fire-team Shar-Kali.

Barsabbas found himself sitting opposite a brother of Squad Hastur. He gave him a curt nod but nothing more. It was known amongst the company that Squad Hastur were 'Muhrites', supporters of Muhr's ascension. Their sergeant, Brother Kloden, was an ambitious aspirant who hungered for conquest, and that did not sit well with the company.

The squads fell into silence as Captain Hazareth pushed back his granite bench with a scrape.

'I could not be more confident in the destruction you will cause,' Hazareth began.

The squads stamped and clapped clamorously, spilling wine and bashing the basalt table with their fists. Barsabbas was so caught up in the excitement he crushed a brass dining plate in his hands and hurled it across the hall.

Hazareth motioned for quiet. 'Our wards on Hauts Bassiq have signalled for our aid. It is our duty to our slavestock worlds that we answer their calls, so it has always been.'

He brought up a hololithic display from a vertical projector. 'This is an aerial surveillance pict from the last time we harvested genestock. That was close to sixteen cycles ago, or almost eighty years standard. As you can see, the terrain is largely open, flat country. The Adeptus Mechanicus blasted the land prior to settlement. In doing so, the ensuing firestorm depleted the atmosphere causing temperatures to scale intolerable heights within years.'

Barsabbas took a sip of his wine and realised it could be the last time in months that his hydration levels would be optimal. The furious loss of sweat and Hauts Bassiq's scarcity of water had driven the Imperial colonies away and turned the planet into a ghost desert.

Spilling a cartographer's chart over the table and cutlery, Hazareth tapped the map with a blunt, armoured fingertip. 'Of all our sixty-two recruitment worlds, Hauts Bassiq breeds one of the hardiest stock due to its borderline inhospitable climate. Minerally, it is one of the richest in resources–'

Brother-Sergeant Kloden frowned and rapped the table in-between mouthfuls of beef tendon. 'What use do we have of mineral resources? We have never been ones to hoard.'

Sargaul interjected tersely. 'Warp-iron. Kloden, do you know what warp-iron is?' he asked coldly.

Barsabbas nodded to himself knowingly. Although he was too young to have ever visited Hauts Bassiq, he had researched the catacombs for archived intelligence. Due to Hauts Bassiq's proximity to the *Occularis Terribus*, its surface was marked with warpstone impacts that had compressed over the ages into a compound similar to uranium. This warp-iron was what kept the *Cauldron Born's* fusion reactors running. Ever since the Chapter had claimed the ghost ship as its own, a piece of irradiated warp-iron almost three hundred metres in length had powered the reactor core.

Before Kloden could respond, Captain Hazareth pointed at the map again. 'Enemy threat disposition is unknown.'

'Xenos, Khoitan?' Sergeant Sica asked.

Hazareth shook his head and drained his wine cup before answering. 'Entirely unknown. The signal beacon from Hauts Bassiq relayed no other information.'

'Try not to retreat if shot at again,' Sergeant Kloden snorted.

Sargaul stood up, clattering dishes and spilling a goblet. His naked blade was drawn.

'Brother Sargaul! I will not have blades at my table,' Captain Hazareth shouted, quick to quell the violence.

Slaves frightened by the outburst scurried from the alcoves to refill wine goblets and placate the warriors with loaded plates of cold meat and spiced offal. The squads fell back to eating, shooting hard glares at each other across the table.

Hazareth rotated the hololith and zoomed in close. 'Your main objective is to reach the city of Ur. This is the last bastion of technology on Bassiq. The remaining Imperialists have sequestered themselves there, in a sealed city. They no longer maintain much contact with the nomads who we use as genestock. If any campaign were to be mounted, it would commence here. There are few other strategic targets amongst the major continents. The plainsmen dwell in semi-nomadic bands elsewhere.'

'Why have our brother-ancestors not conquered Ur already? Why leave an Imperial bastion to blight the landscape?' Barsabbas asked.

'Because we pick and choose our fights carefully. There is nothing to be gained from overthrowing the Barons of Ur. They are an isolationist cult. Yet they protect the world from xenos raids and minor threats when we cannot. They do not even know of our existence or our sovereignty over their lands.'

'Also,' Kloden said, sneeringly, 'we would risk too much. Our Chapter would have a difficult time overwhelming even that little dirthole,' he said to Barsabbas. 'They use a fusion reactor much like our own to power void shields thicker than your skull.'

Captain Hazareth remained impassive, but Barsabbas could sense his Khoitan's seething resentment for the Muhrites.

'What you may not know,' said Captain Hazareth, 'is that Ur sits upon the largest deposit of warp-iron on the planet. There's estimated to be enough warp-iron there to fuel the *Cauldron Born's* fusion plant for no less than six hundred thousand years, standard.'

Nothing in the archives had mentioned this. Barsabbas craned forwards. 'Why have we not claimed this warp-iron as our own?'

Hazareth shrugged dismissively. 'Because, as Sergeant Kloden has said, we are not hoarders. We have all the warp-iron we need to feed the *Cauldron Born's* reactor. We simply do not need more. We are free that way, and untied to the trouble of earthly possession.'

Kloden exhaled derisively. 'We are a poor man's Chapter. Peasant ignorant.'

Finally, Hazareth turned to Kloden. Only then did Barsabbas realise how imposing his Khoitan appeared. At well over two metres eighty, when Hazareth faced Kloden square on, he cast a shadow over Kloden's face.

'Sergeant Kloden. I will strip you of your rank and the skin from your sword hand if you cross me once more. I consider myself a tempered commander who judges his men not by the candidate of their allegiance, but by their merits as soldiers. If you befoul this mission with politics I swear I will eat your bones. You will go to Ur, you will report your findings, you will return here with all your men alive. Otherwise, Kloden, I sup on your marrow.'

Kloden nodded quietly and slowly, afraid to meet Hazareth's level gaze. He threw down a half-chewed haunch on his plate with a sullen clatter. His appetite, evidently, had gone.

Despite Kloden's chastisement, Barsabbas oddly felt no better. He too put down his eating knife. They were supposed to be Blood Gorgons, joined in feasting, shoulder to shoulder before their battle. It was not meant to be like this. Barsabbas was too young to remember the Chapter wars, but the thought of internecine conflict disturbed him in the most intrusive manner.

CHAPTER SIX

On the day the Red Gods descended to Hauts Bassiq, the weather was angry.

A high-pitched wind on the lower part of the south continent built up its strength. By the time it jettisoned itself across the North Territories it was a bellowing dust storm. Grit tore the bark off trees and gales uprooted even the hardy dwarf bushes from the sands. The sky darkened so hungrily that it became black at the height of noon and stayed that way for some hours.

In the central interior plains, a plains herdsman fleeing towards shelter saw several lights in the sky. They winked like stars, but they plummeted, moving too fast across the black sky to be distant astral bodies. He saw them break away from each other, like flowers caught in an updraught, and scatter across the horizon. Peering out from beneath the shuka he had drawn around his face as the sand whipped his lashes, he wondered if they were the cause of such portentous weather.

Guide lights winking, fluttering blindly in the sky, the drop pods became trapped in an updraught. Confined within the coffin slabs of bulk plating, Squad Besheba could only watch the topographic monitors overhead as they veered off course. Violent wind patterns shaped like an eye spiralled outwards and pushed the tiny dots of the Blood Gorgons' drop pods further and further away from Ur.

'Forward venting disabled. Guiding fins are losing drift. Prepare for freefall!' Sergeant Sica shouted above the drop pod's death rattle.

Their Dreadclaw was plummeting, freefalling as the thrusters grunted with intermittent effort to slow their descent. Arrest sirens. The crash of high-altitude wind. The stink of loose petroleum. The drop pod became a self-enclosed world of blind confusion.

Barsabbas was pinned against his restraints by G-force as the entire cabin vibrated against the atmospheric friction. In the restraint harness beside him, Sargaul was utterly impassive behind his helmet and entirely motionless. Barsabbas tried to emulate some of the veteran's composure, but the combat stimms he had ingested were agitating him. He was grinding his teeth as the stimms elevated his heart rate. The crushed enamel tasted like wet sand in his mouth.

Barsabbas almost did not feel the crash. The drop pod collided with the planet's surface at high speed and continued to bounce with a loose, jarring expulsion of force. The impact would have shattered any normal human's skeletal structure. Rolling, tumbling, flipping head over heels, Barsabbas gripped his restraint harness as the drop pod swept him along. His neck whipped violently against the arrestor cage and his shoulder popped briefly out of joint before clicking back into the socket. Blood, hot and sour, filled his mouth as his teeth sliced clean through his tongue.

'Up! Up! Up!' Sica shouted.

There was no time for quiet. The alarms were still so loud they beat in his eardrums. Barsabbas shook his head to clear the concussive aftershock. His ears were ringing as the dust settled around him.

'Contact! Multiple massive movement.' Someone shouted the warning into the squad's vox-link but the urgency blurred the words into no more than a sharp smear. He was already up and uncaged from his restraint harness. The drop pod's surveillance systems were baying with alarm. External motion sensors were detecting encroaching movement.

'Bolters up,' Bael-Shura commanded. The squad uncaged their restraints and readied themselves, slamming bolter clips into their guns. A banging came from the outside, a rapid persistent hammering as if a horde were trying to breach the drop pod's shell.

Barsabbas checked he had a full load in his sickle-pattern bolter clip. His helmet HUD powered up, its ocular targeting syncing with his bolter sights. Slabs of system reports scrolled by his peripheral vision: climate, energy readouts, atmospheric toxicity, all of which Barsabbas ignored as the alarms brayed and amber cabin lights flashed. He signalled to Bael-Shura that he was ready.

Sica stood by with a hand over the release button. The hammering outside grew louder, almost wild.

'Deploy!' Sica roared, punching the release button.

The drop pod's hatch unfolded like a flower petal. There was an exhalation of pressurised air. The outside rushed in towards them as if a flood gate had burst open.

Barsabbas crouched and shot on instinct. His first shot punched through a human chest. The body had no chance to fall as others pushed in from behind. It remained upright – jammed by the press of people. The freshly killed male seemed to write. Barsabbas thought he saw its arms raise, but he dismissed it as a ghost image from his concussion. He took aim for a second shot – and paused.

The body continued to walk towards him, lurching with blind, drunken steps. This time Barsabbas removed its head with a clean shot and it dropped. Only then did he realise that they were surrounded by the dead.

Hundreds of dead. Their arms were outstretched and their faces waxy. Corpses swarmed over the drop pod, climbing the chassis and being pushed by thousands more from the rear. Barsabbas saw a naked male in an advanced state of decay, his skin hanging like loose latex garments from his glistening muscle. There was a woman with skin so infected it left fist-sized holes in her belly. Another whose face was grey with mould barely resembled a man.

Recoiling in physical disgust, the Blood Gorgons opened fire with a whittling, sustained volley that fanned out in all directions. High-velocity explosive rounds impacted against a dense wall of naked flesh. Barsabbas's humidity readings reached almost ninety per cent as a mist of blood and fluid rose in a solid, blinding wall.

The fighting became frantic. Hands reached through the muzzle flashes towards him. Something dragged on his ankle and gave way wetly as he crushed his heel into it. A rotting palm clawed at his vision lens.

Crouched low, Bael-Shura released his flamer. An expert pyro gunner, he applied light pressure to the trigger spoon and played a tight, drilling cone of promethium into the wall of walking dead. Several were incinerated by the direct blast, but many simply caught fire and continued to fight. The flaming corpses flailed wildly, spreading the fire until it swirled in the air and churned a rippling backwash of heat into the drop pod.

Barsabbas grew agitated as black smoke began to clog his filtration vents. Bael-Shura was a calloused warrior, but he was frustratingly obstinate. The flamer fulfilled a devastating anti-infantry role within the squad, but right now its area of effect was causing more tactical complications than necessary. The weapon spewed a promethium jet that incinerated most unarmoured targets upon contact, but it was precisely because of its super-heated temperatures that it caused surrounding fabric and hair to catch fire. The tide of corpses became mobile tinder. Despite this, Bael-Shura continued to fire, trying to play as narrow a flame as he could.

Barsabbas, however, preferred his mighty bolter. A standard Godwyn-pattern with its high-explosive bolt-round was his lifeline. The bolter might have been heavy, bulky and had a recoil that could dislocate a human shoulder, but it flattened most targets with one shot. When engaged in a protracted firefight, Barsabbas had learned it was better to shoot a target and see it fall than have the wounded target flee and spend the next few hours wondering if it was now doubling back to ambush him.

'Besheba, switch to melee and fall behind me. We're going to drive a wedge through them,' Sica voxed into the squad link.

Barsabbas had been waiting for this command. Boarding actions had always been Barsabbas's field of expertise. It was in the dense, mauling scrum of breach-fighting that Barsabbas, young though he was, received the greatest respect. His dense, heavy frame was well suited to the wrestling, grinding melee. Ever since his bond with Sargaul and induction into Squad Besheba, Barsabbas had claimed the role of 'fore-hammer': the lead point of a boarding advance.

'Besheba, form on me,' said Barsabbas, wrenching his mace from a waist hook. One and a half metres long, cold-forged from a single rod of iron, the mace was capped by a knot of fused metal.

Sica nodded, pushing Barsabbas to the front. 'Turtled advance.'

They drove forwards, Sica with a boarding pike, stoving ribs and skewering the dead with each thrust. Barsabbas kept his eyes on the sky and cleared the path with wide arcs of his swinging mace. As sophisticated as his suit's auto-sensors were, they had no answer for the blood that congealed over his lenses. Barsabbas tried wiping them with his gloved fingers but it simply smeared the blood, resigning him to seeing through a fog of pink. Beside him, Sargaul slipped on the bodies spilled across the ground, crashing down on one knee. Barsabbas was immediately there, standing over Sargaul and tossing aside body after body. The dead buffeted him from all angles, glancing off his armour, dashing their teeth against his ceramite, climbing upon his back. Although he weighed close to three hundred and sixty kilos in armour, the sheer numbers rocked his heels. Unable to see clearly, Barsabbas felt engulfed by an avalanche of body parts.

'Stay tight and follow me,' Sica repeated. His low, steady voice on the vox-link pierced the jostling, teetering confusion.

Looking over the swarm of undead, Barsabbas watched solitary figures crest the sand dunes on a far horizon. They were more walking dead, attracted by the brilliant contrails of their descending drop pod. Some sprinted, other walked stiffly, others still seemed to follow in confused huddles. Beyond them, the red ferric peaks surrounded them like lowlying mountains, impervious to the furious fight below.

The stratospheric wind had blown them wide off course. The landing zone of Squad Besheba had been locked for the infected north, just twelve kilometres away from the sealed city of Ur. Instead, they had been inserted deep into the south, beyond the demarcation of infection, where the black wilt had not yet developed into a contagious threat.

It was not a portentous beginning to their deployment.

Barsabbas set himself upon a rock, fanning out the great trunks of his legs. He unlocked his helmet and a trickle of sweat sheeted down from the neck seal. Running his thick metal fingers through his damp locks, he sighed wearily as Sica reported.

'All squads were blown off target by the storm. All of them except Squad Shar-Kali experienced a mass assault by the dead.'

'Maybe these walking corpses were attracted by the falling lights,' Bael-Shura offered. Under the orange light of sunset, Barsabbas could see tiny scratches over the surface of his power armour. The undead had literally clawed their fingers to bloody stumps in an effort to break him open. Barsabbas imagined he looked much the same.

'Or maybe our arrival was anticipated and they were sent to find us,' Cython said in a rare moment of insight. The usually loud, boorish Cython and his bond Hadius were placated for once by the post-adrenal slump. Despite their superhuman metabolism and delayed onset of lactic acid build-up in their muscles, the exhaustion of hand-to-hand fighting could be felt by all. Every fibre in Barsabbas's body, particularly his forearms, was sour with strain. Squad Besheba had managed to travel six kilometres from the crash site, pursued by the undead relentlessly. Scattered, broken bodies were left in their wake. Barsabbas counted one hundred and ninety-six kills by hand, bested perhaps only by Sergeant Sica. They had finally been forced to climb the canyon in order to shake off their pursuers.

'We will press on to Ur when the temperature permits. It is far, but that is our objective and no orders were issued to deviate.'

As Sica spoke, Barsabbas was already analysing their situation. According to tact-maps they were rock-marooned almost eleven hundred kilometres from their intended dropsite. The local geography was predominantly arid with a high density of ferrous metals in the dirt. To their immediate south lay a bee-hived range of sedimentary formations, the sandstone and clay appearing ominously scarlet. Barsabbas chose to interpret the red as a good omen, a sign of angry retribution.

Sargaul was crouched a little further away, his bolter wedged vigilantly against a rock ledge. By the set of his jawline, Sargaul's conscious mind was shut off, stripped bare of thought. For now, his body was reduced to cardiac, respiratory and autonomic functions and he knew nothing except the scope of his weapon and the trigger finger of his right hand.

Barsabbas settled on a rock next to his bond. Sargaul turned his head slowly to regard him, before nestling his face back behind the weapon. Together they sat in silence, watching the suns leapfrog each other as they slunk beneath the horizon. For a while, nothing was said as they seeped in the sticky, chest-heaving glow of post-combat.

Finally Barsabbas turned to Sargaul. 'What were they?'

'They were the dead.'

'But I've never seen corpses do that before. It is... is it common?' Barsabbas asked. He often tried not to ask Sargaul too many questions. Barsabbas was conscious of the fact that he was the youngest and his combat experience had been limited to raids and squad-level deployments. Questions were weak, grasping things and he often avoided them.

Sargaul shook his head. 'Once, I saw dead men possessed by the puppet strings of an alpha-psyker. They were much the same.'

Barsabbas thought about this. Sargaul had seen many things throughout his service, but something about the corpses had put the veteran on edge. He could feel that his bond was agitated, of that he was sure. 'You are disturbed by this?'

Sargaul did not try to hide it. He nodded, almost to himself. 'I have never seen the dead rise of their own accord, have you? I try not think about why the dead would become so angry as to rise from their sleep and walk the earth. What could have wronged them? What influence makes these old ancestors restless? The walking dead are a by-product, an effect of influence. The answers escapes me and I am disturbed.'

'Do you think the enemy will fear us?'

'No, Barsabbas, I don't think they do,' Sargaul replied without taking his eyes off the scope.

'That's a shame,' said Barsabbas matter-of-factly. 'We look terrifying.'

At first, Barsabbas had taken pleasure in the carnage of the fight. After so many months of slithering through the cramped training tunnels of the ship, it felt good to finally be uncaged and administer so much destruction. But now he felt hollow. The walking dead were not living beings who feared him, nor breathing creatures who felt the despair at the sight of a charging Traitor Marine. They were 'the dead', a thoughtless horde no more sentient than a tide or the weather. It was a pointless fight. But there would be something else here. As Sargaul had said, the dead did not rise of their own accord. Something was causing this. Perhaps if Squad Besheba could find that cause, then they could put the fear into them.

Muhr had not seen the artificial light of the ship in days, only the darkness of his tower and the glow of his scrying lens. Despite the rituals of deployment and warp transit of the *Cauldron Born*, Muhr remained cloistered, refusing any contact beyond his own sanctuary.

His hair, unwashed and long, hung like a greasy mantle from his armoured shoulders. He was sweating fat beads that ran down his neck. His head was throbbing. Yet still he hung on, wringing the last efforts of psychic strength from his mind.

The mirror was set in a heavy frame, a free-standing structure of sculpted white meerschaum. But the frame was not important, for the mirror itself had had many frames throughout its long existence. It had once belonged to a prophet of the eldar race, or so the story went, and had since changed hands. In the hands of the eldar, it was said to have been an oracle, a scryer and a means of entering the webway, but Muhr dismissed these tales as fanciful. He had never been able to use it for anything more than astro-telepathy, and even then, the image was often poor.

As he waved his hand in an arc, the mirror surface became cloudy and changed. Muhr peered deeply.

He saw a settlement in Hauts Bassiq. A colony of wagons and carts tucked beneath the shade of a red, dusty hill. The image was murky, appearing fractured in some places and layered with ghost images. Muhr tapped the mirror and an image of the huts blossomed across the lens. He saw the corpse of an old man, withered and dry, crouched by the wood frame of a caravan. Periodically, the corpse gnawed on a femur before discarding it, as if it couldn't remember what it was doing, before picking it up and repeating the process.

Muhr tapped again. Now he saw a mass exodus of people. Plodding with stiff gaits, they moved in a single direction as if they were a great herd in migration. Flies settled on their slack lips and eyelids and they did not react. These were the walking dead, victims of the black wilt who spread the disease southwards.

Sudden footsteps intruded upon him. Distracted, Muhr shed the psychic link and turned from the mirror.

'My lord.'

It was Nabonidus, one of his coven. Nabonidus, the Chirurgeon and sorcerer attached to Fifth Company.

'My lord,' Nabonidus repeated. 'I report that the scouting element has been deployed. They made landfall thirty-one hours ago, but you were not present at the ceremony.'

Muhr smiled. 'I have been reviewing a joint operation.'

Nabonidus paused. He was a direct man, blunt and obtuse, and often did not understand Muhr. Like the smooth, faceless iron mask that Nabonidus wore, he was very straightforward. Although Muhr relied upon him as an enormously powerful psyker who had a natural affinity for daemonology, and a deft Chirugeon, there were some jobs that Muhr did not entrust him with, for Nabonidus lacked cunning. Muhr perceived him as no more than an effective automaton. Had his latent psychic abilities not been discovered during his neophyte induction, Nabonidus could have become a squad sergeant or even company captain. As a sorcerer of the coven, he would always be limited by his lack of guile.

'Come, Nabonidus. See for yourself.'

Muhr tapped the scrying glass. The same image reappeared as before.

Nabonidus looked, his iron mask expressionless.

'That is Hauts Bassiq,' Nabonidus announced flatly.

'That is our joint operation. It is partly the fruits of my labour,' Muhr admitted proudly, his eyes glazed with psy-trance.

Nabonidus tilted his head curiously. 'You are the source of the troubles on Bassiq?' His tone was monotonous, devoid of accusation. Nabonidus was linear and so was his question.

'I am not the source, no,' said Muhr. He thought for a while, relishing the act. 'I am more of a facilitator, if you will.'

'You could be seen as a betrayer,' said Nabonidus. Somehow the words were not at all accusatory. If anyone else had uttered such words, Muhr would have slain him outright. But not deadpan Nabonidus.

'Nothing could be further from the truth. I am doing this for the glory of our Chapter,' said Muhr as he stepped away from the mirror. 'Do you see the work I have done there?'

'Perhaps,' Nabonidus replied, choosing his words carefully. Muhr was testing him now and the coven witch sensed it. If he displayed the slightest sign of dissidence, then he would be done.

Rising up, Muhr closed in on Nabonidus. 'My patron is creating a slave force capable of exploiting the warp-iron on Hauts Bassiq. My patron requires this warp-iron to fuel his expanding fleets of conquest, and only I have the wisdom to facilitate this for him.'

The witch sounded delirious, his hands describing grand arcs in the air. Nabonidus tried to step back but his coven master pressed forwards until he was almost standing face to face.

'Do you understand what I do? Why I did this?'

'I do, Muhr,' Nabonidus said cautiously. 'But we are sending our brethren into a trap. Hazareth's company should be told–'

At this Muhr started, grasping Nabonidus's face in his palms and pulling him until they were eye to eye. 'Nobody needs to be told. No one but those that I choose,' he hissed.

Suddenly casting Nabonidus aside, Muhr swung about and manipulated the mirror again. He saw a fleeting glimpse of Ur – a microcosm of civilisation in the wild plains. A dark cloud hung over the city, suffocating its stacked chimneys and settling like fog on its ramparts.

'See this power? The power of my patron? We can share this power. If we give him Bassiq, we can share it. We do not have to be pirates, scavengers, any more. We will all be noble warlords.'

'Blood Gorgons do not have a patron,' Nabonidus ventured.

'We have a pact, Nabonidus. If the Blood Gorgons relinquish Hauts Bassiq to my patron, my patron will strengthen our Chapter. I am a pragmatist, Nabonidus. I know what needs to be done to raise us above our anonymity.'

'I understand,' Nabonidus said, his voice trembling.

Muhr slapped his palm against the scrying mirror. As the images of Hauts Bassiq faded, all that remained on the glass was the ghostly imprint of his hand. 'We need this. I'm not doing this for myself. I do this for the Chapter,' Muhr said with finality. 'Hauts Bassiq is a worthy sacrifice for the prize that awaits us.'

CHAPTER SEVEN

It was not yet dawn but Barsabbas did not think today would be any different from the day before that. The squad crossed another empty creek, leaving gridded prints in loose, dusty clay. They had been moving at a ferocious pace for the past four days, even during the heat peak of midday. They had left the rust and sandhill country of the southern tip far behind and, according to the tact-maps, had penetrated thirty-odd kilometres into the central plains. Strangely, it grew more verdant there. Hauts Bassiq was a land without oceans, yet intermittent rainfall drained gullies and creeks into the central dune fields.

Rust-resistant saltbushes flourished alongside weeping acacias in the red, infertile earth. The remnants of palaeodrainage channels became a refuge for relic plants with ancient lineages. Tall trees in dunefields were perhaps the most striking difference between the central and western territories and their eastern and southern cousins. Following the dry channels, Squad Besheba swept north, ghosting in and out of vox range with their brother squads.

Barsabbas plodded along to the rhythmic hiss of his hydraulic knee suspensors. In such monotonous country, it was easy to fall into a cata-lepsean sleep, purposely inducing partial consciousness. But he remained alert, forcing himself to make periodic environment scans and disseminate the information through the vox-link. His boltgun was strapped like a sash across his chest, his left hand coiled loosely around the trigger. In the past four days, Squad Besheba had learned to avoid the scavenging mobs of walking dead in order to conserve ammunition. Yet aside from wandering corpses and the stray caprid, there were no significant signs of life.

'I can taste a pocket of high atmospheric disturbance. Bacterial organisms,' Barsabbas announced as the line graph in the upper left corner of his vision spiked. A brisk wind had picked up, throwing dust into their faces. 'What say you?'

Although no human disease could penetrate the immune system of a Space Marine, Sargaul vented his helmet. 'I taste it too. Very acidic. Very strong,' he confirmed, spitting saliva out through his helmet's grille.

Cython did the same, but breathed in deeply and immediately coughed, his multi-lung rejecting the airborne substance. 'I can't identify,' he said, his words spurting out between violent hacking. 'This is pure strain.'

The squad halted as Cython continued to hack and gurgle. The fact that the substance could force even a Space Marine's multi-lung to respond so harshly was testament to its lethality. His lung sphincters were constricting as the organ attempted to flood his system with cleansing mucus.

'No more samples,' Sergeant Sica ordered angrily. 'Barsabbas, fade off your environment monitor. You're putting the fear in all of us.'

Barsabbas swore fluently but obeyed. The power plant core of his armour was two thousand years old and its spirit was temperamental if not outright malevolent, but it would not lie to him. He had detected something else on his monitors besides the bacteria. There had been a peripheral spike of detection, an organic pattern that was familiar to Barsabbas.

'Remember what Argol said,' Sica continued. 'Instinct will save your skin where scanners do not. Use your eyes and listen with your ears, and stop distracting yourself.'

With that, the squad peeled off, negotiating their way down the slope of a dry riverbed. But Barsabbas lingered. Argol's words resonated with him.

Suddenly alert, Barsabbas loosened his helmet seal and tested the air with his tongue. It was bitter at first, laced with a ferociously destructive organism that was corrosive to his hyper-sensitive taste glands. But he tasted something else on his palate too, fleeting and subtle. There! Hidden behind the airborne toxins was a familiar taste, a coppery taint that was unmistakable. Fresh blood.

'Blood. Fresh blood.'

'Blood. Blood.' The word echoed amongst the squad with breathless anticipation.

Sergeant Sica waved them to a halt at Barsabbas's warning. Cython tasted again, wary this time. He spat. 'Now that you say it, I can taste it too. You can barely pinpoint it with all the other tox on the wind current.'

'Which direction?' asked Bael-Shura. His augmetic jaw was sutured to much of his upper trachea, destroying the neuroglottis that allowed others to track by taste alone.

'Far from here, at least six kilometres to our north-east,' Barsabbas confirmed.

'We go there,' said Sica. 'Sharp find, Brother Barsabbas.'

The wind gained momentum, forcing the tall acacias to kneel and uprooting the saltbushes in bales. There was something angry and sentient about the viral wind. Barsabbas made sure both atmospheric venting and extraneous seals were entirely locked, a precaution usually reserved for vacuum or space exposure. The wind buffeted and rattled his armour like a cyclone grinding against a bunker.

They turned in defiance of the wind. It punished them with the full force of its gale. Heads low, shoulders set against the rising dust storm, Sergeant Sica led them in pursuit of freshly spilled blood.

Aboard the *Cauldron Born*, Sabtah roamed the old corridors. He rolled and unrolled his neck, loosening the muscles and working out the knots with pops and crackles, pacing the halls with a pensive focus. He did so often when things weighed heavily on his mind, such as now.

The shrine was a place where he came to think. These days it seemed like the younger Chaos Space Marines were too martial, too physical. They seldom tended to their war shrines. It was a quiet place and a place where Sabtah came to brood.

He sat before his shrine and retrieved his most precious prize.

The axe was of Fenrisian make, with a richly decorated brass haft-cap secured the trumpet blade. It was one of Sabtah's own trophies and one he kept at all times within his personal shrine.

Lifting the axe, Sabtah slashed the air with clumsy practice swings. It was not his weapon – it had once belonged to a Grey Hunter, one of Leman Russ's cursed children. Sabtah remembered the time when the Blood Gorgons had been declared *Excommunicate Traitoris* by the Inquisition within six decades of their Founding. He had been a young neophyte then, not even blooded, yet those had been ignominious days. They had been driven from their home world by Space Wolves, a broken Chapter pursued into the warp by lupine hunters. They became thieves: foraging, hiding, always hunted. The brothers had stayed together only for survival, the Chapter divided by minor war-captains and factions who sealed off entire sections of the *Cauldron Born* as their own fiefdoms and baronies. There was no dignity to their name.

It was to be Gammadin who united the warring companies. It was he who waged an intra-Chapter war that left much of the space hulk in devastation, even to this day. But in the aftermath of fratricide, the Blood Gorgons found cohesion. It had been Gammadin who devised the rituals of blood-bonding to ensure that his Chapter would never again fight internally, pledging their very co-existence to each other and the powers of Chaos. No Blood Gorgon would ever turn his blades on his brother again.

But Sabtah believed history came and went in cycles. What was due, would be due. The Blood Gorgons' unity had been constructed and could thus be dismantled.

Yet Sabtah also believed he could change it and map the course of his Chapter; it was his duty as Gammadin's blood bond. After all, Sabtah had been there from the beginning. He had been there the very day the Blood Gorgons rose up, seething and angry after decades of shame, to confront their Space Wolf pursuers.

Sabtah could still remember the fury and pent-up anguish that the Blood Gorgons had released against those loyalist Space Marines. Sabtah had never experienced anything like it since. They had engaged the Space Wolves with Lamprey boarding craft simply to inflict damage, a malicious hit-and-run assault that left their pursuers with severe casualties. Feared though the Wolves were in battle, they did not possess the refined boarding tactics of the Blood Gorgons. Although Sabtah had been a fresh-blood then, he slew a Grey Hunter that day. He had even scalped his enemy's long beard and plundered his axe.

He could not bear to see the Blood Gorgons live such shallow, inglorious existences again. They were a free Chapter, free to travel to the edge of the universe.

The Blood Gorgons knew nothing of restraint. Restraint, to Sabtah, was the bane of human existence. He knew that citizens of the Imperium worked their constant shift cycles until they withered and died, never deviating from doorstep to factorum. That was not existence. No, Blood Gorgons were like the sword-bearing leaders of Old Terra, conquering and plundering whatever they touched. There was substance to that. It was something Sabtah could be proud of.

Suddenly, Sabtah snapped out of his reverie. He felt a tweak in the base of his neck, and a chill ran across his skin. A flutter of nerves made his abdomen coil and uncoil.

Something was wrong.

Sabtah trusted his instincts without hesitation. The veteran pivoted on his ankle. He glimpsed movement as he spun mid-turn. It was fleeting. A ghostly double image in the corner of his vision, disappearing behind the pillars that framed the temple entrance.

He was old, but his eyes did not lie to him.

Sabtah gave chase, exploding into a flat sprint. He did not know what he had seen. The *Cauldron Born* was old and large. He had seen odd things aboard the vessel before. There were rumours of strange, immaterial things that dwelt in the forgotten catacombs and drainage sumps in the lower levels of the ship. Others spoke of a dark terror that lurked in the collapsed passages beneath the rear boiler decks. Those with no knowledge of the arcane would accuse the ship of being 'haunted'. Sabtah knew it was an inevitable influence of warp travel.

Twice more he caught sight of something large yet frustratingly elusive to his eyes. He pursued doggedly, his heavy legs pounding the ground. It led him further and further away from the serviced areas of the vessel. Sabtah chased hard, refusing to slow. He realised he was being led into the forgotten areas. The corridors became unlit. The ground was uneven, broken by rust and calcification, but Sabtah was consumed by the chase. His hearts pulsated in his eardrums.

The thing, whatever it was that Sabtah saw, appeared once more, like a black sheet caught in the wind, and then vanished.

Sabtah found himself in a cavern. Leakage in the overhead pipes had created a curtain of stalactites, some pencil-thin but others as stout as the trunks of trees. A carpet of mossy fungal growth glowed a cool, pale blue.

His lungs expanding with oxygen, Sabtah realised he was still gripping the Fenrisian axe. In his haste, he had left his bolter behind. Despite its brutish appearance, the axe was gyroscopically balanced – but Sabtah lacked the axe-craft of a Fenrisian. Instead, he would have to rely on brute strength to force its leverage, and Sabtah had plenty of brute strength. Clutching the awkward, top-heavy tool in a double grip, he advanced.

The creature had baited him deep. Sabtah knew that, and part of him enjoyed the thrill of a sentient adversary. By his reckoning, he had grown slow and fat on board the ship. He was a specimen made for war.

Slowly, adrenaline drew his muscles tight, the sheaths of his musculature taut with that familiar feeling of pre-combat. His knees and forearms quavered uncontrollably, every spindle of muscle building up with unspent energy.

He saw movement. This time it appeared and stopped, rising to its height less than thirty metres away: a human shape, clothed in shadow.

For no apparent reason, the reknowned words *'and they shall know no fear'* scrolled through his head. Sabtah snorted.

With that, he charged through the stalactite forest. His plate-cased shoulders splintered the drip-rock to powder upon impact. He ploughed through it unarrested, a storm of fragmented stone churned in his wake. Baring fangs through his wild beard, Sabtah howled with joyous aggression. His arms yearned to uncoil and channel all of his strength, all of his momentum and all of his rage through the edge of his axe and into the flesh of his foe.

'Sabtah. Stop!'

Sabtah did not hear anything except the red wash of fury in his ears. He looped the axe in a hammer-thrower's arc, tearing down four or five stalactites in one sweep. The black shadow flickered like a disrupted pict-feed.

Henry Zou

'Sabtah!'

Unresponsive, Sabtah drew the axe far back for another swing.

'Muhr is going to kill you. Sabtah! You have to listen to me.'

The axe froze.

Finally, a hint of recognition creased Sabtah's furrowed, animalistic brow. The feral snarl softened behind the beard. The killing rage ebbed. Sabtah lowered his axe cautiously, peering into the dark.

'Nabonidus?'

A figure walked towards the glow-lights of the ground fungus. It was indeed Nabonidus – chosen of Muhr's coven. The witch-surgeon had shed his power armour and was clad in a hauberk of supple chainmail. His face was painted white and his eyes daubed with ash. The sorcerer clicked his fingers and the shadowy apparition standing before Sabtah dissipated.

Sabtah cursed. 'I could have killed you, Nabonidus. What did you think you were doing?'

Nabonidus pushed a finger to his lips. 'Hush, Sabtah. Please lower your voice.' He ducked his head and peered about the cavern. Finally satisfied that they were alone, Nabonidus whispered, 'I lured you here for a reason.'

Sabtah raised his axe cautiously. Nabonidus was a sorcerer. There was an innate distrust between the coven and their warrior brethren. He watched the witch's hands carefully.

'I lured you here because that is the only way it would be safe. I can't be seen talking to you, Sabtah. It's not safe.'

'Safe for who?' Sabtah asked.

Nabonidus's reply was tinged with a genuine terror. 'For me,' he admitted.

Still unconvinced, Sabtah remained silent. 'I will give you one chance to explain yourself.'

'Muhr is behind this. It is part of his power game. The troubles on Hauts Bassiq are his doing. It will cause a Chapter war from which Muhr is positioned to emerge the victor.'

Sabtah shrugged. 'I suspected this. But he has nothing I cannot deal with.'

Nabonidus shook his head. 'It is more than Muhr. There is another force at play here, more powerful than Muhr. There is some sort of pact between them.'

'Who is that patron?'

Nabonidus took a step back. 'I don't know, Sabtah. All I know is that Muhr is a mere minion. This patron is destroying Hauts Bassiq, and in return for Muhr's role, this patron is willing to aid Muhr in his ascension to power. That's all I know.'

'Why are you telling me this, witch?'

'Because I am frightened, Sabtah. I am seven hundred years old and I am frightened, not for myself but for the Chapter. I do not want a Chapter war. It's your duty now, Sabtah. You are his only obstacle.'

The blood wind led them north-east, trembling across the lowlands. It led them to a ravine, a shallow cleft that revealed the headframe of an ancient mine. It was partially sealed by the wreckage of a collapsed hoist, like a steel spider web crushed into the entrance.

Such delving was not uncommon. The landscape was porous with such abandonment. Some were large scale constructs, open shelf mines that sliced slabs of the continent away from its crust. Others were smaller shaft mines, long forgotten and extinguished by collapse.

This one – according to the squad's pre-deployment briefing – fell somewhere in-between the two extremes. A perfect circle, jagged with cog's-teeth markings, had been cut into the ravine's coarse-grained sandstone. Wide enough to accommodate seismic earth-tractors, the severed remains of a rail system led directly into the worm's-mouth entrance.

Much of the shaft entrance had become buried beneath thousands of years of sand, dust and clay, forming a natural ramp that descended into the flat, black depths. Lobed spinifex grass lined the natural stairway, covering the flaking fossils of frames and sheave wheels.

There was blood amongst the spinifex too.

Here and there amid the tufts of coarse grass could be seen bright dashes of red. From the pattern and volume, Barsabbas knew this was not the spotted trail of a wounded animal. Strong violence had occurred there.

The squad skirted the ravine warily, appraising the area from a tactical perspective. Below them lay an irregular basin of yellowing grasses and crumbling clay. The rough terrain provided plenty of hiding space for unseen predators, but little meaningful cover for a Chaos Space Marine. Across the basin floor, the mine entrance was an edifice of sagging, oxidised framework, a perfect circle cut into the side-wall of the ravine. Even with his enhanced vision, Barsabbas could not see into the girdered depths.

Sica studied it for a while, not moving, not speaking, simply sitting and watching. After what seemed like an eternity he finally spoke. 'There is no cover. We will cross the basin in pairs. First pair moves across with the others covering. Once the first pair reaches the headframe, turn around and provide cover. Clear?'

'Clear,' Barsabbas repeated with his brethren.

They only discovered the carnage once they reached the bottom of the ravine.

The giant spinifex grass was much thicker than Barsabbas realised, dragging at him with thorny burrs. The megaflora formed unusual growth patterns where the inner grass died off and new stems sprouted from the outside forming concentric circles of various sizes.

Barsabbas mowed through the giant spinifex, flattening it with great sweeps of his metal paws. Sargaul prowled at his side, bolter loose but ready. They crunched through the loose threads of ochre grass, stopping sporadically to study the blood that flecked the area. Behind them, the rest of the squad kept an invisible watch.

Sargaul's voice suddenly came over the squad vox-link. 'I found a dead one.'

By his tone, Sargaul was anxious. Moving over to him, Barsabbas parted the grass to see what Sargaul had discovered.

There was a plainsman. Dead. A warrior, judging by the way he wore his red shuka and the quiver resting on his exposed spine. Two parallel impact hits had segmented him and smeared him into the clay. Barsabbas stopped and marvelled at the freshly slain corpse. It always amazed him how soft and easily broken was the normal human body. Mankind was not meant for war – a pouch of soft, vulnerable tissue encased in pain-receptive skin, all reinforced by a skeletal structure no more durable than pottery ceramic. Mankind was too mortal for war.

'The walking dead don't have the combat capacity for that,' Sargaul concluded.

The pair swept the area, realising the full extent of the violence. There had been combat, a fight of some sort. A broken hatchet with its edge blunted by heavy impact. Broken arrows lying in the grass. Pieces of humans thrown far and wide by the tremendous force and violence.

They found another plainsman tossed some distance away, a jumble of filleted flesh and splintered bone barely held together by skin and sinew. Barsabbas knew there were more – he saw enough hands and broken parts to know there were others, but they could no longer be found. Just pieces.

For a moment, Barsabbas was overwhelmed by the urge to spray his bolter wildly, directly into the mine shaft. But the frenzied urge was fleeting and the Chaos Space Marine's discipline held. They reached the sloping wall on the other side and took a knee, covering the area as the next pair made their way across.

A brief, keening cry echoed up from the mine shaft, causing Barsabbas to turn quickly, his bolter heavy in his hands. Despite switching to thermal version, Barsabbas could see nothing down the rocky throat. The angled shaft simply slipped away into lightless, visionless nothing. The scream came again.

'Besheba, move on!'

The last pair, Sica and Bael-Shura, had crossed the basin. It was time to confront.

'Divide into bonds. Sargaul and Barsabbas to head east, Cython and Hadius to the west, we'll spearhead north. Keep constant vox-link at both high and medium frequencies. Explore the facility and report. Stay fluid,' ordered Sica.

With that the six Chaos Space Marines descended the shaft slope at a sprint, their footfalls rumbling like the infant tremors of an earthquake.

A shadow fell across the wallowing blackness of the entrance shaft. Not a physical shadow, for nothing could be discerned in the pitch dark, but a shadowed presence.

It walked quietly, yet each step crushed calcite into mineral dust. It moved softly in the shadows, gliding and shifting, yet its girth eclipsed almost the entire passage. Its heart did not beat, but it was not dead.

It followed Squad Besheba for a time, stalking warily out of auspex range. As the Blood Gorgons split off to sweep the stope tunnels, it followed too.

Cython and Hadius followed a railed tunnel for several kilometres. The railway was old, with much of the wood disintegrated and the metal a crisp, flaking shell. Yet amongst the crumbling dust, Cython could see fresh footprints. Fresh humanoid prints, some bare-footed but others in heavy-soled shoes.

It would be eighty-six minutes into their descent before Squad Besheba encountered the enemy on Hauts Bassiq.

The tunnel widened into a large, yet low-ceilinged chamber. Huddles of men and women were digging at the walls with their bare hands, scraping the soft chalk with their nails and scooping the powder into mine carts. There were perhaps two hundred of them, working in unison, yet none of them registered any heat signals under thermal vision. They were already dead.

Standing guard over the work detail was a trio of men. These three were alive, their living signatures throbbing with vital signs in Cython's HUD. Their heads and necks were hooded in loose bags of canvas. Their faces were hidden but for the pair of round vision goggles, wide like the eyes of a monstrous doll. Their bodies were armoured in cheap, mass-moulded segments of rubberised sheathing the grey colour of arsenic – bulky, overlapping and lobster-tailed. None of the men bore any military insignia or heraldry that Cython could recognise.

The three men gave monosyllabic commands to the labouring corpses – carry, retrieve, dig, lift. Already an entire section of the chalk wall had been cleared away to reveal a system of pipes like exposed muscle fibre. It was evident that the dead were re-excavating the ancient mine networks of Hauts Bassiq.

Cython fired a single shot. In the distance, no more than eighty metres down the stope, one of the men spun right around and fell. Hadius felled the other two with such speed that they never uttered a cry. *Bam-Bam-Bam*. Three shots in a semi-second and it was done.

Cython and Hadius pressed on, through the chamber of slave-corpses. These, however, did not attack them. They did not even look up from their work. Without the three men to give them commands, the slaves simply continued to work in their shambling, methodical fashion. The chalk was red with blood as the slaves scraped their fingers down into stumps.

The moment before a firefight is an oddly awkward affair. There is a fraction of a second when opposing forces meet and strain to recognise one another. A slight hesitation as the human mind reconciles the concept of shooting down a stranger before actually doing so.

But the Blood Gorgons harboured no such hesitation. Sica opened fire from behind the cover of a gas main.

The procession of hooded men advancing down the tunnel was caught by the ferocity of the sudden ambush. The hooded men fired back. Their shots were surprisingly rapid and precise, solid slugs hammering Sica's chest plate and helmet with percussive shocks, pushing him back. These men were soldiers, or at least fighters of some discipline, Sica could tell. Bael-Shura fell amongst them, an almost platoon-sized element of these cumbersome-looking soldiers. He washed them with his flamer and scattered the survivors with his spiked gauntlet. Although the men were large, imposing things, Bael-Shura made them appear frail and undersized.

The tunnel was large and chaotic. Hundreds of walking corpses were digging, scooping sediments away from the porous shell of an ancient gas main. Hundreds more dragged a monolithic length of plastek piping down the passage, evidently to replace the older, semi-fossilised piece.

Despite the shooting, the walking dead did not seem to notice the Blood Gorgons in their midst. Some looked up almost lazily, like bored grazers, but none reacted. Some were caught in the backwash of Bael-Shura's flamer, but they did not stop work, even as they burned. Their fat boiled and their skin peeled but they continued to drag on the ropes of the replacement pipe. These were obedient workers.

Hooded figures charged down the stope towards Sica. They were shouting orders, shooting down any corpse who did not move out of their way. Sica made sure to recognise them, blinking his eyes to capture file-picts of the enemy. It would provide valuable reconnaissance should the Blood Gorgons have to deploy in greater force. He zoomed in on their armaments, blunt-muzzled autoguns with trailing belt-fed ammunition; not of Imperial issue, but a distinctly human design nonetheless. They fought in loose platoon formations, but their arsenic-grey armour was too thick for light infantry: a rubberised synthetic moulding that would be simple to manufacture but inferior in quality. It offered no protection against Sica's bolter.

Bael-Shura moved next to him, the tunnel wide enough to allow the Traitor Marines to fight shoulder to shoulder. They laughed as they worked, a dry wicked laughter that was frightening in its intensity. From behind the circular saws of an industrial rock cutter, a hooded man lobbed a rock at Sica. He heard a whistling sound and he turned the slab of his shoulder pad towards the missile. There was a flash of light. Even with his eyes closed, Sica's vision strobed red and bright yellow. It had been a grenade. The explosion pushed Sica slightly and made him grunt with annoyance at his own carelessness. He shot the man off the industrial saw, quickly, as if ashamed.

What seemed like two or three full platoons of the hooded men flooded the tunnel. Perhaps seventy or eighty men, by Sica's estimation. He reported the situation over the squad vox-link in-between shots. It was confirmed without concern. The hulking, rubberised soldiers swarmed over them, firing their underslung autoguns, brass casings flickering rapidly into the air. Sica's armour registered some minor damage in the extremities, particularly the forearms and shoulder regions as bullets chipped the external ceramite and hypodermal mesh.

Laughing, Sica backhanded one of the hooded men with the ridged knuckles of his gauntlet, snapping his neck and throwing two hundred kilos of brutish soldier back into his comrades. Bael-Shura expelled the last of his promethium and did not bother to reload; he crashed into the enemy with his weight, slashing with his studded fists. Bones broke and rubberised armour split like melon rind. There was no stopping them. Panic finally setting in, the hooded men turned and fled.

The vox-links were dead. Partitioned by solid bedrock, Barsabbas and Sargaul knew nothing of their brethren's conflict. The pair skirted east at Sica's command, following what seemed to be a recent delving. The rock was freshly cut, as if expansion of the ancient mines had began anew.

Barsabbas and Sargaul descended on a chain-belt platform down hundreds of metres. Despite the oxidised state of the iron elevator, the chain belt was of newly galvanised steel and still smelt sweetly of greasing oil. Something had been reconstructing the mine. Perhaps the same things responsible for eviscerating the plainsmen braves above ground.

The elevator came to a clattering halt, fifteen metres above the shaft bottom. They hung there, suspended like a bird cage. Below them, the vault at the pit of the mine was not what they had expected.

There were hundreds of walking dead down there, packed like meat in a storage facility, a dense grid of scalps and jostling shoulders. The cooler temperatures ensured they did not rot or bloat from the surface heat. They did not move and they did not respond. The frigid air rendered them stiff and sluggish. Some moaned and rocked gently on frozen limbs.

'An army of the dead,' Sargaul whistled appreciatively.

'A workforce,' Barsabbas observed.

'But they would make poor slaves. I would not eat food prepared by these creatures.'

'No. I do not think they can do anything except menial labour. No dexterity or cognitive capacity,' Barsabbas suggested.

As if on cue, several of the closest corpses looked up and began to babble nonsense. Their vocal cords had stiffened and gases exhaled from their lungs in a strained, raspy cry.

'But they will work,' said Sargaul.

The walking dead needed no food, no water. They did not suffer under the intolerably harsh climate, and they did not sleep or rest. They would simply work until they rotted apart.

In a way, Barsabbas was awed by the simple logic. It was almost impossible for Hauts Bassiq to host a living workforce – this was the primary reason behind the Imperial exodus. Bassiq lacked water or arable land. The climate could not sustain a proper agriculture. Despite his post-human fortitude, Barsabbas felt the sting of the heat and the fogginess of extreme dehydration – he could not imagine what the conditions were like for natural-born men. In the end, the Adeptus Mechanicus left their great earthmovers and machines to rust and the rich mineral seams unclaimed. It had simply been unworkable.

A standard healthy human forced to toil in the mines or above-ground refineries would not last long. Extreme surface temperatures combined with a lack of available water was a simple yet logistically impossible obstacle. Barsabbas calculated a normal human constitution could withstand no more than an eighteen-hour work shift before death – unless heat stroke, dehydration or muscular contractions put them out of commission first.

'A long time ago, when I was still young, Gammadin had once considered harvesting Bassiq for more than just genestock,' Sargaul said, even as he studied the corpse ranks below them. 'There are enough resources and repairable facilities to equip and power a Naval armada, buried just beneath the sand.'

Barsabbas shook his head. 'And Gammadin...'

'And Gammadin was wise enough not to attempt anything so foolish. This world is borderline uninhabitable. Nothing living can really thrive here,' Sargaul said, gesturing at the dead to emphasise his point.

Below them, the dead shuffled on the spot, moaning and occasionally expelling a bellow of bloat gas. There was something developing on a much grander scale, much more than a mere outbreak of pestilence. Of this, Barsabbas was sure.

* * *

The hooded men thought they had the intruders isolated. These were, after all, their mines and their domain. Slinking within the shadows, they had hunted Cython and Hadius quietly, waiting until they were trapped within the gantry-maze of a bauxite cavern.

But when the fighting erupted in the old mines, the Blood Gorgons did not fall as expected. Instead, the intruders seemed to enjoy the game.

Cython and Hadius, whooping with glee, sprinted down a gantry frame, gunning as they went. They were an old pair, a veteran bond who genuinely enjoyed the business of war. There was a flippant creativity to their murdercraft and it came as easily to them as walking or sleeping.

Hooded silhouettes rose from the numberless tiers of rock shelves and walkways. The Blood Gorgons blasted them back down, calling out targets to each other in perfect rhythm.

Suddenly Cython barked in laughter. In the upper tiers of the gantry he saw the reflective glint of a gun scope. He turned to warn Hadius, but his bond was already aware. They fired and a grey-clad body plummeted down, bouncing off gantry spurs twice.

'This is bad. I'll wager Sica and Bael are carving up a hellstorm and we're missing out on all the kills,' Hadius said, breathing through his vox-grille.

'They're too afraid to engage!' laughed Cython. He spotted movement to his left and fired on instinct. He worked on drill-conditioned reflex, aiming and shooting before he thought to. Another hooded man died, the bolt-round punching through the metal drum he was cowering behind.

Cython was still laughing when Hadius's helmet exploded in a plume of blood and metal wreckage. It was a definitive kill, the only injury that could truly put down a Traitor Marine. Hadius's body continued to move on muscle memory. He fired twice in a random direction, reloaded his bolter clip in one fluid motion, sank to his knees and died.

Cython stopped running, suddenly mute with shock. He felt the death keenly, as if something had been severed from his physical self. He stood still for one whole second, a momentary lapse in his surgically-enhanced combat discipline, as he looked at his blood bond. It was one whole second he could not afford.

Cython tried to move but he realised something hot was pulsing down his throat and soaking the front of his chest. He put a hand to his throat, trying to stem the flow of blood. Even in the darkness, he could see the arterial sprays spit between his fingers. He aimed his bolter with his free hand but by then he was already falling, the entire left side of his torso, abdomen and arm disintegrating in a blizzard of superheated ash. He hit the bottom after a forty-metre drop and died wordlessly.

Forty metres above him, in the upper crane of the gantry, the stalkers melted away, leaving only the faintest trace of gun smoke in their wake.

* * *

A rapid data pulse ran through the squad sensory links. Hadius was dead. His life monitors blanked out with a surge of white noise, then nothing.

A mere moment later, the squad link was disrupted again. Cython was dead. Two dead.

Sergeant Sica had always been in control. It was the only state that he had ever known. Now, crouched in the dark, attempting to re-establish a vox-link, Sica no longer felt in control. The enemy were in the shadows all around him. Shots tested the air, hissing past him and promising more to come.

Slapping the side of his helmet, Sica swore at himself and at everything around him, cursing himself for his lapse in judgement.

Trembling with rage, Sica tore off his helmet. A heavy-calibre round thrummed past his ear with meteoric speed.

'We need to regroup with Sargaul and Barsabbas!' roared Bael-Shura. He was crouched before the bend in the mine shaft, his flamer wedged against the corner. More of the enemy spilled from the surrounding stope tunnels, clattering down staircases with thickly soled boots. Shura forced them backwards with an enormous belch from his flamer. 'We need to regroup,' Bael-Shura repeated urgently.

Sica shook his head. It was too late. 'I don't have coordinates for them. My auspex is jammed with interference.'

Bael-Shura stood up and sprinted over to Sica. He had not taken three steps before his right arm exploded at the elbow. Reeling from the blow, Bael-Shura rocked back on his heels like a teetering fortress. His body was fighting the trauma, flooding him with endorphins as he fell to one knee.

'Not now,' Sica hissed.

A dark shape rose up behind Bael-Shura, engulfing him in its shadow. It stood head and shoulders taller than either of them, a monstrous specimen. A great distended gut, studded with barbs, eclipsed Sica's vision. Its power armour was off-white and marbled with fatty threads of lime green. There was a heady aura of disease and the odour of stagnancy. It clutched a leaf-bladed dagger, slick with the blood of Bael-Shura.

'Plague Marine,' spat Sica.

Sica remembered meeting their kind in the Gospar Subsector. Sica had ram-boarded the cargo fleet of a Nurgle warlord, and the bastards were exceedingly difficult to kill. Their plunder had been tainted too – the gold tarnished, their manuscripts rotting and their slaves sickly.

'Pest,' the Plague Marine replied with a shrug of his massive torso.

They clashed then, colliding head to head, shoulder to shoulder. The rotting monster was inhumanly strong and he was larger than any other Chaos Space Marine Sica had ever faced. Tying up the back of the Plague Marine's head with one hand, Sica began to deliver a series of hammer fists with his other. The reinforced, pyramidal studs on his gauntlet cracked his enemy's cyclopean visor. In answer, the Plague Marine hacked with his heavy, chopping knife. The seax slid into the joint between Sica's chest guard and abdominal plates. Roaring, both combatants broke from their clinch with a burst of blood and ceramite fragments. There was a momentary lull in violence as Sica shouldered his bolter and the Plague Marine raised his bolt pistol.

Then they shot at each other repeatedly at point-blank range.

Shots pounded into Sica, crazing his vision, punching through ceramite, jolting the ground out from beneath him. They exchanged shots on automatic, drilling each other from no more than five paces apart. Seismic vibrations rattled his teeth and dislocated his jaw. Sparks flew and metal fused. Sica's bolter was stronger, larger and its stopping power considerable, popping a trio of gaping holes in the Plague Marine's stomach and tearing a line of ragged shots vertically up into its neck. Simultaneously, the enemy's bolt pistol skipped fat explosive slugs across Sica's groin, chewing the ceramite deeply before penetrating the weaker armour of Sica's upper thigh.

Sica fell to his knee as his femur was shot clean through. The Plague Marine folded, stumbling backwards and recoiling away like a wounded animal.

Bael-Shura, finally seeing a clear shot, enveloped the Plague Marine with a splash of fire. Dying, the monstrous specimen crashed to the flowstone in a mountainous pyre. Even as it fell, another Plague Marine appeared at the end of the tunnel. Then two more appeared in the gantries above them. The Blood Gorgons were surrounded.

Bael-Shura dragged Sica's heavily bleeding form against the rock wall with his remaining arm and crouched next to him.

'I think we're going to die,' Sica said quietly.

'Your leg. It's going to need attention,' Bael-Shura said to Sica as he kicked his own severed arm away to make room.

Sica looked down at his leg and swore. There was a clean hole through his left thigh and the middle section of his femur was no longer there. His entire leg was twisted ninety degrees and attached only by threads of muscle and ceramite plating.

'No time,' Sica said, struggling to sit up.

The Plague Marines began firing. Muzzles flashed in the distance, and nearby rocks and scaffolding crumbled as if scored with an invisible drill. Sica fired two shots and opened the squad vox-channel.

'Sica to Besheba. Threat identified as Chaos Space Marines of Nurgle. We are outnumbered.'

It was the last transmission he would make. As shots barked and snapped around him, Sergeant Sica calmly ejected his spent magazine and clicked a fresh one into place. By his side, Bael-Shura balanced a bolt pistol across the stump of his arm. They began to fire, determined to spend their ammunition while they still could.

* * *

Eight levels up, driven into the dead end of a rock grotto, the remnants of Squad Besheba fought. Barsabbas sprinted across a sloping shaft, racing upwards. He fired his bolter to the left as he ran, raking his field of vision. The enemy answered with their own fire, shooting so fiercely that the stalactites trembled from the ceiling. A shot glanced off Sargaul's elbow. Angry, Sargaul risked stopping for a moment and hurled a frag grenade.

The pair were running. What had begun as a coordinated sweep had degenerated into slaughter. The Plague Marines had ensnared them. They had exploited a Traitor Marine's lust for violence by using auxiliary cultists as bait, luring the squad deep.

Barsabbas could barely keep track of enemy positions. They were everywhere. Gunshots exploded back and forth. They came and went, a rapid barrage of small-arms fire, sudden and sharp, the whine of cyclical shots, then the singular shocking roar of rockets.

'We have to go now,' Barsabbas shouted to Sargaul. 'We have to go.'

'No, we stay,' Sargaul replied.

'They're everywhere,' Barsabbas argued. The violence was overcoming his deference to Sargaul's seniority. 'We can't do anything here. We need to link up with another squad.'

The explosions and detonations threatened the integrity of the tunnel. Drip-rocks above them rattled, shaking down a raft of dust and loose grit.

'We have to go, brother,' Barsabbas repeated. A missile launcher slid out from behind a support girder, almost directly in front of him. Barsabbas swung up his bolter and fired four times. A Plague Marine fell out from behind cover. The warhead fired and went wild, detonating overhead.

'Sargaul!'

An overhanging shelf of sandstone weighing at least twenty tonnes cracked above Sargaul's head. Oblivious, Sargaul traded shots with their pursuers. The stone above gave way. There was a whiplash *snap* as the sandstone split, before it dropped with a tectonic rumble. It missed crushing Sargaul by less than a metre. Unfazed, Sargaul spared the rock a curious glance before sprinting behind it for cover.

Fighting the urge to avoid being shot, Barsabbas waded back out into the open. He was low on ammunition. He locked onto a Plague Marine and shot at him, buckling him. In return, a bolter round exploded against his right chest plate. He felt the lancing pinpricks of shrapnel. The machine spirit of his armour recoiled in seething displeasure.

'I'm getting hit. Absorbing shots and taking hits!' Barsabbas voxed.

Boltguns barked, overlapping shots. Coarse screaming. The stampede of steel-heavy boots. More shots.

'Hold on, brother. Hold on,' Sargaul replied.

Barsabbas saw Sargaul swim through the barrage towards him. His bond-brother was missing a hand. Rounds drilled against his glossy hide. Sargaul ran.

Then the tunnel collapsed.

Creaking girders could no longer support the ancient mine shaft. The entire tunnel buckled, warped, as if the sandstone was momentarily liquefying. Steel girders snapped. The ceiling imploded with a puff.

As the weight of a planet's crust fell upon him, the last thing Barsabbas thought about was the shame he had brought to Squad Besheba.

CHAPTER EIGHT

Sabtah was sleeping when they came for him.

They dispatched his black turbans quickly and without alarm. One slave-guard was decapitated and hidden in a path of filamentous bacteria, just outside Sabtah's chamber gates. His throat was cut and the blood absorbed into the gossamer hairs, leaving little trace of his murder.

The other sentry was less fortunate still. Standing guard outside Sabtah's vestibule, he found himself unceremoniously rolled down a venting chute. The chopping fans coughed only slightly as his body was fed through them.

Although the iron-bound gates were sealed by sequential trigger locks, the intruders knew the numeric codes and slid them open manually. Once inside, they severed the power cables that veined the ceilings above. Vox-channels, motion sensors and trip lasers were all disconnected. In one quick act, Sabtah's proto-fortress became vulnerable and isolated. Even the phos-lights dimmed to black.

But Sabtah heard it all.

He sat upright in his circadian cradle – a high-backed throne of leather and iron. Spindles of wire sprouted from the cradle and interfaced with the black carapace beneath Sabtah's naked torso. He pretended to be in a drug-induced comatose state. He was unarmoured, wearing nothing but a leather kilt. His chin rested against his chest and his eyes were closed. But in his mind, Sabtah was wide awake.

He kept his eyes closed even as he heard the soft click of his chamber door.

In his mind's eye, Sabtah drew a mental map of his vault. The vault was high-ceilinged and circular, a silo of vast but empty proportions. Ringing the walls were racks of disused boarding pikes – hundreds, perhaps thousands of spears, among them Adulasian harpoons, Cestun half-and-halfs and even Persepian marlin-pikes. Dusty and antiquated, the pikes huddled like clusters of old men, their shafts brittle and their tips toothless.

To his right, at the opposite end of the empty chamber, was his MKII power amour. Erect on a dais, the suit watched the vault like an empty sentry. The only other object in the vault was a tiny necklace, a blackened, withered scrap of coarse hair and leather. It was suspended in a glass pillar, floating like a tribal fetish. Sabtah had worn it once when he had been a mere boy, thousands of years ago, in the darkest caves of his memory. Capturing the image behind his eyelids, Sabtah waited.

He allowed the intruders to step closer. He counted two, judging by their movements. He heard the rasp of metal being unsheathed. It was a good draw, smooth and unhesitant. He restrained his battle instinct and kept his eyes closed.

He heard the final whine of a blade as it cleared the scabbard, so soft it barely disturbed the cool, recycled air.

That was when Sabtah burst into life.

He leapt. His explosiveness was incredible, clearing four metres from a standstill. The spindle wires snapped painfully from his torso plugs but Sabtah didn't feel them.

He seized the knife arm in the dark, wrenching it into a figure-four lock and dislocating the elbow with a wet snap. He judged where the intruder's throat would be in relation to the arm and punched with his fingers, jamming his gnarled digits into the larynx. He was rewarded by a wheeze of pain.

Suddenly an arm seized Sabtah from behind, constricting around his throat. It snapped shut around his carotid arteries like a yoke. The arm was exceedingly strong and corded with smooth slabs of muscle. No normal man could possess such tendon strength; Sabtah knew he was fighting Astartes. It was something he had suspected when they first attacked, but now he was sure. Pivoting his hip, Sabtah tossed the assailant off his back with a smooth shoulder throw. The intruder crunched through his circadian cradle with a clash of sparks and broken circuitry.

Under the fitful, hissing glow of his wrecked sleeping capsule Sabtah caught a brief glimpse of his assassins. They were both Blood Gorgons, and Sabtah knew them well.

Both wore bodygloves of glossy umber; compression suits utilised for rigorous hand-to-hand combat, strength and conditioning drills. Both were young, their faces lacking the mutations of warp-wear. They were newly inducted warriors from Squad Mantica, a unit from the ruthless 5th Company.

'Voldo, Korbaiden, desist!' Sabtah ordered. His voice was sonorous, a blaring wall of sound.

The young warriors faltered, stiffening for a second. But their training, their clinical drive to complete a mission, overtook any fear they held for Sabtah's seniority. They were here to kill Sabtah and they would finish the job.

As Voldo rose from the smoking wreck of the cradle, he lunged at Sabtah with a shard of broken panelling. Sabtah deflected the stab with the palm of his hand, a manoeuvre he had repeated millions of times in the drill halls. The younger warrior's strike was slow in comparison, not yet honed through centuries upon centuries of combat. The trajectory was inefficient by ten degrees to the right and he did not roll his shoulder into the blow. Sabtah was faster and rammed his chin into Voldo's eye. As Voldo reeled from the blow, Sabtah followed up with a rapid flurry of upper-body strikes. An elbow that crunched the orbital bone. A straight punch that dislocated the jaw. A knee that collapsed the sternum. Fists, knees, forearms and elbows, anvil impacts that thrashed Voldo back onto the floor.

'Did Muhr send you?' Sabtah asked forcefully, turning to face Korbaiden.

The younger warrior backed away, his eyes darting left and right for a weapon. As old as Sabtah was, the hoary veteran's body did not show any signs of mortal ageing. His torso was ridged and his legs were deeply striated, quadriceps bulging like hydraulics made flesh. He was short and compact for a Traitor Marine, but he carried the scarred, calloused pride of a weary predator. He could tell Korbaiden was frightened.

'Did Muhr send you here? For me?' Sabtah asked again.

Korbaiden did not answer. He simply closed the distance, stepping to punch with his dislocated arm. Sabtah felt oddly proud of the young Blood Gorgon's determination, but it did not deter him from sidestepping the punch and driving his knee into Korbaiden's liver. Once. Twice. Sabtah wrapped his large, coarse hands behind Korbaiden's head in a tight clinch and continued to knee him over and over again.

He laid out both assassins on the floor. Voldo and Korbaiden were broken. They had suffered massive internal trauma that would have killed any normal human. Bones were split and organs had been ruptured. All of Korbaiden's lungs had collapsed and part of Voldo's face folded inwards.

'Does your squad know of the shame you've brought them?' Sabtah asked, softly this time.

The assassins from Squad Mantica remained silent. Voldo tried to crawl towards a discarded knife, but his broken thigh would not hold him and he slid onto his stomach, eyes wide open as he breathed long, jagged breaths. Sabtah knew there was no sense in interrogating a Traitor Marine. They would not yield.

Crossing over to a wall panel, Sabtah placed his palm on the scanner. The wall emitted an obliging chime and slid open. From the alcove, he retrieved his bolter and a fresh, heavy clip.

As he loaded the weapon and crossed to the two injured Blood Gorgons, Sabtah sighed. He was profoundly sad. He had long feared that history came and went in cycles. The Blood Gorgons looked up at him, eyes wild and face muscles clenched in defiance.

As his bolter banged twice, tremendously loud, it seemed his fears had been proven true.

Barsabbas regained consciousness, but it made no difference. He could not move and he could not see. The only thing he could make out was a hairline crack on his otherwise blank, black helmet lens. There were no system reports, squad data-link or auspex monitors. Nothing.

He tried to wriggle his fingers but they were wedged by stone. He tried to turn his neck but that too was viced under the avalanche.

Unable to rely on his machine spirit, Barsabbas closed his eyes to mentally recompose himself. He felt no pain, which meant he was still operational. Except for some minor internal bruising, his major organs and skeleton remained intact. The concussion in his head was already fading, and it seemed his armour sensed his stirring consciousness. Slowly, the armour's power plant roused from dormancy. Systems came online, one after another. His vision flashed, flickered and then became backlit by a luminous green as status updates scrolled across his helmet lens. The power plant would run on standby, slowly regenerating to full power, awaiting Barsabbas's command.

But Barsabbas simply opened his mouth and screamed in rage.

They were defeated. It had never happened before. Barsabbas found it difficult to comprehend.

The retreat on Govina against the tau had been just that: a retreat. It had been shameful, but it was nothing more than a blemish on what should have been an immeasurable history of warfare. But now Squad Besheba would gather no more history. Each warrior had been an invincible, terrifying warmonger. They were the horror stories that quelled unruly children. They were ruthless, clinically developed post-humans.

And now they were all dead.

This concept was something the Chirurgeons had not mentally processed him for. He felt dazed. He had fought Astartes before, both loyalist and renegade. He had repelled a boarding action against Imperial Fists; they had been linear and predictable, tactically sound but uncreative. The Salamanders had possessed heavy, static firepower, but had been susceptible to the Blood Gorgons' guerrilla doctrine. They had even skirmished with the Black Legion – Abaddon's own – over the spoils of a raid and escaped relatively unscathed.

His power armour stirred impatiently, the power-plant surging static into his earpiece. *Sargaul.*

Suddenly Barsabbas jolted. His bond. Where was his bond? Triggering the suit's sensors, Barsabbas attempted to log on to the squad link and search for life signs. His systems were badly damaged. No read-outs or tact-visuals. No squad link. The vox was grainy with static and he had no status monitors on his squad.

Where was Sargaul?

He did not feel the pain of separation experienced by the survivor of a broken bond. The death of a bond brought great mental and physical anguish, but he felt none. Sargaul was still alive, Barsabbas was sure of it.

Again his power armour growled, its power plant surging. The machine spirit of his suit was rousing him to action. He was an operational Traitor Marine. He needed to proceed to Ur, for that was his primary objective. Mental conditioning took over, stabilising his rationality despite the neuro-toxicity of depression and hopelessness. Everything else had become secondary. But first he needed to free himself.

Slowly, millimetre by millimetre, Barsabbas shifted his fingers. Calculating rest periods, it might take days to free himself, but he needed to proceed to Ur. Nothing would stop him while he still lived.

Muscles tensing, suit hydraulics coiling, Barsabbas began the long, agonising process of clawing his way through the avalanche of rock.

Mental conditioning was the cornerstone of an Astartes warrior. It was not their explosive strength, or the speed of their muscles. What made a Traitor Marine so terrifying a prospect was the conditioning of his mind.

These were the thoughts that Barsabbas focussed on as he worked his way upwards from his burial. Beneath the suffocating weight of multi-tonne rock, Barsabbas thought of nothing else. He remembered the tale of Bond-Sergeant Ulphrete who fell comatose after a shell-shot to the temple. For ninety-two years, he lay in a coma, unable to be coaxed into wakefulness. Unknown to his brethren, Ulphrete had been awake the entire time. He had simply been unable to control his body. There he lay, trapped inside his own unresponsive form. For almost a century, he was left to his own madness as respirators nurtured his physical frame. The claustrophobia devoured him. What thoughts did one keep to close one's eyes and simply think for one century?

After almost a century, the bond-sergeant finally broke from his coma. To the disbelief of all, Ulphrete had clear memory of the conversations the Chirurgeons had held while they had thought him paralysed and brain dead. He had been awake and he had not gone mad. The mental conditioning of an Astartes had steeled his mind.

For days, Barsabbas thought only of Ulphrete. Sensory deprivation for the first few days was bad. But then afterwards, he became accustomed to the kaleidoscopic scenes behind his eyelids and the utter lack of sound. He wriggled his way, easing out his fingers, creating room for his wrist, slowly pushing and shrugging his shoulders until finally he could move his entire right arm.

He did not know how long it took him. Two days perhaps? Seven? Barsabbas had no way of telling. Painfully, bit by bit, he clawed his way up and out.

Dragging his lower body free of the rockfall, Barsabbas stood up and stretched his limbs. The sensation of movement felt unnatural to him. Looking around, it took him some time to take in his surroundings. He stood atop the slope of an avalanche, the tunnel collapsed beneath crumbling sandstone. Above him, the upper tiers of the mines had fallen through, the rusting girders finally giving way. Patches of sunlight speared down from the remains of the mine shaft entry.

In the back of his head, Ur still called. Barsabbas knew, if circumstances so required, he could stop thinking altogether and his body would take him to Ur – such was the mental conditioning of the Astartes.

He retraced his steps, clawing his way up the shale slope. Enraged and despondent, the world became disjointed. He followed a trail left by the enemy, a spoor in the dirt. Something was leaking fluid, condensation from the damaged temperature control units of their power armour suit. It was unmistakable. Someone in damaged power armour had walked these same tracks.

Barsabbas followed.

His mind was a blank ocean of fury. Barsabbas's entire world became a thin stream of fluid leakage that he followed. Occasionally, he sniffed the air. He tasted the decaying stink of the Plague Marines. Chasing them like a desperate hound, Barsabbas pushed himself. He crawled on his knees up sand dunes and sprinted where the ground was flat. He was maddened and did not know where he was. He no longer cared. It only mattered that he followed the scent and trail.

When Barsabbas regained his senses he did not know how long he had been walking. The trail petered out, soaking into the sand. He found himself in a field of cenopods. The heat was fading from the day, and the burning light of the sequential twilights had begun, shading through white, red, orange and purple. If he looked to the dune crests behind him he could gauge the hours of remaining light. Already the dune faces were in shadow, the driftwood blue of canegrass contrasting with the sepia of the desert sands.

But he no longer needed light to guide his way. He could see boot prints in the sand, the unmistakable prints of steel-shod boots like small craters made by giant feet. The wind had barely disturbed them yet, tracing fine whorls into the griddled prints, which meant they were fresh.

* * *

Squad Shar-Kali did not receive. Squad Yuggoth did not receive. None of the squads responded. Only Squad Brigand made contact with a two-second signal. They were ambushed and dying.

Finally, Barsabbas blanked his vox-bead and consigned himself to its soft static. His vox-systems were far too heavily damaged, and even the armour's self-repair systems could only rewire the transmission to other non-damaged but already overloaded data fibres.

As far as Barsabbas knew, he was on his own.

CHAPTER NINE

Hepshah was a capricious one who did not fear the mon-keigh. He did not even fear the hulking war machines those mon-keigh called the Space Marines. No. Hepshah was too fast, too clever to ever feel the delight of an adrenal dump when confronting the hairy, ponderous anthropoids of humanity.

He certainly did not fear them now, as they ran from him. There was a shocking honesty to a human's terror that Hepshah found strangely endearing. When a man was pushed to the absolute limits of desperation, when the horror of death became impending, a human acted in comical ways. Arched eyebrows, gaping mouth, facial muscles contorted, limbs stiffening as they ran. Hepshah did not laugh often, but their fear was irresistibly amusing.

That was how he came to be hunting humans through the burning settlement, playing with them and extending his victims' misery to the heights of uncontrollable panic. Hepshah even held aloft his aperture, a crystalline shard prized amongst the kabal. Upon exposure to light the stone would record sounds and images, so that he could relive this day's festivities in luxury, much later.

He held up his aperture shard, panning it to record a clear panorama of the settlement. There was not much of the settlement left. The road train was upturned and twisted, its silver belly ruptured and spilling bloodied furniture. Its sacred engine was wisping with fire. The tents and lean-tos that cuddled around its protective girth had been flattened into the dirt. The settlement had been camped at the edge of a saltpan and many of the occupants had tried to flee across its basin. Their bodies still lay there now.

Hepshah made sure to catch images of the dead, focussing his warp-stone to record close-up shots of their slack faces. Here and there, amongst the livestock pens, rubble and caravans, survivors still hid. Hepshah caught glimpses of his fellow dark eldar hunting in the ruins. They were dark flashes, quick movements that seemed to elude a clear image.

Hepshah's victim suddenly ran across a caprid pen. He was hunched over and sprinting. His skin was dark and his woollen shawl was bright red. Hepshah had never seen the man before, but he had decided there and then that he was curious to see the man die by his hand.

Hepshah scuttled behind low rubble and ran parallel to the man. His indigo carapace was almost weightless and he easily outpaced the human with long, bouncing strides. As if sensing his danger, the human looked up. He was an older man, his skin prematurely aged by sun. He was crying, his thin shoulders bobbing in the supplicating way that seemed habitually human. Fire burned around him. The bodies of his kin poked out from beneath scattered furnishings and dismantled homes. Hepshah took a moment to savour the carnage.

Suddenly, the man sprinted in the opposite direction. Sensing an end to his pursuit, Hepshah armed his splinter pistol with one hand and held up his aperture for a clear recording. He fired. The splinter barb impacted against a wooden pen-post, punching a nail-sized hole through the wood. The man was still running, weaving between the narrow gap of two punctured train carriages. Laughing, Hepshah pursued.

He only ran five steps before something arrested his momentum hard. His thin neck whiplashed, his laughter choking in his throat, Hepshah's back slammed to the ground. He found himself looking up at a brown, monstrous face, a bovine snarl, branching antlers. A helmet, Hepshah realised.

The warrior towered over him, filling his aperture with images of dark armour, amour like bloodied earth pigment. 'This is my home, little creature. These lands belong to the lineage of the Blood Gorgons.'

Hepshah gave a shrill yelp of surprise. He never realised how tall and thickly built the mon-keigh could become. He had known Space Marines to be cumbersome flocks of tank-like infantry. Now he realised they were not.

As Hepshah struggled to regain his breath, the Chaos Space Marine gripped him firmly by the face, pinning his head with a delicate grip. His other hand darted, whisper quick, tapping him on the temple with a long mace. No more than a light double tap.

Hepshah stopped struggling. The dark eldar was no longer recognisable from the neck up. The encounter took just seconds and by the time Hepshah's body was discovered, Barsabbas was already gone.

Moribeth found Draaz hung from the rafters. She found Fhaisor and Amul-Teth reclining behind a bombed-out dust buggy. In the open, tossed amongst the debris, was a stove boiler that leaked blood. She did not open the coal hatch, but presumed it to contain the remains of Sabhira.

She did not feel fear – only indignity. Snarling, she stalked through the ruins. Occasionally she stopped to crack her whip meaningfully, with a belligerent pop. It was a declaratory snap and most knew to run when they heard it.

'You can't hide from me,' she sang.

She had always been the predator. Ever since her young maiden years, Moribeth had accompanied her cousins on slave raids. This was second nature to her. In her free hand, hidden behind her back, was a neural blade gifted to her by her kabal's mistress. The poison it secreted overloaded the pain nerves in living creatures. She pitied anything that crossed her path.

'Come out, come out,' she cooed.

'Here I am.' The voice sounded like slabs of rockcrete grinding together. A shadow fell across her.

Moribeth turned and her confidence dissipated. She slashed her neural whip low, but the tip snapped listlessly as it connected with ceramite.

With a speed that surprised her, the horned warrior slapped the top of her head with his palm. There was a pop as her spine compressed and vertebrae slipped out of joint. Moribeth died still believing herself a predator.

Vhaal, second-born son of Gil'Ghorad's Kabal, heard the death-screams of his fellows. They were loud, even though he was inside the road train's sealed interior. The sound rattled the iron walls, producing an eerie, acoustic vibration. In some parts, the train's ancient glass windows had been replaced by wooden frames with hand-painted paper awnings. The paper fluttered fitfully, the watercoloured scenery shaking ever so slightly.

Vhaal had been skinning trophies with a scalpel when he heard it, but the sound spooked him. Carefully he placed the scalpel on the floor and pulled a blanket over his project.

With a snap of his hands, wrist blades swung out from his vambraces like unfolding guillotines. He retrieved his splinter rifle, propped up against the iron carriage, and hopped down the short rungs. Outside he could see no signs of life. Not his father's soldiers, and certainly not plainsmen.

'Show yourself!' he commanded.

He knew something was out there. He began to fire his splinter rifle.

The gun's purr grew into a shrill whine as it spat a tight spread of toxic barbs. It threw up a line of powdered dirt to his front, knocking down the remains of a painted hand cart.

'Come and face me! I am second-born!' he howled.

Pride and familial name were things most fiercely venerated in his society. Vhaal imagined himself to look quite intimidating. Hooked armour curling on his skeletal frame, swing-blades creaking from his forearms, he was in the full regalia of a dark eldar raider. His hair was brought up into an oiled topknot, laced through with silver filigree and virgin sinew. He wore a cape of sewn skin fashionably off one shoulder, stitched together from the faces of vanquished foes. He was second-born of Gil'Ghorad.

'Face me!' Vhaal howled, raising his arms into the air in challenge.

A muzzle flashed in the distance. Low and muffled. The bolter's bark.

Vhaal, second son of the kabal, fell unceremoniously through a screen paper window, his feet stiffening awkwardly in the air. He was already dead before he landed, felled by a single shot.

Sindul hissed, baring his teeth. He crouched low on his haunches, his arms spread for balance, lacerator gloves rearing like coiled serpents.

The mon-keigh warrior appeared indifferent to his threats. He walked into and through the caprid fence that separated them, splintering the wood with his shins and thighs.

'Catch me to kill me!' Sindul spat. He leapt up against the sheer rock wall behind him, limbs splayed against the surface, and began to scarper up the vertical drop. He used his lacerator gloves, dragging the hooked claws of his fists for purchase. He shot up the wall like a rodent, scaling twelve metres in a matter of seconds before bounding backwards into the air.

A bolter round missed him as he leapt. He landed behind the mon-keigh, slashing his lacerators as he sailed overhead. But the horned warrior was faster than Sindul had estimated. It was a grave error. The mon-keigh spun with practiced fluidity, pouncing with all the weight and drive of a quarter-tonne primate. Sindul rolled aside, but not fast enough. The mon-keigh snagged him with its paw and dragged him to the ground by his ankles. Sindul tried to regain his gyroscopic balance, but his thin ankle was locked in a hammer grip of ceramite.

'I don't need to kill you yet,' growled the Traitor Marine as Sindul thrashed like a hooked fish.

Dragging his splinter pistol free from its chest holster, the dark eldar began to fire. The first shot hammered a toxic splinter into heavy chest plate. The mon-keigh dodged the second with a little dip of his head.

'Stop, now.'

With that, the mon-keigh backhanded him with steel-bound hands. Sindul's head snapped violently off to the right and he blacked out.

* * *

When the dark eldar came to, he began to curse in his sepulchral tongue.

He was bound, his wrists anchored by heavy chain that looped up to his neck and head. A muslin bag used to ferment milk curds was wrapped around his face and the chain tightened around it, biting into the flesh of his cheeks and forehead. The bag reeked strongly of sour, human smells that disturbed him.

When the captive tried to move, Barsabbas placed a boot on his chest. 'Tell me your name, darkling.'

The captive tried to writhe. Barsabbas stepped harder. The pressure elicited a mild curse from the struggling captive.

'I am Sindul,' he gasped as the air was pushed from his lungs.

Barsabbas knelt, peering closely at the dark eldar, studying the odd shapes of his insectoid carapace. Everything about the creature was alien, as if the angles and planes of his attire were beyond the conceptual design of a human mind. He did not belong on Hauts Bassiq.

'Why do you trespass, darkling?'

'I will not speak to you,' Sindul replied, his words muffled by the muslin.

'That is not your choice to make.'

'There are others,' Sindul began. 'There are more of us. We will come for you.'

'I've made them all dead, you know,' Barsabbas replied flatly. He stood up and walked to where a row of thin, frail corpses lay amidst the ash and charred earth. The carrion flies were already swarming over their glazed eyes and open mouths. 'I count fourteen. There are no more. Is that true?' Barsabbas asked.

The fact was confirmed by Sindul's silence.

Barsabbas walked back to his captive. 'You will talk,' he said. He released and slid open a hatch on his thigh plate, revealing half a dozen steel syringes, stacked like rocket pods.

Upon hearing the metallic click, Sindul began to laugh. 'You can try to torture me. But you are truly of diminished wit if you try,' the dark eldar declared in stilted Low Gothic. 'We relish pain.'

Barsabbas already knew this. The dark eldar species was entirely devoted to the cult of pleasure. Psychologically, they were nihilistic, pleasure-driven and irrational. Heightened sensations such as pain would only elevate them to a state of adrenal euphoria. For once, violence would yield nothing.

'Do your worst,' Sindul goaded, almost tauntingly.

Barsabbas extracted a syringe from its sheath. It was a barbarous thing, a pneumatic-gauge needle designed to punch through the thick skin of a Space Marine.

'This is tetrotoxillyn. An anaesthetic, a nerve-killing extract. My constitution inhibits the majority of chemicals from affecting my body. But this...' Barsabbas said, holding up the syringe. 'A dose of one-sixteenth is potent enough to serve as a local anaesthetic for a Space Marine. One quarter dose is enough to cause permanent paralysis in a young adult human.'

'We may not be robust in stature, but I assure you, we eldar are very chemically resilient,' Sindul retorted.

He was right, and Barsabbas knew this too. The dark eldar, despite their frail appearance, had a certain tolerance for toxins and chemicals, a tolerance built up through a dark culture of substance abuse. By his calculations, Barsabbas would need to quadruple the human dose.

Without warning, Barsabbas wrenched his captive up by the head, exposing his neck, and drilled the needle deep into the carotid artery. He injected a fractional dose, a mere droplet.

'This is an ion channel blocker. It is not meant for non-Astartes. It will stop your brain from receiving nerve signals. Can you feel numbness running down your spinal column? It will only be temporary but it signifies the early stages of nerve damage,' Barsabbas said.

Sindul screamed. He began to thrash, his legs windmilling for purchase as Barsabbas restrained him with a knee on his back.

'I could inject you with more. A triple dose and you may begin losing finger dexterity. I'm afraid that would be permanent.' Barsabbas placed the cold steel of the pneumatic needle against Sindul's neck. 'I ask you again – what are you doing here?'

His face pressed into the soupy clay and dung, the dark eldar finally relented. 'Collecting slaves. Nothing more,' Sindul spat.

Barsabbas detected the slightest tremor of panic in his voice, but also defiance. The dark eldar were a notoriously proud race and dignity meant more to them than death.

'There's so much more,' Barsabbas said, injecting him again. 'You are in league with the Death Guard.'

Sindul writhed in numb agony. Although the dose of anaesthetic was considerably less than a Space Marine's standard amount for field application, it was enough to cause him significant nerve trauma. Already Sindul's left arm had begun to twitch involuntarily.

'They allowed us here. They let us take the slaves.'

'Your reward was to plunder the land? Our land? What right have the Death Guard to reward you with property that was not theirs? These slaves are *our* slaves,' Barsabbas barked, withdrawing the needle.

'Mercy. Mercy. Do not inject me any more,' Sindul whimpered.

Barsabbas ignored him, his attention already drifting away from the pathetic thing writhing in his grasp. The notion that the capricious dark eldar raiders would ally with the Sons of Nurgle was monumental. It did not bode well for the Blood Gorgons. He would need answers. Almost carelessly, Barsabbas began to pump anaesthetic into his captive.

The dark eldar's pupils dilated with chemical shock.

'We are mercenaries, no more! We want nothing of the fight between you and your brethren.'

'Why are you here?' Barsabbas roared, suddenly forceful. The needle snapped. He unsheathed a new one.

Sindul shook his head. 'I can't...'

'If I overdose you, it will cause permanent muscular paralysis. You will not feel anything. You will not move anything. You will become a slab of meat. Imprisoned within your own body until you wither away.'

At this, Sindul began to howl, like an animal caged before slaughter.

That was no mere threat for a dark eldar. They were a long-lived race, and that could mean thousands of years, trapped within his own unresponsive body, unable to move or feel. During the Chirurgeon's initial experiments a slave subject had been induced into a paralytic coma for twenty-two years, unable to even open his eyes. The slave had gone mad, of course. But several thousand years of physical and visual deprivation...

A dark eldar could suffer no worse fate than that.

'We were paid by a person called Muhr.'

'Muhr? What does Muhr know of the Plague Marines?'

'I don't know. But they are allies, in league. They paid for the head of Gammadin, they needed a neutral third party to dispose of your Champion. That was us.'

Barsabbas considered injecting the entire tenfold dose into the creature then and there.

'*You* killed Gammadin? How could you kill Gammadin?' Barsabbas asked accusingly. He kicked the dark eldar dismissively, as if disgusted by his lie.

'Not I! Not I! The kabal disposed of him. I know nothing of that! I am only here to claim the kabal's reward. Slavery rights on Bassiq.'

'The right to harvest slaves from *our* territory? You slew Gammadin for that?' Barsabbas was possessed by sudden fury. He punched the needle into the dark eldar's wrist. Sindul would never again feel anything in his right hand. No pain, nor cold, nor heat or any sensation.

'That is my luchin hand! I will never ply my craft again!' shrieked the captive.

'And I will take your other hand for good measure,' Barsabbas stated calmly.

As his captive began to hyperventilate, almost choking in discomfort, Barsabbas sat down and began to think. Muhr, the dark eldar and a cult of Nurgle were in allegiance; they were somehow the source of strife on Hauts Bassiq.

'What did the dark eldar have to gain?'

'As I said. We took slaves. We are not a large kabal. We only sealed our part of the deal in disposing of Gammadin. Hauts Bassiq means nothing to us, except for raiding rights granted by the Plague Marines.'

'Rights. They have no rights.'

'They say Hauts Bassiq is their world.'

'You must have contact with them then. Where are they?'

'I don't know.'

'Where?' Barsabbas said. He approached Sindul and placed the cold steel of the syringe against the nape of his neck.

He felt Sindul's shoulders slump and his body sag in defeat. 'North. They are gathering for a great war to the north. The native mon-keigh prepare for war against the decaying ones.'

War. That was exactly what Barsabbas needed to hear. War meant the forces of Nurgle would amass. It was not much, but it was better than nothing.

'Good. You will take me there.' With that, Barsabbas hauled on his captive's neck chain, dragging him up like a disobedient dog. 'We go north.'

The shame of defeat was a heavy mantle and one that Barsabbas could not shake off. He stood in the heat but did not seek shelter. He did not deserve it. The discomfort reminded him of his mistake. Everything he did reminded him of his mistake.

The captive was staked down a distance away, under the shade of a lean-to, a blanket that was secured to a carriage window and pegged to the dirt. As much as Barsabbas would have preferred staking him out under the sun, for now he needed the creature alive. His leash chain was bound to a carriage wheel and his head was secured with yet more chain. Every so often, the captive tested his patience with whimpers of pain.

Barsabbas ignored the dark eldar's pleas and drew a long-distance voxsponder, a small, hand-cranked device, from a flak pouch on his waist. He only logged several words into the machine, for the micro-device could not hold much in its memory and the transmission had to travel far.

'The soldiery of Nurgle has taken Hauts Bassiq, and Muhr has sold us to them. Muhr has sold Bassiq to them. He has betrayed us.'

It was a simple message. There could be no mistaking it. Even in his desperate state, Barsabbas remembered to encrypt the message for Sabtah only. He could not be sure that any other Blood Gorgon could be trusted.

By nightfall, the tiny voxsponder had received a return transmission from the orbiting Chapter hulk. The distance it travelled had been great and interference had robbed the spoken message of much clarity. Through the garbled static, Barsabbas could make out the words.

'Return to dropsite. Return to Chapter. Immediate.'

The vox message had been sealed with Sabtah's personal decryption code.

Barsabbas stared at the voxsponder for a while before he crushed the device in his palm.

CHAPTER TEN

Behind the moon of Hauts Bassiq, the *Cauldron Born* remained a lurker, its leviathan bulk anchored behind the rock's spheric shadow. The hour was past end-night and the halls were still but for the tread of sentries. Night menials emerged to prepare the morning gruel and the ship's sleepless maintenance crews worked softly, but it did not dispel the quiet. All the blood brethren had retired for their nightly circadian rest, allowing their bodies to knit and heal for another day's training. All, except a few.

Sabtah awaited the reports of his deployment, poised with the apprehension of a predator in hiding. He knew the Dreadclaws had missed their dropsites by a wide margin. He knew the five squads had engaged enemy combatants: plague victims as the reports confirmed. But then he heard nothing. Sabtah began to fear the worst until Captain Hazareth requested his presence.

In one of the many exterior citadels that studded the ship's upper deck, Hazareth had taken charge of the foreship's amplified vox-transmitter. It was a frontier-grade machine, capable of burst transmissions to surrounding, intra-system receivers.

'We have a long-burst data receipt from Hauts Bassiq, Squad Besheba. It is coded urgent and encrypted to you only, Brother-Master,' Hazareth said, keying the console.

Sabtah ungloved his hand and placed his palm flat across the vox's mainframe panel. There was a compliant click as the vox-transmitter accepted Sabtah's genecode and began to unscramble the data burst.

'I will take my leave,' Hazareth said, bowing.

'No, captain. You can stay for this,' Sabtah said as he adjusted the volume dial on the transmitter. Trust was not much of a concept amongst Chaos Space Marines, for whom abrupt violence was an integral part of their warrior culture. But Sabtah knew Hazareth had principles. He was a soldier who would not fail his brethren.

There was a gurgle of audio, almost completely buried by interference. The *Cauldron Born* lay at high anchor ghosting the orbit of Hauts Bassiq, but the moon they hid behind was causing the transmission to lose clarity.

Sabtah adjusted the volume higher and played the message again. The vox squeaked with feedback.

'The soldiery of Nurgle has taken Hauts Bassiq, and Muhr has sold us to them. Muhr has sold Bassiq to them. He has betrayed us.'

Sabtah punched the metal casing of the trembling vox. He replayed the message, dissecting every word.

Captain Hazareth's face was dark and serious. 'I see why the witch has been so reluctant to deploy on Hauts Bassiq. He has some stake there.'

Sabtah ran a hand through his beard, his eyes closed. He breathed deeply before opening them again. 'Transmit a message back to Bassiq and all units. Tell them to withdraw immediately with all squads. We need more answers.'

Hazareth began to key the sequence from receiving to transmit. He looked up from his work, the sharp quills on his scalp bristling with anger. 'Give me the honour of removing Muhr from our Chapter,' Hazareth growled.

'No.' Sabtah shook his head. 'If we kill Muhr now, there will be intra-Chapter war. I can't allow that to occur under my wardship.'

'Then we will watch him,' Hazareth countered immediately. 'Let me activate Squad Murgash. They are old and will not fail you.'

'Make sure they do not. I always knew those witches were of coward's blood. They are not bonded,' Sabtah said. 'That makes strangers out of them. I'd sooner put my life in the hands of the devious sons of Alpharius than call a witch my brother.'

Sabtah locked the doors to his citadel. He shut the double gates of his interior courtyard and posted a double sentry of black turbans outside them. The blast shutters to his central tower and barracks were thrust into emergency lockdown. Finally, the interior wheel locks were turned, sealing the entrance to Sabtah's bed chambers behind eighty centimetres of psy-dampening plasteel.

Only then did Sabtah listen to the captured transmission.

The transmission from the atmospheric vox-caster was soft and cut with static. Words were clipped, stilted and stuttering, but the gravity of their accusations and the stern deliverance of Bond-Brother Barsabbas was not lost over distance.

'The soldiery of Nurgle has taken Hauts Bassiq, and Muhr has sold us to them. Muhr has sold Bassiq to them. He has betrayed us.'

Sabtah reclined in his throne, resting his back against the solid interior of his power armour and bracing his chin between the fork of his fingers. He thought deeply of Bond-Brother Barsabbas's accusations. It did not surprise him that Hauts Bassiq was the target of foreign conquest. It was a mineral-lush planet and had once been an Imperial mining colony. So close to the Eye, it could serve as a strategic staging post for the first major leg of any campaign, if one were so inclined. The Blood Gorgons had always preferred the freedom of nomadic flight and had never seen the utility of devoting so much infrastructure to the extraction of earthbound resources. But it made sense to Sabtah.

Despite the blunt clarity of Bond-Brother Barsabbas's intelligence, Sabtah could not act hastily. Any provocation of Muhr and his small yet influential faction could spark the tinders of a second Chapter war. The memories of the first fratricidal conflict had faded but never dimmed for Sabtah. He had executed eight of his own brethren in that dark period and still bore the millennia-old scars across his abdomen. He had no wish to fight through another.

Muhr was a cunning creature, and if Sabtah were to confront him, he would need to pick his time judiciously.

Sabtah's ruminations were interrupted. The abrasive howl of a breach siren and the rhythmic pounding of tripwire alarms jolted him. He leapt from his oaken throne and crouched low without thinking. Simultaneously, the phos-lanterns winked out with a crackling hiss of electricity.

The room was dark, but he could still hear the crashing pounding of his alarms. Slipping his war-helm over his face, Sabtah loaded his bolter's underslung flamer with a gilded canister from his oiled leather belt. The world lit up a lambent green behind his visor, his flamer held out before him, like looking through the vision-slit of a tank turret. Beyond his field of vision, pitch-black shadows leaned out across the room like lunging spectres.

Sabtah erased the transmission from the atmospheric caster with a squeal of the turn dial. He slapped a side-mounted magazine into his bolter, made sure the transmission had been cleared, and rose from his seat.

Raising the muzzle of his underslung flamer, Sabtah released the blast seal to his bed chambers. The lighting in the wide, steel corridor outside had been cut. Emergency glo-strips flickered weakly along the mesh decking.

As was his practice, Sabtah hollered for his guard hounds. They were each three hundred kilos of vat-brewed muscle, a mutant species of the bearded crocodilian. Aggressive and unseeing, the guard hounds always answered his calls dutifully but now there was no sign of them.

Edging slowly down the corridor, Sabtah tried to remember the basic foot patterns of silent movement. It had been many thousands of years since he had practised the steps as a neophyte but the neural programming came back to him. Sinking his weight with each step, Sabtah crept softly, although he had not felt the need for stealth in many centuries. As a champion of the Chapter, he could usually afford the luxury of charging from the fore, gladius in one hand and combi-bolter in the other.

But there was an unsettling darkness and quiet that warranted a vigilant approach.

Sabtah swept quickly through the crumbling ruins of his tower's lower levels. Over the years, the plunder and loot of his many campaigns had lain forgotten in his dominion. The hilts of swords and gilded treasures peered from between the cloth-like sheets of spider webs and dust. He swung his weapon at each corner, hunting furtively through the statues and stacked chests for a target.

Sabtah swept out into the interior courtyard. He could smell blood and entrails. His suspicions were confirmed when he saw his gutted sentries, quite dead and sprawled in his garden.

There was a soft ping from his MKII suit's internal auspex.

Sabtah looked up reactively. He spied a large, imposing figure scaling a ceiling cable. It was already disappearing into the smoking, gaseous heights of the *Cauldron Born's* upper ceiling shafts. Guide lights reflecting off the overhead network of pipes turned the deck's upper reaches into an interior atmosphere of smoke clouds and electric stars. Squinting upwards, Sabtah fired a ranging shot with his bolter as the figure was winched up. He fired again, but the figure scrambled onto a nearby gas main and disappeared into a canopy of steam hoses and cables.

Sabtah scanned the courtyard. One of his bearded croc-hounds lay on its side. They had cut the reptile by its throat flaps. One of its clawed hind feet still twitched spasmodically.

His pet's eyes had been cut out and its tongue severed from its gaping maw. The symbolism of the croc-hound's death was not lost on Sabtah. He knew what it meant. The intruders had tried to breach his citadel again but failed, and this time had chosen to leave him a warning.

Sabtah realised Muhr and his patron knew. He did not have time on his side.

On the horizon of Bassiq, an undulating red plain broken only by occasional boab trees, two figures could be seen. They plodded, slowly and methodically, but forwards, always forwards. One was big and broad. Trailing behind, lashed by a chain, dragged almost on all fours, came a smaller figure bent double. A Blood Gorgon and his dark eldar.

They went north, following the multiple dawns and sunsets on the horizon, always northwards. For five full days Barsabbas walked, leading his captive.

The interior of the central plains was a vast, empty space of bushland and drying river beds where the pockets of wildlife slowly withered to meet the dune systems of the north, the largest longitudinal dune systems on the continent.

The earth had a higher ferric content here, coloured a deep red. Here and there, slivers of water boiled on silty tracts of old waterways. Dunaliella algae lent the lakes a pinkish hue. Barsabbas knew the plainsmen would eat the fish that were preserved in the salt on the river beds, but how he came to know, he could not remember.

Barsabbas and his captive did not talk. They simply plodded along as Sindul pointed the way.

The heat was shocking. Even sealed up in the climate vacuum of his armour, Barsabbas could feel the prickly heat. He made sure to stop and water his captive regularly. When Sindul collapsed from exhaustion, Barsabbas simply draped him across one arm. The dark eldar weighed little more than his bolter.

They did not stop walking, even during the short nights. Barsabbas needed no rest. Inquisitive predators stalked them, but none dared attack.

Soon the land became indistinct and the days merged into one. No matter where he looked, the land stretched outwards and onwards, disappearing eventually into a flat, featureless line. Even the low mountains and dunal corridors that bobbed on the horizon became a regular, rhythmic occurrence, a steady flatness interspersed by humps like the predictable graph of his suit's heart monitor.

Occasionally, in the distance, Barsabbas would spot the silhouette of a lonely wanderer. He knew those to be the dead. No plainsmen would ever be so foolish as to brave the climate alone. Sometimes he encountered larger flocks, but a signal flare in the opposite direction would send the dead sprinting towards the brightness in the sky.

Finally, as they left the interior behind them, Barsabbas heard the bray of war horns. He hoped the battle was nearby.

Chief Gumede sounded the war horn, rousing his small kinship from their high-noon rest. 'Small' was perhaps an inappropriate term, but Gumede had always considered his family a modestly-sized yet intimate gathering.

Already, the caravan trains were being warmed, the ancient gas engines grumbling as shamans began to rouse the old gears and goad the arthritic pistons to life. At least fifty of Gumede's kin were rising from their makeshift beds under the shade of the wagons and carriages. Another thirty were spreading down to the creek to wash their faces and rinse the sand from their mouths. Outriders, having already mounted their giant bipedal birds, were racing impatiently as the kinship prepared to mount up and move.

Gumede blew his brass war horn again. Although the horn itself had once been the steam valve of a gas engine, it represented his seniority within the kinship. He was the patriarch and his family looked to him for guidance. He was young for such a role, but he was tall and well made and he had a presence that he carried easily with his height and stature.

Amongst the short, wiry plainsmen, Gumede was an imposing figure with a thick neck and a narrow, athletic waist. The kinship had never questioned his leadership, nor his father's before him. Gumede came from a direct lineage of elders, and wisdom was considered his birthright.

Perhaps it would have been safer to flee southwards, away from the troubles. Already the skies to the north had darkened visibly and the horizon appeared as a sick rind of black that settled along the furthest ridges. It would have been safer to travel south, hugging the dust coast, but Gumede knew that it would not be right.

Other kinships were travelling north too. A war host was gathering to repel the spreading evil. They had all heard the echoes of drums and horns and read the plumes of smoke signals from nearby kinships. It was a muster call.

They did not know what evil it was. The simple-minded claimed them to be ghosts, but then again, all disturbances were blamed on restless spirits. Others, more astute, remembered the days of raiders who came from the skies. Gumede was not certain, but he felt compelled to act. It was clear the plainsmen were gathering on the Seamless Plains, the great dividing range that separated the interior from the Northern Reaches. Thousands had already gathered there, to confront the 'evil' with hatchets and shamanic superstition. Now his family would join them.

Gumede had barely saddled his talon squall before his riders came to fetch him.

'Chief! Chief!' they cried, sprinting across the hot sand on their lurching, thudding birds. His braves were in full war regalia. Their red shukas were decorated with squall feathers, braided hair and brooches. Some preferred breastplates of latticed bark while others preferred salvaged tin. They all balanced recurved bows across their saddles and brandished hatchets over-head. Many brandished las-weapons, traded from distant Ur.

'The Godspawn has come! Quickly, see this!' cried Tanbei, riding at the fore.

Gumede had heard that the Northern Kinships in desperation had summoned the ancestral Godspawn. But he had not believed it. He had not wanted to give himself false hope. But now he was overwhelmed.

'Truly?' asked Gumede, his heart suddenly racing.

But Tanbei had no reason to lie. His face was flushed from a mixture of excitement and awe. 'He comes! He comes!' he shouted.

The commotion stirred the kinship. Children emerged from their household carriages and wagons, throwing aside blankets and creeping out from hiding places. Women and men paused from their task of packing, craning their necks curiously.

'Tanbei.' Gumede's quiet tone commanded silence. 'The Godspawn, Tanbei? Where?'

The young rider reined his bird to a sharp halt, almost startling Gumede's own mount from his hands. Tanbei turned in his saddle and jabbed his finger to the high dunes beyond. Sure enough, Gumede could see a figure cresting the dune spines. Even at a great distance, Gumede could tell that the figure was large, with a long stride that was as sure and as steady as a rising dust tide.

Gumede hurriedly tightened his saddle and vaulted atop his bird. 'Prepare offerings!' he shouted, his tone rising with excitement. 'Gather the shamans! Spread the word to the tribe!'

Wheeling his bird around, Gumede led his flight of outriders to greet the Godspawn.

When the Godspawn came to Gumede's kinship, it was as if the war had been forgotten. All the people gathered in nervous clusters around the road train. They were keen to catch a glimpse but afraid of what they might see. They huddled closely, jostling to be in the middle.

He came to their camp, escorted by Gumede's outriders.

The warrior was so big that a hush fell over the kinship as he approached. The people actually shivered. He resembled a mountain, his armour craggy and pitted, from the solid base of his boots to the sloping swell of his shoulders, all the way up to the branching antlers of his head. Although he was a Godspawn, his armour was not at all like the bright red of their shukas. It was the colour of ferric earth after hard rain – a muddy, burnt orange. Radiant with martial aggression, he appeared to them as an angry golem that had been birthed from a rock womb.

Almost as an afterthought, he dragged a blackened, stick-like captive on a leash. The beast was bound in layers of chain and could barely stand upright.

'I am Barsabbas,' he said. 'The Blood Gorgons have answered your summons.' His first words, loud and metallic, startled the children. But they didn't cry. No one dared to disturb the resonance of his declaration.

Half a dozen shamans, all of them elders of venerable years, hesitantly came forwards. They sacrificed a caprid for him, draining its neck of blood. Another began to pray to him, falling to his knees and touching his forehead to the hot sand.

'My kin are honoured to receive you, Koag Barsabbas,' said Gumede. He rode until he was side on with Barsabbas, reining in his mount a respectful distance away. Tall as Gumede was, and mounted on his talon, Gumede was still barely on eye level with the visitor.

'I've come to find your war. Where is it?' asked the Blood Gorgon. His words were clipped and impatient.

'Over there, beyond those mountains,' Gumede replied. 'You have come to lead our crusade to drive back the evil?' he asked, his face openly honest with hope.

Barsabbas snorted. 'I can lead a mount to a watering hole, but I cannot force it to drink. If you do not want to fight, then I cannot force you to fight well.'

'We are willing,' Gumede replied. 'Many of the kinships of the south and central territories are gathering beyond the Seamless Plains. It is an army that will rid the land of the evil and dead. Can you lead us, great koag?' Gumede asked.

'I will,' answered Barsabbas.

At his words, the kinship erupted into jubilance. The tense mobs dispersed, as if their battle had already been won. Some sprinted down to the creeks to dance in the water or scaled the road train to scream relief to the skies. Those more daring encircled the Blood Gorgon, thrusting offerings towards him – bead quilts, necklaces, empty tins with exotic off-world labels. The shamans cavorted, clapping hand cymbals and tiny percussion drums. All the while, Barsabbas stood immobile amongst them, unable to comprehend their behaviour.

Barsabbas felt nothing towards these people. They were genestock, they were slavestock. In truth, he loathed them for their ignorance and their dependency. As the plainsmen groped his armour, tapping him for luck and trying to push votive offerings into his hands, Barsabbas curtailed his urge to strike out.

He knew they would all die. He held no illusions about the outcome of a battle between bow-armed plainsmen and Plague Marines of Nurgle. But he could not conceive of a better diversion to allow him to infiltrate into the northern territories. With the war host on the march, Barsabbas would be free to head north, ever deeper into the enemy territory.

They were all expendable if Barsabbas could find Sargaul. He would need them to take him into the deep north. Alone he might fail, but with a mighty war host as a diversion...

That night, Barsabbas dreamed of Sargaul. A Chaos Space Marine did not often dream. Rather, their catalepsean nodes placed them in a state whereby the resting portions of their brain relived memories throughout the day. Memories of drill, memories of field tactics, memories of war.

Decades or centuries of memory that would otherwise be forgotten in the sieve of a human mind.

But that night, Barsabbas dreamed. He dreamed that he visited Sargaul. His blood bond was tinkering with the wreckage of a Rhino armoured carrier. The desert plains stretched out on every side and the tank was beached in the centre, its paint scorched to cracking by the sun.

Sargaul was muttering softly to himself as he worked on the broken tank. But as Barsabbas approached he saw that there was nothing to fix. The tank was an empty, burnt out shell.

'Brother, what are you doing?' Barsabbas asked as he drew close.

Sargaul looked at him but did not seem to recognise his battle-brother. He started vacantly at Barsabbas before turning his attention back to the wreckage, muttering ceaselessly.

Barsabbas knew his brother was lost. Sargaul was tapping away at a crumpled panel of plating with a tiny work hammer, utterly focused on the task.

'Brother, where are you going?'

At this Sargaul drowsily raised his hand and pointed to the north without even looking at him. Far away, hazed by the glare of background suns, Ur shone on the horizon.

For a while, Barsabbas attempted to speak to Sargaul, but his bond did not acknowledge him. It was almost as if he did not exist. Only when that seed of doubt was nurtured in Barsabbas's mind, did he think it a dream.

He awoke then.

The final sunset was two hours away when Gumede began the final preparations for departure. The arrival of a Godspawn had been an unexpected delay and the temperamental gas engines of the road train had to be refired. Despite this, he believed the Godspawn was a good portent. As the last of the kinship tied their possessions to the roof and side racks of the convoy, Gumede needed only one more thing before he was ready.

He took from his carriage rack a lasrifle. It was an heirloom, handed down between the elders of the kinship. The gun had always belonged to the family and none knew its precise origins. Some cousins claimed it had been simply traded for two dozen caprid from the city of Ur by a long-lost uncle. But Gumede had also been told by an aunt that it had been given to them by missionaries of the *eagle-headed faith*. Those missionaries did not come to their land any more, but the cells that powered the weapon continued to be recharged by the solar heat of their many suns, even after so many centuries. The use of the lasrifle was a rare skill and something that Gumede had learned from an early age.

He wiped the rifle's metal exterior with a cloth and slotted a rectangular cell into its housing. He chanted a mantra and dialled up the weapon's charge. It hummed softly. He thumbed the well-worn slide down to idle.

'I am ready,' he said to himself. Climbing atop his bird with slow deliberation, he made one last survey of his convoy and began to ride.

CHAPTER ELEVEN

It was just a rumour, but Sufjan had learned to take rumours very seriously.

Sufjan Carbo had earned his black turban by keeping a clear head and open ears. Being a slave to the Traitor Marines was usually a short and very brutal existence, but there were those such as he who had learned to thrive in such volatile environments. Men like him had learned to listen and glean every scrap of information to survive. Everything on the *Cauldron Born* happened for a reason, and everything that happened had consequences, even for the lowliest slave.

Things had not always been this way. Sufjan Carbo had been a janitorial factotum for a district scholam. His life had involved distilling the right combination of bleach and water for the cork floors and tightening the scholam's faulty plumbing. Such things were a fading memory. He had come to accept life as a volatile thing, from the moment they took him away from his world, to the dangers of life as an expendable servant of the Chaos powers.

And things, he had learned, had become very volatile lately.

There were rumours amongst galley slaves and the warp engine crews that rival factions were on the verge of intra-Chapter war. The slaves were scared, even more so than usual. They walked timidly, keeping their eyes down, hoping to avoid the attention of their Blood Gorgon masters. Some saw the strife as a good thing, as an opportunity, perhaps, for liberation. But Sufjan knew that nothing good would arise out of it.

If the Chapter were to go to war with itself, the slaves would be the first to suffer.

Sufjan did not intend to suffer. He had earned a trusted position standing sentry outside a little-used staircase from strata 23/c that led to the upper spines of the ship. His familiar staircase 23/c, with its rusty spiral stairwell and the globe-lamp larvae that hung in small, grape-like clusters. Compared to other slaves, his job was simple: to keep order amongst the menials and lower caste servants. In doing so, he earned a double ration of protein strands and a billet in the guard barracks. It was not something he intended to relinquish easily.

The vacuum hiss of blast shutters opening woke Sufjan from his fretting. Suddenly he felt nervous, as he fussed over his orange silks and began to buff the brass etchings on his breastplate. Although the Blood Gorgons were piratical by nature, they enforced uniform infractions amongst the black turbans with a heavy hand.

Thudding footfalls echoed down the corridor. Sufjan bladed his shoulders and stood to attention. His horse-headed halberd was angled in salute, planted forty-five degrees out from his upcurled boot toes.

'None may pass…' Sufjan began to say.

The Blood Gorgon's shadow fell across him. It was Sabtah the Older. The slaves knew him as the *old brown wolf*. Sabtah was followed by a squad of Blood Gorgons that Sufjan did not recognise. They were heavily armed, unusually so. Perhaps the rumours were true.

'Step aside,' Sabtah said in a weary, almost languid tone.

Fighting against his sense of self preservation, Sufjan remained at attention in front of staircase 23/c. 'My apologies, master… but Master Muhr has ordered me to refuse entry at this time.'

'I am countermanding those orders. Step aside.'

Sufjan felt the prick of sweat on his scalp. Master Muhr had been very specific in his instructions that no black turbans were permitted to allow access for anyone to his spire chambers. It had seemed straightforward at the time, but Sufjan had not expected this.

'Master Muhr was very specific,' Sufjan said timidly.

'Why are you even looking at me?' Sabtah asked, his voice remaining even.

Sufjan dropped his gaze to the floor. He realised he was trembling. In his mind, he tried to weigh up the danger of disobeying Master Muhr with the danger of antagonising Master Sabtah, but he could not think properly. All he could think about was the calibre of a boltgun. Zero point seven five. It filled his mind like a void.

'Master Muhr does not wish to be disturbed,' Sufjan murmured into his chest.

'I will kill you, then,' Sabtah said, his hand shooting out to clamp Sufjan's throat. 'Hold still, you won't feel it.'

'No, master, please!'

The bolt pistol swung down to his forehead like an executioner's axe. Cold steel pressed against his skin. He heard the round being chambered. It vibrated through his skull with finality.

'I know things! I've heard things!' Sufjan screamed, his words overlapping each other.

The gun wavered.

'What do you know, slave?'

Sufjan felt weak. He leaned against his halberd for support, his rigid salute collapsing as fear shook his body. 'Muhr, he talks. Other slaves can hear it in the air vents from corridor 25/Upperlevel-32 and in the lavatories of the guard barracks if the warp echo is strong.'

Sabtah seemed interested. He smiled, a flash of curved fangs parting his beard. 'More.'

'Muhr talks constantly with someone he calls *Overlord*. He wishes to merge the Blood Gorgons with his new master. That's all we know!'

Sabtah seemed to ponder that. His eyes took on a glazed, distant look. But his grip on Sufjan's throat did not loosen and the boltpistol did not waver.

'Slaves heard this?' he said finally.

'I am sure,' Sufjan croaked. 'They listen. Not me personally. But others do.'

Sabtah unlatched his grip from Sufjan's throat. He smoothed the slave's collar with a delicate finger. 'That may be so. But we can't have eavesdropping slaves. You understand?'

The boltpistol clinked. It was the firing pin. Sufjan had never fired a gun before, but somehow he knew it was the firing pin.

The blast shutters that sealed off Muhr's sanctuary were barred from the inside. Behind Sabtah, the six Blood Gorgons of Squad Pharol wedged their wide shoulders into the cold, wet corridor.

'Sergeant Orchus,' Sabtah said, turning to the squad. 'Breach this door.'

Orchus lumbered his way to the front. 'Milord,' he said, patting his power maul against his palm. The weapon's energy field activated with a crackle of compressed oxygen. The corridor's stale air was cut with the smell of ozone.

Hauling back for a wide backhand, Orchus collided his power maul into the blast shutter. The boarding weapon sank through with a liquid *pop*. Bubbles of molten metal boiled to the surface as the power maul was torn from the shutter. It peeled away a long strip of armoured door, leaving it to slough off like a wilting petal. Orchus struck again, throwing his hips and torso into the swing. Again and again. Droplets of liquefied steel flew.

'That's enough, sergeant,' Sabtah said as the solid steel became doughy, melting in puddles across the decking.

The group entered Muhr's sanctuary proper. They pushed on in a tight formation into Muhr's laboratories. There, the walls were peeling, the cracked paint revealing cryptic designs underneath. Slab-like operating tables lined the wide hall. When Sabtah looked closely, he could see the tables were scarred with irregular human tooth marks. The witch conducted many of his live experiments here, and the pain of his victims had driven them mad.

Four black turbans, unaware of the squad's identity, charged out from behind amniotic tanks and curing shelves with their halberds raised. They realised their mistake too late. Sabtah and his retinue shot them down before they could protest.

Others appeared on the mezzanine steps. Sabtah could not tell whether they were menial servants or armed guards. It did not matter. They shot them all down, chopping down the silhouettes until none appeared above the banisters. The squad stormed up into the unlit upper levels, moving by the muted shades of night vision.

They found Muhr in the upper tip of his tower, a conical chamber with a thin, fluted ceiling. He was stooped over his mirror, his hair matting his face and trailing to the ground like a torn shawl. He stood up quickly, forcefully.

'What is this?' he shrieked.

His outburst stopped even Sabtah in mid-sprint. Muhr had changed. He was unarmoured, but somehow he looked larger. Muhr had always been pallid and thin compared to the others, but now he looked distended, as if his bones, like his nails, had been painfully lengthened.

'Muhr. We have come to detain you,' Sabtah announced from behind the barrel of his bolt pistol.

Muhr laughed aloud. 'On what grounds?'

Sabtah's tone was expressionless. 'You are a traitor, Muhr. Hauts Bassiq, Gammadin's death, it was all your doing, witch. You sold us to Nurgle.'

'I accuse you of the same!' Muhr retorted, his voice rising. 'As do my brothers in arms.'

Above them, high amongst the viewing balconies, warriors of Squad Agamon and two Chirurgeons of Fourth and Ninth Company emerged. They were resting with their boltguns against the balustrade. Sabtah found himself staring into the barrel of Squad Agamon's autocannon from a second-storey knuckle balcony.

'Brother-Sergeant Phistos. Lower your weapons. I am your superior,' Sabtah commanded. His voice was calm, but inside he seethed. Sabtah knew Phistos as a promising young prospect, a ruthless raider with many years of service to the Chapter. But now he had been led astray by Muhr's promises of change and power, as Sabtah had always feared. The Blood Gorgons were already straining under the first cracks of intra-Chapter war.

Phistos of Agamon hesitated at Sabtah's command. His barrel dipped. 'Weapons trained!' Muhr shouted. 'He is the traitor! Detain him.'

Sabtah knew it was an empty charge, a counter-accusation simply to buy Muhr time.

Muhr knew he had been caught and he was desperate, cornered and crazed. Behind Sabtah, Squad Pharol's guns did not stray from Muhr. Optic scopes chimed and auspexes pinged with feedback as they refused to lock on. To prevent friendly fire in the tight confines of a boarding action, their bolters' machine spirits had been forged to seize up when targeting Blood Gorgon power armour.

There was a brief moment of stillness. The squads were locked, both unable to act, their weapons trained on one another.

Sabtah thought about finishing it. He could kill him now, execute him and be done with it. But such an act would open the floodgates of utter chaos. Muhr's factional supporters would grow uneasy – there would be repercussions. Those rogues who harboured their own ambitions would fear for their own safety. Above all, Sabtah would be viewed as an indiscriminate tyrant. They would never accept him as a rightful Champion. The fabric of Blood Gorgon unity would erode through mistrust and paranoia. Brother would turn against brother, blood bond against blood bond. It would force history to repeat, and that was what Sabtah feared the most.

'All squads, lower your weapons,' Sabtah said quietly. Both squads continued to threaten each other with their guns. 'Now!' Sabtah warned, spiking his vox with amplitude. Once the squads cowled their weapons, he approached Muhr with open palms.

'This can only be resolved by invocation.'

Muhr bared his teeth. 'You dare rouse Yetsugei for this?'

'Why, are you frightened of judgement? The Prince sees all,' Sabtah snorted.

Muhr licked his lips with a serpentine tongue. 'Then we will summon him. The one who survives judgment will stand as ward of this Chapter.'

'You should be dead, Muhr,' Sabtah spat. 'By all rights you should be dead. I should kill you. Now the Prince will have that honour.'

'We shall see, Sabtah. We shall see.'

The warp. The warp was no place to walk barefoot.

There, the sky was constantly expanding, allowing him to glimpse overlapping time loops of the universe's ending. The land curved away from him, never-ending. Crushed stone bit his soles. He could see a citadel. Its towers and parapets sat atop the shell of a turtle like a hive stack. The turtle was ponderous, marching tirelessly across the horizon. How large was it? A thousand kilometres long? Perhaps a million? With each lethargic step, it levelled mountains and bevelled cliffs into biting, crushed stone shards. The scale was hypnotic.

Muhr knew he was dreaming. He was dressed in a cloak of black velvet, but nothing else. At his hip was a sword he did not remember owning.

Sabtah's threats still rang in his ears. Muhr had been thinking about them before he drifted into his psy-trance. Now, even as his spirit waded through the warp, the troubles of the physical world followed him.

He knelt down to pick up a flint. It crumbled at his touch, exploding into powder as if age had stolen its integrity. Muhr stood up quickly, his black cloak snapping. The simple movement caused a rippling wind that puffed a stand of dry, leafless trees into ash. Everything in this world was dead, preserved only by tranquillity.

'Welcome to my home,' said a hollow voice. 'It is as much yours as it is mine.'

'Opsarus! My Overlord!' Muhr gasped. He fell to his knees, pressing his forehead to the powdered stone.

Opsarus appeared to him as old as the world itself. His power armour had a petrified, granular texture, as if a mantle of minerals had risen from the ground to streak it with opaline, jade and sickly lime and white. Its surface was studded with bolts, weeping with rust. Looming over Muhr, Opsarus was a rising ocean wreckage, dragged from the bottom of a powerful sea.

'Get up, Muhr. Act like my lieutenant for once.' The turbines of Opsarus's power pack whirred with a rhythmic hum, constant and powerful. His face was a deathmask of sculpted turquoise, its moulded features noble, almost angelic in bearing and set in the middle of his hulking shoulders. When he spoke, the voice that issued through the metal lips was garbled and distorted.

Muhr got up quickly. 'Why do you bring me here, Overlord?' he asked.

'Be quiet, sorcerer. Listen first, then ask questions,' Opsarus snapped impatiently. 'Too much talking, that's your failing, sorcerer.'

Muhr lowered his head.

'Sabtah seeks to invoke Yetsugei to reveal your true ambitions?' Opsarus chuckled.

Muhr nodded.

Opsarus chuckled again. 'And you are frightened? Yes?'

'Of course, lord. Yetsugei sees all, and the Chapter will listen to the daemon's words. They will discover the truth. It will lay bare our plans.'

'Yetsugei is a jester. A king among men, but a fool among daemonkind.'

'Yet the Chapter heed his words. They will know.'

'Another failing of your Chapter and your gene-seed, sorcerer.'

The words stung, but Muhr knew it was the truth. The Blood Gorgons lacked the favour of the gods. While Opsarus could invoke the power of the Great Unclean One, the Blood Gorgons were left to grovel to some petty daemon prince. It reminded him of their inferiority.

'What can we do, Overlord?'

'All part of the plan,' Opsarus said, laying a hand on Muhr's head. 'I have known this for some time.'

'I'm sure, Overlord. Your wisdom has never led me astray.'

'Take this.'

Opsarus pressed a small, hard object into Muhr's palm. It was a crystal. Unremarkable and entirely mundane. Yet when Muhr peered closer, he saw a scintilla of movement within. When he squinted, Muhr could see a peculiar little thing – a tiny figure was trapped in the fragment. Sure enough, the creature moved again, dancing and prancing inside the crystal. Although Muhr could not see the microscopic expression of the creature inside, there was a malevolence that exuded from it. Muhr was sure the thing was sneering at him.

'Thank you, Overlord. What do you–'

Opsarus cut him off. 'Listen first, Muhr, then questions. Use this shard to disrupt the summoning. Cast it into the wards as you invoke. It will release the daemon within. Yetsugei will not heed the call.'

'Overlord...'

Opsarus turned away. 'Leave.'

Muhr blinked and felt his consciousness resettle in the physical plane. When he opened his eyes, he was in his tower again, surrounded by the familiar pipes and boilers of his laboratory. He rubbed his eyes blearily. As he did so, he realised he clutched something in his palm.

He opened his hand slowly. There, cradled by the folds of his flesh, was a crystal shard.

CHAPTER TWELVE

The plainsmen took Barsabbas northwards. They left the lowlands to spread out behind them, heading towards the darkening skies and the ruins of the deserted north. Soft sand gave way to a barren, rocky topography. The planet's surface here was scoured dry.

The great muster of kinships was spread beneath the shadow of dormant volcanoes, a range of mountains they called the Weeping Sisters. Acres of tents and shade awnings surrounded the basking silver snakes of various road trains. In the dunes north of the encampment, a kilometre-long stockade of wagons had been drawn up to protect the exposed flank. What few firearms the plainsmen possessed were there, facing the enemy. Flocks of outriders on their birds roamed there, patrolling up into the mountains themselves to crow's-nest the region.

They spotted Barsabbas and his convoy winding their way through the narrow mountain shoulders. A dozen riders were dispatched to meet them. Together they rode down into the encampment.

Barsabbas counted the numbers with a cursory auspex sweep. He calculated the readout in his head, subtracting an estimation of non-combatant families and livestock signatures. The total, even with a generous estimate, would be no more than twenty thousand fighters. It was a gathering of road trains, women and children. A mass exodus, not an army.

He had hoped for more. Twenty thousand men would amount to little more than a speed bump against a well-drilled company of Chaos Space

Marines. He needed the plainsmen to occupy the enemy in order for him to infiltrate unnoticed into the deep north. But they would have to do. He would adapt.

The road train pulled to a steaming halt. Barsabbas alighted from the road train's cab, dark eldar in tow. Outriders had ridden in advance to bring news of his arrival. Plainsmen rose to meet him, jostling crowds in bright red shukas. They chanted his name. Children spilled from their parents' tents, eager to claim first sight of the Red God. Women wreathed in brightly coloured neck rings peered sheepishly at him from behind drawn shades. The plainsmen braves, trotting on their predatory birds, came out to regard him with a martial suspicion. They looked like savage men, and Barsabbas understood how his Chapter came to use their ancestors as genestock. Lithe and narrow-waisted, they donned war crests of feather and hauberks of woven bark strips. He recognised the lineage of bronze skin and high cheekbones on many of his fellow brothers. Drovers, hunters, stock tenders, shamans, they all came to see him and exult in his coming.

As they threaded through the throng, Barsabbas could see a massed ring of hand-painted caravans shaded by a large canvas awning. That would no doubt be the command centre. Its conspicuousness annoyed Barsabbas. It was a large, vulnerable and easily identifiable target. The plainsmen may have been brave, but they certainly did not know war.

A procession of chieftains from the gathered kinships rode out to meet him. They were all elders, men with sun-creased faces, long and wizened as if etched from aged wood. Their shukas were freshly re-dyed and left traces of red pigment on their shoulders and arms. At their front, riding several paces ahead upon a black and grey talon squall, was the elder of the entire gathering. Gumede had told Barsabbas of his name, Ngokodjou. Gumede had also warned Barsabbas of his insufferable superiority.

'I am Ngokodjou Akindes, the elder of elders, wisdom of the dunes to the west. You may call me Ngokodjou,' said the elder as he drew closer. He lazily swatted a fly from his face, seemingly unimpressed by the Chaos Space Marine.

Barsabbas did not reply. He studied the haughty chieftain. The elder of elders was a fat man, thick with meat, while those around him were gaunt and emaciated. He was tall too, and carried the arrogance that came to those who were imposingly tall and knew it. Pendant earrings hung like heavy tendrils of gold and onyx from his ears and he carried a recurve bow across his lap. Barsabbas decided he did not like the man. There was a shrewdness to his crescent eyes, an animalistic cunning that told Barsabbas he would be difficult to deal with.

'I have heard of you already,' Barsabbas replied bluntly.

'My reputation precedes me wherever I go,' said Ngokodjou, choosing to take the words as a compliment. 'I too have heard of you. We are equals, you and I, and more similar than you would know.'

Barsabbas snorted. The man had grown accustomed to speaking to his kin as if they were ignorant. 'We are not the same, human. Do not speak to me like that.'

Ngokodjou's eyes flashed with anger. Barsabbas detected a trace of vehemence, fleeting and then gone. But the smile never wavered on Ngokodjou's face. 'Of course, koag.'

In any other place, at any other time, Barsabbas would have shot him through the throat and taken his necklaces as trophies. His trigger finger twitched involuntarily. But he needed the plainsmen. They thought him to be a benevolent and godly spirit, and he needed to exploit that for now.

As if sensing the enmity between them, Gumede stole close to Barsabbas and bowed to Ngokodjou. 'We should bring the koag into the house of elders. Times may be hard but we must not neglect hospitality.'

They brought him bowls of gruel. They gave him jugs of curdled caprid milk. A dancing file of children brought them dishes of dried apricots and small, tart berries.

Barsabbas consumed only a small amount of milk to replenish his protein stores.

Wrestlers entered the tent to perform their ritual matches. Young dancers with supple waists danced and chanted in unison.

Barsabbas grew impatient.

He sat awkwardly on a spread of beaded blankets, his hulking form barely contained by the low awnings. The tent was filled with clapping elders. It seemed that the arrival of a 'Red God' was seen as a portent of victory.

'We should plan our attack,' Barsabbas said finally.

'We defend here,' announced one of the chieftains proudly. The others agreed with him by clicking their tongues and nodding sagely.

'No. We need a strategy, supplies, logistics, reports of enemy disposition, structured formations,' Barsabbas said.

Ngokodjou sneered at him, as if he had been waiting for those words. 'But if you are so powerful, then why do we need to do so? With the powers of a god, surely the dead will fall,' said Ngokodjou. It was a direct challenge.

Barsabbas imagined choking the man's jowls with his hands. 'You will face more than just the dead. There will be human fighters with guns. Other threats too, warriors like me, but many times in number.'

The tent grew very quiet. The dancers ran off in a hurry, leaving their hand chimes and tall drums.

'Warriors like you?'

'They follow a different path, but yes.'

'Tell us what to do, koag.'

'Is there disease in the camp?'

'Very little,' said one of the southern chiefs. 'These gathered kinships are mostly from the deep southlands. When they fall ill, we tie them up.'

'Tie them up?' Barsabbas burst out with deep, bellowing laughter. 'Why do you not just kill them?'

'The families will not allow it,' said another. 'But before the plague takes them, we bind their hands and feet. That way, when they...'

Barsabbas shook his head. He could not understand the strange attachments these humans seemed so adamant to cling to. Why risk infecting the entire camp, hundreds of thousands of people in close proximity, when it would be more efficient to leave the infected to die under the sun? There was no logic to it. Why leave someone infected to the care of healthy and vulnerable kin?

A Chaos Space Marine would have been efficient. They would sever an arm before infection set in, and would certainly execute a comrade if sparing him meant compromising the effectiveness of the Chapter. Barsabbas was disgusted by the humans' weakness.

'We must preserve our strength. Your army is small and we cannot afford the numbers to dwindle under a plague. We will bring the fight to them. We will push north. The enemy will come, I know how they fight.'

'What about our great conveyors? Or our kin?'

'Take them with us,' Barsabbas said. He did not relish their slaughter. But he needed their diversion, and twenty thousand warriors alone would not be enough, especially with plague slowly but steadily spreading through the camp. It would be a sacrifice, but a necessary one.

There had been a time when the *Cauldron Born* had been many different ships. There had been a collision of abandoned ghost drifters that had welded the superstructure together by the grinding pressure of megatonnes. Gradually, the hulk grew larger, gathering a gravitational pull by virtue of its fattening girth.

Drifting into the Eye of Terror – that legend-haunted region of space – the space hulk began to take form. Daemons and malevolent spirits of the Eye found a home in its cavernous catacombs. There it drifted, a shapeless wreck forced into perpetual motion, gathering size like a ghosting ball of dust.

It was eight thousand years before Gammadin found and tamed this vessel, grafting his own flesh tissue into the drifter's heart and binding it with Chaos witchcraft. From there, the ship grew organically, shaping itself to Gammadin's will. Flesh cauliflowered over the skeletal metal and fused with the dormant engines. It became a living creature, long and lithe. Its daemon spirit made it receptive to the warp, a conduit of energy.

A sacred place to open the warp to the material plane.

* * *

It would take many days for the temple to be prepared for summoning.

First, the temple would need to be swept and cleaned, the wards redrawn and rechecked. Teams of menial slaves climbed scaffolds, using their bare hands and feet to scale sixty metres on yielding wooden supports. The walls were scrubbed clean of psychic residue.

Working vigorously, the slaves did not look at Muhr as he entered the chamber. They did not even dare to acknowledge him. The witch ghosted up the dais's steps and across its marble surface. Set in the centre was a bowl filled with mandrake roots in fresh blood, drowning like swollen dolls. When the warp rift was invoked, the offering would draw daemons like a droplet of blood drew sharks. Every daemon had their own preference. Yetsugei would only answer to a summons of blood and mandrake. Even the slightest change in offerings could result in unwanted visitations.

Muhr cupped the bowl in his hands and began to chant. He was not meant to be here and he rushed the words, almost stumbling over the syllables in his haste.

The bowl contained three large mandrake roots, the roots resembling pudgy human limbs and torsos, sitting in a thin pool of blood from a suffering human. It was a very specific ingredient that could lure many minor warp denizens. This blood had belonged to a slave called Sufjan, or so he had been told. The slave had apparently died an insufferable sort of demise.

Muhr finished his chant and drew the crystal shard. The tiny figure inside, like a painted doll, did not stir. Muhr dropped the gem into the bowl. It hit the surface with a guilty plop, before sinking to the bottom.

Hiding his intentions behind an air of solemnity, Muhr descended from the platform, nodding with satisfaction.

CHAPTER THIRTEEN

Sabtah picked his way through the armoury, shifting apart a quagmire of discarded weaponry. Kicking aside a tower shield, Captain Hazareth stood in agitation, waiting for Sabtah to speak.

'What do you mean, betrayal? Hazareth asked finally.

'Muhr has too much at stake to be undone by this summoning. He will do something to prevent its execution. It's only logical,' Sabtah replied.

Sabtah watched Hazareth's reaction carefully. The captain continued to make his way down the vault, pushing over another shelf of weapons as if to dispel some nervous energy. A wave of short stabbing swords and daggers spilled onto the ground. Hazareth picked through the mess thoughtfully before giving Sabtah a solemn, appraising look.

'What does he stand to gain?'

Sabtah knew the captain had a right to be curious. Feared and accursed, Hazareth was considered neutral. He supported neither Muhr, Sabtah nor the minor factions that struggled for power. Hazareth was the consummate warrior and he cared not for Chapter politics. But Sabtah trusted Hazareth. He knew that the captain valued martial capacity above all else, and Muhr's betrayal would be a direct impediment to the combat abilities of the Chapter. This argument was the only way to get Hazareth on his side.

'Muhr has always advocated a patron. First it was Abaddon, two centuries ago. Muhr had suggested to Gammadin that we pledge our allegiance to the Destroyer. Gammadin would have none of it. He has always been hungry for greater power, greater recognition.'

Hazareth thought judiciously. 'What is wrong with power?'

'It will come at the cost of Blood Gorgon autonomy.'

The captain nudged a pile of swords, but had clearly given up searching for anything.

'It will cost us our identity,' Sabtah continued. 'We may not be a Legion, we may not have a dominion, but we are free. We have always been free. Alliances with any greater force would not bode well for our independence. The Death Guard, the Black Legion, the Renegades Undivided. It would all be the same.'

Sabtah could tell Hazareth was still suspicious. 'But why would he harm Hauts Bassiq?' asked the captain.

'Because his patron wishes to claim Bassiq for himself. Muhr is simply serving a purpose, weakening us from the inside, so that his Overlord can claim the world with minimal losses. In exchange for his aid, his overlord will accept Muhr under his patronage. It is a pact, but not one that I wish this Chapter to fall under.'

Hazareth didn't reply. He had spotted something amongst the disorganised piles. He picked it up. 'Is this it?' he asked.

He held in his hands a dagger. Its handle was polished black wood and its blade was dirty steel. Chipped and worn, the serrated blade was engraved with an arcane script. Sabtah had claimed the weapon six centuries ago from an agent of the hated Ordo Malleus. With its ordinary appearance, Sabtah had initially regarded the piece as nothing more than a trinket. It had taken some four centuries before he ascertained its true nature, and since then it had collected dust in Sabtah's weapon vault, lost between forty-metre-high stacks of plundered weaponry.

'That's what we came here for,' Sabtah said. He kicked his way through the vault and took hold of the knife. Rifles and lasguns scattered like dry leaves before his boots.

'A fine weapon,' Hazareth said, handing it to him.

'A daemon weapon. A she-bitch,' Sabtah said, tossing the knife from palm to palm. The haft vibrated as the daemon within became agitated.

'You think you will need it at the summoning?' Hazareth asked.

'I believe Muhr will show his hand there. Yes.'

Hazareth plucked a warhammer down from a nearby wall mount. 'Then you have First Company's support, Sabtah. You were Gammadin's bond and I uphold my fealty to you.'

Sabtah smiled. 'If something should happen to me, Hazareth, I need you to kill Muhr. The Blood Gorgons must remain as we are and always have been. We are nothing without our history and our tradition. Don't let Muhr change that.'

'I will punish him,' Hazareth promised.

'Good.' Sabtah drew from beneath his nail a sliver of black, no larger than a splinter. 'This is my genecode. It will access most of the vessel's defence systems and security scans. I am bonded to Gammadin and whatever Gammadin can access, you will be able to too.'

Hazareth received it in the tip of his index finger. The splinter curled like a dying earthworm before burrowing beneath his cuticle with a slight sting. 'When will I need this?'

'As long as I live, never,' Sabtah began. He paused, his brows knitting. 'But one day, I have no doubt you will. Keep it close and tell no one.'

The ship's bay sirens wailed with the passing of a new cycle. A new day.

Deep in the temple pit, Muhr and his nine were completing the last of their monophonic liturgy. The coven surrounded the wide dais, their vox-speakers generating a constant, steady drone of plainchant. The rims of silver bowls were rubbed, letting their harmonics peal and stretch.

The wards had been drawn by morning. A spider's web of interlocking, overlapping polygons and flat geometry radiated outwards in mutually supporting glyph work. Several external seals, large pentagrammic stars, reinforced the initial containments and spread up into the walls with sharp, linear lines.

Only thirty hand-picked Blood Gorgons and their slave retinues formed a circle around the pit. They each carried a black tapestry. Thirty black tapestries in all, one for each of the warriors lost on Hauts Bassiq.

Slowly, the air grew cold. A wind began to gather as the chants climbed in rhythm. Frost settled down on them like a coarse fog. The wind boomed, thrashing against the interior.

The chanting stopped. The wind stilled abruptly.

Slowly, at the centre of the dais, the air began to bend and tear. It buckled.

Wet frost was coating the dome, running in sheets down the walls and collecting in droplets across the domed ceiling. The coven of Chirurgeon-witches sounded their singing bowls with odd, polyrhythmic melodies. Haunting and drawn, they channelled the psychic focus of the coven.

Slowly and deliberately, Sabtah stepped onto the dais. He was alert, his eyes darting, but his body was fluid and relaxed. He turned and gave the surrounding Blood Gorgons a salute, extending his power trident horizontally before him.

Opposite him, Muhr also stepped onto the dais. The witch's armour was polished clean. New iron studs had been riveted over the polyps that clustered on the shoulders and chest plate. A black cloak poured from his shoulders and a sword that Sabtah had never seen before sat at his hip.

Both were ready for judgement.

Sabtah knelt down, murmured his devotion to the gods and threw fistfuls of rock salt over his shoulders. The coarse grains cascaded down his back as he prayed.

'We invoke you for judgement,' intoned one of the coven. The air continued to distort, warping itself to bursting point. Patterns solidified in the air as overlapping dimensions within the warp became lucid to the human mind. The air became so cold, it carried particles of frost.

Muhr looked at Sabtah, curiously confident despite his impending judgement.

Inside the sacrifice bowl, Muhr's crystal shard rocked gently as the warp energy was invoked. The creature within became animated, thrashing its microscopic arms and dancing with an eerie vigour. As it cavorted, minute cracks appeared across the tiny shard. The crystal cracked and began to weep a black fluid. Oozing like treacle, it was pushed outwards from the crystal shard, discolouring and mingling with the blood. Bubbling and frothing, it released an absurd amount of liquid that the tiny crystal could not possibly contain. It filled the bowl until the black fluid gathered along the edges and poured down in a solid curtain. With one final shudder, the bowl rocked and tipped over, spilling a low tide across the marble.

The Blood Gorgons gathered at the edge of the pit touched their bolt-guns in trepidation. The invocation was a common ritual but they had never seen this before.

Sabtah looked up. Across from him, Muhr had crouched with one knee on the ground. The witch's head was bowed. His hands were nonchalantly pressed against the marble. His fingers, subtle and almost unseen, were scraping away at the painted wards.

Sabtah rose urgently. He opened his mouth to shout a warning. Muhr looked up and smiled at him.

Something was wrong, but it was too late.

Reality began to buckle. The walls of the temple appeared to liquefy, the particles of its structure becoming loose. The floor and ceiling tilted at an angle that was nauseous to the human mind. The three dimensions of the material plane and the numerical perfection of existence was disintegrating as the warp hole began to expand.

And then the world went black.

Yetsugei was awakened. His playthings were pleading for his presence again. The warp was shifting. Beyond any concept of distance or time, a rift was opening. He could sense his invocation. But there was something else there too – a baleful malevolence, strong and reeking. Yetsugei knew better. He curled himself away, folding himself up and squirming into the darkest regions. The presence was too much, even for him. He ignored their call and tried to flee.

There was an atom-splitting howl. They all heard it.

It was followed by a sudden and ominous blackout. Every single sconce torch fluttered out.

As a matter of automatic reaction, the Blood Gorgons switched to thermal vision. Nothing. Night reflection. Nothing. Multi-light overlay. Nothing. It was an unnatural darkness flooding in from the warp.

Then the screaming began.

It killed quickly. Brother Talus was disembowelled. Brother-Sergeant Arkum fell in sections, blood drizzling like fine rain. Muzzles flashed.

Inexplicably, the torches fluttered back. A daemon was amongst them. The containment wards had failed. They were scorched into the marble itself, burning like a racing promethium flame.

It towered above them all, thirteen metres tall. Its body was flaccid, covered with sparse, wiry hair. Its eight-dozen arms whipped sickles like a threshing mill. Its maw was ringed by blunt, chiselled teeth.

'Daemon of Nurgle!' shouted one of the coven.

'Basho Eeluk has come for Sabtah,' gurgled the daemon.

Before the coven could banish it, Basho Eeluk shouted a single word, a syllable of power. The warp gate expanded rapidly until it encompassed the entire dais before collapsing with a surge of static. There was a rolling boom like thunder, as air rushed in to fill the vacuum.

The marble dais was gone. The sacrificial bowl lay upturned. Sabtah was gone. Muhr was gone.

Sabtah did not know where he was. His surroundings were dark and insubstantial. The marble dais seemed to be suspended in mid air. He saw only the daemon and moved to flank it. The daemon sensed his intent and swung to meet him. It crashed down onto the dais, splitting the marble, as it bellowed.

Sabtah held his trident in a loose hammer grip, winding his arm back like a javelin thrower. He cast it with all his superhuman strength, pivoting on his toes to wring out every shred of momentum. The weapon punched deep into the daemon's paunch and quivered there like an arrow. Recoiling from the wound, Basho Eeluk began to pull at the protruding weapon shaft even as a conical swarm of bone hornets belched from the daemon's mouth.

Like sharp-edged darts, the swarm richocheted against Sabtah's plate. They slashed his face open, drawing hundreds of tiny, piercing cuts through skin, fat and flesh. Garbling a howl of elation, Basho barged forwards, driving off its powerful legs. Standing his ground, Sabtah sprayed his bolter on automatic. Yet the daemon's multiple hands moved so quickly it seemed as if it fanned out hundreds upon hundreds of arms, catching the bolt-rounds and exploding them in mid-air. His bullets foiled by dark magic, Sabtah pivoted to the side as the daemon pounced. Rolling off his shoulder, Sabtah came up in a crouch, his bolter already tracking.

'Is this what you wanted, Sabtah?' asked a voice from behind his neck.

Spinning quickly, Sabtah saw Muhr. The sorcerer stood at the edge of the marble disc, aiming a bolt pistol. He fired from almost point-blank range.

Sabtah had no choice. He slapped the round away. His left hand exploded in a concentric swirl of blood and armour fragments. Circling away, Sabtah returned with a triple burst of his boltgun. The shots sent Muhr ducking for cover.

And then the daemon was all over him.

Teeth. Fangs. Glistening skin. Sabtah was mauled from all directions at once. He let his boltgun fall on its sling. Basho Eeluk used its bulk, pushing the old warrior to the edge of the marble disc. Solid, black nothingness plummeted away beneath him. Hands slapped at him. Tremendously powerful palm slaps that jostled Sabtah's heavy bones against their ligaments.

Sabtah barely reached the daemon's thigh height, but he clinched up with it. Power armour servos whirring, Sabtah locked up Basho Eeluk's thighs with his arms and began to drive forwards. Blood draining from his severed wrist, Sabtah relied on his arms alone, sucking the daemon's knees towards his chest by tucking his elbows in. Pushing forwards, Sabtah began to lurch the daemon over its centre of gravity, worrying it like a game hound. Basho Eeluk toppled, stretching out a choir of arms to break its fall.

Sabtah muscled the daemon onto the ground and began to climb up its supine form. Basho Eeluk shook its monstrous body, trying to dislodge the old warrior from its torso.

Finally, Sabtah found purchase on the daemon's enormous throat. He wrapped his steel-shod legs around the daemon's neck and constricted his thighs like a lariat. Rearing its greenish bulk, it jerked, suddenly rising. Sabtah dangled off the neck upside down, like an oversized necklace.

With a creak of scraping metal, Basho Eeluk clawed at Sabtah with a forest of hands. Another two-dozen hammered his armoured shell, wrenching him like a struggling crustacean. Sabtah locked his legs tighter and curled his abdomen, pulling himself upright despite the suffocating wave of attacks. He found himself staring directly into the daemon's face. The head was almost as large as Sabtah's torso. Disc-like fish eyes returned his stare with a dull, silver gaze.

A sickle chopped into his side. One of the daemon's many weapons had found a gap in his torso plate. The razor cut deep into his liver, exploding toxins into his bloodstream. Another finally punched through his battered thigh plate.

Gritting his teeth against the accumulating wounds, Sabtah unsheathed the knife. Basho Eeluk rolled, wrenching its body like a surfacing whale. Sabtah swung on the daemon's neck, but his legs only hugged tighter. Reaching up, Sabtah rammed the knife into Basho Eeluk's eye. It scored open like firm fruit.

Basho Eeluk spasmed. It gripped Sabtah with all of its hands, hundreds of clawed fingers grasping and worming away him. Prying and pulling, Basho Eeluk tried to drag Sabtah off its neck like a stubborn leech. Sabtah slashed the knife again, paring away a long strip of daemon flesh. Where the ensorcelled blade made contact, Basho Eeluk corroded, bubbling like acid on metal.

Yet Eeluk refused to die. It reared up and dived back down, head first. There was a sharp, jarring impact. Sabtah's back slammed back into the marble dais. He felt his spine shatter, vertebrae twisting. His legs loosened, flopping aside as his nervous system seized.

Sabtah had one last window of opportunity and he took it. As Eeluk pulled its head free, Sabtah's knife hand followed it.

Basho Eeluk was still bellowing victory as Sabtah blinded its other eye. The daemon reeled. Completely sightless it lurched, limbs awkwardly flailing. Its cry became one of despair. It dragged itself over the edge of the marble dais and slithered over the edge, banishing itself back into the rolling clouds of the warp-sea. It roared one final time, fading cries marking the depth of its descent.

'Muhr,' Sabtah said. He tried to rise, but he no longer had control of his lower body. Given proper clinical treatment and augmentation, the spinal severance would only be a minor injury.

Muhr drifted into view. He stood over Sabtah's splayed body.

'Sabtah. How sad it has come to this,' Muhr said.

'Betrayer,' Sabtah accused hoarsely.

'Not so,' Muhr replied. 'I only have the glory of our warband in mind. I can make the Blood Gorgons a proper Chapter again. Not renegades, but an army.'

'We've always been who we are, Muhr.'

'Vagabonds,' Muhr finished testily.

'We have a name. The Imperium does not wish to fight the Blood Gorgons. We have a history.'

'Under Opsarus and the Legions of Nurgle we will achieve more than we ever could alone. We will raise empires. Empires, Sabtah. Hauts Bassiq is a small price to pay in return for Opsarus's patronage.'

'But we won't be Blood Gorgons any more,' Sabtah concluded bluntly. He was beginning to feel drowsy. His body was fighting the massive trauma he had sustained: a severed hand, a ruptured liver, serious cuts, a broken back. Endorphins flooded his brain as the Larraman cells in his bloodstream coagulated the wounds. His sus-an membrane began to slow the beating of his hearts. His breathing became shallow.

'Nothing you have to worry about, Sabtah.' Muhr cocked his bolt pistol. 'I never wanted to do this. You are a good warrior and a sound tactician. But our ideologies are irreconcilable.'

Sabtah shook his head as blood bubbled into his beard. A *dowry*. That was what they used to call it.

In order to cement the Blood Gorgons' alliance to greater powers, there needed to be a gift, a token. That was Hauts Bassiq. Mineral-rich, resource-rich, a staging post of conquest that would become the jewel of Opsarus's dominion. In ancient days, humans exchanged livestock, beads, even precious stones. Hauts Bassiq was no different. It was a valuable gem for those who could exploit it.

Meek. That was the accusation Sabtah wanted to use. Muhr was meek. He was selling Sabtah's bond-brothers to the Cult of Rot and Decay merely for the promise of power. Amongst soldiers such as themselves, the word *meek* was the gravest insult.

But the witch had sold the warband like a bride. There was no allegiance here. Muhr was trying to buy his way into power by offering Nurgle both a Chapter and a world. For a moment, Sabtah was overwhelmed by the hot rush of anger and the contrasting cold of his wounds.

'You are a bondless witch,' Sabtah murmured. He invoked the last of his bleeding strength. 'Muhr the Meek. That is how history will know you.'

Muhr flinched at the accusation. 'I may not have the blood bond but I have devoted myself to this Chapter all the same. You just can't accept it.'

Muhr pressed the pistol against Sabtah's head.

The marble dais reappeared in the Temple Heart with a clap of expanding gas. The fifty-tonne disc slammed back onto the decking with a force that caused earthquake tremors across a third of the space hulk.

As the dust cloud parted, Muhr was the only one remaining on the dais. Blood and fragments splashed across the white marble. The assembled squads had formed a ring around the dais, weapons primed and aimed. Muhr waved them back.

'The waves and tides of the immaterial realm have cast me in the role of guardian,' he declared.

Some of the Blood Gorgons reacted more slowly than Muhr would have liked, giving him a hesitant salute. There were those among the assembly who did not react at all. Beneath the screaming face-plates of their helmets, there would be surprise and perhaps some measure of fear. Muhr made sure to remember those dissidents who now disrespected his rank; they would need to be quelled soon.

But for now, Muhr had other things to attend to. The air of the warp clung to him and he would need to exorcise his body. Perhaps he would even allow himself some rest. He could afford the time, now he was Chapter Master.

Barsabbas had not commanded humans in combat before but if their travel discipline was a measure of their soldiering, then it did not augur well for the campaign. Slow, disorganised and soon needing rest, the humans were incapable of travelling at a competent pace.

The muster travelled for four days and five nights before reaching the baked clay flats of the north. Accompanied by the rumble of motors, a line of dust almost two kilometres in length meandered across the terrain. Road trains forged the way, escorted by talon outriders. Herds of caprid straggled behind, trailing like a spillage of shaggy brown coats in their wake. The convoy was a mess. It was a wonder that the enemy did not attack.

Barsabbas rode at the front. His frame was too big to fit comfortably in the engine cab, so he sat on the tin roof, surveying the lands with an old retractable telescope.

Hauts Bassiq had once been an industrial world. He saw, interspersed between mountains, the artificial outlines of human structures, half buried by sand and rust. The infrastructure, old as it was, still remained. There were foundries, gas refineries, open cut mines and millions of kilometres of pipeline that had been laid down. They remained like buried mausoleums, preserved by the ferric sands.

They encountered the walking dead too, but only in small, wandering packs. The outriders lured them away from the main advance and dispatched them from the saddle with well-placed bowshots.

At one point, during their third day of travel, mounted scouts returned in a panic. They had spotted a patrol of large men in hoods, shod in bulky grey: a twenty-man platoon of Septic infantry. It was a convenient opportunity for Barsabbas to show the natives what he was capable of. He halted the convoy and asked the scouts to lead him to where the enemy were camped. There, from a distance of five hundred metres, Barsabbas gunned down the entire platoon of enemy auxiliary as they slept. He slew six before they even realised they were being fired upon. He downed another four more as they struggled to locate his muzzle flashes. By the time the Septic returned feeble, hesitant counter-fire, Barsabbas had put down the rest with precise, clean shots to the chest. The entire engagement took less than a minute and Barsabbas did not even change his thirty-round magazine.

By the time he returned to the convoy, word had already spread about his exploits. Outriders brandished the enemy guns as trophies, even though most did not know how to use them. The plainsmen seemed unduly occupied with deifying him. They truly believed Barsabbas would lead them to victory.

They made camp in the badlands, surrounded by fields of dry organ pipe cactus. Two hundred thousand people spreading out to prepare for the coming war.

While the kinships rested and watered, Barsabbas did not. He debated plans of attack with the chieftains long into the night.

According to the tact-maps and scout reports, they were in the heart
of enemy territory. With such a large force, it would only be a matter of
time before the enemy responded to their presence.

Barsabbas knew they could do nothing but prepare their defences. He
knew they would be overrun, but at least they would cause significant
damage to the enemy plans on Hauts Bassiq.

The suns were at their highest ascension. The Celsius gauges peaked at
the high fifties. Bare skin seemed to strip and crack upon exposure to
the glare.

The camp was alive with the sounds of urgent activity. The cactus fields
formed natural fortifications for the camp and the plainsmen went about
their daily business of cleaning, washing and cooking. Several of the
chieftains attempted to send their closest family members to feed and
bathe Barsabbas, perhaps in the hopes of receiving good fortune.

Barsabbas dismissed them all. He gathered Gumede and two-score
mounted braves. He ordered them to pack a day's worth of supplies and
to travel light. While the camp braced itself for the inevitable assault,
Barsabbas intended to ride forth and survey the region.

He also requested a vehicle, something fast that was capable of carrying
his significant weight. The braves scattered, eager to be the one to fulfil
the Red God's wishes.

Upon their return, a vehicle waited for him, draped under heavy woollen blankets. Underneath was an open frame chassis mounted on four
muscular wheels. The rail frame itself formed an integrated roll cage with
an exposed gas engine. Barsabbas did not know its age, but he guessed
it was pre-colonial, a relic from the planet's prospecting era. Despite the
plainsmen's efforts to preserve its condition, the centuries had taken their
toll. Much of the roll cage was corroded to a mottled orange, and the
exposed engine block was fused together by rust in some parts. Somehow
the shamans, with their rote knowledge of machinery and rudimentary
repair skills, had managed to keep the engine alive. Rope actually held
parts of the vehicle together.

When Barsabbas eased his weight onto the cracked leather seat, the
quad groaned under his weight, yet the engine purred responsively to
the ignition. Given the situation, Barsabbas considered the quad quite a
fortunate find. Nestled within the motored cage, Barsabbas left the camp,
a single file of outriders following his dusty plume.

CHAPTER FOURTEEN

The badlands of the north appeared as a monotonous, featureless land to Barsabbas, an uninspired painting rendered in a repetitive sequence. But to the plainsmen braves, the terrain was an open book, every tree or stone a page mark for another narrative.

They rode for six kilometres with desperate haste, until they reached the stump of a brittle acacia. The tree looked no different to the sparse, withered things that he had seen standing like lonely fence posts on the horizon. Yet the tree was of some significance to the plainsmen. Barsabbas listened patiently, logging pieces of intelligence into his helmet's data feed.

The tree, he was told, marked a well-known walking path – a line in the sand that was barely visible until they pointed it out to him. Apparently satisfied that neither the walking dead nor the Septic had used the track for some time, they continued on.

As they scouted, the braves, some as young as ten, began to point out the prints of various animals: the splayed bird feet of talon squalls, the crescent prints of the caprid, curving belly marks of a brown-backed serpent. Simply from the depth and size of the tracks, they deduced the animals' gender and age. From this tiny fragment of information, they could tell whether the animals' natural habitat had been disturbed and, if so, in what way.

Two hours into their patrol of their surroundings, Gumede indicated a series of splayed prints in the sand, sprinting in the opposite direction.

Judging by the spacing of their strides, Gumede knew many of them
were injured by the way some of them left unevenly distributed prints,
or dragged the knuckles of their feet.

'Injuries,' Gumede said, running a finger through the prints. 'Many
injuries.'

'Tell me what that means,' said Barsabbas, deferring to the plainsman's experience. Barsabbas was an expert tracker. Memo-therapy had
imparted into his hippocampus knowledge of wilderness survival across
seventy-eight different forms of terrain. This, however, was beyond even
his considerable skill.

'Birds are predators. They are rarely injured, and if so, never so many.
They were attacked,' said Gumede. 'See here? Running tracks. The birds
are running away from something to the north. There are fewer males
running with the flock too, far too many chicks and females. It tells me
that many of the males were killed protecting the flock.'

'These tracks are fresh?'

'No more than one day old. I would guess whatever attacked the birds
is roughly two days' travel from here. Maybe less.'

Barsabbas understood. Out in the badlands, nothing would attack a
flock of apex predators, except for something far more dangerous. It was
likely something had fired upon the flock, or engaged them in a brief
skirmish. The predators, defeated, had fled southwards, away from their
attackers.

'Then we do not have much time. The enemy are close,' Barsabbas said.
'We should warn the camp.'

Barsabbas smiled and hefted his boltgun. 'We will return to the muster.'

The plainsmen were ready when they came. Through the low, bulbous
fields of cacti the enemy approached. Four thousand Septic infantry,
accompanied by light, sand-trawling gun platforms. The keening squeal
of hydraulics and the clatter of engines echoed across the badlands.
Behind them, with almost no urgency, marched a company of Plague
Marines. Twenty-eight warriors in all, a procession that followed the
heavy banner of Nurgle.

Barsabbas had brought the road trains into a crescent-shaped wall,
a silver ridge of carriages almost one kilometre in length, girded by
mountains on either flank and fields of cacti to the fore. Behind them
the sprawling tents and lean-tos of the kinships took shelter. Barsabbas
did not expect the line to hold. The thin skin of a steel carriage would
not resist bolter shot.

Drawn out in front of the camp, standing in a thin line, came two
thousand Bassiq braves. They faced the enemy, standing against them
with bow and arrow, throwing hatchet and firing their heirloom rifles.
They were crested with massive feathers, quivering fans of squall pinion

atop heads and shoulders. Their faces were painted red, like their brightly coloured shukas. The red would make them fearless, or so Barsabbas had been told.

The enemy advanced steadily. Their boots and tracks crushed the cactus fields. The engines became a monotone growl.

Anxious and rightfully frightened, the kinships dug deep within the sheltered encampment. They were vulnerable. Mothers hid their children under beaded blankets. The old men sat together and spoke of younger days and death. Many more – tens of thousands of people – crowded behind the parked road trains, peering between boarded windows and carriage gaps for a glimpse of the battleline beyond. Far deeper into the camp, the sickened and infected began to spasm, as if sensing great evil.

Higher up, on the lower ridges of the mountain, Barsabbas signalled for Gumede to raise the totem standard. Each of the waiting flocks returned signal with their own kinship totems. There were almost sixteen thousand riders up there. Sixteen thousand birds clacked and cawed, waiting to stampede down the slope.

'Weep not. Everything must have its day,' said Barsabbas, leaning down from his quad-cage to shout at Gumede above the stormy clash of sound. 'The mettle of your entire culture will be measured in this one engagement.'

The chief seemed to understand. He raised his lasrifle and lanced the signal upwards. A red beam, straight and true, pierced the sky. With a roar, sixteen thousand voices raised as one, the plainsmen charged down the mountain.

The Septic infantry began to fire, just three hundred metres distant from the plainsmen. Las-shots and solid slugs came whistling through the organ pipe cactus. They were horrible, rapid fire volleys that cut through the braves in droves. A line of dust plumes kicked up in front of the road trains as dozens upon dozens of unarmoured braves writhed and buckled beneath the firestorm. Support weapons punched clean holes through the carriages behind them, landing ordnance and incendiary directly into the camp itself.

For the first time in his life, Barsabbas felt the fear of facing superior forces. He understood now what his foes had felt when they faced the overwhelming might of an Astartes battle force. Yet he waited, despite the carnage, waiting for the enemy to grow eager, to become lustful in the excitement of slaughter. On the slopes below them, braves continued to die, odd arrows hissing fitfully in reply. Barsabbas waited, waited more, until the enemy drew level in the fields below.

And then they charged.

They charged, and what a stampede it was. Like a rolling avalanche, sixteen thousand talon squalls came. One-tonne beasts, axe-beaks snapping, pumping thighs slamming the dirt with black avian nails. They gathered a wild, heedless momentum.

A rolling tide swallowed the Septic battle line from the flank. The talon squalls crashed into and over the infantry platoons, rolling, tumbling, thrashing. Bodies were trampled. Shots were fired at close range. Hatchets rose and fell. The men in ghastly hoods fought back with bayonets and pistols, but the crushing juggernaut birds simply ran over them.

Talon squalls sprinted onto the gun platforms. The birds began to peck at the fighting vehicles like shelled prey, clambering atop the chassis to snap at the crew compartments with their long necks and plucking them out like morsels with their clawed feet.

Engaged to the front and suddenly outflanked, the companies of Septic infantry buckled. Their firing lost all focus and coordination. A young brave, no more than sixteen, pounced his bird atop an autocannon trailer, holding two bloodied sacks in one hand as trophies, a slick hatchet whirling in his other.

Surveying the field, Barsabbas dared to think that perhaps the braves might yet send the enemy into retreat.

Then the Plague Marines engaged.

They waded into the fray slowly, as if boredom had finally compelled them to action. They were massive, as tall as a mounted rider and broader than the breast of a talon squall rooster. Incarnations of pestilence, they seemed invincible. Hatchets and arrows skipped off the dirty white surface of their plate, barely scratching the lime green bacterial colonies that beveined the enamel. Helmets with wide, trumpet-like rebreathers and ugly, mismatched goggles encased their heads. They leaked grey and yellow fluid when pierced but showed little reaction to any wounds inflicted.

In their plated gauntlets and thick, rubberised combat gloves, they fired boltguns. They favoured knives as heavy as short swords; rusted chopping blades that parted flesh crudely. Every stroke of the knife or squeeze of the trigger killed men. Onwards they came, and Barsabbas moved to meet them.

Barsabbas vaulted off the quad-motor as las-shots raked across its fender. The flimsy vehicle was not fit for a bond-brother. He kicked the roll cage away and began to pick careful shots with his boltgun. His leash chain looped around Barsabbas's wrist, Sindul began to shriek in panic. Hooded and bound, the dark eldar could only squirm in terror as the battle raged blindly around him.

A platoon of Septic infantry appeared out of the rising dust. Thirty or forty soldiers in baggy, hooded masks, advancing in a loose spread. He heard their shouts of alarm as they spotted him.

Barsabbas reacted as he was drilled, pressuring them with a wide spread of automatic fire. The sudden volley of crackling bolt shells cut out in a semicircle. Rounds so heavy that even their passing shockwave haemorrhaged the brains and organs of any target in a one-metre radius. Enemy infantry sprawled, fell and dived under the burst of fire. It was what Barsabbas needed to close the distance.

As the enemy went to ground to escape the initial onslaught, Barsabbas charged and fell amongst them. Now he was in his element and superior enemy numbers did not faze him. At the edge of his visor, he saw a Septic thrust a bayonet towards him. Using his great armspan, Barsabbas lashed his mace over the Septic's rifle and caved in his hooded mask. He fell sideways, lurching into another Septic. Barsabbas killed that one too, breaking his neck with a quick backstroke. So absorbed was he in the practice of death-dealing that Barsabbas had to remind himself that this was not his fight. It was a diversion for him to slip north, past the bulk of the Nurgle armies. He had to keep himself alive. Finding Sargaul was the objective. He had to remind himself of that just to keep his battle rage in check. The nostril-flaring lust to kill almost overwhelmed his logic and conditioning.

'Attack the gaps in his armour!' shouted a Septic officer.

But Barsabbas would not stand still long enough to allow it. Three Septics harried him, surrounding him and trying to slip a bayonet into the gaps of his knee joint. Barsabbas moved faster than they thought he could. Over three hundred kilos of an explosively-moving steel-shod body crushed the nearest Septic. Sindul was dragged along with him, the chain snapping taut and almost decapitating another Septic. Barsabbas felt bayonets snap against his unyielding plate.

Glancing sideways, Barsabbas saw the charge of the mounted braves stalling. They were engaged in a grinding close-quarter melee. Gun shots ruptured the air. Above that could be heard the distinctly hollow chopping of hatchet through bone. Garbled screams rose from both sides and the warm-blooded croak of dying birds floated above the clamour.

It was a messy, discordant battle and Barsabbas allowed himself to indulge slightly, exulting in the violence that he had created.

CHAPTER FIFTEEN

Luren Menzo lived as comfortably as a supply slave could. His quarters in the warrens of the undercellars were exceptionally large, almost three times the cotspace of any other. He had the luxury of curtains that separated his living space from the squalor of the others. Battered cushions, thin blankets, old pict frames and even books littered his den. His possessions were valued amongst slaves, but not stowed securely, for no one would dare to touch them.

Menzo had come to all of this thanks to hard work: hard work in blackmail, extortion and a highly lucrative black market. As a supply overseer, Menzo took charge of a load-bearing team in the ship's cavernous docking hangars. He had a mob of servitors, haulers, riggers and packers who processed and stored the plunder and stock of the Blood Gorgons' raids. Through that, he had built a business of sorts. A cadre of close thugs to do his heavy work, a network of informants and many, many in need of his wares. They called him Mister Menzo and he offered them a service no one else could.

Of course there was no money, but amongst slaves, there was always barter: extra rations for pilfered liquor, a debt to Menzo for a loan, perhaps some information in exchange for a satch of obscura. It was surprising what slaves would do in exchange for a single hit of a narcotic to drown their sorrows.

There came a voice behind his curtain.

'Mister Menzo?'

Menzo drew back the curtain to his den. Bleary from sleep, he rubbed his eyes and checked his chron. It was still four hours until dawn cycle but the slave dens were raucous with activity.

'What? Quickly,' snapped Menzo. He did not like to receive visitors before his shift began.

'Sabtah is dead!' cried the man. Menzo recognised him by his matted hair and the dried, flaking corners of his mouth. It was one of the drug-dependent menials. Culk, or whatever his name was. His eyes were ringed with black from insomnia, the sign of a man who had spent eighteen hours labouring and the following six in a drug-tranced stupor.

'I know that. Quieten your voice,' Menzo said. He threw back his blankets and smoothed down the front of his canvas tunic.

'Will this... this affect your trade?' Culk asked pathetically, wringing his hands with worry.

'Why would it?'

'You always said Gammadin and Sabtah didn't care enough about the slaves to mind what we did with our sleep shift. You said Muhr'd be a hard bastard to try to sneak by.'

'Shut your mouth!' snapped Menzo. He glanced around to make sure no one had heard. Muhr was now the helmsman of the ship, so to speak. Insolence towards any bond-brother was punishable by torture and death, let alone the Witchlord. He could not imagine what harm Muhr would inflict on an insolent slave.

Culk didn't seem to understand the danger of his words. His speech was slurred and his eyelids hooded. Chemicals seemed to have addled his mind. 'But you said that. You said Muhr would be a right stiff pri–'

Menzo cut him off, clapping a palm to Culk's mouth and shoving him against a bulkhead. Culk's glazed eyes suddenly widened. Menzo had stabbed him with a shiv, a screwturner for unpacking sealed crates. He twisted and Culk shuddered all over before falling slack.

As Menzo lowered Culk's body to the floor, he heard footsteps behind him.

It was a trio of slave loaders, judging by the curve of their backs and the slump of their calloused shoulders. The men had just completed a toil shift and were hurrying back to their dens for a flicker of sleep before their labour began anew.

'Long live Lord Muhr!' Menzo shouted to them, his bloodied shiv hidden in his palm.

'Long live Lord Muhr,' they chanted wearily without even acknowledging him with a look.

Pounding drums and the squeal of a viol penetrated the citadel decks of the foreship, a constant babble of sound that suggested relentless energy.

It echoed in the abyssal halls with a timbre that did not belong in the pages of man-made music. The citadels themselves were unbarred, their masters and slaves trickling out to cavort on the wide causeways that connected them.

On the stone walkway, Brother Skellion glanded a concoction of industrial chems. The abrasive substance scoured his superhuman fortitude, lapsing him in and out of consciousness. Skellion was naked, except for a loincloth of chain; today was not a day for war. He allowed himself to sink down on his palanquin as menials massaged his keg-like quadriceps. Other menials filed and polished the stubbled horns that grew across his upper back.

Since his ascension, Muhr had declared a day of celebration. For a Blood Gorgon, that meant an orgy of chem-based alcoholics, savage pleasure and pit-fighting. The young warriors of Squad Akkadia indulged themselves. The air was thick with incense, and wine had sluiced in sticky rivers across the floor.

In truth, Skellion did not care whether Sabtah or Muhr ascended. He was a young warrior, inducted two years ago, and he barely remembered Gammadin. Skellion and many other new youngbloods in the Chapter shared the same nonchalance towards the leadership struggle. As long as Muhr promised him plunder and war, Skellion cared nothing for history.

Aboard the *Cauldron Born*, Vigoth locked himself away in his tower, high up in the eastern shelves of the citadel deck. A sagging gambrel roof capped the iron fort that was anchored into the bulkhead, clinging to the wall like a barnacle.

Sheltered within, Chirurgeon Vigoth was left to his brooding. He was not pleased with Muhr's ascension. He was one of the coven, a witch too, but that did not make him one of Muhr's own.

Casting the bones again, he watched the runes tumble in the darkness of his vault. They landed on the sign of the Ophidian – a bad omen.

He feared for the old ways, for Vigoth himself was old. He remembered a time when the Blood Gorgons had roamed freely. There had been no limits, not physically, nor of time in their immortal age, nor of law or code to restrain them. It was precisely that which made them Blood Gorgons. It raised them above the loyalist Slave Marines who were no better than menial servants of the enthroned Emperor.

There were others within the coven who shared his views: Nabonidus, for one. They had scryed. They had cast the bones. They had prayed to the gods.

Picking up the Ophidian tablet, Vigoth traced the rune with his fingers. The serpentine lacuna was a portent of cycles, resembling a snake devouring its own tail. It symbolised destruction and the rebirth of history.

Muhr would be a new beginning. But to create anew, Muhr would dismantle the old. Vigoth feared for the old with a deep conviction.

Autoloaders clicked on cyclical. He swivelled, and the paralysed bulk of his lascannon arms tingled gently where machine fibre was sutured to flesh nerves.

His name was Gunner-156X, but the maintenance slave jokingly referred to him as 'Sternface'.

The world outside was boundless and black, impossible for him to understand. Cocooned against the universe, human eyes attuned to nothing but signature scans.

He locked onto a target, a sudden blip on the auspex. He framed it under target lock for a brief second, and then it was gone.

Wires thrummed and electricity coursed through his veins. His focus was singular. In the distance, he heard the deep throb of celebration as the Blood Gorgons revelled. There was the sound of the ship's auspex systems sweeping the regional asteroids, bypassing debris and the looming nearby moons. He heard all these things, but his focus remained singular.

Gunner-156X was a gun servitor. His sole reason for existence was the functioning las blister 156X, a six-stack lascannon turret. A tiny pore on the oceanic hide of the *Cauldron Born*. He was hard-wired, his fleshy torso plugged at the hip into a swivel turret and his arms amputated by the triple pod lascannons affixed to his shoulder sockets.

There. A target again.

Multiple targets. Sizeable threat. Cruiser-sized craft and shoals of escorts. A swarm of unknown predators encircling the leviathan bulk of the *Cauldron Born*.

With a domino effect, defence blisters and lance ports all reported the same active reading. The entire starboard sector came alive with warning.

Gunner-156X suddenly felt alive. This was the only time that he remembered the human concept of excitement. He swivelled his lasstack, locking onto the approaching fleet. They were too far away for him to see, but he could feel them like cold pricks on his skin from the ship's hardplugged monitors.

++All automatic defences stand down. All automatic stand down.++

Gunner-156X paused. His muscles twitched. Where the locking clamps of the turret connected to his shoulders he itched. He waited for the override authorization.

++Defence system down. Authorisation: Lord Anko Muhr.++

Muhr...

Gunner-156X brought up his memory banks. Muhr was the master now. He knew this had not always been the case. There had been another, but the information had been blanked out. Changed. His machine mind could never bring up that data again.

++Authorisation cleared.++

As the unknown fleet lurked closer, Gunner-156X powered down simultaneously along with all the ship's defences.

The fleet of Opsarus stole upon them suddenly, ambushing them from behind the flare of a gas giant. Skulking cruisers of rusted white, great shambling things, drifting together like listless corpses. They entered the *Cauldron Born's* docking bays without challenge.

No strike fighters were scrambled to intercept the intruders even as eight Light-class cruisers berthed themselves inside the Gorgons' fortress. Neither did the space hulk's lance batteries and gun towers and defence blisters fire upon them. The alarms within the docks did not sound. Void seals did not activate to trap the invaders within the exterior bulkheads.

Most Blood Gorgons, lost within the depths of their delight, did not know what had occurred. Many were still pleasure-drowsed and heavily intoxicated. After all, Lord Muhr had granted them permission – nay, he had encouraged it.

Within eight minutes of landing, squads of Plague Marines prowled the lower decks of the floating fortress. The cruisers disgorged almost five full companies of Plague Marines and several regiments of Septic infantry.

Reports were mixed as to what followed; there was considerable confusion. There were a minority of squads who had remained vigilant in the wake of Sabtah's death, Muhr's dissenters. They engaged the invaders in a brief, sporadic firefight in the Maze of Acts Martial and the slave barracks of mid-level 42. Other reports held that armed Blood Gorgons, surprised by the swiftness of the Plague Marine boarding action, could do nothing. Muhr declared on mass broad-speakers that the Nurgle Marines were allies and brothers. In any event, the invaders seized the *Cauldron Born* with minimal resistance and no casualties.

All after-action reports agreed, however, that Muhr welcomed the invaders on the mezzanine level of the ship's helm. In the vast bowels of the armoured prow, the Lord-Sorcerer knelt and greeted the captains of Nurgle. They removed their helmets and clasped forearms.

From around the ship, most of the Blood Gorgons were rounded up and herded into the ship's mezzanine prow. Disorientated and naked, they were forced to obey at gunpoint. The shamed Chaos Space Marines were manhandled, pushed and kicked like animals. The only casualty was Brother-Sergeant Kroder of Squad Zargos, shot through the skull as an example for his squad who assaulted the invaders with their bare hands. A minority managed to flee into the forgotten bowels of the ship, but it was a Pyrrhic victory. The shame was overwhelming.

Under the glittering chandeliers and candle tiers of the mid-prow, Muhr addressed his fallen Chapter, or at least those who had been shepherded there. The Lord Sorcerer pledged his allegiance to the Plague Marines and to Nurgle and grovelled. There was a sickness to his enthusiasm that was utterly at odds with the indignity and fury that raged amongst his Chapter. Even those who had supported his ascension began to doubt the wisdom of their decision.

But it would amount to an impotent rage. There was nothing the Blood Gorgons could do. Two-thirds were unarmoured and shamefully naked. They had been stripped of their weapons. Already, the Plague Marines mocked them, taunting them about desecrating their sacred suits of armour. Surrounded by a thousand Plague Marines, the Blood Gorgons became hostages aboard their own ship.

As a final shame, Opsarus the Crow appeared before them. In his Tactical Dreadnought Armour, he was a living totem of Nurgle's corpulent aesthetics. Hulking and leviathan, his every movement was like the slow grind of a tectonic plate. His head was miniscule in comparison to his mountainous body, a hooded face shaded from light, set in the centre of his torso case. Spores, chittering parasites and entire hives of honeycombed growth glowed an almost lambent green against the ivory surface of his plate. He placed a hand on Muhr's bowed head and raised the other.

'This is my conquest,' Opsarus began. His voice throbbed like a migraine. 'I will carve an empire in the name of Mortarion, and Hauts Bassiq will be the foundation for my fleet. A stepping stone. I thank you for giving me your world, and be assured I will repay you in time. But for now,' he laughed, 'I must subjugate the Blood Gorgons.'

The Plague Marines turned the battle into a massacre. A seven-man squad of Plague Marines broke through the main line of fighting and overran into the camp itself. They clambered over the carriages, spilling the heavy steel structures onto their sides, belly-up, tracks whirling. The plainsmen's screams were driven to hysterical heights. Grenades flattened tents and wagons.

Upon hearing the wails of their relatives, a flock of mounted braves broke away from the main battleline. Barsabbas cursed their lack of discipline. The enemy pushed through the gap that had opened up, punching through the Bassiq muster. Plague Marines spearheaded the rush, tearing braves off their mounts and snapping them with their big, broad hands.

Barsabbas tried to manoeuvre his flanking forces to plug the hole in the line, but his voice was lost under the war clamour. Three squads of Plague Marines, twenty-one warriors, punched through and doubled back to hit the mounted plainsmen from behind. Shambling, horned, heavy with fur and mould, solid like steel-cased ogres, they tore into the braves. The line threatened to break as the solid phalanx of mounted riders became disjointed, fragmented and slowly isolated.

Frustrated, Barsabbas tried to fight his way towards the gap. A bolt shot smacked off his shoulder pad and a small-calibre round cracked his visor. Ahead, he saw a talon squall rear up and kick a Plague Marine in the pelvis with its powerful legs. It staggered the Traitor Marine. Another talon squall seized the momentary advantage and leapt onto his chest, the one-tonne beast driving the Chaos Space Marine into the ground and worrying his chest plate with a hooked beak. Others piled on, snapping and kicking at the downed enemy. A brave drew his recurve smoothly and unleashed an arrow into the Plague Marine's throat, piercing the rubberised neck seal. The Plague Marine died. It was an island of triumph amidst a rolling ocean of slaughter. Four squads of Plague Marines were too many.

The braves broke. It began at the edges first: a tense, hesitant withdrawal as the screams of the camp became too much. The braves had accounted for themselves longer than Barsabbas had expected. After all, the Plague Marines were gods to them. Malevolent gods, but no less awesome for that. In their retreat, the braves were butchered. Autocannon and heavy bolter fire chased them, chopping them down as they fled.

The camp had been overrun. Plague Marines and their Septic minions were putting the settlement to flame. Hooded men with canister packs and nozzle guns hosed the area with gas. Native kinsmen wandered about, half-dressed and confused. Some did not even try to run, for there was nowhere to go. Clothing and household items were scattered into the dirt. Black smoke and poisonous gas gathered in thick plumes.

The moment had come for Barsabbas to steal away.

He churned across the cactus fields. He stepped amongst the dead and crushed succulents, running ankle-deep through a mire of mud, gore and crushed pulp. Hobbling several paces behind, Sindul was trawled through the fields. He ran several steps and fell, dragged along by his knees, before he regained his footing and tripped again.

A rearguard of Septic infantry spotted the lone Blood Gorgon and his captive. He was a prime target, a proud trophy. They gave chase. It was a stupid thing to do and a trained officer should have known better, perhaps voxed for reinforcements or a gun platform, but their commander was riding the high of a victorious slaughter. They gave chase and Barsabbas shot them all down. He turned and emptied the last of his clip, auto-targetters skipping from one head to the next.

Without turning, Barsabbas set a hard pace up the mountain pass, heading ever north. The sounds of the massacre echoed up the valley, but Barsabbas did not look back.

The Funeral Mountains were a desolate place. Creosote bushes squirmed from between the cracks of dolomite slabs and pupfish dwelled in the alluvial salt pans. Even the mountains themselves were small and steep, squeezed together to form telescopic peaks that fell away into vertical chasms. The plainsmen interred their ancestors here, marking their resting places with petroglyphs and stick-like carvings.

The rocks were soft and crumbled dangerously beneath his grip. Yet Barsabbas climbed on with an urgent recklessness. He vaulted onto a narrow ledge and dragged Sindul neck-first up the slope after him.

'Please,' choked Sindul. 'Slower.'

Barsabbas ignored him. The enemy were still giving chase. His auspex imprinted the ghostly contrails of their pursuers across his visor.

'Let me free. I can fight. Just let me see the daylight. I can fight,' Sindul wheezed.

Barsabbas tugged the chain leash sharply. 'Be still.'

He settled beyond the ledge, crouching down to minimise his profile. If the enemy insisted on pursuit, then he would give them something to find. He plucked forth one of the frag grenades that hung from chain loops across his left shoulder pad. Stilling his breath, he waited.

Beneath the rock ledge, on the rock-strewn escarpment, a single solitary reading flashed across the auspex. The target was nimble, fast, scaling up the mountain with sure-footed speed.

'Are you stupid? You don't need that,' Sindul murmured from beneath his hood.

'Quiet,' hissed Barsabbas, yanking the chain taut. The target scrambled closer.

'Are you scent blind? That doesn't smell like a cultist of Nurgle. This one stinks of milk curd.'

Barsabbas paused, testing the air with his olfactory glands. Perhaps the dark eldar had a keener sense of smell than he realised. Heightened sensory perception was a trait of the eldar species, but Barsabbas had not expected anything so acute. Although he heard the skitter of pebbles bouncing down the slope, he could smell no distinguishable scent except for the blood and gunsmoke as the updraught carried the stench from the valley below.

'Plainsman!' Sindul shouted out.

Before Barsabbas could silence the dark eldar with a swift repercussive strike, a voice answered from below. '*How de bod, koag!*'

A long-limbed man scuttled up the ledge with his hands and feet gripping the rock with practiced ease. The shredded remains of a feather crest flapped from his head. It was Gumede.

'Why did you follow me?' Barsabbas growled. His hand fell to the mace looped at his hip.

'Why did you abandon us to die?' Gumede asked. His voice cracked. He sounded wounded although he had suffered no physical injury.

'I have plans you would not understand. You have served me well, slavestock, and for that I will give you mercy. But do not seek to follow me. Leave now before I kill you.'

Gumede collapsed onto his knees. 'My people are gone. I have nowhere to go. You may kill me if you wish, Red God.'

Barsabbas began to think tactically, an instinctive cognitive process that was the product of intense psychiatric therapy. He could kill Gumede now and be done with it. It would give him little satisfaction but it would minimise further complications. Or, he could exploit Gumede as his guide. Traversing the northern badlands would be significantly more difficult without the aid of someone who knew the land. From his brief encounter with the Bassiq, Barsabbas had learned to value their connection with the land. Perhaps this would be the most tactical choice.

'You will come with me, Gumede. I need your knowledge of these lands,' Barsabbas said.

'I will not,' Gumede said, staring vacantly. 'You are a betrayer. You left us to die. I saw you run.'

'I am a god to you,' Barsabbas reminded him, rising to his feet.

'You are a cruel god.'

Barsabbas could not understand the human's misgivings. He knew of them, but he could not understand them. Humans formed emotional connections to things, objects, people, animals. It weakened their minds. Barsabbas knew no bond but the blood bond. The blood bond was a pragmatic thing, a multiplier of combat effectiveness. He felt no love for Sargaul, only a need to recover him, like a swordsman who was missing his swordarm. There was no place in Barsabbas's consciousness for attachment. He did not understand Gumede at all.

'Battles will be won and some will be lost. Today, you lost,' Barsabbas said.

Gumede seemed to wither physically. He shook his head with a grimace. 'I've lost everything.'

'You were born naked and as you are. You have everything. You have simply lost everything you grew attached to,' Barsabbas replied. He crossed over to the rock ledge and surveyed the boiling flames of the camp far, far below.

Gumede's shoulders began to tremble. 'I lost my sons.'

Barsabbas pondered this. Finally he nodded. 'They have no gene-seed. You can replace them,' he answered, finally enjoying his discourse with the simple-minded human.

When Gumede did not answer, Barsabbas continued. 'You will come with me. I calculate that, with your field expertise and knowledge of terrain, you will reduce my travel time by approximately thirty per cent.'

'Leave me be, Red God. There is nothing else you can give me.'

'I have condemned your people. But I can still save your world.'

It was a lie, of course. Barsabbas did not believe that. But lying was another thing that humans did not understand. To lie was to weave reality. Barsabbas did not know what stopped humans from lying – some obscure social contract to their fellow man? Another self-imposed limitation that reduced effectiveness.

'How?' Gumede asked, finally looking up. To see a grown man slack-mouthed from crying disgusted Barsabbas. The Chaos Space Marine was not even sure he possessed tear ducts any more. Hiding his distaste, Barsabbas put a hand on Gumede's shoulder.

'I am a god, remember? I have plans.'

CHAPTER SIXTEEN

And so they marched together, Gumede of the Plains navigating, the Blood Gorgon striding behind with his chained, captive dark eldar in tow. They followed the trails through the cracked, stony desert. The ground resembled the skin of a blistered heel, dry and flaking. Caprids never grazed here, for the stone wore down their hooves. Between the badlands and Ur, the nomadic kinships were considered poor due to the absence of large herds. But it was also a common tale that the denizens of Ur were shrewd traders and tricked the herdsmen of the north.

There was no trade now.

The days were dark and overcast with clouds of mustard yellow. Humid gases sluiced from the atmosphere, a weak corrosive acid that only scoured the earth. The landscape looked prematurely aged, as if the cycle of seasons, renewal and ecology had ground to a halt. New roots did not sprout from the wilted remains of the old.

During the high noon, when the suns were at their harshest and Gumede and Sindul became fatigued, Barsabbas found shelter in the deathly settlements of the northern plains. The wagons and trailers were empty but stank sour with stale air. Many were marked with the white palm-print of plague. Of the dead, however, there was no sign. It seemed they did not linger in their homes.

Finally, having found some momentary peace, he unhooded the dark eldar. Blinking weakly, Sindul flinched at the sunlight. His weeks of sensory deprivation had left him dazed and psychologically depressed.

The chains on his wrists, however, remained, a tightly wound knot of heavy links.

They rested in the settlement for two nights and left on the third dawn. Gumede and Sindul slept in borrowed beds, the sheets still smelling of death and their previous owners. They ate what they could from the abandoned larders, touching only the knots of chewy dried caprid and some dry sugar fruits. Barsabbas did not sleep, nor did he eat anything more than a handful of jerked meat once a day. He spent his hours watching the distance, plotting his course and cleaning, always cleaning his weapons.

As they trekked, Gumede tried to point out the shimmering silver mirages that steamed from the hot clay ground. He gestured at the exposed coal seams that ran like black blood through the gullies and ravines. Barsabbas was unimpressed. He did not even seem to be listening. The plainsman's attachment to his land irritated him and distracted him.

Sometimes, when the march became weary, Gumede even spoke of his kinship. His voice would be heavy with bitterness. He spoke fondly of his kinship and the pain his loss caused him every day.

The Chaos Space Marine simply could not understand how Gumede could come to feel emotionally involved with rocks and soil or other people. Home and family was not a concept his mind could appreciate. His lack of comprehension irritated him. It made him angry, and Barsabbas reacted to anger by killing and breaking.

Everything seemed to matter to these humans. Barsabbas wondered how their fragile intellects could withstand the emotional assault. The Blood Gorgon knew only training and fighting. There were events in-between, but those things did not matter to him. His mind had been sharpened to a singular focus. Barsabbas felt no remorse or guilt at the death of Gumede's people. There was no right or wrong, it had been an act of will in achieving a goal. He simply found no logic in the man's reasoning.

Four more days in the empty badlands brought them to a broad basin of split clay. The cracked minerals tessellated with regularity like brown tiles. The basin was endorheic, an evaporated ocean floor littered with fossil and coal.

There was a familiarity to the landscape that gave Barsabbas hope. He felt a sense of recollection, and yet he knew he had never seen this place with his own eyes. Without a doubt, Sargaul had been here before, for the feeling of paramnesia was too compelling. Barsabbas remembered the smoke stacks that rose from the hard ground, fluted chimneys that belched smoke. When he peered at the furnaces through his bolter scope, he could see the barbed gravitational tanks of the dark eldar framed within his crosshairs. They were narrow, sword-shaped vehicles that hovered above the ground.

'This is the location?'

Sindul shrugged. 'This is the only place where we strike out on raid, yes. We have herded our captives here.'

Nodding, Barsabbas breathed deep, reliving the sense of familiarity that he had not really experienced firsthand. He felt Sargaul's presence, he was sure of it, as his heart rate began to rise.

'My kabal will still be here,' Sindul said, pointing with his chin.

'Then I will kill more.'

'Give me a blade, let me fight.'

Barsabbas rolled with laughter. 'You think I am stupid? Let you go and you will fight for me?' Barsabbas laughed again.

But Sindul did not. The narrow, slitted features of his face remained gravely serious.

'I cannot allow the kabal to see me captive. I would rather be a traitor.'

'I will not release your chains, eldar. Save your tricks.'

'In my culture, we have a different word for traitor. *Muri'vee*. It means gambler, or opportunist. But its meaning is more subtle than that. It means the "warrior who outplays".'

'You wish to be a traitor.'

'Of course. Otherwise I will be a slave in their eyes forever. Even when I am dead I will be remembered as a slave.'

On some level Barsabbas understood. Shame and pride were the foundations of character. Oddly, the dark eldar way of thinking made sense to him. Sindul could not return to his people a captive, a slave or a neutered warrior. The dark eldar would rather be remembered as a traitor. His people valued guile and cunning so at least there was conviction in that.

'Then it will be so,' Barsabbas agreed. Shame was not something that he wished his enemies to feel. He preferred they died fighting him, with a blade in their dead hands.

Barsabbas lunged forwards without warning, seized Sindul and hauled him into his lap by his hair. Sindul squirmed in response, cycling his legs in the air. Pinning Sindul's head with an elbow, Barsabbas began to unscrew the extractor cap hidden inside his mace.

Sindul's legs continued to kick as Barsabbas started to work. It was a long and relatively painful procedure, especially given Sindul's defiant thrashing. By the time Barsabbas had coaxed the larva into the extractor, Sindul's face was slick with blood. A weeping, gaping hole the size of a thumbnail puckered the flesh beneath the dark eldar's cheekbone.

Even as Sindul sulked at the indignity of his manhandling, Barsabbas hauled him up by the arm and yanked at the padlock around his neck, loosening his leash chains.

'Let me make this clear. I do this because I choose to. You present no threat to me, armed or unarmed. A traitor may be martyred in your culture, but in mine, we punish them severely.'

The lower dungeons of the *Cauldron Born* were honeycombed with oubliettes. They were no more than a maddening burrow of penrose stairs, ascending and descending while never appearing to end, each leading to a dingy grille hatch. The narrow, uneven steps meandered aimlessly, unlit and moist from the coolant leaks.

It was here that heavily armed Plague Marines escorted the Blood Gorgons into the dungeons. The action was executed with a façade of cordiality almost as if the Plague Marines were extending their hand in alliance, and the captivity was only an unfortunate side effect. Yet there was an undertone of veiled aggression. Lord Muhr had assured his brethren it was only a temporary relocation, until order was restored and his new leadership firmly cemented against dissenters.

Resistance was piecemeal, as the squads had quickly been separated upon boarding to prevent any cohesive counter-attack. Many were too drug-fugued to stand. Despite this, many rioted against their captors, fighting back with teeth and fists. But their armouries had been seized and the Plague Marines had the advantage of full combat riggings. Bond-Brothers Gamsis, Paeton and Himerius were shot before order was restored.

Some, including Squad Hezirah, escaped into the uncharted burrows of the space hulk.

Over the coming days, order aboard the *Cauldron Born* continued to deteriorate. Disease spread from the Plague Marines to the sheltered immune systems of the Blood Gorgons' slaves. Within a week, hundreds within the slave warrens, barracks and engine galleys had fallen ill: fevers, dysentery, pneumonic viruses, dermal infections. Even servitors began to glitch as ailments began to affect their biosystems. Without the menials who maintained the inhabited sections of the space hulk, the vessel ceased to function effectively. Circulation systems became blocked as drainage pipes leaked. The lanterns remained unlit and food rotted in storage, untouched.

The touch of Nurgle was everywhere. Like a virus incarnate, the Plague Marine intrusion had weakened the Chapter from within. Rapidly deteriorating, it seemed Sabtah's fears had come true. The Blood Gorgons had become fractured again.

The undercellar was dark and cold but this did not matter to Sergeant Krateus, who preferred being cold and free than warm and captive. Squad Hezirah had done well to elude the round-up, processing and lockdown. They had escaped to the infirmary wards during the boarding action and smuggled themselves through a large drainage tunnel during the rioting.

Used to circulate waste, the undercellar was a series of sealed tunnels that laced the lowest sectors of the *Cauldron Born*. They had hidden there for nine days, finding a sanctuary amongst the stinking tubes and low ceilings. Waste matter sluiced through overhead grates, and the ammonia and faecal stink was stinging to their acute senses, but they bided their time.

They were weaponless, but they had escaped fully cased in their power armour. The suits aided them, sealing them against the filth. Rebreathers circulated fresh air. Glucose solutions from med-dispensers fed their bodies. But they could not continue in this way. A Traitor Marine's instinct was to fight and although they had no armaments, they felt compelled to do something.

Nine days after the seizure, Krateus finally decided they could hide no more.

Squad Hezirah headed out, following the disposal tubes. Besides Krateus, there were Brothers Cambysses, Zagros, Magan, Khabur and Ngirsu. Retrieving tact-maps from their suit databanks, they followed the blueprints towards the starboard sub-hangars. They made good progress following a sewage main that ran for almost half the length of the space hulk. In some parts, the partition grates were so thin they could hear the scrape of heavy boots above.

Somewhere between mid-sublevel 12 and some unclaimed corridors, a patrol of Plague Marines strode directly overhead. The squad froze, the shadows of the patrol ghosting across the tops of their helmets. Risking an upwards glance, Krateus counted seven Plague Marines, the sacred number of Nurgle.

They waited until the steps had faded before they began moving again. Krateus thought briefly about moving ahead and ambushing the patrol. They would need the weapons once they reached the docking hangar, but he dismissed the thought. They were too far away and the alarm would be raised too early.

Leaving the sewage main behind, the squad began to pick their way through the smaller, upward-slanting sluice pipes. It was tough, the drainage systems tight and narrow, and for once their bulk did not aid them.

Krateus led the way, as he would need to disable the high-torque circular saws that lined the tunnels at the entrance. The fan blades shredded organic waste with powerful motors, buzzing to life when their sensor pads came into contact with any material. Being 'disposed' was a common method of culling unwanted slaves through the torque-saws.

Krateus reached out. Sensing movement, the saw began to spasm, oscillating back and forth with jerky, vicious chops. Jamming his fingers into where the blades connected to the motor, Krateus began to fidget the central shaft with his free hand. Sparks hissed like water droplets as the motor began to grind Krateus's armoured fingers. He worked quietly, trying to tear out the wires from the axial casing. The torque-saw squealed as his wedged digits began to give out. Finally, Krateus found the wires and clawed them out with the tips of his fingers, breaking their fibrous bunches.

The torque-saw died. Krateus pulled his hand from the blades. Four of the fingers on his right hand were missing. Blood drooled down his forearm and leaked from his elbow. Proud of his work, the sergeant waved his squad onwards with the stump of his right hand. There would be a time for healing later, perhaps even some augmetic implants, but for now he gave his fingers no second thought. The body was a tool to survive and preservation of non-vital body parts was mere social conditioning.

The Traitor Marine was functional as long as his primary heart still beat. As his wounds began to coagulate, Krateus had already forgotten how many fingers on his right hand he once had. He knew only to keep moving.

It was not long before Squad Hezirah reached their intended destination point. Sub-hangar 6 was a minor docking berth. It was essentially a void-shielded section that held a trio of Hag interceptors and a lone Thunderhawk: the *Sleepwalker*. The armoured compartment was lightly guarded by two Plague Marines, their silhouettes murky and indistinct under the low, red phos-lights.

Hezirah fanned out wide, sprinting behind the heavy fuselage. Keeping to the shadows when they could, shifting their weight lightly despite their size, they crept past the interceptors. The Hags were servitor-crewed, a swarm of vector-thrust light strikers utilised to hunt down incoming space ordnance. These would be of no use to Krateus.

He moved on to the larger *Sleepwalker*, signalling for his squad to remain stationary. The gunship was heavy-muzzled, with a brutishly stubby wingspan and thickly plated fuselage of scratched umber. Using the gunship's pectoral fins for purchase, Krateus pulled himself up by his arms until he was almost chin-level with the cockpit. The gunship squealed softly as he did so, the tiny creak of metal on metal. Krateus held his breath. But the Plague Marines did not seem to notice. Krateus closed his eyes and counted to five before he dared to move again.

Peering into the cockpit bay, he checked the console and almost swore aloud. The fuel gauge sat on empty.

Empty. Krateus felt much the same as he lowered himself down to the decking. Refuelling would be difficult without fuel servitors, and that was assuming the supply lines had not already been locked.

'Empty as we feared?' His bond, Cambysses, appeared next to him.

'Contingency,' Krateus affirmed.

Flexing the piston muscles of his forearms, Krateus with Cambysses at his side rounded the Thunderhawk and stole closer to the Plague Marine sentries. The enemy stood impassive, their backs against the wall, bolt-guns snug against their chest plates. Auspexes hung from their war belts, the screens greened out on standby.

Krateus knew what to do.

Without warning, he burst into a sprint, darting out from behind the *Sleepwalker*. He rushed for the cover of a Hag interceptor. He felt something clip his shoulder and heard the slamming bark of bolt shot. The Plague Marines gave chase, shouting into their vox-links as they did so. Both sentries ran past the *Sleepwalker* in pursuit.

That was when Cambysses struck. He launched himself out from hiding as the Plague Marines rushed past. He came out low in a wrestler's prowl and tackled the closest sentry into the decking. They were struggling for control of the boltgun before they hit the ground in a crashing roll. Both hands hanging on to the weapon, Cambysses summoned every shred of his upper body strength. But the Plague Marine held on. They butted heads, grunting with animalistic exertion. Shots went off.

Suddenly, Zagros and Magan were there too. Magan coiled an arm around the Plague Marine's throat from behind and Zagros began to drag on his ankles, sweeping his legs out from underneath him. Khabur and Ngirsu rushed the second sentry. The Plague Marine brought up his weapon but could not shoot before Ngirsu closed the distance and clinched up with him.

There was a brief, intense struggle and loud shouting echoed in the armoured hangar. Another shot rang out. A moment of confusion. Cambysses had shot the Plague Marine. He had finally wrestled the boltgun free. It was more awkward than the Godwyn-pattern boltgun Cambysses was familiar with, with pitted wood panelling and an archaic pre-Heresy sliding track mechanism, but it was a boltgun nonetheless. The shot tore a gaping hole in the Plague Marine's neck. Cambysses's next shot killed the Plague Marine who grappled with Ngirsu outright, with a point-blank round to the back of the head.

By then the alarms had began to wail. The low, red phos-lights were strobing to a regular heartbeat. Shot through the neck, the last sentry continued to struggle against Magan and Zagros. Cambysses pushed the stolen boltgun against the bleeding wound on his neck.

'Take him with us,' said Krateus. 'We need him.' The sergeant had retrieved the boltgun from the slain sentry and was checking the magazine.

Magan pulled the wounded Plague Marine to his feet. The neck wound was bad, a wheezing entry hole that gaped like a skewed mouth. The exit wound was even worse, a fist-sized crater that punched out between the Plague Marine's shoulder blades.

The sentry breathed in short, ragged gasps. The serious wound made him appear slow and lethargic, but he did not seem to be in pain. He even insulted Cambysses's blood lineage as he applied pressure to his neck with his hands. The warriors of Nurgle were notoriously hardy, even by the superhuman standards of the Space Marines. Their corpulent state killed their nervous system, numbed their flesh and thickened their blood. Essentially, they became immune to pain and shock trauma.

Pressing the boltgun to the Plague Marine's head, they marched him on. Moving quickly, at a jog, prodding their hostage with the muzzle of their boltguns, they left sub-hangar 6 behind.

Ship alarms all along sub-hangars 6, 12 and their corresponding sub-levels were keening, changing in pitch from long and wailing to short, pulsating howls. Yet on the command deck, all was quiet. Except for the constant throb of air circulators, there was no noise.

Opsarus lounged in the deck's command throne without moving.

Wire spindles and optic thread were interfaced directly into the incisions in his spinal cord. It was a crude surgical method, courtesy of Muhr, which allowed him limited access to the ship's command functions. The spindles squirted visual data into his cerebral cortex, allowing him to view the vessel's many surveillance systems.

But it was precisely the crude nature of the surgery that limited his command. He was not Gammadin, and without Gammadin's genecodes or the ship's proper acquiescence, Opsarus did not have full command of the ship's defence systems. The ship was a predatory steed, but Gammadin's steed. It had a wild sentience, whether artificial or daemonic, that recognised only Gammadin.

Opsarus could observe, but he could not control. His frustration was obvious as his fingers fidgeted, spasming every so often.

He watched impatiently as ghost images flashed behind his eyelids. He saw a rogue squad of Blood Gorgons, mostly unarmed, sprinting down a flashing red corridor. He saw his own, Plague Marines he knew by name, hesitate to shoot. Stalemate.

'This is not right. They need to shoot.'

Opsarus opened his eyes and the images faded. Muhr stood some distance away, watching the console banks that honeycombed the high walls.

'They need to shoot,' Muhr repeated, shaking his head.

'You are a strange soul, sorcerer,' Opsarus chuckled throatily.

Muhr turned away from the consoles, his voice faltering. 'Master?'

'Shooting at your own warriors? I feel no loyalty to your Blood Gorgons, but you should.'

'If we do not shoot, they will escape. We can't afford such mistakes so early. It will weaken us in the eyes of our Chapters. We have to kill them all.'

'That is Brother Hepsamon. Mine. He is a warrior with a good campaign record.'

'Master...'

'We spread lengthy misery, but Grandfather Nurgle is deeply caring towards his mortal and daemonic servants,'

Muhr did not seem to understand.

'That is where you and I differ, Muhr. Your warriors hate you, but they fear you. Mine...' Opsarus did not finish, he simply gestured to the consoles.

On the grainy pict screen, they saw Brother Hepsamon turn on his captors. There was a brief struggle. The hostage threw himself before the flashing boltguns of Squad Hezirah. He sacrificed himself, the black and white image falling jerkily to the ground. Waiting Plague Marines swept in for the kill.

'Loyalty. Above the carnage, the slaughter, the violence and the lust, there must exist loyalty. The backbone of a fighting force, tasty marrow. You can't make soup without marrow. Did you know that, Muhr?'

Muhr watched the screen as the last of Squad Hezirah were chopped down by bolter fire. Executed. Had the Plague Marine not given up his life, then the plan might have succeeded.

'If I give an order for my own warriors to kill their brethren, what sort of master would that make me?' Opsarus asked. 'A fat one without trust. No trust. No army,' Opsarus said, blossoming his fingers as if a plume of dust had puffed up.

'That's your flaw, Muhr. You do not know how to foster your brethren,' Opsarus said, chortling with delight.

Muhr strode down the length of the dungeon cells, clattering the cage bars. 'Who here does not swear allegiance to me?'

He pounded the metal grates for emphasis. 'Who?'

Blood Gorgons he had known for decades, some for centuries, stared at him with hatred in their eyes. Muhr knew he was a traitor to them. He was their lord, but they would not follow him.

'Who does not recognise my place within this Chapter? Who?' Muhr repeated. He struck the cage bars with the back of his armoured fist, lashing out in his anger.

None of the Blood Gorgons answered him. They seemed unified by their animosity towards him. The thought made Muhr angrier. Even imprisoned, stripped of their wargear, the Traitor Marines were resolute. They would not give up any ground.

'I do not.'

Muhr turned, finally finding a target for his wrath. It was Captain Zuthau, Commander of Fourth Company, a towering giant of a Chaos Space Marine, horned and plated from centuries of warp travel, the skin of his arms and torso pinched and ridged into chitin. Zuthau who had conquered the sea fleets of Shar. Zuthau, the very same who had orchestrated the capture and ransom of a tau caste leader. Zuthau who slew eleven Ultramarines at the Brine Delta Engagement.

Muhr stalked towards Zuthau slowly. The captain stood at the front of his cell. He wore only a breechcloth, yet he stood proud, almost a full head taller than Muhr. Zuthau. A war hero.

Muhr shot him in the belly and then the head. The gun-shots were so loud and so sudden that Zuthau never reacted. Muhr shot him three more times as he lay in a spreading pool of blood. Zuthau's blood bond, Brother-Sergeant Arkaud, screamed in rage. He threw himself at the cage bars, spittle flying from his mouth. Muhr shot him too, emptying the rest of his bolt pistol.

Arkaud was a veteran, but Muhr reasoned it was a small sacrifice to pay for the greater good of the Chapter.

The dungeons remained quiet. No one shouted from their cells. Even those who could not see what had occurred, knew by the rusty scent of blood and the methane stink of gunsmoke.

CHAPTER SEVENTEEN

As Barsabbas approached the dark eldar encampment, he could hear the bark of warp beasts. The creatures could scent his soul. They were restless, excited, their yaps and wails carrying across the darkness of the night.

But Barsabbas could scent them too.

'Warp hounds,' Barsabbas said softly.

'*Illith-rauch*,' Sindul whispered. 'Hounds of the Arenas. Slave-maulers.'

'Tell me how to get in,' Barsabbas said.

Across the horizon, a field of spined, xerophytic grasses sprawled out for many hundreds of metres, bald patches of clay interspersed with coarse continents of low brush. Beyond that, the chimney stacks of the facility could be seen against a purple sky.

'You can't. My kabal dispatched a large raiding force here to claim our rights of plunder from the Ner'Gal. Dozens of them. My people are vigilant when slaves are involved.'

Barsabbas narrowed his eyes at the xenos. 'Remember not to run.' The Traitor Marine rubbed his thumb across the scarred bump on Sindul's cheek.

'Watch him,' he told Gumede. Bobbing his head obediently, the chief slid a long arrow from his quiver and notched his recurve bow. Barsabbas doubted the human was any match for the dark eldar in combat, but that didn't matter. Although the dark eldar's capacity for treachery was well known, they were almost painfully predictable.

As Barsabbas turned to go, Sindul seemed to have a change of heart. 'There is one way,' he began.

'Speak. Quickly.'

'Warp beasts are blind. Or at least they do not see in the way that humans see. They sense fear, even the slightest quaver of the heart. My people use them to run down escaped slaves. It doesn't matter when the slave escapes. If you have fear, or doubt, or hesitation, they will find you.'

'So I must not regard them with any measure of emotion.'

'Yes. If you can look upon a warp beast without emotion, then they will not attack you. The warp feeds on emotion.'

Barsabbas was not sure how he could do this. A warp beast was a daemonic creation from another plane of existence. He had never seen one before, but to look upon them and feel nothing seemed an obscure challenge.

'Sindul will guide me in. Gumede, stay here,' Barsabbas ordered.

The plainsman looked hurt, as if his courage had been questioned, but Barsabbas did not care. Humans felt too much emotion, it seemed they were predisposed to hysteria just from being left in the dark. Petty things quailed the human spirit too much. Gumede would definitely be a liability.

'Stay,' he repeated to the plainsman, as if humans were particularly dull.

Barsabbas set off at a low crouch, trying to muffle his heavy footfalls in the clay soil. Sindul ghosted nearby, sliding through dry grass and salt-bush without noise. The xenos could move shockingly quietly. Barsabbas had to rely on tactical training: rolling on the soles of his feet, tight control of his muscles, controlled breathing. Sindul seemed effortless. There was a springiness to his movement. The dark eldar was in total control of his body. When he needed to leap from one grass patch to another, he did it, flashing, bobbing and weaving. He moved so effortlessly it was difficult for Barsabbas to understand how it happened. If it were not for the metronome sweep of his auspex, he would have lost the dark eldar in the shadows.

As they neared the facility, Barsabbas pulled them to a halt. Ahead, prowling in front of the power station, were three warp beasts. They circled the perimeter of the main station block, guarding the drawn roller shutters. Another four drifted in and out of the shadows, guarding the fleet of dark eldar grav-tanks parked in the open. They prowled low like dogs, but shared few other canine traits. Their shoulders were thick and almost humanoid, loping arms connected to round deltoids.

'Remember what I said,' Sindul whispered.

'You are distracting me. Be quiet,' Barsabbas said flatly. He focused himself. Traitor Marines did not easily suffer from fear, but they were no emotionless servitors. The canine creatures made him tense. Although they posed no physical threat to him, they could raise the alarm and that gave him doubt. Breathing deeply, he suppressed it. He felt his heart rate and pulse dull, drawing out to a slow cadence.

Without hesitation, Barsabbas strode out into the open.

The warp beasts started and craned their muzzles skywards, snuffling the air. Barsabbas saw them up close. They were wet, skinless creatures, pulsating with exposed arteries and ridged muscle. As he stole closer, he could smell warp sulphur on their hides. It reminded him of Yetsugei, and he felt his heart rate spike. As if catching a sudden scent, the warp beasts sniffed the air in his direction. Their milk-white eyes saw nothing but their muzzles curled back in a growl, unsheathing strong sets of teeth.

Sindul slid past him, shaking his head with a haughty manner. He walked past the warp beasts, even putting out a hand to skim the muzzle of one, almost touching them. The hounds did not react. Emboldened by Sindul's manner, Barsabbas reached the armoured shutters without acknowledging them. Once there he turned and saw the three warp beasts licking their paws and gazing out across the horizon.

To his fore, the power station seemed empty beyond its half-drawn shutters. Through the dim green of his visor display, Barsabbas made out ancient machinery trapped beneath the woven fabric of thick dust. There were ripples of disturbed dust on the rockcrete ground, kicked-up tufts of floss that showed recent activity. He nodded at Sindul, a meaningful nod that reminded him of their pact.

With a soft click of his boltgun's safety, Barsabbas ducked underneath the shutters. They shuffled through the dust carpet, dragging their feet along the woolly filth to muffle their entrance.

They found themselves in some sort of workshop, dark and cavernous. Cogs, motors, pipes and power blocks were stacked like tetric sculptures, promising dark hiding places for the enemy.

'This way,' Sindul said, flitting up a short flight of metal steps that led into a porthole door. 'The slaves are beyond there.'

Wary of his captive but needing his guidance, Barsabbas rescanned the area with his auspex. Despite the high metal interference in the area, the dark eldar did not seem to be lying. The Blood Gorgon saw the distinct bumps of life signs overlaid with the contoured graphics of crowded machinery.

'Stay within my view, or I will shoot you. Give me any reason to suspect deceit, I will kill all your comrades first and then I will bury you alive,' Barsabbas promised.

Sindul did not seem fazed. 'Better a proud traitor than a shameful slave,' he replied.

Barsabbas's knotwork mace flashed in the dark. 'Then go.'

Barsabbas climbed a low walkway above furnace vats. Corrugated iron and brittle board shored up gaps in the rusting mesh platform. Below, he could hear the delirious drone of voices, shrill from panic and distress.

Four dark eldar raiders stood guard over the slaves. Close to two

hundred prisoners slept on the rockcrete floors, miserable huddles of
bodies swathed in rat's-nest clothing. The dark eldar were taking their
time to process the slaves, separating any with signs of the black wilt.
Three squat furnaces were firing up for the first time in centuries. Barsabbas could imagine what the dark eldar did to dispose of the sick and
infected. Further down the power station, separated by a chainlink fence,
healthy slaves were being loaded into cubed shipping containers, ready
to be shifted off-world.

Barsabbas fired from his vantage point. One of the dark eldar fell away,
his torso ruined. Another was chopped down at the shins. In one fluid
movement, Barsabbas rolled off the gantry, firing as he went. Sindul
followed, landing on his knees and spinning into a forward roll. At the
sound of gun-shots, the slaves rose up in one panicked tide. Confused by
the sudden chaos, the dark eldar guards fired randomly, spraying splinter
fire into the oncoming crowd.

Like a herder, Barsabbas fired his boltgun into the dense, mass of
slaves. He switched his vox-casters to maximum amplitude and screamed
so loud that the rafters rattled and the dirty-paned windows blew out.
Terrified of the braying giant in armour, the captured plainsmen overran their guards. Hundreds of slaves ran amok. People began to shriek
in terror.

Barsabbas blasted his voice at Sindul. 'Release the chainlinks, traitor.'

Sindul made his way across the station floor. He knifed any slave that
came too close, his pair of hook swords drizzling blood. Crossing over to
the holding pens, he struck the greasy padlock with a downward stroke,
cutting straight through the soft iron. As the cage door swung open,
Sindul had to vault up on top of the chainlink roof in order to avoid the
stampede of plainsmen gushing out.

From the side doors and connective rooms, dark eldar raiders emerged
from their sleep. Some were half-dressed in kimonos of dark silk. Bleary
and dazed, they nonetheless began to lay down indiscriminate splinterfire.

Snatching Sindul by the back of his cuirass, Barsabbas snapped at him,
spitting behind his helmet. 'Lead me to him,' he shouted. 'Lead me to
him now.'

Sargaul was close by. Barsabbas could feel the old pains returning, the
familiar shared aches and throbs of blood binding. He was sure of it.
Sargaul's presence was a tangible thing.

Almost irrational, Barsabbas began to wade through the rush of escaping slaves. Splinter shards drummed off his ceramite plates but he did
not care. He fired his boltgun but his mind was not there; the targeting
systems locked onto incoming muzzle flashes, framing them with trian-
gular icons, and Barsabbas simply went through the motions. Years of
incessant drilling had prepared him for such a moment.

'Where is he?'

Sindul lifted a trembling finger to the metal balconies on the second storey. 'They store personal slaves up there. Hand-picked ones.'

Barsabbas climbed onto a hydraulic elevator and ascended to the mezzanine level. Dark eldar waited for him there in various states of undress, shooting him. The boltgun fired heavy-calibre, self-propelled explosive rounds into their frail naked flesh, a scattering of tiny detonations that misted the air with fine blood. Barsabbas surged past and ran shoulder-first into a locked metal door. It flipped off its hinges, buckled by the impact.

In his rage, he found himself in the generator room. His rush to find Sargaul made him careless. He barely knew where he was. He only noticed fragmentary details, as if his mind was clouded. The room was well-appointed, for the derelict power facility. Dark eldar were purveyors of fine living, and satin sheets lined the wooden floor boards. Incense burned.

He saw warlike dark eldar soldiers, not mere raiders but heavy infantry, in the periphery of his vision but he ignored them. He saw slaves: human females that others would consider facially attractive, robust warriors, a plainsman child with amber eyes. He saw all these, but none of it mattered.

At the far end of the room, chained to the behemoth silos of coal generators, he saw Sargaul.

The bone tablet was small. It was no bigger than a thumb, and upon it was carved a single ophidian coil. Even those within the Chapter who were prophetically obtuse understood the symbolism of the bone.

It was an unsettling portent and one that could have only come from the coven. The bone had been passed through the dungeon cells, slipping into the tiny venting grates at the top of their cubicles.

From there, the tablet had been passed between cells. Each receiver understood full well the meaning of the message. It was a rallying call, a message that reassured the fragmented brothers that there was still cohesion in their ranks.

Reassurance of their cohesion was what the Blood Gorgons needed to spur them into action. Captain Hazareth was of the opinion that he could access the central security block if they could provide some form of distraction to occupy their guards. Baalbek was not sure how Hazareth could break free from his cell, but the captain was adamant he would be able to, and he had never been one to make claims he could not honour.

Baalbek began to push the bone tablet through the venting grate.

A Plague Marine strode past, peering closely through his bulbous goggles at the occupants of each cell. Hearing the rubberised clip of his boots, Baalbek wadded the bone tablet tightly into the meat of his palm.

'What have you got there?' the Plague Marine asked, stopping at the Blood Gorgons' cell.

Before Baalbek could answer, his bond, Brother Hybarus, cut in. 'We're bored, brother. Our bodies should not be bound like this. Let us out to stretch our limbs.'

The Plague Marine ignored Hybarus. 'What's that in his hand?' he asked, pointing at Baalbek.

Baalbek was suddenly very conscious of the tablet clenched in his fist. They had no means of distraction yet, and now the plan would become undone. Baalbek's face remained impassive, but he cursed fluently in his head.

The cell door slid back and the Plague Marine squeezed his bulk through. 'Show me your hand,' he ordered, raising his boltgun.

Stepping in-between them, Hybarus shoved the Plague Marine on the chest. 'You dare threaten us in our own home?' he growled.

The Plague Marine struck Hybarus across the jaw with the pistol grip of his bolter. The clash of metal on bone was clearly audible. Reeling from the blow, Hybarus spat teeth. He could only turtle up, splaying his fingers across his head and keeping his forearms tight to his ribs as the Plague Marine struck him again and again with the pistol grip and solid, reverberating backfists.

In the brief episode of violence, Baalbek slipped the shard under his tongue.

'Show me your hands!' the Plague Marine shouted, snapping his attention back to Baalbek.

Freezing, Baalbek dared not swallow under the Plague Marine's stare. The Plague Marine stood over Hybarus, pressing his boltgun to the back of his skull. Even the bob of Baalbek's throat would likely admit their guilt. Slowly, deliberately he opened his hands and held them out before him.

'Mouth!' shouted the Plague Marine. 'Open your mouth!'

Baalbek hesitated. He opened his mouth slowly.

'Under your tongue!' the Plague Marine shouted.

Baalbek lifted his tongue slowly in defiance. But bared for all to see, there was nothing hidden beneath. Hybarus snorted up at their tormentor through a mouthful of blood.

The Plague Marine pressed the bolter barrel into the hollow of Baalbek's throat. 'You had something,' he said slowly. 'I saw.'

'You saw what you saw,' Baalbek replied unflinchingly.

Behind his goggles, the Plague Marine slitted his eyes. He thumbed the well-worn nub of his bolter's safety.

'Shoot me,' Baalbek dared. 'Execute an unarmed Blood Gorgon without evidence or explanation. Do it and see what riot ensues.'

'Maybe I should. Your mob is nothing more than genetic waste,' the Plague Marine hissed.

But Baalbek knew their jailer wouldn't shoot; such an act would have consequences. Although they were captives, their state of confinement was made under a pretence of eventual allegiance to the Nurgle Legions. Muhr had declared that once his rule was cemented and his dissidents disposed of, the warband would be accepted within the Plague Marine fold. Bond-Brother Baalbek would prefer death than the corpulent existence of a Plague Marine, but for now, that pretence worked in the Blood Gorgon's favour.

'I'll remember you,' the Plague Marine said silkily. 'I have a good mind for faces. You are dead. Nurgle whispers me this.'

The bond-brothers waited until their captor's footsteps drifted off down the corridor. 'Betcher's gland,' Hybarus nodded knowingly. He wormed a finger into his mouth and twisted out a loose incisor.

Swallowing the last remnants of bone, Baalbek ran his tongue along the roof of his mouth. Using the poison glands made his mouth furry and thick with mucus, as if he had eaten something highly acidic. Surgically implanted into their salivary glands, the Betcher could release a limited amount of corrosive and highly toxic venom each day. It was a practice rooted in the traditions of pre-Heresy, when the primarchs' Legions had not only been warriors but crusaders. The Adeptus Astartes were preachers of the God-Emperor and their words burned with righteousness. Symbolically, they had spat on the heretical texts of old, wiping them blank through the teachings of the Imperium.

The bone tablet had corroded into a fine grit that left Baalbek swallowing saliva gingerly.

Bouncing his tooth off the cell wall, Hybarus stood up as if possessed by a great revelation. 'Our distraction,' he said, crossing over and patting the round gas pipe that provided thermal heat for the cell.

'It will be difficult, those gas mains are reinforced,' Baalbek replied. The volatile gas mains and petrochemical pipes that carried the ship's interior energy systems were sheathed in rubberised skin almost a quarter-metre thick and laced with steel thread.

'It will take some time, but it can be done,' Hybarus concluded. He laid a hand on the pipe's python-like body, testing the smooth, solid surface. Without warning he spat on it, ejecting another broken tooth.

As Baalbek watched, the streak of clear saliva started to hiss, the chemical reaction beginning to froth the rubber sheathing. It would take some time, but it could be done.

CHAPTER EIGHTEEN

Time could not be marked with any regularity in the dungeons. Each day cycle blurred with end-night as the Plague Marines attempted to distort their captives' senses through temporal isolation.

Captain Hazareth no longer knew how long they had been confined. Locked up and separated, he knew very little and as a commander of men, that bothered him. He knew not of the disposition of his men, their general morale or even their exact locations. But he knew they would follow him when the time came, and that was all he needed to be sure of, at least for now.

Hazareth slid the genekey out from beneath the nail of his index finger. The splinter was small and his fingers thick and flesh-bound. It took some time to coax and dig the micro-worm out but with practice, Hazareth could now do it with some ease.

He closed his eyes as he fidgeted with the genekey and resumed his count. There was no chron in his cell and Hazareth had taken to marking the passing of time by the beat of his primary heart. Forty-eight beats was one minute, 2,880 was one hour. Over thirty-four thousand for one ship cycle. Only five ship cycles until the plan was under way.

'You are distressed?' asked Blood-Sergeant Volsinii.

Hazareth opened his eyes. Volsinii was his blood bond; a warrior of four centuries. Grey-skinned and contemplative, there was little that escaped the gaze of his jet-black pupils.

'I am impatient,' Hazareth replied. It had already been two cycles since he had received word, whispered through venting grates from cell-block 22D – Baalbek and Hybarus's cell – that they would provide a diversion. Details were not shared for fear of discovery, only that he would know the diversion when he saw it. Hazareth only had to rely on the word and competence of his men. As their captain, Hazareth knew he owed them that, but it did not placate him. He could not see them, nor could he aid them.

Hazareth, Horned Horror of Medina, sat and waited.

'Do you think the genekey will work?' Volsinii whispered, drumming his fingers on his thighs.

Hazareth slipped the flesh-worm out again. It thrashed its tail like a furious eyelash. 'It is fused with the genetic structures of Gammadin and Sabtah. Of course it will,' Hazareth replied, in low, hushed tones. Volsinii was the only one who knew of his genekey, he was the only one Hazareth trusted with such information.

The gas main was porous with holes along its inside edge. Tiny craters pockmarked a rubbery mass of melted sheathing.

'Is it clear?' Hybarus asked.

Baalbek, crouched near the sliding cage door, pressed his face to the bars and scanned the corridor. He signalled the affirmative.

Working quickly, Hybarus collected the venom from his Betcher's gland beneath his lip. There was not much left. Over the past thirty-six hours, he and Baalbek had been steadily corroding the gas main. Their venom ducts were raw.

A thin trickle of acidic venom hit the pipe with a hiss.

'They're coming!' Baalbek hissed urgently. He lumbered over to the steel bench and sat down, waving Hybarus back to his own.

A pair of Plague Marines swept past. One of them turned to stare directly at Baalbek but they did not stop.

They waited awhile, sitting in dehydrated silence. Slowly, Baalbek got off his bench and crossed to the gas main. Their corrosive fluids had chewed through the sheathing and revealed the chrome metal beneath like bare bone. They were almost through.

Desperate, Baalbek scooped some water from a watering dish their captors had left them. It tasted of bleach and ammonia, but it wet his parched mouth. Rinsing his mouth, Baalbek spat venom, aiming for the exposed metal piping. The venom settled into a pocket crater of melted rubber, sizzling with caustic froth.

With a gaseous pop, the metal disintegrated. It was only a pinprick hole but it would be enough. Baalbek stabbed his finger into the thick piping in an attempt to crack the corroding metal. There was a metallic click. Eagerly, Baalbek prodded the pipe harder. Thermogas shot up from the breach.

'We're through!' Baalbek roared as he threw himself flat.

Then the world seemed to explode in brilliant, blinding whiteness.

The explosion expelled a bow-wave of pressure through the dungeon. Funnels of chemical smoke ripped through the air, rippling and superheated. The eruption shook the squalid cells, loosening brickwork and hatchways with over-pressure.

A squad of Plague Marines clattered down the stairs from the upper levels, issuing commands through vox-grilles. Hazareth was on his feet as soon as the Plague Marines stormed by. He was digging at the gene-worm. Wrenching it out between thumb and forefinger, Hazareth placed the genekey against the cell's gene scanner.

Despite the rusting condition of the hatchway, the gene scanner across the bolt had been meticulously cleaned and oiled. The cogitator scanned the vein structure, layout, and blood flow with an infrared sweep. A layer of light swept up the scanner, passing over the genekey and magnifying its helix structure.

There was a compliant *clunk* as the hatchway's iron bolt retracted.

Out in the corridor itself, a dense cloud of smoke reduced visibility to a pall of featureless grey. Shielding his eyes against the sting, Hazareth sprinted up the nauseating course of stairs. Volsinii followed him, scanning the corridor for signs of their guards. In the confusion, Blood Gorgons began to bray and roar, making as much noise as possible. They pounded on their cell walls as Hazareth made his way towards the guard rooms.

There was a single Plague Marine patrolling the metal stairs that led up to the central control unit. He was crouched low against the smoke, scanning the corridors in both directions as he stalked with his boltgun.

He approached the blast door of the dungeon warily. It was ajar. The forty-centimetre-thick vault door had been opened, its wheel-lock handle had been unwound, unclamping it from its seal. The Plague Marine opened his vox-link to enquire.

Hazareth got to him first. Appearing out of the smoke, sudden and murderous, Hazareth rammed the Plague Marine against the wall. Steely fingers clamped over the Plague Marine's neck seal, between the underside of his helmet and the protective parapet of his chest plate's gorget. With desperate savagery, Hazareth dashed his enemy's head against the rockcrete. Intense pressure split the ceramite casing, stress fractures spider-webbing the armour immediately. Hazareth tensed. The helmet gave way under the pincer, crunching wetly. Yet even headless, the Plague Marine stumbled, muscles twitching. He brought up his boltgun as if to shoot, stumbled again, lashed out with a desperate fist and then toppled.

'Leave that,' Volsinii urged. 'Follow me and stay close behind.'

They forged their way up the final flight of steps towards the control room. No alarm had been raised yet. Through the glass viewing blister, they could see the control room was empty. The Plague Marines had responded to the diversion as they'd hoped, leaving their posts to deal with the threat of a mass-scale riot.

Hazareth pushed open the ironclad door and stormed inside reaching for the intricate gilded console. He could hear the distant, muffled shouts and hammering in the dungeon cells. He pulled the accordion-lever to unlock the entire cell-block.

Nothing. Not even a click.

'I had no choice,' Volsinii said knowingly from behind Hazareth. 'I had no choice, Captain Hazareth.'

Desperately, Hazareth pulled again but the lever had no resistance, as if connected to nothing. It came away loosely in his hand.

'He apologises profusely, but if he truly meant it, why do it at all?' chortled a low voice.

Opsarus. Hazareth saw him ascend the stairs. His footfalls were death knells upon the metal steps. The deathmask seemed to smile at him with a tranquil serenity. In his left gauntlet, he grasped an autocannon as a man might hold a rifle.

'Why would he warn us of your escape if he is sorry? He's not sorry,' said Opsarus.

Hazareth hammered his claw across the console. Volsinii would not look at him. Staggering back, Hazareth slumped down. Trust was not a concept between the minions of Chaos, but Volsinii had been his blood bond, an extension of himself. It was the foundation of unity between an otherwise dissident Chapter of raiders. Hazareth bayed like a wounded bull, shaking his head unsteadily.

'Perhaps the blood bond is a mere placebo. You give it more meaning than it truly holds,' Opsarus laughed. It sounded forced, garbled and sudden behind his reinforced helmet.

Hazareth attacked without warning, spearing through the air at Opsarus. His claw bounced off the unyielding plasteel of Crusade-era armour.

Opsarus did not even move. There was a low whir as the autocannon rose into place, traversing like a linear siege battery. Hulking down behind the thick walls of his plating, Opsarus braced himself. He fired.

The blast in the confined space of the console blister was like a firestorm. A wash of flame engulfed the room. Tearing through the foundations of the room, the shell blew out the ceiling, disintegrated the cell-block console and atomised the glass viewing bubble. The expanding pressure pulled Captain Hazareth apart, and what remained was swept away by the whirling flame.

Volsinii, too, was caught in the backblast. His reward, although Opsarus had not intended it, was a death that would not be remembered. Behind the external bulwark of his suit, Opsarus breathed cooled, internal air as ambient temperatures lingered at the high six hundreds.

The room was now a blackened hole in the high, vertical bulkhead. Scraps of fire still flickering against his external layers, Opsarus made his way down the stairs.

Barsabbas crossed the room, emptying two bolt clips within the span of ten seconds. His sole focus was to destroy everything in the room that stood between himself and Sargaul. Everything.

The dark eldar warriors, however, did not give ground. They were different from the raiders: they were incubi, proper soldiers with good firing discipline and martial bearing. They wore heavier form-fitting armour that hugged their slender frames like the black-blue of an angry hornet, and formed a solid protective block around the prize slaves.

Barsabbas had not been hurt in a long time, but his attackers hurt him now. They punished him with electrified halberds, pivoting and striking with precise, practiced strokes. Static shocks wracked his body, threatening to seize his hearts. Warning sigils and power overload warnings flashed across his visor in urgent amber. His blood began to boil. His muscles spasmed.

But his eyes were fixed on Sargaul and his finger glued to the trigger. The bolter bucked like a jackhammer, ripping out the entire clip in one continuous and sudden belch. But the incubi were too many, too hardened. A halberd bounced off Barsabbas's thigh plate, shocking his femoral nerves. Grunting, the bond-brother fell to a knee as his leg cramped and spasmed violently. Another strike chopped into his bolt-gun, denting its brass finish and almost wrenching the weapon from his grip.

Vomiting into his helmet as his pain receptors fired, Barsabbas raised his head to see Sindul sprint through the door. The dark eldar raider had salvaged a splinter rifle and fired it on automatic, whistling splinter shots into the room.

It was not much, but it gave Barsabbas the brief opportunity he needed. Reeling, he withdrew from the maul of incubi, ejecting his spent clip and slamming home a fresh one. Vomit drooled from his muzzle grille. He cleared his head and unhinged a grenade cluster from his chain loops.

'Down, Sindul, down!'

Tugging out the top pin, he allowed the grenades to cook off for a half count. The delay cost him a splinter shot to the neck seal. Hissing with agony, Barsabbas launched the grenade as a reflex action, skipping it across the rockcrete at an awkward angle. Turning his back to the grenade, he hunched down to make himself a small target.

There was a string of clapping eruptions. It felt like someone had pushed him from behind. He turned into the smoke and began firing. But there was little need. The half-dozen incubi had been crumpled, their bodies contorted on the ground, their limbs rearranged and pockmarked with shrapnel holes.

Above the muffled quiet of the aftershock, Barsabbas heard Sindul stir some distance away, coughing and spitting words in his harsh language. Parting the smoke with his hands, the bond-brother staggered towards his captive. Although he had taken multiple lacerations and some minor internal injuries, Barsabbas felt no pain. He could only concentrate on the pain that ached in his primary left lung – Sargaul's pain. The cold often made it worse. It was a good pain, for without it, there would be no Sargaul.

'Brother Sargaul,' Barsabbas called out.

The solitary figure in the distance raised his head, as if startled from sleep. Even at a distance, Barsabbas could recognise the deep-set eyes, the heavy brow and the missing ear.

'Sargaul,' Barsabbas said, drawing closer. He peeled off his helmet, sucking in deep breaths of dirty, smoky air.

Sargaul looked at him vacantly, expressionless. Finally, he opened his mouth as if finding the right words was an intense focus of will.

'Who are you?' he asked.

Shafts of sunlight, paper-thin, glowed between the cracks of the boarded windows. They rendered the room in shades of brown, black and a hazy, egg-yolk yellow. The generator silos waited in the back, sleeping giants that had not stirred for centuries, their turbines suffocating under bales of dust. There, chained between two iron cylinders, sitting upon the tiled floor, was Bond-Brother Sargaul.

His armour had been shed in a dismembered heap nearby and a red shuka, salvaged and ill-fitting, was coiled around his waist. Track marks – bruised, ugly holes that scarred his neck, abdomen and wrists – contrasted with his white skin. Parts of him had been surgically tampered with, the sutured slits in his skin still clearly visible. The stitch marks were long and some were infected. Barsabbas could feel his own skin tingle in sympathetic horror.

'Who are you?' Sargaul repeated, words slurred by a swollen, irresponsive tongue.

'It's me, brother,' Barsabbas answered tentatively. 'Barsabbas.'

Sargaul's eyes rolled lazily in his sockets, losing interest in his bond-brother. 'I have to find their gene-seed,' he muttered to himself.

Barsabbas shook his head in disbelief. Sargaul was a veteran Astartes. His mind had been clinically, surgically and chemically conditioned. His mind had been tested through constant, rigorous stress for years before his induction. In fact, most Astartes were, to a minor degree, psychically resistant. Surely, this would be a temporary, a fleeting illness, for nothing could break Sargaul's mental wall for good.

'Reverse it!' Barsabbas shouted, grabbing Sindul by the arm and pulling him close. 'Reverse it!'

'I cannot!' Sindul squealed. 'His mind is ruined. There is nothing I can do.'

'Look at me,' Barsabbas commanded Sargaul, but his bond wasn't listening. Fitful and barely lucid, Sargaul seemed oblivious to his environment. Physically his body was there, but his mind was broken.

'Where is the gene-seed?' said Barsabbas.

Sargaul's eyes widened. 'You found the gene-seed! We can return, then.'

'No, brother. I have not. I need your help.'

Sargaul didn't seem to be listening any more. 'I must find the squad's gene-seed. We need to report back.'

'The haemonculi would have been thorough,' Sindul observed.

Barsabbas punched the ground. 'Impossible. We are Astartes.'

'Especially Astartes. Your pain thresholds are so high, you are every haemonculus's greatest fantasy.'

'What did they do to him?' Barsabbas asked quietly.

'I don't know. It is dependent on the creativeness of the torturer and the hardiness of the recipient,' Sindul said, licking his lips. 'Injecting mercury into the liver, pumping glass filings into the lungs, stimulation of exposed nerves with contact acids, selective lobotomy–'

Barsabbas startled Sindul with a roar, sending the dark eldar scuttling for cover. Enraged, the Blood Gorgon hammered the floor tiles with his fists. The tireless banging split the ceramic and brought down scuds of dust from the rafters. Still howling, Barsabbas rose to his feet and began to beat his own naked face against the generator's iron bearing covers. The ridged metal scored his cheeks and opened up raw, bleeding lines across his forehead. Sargaul began to bawl too, stimulated by the loud noise. His eyes were fixed upon the ceiling and his clumsy tongue worked in a muted, stifled yell.

Barsabbas raged long into the night. He did not stop. Seized by an anguish that had no release, he began to tear down the processing facility with his bare hands. Bones splintered wood, boots dented metal. He raged until his fists were black and bleeding and the ceramite of his gauntlets was textured with scratches. Dust clouds fumed as he broke through the walls.

Sindul sheltered behind a storage locker as the world crashed and shook. The Traitor Marine was like an earthquake or a storm. Sindul had little hope of escaping and was helpless to stop it. Instead he hid and hoped it would pass quickly. The noise had promised such fury that even the warp beasts had fled the area, balking at such raw power.

Gumede, hiding far out in the grass fields, prayed. He thought the end of the world had come. He prayed through the night and did not stop until the first sun crested the horizon.

Finally, as the suns reached first dawn, Barsabbas grew tired. By then, he had levelled almost a third of the abandoned facility. He collapsed as the lactic build-up in his muscles reached toxic levels, beyond what even an Astartes could ignore.

Throughout all of this, Sargaul was oblivious. He sat with a look of contentment upon his face as his mind drifted.

Sargaul lay supine before Barsabbas. Where once Sargaul had been full of martial vigour, the mindless wreck that shivered on the ground could barely be recognised as him.

'Brother. I have failed.'

Those were the last words Barsabbas said to Sargaul as he stood before him. It was hard to believe there was anything left of Sargaul. Although his body was whole, his mind had been stripped bare.

They had been warriors together. Sargaul who had burned an entire township at Port Veruca just to goad the local garrison into battle. Sargaul who had claimed over a hundred and twenty heads at the Siege of Naraskur. The very same Sargaul who culled slaves unable to lift more than a twenty-kilo standard load.

Barsabbas unchained him and lifted him unsteadily to his feet. He had almost forgotten how much taller Sargaul stood than he, and for some reason that pained him. Tall, venerable Sargaul.

Although Sargaul had no equilibrium to stand on his own, Barsabbas helped the veteran into his salvaged battle dress. He slowly dressed him in his beaten power armour, a painstaking process without the aid of servitor and retinue.

Barsabbas activated Sargaul's armour and as the suit hummed to life, the squad-linked data feed connected between the surviving members of Squad Besheba. Its initial system sweep detected almost no cognitive activity in Sargaul's brain, as if entire portions of it had been excised.

'Gene-seed. I can't go home without the gene-seed.'

It was the same monotone phrase. Barsabbas decided it must have been Sargaul's last lucid thought, the last thing on his mind before the dark eldar took it.

Barsabbas pressed Sargaul's boltgun into his hands and took one step back. In his full battle dress, Sargaul looked whole, if Barsabbas did not look into his eyes. Except that he stood upright only by the power of his armour's servo motors.

'Brother, I have failed.'

Barsabbas unscrewed the hilt of his mace. Holding the pommel he slid a slender metal tube from the shaft of the weapon, a device to extract gene-seed. The removal of the gene-seed was a duty of the Chirurgeon or Apothecary, and so it had been since the early days of the Crusade. But the progenoid gland, as the conduit of genetic data, was held in even greater reverence by the Blood Gorgons. To the bond-brother, the gene-seed was one half of their own lifeblood and each carried the device capable of executing the final duty.

He stabbed the tube into Sargaul, in the pit above the collar bone just over the lip of his neck seal. There was a tearing, agonised shudder. Sargaul's eyes opened, and suddenly they were his again. 'Reclaim our gene-seed, brother,' he said.

There was a flash of lucidity, of consciousness in those eyes. A brief return of Sargaul. For a moment, Barsabbas almost believed he'd needlessly killed his bond. But then Sargaul faded fast, descending into a dazed stupor before expiring quickly, his life signs fading on the squad link.

CHAPTER NINETEEN

The decision had been made for Barsabbas. There was no other option but to continue to Ur. Try as he might, he could not turn back. Like the southward bird in winter, Barsabbas was drawn to his objective. It was the behavioural pattern of a Space Marine that he could not have stopped had he wanted to. The impulse to go north lingered over his every thought and action. The original objective was Ur, and until Barsabbas received express orders to desist, his mind would allow him to do nothing else but tread step after step in the direction of that cloistered, faraway place.

Strangely conscious of his mental conditioning, Barsabbas did not resist. The ability to execute their objectives until death made Space Marines the most effective military formation known to man. If Hauts Bassiq had a sea, he would walk along the ocean bed to reach his destination.

Behind him, the power facility burned. A high afternoon wind lifted the flames, taunting them higher and higher. None of that concerned him. In his mind, Barsabbas could only picture the city of Ur – a solid polygon at odds with its environment. Sealed, impervious and smooth-walled, harshly artificial amongst the softly undulating clay plains. A segregated island of man amongst an oceanic spread of feral, unculti-vated wilderness.

'What now?' Gumede asked, the roaring fire reflecting off his promi-nent cheekbones.

'To Ur. It is what Sargaul would have done. Besides, there is little left for me. In Ur, I will find my death or my redemption.'

'You cannot enter Ur. There is no way in,' Gumede replied.

Perhaps not for a plainsman, Barsabbas accepted. Ever since the Blood Gorgons harvested the first plainsman stock to replenish their ranks, they had known of the existence of Ur. But even the Blood Gorgons had never entered the city. It was sealed, a hive world with no entrance nor exit; a ziggurat that could not be entered. In turn, the Blood Gorgons had plundered more vulnerable targets, content to claim the planet of Hauts Bassiq as their own and leave the insulated bastion to itself.

'I have entered Ur,' Sindul proclaimed smugly. Content with himself, the dark eldar lay in the dry grass. He flicked his blades playfully, tossing them and catching them.

Barsabbas remained impassive. 'Tell me how you got in.'

'It is not ruled by the Barons of Ur. The Imperial cult has fallen,' Sindul laughed.

'Don't ignore my question,' Barsabbas growled, shifting his weight menacingly. 'How did you get in?'

'I was in the retinue of my lord's firstborn son. We were guests of the Ner'Gal warlord.'

'Then we will not be welcome. You cannot enter Ur. Not in all of our stories has anyone entered Ur,' Gumede concluded, shaking his head.

'Then you have resigned yourself to following history,' said Barsabbas. 'But I have a plan.'

It was not right for an emissary of the kabal to be treated like a pet hound. The humiliation sat like the cold edge of a rock in Sindul's boot. Although the *mon-keigh's* thrall-worm had been excised from his flesh, it would leave a humiliating scar for the rest of his days. Holding a shameful hand to his face, Sindul harboured the resentment deep in his belly.

The three had walked for six kilometres north and made camp in a high cave overlooking the alkali flats. When they looked south, black storm clouds had crept up behind them, promising a heavy afternoon downpour.

Barsabbas departed without explanation, disappearring into the storm as the curtains of rain fell over him.

It was the opportunity that Sindul had been waiting for since his capture. Only Gumede remained to watch over him, an arrow notched loosely inside his bow frame. The plainsman sat cross-legged across from him, watching the sky swirl darker.

But Barsabbas had grown careless. By extracting the slave-seed, he had removed the last reason for Sindul to stay.

The dark eldar was no longer trapped. Barsabbas had slain the survivors of their raiding party and with it, any trace or evidence of Sindul's disgrace. Alone, Sindul could return home as the sole reminder and the events on Hauts Bassiq would be his words, and only his words. To his great fortune, the Blood Gorgon had, in a fit of human carelessness, even removed his thrall-worm.

Seizing the narrow window of opportunity, Sindul wasted no time. Although Barsabbas had confiscated his hook swords, Sindul knew the plainsman would provide little sport. Every dark eldar, no matter their status, spent considerable hours drilling on the *atami* mats of their kabal's fighting master. Even without weapons, Sindul could use the barbs and edges of his armour to vicious effect.

Sindul coiled himself into a crouch, tentatively watching the slopes for Barsabbas's return. He waited until the rain was thick and nothing could be heard except for the hollow roar of droplets hammering the clay.

That was when he attacked Gumede. The plainsman fought back gamely with clumsy fists and ill-balanced kicks, but Sindul side-sauntered and slipped them almost lazily. He struck Gumede unconscious with a flurry of pinpoint elbow strikes. Briefly, he considered killing the human for sport, but there was no time. Barsabbas could return at any moment.

As the rain began to cease, Sindul skidded down the slope. He knew the location of the kabal's lander was not far. If he recalled correctly, and his memory did not fail him, the vessel would still be docked at the power facility, hidden by now beneath metres of ash and ember.

Retracing the steps he took, slim boots churning in the clay-turned-mud, Sindul fled the way he had come.

A broken nose was a painful thing. It obstructed breathing, forcing Gumede to take in jagged mouthfuls of air. Blood and snot simmered in his sinuses, bubbling forth to drool in thick strands down his face. Worst of all was the humiliation, a bleeding, unavoidable token of his failing. An abasement of Chief Gumede's pride.

When he heard Barsabbas crunching up the rock slope, Gumede tried to wipe the blood off his face with his wrists. There were abrasions on his chin and forehead too but his nose was still dribbling blood.

'What happened here?' Barsabbas asked as he ducked underneath the cave entrance.

Gumede backed away, apprehensive of the punishment that would be inflicted upon him. 'He escaped,' the chief admitted.

The Chaos Space Marine stood at the cave mouth, his shoulders barricading the entrance from edge to edge.

'I fought back but I couldn't hit him,' Gumede stammered, reaching for his recurve bow.

Barsabbas seemed to rumble with a throaty hum of satisfaction. 'I know, I saw him run,' he said finally. 'We can follow him now.'

'You let him escape?' Gumede asked, deeply concerned.

'Of course,' said Barsabbas. 'Where would the dark eldar go?'

Gumede shrugged, uncertain of whether it was a trick question. 'I don't know.'

'Sindul came here by ship. It means Sindul must leave the same way,' Barsabbas said, speaking slowly as if the chief were particularly dim. 'When I track him, he will lead me to that ship.'

'You will use it to enter Ur!' Gumede said, his eyes widening with revelation.

'The dark eldar ship. Guests of Ner'Gal,' Barsabbas purred. 'Sindul is a vindictive and deceitful creature, but predictable.'

'Then this was planned,' Gumede said, pinching the bridge of his nose to stem the blood. 'He could have killed me.'

The Chaos Space Marine chortled as he strode out into the rain, already checking the wet clay for prints. 'I'm surprised he didn't,' Barsabbas said.

Sindul was breathless. He sucked in deep lungfuls of air to introduce some oxygen back into his burning arms. The sprint from the cave had wearied him but he could not afford to rest. Digging with his bare hands, Sindul was frantic, spurred on by the ever-present threat of discovery.

Despite the rain, the ashes were hot. As the water hit the charred framework, it hissed with steam. Sindul scooped with his palms, scraping at the ashes with his fingers. Like coals, it burnt through his kidskin gloves, but Sindul didn't feel it. He was running out of time.

Pushing aside a burnt sheet of ply-wall, Sindul uncovered a trapdoor in the ground. The metal hatch had withstood the inferno but the lock had warped and buckled in the heat. Tearing at the trapdoor in his haste, Sindul scrambled down below.

He almost fell directly onto the hull of a ship beneath. Scrambling for purchase he swore and then began to laugh.

The *Harvester*.

An Impaler-class assault ship. Thin and spear-shaped, barbed and tapering, the ship could carry an entire crew of raiders through atmospheric entry. The thin, bat-shaped wings were underslung with pods of shardnets and a trio of dark lances jutted pugnaciously from beneath its needle prow.

It would also be Sindul's only way home.

The ship was berthed in a low, underground hangar. It had probably once been the storage cellar for the power facility, centuries ago. Sagging shelves loaded with dusty tools and pipe ends filled the surrounding walls. Empty slave cages were stacked in along the far wall, ready to be loaded into the *Harvester's* yawning rear ramp.

The ship reacted to Sindul's presence, display consoles becoming suffused by soft purple, blue and white lights. Hololithic displays were projected into the air, displaying the ship's status in rolling eldar script.

With deliberate, practiced movements, Sindul delicately placed receptor fibres. The thin threads interfaced directly with his fingertips, trailing translucent optic thread from each of his fingers. He contorted his fingers like an orchestral maestro and the ship responded with an agonisingly slow whine, the Impaler's thrust engines building power.

Then an object whistled past his ear, hard and fluid-quick. Sindul flinched, thinking something on board had malfunctioned. But when he glanced sidelong he realised it was not a malfunction at all. An arrow had thudded into his pilot cradle. A wooden shaft protruded out of the soft polyfibre headrest, a shaft fletched with a red and black feather.

Shrieking with rage, Sindul saw Gumede drop from the hatch and behind him, Barsabbas.

Wretched Barsabbas. The Blood Gorgon crashed through the hatch and landed on the thin prow. His weight made the large ship dip forwards. Steadily, hand-over-hand, Barsabbas began to climb towards the cockpit.

Sliding back the Impaler's outer viewport like an eyelid, Sindul drew a splinter pistol from beneath the seat. He loosed a volley of choppy shots at the Traitor Marine, the splinter fire dancing off his ceramite like solid rain. He did not manage more than six shots before Barsabbas reached him.

Barsabbas tore away the canopy and his hand shot for Sindul's throat, clamping tight and dragging him out, tearing him out of the seat restraints. He shook the eldar, knocking his limbs loosely about the air, shaking the pistol out of his hand.

'Look how senseless that was!' Barsabbas shouted through his vox-grille.

'Don't kill me!' Sindul managed to gasp in-between his head lashing back and forth upon his neck.

Maintaining the chokehold, Barsabbas unhooked the lotus-head mace from his girdle and he looped it back like a loaded catapult. 'You knew escape would be your death, but you took that choice. I see no other way.'

'You need me to fly the ship!' wailed Sindul.

Barsabbas lowered his mace. 'Why?'

'To take you to Ur.'

Barsabbas let Sindul drop bonelessly back into the pilot seat. 'I'm glad you understand. Fly well, and perhaps next time I will let you escape for real.'

'You allowed me to escape?'

'To lead me to your ship – yes. Ask yourself this, would you have ever told me? No, yours is a patient race. As frail as your physical bodies may be, the eldar have always been patient. You could have waited for years before you tried to escape to this ship. You work differently from the short-lived races.'

The dark eldar allowed himself a gloating smirk.

Barsabbas crouched down and peered closely at Sindul, his helmet almost level with the dark eldar's face. 'I may be of the Chaos flock, but I am not an irrational man. You cannot coerce me through fear alone. Take me to Ur. Do so without delay or deception. In return, when I leave Hauts Bassiq, you will be free to go.'

'*If* you leave Hauts Bassiq,' Sindul corrected.

'If I die, then you die. Can you not see that our fates are intertwined? The gods have made it so.'

The Harvester climbed in altitude rapidly, angled against the land below at a nauseating slant and rapidly leaving it behind. They pierced the atmospheric clouds at mach speeds. Except for the gloss of sun reflecting from the craft's nose, the world around blurred like wet paint: the brown earth, white sky and grey clouds streaking together into a tunnel of streaming colours.

Barsabbas had utilised the most destructive human war machines, but the dark eldar technology left him in a state of jealous awe. The soldier within him could not deny that the vessel was a dangerous beast. It floated, spiralled and levelled out with a dexterity that was weightless. It could change directions without the hauling, air-dragging lunges of an Imperial fighter. Most impressive of all, grav-dampeners seemed to change the interior air pressure and speed. It felt as if they were not moving at all; there was no hint of velocity or momentum. Even standing in the fluted cockpit, unable to fit into any of the seats, Barsabbas did not budge as the Impaler soared.

According to his helmet's onboard display, the craft was travelling at supersonic speeds of Mach four-point-five, but Barsabbas estimated they were going hypersonic; his power armour simply did not register faster momentum.

Gumede, terrified of the ordeal, was splayed out on the decking in the craft's bottom. Face to the padded flooring, nails digging into the soft material, the chief's eyes were closed. Barsabbas guessed he had never seen an atmospheric flier before, let alone been on board one. His cowardice, in Barsabbas's mind, was distracting and the Chaos Space Marine ignored him.

They crossed the northern badlands and overshot a narrow dust lake. From their vantage point, the pollution of Nurgle was revealed in its fullness. The intruders had poisoned, sickened and befouled everything.

The further northwards they flew, the more jaundiced the sky became. It was thick with a mustard smog that left threads of heavy pigmented vapour in the clouds. Sometimes it rained and when it did, the downpour was brown like water from a disused and rusting tap. Even with the air-vents locked and the internal vacuum of the ship pressurised, Barsabbas could smell the faint odour of ageing, the sepulchral smell of organic matter falling apart prematurely, of rocks and plant life disintegrating to dust.

The ship's hololith projection of the topography showed almost zero plant or animal life. The mass graves of talon squall and caprid were illuminated as ghost images of bones breaking the monotony of the plains. Surface radiation was detected by the ship's atmospheric reports, a steep increase the closer they flew to Ur.

As the presence of the invaders grew stronger, Barsabbas felt increasingly disconnected with himself and his Chapter. He was on his own. The Traitor Marine let that thought seep in. He had hoped to find Sargaul, but with Sargaul gone, Barsabbas was entirely alone. He allowed the feeling to enrage him, to nurture the despondency into a vengeful rage. Gammadin had preached about harnessing emotions as opposed to wasting them. He nurtured his hate and soon he forgot all about the dust and ageing and emptiness of the plains. Thinking only in terms of kill count and ammunition ratio, Barsabbas prepared himself to enter Ur.

The *Cauldron Born* had been full of life. Its flank had twinkled with the ship lights of activity, from the release of gases, from the over-venting of the engines, the hazard lights of ship dock, The daily test firing of batteries.

But slowly, like an ailing man, the *Cauldron Born* was dying. Section by section, the ship's lights became dark as the vessel trembled. As a living machine, the *Cauldron Born* was suffering. Its ventilation systems were blocked by mucus. The warp engines became weak and lethargic, consuming more and more power just to remain at anchor.

Like the ship, entire galleries of slaves, the backbone of the space hulk, were falling to disease. Their habitation warrens were heady with the muffled heat of illness. Little by little, the lights switched off and the corridors dimmed as sections of the ship fell into disuse. The slaves who lived there were no longer. Nurgle had entered the vessel like a virus, spreading disease and wasting it away.

Many slaves were reduced to eating scraps as the vast food stores rotted supernaturally fast. The ship's hydroponic fungus farms, the mainstay of their diet, mutated, the edible mushrooms becoming pulsating, monstrous things. Stories were told of the vile, psychotropic poisons that affected victims who ate them.

Perhaps the greatest change was the deliberate dismantling of the Blood Gorgons as a functional fighting force. From the dungeons, in slow piecemeal fashion, the Blood Gorgons were released to crew their ship. Unfamiliar with the workings of the ship, Opsarus's Legion allowed the Blood Gorgons back into the fold, not as masters but as crew.

The objective was to divide them, split them: segregate and neuter their ability to communicate, organise and unify. Companies were broken down into lonely squads, dispatched to crew distant peripheries of the ship.

Some squads were relegated to maintain the warp engines, overseen by armed Plague Marines. Many were forced to perform the menial tasks of crewing surveillance systems or maintaining the ship's bridge.

When the Blood Gorgons were not utilising their combat-honed bodies for menial slavery, they attended indoctrination sessions. The high priests of Nurgle delivered fiery rhetoric about the divinity of decay. They forced the Blood Gorgons to kneel and pray for the poxes and plague of the Old Grandfather.

Many outright refused, preferring to die than face the ignominy of slavery. The riots continued. There was an attempt by Squad Archeme to reach the weapon vaults via the air circulation ducts. Several minor resistances were attempted, but without organisational capacity, each was a needless casualty.

The Blood Gorgons were no longer caged, but they were just as imprisoned. Their proud fighting companies fragmented – disarmed, controlled and infiltrated. Under this assault, there were those among the Chapter who openly admitted that the Blood Gorgons were no more.

CHAPTER TWENTY

From orbital surveillance, Ur had never registered as anything more than a rock formation, a mere smudge upon a strata-map.

But as they flew close, dropping in altitude, Barsabbas could see it in detail. From a distance, it had appeared a featureless bubble, merely a contrasting shape on the horizon. Up close it was a marvellous construct with an artistic symmetry that was not lost even on one so militantly linear.

The city seemed entirely constructed of red clay. From the smooth panes of its siege curtains, it rose up and up for eight hundred metres, forming an imposing girdle of interlaced brick art. The wall was so tall it spread out to either side and up, its edges lost to a haze of dust. With such inferior materials, the city stood only by the design of sound engineering. It resembled a termite mound, the top clustered with finger spires and punctuated with mazes of galleries. Its raw size and flat, unyielding facelessness gave it a prominent, intoxicating stature.

The monolithic walls were sealed within a void blister, a hemisphere of shields tessellating from generator pylons at ground level. Amber hexagons overlapped each other in a semi-sphere of paned scales. It was by far the thickest void shield Barsabbas had ever encountered, possibly sturdier than the shields of the Mechanicus Titans. Bronze, amber and tarnished brass, the tessellating pieces reflected the sunlight like tinfoil.

Those shields, Barsabbas reckoned, had been the primary reason that the Blood Gorgons had never taken Ur. It was not that the Blood Gorgons could not break them – they had simply reasoned the costs to outweigh the gains. Ur, in some ways, protected the plainsmen of Bassiq against roving raiders from beyond the stars when the Blood Gorgons could not. Ur had protected Blood Gorgon interests, and in return the Blood Gorgons had chosen to let them live. Fight only when you have to, as Gammadin had always said.

As the *Harvester* levelled out three hundred metres from Ur proper, a vox-signal was received by the ship's tympanum, bringing Barsabbas out of his thoughts.

'Mercenary, this is Green Father. State landing protocol, archon.'

The voice that hailed them came through the *Harvester's* aural fronds. Grating and intrusive, the voice thrummed through the metallic tuning forks set into the console with crystalline audio clarity.

Sindul opened the vox-link on his console by touching the fibres connected to his ring fingers together. 'This is the archon's troupe. Mercenary awaits the Green Father's welcome. Landing protocol sequenced,' he announced loudly into the aural fronds.

Without a second of delay, one of the shield pylons deactivated, winking a hexagonal gap in the city's void blister. They flew in. The city rushed in to swallow them in a haze of sepia. The sudden change in atmospheric light was disorientating. Sunlight filtered through the void shields in honeyed orange. Everything seemed suspended in amber.

The city itself rose in solid tiers. Enormous canvas awnings – perhaps half a kilometre in length – steepled each ziggurat with broad wings. Flat tiled roofs were set with perfect, geometric regularity up the stepped slope. Orthostats, pillars and open courts gave the architecture a palatial bearing.

Barsabbas constructed a mental map of Ur from his briefing, remembering everything to scale and detail. Cross-referencing his coordinates with the dark eldar ship's console display, Barsabbas remembered the ramparts contained narrow docking chutes heavily guarded by aerial defence silos. Measuring trajectory and angles of entry, he began making swift calculations in his head. 'Zoom in there,' he commanded, tapping the hololith display of the city's rampart.

Sindul's fingers danced across his console, nimble and quick, and the image magnified. There amongst the brickwork was an aperture like an archer's slit, a mere crack in the leviathan wall.

'Take us in there,' said Barsabbas.

Sindul banked the Impaler into a lazy roll and dropped level with the rampart wall. Along the port side, they saw multiple box-battery missile systems swivel to track their descent. The accusatory finger of a turbo-laser tracked them, traversing on a railed track.

'It's time, then,' Barsabbas intoned. He stowed his boltgun, mace and falchion in the storage bays and held out his wrists to Gumede. 'Bind me,' he ordered.

The plainsman hesitantly looped one of the dark eldar's barbed slave cuffs around Barsabbas's forearms. His movements were clumsy and fearful, as if he did not want to touch the Godspawn. He cinched the noose tight around both of Barsabbas's hands.

Gumede peered outside the ship's viewing ports as Ur rose above them. 'I am not sure this will work,' he said wearily, with the voice of a man resigned to death.

Barsabbas shook his head. 'It will work, as long as you both play your part.'

The plan was simple. They would enter Ur and tell the truth, or at least a version of the truth. The dark eldar mercenaries had ambushed a lone Blood Gorgon survivor and captured him. Sindul, acting on behalf of the kabal, had come to negotiate a price for their Traitor Marine captive. Gumede, of course, was Sindul's personal slave, a trophy from Hauts Bassiq.

The plan was not without risks, but Barsabbas saw no other way of locating the gene-seeds or any other Blood Gorgon survivors. Ur was vast and to find a prisoner he would have to become one. Once imprisoned, Sindul would have no choice but to find and free him, lest he risk birthing a slave-scarab.

Crossing over to the pilot's seat with his hands bound, Barsabbas slapped the side of Sindul's face. The dark eldar screamed in shock, the craft jinking as he flinched. A flesh scarab latched onto his milky skin and burrowed under the flesh, creating a bulge before disappearing into the muscle layers.

'Why?' Sindul hissed.

'Do you need to ask?'

'How can the plan work if I die? You need me to free you once you are captured,' Sindul shot back.

'That's exactly why I've marked you. To ensure you do come back for me,' Barsabbas replied.

Sindul had nothing else to say. He simply touched his cheek where the flesh scarab had left a neat, red incision in his white skin.

'You are a traitor, like all of your kind,' Barsabbas said flatly. 'You have five hours to come for me. So you best keep alert.'

Those were the last words he said as the Impaler shot into the wall and into the city of Ur itself.

Compared to the plains of Hauts Bassiq, the city of Ur seemed like a different world. Sealed within its void shields and walls, it existed as a self-contained ecosystem.

Long ago prospectors, those who did not wish to wander the wastelands as nomads, had retreated to this place. They hoarded the last of the industrial engines with them and constructed the ziggurat – an ancestral symbol of human engineering. It was a construct of simple necessity, a sturdy monument of utility that has held a place within human history.

They hid there. Away from the agonising climate, away from their wayward kin. Hiding, even, from the Imperium itself who had long since assigned the status of Hauts Bassiq as 'inhospitable' and tucked the notation away in forgotten archives.

There, left to isolation, the ancestors of Ur devolved. Insular and inbred, her people became sickly and viciously paranoid. They diverged into their own puritan Imperial Cult, believing the preservation of their isolation the key to resisting corruption.

They became obsessed with locking out the exterior. They raised mighty walls and developed stout shields. All their industry, their resources, all of their salvaged technology was devoted to isolation. To them, the world outside Ur was a hellish, primordial place.

They emerged intermittently to trade with the distant nomads, and even then only for necessities which could not be synthetically produced in Ur's industrial mills and foundries. Beyond that, Ur had remained sealed to the outside.

Refineries in the lowest portions of the city-stack fed power and fuel into the city above, appropriately serving as its foundations. Pipe systems large enough to convey battle tanks coiled around the bottom stacks like a nest of metal pythons. The refineries cooled the city with cyclopean turbines, recycled water and powered the void shields. The columns of smoke stacks coughed exhaust into the atmosphere, steaming the void shields with their pollutant heat.

Above this, the city itself rose in neat, geometric stacks. Brown, red and dust coloured brickwork rose up in tetric tessellation, as if the buildings were blocks that slotted into each other. No bolt, nail or adhesive could be found. Like the sealed city itself, the architecture was raw and unadorned, shocking in its gigantic scale – blunt and imposing and entirely interlocked.

The Harvester landed in the open plaza of the apex palace. From within emerged the dark eldar slaver and his servant, a gold-skinned native. The shambling Traitor Marine was dragged out of the ship's hold by means of anchor chains and barb cuffs. It took an entire platoon of Septic infantry to get him out, hauling taut on his collar, wrist and waist chains as he bayed and roared at the indignity.

The interior of the palace was broad and high-ceilinged. Ivory tiles lined every surface, cool and sterile. Some were arranged in concentric spirals while others formed hypnotic helix patterns across the ceiling. It might have once been beautiful, but there was an air of darkness that spoke of its new occupiers. The tall windows were muffled by dark, heavy drapes to seal out the golden light. Septic soldiers patrolled the corridors or stood sentry in the galleries.

The monstrous captive was led to the council chamber, where the barons of Ur had once held court.

Much had changed since the coming of Nurgle. The tiled walls were scummed with gangrenous mould and mildew. Although the High Baron still sat upon his basalt throne, his face was haggard and his hair white. He was only thirty-two years old, but had aged forty years since the invasion. He was surrounded by his subjects – courtiers, advisors and scribes. They were all dead, their skin grey and their eyes white, but some still stood upright, locked in grovelling poses. Others still had been afflicted with the black wilt. Dirty nobles in filthy finery lurked in the corners like rodents, their wrists chained to the walls as they gnashed hungry teeth and wailed from dead lungs.

As a reflection of the city itself, the court still stood as a dead shell of its former self, unchanged from the outside but decaying from within.

Next to the High Baron stood a warrior-captain of Nurgle, a Plague Marine with a rhinocerine helmet and large, swollen hands that could not fit into armoured gloves. He leaned down to whisper into the ear of the High Baron, 'You may speak.'

And so the dark eldar slaver negotiated for the price of his captive. The High Baron responded, but each time at the behest of the Plague Marine. He was a mere puppet, his eyes wandering aimlessly as the Plague Marine prompted words into his mouth.

They settled on a sum of two hundred slaves, of which at least one hundred would be strong, human males, to be paid immediately. In addition, two tonnes of high-grade adamantite from the newly reconstructed mines would be paid later, once the infrastructure was completed.

The deal done, the High Baron bowed low and said, 'May the Emperor protect,' with a bored expression that spoke of thoughtless monotony.

His words incurred a slap from the Plague Marine, his large, black palms knocking the High Baron to the ground.

Without paying any attention, Sindul strode out of the chamber. The belay team of Septic soldiers following him strained against the chains of a raging Blood Gorgon.

A procession descended into the hab quarters. The Septic had yoked Barsabbas to a stone chariot, chaining his limbs tightly against the basalt frame and pulling the ponderous platform on grinding stone wheels. The denizens of Ur mobbed the streets to catch a glimpse of him. For hours, the city's address systems had announced the capture of an invader. Horn speakers from the ramparts promised the 'bringing to heel of distant enemies' – in turn, the survivors of Ur, those not too sick to show fealty to their new rulers, came to see him.

They dragged the slow and trundling carriage through the neatly ordered industrial tier with its smoking foundries and running rivers of molten metal. The air there was cooled by turbine fans the size of small hills that whooped with a constant urgency.

Barsabbas was taken up into the residential tiers, past layer upon layer of stacked, multi-storey villas. Although several children picked despondently through the street litter, the tiled streets were dominated by Nurgle infantry who patrolled in squads.

They led him up and up, towards the apex palace and where the chimney columns protruded through the void shields to belch black clouds into the atmosphere. There, the nobles and prestige castes of Ur, those who had sworn obedience to their Nurgle overlords, now waited to see him: the captured trophy.

Barsabbas had expected more of the barony. But the denizens of Ur were a sad, sick group, milky-skinned from the sun protection of their void shields, their faces wrapped in glare shades. Their clothes were crumpled and filthy. Their isolationism was evident amongst their fading finery; the textiles once rich and well made were now thinning into thread. The men preferred tabards and cloaks of coarse hessian for their resilience, while the women wore shawls of blues, greys and blacks for their ease of dyeing. It seemed the barony held a monopoly of the planet's resources but had nothing to spend it on.

The isolation had eroded their health too. Even a visitor such as Barsabbas could plainly see the effects of inbreeding and an indigenous immune system which hadn't been in contact with the pathogens of an outside world. There were not many children, and many people balanced upon crooked limbs and crutches. Rarer still were those of an older age, for it seemed the elderly did not live long in Ur. Barsabbas imagined that the arrival of Nurgle would have devastated their sheltered existence through mere contact with bacteria alone.

They stood with the inattentive wistfulness of forlorn prisoners. The fusion reactors had been made to leak on purpose, allowing Ur to irradiate its surrounding land and slowly kill its inhabitants. The Plague Marines with their supernatural constitution and power-armoured containment were immune, but these people were not.

Nurgle was poisoning them slowly, yet still they jeered Barsabbas as his open-topped carriage trundled past. They shouted and hurled pebbles although their taunts lacked conviction. Barsabbas had the sense that these people performed their hate simply to curry the favour of Nurgle. Many simply watched him with sullen looks, empathising with his state of captivity.

In truth, the decay of Ur had begun long before the coming of Nurgle. It could be said that by some strange, or perhaps divine, consequence, Nurgle had chosen to conquer them and accelerate their process of decline.

Once, the citizens of Ur had been men of a mono-segregationist

Imperial cult. They had believed Bassiq was a trial for the colonists and the God-Emperor had wanted them to remain pure, to shore up their city-state as an island of salvation amongst a sea of godless sin. They believed, in short, that Bassiq with its fire and heat was the canonical damnation of the warp.

But they had devolved over the centuries. Sealed away in their city, the people had atrophied, withering like an unused muscle. The Barons of Ur, once Imperial cultists, had quickly relinquished rule to Nurgle.

Now the Barons of Ur attended their sumptuous courts, in a dining gallery in the highest tiers of their clay palace. The woven rugs that adorned the walls were threadbare with silverfish. Men roosted on ceremonial tables whose gilt was flaking to show the worn, chipped wood beneath.

High Baron Matheus Toth sat in his fading chiffon. His ring-clustered fingers darted as he pantomimed the act of eating. The table was bare but he supped on a spoon delicately and drew deep breaths from a hollow goblet.

The full court had been summoned by their Plague Marine overseers. Some guests were living, while others, quite dead, were dragged unceremoniously from their coffins. The unliving sat in their high-backed chairs, their hands curled into stiff fists and their faces unmoving. Some were bloated with corpse gas and slumped awkwardly in their seats. The aggressive ones had to be tied down by rope, their dignity long faded as they shouted garbled words from black lips.

A full court of dying nobles, eating dust and attended by the dead. The richly dark humour of Papa Nurgle was evident in the actions of his followers. A royal guard blew on a horn with flaking lips and the celebrations began.

Sindul scratched his cheek, fidgeting incessantly at the mark. If he probed with his fingertips, he fancied he could detect the hard lump buried in his flesh. He was insufferably bored.

The human architecture did not at all interest him. The walls were too neat, too vertical and bared brick. Ugly, wrought-iron torch brackets were fixed to the walls, but their flames had been replaced with phosphor lighting. Sindul supposed the sconce fixtures were meant to complement the dining hall but they didn't. The placement of the long trestle tables was not quite symmetrical and everything about the chamber was linear and claustrophobic. Sindul had not wanted to accept the barony's invitation to be the guest of honour at their banquet. He felt like a vulture dining alongside rodents.

For a moment, it seemed as if the barons were watching him. Playing the part of a willing guest, Sindul's hand drifted back to the table and he picked up a fork. But then he cursed himself inwardly for he remembered they were mostly dead. Those sitting around him were mere carrion kings, propped up between living vassals. Among the hundreds of guests, more than half were corpses set into place by their household servants.

Those who were yet living regarded the xenos in their midst with weary resignation. He remembered that these barons had once been puritanical men. Now they were nothing but puppets of Nurgle. They regarded him with suspicion, and rightly so.

One of the barons leaned over and laid a chubby paw on Sindul's shoulders. His nails were yellowed from malnutrition. Sweaty, yet oddly soft with fat, he smiled at the dark eldar. When he did so, a varicose ulcer on his cheek fluttered tentatively like the heartbeat of a tiny bird.

'If you are hungry, feel free to dine on our departed guests,' the baron suggested, handing him a carving knife.

For a second, Sindul contemplated driving the fork in his hand straight into the man's face. He pondered the after-effect of fork against flesh. The baron was a moist, breathy man and Sindul wondered if he might simply deflate with a burp of corpse gas. The concept intrigued him.

But before Sindul could be tempted to respond, a sentry of Ur began to blast discordant, human music from a crude horn. At the summons, Barsabbas was wheeled in on a stone carriage, his limbs bound to the edges of a circular yoke. They had cleaned him and polished him like a trophy, scouring away the dirt to reveal the rich umber ceramite beneath.

Sindul looked away, feigning disinterest, as other nobles rose from their seats and stole closer to the living trophy.

Finally, almost reluctantly, Sindul mopped the corners of his mouth with coarse cloth and pushed his chair back with a squeal. Now was his chance.

Sindul stole close to Barsabbas. He pretended to marvel at the Traitor Marine's power armour, tracing the enamel and filigree with his hands. Deftly, he slipped a filing spike down Barsabbas's elbow joint.

'I'll find you in the asylum,' Sindul whispered.

Barsabbas nodded imperceptibly.

Touching his cheek gingerly, Sindul moved away from Barsabbas as the nobles closed around him, touching, prodding and gasping in fascination.

After the ignominy of the banquet, Barsabbas was wheeled into a low-ceilinged room. They closed the door behind them with a *krr-chunk* of a wheeled lock, sealing him in a cubicle of stone. Claystone floor, the same ruddy red on the walls. Marks had been made there, the ant-like scrawl of previous prisoners, scratched, chipped and scraped into the clay brick. He could make out Imperial prayers in the mortar, written in a bastardised Low Gothic. Last testimonies, letters to loved ones, lamentations.

It very slowly dawned on him that those words etched in the stone were the scrawls of dead men. There was a finality to the lines that sat heavily on Barsabbas's heart as he read them. He became convinced, by virtue of those lamentations, that he was now in an execution chamber.

This was where many had spent their last hours.

Renewed with sudden urgency, Barsabbas began to work the file out from his gauntlet. He wriggled his wrists, nudging the blade file out by friction, trying to bend his fingers towards his palm to catch its tip.

It slid out ever so slightly. Barsabbas changed the angle of his wrist, allowing the file to slide further out from the vambrace. It shifted, slipped out of his grasp and, to his sinking horror, fell to the floor. Barsabbas blinked in disbelief, looking at the file. He struggled for a while, straining against the shipping chain, whipping taut the bindings of his wrist. On board the *Cauldron Born*'s palaestras, it was not uncommon for Barsabbas to press three hundred and eighty kilograms of loaded kettles overhead, unarmoured. Yet the chain did not yield in the slightest.

Finally, with a last look of resignation, Barsabbas began to bite at the chains on his wrists. They were thick industrial links. At first the shock of cold metal against his teeth alarmed him, but he worked through the pain and continued to chew at the metal. A Space Marine's teeth, although heavy and calcified in order to chew indigestible proteins and fibre, could not manage iron. But by the time his calcified enamel was beginning to crack, Barsabbas had mostly lost feeling in his mouth anyway. He salivated, allowing his Betcher's gland to drool acidic mucus as he worked. He savaged the links at his wrist.

Finally the metal, softened by acid, gave way with a snap that split all his remaining molars. Spitting out flakes of iron and fragments of his own teeth, Barsabbas tore his way out of his restraints and began to recouple the power cables to his reactor pack.

The throbbing pain of shredded nerves was forgotten as his power armour hummed to life. Suddenly elevated by euphoria and the surging strength in his limbs, Barsabbas ran his tongue along the jagged rubble of his teeth.

Sindul climbed the stairs to the palace through the darkest of routes. Humans were hostile to aliens as a rule, and the sight of a dark eldar, especially the mercenary guest of their new overlords, would not invite good intention. He shied away from the lighted puddles of street lanterns and glided along the narrow side lanes. Gumede followed a respectful distance behind, as befitted a slave. He too carried a weighty medallion of Nurgle to display his favour.

With his body swathed in a hooded cloak of steel thread, Sindul passed the palace sentries with a wave of his copper crest of Nurgle.

The servants and house boys averted their gaze as he passed them by, frightened by the spectre that brandished the favour of their Nurgle overlords. They knew of stories, passed through hushed whispers in the kitchens and launderettes, that the dark eldar slaver had single-handedly captured a great beast of Chaos. A Space Marine.

Finally, Sindul came to the asylum of Ur, a fortified wing of the palace itself. It was connected to the spires of the palace by means of a narrow sky bridge, but it seemed distant and forlorn, a finger of clay balanced on a low tier that overlooked the gas and chemical plants of the lower stack. Even from a distance, Sindul could see the asylum had no windows and despite its proportions, the only entrance was a remarkably ordinary door of very ordinary height. It almost seemed like the door had been added as an afterthought, as if the asylum had never been intended to have any windows or entrances.

A pair of sentries stood guard. They were largely ceremonial, if all that Sindul had heard of the asylum were true. The Barons of Ur, paranoid as they were, incarcerated many. Political dissidents, illegitimate noble births, heretics – any who might threaten the stability of their cloistered, pocketed existence.

But the asylum's reputation had been built upon its most dangerous inmates – psykers, mutants and killers of men. Ur was an unwholesome place and it bred strangely unwholesome deviants. If these were to escape, the pair of sentries, Sindul reckoned, could do little. But then, where would the inmates flee? Into the thirsty death of the desert sands?

Sindul waved Gumede ahead and the chief played the part of slave well, bowing subserviently. He scampered forwards and brandished his emblem of Nurgle at the door. Overbright sodium lamps mounted overhead shone directly into his eyes.

The guards studied him before shaking their heads.

'No,' one said shaking his head dismissively. The man was the younger of the pair, with a pugnaciously set jawline.

Gumede thrust the emblem before him again.

'No, the emblem does not allow,' snapped the sentry in his stilted, idiomatic tongue. His older companion nodded sleepily.

Sindul gritted his teeth. His left hand, hidden within his cloak, closed around the hilt of his needle blade. He stepped out of the shadows and waved Gumede aside. 'I am a guest of Opsarus the Crow. His captains host my stay.'

'Are you stupid?' snapped the sentry. 'Opsarus cannot be pleased by entry here. No one. No one ever enters. If you enter, you do not leave. This is your last home.'

Sindul still held out his hand with the emblem. But he was no longer showing them. He was distracting them. The guards stared at the emblem, then back to Sindul, before returning their gaze to the emblem again.

Suddenly frustrated, the younger sentry tapped Sindul's forehead. 'No access!' he said. He poked Sindul's forehead again. 'No access.'

Upon seeing this, the older sentry took several quick steps backwards.

He was wiser with age and did not have the ego of a younger man. He knew when to be quiet.

As the younger sentry continued to harass Sindul, the dark eldar clenched his jaw. The needle blade flicked out four times. It punctured pressure points and the sentries stiffened and died, their hearts stopped by poison, yet they remained standing. The young man died while pointing pugnaciously at Sindul.

The older sentry, for all his wisdom, died with his face to the wall, the dark eldar knife finding his back again and again.

Their voices were frantic. 'He is out! The monster is out!'

Barsabbas could hear them echo in the corridors. He could hear the clumsy drone of footfalls as the sentries gathered to find him. They would be checking each of the doors along the passage, checking their prisoners were still contained, all of the mutants, the murderers – the high threats. In their voices he heard panic and the slowed vowels of confusion.

Barsabbas knew the sentries were outmatched. This was not their game. Until several months ago, before the taking of Hauts Bassiq, these men served cloistered military tenures. Raised within the sealed city, most of these men had never heard of a Traitor Marine before, and could have no idea of their capabilities.

Barsabbas rounded a corner, looking for a weapon. He almost walked straight into a quartet of sentries. Before they could finish their initial screams of surprise, Barsabbas swept his forearm and pinned the closest against the wall, crushing his spine. The rest backed away, yelling loud, panicked words. One of them began to fumble with a lasrifle, but he was unfamiliar with it beyond ceremonial purpose. He attempted to fire on Barsabbas with the safety still caught.

Like a great fish breaking the surface, Barsabbas tossed a sentry away and flung him down the corridor. Hastily lashed shock mauls bounced off his unyielding hide. The remaining three men were tossed about like bushels of grain. Each surge of Barsabbas's steel-bound limbs threw them from wall to wall, bouncing them, breaking them. The Blood Gorgon was simply playing with them.

Finally tired of his sport, Barsabbas left the four broken sentries and kicked down the nearest door. The asylum inmates were agitated by the commotion and they had begun to keen and howl, making nonsense noise through the tiny slits of their armoured doors.

Within the cell Barsabbas had opened was a bookish-looking man. Slender from malnutrition and pale from confinement, he had a dash of handsome white hair punctuated with almost neon blue eyes.

As Barsabbas lowered his head to peer through the door, the man struck at him, hacking at his neck seal with the snapped handle of a

chamber brush. Before his attack landed, Barsabbas pushed him aside
contemptuously.

'Do that again and there will be no turning back,' Barsabbas growled.
He should have killed the man for his mistake but he had a use for him
yet.

'You are free. Go and kill. Now,' Barsabbas commanded.

Go. Kill. The slender man understood him perfectly. Without another
word, the man squirmed through the door past Barsabbas and disappeared, screaming in glee down the hall.

By now the asylum was ringing with the shrill bells of disaster. Sentries
huddled behind shields and shock mauls advanced in formation down
the hall, three abreast. It would not be long before the Plague Marines
responded in force. Barsabbas heard the sentries yell warnings. Something about 'priority inmate'. He did not know who the priority inmate
was, but he noted the consternation in their tone.

He began to bash through each door he came across, punching the
metal plates off their hinges. There were all kinds in there: murderers,
lunatics, an ox-necked man with a hammerhead for a hand, an elderly
female who appeared entirely harmless. None attacked him, as if they
were minor predators cowed by a far greater threat. Some paused to
thank him briefly, awed by his physical size and appearance, before
sprinting away to wreak havoc on their gaolers.

Barsabbas followed a sandstone drawbridge that extended across to
an otherwise inaccessible door high in the wall. The door was almost
invisible in the brickwork, placed in the centre of a wall perhaps forty
metres high, as if the sentries had wanted to forget about the inmate
within. Judging by the hysteria of the sentries that pursued him, Barsabbas guessed the door to be of some significance. The guards tried to
retract the drawbridge, grinding the ancient mechanical gears slowly.
Barsabbas leapt the gap with ease as the drawbridge continued to edge
back. A las-shot sparked over his head and another missed him by a wide
berth. Snorting with disdain, Barsabbas ignored the sentries.

Beyond them, the last door was reinforced with thick brass bands.
Not a door but a true vault seal much like the one where he himself had
been confined. A coiled nest of pipes was funnelled into the door. They
writhed with pumped gases, and Barsabbas scented the sugary smell of
nitrous oxide and barbitane. Whatever was inside was kept in a state of
controlled sedation.

For a moment, he considered the beast that lay within. He was not
prone to fanciful thinking, but the occupant must have been a dangerous one, at least the equal of he. Grasping the locking wheel, Barsabbas
turned it, retracting the bolts that anchored the vault seal to bolt locks
in the walls. The vault popped with a hiss as the sedative gases were
expelled.

The explosion caught even Barsabbas off guard.

Barsabbas was blown backwards off his feet immediately and thrown against the far wall by a wave of pressure. Light poured through the opened vault. The clay walls were melting, dripping with condensation and ice crystals. A voice so deep it was slurred issued from the light.

'I am death!'

A toddler emerged, wild-haired and chubby. He had a mole on his left cheek but besides that was unremarkable. Barsabbas rose to his feet and the boy did not reach past his shin.

'Do you know who I am?' asked the boy in fluent Low Gothic. 'I am death!'

Barsabbas smiled. He had not found a Blood Gorgon but the potential for destruction nonetheless excited him. 'I am a god and I have freed you. Go do your work.'

It amused Barsabbas that the young, crazed psyker thought himself to be an incarnation of death. A juvenile imagination combined with limitless destructive potential would always be entertaining. Moreover, the child seemed devoid of any sanity whatsoever.

He could already hear the horrified shrieks of the sentries across the chasm of the now retracted bridge. The child psyker curled his chubby arms in an upward direction. There was a snapping of chains and the walls shook as if someone had loosed a succession of bombs. The drawbridge slammed back into place as if it were a mere toy. Clapping, the child skipped across the bridge.

The monsters had escaped, cried the sentries. All the monsters had escaped.

CHAPTER TWENTY-ONE

The monsters left a trail of mangled bodies in their rampage. Even in their execution of violence, there was no order, only pandemonium and a sense of reckless savagery. Dead men lay amongst the rubble of broken walls, askew and half-buried.

A mezzanine of the second gallery had buckled over its support columns. Sentries of Ur sought shelter under the collapsed walkway, holding their shields timidly above their heads as inmates sprinted through the corridors screaming in their delirium. Far away, in the other wings of the asylum, there could be heard a low banging that was jarring in its reverberation.

Sindul danced over the remains of a sentry, delighting in seeing patterns within the blood fall. Several respectful paces behind him, Gumede stepped gingerly around the carnage. For Sindul, the asylum was festive with the sounds of pandemonium and he felt the flush of excitement. He hurried his pace at the jubilant sounds of screaming.

The pulsating beneath his orbital bone had dulled and the searing pain was beginning to numb as the slave scarab grew calm. It meant Barsabbas was nearby. Perhaps the mon-keigh would remove the creature for good once he kept his part of the bargain. Perhaps not. By his adolescence, Sindul had already murdered his own eldest half-brother over a modest gambling debt. To 'promise' was not a concept that Sindul fully understood. He knew of its existence but had never seen a proper use for it.

He followed the banging sounds. Even at a distance, it seemed the very walls were being clapped together. He hugged the walls for cover, a splinter pistol now holstered against his ribs. High overhead, hooded lamps swung fitfully with each tremor. Crushed clay, red and soft, covered the tiled floors. Metal doors and entire sections of wall had been cast to the ground, discarded like wind-torn debris.

Gumede followed behind him, his steps frustratingly loud to Sindul's ears. His bow was notched, his sinewy forearms tensed against the string. Despite the muffled, indistinct sounds of destruction, the air was still and tense. Sindul did not have the firepower to deal with one of the *Ang'mon-keigh*, especially those half-corpse giants of Nurgle. At his side, the high-velocity splinter pistol seemed terribly meagre. As a species the eldar knew no equal – subtle, savant and entirely beyond human in their intelligence and philosophy. The eldar had developed and proven theories of universal creation and expansion before humanity had invented the wheel. But even the fearsome eldar warriors in full battledress had learned to respect the savage rage of humanity's Space Marines. They fought with a fearless ignorance that the eldar could never hope to replicate...

'Sin... dul,' Gumede whispered. The chief's eyes were saucered in consternation. 'Do you feel that?'

Sindul turned on the chief, ready to lash out at him for disrupting his thought process. But he stopped himself short when he felt it too. A continuous tremor in the very walls. He placed a palm to the clay and it vibrated loosely.

'What is that?' Gumede asked.

'I–'

Sindul did not finish his sentence. The hall shook so violently that the lamps shorted out, burying them in darkness. The ground heaved underneath them as if the world had been tilted onto an angle. Sindul could hear tables and other unbolted furnishings slide across the tiles.

'Get away from the walls,' Sindul managed to shout before his voice was lost to a thunderous clash. Covering his head, the dark eldar curled up and let the world rock him back and forth. The sensation continued for some time, a violent shaking that hummed in his skull and loosened his joints.

By the time he opened his eyes, the light had returned. Or rather, light now pierced where none could before. As he opened his eyes and adjusted to the haze of brick dust, he could see that he lay on the broken edge of tiled flooring. The ground plummeted away from him, along with the entire left-hand wall and structure. An entire portion of the asylum had collapsed.

Beyond the rubble of the destroyed wing, he saw a child standing atop a stone plinth, flinging up his arms like an orchestral maestro. With one lift of his left arm, a surge of clay rose like liquid, radiating outwards with seismic tremors. With a sweep of his right wrist, a wall burst into constituent bricks. Up went both his arms in crescendo as a column of spiralling sandstone spiked from the ground to pierce through the skin of the ceiling. From behind the cover of dog-toothed rubble, sentries of Ur as well as a formation of Plague Marines hammered him with volleys of shots. The ammunition sparked harmlessly off a bubble of kinetic force around the child. It was the most terrifying performance of telekinesis Sindul had ever witnessed.

He might have remained there, mesmerised, had a hand not dragged him away from the edge. Sindul turned, expecting to see Gumede, but found himself staring into the face of a stylised gargoyle – Barsabbas.

'It is *ever* glorious to meet you,' Sindul said, scratching his cheek.

'No, it's not,' Barsabbas refuted, entirely ignorant of Sindul's sarcasm. 'You lie too much.'

Behind them all, the wall ruptured, silencing their exchange. They moved then, darting through the open storm of rock shrapnel and stray rounds. Barsabbas only paused to pick up a weapon, a stray bolter lying next to the body of a fallen Plague Marine. While the power armour of the corpse was unmarked, ugly wounds marked the bare flesh at its joints. The 'monsters' had done their work well here.

Weaving through broken remains of masonry, they left the skirmish between the inmates and their keepers behind.

The central blockhouse was empty. Without fuss or ceremony Barsabbas, Sindul and Gumede made their way down the three-hundred-metre hall to the one door at its end. They followed a trail of dead and dying sentries and inmates alike.

The final door was high priority indeed. Despite the rumbles of a not-so-distant fight, a phalanx of twenty Urite sentries crouched pensively by the nickel-plated door. Their collective fear became tangible as they spotted Barsabbas approaching, as if each man were literally shaking from fright. The Traitor Marine's horned helm clapped against the ceiling and his massive, plated shoulders chafed the walls. The tiny, flitting black ghost of the dark eldar was barely noticed and Gumede, eager to indicate his apartness from the group, trailed behind nursing his bow.

At first they panicked. Their sergeant, a wilting man of middle years, flapped his arms in some sort of command or pre-drilled order. 'Release our hound!'

The phalanx remained fixed, no one willing to break away from the protective formation as the Traitor Marine drew closer, towering above them. The sergeant executed the same hesitant command signals. 'The hound, damn you. Babalu! Unlock Babalu!'

Willing themselves into action, the soldiers began to pry open the weighty door, taking two men to haul on the steering lock and three of them to scrape it open against the suspension hinges.

Barsabbas paused. He staggered his stance into a low crouch ready to receive an oncoming charge. The door edged upon. From beyond came a roar, a challenge.

Stepping under the door frame rose the largest non-modified human Barsabbas had ever seen. At first the man seemed naked: so much flesh did he possess that his bib-and-brace did not trail down past the rolls of his knees or cover the fleshy mountains of his breast. He was easily shoulders, traps, neck and head taller than the guards and weighed perhaps in the mid-three hundred kilos. They had housed most of his torso in riveted metal sheets like a submariner's rig and his paws ended in studded spheres of solid black metal – wrecking balls, pitted, spherical and brutally physical. Barsabbas gathered that this was 'Babalu' – the thing responsible for their so-called 'tier market massacres'.

Babalu turned on his gaolers first, crashing his sledgehammer fists into their soft, yielding bodies. It was only then that Barsabbas realised the guards had been terrified not of him, but of their own weapon. Cringing, the Urite sentries pressed themselves against the walls as Babalu crushed his way through them to lunge at Barsabbas. Some Urites drew their knees to their chests and simply lay down, their will to fight having long deserted their hands and hearts.

The killer issued a challenge, unimpressed by Barsabbas's stature. He clashed his kettled hands together, sounding out his strength and stomped his legs to establish his girth. He postured, flexing the rolling orbs of his biceps. He had the gall to roar at Barsabbas with his quivering jowls.

Barsabbas slapped Babalu's head: a casual, insulting blow that bounced his skull against the wall and it cut the killer's raging screams short. Pressing up close, Barsabbas slapped him again, snake fast. The blow broke Babalu's jaw and he fell, his insensate head lolling to the side. His fat bunched obligingly as he dropped, his bulk jammed against the corridor. Dragging him by his belt, Barsabbas hauled the feared killer aside and did not bother looking at him again. He guessed the man was dead, but he did not really care.

Unnerved by Barsabbas's warpath, Gumede and Sindul followed behind, cautious of the Traitor Marine's volatile strength. As they picked their way through the antechamber, the chief stole glances at the cowering sentries and felt a deep understanding of their fear.

Barsabbas was not an enemy, yet Gumede's manner was nonetheless furtive in his monstrous presence. Barsabbas was running roughshod over everything that stood before him.

The room beyond was a cavernous cell plated in sheet alloy. The reflective floor stretched far out into the distance and the inward-slanting walls warped the reflections back and forth in a nauseating mess of images.

There were no seams nor rivets to the coppery compound; the chamber appeared as if it had been hollowed out from a monolithic block of metal, and the asylum had simply been built up, brick by brick, around the maddening metal core.

The prisoner, large though he was, was buried in a cocoon of chains. They had bound him from his head to his shins in the centre of the chamber, anchoring him in mid-air with an archaic winch. Glyphs and ward runes radiated out from him in concentric circles and overlapping hexagons, poured onto the floor with red sand. Barsabbas was not well versed in daemonology, but he recognised the runes of binding and psychic dampening directly beneath the oubliette.

+*Who is that? You are familiar. I have met you before, brother.*+

The words brushed across Barsabbas's mind in a quietly commanding manner. He felt compelled to answer, but realised the prisoner would not be able to hear him through the solid ball of chains.

Possessed by a sudden conviction he could not rationalise, Barsabbas kicked and brushed through the wards, sweeping the red sand away. He felt the psychic power emanating more strongly from the prisoner.

+*Lower the winch, brother*+

The voice resonated with Barsabbas. He felt compelled to obey, and indeed found himself doing so on muscle impulse. Eagerly, Barsabbas began to unwind the chains.

Outside the chamber, the pandemonium sounded like the roar of ocean waves. The military force of Nurgle would respond soon if they had not already. Barsabbas knew his time was limited.

+*Yes. We do not have long. I can feel the Plague followers coming closer now. Many of them, like a seething tide.*+

Barsabbas tore at the chains with his fingers, snapping the links and shredding the metal fragments with his gauntlet tips. An involuntary cry of triumph escaped his lips: beneath was a corpse-white powder that was familiar to him, the very same pigment with which Blood Gorgons dyed their skin.

He tore at the cheeks to unveil kohled eyepits and a high forehead. The brow ridge was scarred and shelf-like, furrowed over a long, battered face. The bare skin was pitted like gravel. Dark eyes squinted at the light, as if breaking the wards had awoken their owner from some deep, dreadful sleep.

'Lord Gammadin,' Barsabbas cried, falling to his knees.

'None of that,' Gammadin intoned. The Ascendant Champion seemed to flex beneath his cocoon as his dampened mind began to rouse. In a rapidly unwinding spool, the chains fell away. Beneath was the leviathan bulk of horn and plate – the hulking body of Lord Gammadin, thick in the shoulder and heavy in the hands, with its ursine profile. The recognition brought a flutter of thrill to Barsabbas's stomach.

'It is I, Bond-Brother Barsabbas,' Gammadin replied in measured tones. 'Lower your weapon.'

Outside the vault, the sound of footfalls became urgently incisive. A great number of hostiles was gathering outside, yet Gammadin was not at all hastened. Sighing slowly, he shook his head. 'Squad Besheba have fallen, then. I do not feel their presence.'

'They have. I carry the name of Besheba on my shoulders.'

'That is a heavy burden, Barsabbas. After the shame of Govina, the other squads already see you as a weaker pack,' Gammadin said, his neutral tone not at all accusatory.

A small detonation shook the adjacent chambers. Shouts and commands, closer now. Barsabbas heard the bellow of Nurgle trumpet voxes, crackling with coordinates and field reports.

Yet still Gammadin seemed unaffected. He shook out his arms, flexing his one hand. 'How did you arrive?'

'By aerial craft. I have memorised the route from the hangar by retina overlay–'

Barsabbas was cut off as a gunshot echoed from the entrance hall. An arm-sized sliver of wall was gouged out by the slashing bolter-round. Sinking to one knee, Barsabbas returned two shots on instinct.

Ponderously, almost like a mountain harassed into motion, Gammadin met the enemy.

When Gammadin moved, he did so with an unstoppable momentum. He housed so much physical power that it took him some time to pick up speed, like a rolling avalanche, but when he began to move he did not seem capable of slowing.

Plague Marines shot at him. Those shots that Gammadin did not slap out of the air, he took against his shoulder plates. Shrapnel puffed against him. He rose in his full armour, for it had become fused to his muscle and bone, the ceramite laced throughout his entire body. Barsabbas could not even tell where Gammadin's armoured suit ended and his own flesh began. According to Barsabbas's thermal imaging, Gammadin simply appeared as a solid block of ceramite with arterial warmth running through the deepest core. The data calculated Gammadin at seventy-six per cent metal density. By his memory, even a standard template Rhino tank stood at only sixty per cent metallic composition.

As Gammadin howled and bolt shot powdered against his thickened hide, Barsabbas realised how truly destructive his lord could be.

Bodies were tossed aside. Flesh impacted violently with stone. Gammadin simply walked into and through the walls. Small-arms fire glanced against him. Contemptuous, Gammadin pushed his hand through the brick walls like damp card. He was entirely fixated upon moving.

'Lord Gammadin,' Barsabbas called. 'I have an escape route prepared in the city's flight docks.'

With grinding deliberation, Gammadin wrenched a vault seal off its hydraulic hinges. 'Go then, brother. I will follow.'

A changing of heart. Perhaps that was the one true flaw of the dark eldar race.

Try as he might, Sindul knew no other way. Deceit was like a game to him. It was a constant, never-ending puzzle that he constructed in his mind, whenever he felt himself drifting away. As a culture, the eldar saw cunning as a manifestation of culture and intellect. It was a desired trait in any courtship; indeed, an evolutionary aspect of their entire culture.

Those who could not scheme were seen as dull-witted, *pen'shaar'ul*, which meant 'waiting to be murdered'.

Sindul did not consider himself *pen'shaar'ul*. He had been scheming the moment he and Gumede reached the *Harvester*. The vessel was docked in an open courtyard and had been left unguarded. Septic foot squads passed them, too rushed to give Sindul and his slave any notice.

By Sindul's reckoning, Barsabbas was free. His thoughts were confirmed when there was a distant thrum a hundred metres above. Looking up, Sindul saw puffs of gritty smoke drifting from the distant minarets.

'We must stay and wait for the koag,' Gumede declared, as if sensing Sindul's intentions.

Sindul cast him a sidelong glance, smiling softly.

'We wait,' Gumede repeated firmly. 'You will not do to me again what you did last time.'

The chief stepped back and pointed a lasrifle at Sindul.

'This is awkward,' Sindul began. He shot forwards and parried the lasrifle aside with the blade of his hand. His left hand shot out and seized Gumede's throat.

'You made it easier than last time,' the dark eldar hissed through his teeth. He stepped inside and pushed Gumede against the ship's fuselage. With two strokes, fast and deft, Sindul severed the chief's vocal cords and collapsed his lungs.

Turning swiftly from his act, Sindul looked for any witnesses but saw none. The hangar was empty but for his own long shadow.

Satisfied that he was alone, Sindul began to pare off his own right cheek. He placed the blade against his own face and sliced deep. Startling, blinding pain almost blacked him out. The trauma would have sent a human into shock, but the dark eldar was a connoisseur of pain. The sensation, bright and heated, paralysed him temporarily. For a brief second the wound was too much even for Sindul, and he wobbled on his feet before he regained his senses. He forced down the pain and embraced its sensation until adrenaline numbed it.

Stumbling, leaking a trail of blood, Sindul lurched towards his wait-ing vessel.

The city was a vast place of unfamiliar angles and planes. A lesser man would have been disorientated and lost, yet Barsabbas moved with a sure-footed purpose. The broad plazas, walkways and mezzanines were mapped to hololithic precision in his mind. Retracing the route of his stone chariot, Barsabbas drew upon his short-term memory banks and the pict-captures from his iris.

Bullets fragmented the stone around him as the enemy tracked his escape, but he was unfazed. Barsabbas ran point, snapping back shots when it suited him. He depleted the last of his ammunition, draining clip after clip. City wardens and Septic infantry soon discovered that lattice bricks did not stop bolt shells and fled at the accuracy of his fire. Automatic targetters jumped from victim to victim. Barsabbas fluttered the trigger, coaxing a constant burp of bolt-shot into the overhead ramparts and alcoves. The brickwork was chewed up, forcing the enemy deep into cover.

Behind, Gammadin strode through the smoke. His head was lowered, the antlers of his forehead pointed forwards.

'I've seen this before,' Barsabbas said, gesturing at a stone arch that framed a causeway.

They turned a corner and the view opened before them, an open court-yard framed by inverted columns. Several bodies were strewn across the flagstones – among them was a figure swathed in a red shuka.

Barsabbas recognised Gumede. His bolter flashed up immediately, looking for Sindul. Stepping past the plainsman's body, Barsabbas afforded Gumede a brief glance. He felt a curious sensation, like a man who had lost a valuable tool, but he dismissed the thought immediately.

Some metres away, the *Harvester* was already powering up as incandes-cent light speared from its rearward engine pods. Barsabbas tensed up at the sound. Something was wrong, or so his instincts told him. Running into the open, Barsabbas waved towards the *Harvester*'s cockpit.

In response, the ship swivelled to face him, its engines flaring. Behind the glass viewing shields, Barsabbas could see Sindul's face.

The dark eldar actually smiled at him. He smiled through a face slick with blood.

At first, Barsabbas only noticed the stone pillars around him toppling. Only a second later did he hear the *Harvester*'s nose-mounted cannons shriek into life.

Barsabbas was already rolling backwards as flagstones around him liq-uefied, rolled and rippled under the impacts of a hyper-velocity cannon. He banged back three or four shots with his bolter, feeling impotent as he did so.

As he dived for cover, Barsabbas could hear the increasing whine as the ship's vector thrusters built up to full power. The *Harvester* levitated unsteadily as its landing struts folded into its hovering belly. The cannon continued to shred the surrounding area, felling walls and flattening nearby habs.

+*Desist.*+

A sudden wrench of neural pain tingled up Barsabbas's spine and into the back of his head. Screaming, Barsabbas fell into a crouch.

Simultaneously, the *Harvester* seemed to lose balance. Its starboard wing listed and tipped, grazing the flagstones. It righted itself then lurched the other way, its portside wing scraping the tiles with a flash of fat orange sparks.

Barsabbas turned around just in time to see Gammadin raise his hands and hurl another mind bolt.

+*Desist*+

This time, Barsabbas tried to duck, but ducking did nothing to protect him. The psychic pain exploded again. The word 'desist' echoed in his brain. Barsabbas almost dropped his boltgun and lost control of his hands as the muscles spasmed. Although Gammadin's will was focused on Sindul, such was the power of his psychic echoes that Barsabbas was compelled even by their residual fury.

To his front, the *Harvester* tried to thrust up into the air. It rose hesitantly, stalled and then slammed back down. It came down so quickly that the landing struts snapped and there could be heard the bestial friction of forty tonnes of metal squealing against stone.

+*Show yourself.*+

The cockpit hatch popped open with a vacuum hiss and Sindul crawled down the ledge. Blood ran down his face, into his chest and down most of his legs. His hands were clawing his head, his topknot frazzled and wild.

Gammadin crossed the courtyard and bodily lifted the dark eldar into the air with one arm, holding him face to face. 'Twice I have been betrayed by the dark eldar. Twice,' Gammadin said with disgust while studying the specimen in his grasp.

Sindul screamed. Gammadin tossed him onto the hard ground. A boot, wrought like a cloven hoof, was brought down onto Sindul's femur, breaking his leg cleanly. Gammadin stomped again and broke the eldar's other leg.

'We still need him,' Barsabbas gasped as he limped across the courtyard. He could already hear the familiar shouts of soldiers being mustered to find them, and the *crump* of approaching footsteps.

'We still need him to fly his ship.'

Gammadin nodded sagely. 'Well, he can fly without the aid of his mischievous little legs.'

At this, Sindul raised his head with a bloodied grin. When he smiled, the missing part of his right cheek twitched with exposed fat and sinew. Blood stained his teeth and drooled from his lips. 'Well, we better go, then. The enemy are coming for you,' he taunted defiantly.

CHAPTER TWENTY-TWO

Anko Muhr had not expected the influence of Grandfather Nurgle to pervade so quickly. The God of Decay was generous to those who gave worship. The *Cauldron Born* was ailing, its ventilation wheezing like great bellows. Even the Witchlord's own brothers would one day succumb to the persistent corruption of Nurgle when their wills were sufficiently broken. Muhr, however, had welcomed the Lord of Decay openly.

Had his hand always been so black? He was certain it had not.

For as long as he could remember, Muhr's ungloved hand had been that of a Blood Gorgon: pale white and deeply striated, with thick bones and the wiry muscle that bound them. It was not like that any more.

Muhr's hand, when he held it up to his face, was entirely black. The skin itself was so dark it was almost waxen, but not the smooth beautiful black of ebony, it was the black of rot. He had not even noticed the change in colour until his fingernails had slid off his fingertips. Now his hand pulsated, the veins engorged with tarrish blood and swelling the walls of his skin. The changes Muhr had undergone were mesmerising. The gifts of Father Nurgle, the beautification of decay, were endlessly fascinating...

'My sorcerer. That has a measure of dignity to it, does it not? Sorcerer. Advisor. The second of the Crow.'

Muhr turned to see Opsarus standing in his chambers without announcement. The Crow had a habit of doing so.

'Nurgle favours you,' Opsarus continued. 'See the attention he invests in you?'

'Yes,' Muhr replied, hypnotised by his own hand.

'Behold the floral magnificence of Nurgle. Budding flowers of flesh growth, the tessellating landscapes of mould spore. There is no beauty to the unadorned,' Opsarus declared. 'Nurgle is first and foremost an artist. Tzeentch, he is a mere mischief-maker, and young Slaanesh no more than a libertine. Let us not even begin with the linear, narrow-minded aggression of Khorne.'

'Nurgle nurtures,' Muhr said. 'But I do not know how openly my bonded brethren will appreciate the artistic mutations of Nurgle.'

Opsarus's delighted tone changed suddenly. His voice lowered. 'What do you mean?'

Muhr shook his head quickly. 'I did not mean anything by it,' he stammered. 'But the Blood Gorgon companies. They may not be impressed by the physical changes that Nurgle has planned for them.'

Opsarus rose to his full height, his voice a slavering growl. 'Of course they will. You would like it. Soon they will become like you. Like me. We are one. Nurgle will take the Blood Gorgons into the fold, whether they choose it or not.'

Muhr nodded. He stared at his black hand. Nurgle was claiming him because he had allowed Nurgle into his soul. But sooner or later, whether the Blood Gorgons wished it or not, the deathly presence of the Plague Marines would change them. The spores would spread into recycled air, the viruses would consume the space hulk. The very presence of Nurgle himself would eventually change them all.

Opsarus appeared to calm down, his breath slowing to a rasp. 'Good,' he said. 'We can be brothers in Nurgle together. You, I and all your brethren. There will be peace then.'

'Of course, lord,' Muhr agreed. 'Of course.'

The moons of Hauts Bassiq were not distant beasts. They lingered shyly on the fringes of the sky, sulking behind the fiery light of their solar cousins. Small, brown and fretful, the half-dozen moons fussed across the sky, attempting to find any space, any gap that was not dominated by the harsh glare of day just so they could be seen.

It did not take long for the *Harvester* to locate the secondary moon of Hauspax once they left Bassiq's toxic atmosphere behind. The moon was a slow-moving orbiter, a fat disc that crawled across the sky when viewed from below. What could not be seen from below, however, but became clearly visible on the *Harvester*'s sensor, was the leviathan bulk of the *Cauldron Born* hiding behind the moon's unseen side. Its massive energy output and warp engines lit up its presence like a miniature star. Even lurking behind the dark side of the moon, its energy signature was so radiant that it could have been picked up almost a subsector away by any armada scan.

It was a slow, steady affair to navigate the vessel by sensor scans alone.

The ship's glare shutters and void shields locked them in a cabin of low blue lighting. Cocooned by insulation, it shielded them from the boiling temperature and the retina-scalding brightness of the proximate suns.

Despite their blind flight, Sindul proved to be a pilot of finesse. They circumvented the locust swarms of micrometeors that obstructed them. The xenos ship was light and comparatively fragile. Its void shields were not the thick-skinned energy-draining monsters favoured by human technology. It floated and spiralled away from oncoming high-velocity rock fragments rather than meeting them head-on, its shield shuddering briefly from hypersonic impacts with dust particles.

As they crested the moon's hemisphere, the *Cauldron Born*'s shadow eclipsed the sky. Here, even amongst the depthless expanse of space, the term 'space hulk' was entirely apt. Like the hand of a god it reared its fingers across the moon's horizon. Four thousand metres away, the cityscapes of twinkling lance batteries, torpedo banks and gun turrets welcomed them with a taut, breathless tension.

Although the broadsides were capable of dismantling continents, they were far too ponderous to harm the *Harvester*. Cloaked by refraction, the dark eldar ship pierced the *Cauldron Born*'s scans, registering as nothing more than tiny space debris.

As they approached the tectonic flanks of the *Cauldron Born*, Sindul sped up. Launch tubes that clustered the vast underbelly closed rapidly. The raiding craft darted into a tube like a mosquito, swallowed up by the enormous metal hide of the floating fortress.

It was too fast to fly by sight.

The inner launch tube of the *Cauldron Born*'s flight passages became a blur, interrupted only by the strobe of overhead lights. Constructed to catapult raider craft from within the docking hangars, the tube's guide markers were not clearly visible as the dark eldar vessel reduced speed to subsonic. Sindul navigated only by the sonic projection of his Impaler, guiding the craft with whisper-soft touches.

By Barsabbas's estimate, the *Harvester* was still going too fast. It was not meant to fly at such speeds. The wingtips barely cleared the tight confines of the entry valves. They banked hard, swerving as they flew deeper into the *Cauldron Born*'s sealed hangars. A human craft could never have matched the sharp brakes and switches in air pressure.

Impressively, Sindul guided the craft in blind within the pitch-black chute. As Barsabbas watched, he realised that perhaps the folklore was true. Perhaps all eldarkind, to some extent, were possessed of psychic abilities. Even looking two or three seconds into the future would allow Sindul to pre-empt each turn, bend and elevation in their flight.

A gas main flashed over the cockpit. The overhead ceiling skimmed so close that it felt like they had hit an oil slick.

It seemed as if Sindul was fading. The dark eldar was shaking uncontrollably in his pilot's sheath. As a Traitor Marine, Barsabbas had overlooked the physical and psychological ordeal he had forced upon his captive.

Yet still Sindul laboured on.

The *Harvester* finally slowed as it neared the *Cauldron Born*'s first atmospheric seal. It crashed then, as if entirely spent. It dropped, steadied and dropped again like an injured bird. Sindul only just managed to level out before the *Harvester* collided belly-down. It bounced once and skidded, wings sheared by a wall as the ship spun axially on its underside.

Finally, with its rearward engines trailing flame, the ship came to a final, shuddering stop.

Barsabbas pushed the side hatch open and manoeuvred his shoulders out from the frame. Gammadin strode out after him, his ceramite-fused body entirely unaffected by the landing. Without a word, the Ascendant Champion disappeared into the darkness of the launch tube's hangar seal.

Pausing briefly, Brother Barsabbas stole one last look into the *Harvester*'s interior. Under the flickering cabin glow, he could see Sindul's body slumped in its cradle. As much as the creature had irked him, the dark eldar's instinct to survive had impressed him. The utter lack of social conditioning, much like that of a Traitor Marine, meant the dark eldar could operate ruthlessly and without inhibition. That much at least was to be admired. Giving Sindul an almost imperceptible little nod, Barsabbas left, following Gammadin into the dark.

Sindul breathed unsteadily.

If he could see himself now, Sindul imagined he would not be the handsome creature he had once been. His pared-open face was smeared with a synthetic gel. Dried blood aproned the front of his chest and thighs. His hair framed wiry strands across his shoulders.

He did not want to look down. He already knew his legs were a mess. The grating pain in his femurs had dulled now, one of the last feelings he would remember.

Shaking uncontrollably, Sindul powered down the *Harvester*'s systems. Interior lights dimmed. Resting his head against the pilot's cradle, he fought to stay awake.

The Septic infantry squad clattered down the lightless launch tube, unmasking the shadows with clumsy floodlight. Striding ahead of the human infantry came Brother Pelgan, a shambling, rusting behemoth of Nurgle. Despite the calls and clicks of animals that lurked in the subterranean depths, Pelgan was by far the most fearsome thing in the region.

They made their way down into the abandoned extremities of the floating fortress. It was too dark to see what purpose these corridors once served, or where they led. In many parts the ceiling had collapsed or the mesh decking simply fell away like a cliff-face. Men stumbled often, sometimes a mere step away from some bottomless drop. It was difficult to imagine how large the *Cauldron Born* appeared from orbit, but within, Pelgan had learned to hate the enormity of its landscape. It was so easy to get lost.

It was for that same reason Pelgan had bemoaned his ill-fortune when his squad sergeant forced him to investigate a foreign object that had breached the ship. It was likely no more than a small meteorite, attracted by the gravitational pull of the floating fortress. Nonetheless, the Septic subordinates could not be entrusted to such a task. With the recent riots in the dungeons, Opsarus had become even more wary, ever more alert.

'Bring that floodlight over here,' Pelgan snapped impatiently. The Septic hauled the heavy lamp over to where Pelgan indicated and began to pan the light back and forth.

At first they saw nothing. The walls were caked with a patina of organic decay. Like an ossuary, the oxidised metal was honeycombed with fossilised plant life. Yet if Pelgan looked closely he could see gouges in the walls – high-impact damage to parts of the ceiling where flora and decay had been ripped away to reveal the raw metal of the ship's infrastructure beneath.

'Over there,' Pelgan said, checking his auspex again.

The floodlight captured something reflective in its beam. A long and fluted silhouette three times the length of a battle tank, yet organic in its sweeping profile. Its skin was the colour of a fresh bruise, mottled purple and black.

It took Pelgan a moment to recognise the unfamiliar shape of an alien vessel. Lying tilted on its side, exposing its wounded stomach with one snapped wing saluting upwards, the craft looked severely vulnerable.

Pelgan chortled. Finally, he thought, something worthy of investigation. He beckoned for the Septic infantry to follow. 'Hurry now,' he said as he closed in on the stranded craft.

Pelgan entered the gaping spacecraft slowly and cautiously. Nurgle had a peculiar method of execution in all things, which was evident in Pelgan's approach. The Plague Marines proceeded slowly, creeping through the xenos craft's unlit interior. Entering through the rear cargo ramp, Pelgan sent his Septic infantry ahead to probe for traps.

Judging by the residual stink of excrement and musk, Pelgan guessed that the hold of the craft had once been used to transport prisoners of war, perhaps even slaves.

As Pelgan edged forwards, the interior was rendered by his thermal imaging into unsettling alien shapes. There was an organic feel to the ship, as if its composition had been grown naturally from bone.

Sweeping arches, ridged framework and smooth floors. Pelgan saw no sign of the carving, chopping and bolting so unique to human and orkoid construction.

Boots clopping softly, Pelgan entered the cockpit.

'I was counting how long it would take you.'

The voice came from the pilot cradle facing away from Pelgan. His finger hovered over the trigger of his boltgun.

Strapped into what appeared to be a command seat, Pelgan recognised the figure of a dark eldar. But not like any eldar that Pelgan had encountered in the field of war. This one was dishevelled – pale, weak, bloodied. He did not need to know much about xenos physiology to know that the eldar was in significant pain.

'I can't believe you were stupid enough to come in...' the dark eldar wheezed.

Pelgan stepped back. 'Your employment is no longer required, mercenary. Your payment is to be claimed on Hauts Bassiq. Why are you here? Answer me well, or I shall cut you up.'

The dark eldar's head lolled weakly. His chest heaved up and down with each laborious breath. 'You have less time than I...'

Pelgan's honed battle instinct made him take another step back. 'I will shoot now, mercenary. State your business.'

Suddenly, the ship's power systems hummed back into life. Consoles blinked and overhead lights fluttered brightly. Garbled alien words were emitted from the cockpit.

The dark eldar fixed his gaze on Pelgan. His pupils were enlarged, indicating severe concussion or psychic brain trauma. 'Better to die a traitor than die a slave. The Blood Gorgons, I'm sure, share that sentiment with me.'

The realisation startled Pelgan with a jolt. As far as he knew, eldar guarded their technology with a sacred reverence. Many of their machines were inhabited by the spirit stones of ancestors, eternally bound to the machine's circuitry. No eldar would die and leave their ancestors in human hands. There must be a rational reason for the creature to come here and die.

The command console displays changed rapidly. There was a sequential pattern to the display. Numbers. Numbers counting down.

Pelgan turned his enormous bulk to run.

The console's display blanked out. It blinked three times.

The ensuing explosion made the *Cauldron Born* cry in distress. The iron skeleton of its frame gurgled with a sonorous, keening protest. The blood vessels and throbbing capillaries that wound around the cables and pipes squirmed in agony.

On a gangway high up in a venting shaft, Barsabbas looked down.

He knew, without any doubt, that the explosion was the *Harvester*'s self-destruction. Far below, he saw a tiny ball of flame puff up, brief and exhilarating, before burning down into a tiny, flickering speck.

Sindul had played his part, Barsabbas at least could give him respect for that. As strange as the dark eldar species were, they had principles. Sindul preferred death over the shame of returning home as a scarred, branded slave. There was never hesitation or doubt. Sindul knew he could never escape Barsabbas. In a strange sense, Barsabbas considered Sindul had simply given up hope and preferred suicide.

'These fanatic templars of Nurgle will respond in full ponderous strength, as they always do,' Gammadin said. 'Our one advantage is terrain and knowledge of our own home. For once, I do not know if that will suffice. '

Barsabbas counted thirteen shots left in his clip and an empty ammunition sling. Sliding out his knotwork mace, Barsabbas climbed the gantry after Gammadin, leaving the twinkling wreckage of the *Harvester* behind.

CHAPTER TWENTY-THREE

Lance-Naik Dumog of the Third Septic Infantry considered himself a superstitious man, so it was little wonder that he felt ill at ease.

At the first trumpet, Dumog had woken from his sleep, groggy with phlegm, as he did every other day. But upon rising, he saw – curiously – his own uniform folded neatly at the foot of his cot and his helmet placed on top. Dumog shook his head, not remembering folding his uniform. Nor did he remember polishing his helmet. Routine and tidiness were not cultivated amongst Nurgle's followers.

Stranger yet, Dumog remembered a time before his induction into Nurgle's ranks. Of these distant, diminished memories of a previous life, the clearest image Dumog could recall was that of neatly folded clothes and a hat, placed at the foot of his grandfather's deathbed.

Ever since then, Naik Dumog had associated death with that eerie pastiche of clothes pressed on a bed, with a hat placed ever so hauntingly atop.

The unsettling conclusion, which had been intruding upon his baffled and hesitant mind, was that he was going to die.

That deep sense of foreboding burdened his shoulders heavily, even as he attended systems operation on the *Cauldron Born*'s command bridge. Although his eyes were fixed upon the console monitors at his bay, his mind was elsewhere.

His paranoia seemed to be confirmed with a final, awful certainty, when alarm sirens began to bray. Slow at first, then loud and urgent – *To arms! Children of Nurgle, to arms!* Dumog had panicked then. None of the ship's command consoles registered enemy activity either externally or on board the vessel. There had been signatures from a small foreign object piercing the vessel's dermal bulkheads, but such was its fractional size that the bridge commanders had dismissed it as nothing more than standard space debris.

Perhaps, Dumog thought with the sinking regret of hindsight, the object had been more.

The alarms continued to sound as the command bridge erupted with frantic action. The sudden surge in activity quietened Dumog's fretful nerves. The security protocols aboard the command bridge were matched by its fearsome troop disposition. Amongst the hundred-odd bridge crew and officers were three platoons of Septic heavy infantry. Overall command, however, rested with Captain Vyxant, a revered veteran who now snapped at his subordinates from a shrine-throne.

When Dumog looked up at the overhead surveillance slates, he espied panic in the decks. Septic heavy infantry were scrambling to respond, yet to what threat, they did not know. The command bridge had no answer. Neither surveillance pict nor auspex could locate any intrusion.

Through watching the hapless preparations on surveillance, the panic began to infect those crewing the bridge by osmosis. Alarms continued, yet the command bridge could give no commands. Crewmen hurried about, attempting to look occupied, but they had no direction.

Suddenly, Dumog heard a rash of gunfire beyond the command deck's blast doors. Feeling the bile rise in his gorge, he scanned through the pict feeds, trying in vain to bring up a view of the confusion outside.

'Gunfire, sir,' announced a Septic officer, stating the obvious. Muffled shots crackled.

Captain Vyxant shouted through his vox-grille for silence. 'Everything is reined in. Maintain control and keep your wits,' he began, relaying information through his squad's external comm-link. 'There has been an explosion in the lower quarters, likely a result of faulty fuel mains. The fires have been contained by control teams.'

As Vyxant spoke, Dumog coughed in relief. Tapping on his porcelain console, he began to relay Captain Vyxant's squad link through the ship's vox-casters.

'This ship is as old as the bottom of Terra's muddy sea and no sturdier. The sooner we abandon this wreck–'

Captain Vyxant did not finish his assessment. The blast doors peeled outwards with a resonant clap of expanding air. A hard wind, frost-churned and biting, slammed into the command bridge, staggering those caught in its ferocity.

What followed sent Naik Dumog diving for cover. He hid, ducking his limbs awkwardly beneath a command console. He drew his limbs in tight and could think only of his uniform, folded at the foot of his bed.

A white-skinned daemon in power armour charged through the entrance. Or rather, it was no true daemon, but a scarred and warp-fused monstrosity, more daemon than Astartes. It bellowed with an anguished, vengeance-hungry howl. It had the bottled rage of a returned king. Indeed, Dumog knew without a doubt that before him rose an ancient, regal monster. He could brand it no other word but *monster*.

The command bridge erupted with the crackle of small arms. There was a ferocity to the counter-fire that spoke of a pressing urgency. It was indiscriminate. As if they were frightened of the warrior in their midst.

And rightly so. The Blood Gorgons patriarch sent out ripples of psychic shock through the atmosphere. Every console screen blew out along the eastern bank. With his spined pincer, he pierced Captain Vyxant's chest and pinned him against the bulk of a cogitator.

Behind him, almost as an afterthought, came a Chaos Space Marine with bolter in hand. Like a retainer to his knight, the bond-brother guarded his lord's back, firing stiff single shots.

Dumog could only hide his face and recite the *Canticle of Seven Plagues*. He had a laspistol at his hip, but he considered it worthless. There would be no point.

As the pandemonium continued, Dumog's chest became taut with fright. He could only think that Father Nurgle had reached out to warn him, when he had woken up on such a portentous day. Nearer and nearer he could hear the grinding crunch of the Ascendant Champion. Gurgling and abrupt screams of death accompanied his approach. Dumog tried to reach for his laspistol but the resolve melted from his fingertips. He could do nothing but stay hidden.

There was another crunch. Somewhere close by, a Septic soldier fired a single shot before the crunch of bone could be heard. Dumog could almost hear the presence of his killer – a deep bass rasping of his expansive lungs. He could smell his nearness – the ozone stink of psyk-craft and oiled leather.

Suddenly, Dumog was travelling through the air, horizontally at first and then vertically, with a speed that whiplashed his neck.

He could feel the sores on his face open and weep, a natural response. His killer stared at him, face-to-face, pinching him up by his collar.

It spoke with a voice like slow-moving magma. 'Did Muhr deactivate my *Cauldron Born*'s defence grid?'

Dumog nodded three times. He was unable to verbalise, for his tongue was too heavy to obey. So great was the Blood Gorgon's presence that Dumog felt compelled to grovel before one so favoured by the gods. By the time the Arch-Champion released him, Dumog's hands were trembling too much to even key the proper sequence into the command consoles.

'Lord Opsarus has shut down the defence grids. We could not control the ship's machine spirit. It turned on us,' Dumog gasped.

'I thought so. Faithful hound. This is a part of me, we are bonded, she and I. It almost boils my blood that you would so dismiss the strength of our bindings,' his killer said. He was already lowering himself into the command throne. A net of neural cords slithered up to connect him to the ship.

As Gammadin left him cowering, Naik Dumog saw that he was the only survivor in the command bridge. The bodies of his comrades were discarded across the floor and cogitator bays. Wiping the pus from his weeping sores, the Septic Naik tried not to move, lest he incur his killer's attention again.

'What do we do with this one?'

Dumog started. He realised his killer's retainer, the Space Marine, was indicating towards him. There was an impassive yet menacing air to his voice, as if Dumog did not really exist.

By now, his killer was nestled in his command throne. The neural cords that had attached to him in rubbery tendrils began to writhe, responding in a way that Captain Vyxant or even Opsarus could not replicate. The *Cauldron Born* was trembling, as though waking from slumber.

'Leave him be,' his killer commanded.

Dumog collapsed to his knees in supplication. 'Praise be, great Lord Undivided!'

So preoccupied was Dumog in his displays of appeasement that he never saw the ceiling-mounted bolters perk up with mechanical vigour. He was still on his knees, prostrate, when the sentry guns fired upon him, killing him, as he had feared all along.

The alarms invoked Opsarus's uncontrolled temper. Each whoop and bray was like a taunt to him, a personal taunt that burrowed its way deep into his ego and ate away at his ability to contain the anger.

Opsarus did not consider himself a furious being. He had an infectious laugh and a deep sense of glee. He often took pleasure in surprising his followers with small gifts – a curious pox, a rash to scratch or a boil to pop – and chuckling warmly.

But he had a serious side too, a cold anger that possessed him when he was enraged. A silent fury that rendered him dark and mute. He would move then almost at a prowl, entirely focussed on eliminating that dark spot against his mirth.

When the rapid series of alarms and reports flooded the hulk's navigation helm, Opsarus settled quietly into that very same state.

Everywhere, the Blood Gorgons were rising – a broken beast that was gradually rousing, shaking its head against the fog of fear and confusion as it woke. It built momentum rapidly, a swift devolution and breakdown of order. First he heard Gammadin's voice on the vox exhorting the meticulously divided Gorgon companies to retaliate. That alone had caused Opsarus some concern. The division of the Blood Gorgons had been tenuous, relying solely on isolation of communication between the squads and an absence of central leadership.

Soon after there were sporadic vox reports of Blood Gorgons squads retaliating against their Plague Marine custodians, of older, veteran Blood Gorgons squads rebelling from the slave galleys, lashing out against their captors with chains and tools. The fighting was quickly suppressed by gunfire.

The last report, issued from the diseased and venerable Sergeant Kulpus, was that the sentry force at the mid-decks had been lost and the Blood Gorgons had reclaimed an unsealed weapons vault. The regular patrols had been forced back by heavy Blood Gorgons fire. They were losing ground to the abrupt nature of the uprising.

Opsarus was not pleased. He had almost been driven into a spontaneous and uncharacteristic outburst of rage. Instead, he calmed himself with jags of breathing. His brass respirator tanks throbbed with exhalation from his chest vents.

'Can you account for this? Is this your doing?' he asked Muhr accusingly. The sorcerer, as always, stood by his side and behind him.

'No, my lord,' Muhr answered, startled. 'Never.'

'How did it come to this? This mess. I hate mess. Nurgle is decay, but there is an order to that. A process. A graduation. It is slow and inevitable but never a mess. This,' Opsarus said, gesturing at the stilted surveillance images on the console banks. 'This is a mess.'

'Shall I summon the bearers?' Muhr asked. He had already drawn his bolt pistol from his holster and was checking the clip.

'No,' Opsarus replied, waving him away. 'I'll do it myself.'

With careful deliberation, he unlocked his gauntlet. The hand within the shell was black and swollen. From the unintrusive shadows, a servitor of melting flesh and rusting metal scuffled forwards and affixed an auto-cannon over Opsarus's hand like a weaponised glove. Another servitor coupled the dense ammunition belt to the Terminator suit.

'We go then. To fix this mess that you've created,' Opsarus said. 'As a matter of principle, Muhr, you should do this yourself. But Nurgle is generous.'

With that, the Crow and his witch made for the command deck, weapon servitors clattering in tow.

The war had begun. The five hundred and fifty Plague Marines and four companies of Septic were recalled to battle formations. They rushed back through the space hulk's labyrinth, collecting in massed, company-strength formations. In congregation, they were a formidable force. Solid phalanxes of fortified armour and massed firepower – the slow, grinding combat doctrine of Nurgle. Boltguns and shoulder-mounted autocannons were brought to the fore.

They beat their pitted gauntlets against their chest plates. They shouted in unison, a mocking bark that was carried by a thousand voices. They thundered their feet against the metal decking, raising a clamour that sounded like the march of legions.

Opsarus the Crow, towering tall in his Terminator plate and shroud of skin-mail, advanced amongst his warriors. They cheered him as he passed. The sorcerer Muhr followed in his wake, his blackened face bearing his allegiance to Nurgle. They cheered him too, for he was now one of them.

Opsarus gave no orders, except to raise his fist. The companies of Nurgle, in reply, held aloft their standards and totems, clinking with skulls, effigy dolls and the fluttering flags of skinned tattoos. Beyond the grotesque savagery of their formations, there was also a tightly ranked discipline. With a final clash of kettle drums, the Plague Marines went forth to crush the Blood Gorgons' rebellion.

The decks quaked. From the lighted halls to the dimmest marshes of the basement sewers, the ship trembled. The *Cauldron Born*'s fusion reactor scaled from standby to its highest output potential. Monstrous turbines spun with cyclonic force as the reactor core expanded with solar heat.

Gammadin's reclamation of the ship's defence grid could be felt everywhere.

Sentry guns, previously limp and toothless, resumed their methodical scanning. Positioned in high ceilings and bottleneck corridors, the twin-linked bolters and scatter lasers fired on anything that was not slave-marked or of the Blood Gorgons gene-code. Septic officers broadcast frantic reports that the walls themselves were attacking, spreading confusion throughout their ranks.

Gun servitors – chem-nourished reptiles of hulking shoulders, piston limbs and arms of reaper cannon – resumed their patrol of the ship's main decks. Eyeless and drooling, the previously placated beasts relied purely on the ship's defence grid to sight their targets and receive patrol orders. Now, packs of gun-servitors engaged Septic heavy infantry at close range. Their sole task was to seek, engage and eliminate.

Throughout the ship's labyrinthine passages, void shields and lock shutters locked into position. The Nurgle forces, already disorientated by the ship's layout, were confronted by road-blocks and impasse at nearly all the major routes.

By itself the *Cauldron Born* could not win the war. Already the sentry guns were low on ammunition; the linear patrol servitors were outmanoeuvred by animalistic cunning. Plague Marines breached the sealed corridors. Yet the ship itself was turning against its oppressors. It gave the Blood Gorgons the respite to regroup, re-establish lines of communication and rearm.

The ship's reclaimed defence systems could not win them the war, but they gave the Blood Gorgons the small respite they needed to cobble together some semblance of an offensive.

Plague Marines were accustomed to fighting wars of attrition where they could use superior combined arms to overwhelm an opponent over a long, protracted campaign, grinding them down with disease, illness and misery. On marshes, mudfields and bloodied beaches, the Plague Marines could use their numbers.

But the cramped confines of ship-to-ship boarding were the domain of the Blood Gorgons. They were used to using their small numbers to maximise effectiveness in boarding raids.

At the Maze of Acts Martial, standing before its sacred gates, Bond-Brother Kasuga fought on his own. He had no guns, only the spears, swords and maces of the armoury, yet he fought with the gate's wooden posts buttressing his flank and the lintel over his head. Denying the packed Plague Marine squads room to use their massed ranged weaponry, Kasuga broke his spears and blunted his swords across their armour. Wound after wound he sustained, yet there was no other recourse. He fought or he died: the instinct of self-preservation had long been expelled from his psyche.

Sergeant Hakkad moved his squad out of their billet in the first moments of confusion. They were unarmed, but well armoured, but that did not matter to him. Hakkad had killed men with less.

He ordered his squad to stay low, creeping through the quiet, disused corridors and guided only by the lambent glow of bacteria colonies. From the main tunnels and gangways, he could hear the distinct whoop of alarms and the high-pitched squeal of automatic scatter lasers. There came muffled, indistinct shouting and the rumble of movement.

Yet, above it all... Above all the noise and disruption, Hakkad heard the voice of Lord Gammadin. That voice urged him onwards. He was compelled by the familiar, rasping tones. The long, drawn-out vowels of a commander who was entirely in control.

'Brothers, I am Gammadin returned.'

That was all he heard – Gammadin's voice over the ship's vox.

There had been a call to arms somewhere, but Hakkad had not really heard anything else. With those words, the rebellion that had simmered in his blood had been brought to the boil. He no longer cared if the other squads and broken companies would join him. It no longer mattered that his squad might be the only one to attempt a resistance. It did not matter because Gammadin had returned in the treasure vaults of the lower decks.

But the other squads did join him. Four members of Squad Hurrian had overpowered their keepers and found Hakkad and his men. Together, the ten Blood Gorgons had entered the unlocked vault and seized anything that could be used as weapons. Ancient relic swords, ceremonial sceptres plundered from ecclesiastical coffers, the gilded pistols of distant kings. These were no real weapons, but Hakkad was glad they had taken them.

Gammadin's declaration was neither magic nor sorcery. In its most basic terms, Gammadin's call gave them a conviction they had previously not possessed. Until then, there had been doubt amongst the Blood Gorgons – separated, betrayed and infiltrated by the enemy, they had lost their trust. Without that trust, they lost the ability to act cohesively. They had ceased to exist as a functional fighting force.

Plague Marines poured into the lower decks to maintain order. With no more than ten Blood Gorgons, Sergeant Hakkad engaged them. They fought at close quarters, a furious hurricane of muzzle flash and glinting steel. The Plague Marines overwhelmed them, but by then Hakkad did not care.

On the vox-link he could hear the reactivation of multiple squads – Squad Khrom, Squad Lagash, Venerable Nysus. One by one, the Blood Gorgons reunited.

Every slave dreams of liberation, but when liberation becomes an impossibility, the human spirit has remarkable ways of adapting. One finds comfort in small things – stability, shelter and a bed to sleep in.

The diseased legions had taken even that small comfort away from the slaves of the _Cauldron Born_. What little the slaves had managed to amass for themselves had wilted under the sickness and neglect visited upon them.

So it was no surprise that when the slaves heard Gammadin's call to arms, they too rose up. There were thousands of slaves in the warrens, engines bays, loading docks and storage vaults. The belay teams, scullery serfs, custodials, black turbans. All of them. Thousands upon thousands, like soldier ants swarming from the darkest crevices.

They came out of the darkness, vengeful and exhilarated. They harboured no love for the Blood Gorgons, but it was the only life they knew. Men, women, families, children, even the elderly. Out they came, clattering tools, utensils and whatever blunt, heavy objects of revolt they could find.

They were cut down in their hundreds, yet still they forced one foot before the other. They threatened to overwhelm several key positions in the primary decks held by Septic guards. Black turbans wielding halberd and crossbow led the assault against automatic guns.

Although the slaves died in great numbers, they delayed and harassed the Nurgle counter-offensive. They blocked off tunnels, barricading corridors with pyres of wreckage and gas fires. Some barricaded the enemy with their own bodies. The ones who were not fighters, those who knew the futility of fighting, linked arms and sat, their voices raised in song. In doing so, they forced the Plague Marines to gun their way through a morass of living bodies. Each sold their life for the price of one bolt shell, but they died with a dignity that would otherwise have eluded them.

Bond-Sergeant Sharlon fumbled through the steaming carcass of a Plague Marine. He found a coil of access keys hooked around the Traitor's war belt.

His squad, only five strong now, settled down in the entrance to the Maze of Acts Martial. They used the cover well, lying belly-down between the frond growths and honeycombed calcium deposits. Each had claimed themselves a bolter from the newly opened vaults on access-level 45. Their ammunition, however, was low and they picked cautious shots.

Across the access corridor, at the top of an iron stairwell, Plague Marine squads hammered them with automatic fire. Spitting bolt shot sparked off the walls and ate hungry mouthfuls of metal from the surfaces. The angle of fire was awkward and the shot inaccurate but the sheer volume of ammunition thrown down from the stairwell caused Bond-Sergeant Sharlon to bend double and sprint across the open, the access keys jingling softly against his wrist. Plumes of dusty shots traced his footsteps.

The enemy had sighted him now, calling out warnings from the upper gallery. From Sharlon's right fist sagged a cluster of melta bombs. The enemy saw this too and began to shoot with urgency. A bolt shot exploded against the bond-sergeant's ceramite neck guard, spreading fragments into his face-plate. Another struck his hip, punching him with hot lancing pain. Sharlon staggered up the stairs, taking one faltering step on his injured hip as another bolt tore through his thigh. The Plague Marines stood resolute at the top of the steps, refusing to give ground. They were no more than twelve metres away.

Sharlon took several more stubborn steps upwards. The clustered bombs swayed precariously around the storm of fire drilling through the bond-sergeant. Trembling, Sharlon rested a hand against the banisters. The upper right of his torso had become a porous mass of chewed ceramite and open bleeding. He climbed one more step, out of spite.

The primed melta bomb ignited. It detonated every grenade in the half-dozen cluster so brightly that Sharlon's squad could see nothing as their visors automatically blacked out to protect their retinas from the flare.

It took exactly two seconds for the flare to settle and the squad's light-sensitive lenses to recalibrate. By then, a perfect sphere had been cut into the partition bulkheads. Of the balustrade and upper gallery, there was no sign, nor any evidence that they had once existed. Almost an entire section of the bulkhead and upper mezzanine level had evaporated. The only evidence of the destruction was the smouldering red glow at the very edges of the blast.

If the Blood Gorgons did not have the *Cauldron Born* then nobody would, this was Sharlon's parting message. The *Cauldron Born* existed only with them, and they could not live without the *Cauldron Born*. There was a symbiosis there.

The bond of the Blood Gorgons went beyond that of blood brother to blood brother, it bound them all as one single organism. A squad was nothing without its company, a company nothing without unity. Even the slaves co-existed in reciprocity with their Blood Gorgon masters. Every aspect of the Chapter existed as a unified whole. They would stand and fight together, or they would die alone.

A single Plague Marine stood on a dais, overlooking the sleeping dens of over two hundred slaves. The slaves, some so sickened that they could no longer stomach water, lay in lethargic heaps before him.

Yet when Gammadin's declaration broadcast over the vox, the slaves began to stir. As one, they began to move.

The Plague Marine was disquieted. He checked the magazine on his bolter and braced it against his hip. He shouted for the slaves to remain supine, but some, he noticed, did not obey him. They stood up – pale and trembling, yet they defied him.

By the time Gammadin's voice was heard a second time, the slaves surged. Their collective minds had been spurred. They rushed up to overwhelm the Plague Marine.

Determined though the slaves were, the Traitor Marine was a killer. With one shot, he killed. He had calibrated his methods of execution to the heights of efficiency. There was no warrior who could match him. But he could not withstand the combined savagery of two hundred desperate humans with nothing left to lose.

They drowned him with the weight of their bodies, tearing at his impervious armour. They crushed the Plague Marine, dying as they did so. For the slaves, it was a dignified end. To be slain in that final thrust of valour, to try but to fail nobly – it was a death they clambered to receive.

Tightly confined violence bubbled up from the lower levels and onto the command deck.

At the supply vaults, Sergeant Nightgaunt of Squad Hekuba succeeded in retaking the entire complex after finding it lightly defended. Heavy numbers of Plague Marines supported by Septic heavy infantry continued to press upon their position. The Blood Gorgons utilised the tight confines of the corridors to their advantage, repelling enemy attacks through their knowledge of the maze-like halls and their tunnel fighting expertise. Nightgaunt himself was killed approaching the third hour of combat, slain as he covered the approach against enemy advance. Yet the remaining five brothers of the squad secured the complex until fragments of the Ninth Company reinforced their position and established a line of supply, including ammunitions and weaponry, to those skirmishing in the lower decks.

Only thirty-six minutes into the uprising, two black turban slaves arrived in the Temple Halls, where the fighting was heaviest. The black turbans advised most senior Captain Zothique that slaves had reclaimed significant portions of the lower slave warrens and basements. They had driven out the Septic overseers through sheer numbers, forcing the enemy to reconsolidate their positions. Although it provided little strategic advantage, it renewed the Blood Gorgons' fighting vigour.

Bond-Sergeant Severn, leading the remains of Sixth Company, brought the fight to the interior citadels. Assuming command in place of his slain Khoitan, Severn led an eighty-strong contingent of bonded brethren into a frontal assault against dug-in Plague Marines. With the aid of a veteran heavy weapons team in the overhead bulkheads, Severn was able to dislodge a company-sized element of Plague Marines from their personal quarters and scatter them into the narrow catacombs that housed the black turban barracks.

Nurgle battle tactics were little-changed despite the unfamiliar terrain – they relied on solid, frontal advances supported by heavy ordnance. They set up road blocks and static gun pits in an attempt to entice the Blood Gorgons into open warfare. But against a mobile Blood Gorgons force that refused to engage, they were frustrated in any attempts to counter-attack meaningfully. Perhaps by fault of their obstinate nature, the static Plague Marine formations endured ceaseless hit and run attacks that eventually drove them lower down the *Cauldron Born*'s extremities.

Two very powerful entities were approaching the command deck, beings of raw Chaos power. Gammadin could feel their psychic imprint and sense their approach through the ship's neural link.

'They are coming,' he said. The Ascendant Champion's eyelids flickered open as he severed neural links with the *Cauldron Born*.

'Can you hear that?' Gammadin asked.

There was a low keening in the air. Barsabbas strained to hear. Low on the wind, almost inaudible, he heard the acoustic echoes of an ancient metal fortress, a monolithic megastructure creaking as all the pressures of the universe pushed against its iron flanks.

'The *Cauldron Born* is warning me of their approach,' Gammadin said. He brushed the neural fibres from his temple and stood up from the command throne. His pincer arm began to click involuntarily in slight agitation.

Barsabbas took a deep, steadying breath, expanding his lungs with much-needed oxygen. His pupils dilated. There was a static burst of machine-scream through the vox-link as his armour's spirit responded to the oncoming threat. Scrolling overlays of system reports, core temperature and power output streamed across his visor. The power armour wasn't calmed until Barsabbas loaded his bolter with a salvaged clip and clicked the magazine into position. Only then did the machine spirit settle, minimising its report tabs and replacing the data streams with a single targeting reticule that bounced from periphery to periphery.

The entire wall on Barsabbas's left was pushed in. All of it. A thirty-tonne section of plasteel bulkhead peeled inwards. Metal groaned in discordant protest as it was sheared from its structure. Warping and twisting, it finally folded diagonally, crushing the ancient cogitator banks beneath it.

Through the shorn wall came Muhr and the Nurgle Overlord, Opsarus.

For a brief moment, Barsabbas froze. He was occupied by the most curious feeling. Almost foreboding, dashed with a fleeting pall of hopelessness. Was this *fear*? Barsabbas could not be sure. Was this what it felt like, to be a pure human, at all times?

Opsarus crunched through the debris on legs like basalt columns. A behemoth, wading through the wreckage, deliberate and unsinkable. Behind him he dragged a wrecking ball of spherical metal, its solid weight keeping the chain taut.

He seemed to ignore Barsabbas entirely, not even dignifying the battle-brother's presence with a glance. Instead, he crashed towards where Gammadin squared up to meet him. Only then did Barsabbas realise that perhaps he did not feel fear of the enemy, merely fear that he would not be able to do his enemy enough harm.

Gammadin, the Arch-Champion of the Blood Gorgons, was physically smaller. Opsarus stood over him, his Tactical Dreadnought Armour almost eclipsing Gammadin from view. Even his cherubic deathmask, set in the centre of his hunchbacked chest, stood at a higher eye level than Gammadin's defiantly raised head.

Muhr glided to circle Gammadin's left. The witch was stalking him and cutting off his angles of manoeuvre. By his movements, Barsabbas could see that they were preparing to execute Gammadin at close quarters. There was no other way. Mere small-arms would be insufficient against constructs of warfare such as these. Such gods of war could not be felled by the cowardly shot of pistol or rifle.

Almost fifty metres away from Barsabbas, Gammadin adopted a low grappler's crouch, his monstrous pincer raised high like the striking tail of a scorpion. Opsarus circled steadily closer, dragging a wrecking ball on a high-tensile chain with one hand.

Barsabbas knew he could not face Muhr or Opsarus in open combat. His bolter would not fell such flesh of the ancients. But if Barsabbas could not overcome them, he could prevent at least one of them from engaging Gammadin.

Firming his resolve, Barsabbas raised his bolter, took aim and waited.

Ever the aggressor, Lord Gammadin launched himself to meet the Nurgle warlord. There was a brief, glancing impact as Opsarus pivoted, their shoulders colliding. It sounded like a light tank had just collided with a super-heavy on full acceleration. The command bridge reverberated with the transfer of their kinetic force.

Muhr stood aside, his eyes rolling as he began to enter a sorcerous trance. Barsabbas had seen the coven work often enough to know their weakness. The brief seconds before a sorcerer could channel the warp were his most vulnerable. If Barsabbas still had a role to play, his time would be now.

Barsabbas banged off three shots at Muhr. They were straight and true, a tight cluster all connected with the target's centre of mass. Yet, as Barsabbas had dreaded, a shield of force solidified before the bolt slugs made impact. The sorcerer turned, snarling.

His visage almost startled Barsabbas. He could barely recognise the witch-surgeon.

Muhr's skin, once white and taut, had become black and sallow. His rubbery face was framed by a matted shock of white hair. The eyes that transfixed him were yellow, lacking any iris or pupil.

Barsabbas withdrew, hoping to lure the witch into pursuit. He sprinted to a side exit, barging through the carved wood with his shoulder. Shrieking, the witch pursued. Barsabbas dared to turn at the tunnel entrance. Anko Muhr's dead face filled his vision with a maw of long teeth and white hair. Barsabbas fired twice, turned, and without looking back, sprinted off with Muhr on his heels.

Gammadin channelled his vengeance. There was a stranger standing in his home, taking his birthright. When he unleashed his psionic fury, it coalesced into a rolling sphere that rippled the air like an expanding ball of water.

The sound could be heard throughout the ship. The psychic resonance was so loud that Blood Gorgon and Plague Marine alike stopped their combat, their mental faculties overwhelmed by the psychic and sorcerous backlash.

Yet it did nothing to Opsarus. The Overlord simply looked at him and laughed. The jade of his deathmask was white hot and trailing smoke, but Opsarus was otherwise unscathed.

'You are not the only one here with tricks,' the Nurgle warrior chortled. 'Sometimes, methods determine the outcome of fights. and my method is better than yours.'

Gammadin staggered, spent by his one furious outburst. It was something he should not have done but his anger had been too great. Now his forearms were loose and trembling and he could not feel his own legs. His head was throbbing as neuro-toxicity in his brain spiked after his psychic manifestation. Gammadin could only growl drunkenly as Opsarus lunged forwards.

Opsarus buried Gammadin under his weight. At three and a half metres tall and weighing close to eight hundred kilograms, Opsarus mauled the Blood Gorgons champion. He backed up Gammadin with his sheer power. He threw a constant barrage of straight punches. Studded knuckles crunched into the crisp enamel shell of Gammadin's external plates. He gave Gammadin no time to recompose.

Pinning Gammadin against a console bank, Opsarus raised his wrecking ball, loaded to swing. Gammadin rolled to his left, crumpling the cast-iron console. The sphere crunched through where Gammadin had been, bounced a crater in the far wall and swung a pendulum arc back to Opsarus.

Gammadin regained his balance. Distorted images crazed his vision. The psychic attack had been too potent, especially for his weakened state. It would take him too long to recover.

A heavy blow suddenly crushed into his side, sending him over.

The Blood Gorgon Ascendant swiped his pincer like a club, weakly. His vision swam. He should have conserved himself, he should have contained his anger.

Another blow crashed down onto Gammadin's chest. Scrambled lights and warning beacons flashed in his eyes. The fused bone and ceramite of his torso cracked.

Bleeding and dazed, Gammadin could only think that he should not have been so wild with fury.

From the command bridge, the multiple sealed side entrances led into a warren of disused bulkheads in the ship's prow region. Over time they had fallen into a blackened, rotting disrepair. Moisture collected on the scummed floors, ankle deep in some places. The air was toxic with carbon and mould. Gases steamed around him. There was a pervasive quiet, as if the blind faecal worms and water snakes dared not disturb the peace.

It slowly dawned on Barsabbas that here was where he might die. As a Blood Gorgon, he had never thought about death before. Even when driven to withdrawal by the tau, Barsabbas had been the superior combatant, the more fearsome of any singular foe. He had never been outmatched before, not like this. Again that strange feeling which might have been fear crept into his chest.

Yet the notion of death did not trouble him. If he were to be killed, Barsabbas reflected, then better it were by a fellow Astartes, and a venerable

Blood Gorgon at that. There was no shame in confronting Anko Muhr, a villain so feared and dreaded in the annals of Imperial history.

Barsabbas crouched down low behind a pillar of calcite and switched off all non-essential power drains to his armour. He watched his surroundings only by the glow of shelled molluscs that clustered around the base of each pillar.

Grimly, he reflected on tales of slaves who had escaped down here to become lost. Indeed, Barsabbas fancied that he had felt the distinct crunch of bones beneath his boots as he threaded his way through the mire.

Barsabbas did not want to be lost, nor did he mean to hide. His purpose was to engage Muhr and this he intended to do. As he heard a distant elevator clang into position, Barsabbas began to shout, his voice caught and reflected by the unseen catacombs around him.

Almost immediately, he was rewarded by sloshing footsteps. Not incisive steps, but the sloshing of a large shape through water.

'Come out,' hissed the blackened witch. The voice echoed, masking the whereabouts of its owner.

Barsabbas held his bolter, pleading to calm its temperamental spirit.

Do not fail me now–

He shouldered his weapon with a solemn finality. His two hearts beat faster in a syncopated pattern. Yes, fear, Barsabbas admitted. What he felt must truly be fear.

And they shall know no fear–

The clumsy sloshing of the water grew closer. Then, suddenly, it stopped. The air grew cold; according to Barsabbas's visor data, atmospheric temperatures plummeted almost twenty degrees in an instant. A rime of crystals coated his vision. Barsabbas wiped the frost away from his helmet with his fingertips.

He heard a soft swish like a carp gliding through a creek, a gentle lapping sound as if someone were skimming the surface of the water, ever so gently. Barsabbas wondered if that sound was the witch, gliding across the water. The wafting white hair. That slackened dead face, levitating above the ground. The image chilled him. He shifted his grip on his bolter and held it tight.

Gammadin wheeled as the wrecking ball crashed through a set of ornate banisters and into the command throne.

'Come and fight me!' Opsarus called.

The Blood Gorgon Ascendant had regained his bearings. His head still pounded with residual pain but he had enough faculty to invoke his will again.

Opsarus cornered him, forcing him back up against the mono-crystal viewing ports of the bridge. Feigning defensiveness, Gammadin lunged upwards without warning. He struck rapidly with his pincer, the gnarled crescent claw snapping at the Nurgle Champion's Terminator plate, gouging chunks from the ceramite.

Opsarus replied with a backhanded punch that thrust Gammadin several steps back – enough distance for the wrecking ball to be brought to bear. Still lurching on the balls of his feet, the Blood Gorgons Ascendant balanced himself against the viewing glass. Sensing a momentary lapse in his foe's guard, Opsarus surged forwards with his tremendous bulk.

It was exactly where Gammadin wanted him.

The viewing ports detonated, their fragments shooting in straight, linear paths as the vacuum of space stole them away. Gammadin's mind blast was weak, strained from his earlier effort, but he centred the force well, aiming the full psionic focus at the viewing ports themselves.

The sudden vacuum tore out the command bridge. Parchment, data-slates and even the shredded shells of cogitators were ripped outwards and through the shattered ports. Opsarus lunged, overcommitting as the vacuum tugged him. Shooting off his knees, Gammadin threw his entire weight forwards and collided with the Overlord's shins. Such was the speed and force of their collision that armour plates detached from boltings, visors shattered, ceramite chipped and steel dented steel. Opsarus snarled and staggered. Gammadin twisted his body and ripped Opsarus's limbs out from underneath him, spilling him over.

The Nurgle lord fell, out of the empty port space and into the void beyond. His mammoth bulk became weightless as he was pushed beyond the *Cauldron Born*'s artificial gravity. His hand shot out and snagged the port frame, digits sinking into the metal as he fought for purchase.

'Go forth! You are not welcome here. Perish in the seas of space so that no trace of you will remain,' Gammadin bellowed.

He raised his pincer and snapped at Opsarus's anchored hand, shearing it off. Globes of blood drifted from Opsarus's forearm, spilling outwards and upwards in a slow, languid dance. Opsarus spiralled away, silent and still. He pointed at Gammadin, almost accusatory, as the void took him out to drift and drift into a slow, suffering death.

His mind imagined the witch's scalpel fingers sliding across his neck. Still he heard that awful swishing through the water. Taut with energy, Barsabbas shifted uneasily in his crouch.

Gravel skittered under his boots, loud and clattering in the darkness.

'Come out...' a soft voice murmured.

Barsabbas spun out from behind the calcite pillar, squeezing the trigger of his bolter. He screamed something just for the sake of making noise. His neck bulged as he roared, his chest puffed as the bolter flashed ferociously.

Muhr reeled back in surprise. His force shield strobed as a rapid series of impacts exploded around him. One shot after another, Barsabbas aimed for the same spot, attempting to weaken and short out the force-field. Time slowed down. The impacts seemed frustratingly languid.

The force shield fizzed and then popped with a vacuum clap. Barsabbas's bolter coughed dry clicks. Emboldened by breaching the shield, he leapt forwards with his mace.

Muhr lashed out with his hands and drilled the bond-brother in the face with a hammerblow of invisible energy.

The blow rocked Barsabbas so hard he momentarily blacked out. He was compelled by fear and did not feel it. He saw only red. Muscles bunching from frantic tension, he began to swing his mace harder than he had ever struck anything. There was a crazed desperation to his strength: the strength of a madman and the howls of a brain-addled lunatic. The fear Barsabbas felt gave him a primal savagery he had never known.

Muhr's face collapsed under the crunching onslaught. The witch tried to fend off the savage blows with his hands. Undeterred, the lashing mace haft bit off two fingers and slapped meatily into the side of the witch's neck.

Barsabbas revelled in the exhilaration of fear. A loyalist Adeptus Astartes knew no fear, but Barsabbas was impassioned by it. He knew the power of fear, how to control it, how to project it and how to become strong from it.

Yielding under the ceaseless torrent of strikes, Muhr reached for his bolt pistol. Despite all his witchcraft and his daemonic power, Muhr wilted under the pure, pressured aggression of a cornered beast. Slipping to the ground, Muhr fired two shots at Barsabbas. The first shot went wide. His orbitals had broken and they jammed his eyeball at an awkward angle. But the witch resighted and fired off twice.

Barsabbas did not even realise he had been shot. He lashed Muhr once more across the face, flattening the witch's jaw. Only then did he see that the bolt pistol had punched two craters in his abdomen. Barsabbas pushed through the pain and brought his mace down hard between Muhr's eyes.

Blind with pain, Muhr fired up from a seated position. He emptied the rest of the clip point-blank into Barsabbas's chest plate.

You are dying–

Barsabbas pushed the thought aside. He sank to his knees slowly, clutching a gauntlet to his chest to stem the bleeding as he had been trained to. But there was too much. The blood pumped around his hand and drained down his front. His visor dimmed as the damaged machine spirit conserved power. The entire chest plate had been shorn away.

His arm came up weakly, the mace trembling in his tenuous grasp. He swung it down again, with his last effort, bringing it down to bounce piteously off Muhr's armour. The witch lay prostrate, his face no longer recognisable, his white hair drenched dark black and red. He wheezed through his broken mouth.

Dead now–

Barsabbas's vision began to fade. He could no longer feel the mighty beat of his hearts. He eased himself down, leaning his back against the crumbling bulkhead. He became listless as his lips grew cold.

Lying down almost beside him, Muhr stirred slightly, blood bubbling from his mouth.

Barsabbas shook his head. He could not die before Muhr. Straining, Barsabbas dragged himself onto his front and inched his hand towards Muhr's throat. Barsabbas's vision was flickering and fuzzing around the edges, but he kept his focus singular. He reached out and seized Muhr's throat in his grasp.

The witch wheezed and slapped at his hands weakly. Slowly, little by little, Barsabbas squeezed the life out of his enemy.

The fighting continued for nine days and nine nights. Deep in the lightless confines, there was no measure of time but the strobe of gunfire. It degenerated into a siege. Bulkhead by bulkhead, corridor by corridor.

Victory would never be an apt word. Gammadin knew that many Blood Gorgons had died. Many more would follow. Whittled down and fragmented since the incursion, the entire Chapter had been weakened. It was a desperate struggle. But the Blood Gorgons maintained that precious advantage of terrain. They were fighting in their home. There was nothing left to do except fight or die, and armed properly or not, a cornered warrior was a dangerous prospect.

Through the command of hidden passageways, the Blood Gorgons shepherded the Plague Marines into the lowest portions of the ship, away from the command decks and, more vitally, from the supply vaults. If they could not drive them from the ship they would starve them.

By the eighth day of fighting, it became clear that the Plague Marines were consolidating their fighting positions towards the docking hangars, as if in preparation for withdrawal. Their leadership had been decapitated, and the Plague Companies fought on despite the wholesale surrender of their cultist infantry.

Having suffered some two hundred and fifty casualties, the Blood Gorgons nonetheless pursued. Of the remaining six hundred warriors, Gammadin committed two full companies for the final offensive. Among the senior captains, there was concern that two companies would not be enough to force the remaining Plague Marines into defeat. Any loss of Blood Gorgons momentum now would embolden the Plague Marines to continue fighting. Although their schemes lay broken, Nurgle's forces would continue to fight on, out of resilient spite, for such was the way of the Lord of Decay.

Gammadin, however, remained confident in his assessment of the enemy disposition. They were leaderless and fought a symbolic resistance. It would not take much more damage to drive them into flight.

On the ninth day, Gammadin established a number of heavily defended positions around the mid-tier decks and docking hangars encircling the main zone of conflict. Once the perimeter was secured, Bond-Sergeant Severn, now elevated to the honorary rank of *Khoitan-in-absence*, brought the two assaulting companies into position.

After an exchange that lasted some six hours, the Plague Marines finally initiated a fighting withdrawal into their Thunderhawks and strike cruisers. Severn voxed that their objective had been achieved – the Plague Marines were routed.

That was when Gammadin gave the order to unleash the Chapter.

He waited until the Plague Marines were partway embarked and vulnerable. Sweeping from their positions, Blood Gorgons attacked the fleeing ships with heavy weaponry. They pursued the fleeing craft with torpedo and rocket.

Long after their withdrawal, the burning wrecks of vessel carcasses and the drifting specks of Plague Marines orbited the *Cauldron Born*. Pulled by the fortress's gravity, they spun, listlessly, some entombed alive in their armoured casing.

He was Bond-Brother Barsabbas and he carried the weight of Besheba on his shoulders.

That much, at least, was still clear to him in his more lucid moments. But these moments were fewer and fewer now and more frequently punctuated by agony.

The only thing that never changed was the cold operating slab against his back. He had felt that cold metal against his spine for months now, maybe even years, for Barsabbas had no way of measuring time.

Muhr had destroyed his secondary heart and most of the organs in his right side. Steadily, piece by piece, the morass fibrillators and valve pumps substituting Barsabbas's organs were replaced and grafted with the organs of Lord Gammadin. The Ascendant Champion owed a debt to Squad Besheba. A bonded debt.

The Chirurgeons drained and refilled his arteries. They removed parts of his flesh, cutting here, scoring and sampling there. Every time he awoke, he did so to the system shock of extreme physical trauma.

But Barsabbas came to dread his dreams so much more.

The daemons would visit him then. The ghosts of the dead clawed their way back from the warp-sea to cavort in his visions. They tried to frighten him with stories of eternal torment and tempt him with the peace of eternal sleep.

At first the torment was ceaseless, but as time wore on, the daemons became wary of him. They bothered him less and less, sometimes fleeing when Barsabbas's consciousness entered their realms. They began to call him Gammadin.

On the five hundred and eighty-ninth day, Barsabbas was animated from his ritual coma. His remade body felt cold, as if he were not quite accustomed to inhabiting it. Rising from the slab to the click of his atrophied ligaments, Barsabbas placed a hand to his chest. He could feel the pulse beneath his sutured muscles.

Bound in flesh, the dormant volcano of Gammadin's heart rumbled.

ABOUT THE AUTHOR

Henry Zou's Black Library credits comprise the Bastion Wars series: *Emperor's Mercy*, *Flesh and Iron* and *Blood Gorgons*, and a prequel short story, 'Voidsong'. He lives in Sydney, Australia. He joined the Army to hone his skills in case of a zombie outbreak and has been there ever since. Despite this, he would much rather be working in a bookstore, or basking in the quiet comforts of some other book-related occupation.

WARHAMMER
40,000

MASTER OF SANCTITY

GAV THORPE

BOOK TWO IN THE LEGACY OF CALIBAN TRILOGY